"Imagine, we are at the beg ‎ in a quieter voice. "Alaric, the King ⟨ ‎ tiate with the Roman Empire for lan

"Thirty years before, the .‎_‎o ‎ their ancestral homelands, beyond the Danube , by the growing restlessness of the Hun nation. Alaric was born on that desperate march south. His people, homeless refugees, seeking safety and protection within the borders of the mighty Roman Empire."

"For years, the Goth would struggle to survive at the edge of that Empire. Alaric, like many of his Goth brothers, joined the Roman army. He fought for the Emperor Theodosius against the Franks, to protect the Imperial borders. He saw how the Roman Emperor used Goth warriors as, how do you say it in English? Cannon fodder? Thousands of his brothers died in the service of the Empire, all in the interests of Rome."

But," said the Professor, smiling and holding up a finger to his audience, "do not, for a moment, think Alaric was an ignorant ruffian, a barbarian. He was an educated man, a Christian. He was trained, by the Romans, in the art of war. He fought like a Roman, he thought like a Roman, but he was a desperate man, a refugee desperate to find a homeland for his people."

"Alaric and his Visigoth warriors invaded Italy twice," said the Professor. "He laid siege to Rome three times in the space of ten years, in pursuit of his dream."

"The first siege ended when the Roman Senate paid him off. The cost?" he asked, before answering his own question. "Two tonnes of gold. Fourteen tonnes of silver. Four thousand silken tunics. Three thousand hides, dyed scarlet. Three thousand pounds of pepper, and, we are told, the return of forty thousand Goth slaves. This is what the Romans paid for the lifting of the siege."

A murmur rippled through the audience.

"In today's values," the Professor said quietly, "Alaric walked away with eighty-two million dollars worth of gold and nearly ten million dollars worth of silver!"

"Imagine it! The wealth that must have been in Rome at the time for the Senate to be able to pull together sixteen tonnes, nearly one hundred million dollars worth, of precious metal to buy off Alaric and his Visigoths." He waited until a couple of the reporters stopped scribbling in their notebooks.

"Rome was not just wealthy. It was the spiritual heart of the Empire. A city of over a million people. It had not been sacked or looted since the Gauls had devastated the city in 387 BC – almost eight hundred years before. With all that wealth within his grasp, Alaric didn't sack Rome. He lifted his siege and walked away, the first time," said the Professor, with a wicked grin.

From his position at the back of the tent, without even seeing the faces of the Professor's audience, Dan could feel the tension and excitement building.

"During his second siege, Alaric forced the Roman Senate to appoint a rival Emperor. He then marched on Ravenna – the Imperial capital of the Western Roman Empire – to depose the Emperor Honorius."

"Months of on again, off again, negotiations with Honorius followed. Finally, they came to an agreement about a Goth homeland. As a sign of good faith, Alaric deposed his puppet Emperor, but, before the deal with Honorius could be finalised, another Gothic commander, Sarus, viciously attacked Alaric and his men. Did Sarus attack Alaric because of tensions between the Gothic tribes, or did Honorius arrange it and, how do you say - did the dirty on Alaric? We will never know. The outcome though, was tragedy."

"Angry, betrayed, with vengeance burning in his heart, he had finally been pushed too far!" said the Professor, throwing his arms up in the air. "Alaric marched for Rome."

"Think, for a moment, of all you know of Rome, the stories you heard in school of conquest, of those magnificent triumphs that paraded through the streets with the spoils of victory piled high for all Rome to see. Scipio Aemilianus who looted and destroyed the great, and fabulously wealthy, merchant city of Carthage. The Emperor Titus who sacked Jerusalem and brought back the Great Menorah. Augustus Caesar who took control of Cleopatra's Egypt, perhaps the wealthiest nation in the ancient world."

Blood of the Emperors

David Hunn

Blood of the Emperors

David Hunn

Published by David Hunn, 2023.

BLOOD OF THE EMPERORS

First edition. August 5, 2023.

ISBN: 979-8215961995

Written by David Hunn.

Table of Contents

To my best friend, Elizabeth, the other loves of my life Charlotte, Willa and George and the loves of their lives James and Vanessa and to Scipio, my buddy.

Maps

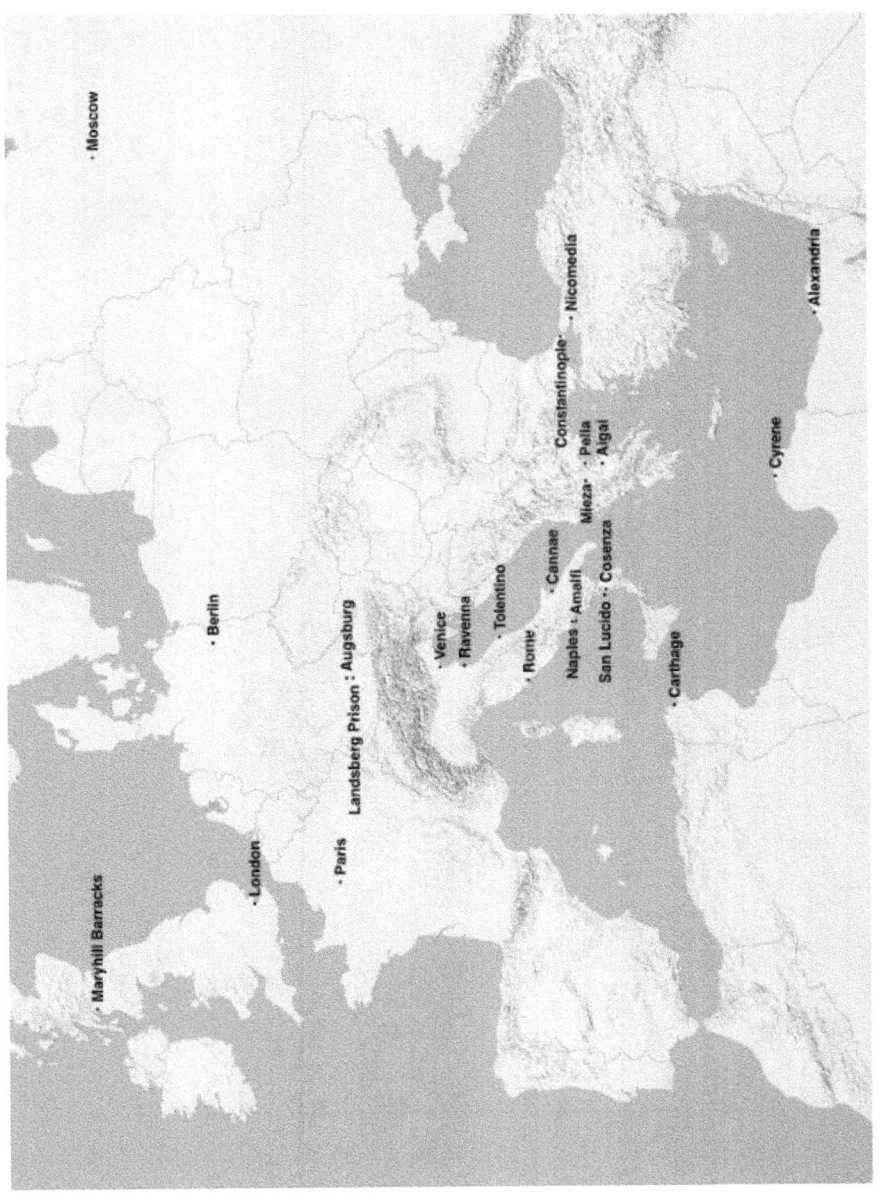

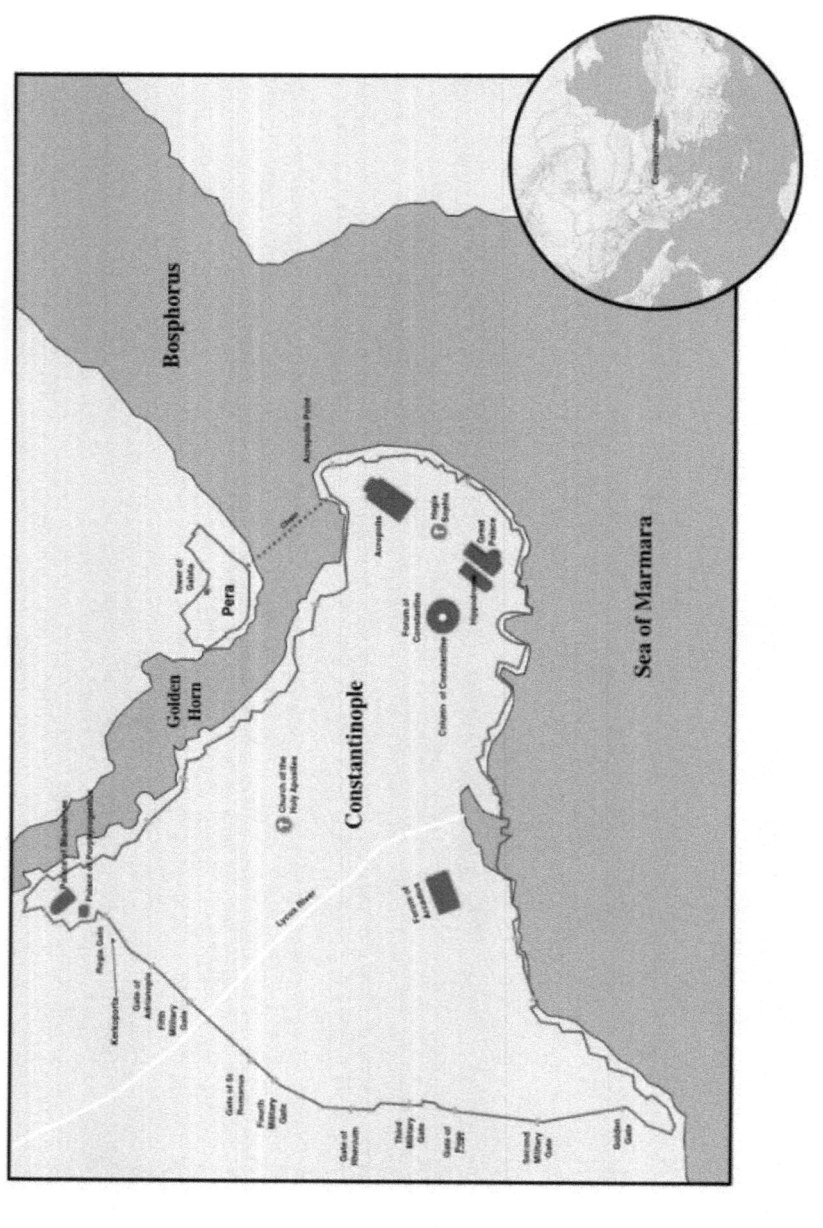

Book 1

1. Calabria - Present day

"We are on the verge of a momentous discovery, my friends. It is a discovery that will rival that of the unearthing of the tomb of the boy king Tutankhamen by the great archeologist, Howard Carter himself!" Professor Lorenzo Pellegrini paused and abstractedly stroked his neat van Dyke beard. He looked around at the eager and expectant faces of the students, volunteers and media that crowded the large tent that had been erected beside the recently diverted Busento River.

The tent was warm and stuffy. The pungent stench from the drying mud outside in the river bed filled the air. Dan Marsh stood watching the presentation from the back of the tent, keeping as close to the opening, and fresher air, as he could.

Dan smiled to himself as he watched the Professor begin to draw his audience in, just as he did with his students at the University. He knew that the small, neat, Italian academic was in his late sixties, but would never have guessed it from looking at him. He had more energy and enthusiam than a man half his age and was widely regarded as the best archeologist in Italy.

The Professor paused a moment longer, to be sure he had everyone's attention, then continued in lightly accented English, "For sixteen hundred years, the waters of the Busento River have concealed the tomb of a great king and the spectacular treasure he plundered from the ancient world's most glorious city!"

"That King was Alaric the Visigoth. The city was Roma." he said dramatically, his accent becoming a little broader in his excitement. He paused for effect; his eyes swept the crowd. He caught sight of Dan at the back of the tent, acknowledging his presence with the slightest of nods.

"For eight hundred years Rome had sat, inviolate, inside its protective walls. For eight hundred years Rome had accumulated the spoils of its conquests. Its generals brought back some of the greatest treasures of antiquity to add to the wealth and glory of their city." He paused again, theatrically, as though lost in thought.

The Professor paused and then spoke in a quiet voice. "Imagine now that you are a Goth warrior, angry, desperate, and about to be given the opportunity to sack the most fabulously wealthy city in the entire world! How would you feel, standing there outside Rome's mighty Aurelian walls, the wealth of the world just beyond your grasp?"

2. Rome – 1st of Augustus 410 AD

"Alaric," said Ataulf, frowning, "we are all growing weary of this siege. Rome's walls have never been breached. Why are we here, wasting our lives away?"

Alaric smiled and put his hand on Ataulf's shoulder. "Brother don't think for a moment that I too have not grown weary of this waiting, but I swear to you we will not be waiting much longer. Do you see that line of young boys down there, heading towards the Flaminian Gate?" he said pointing towards the walls of Rome in the distance.

Ataulf squinted, his eyes shielded against the rising sun. "All I see is a line of a few hundred people walking towards the gate, but I cannot tell who they are."

"They," said Alaric, "are the keys to the gates of Rome."

Ataulf looked confused.

"I have handpicked three hundred of our most beautiful and most educated young boys. I am giving them as gifts to the most noble and influential Senators of the City."

Ataulf looked at him, aghast, horrified. He savagely pushed his older brother's hand off his shoulder. "You have given more of our sons to the Romans as slaves!" he shouted angrily. "Why would you do such a thing? It is bad enough that as warriors we die at the beck and call of Roman generals who care less for us than they do for their livestock!" He paused to catch his breath.

"We waste our lives here in this putrid swamp. Thousands of our kin are being worked to death in the holds of Roman galleys and the silver mines of Britannia and you send mere boys into that charnel house? Why would you betray your people like this?" he asked, incredulous.

By the time he had finished his tirade, his face was red, his beard flecked with spittle and his eyes were fixed angrily on Alaric's.

Alaric reached his hand up and grabbed his brother's shoulder. Ataulf shrugged it off again. "I would not willingly send our sons into such a life, Ataulf," he said quietly. "I have freed more of our kin from

Roman slavery than any man alive, but those boys down there are the means of Rome's destruction."

Ataulf looked puzzled.

"Do you remember the story of the Trojan horse, Ataulf?" asked Alaric.

His brother nodded. "Of course!" he said testily. "A trick by the mighty Greek warrior Odysseus[1] to get inside the gates of Troy." He looked towards the distant city shrouded in its perpetual misty haze. "The Romans would not fall for such an obvious trick, and I see no wooden horse."

Alaric grinned at his brother. "Remember it is said that Laocoön, the Trojan priest, rushed down to confront the crowd that were making ready to bring the mighty wooden horse into the city, warning them about Greek trickery? The Trojans took no notice, too vain, too over confident to recognise the deception. These Roman Senators," he said nodding towards Rome, "sitting safe inside their impenetrable walls, are like the people of Troy! Even if there was a Laocoön among them, they are too arrogant to believe that they could be tricked."

Ataulf looked at Alaric and then down at the small procession making its way towards the Flaminian Gate. He was clearly not convinced.

"I have told our young men to be the best servants, the most helpful and obedient that have ever appeared in Rome. These Romans are as over confident as the people of ancient Troy. I do not even need a wooden horse to get my warriors inside their city."

"I have sent our brothers Sigeric and Wallia, as my ambassadors, to talk to the Senate of Rome. They will tell the noble Senators how much I admire them for their courage and their dedication to their Emperor and that the Goth will trouble them no longer. They will explain that I am giving them this most precious gift as a reflection of the high esteem in which I hold them and in light of their courage in resisting my siege."

"The Romans may be suspicious at first, but we will give them a few weeks to learn to trust their new slaves. In the meantime, we will start to make preparations to lift our siege and march away."

1.   http://en.wikipedia.org/wiki/Odysseus

Ataulf still looked doubtful.

"You will see my brother," Alaric said with a broad grin, putting his hand once again on his brothers' shoulder and squeezing it firmly. "Eleven days after the Ides of Augustus you and I shall walk together into the great Forum of Rome." Alaric pulled his brother towards him and said with a grin, "Come brother. Stop worrying. Let's get something to eat and after that we can tell the men to begin preparations for our departure."

With his arm firmly around Ataulf's shoulders, Alaric led him off in the direction of the nearest cooking fire.

3. Calabria - Present day

Dan stood up and arched back, trying to relieve the nagging ache of a day spent scratching away at the heavy clay that made up the bed of the Busento River.

He slapped at his neck, more out of frustration than any belief that he might be able to kill one of the seemingly millions of mosquitoes that had plagued them since the dig had started three weeks ago. He flinched, immediately regretting his impulsive action, as a stab of pain reminded him just how tender his neck was. He cursed his fair skinned Scottish ancestors, under his breath, for his dependence on sunscreen. Growing up by the beach in Australia had made him careful of the sun, but still he managed to get sunburnt.

Thankfully most of the trench he was working in was now in shadow, but it was still hot, humid, dank and uncomfortable. He looked over his shoulder at the five others who had stuck with him.

Fifteen eager and enthusiastic volunteers had started work in this trench the day after the Professor had given his welcoming speech. A similar number had started work in each of ten other trenches, all neatly carved out of the diverted section of the river by an excavator. The heat, humidity, mosquitoes and, so far, unrewarding toil, had worn away at everyone's initial enthusiasm. Many had given up to pursue more pleasant pastimes.

Dan felt a hand on his shoulder. "Those two dubious looking characters are here again," said a lightly accented Irish voice from behind him. Dan, smiling, turned around and looked into the green eyes of a tall, dark haired woman who stood, trowel in hand, looking up at the far river bank.

Dan followed her gaze upwards to a low stone wall that ran along the edge of the road that followed the winding course of this part of the river.

It had been standing room only, up there, for the first few days. Television crews had jostled with the townsfolk of Cosenza and, seemingly, half the population of Calabria, as well as a good smattering of tourists and day-trippers. The number of spectators had dwindled faster than the volunteers in the trenches. Now only the diehards and the local layabouts seemed to be left.

"Ah, Elizabeth Garvey," replied Dan, smiling and shaking his head, "you have such a suspicious mind. Dark hair, a bad tailor and sunglasses doth not a mafia stooge make," he said, shading his eyes against the late afternoon sun.

He, like Elizabeth, had heard the whispers that, to be able to divert the river, the Professor had, along with getting permission from the Italian Government, the Mayor of the local comune and the city authorities, done a deal with the local mafia. As much as he treated it as a joke each time Liz mentioned it, he had begun to wonder if the rumours might not be as far-fetched as he'd at first thought.

While they were looking up at the road the two men nonchalantly moved off, back towards the other trenches, further up river.

Dan turned back to Elizabeth who arched a perfectly shaped eyebrow at him. "All right, they do look a bit suspicious and they don't seem to like being noticed, but they could be just run-of-the-mill scoundrels looking for an opportunity to thieve something from the dig. Just because we're in Italy doesn't mean they have to be Mafioso."

"Well, maybe not, but I still think we ought to keep an eye on them. Every time I look around, there they are, staring at us, watching everything we are doing. They give me the creeps." she said with an exaggerated shiver. Then, more business like, "Given the amount of money that you donated to this dig, I would hate any scandal to be associated with it."

"I trust the Professor. I am sure everything will be fine," he said, with a smile.

As they got back to work, Dan wondered whether he should have mentioned the possibility that, the more likely explanation for the two men's behaviour, was that she was a beautiful woman, dressed in very short shorts, with very long legs and a t-shirt, and they were two red blooded Italian men, but as usual, he decided against saying anything that might be misconstrued.

As he continued to scrape away at the reddish brown clay, he wondered about Elizabeth's concerns. He knew, from past experience helping to fund other archaeological digs, that there was always the risk that palms would be greased to allow access to sites or equipment. The charitable trust he had established to make donations to this type of project, relied on having a rock solid reputation Over the years they had spent in business together he had learnt to ignore Elizabeth's intuition at his peril, especially when it came to people.

He looked back over his shoulder and saw her hard at work on her patch of dirt. He smiled to himself. He had been thrilled when she'd agreed to join him for a few weeks of treasure hunting. He was just thinking how blessed he was to have her as a friend, as well as a business partner, when he felt the phone in his pocket vibrate just a moment before it chimed to let him know he had received a text message.

He drew the phone out of his pocket and read it. 'Up here!'

He looked up. All he could see was a clear blue sky just starting to darken as the sun sank towards the horizon.

The phone vibrated in his hand. He looked at the screen. Another message had arrived. This one said, 'No, over here Daddy.'

He looked up at the bank of the river. A madly waving arm and a flash of golden hair caught his attention. His face broke into a grin as he got stiffly to his feet. He walked to where Elizabeth was working and touched her lightly on the shoulder as he walked past. "Hey, buddy, look who's turned up!" he said, nodding towards the road.

Elizabeth looked up and grinned. "Well, this is a surprise!" she said, smiling happily and offering him her hand. He helped her to her feet.

Dan raised an eyebrow at her. He looked into her eyes, but all he saw was delighted innocence. He had harboured, for some time, growing suspicions that he was often the last one to know what was going on when it came to Charlotte and Elizabeth. It was highly likely that he was the only one who was surprised that Charlotte had turned up today.

He reached the top of the bank and took in the vision of his daughter. She looked relaxed and casual, in jeans and a long sleeved, striped t-shirt, as she strode across to him, arms outstretched. They hugged. He looked at her, suddenly becoming fatherly. "Is everything okay? I thought you were finishing the last chapter of your thesis this month."

Before Charlotte could answer his attention was caught by a crowd gathering around something at the edge of the road, a short distance away.

The crowd parted momentarily, to reveal a flash of glossy green paintwork.

Charlotte laughed as he drew away from her to look at the car parked by the curb. "Liz arranged for me to pick her up on the way here. She's beautiful, Dad. Marco and the boys did an amazing job on her. I still can't believe it the same car as that tangled mess of metal you bought. She drives like an absolute dream."

Dan stood back and looked at his daughter then across at Elizabeth who was standing a few meters away, smiling. The 'she' in question was a 1991 Aston Martin DB4, Sanction 2. This extraordinary car was one of only four replicas sanctioned by the Aston Martin Company, of their famous early sixties, Zagato bodied, DB4. It was almost impossible to tell the four, so called 'replicas' from the original versions, built as they were on the original 1960's chassis and bodied by Zagato in Milan.

Dan had always loved this type of car and the tradition of independent designers like Pininfarina, Zagato, Ghia, Karmann, Scaglietti and Bertone, that created them.

Dan and Charlotte had bought the car at an auction. It had been in an horrific accident and was damaged almost beyond repair. Badly crumpled and with many parts missing, he had managed to pick up the sorry hulk reasonably cheaply, but he had spared no expense on the restoration. The last time he had been in Milan he had called in to see progress. At that stage, the car had still been in pieces, the chassis laid bare and the body panels, undercoated in matt grey, scattered around the workshop.

Now, in the late afternoon sun, the car glowed.

The small crowd of spectators, mostly men, were having trouble deciding in which direction they should look, the car's or Charlotte's.

With mock seriousness, Charlotte, held the car keys out in front of her. "Dr Marsh, I have great pleasure in returning your Aston Martin to you." Dan grinned, grabbed the keys and started towards the car. Before he reached it, he stopped and turned around, looking for Elizabeth in the crowd. She was a little way off still smiling at him. She waved him on, indicating that she would follow them in their hire car.

Dan hesitated for a moment then opened the passenger door for Charlotte who folded her six foot one frame into the passenger seat. As he did so, out of the corner of his eye, he caught sight of the two men that had been watching them all week. They were still watching.

Dan walked around the car, dusted himself off, opened the driver's side door and climbed in. It closed with a solid, satisfying thunk. He sat for a moment with his hands resting on the beautifully finished wooden steering wheel and breathed in the smell of new leather and the faint floral scent of Charlotte's perfume. With a grin he started the engine.

Ten minutes later, with Elizabeth trailing them in their little, red Fiat Punto hire car, they turned onto the road that would take them to San Lucido, on the coast, where they had rented an apartment. It was a forty minute drive along a road with many bends and very little traffic. Dan, still grinning from ear to ear glanced at his daughter beside him and put his foot down. The Aston Martin, let out a roar as the triple carburettors fed fuel into the engine and they were both pressed back into their seats as the nose of the car rose up and the car leapt eagerly down the road.

4. Calabria - Present day

Charlotte watched her father's face as he concentrated on driving. He looked happy. She often worried that he worked too hard. His short, curly, brown hair had started to turn grey. It made him, she decided, look more distinguished. As she watched she noticed, just for a moment, his expression change. She knew what he was thinking.

She reached over and lightly touched his arm. "Mum would have loved this, wouldn't she?" she said in a quiet voice.

Dan took one hand off the wheel and put it over hers. He glanced across at her and, with a tight smile, tears welling up in his eyes, he nodded.

"Your mum would have really loved this." he said tightly, looking away and concentrating on his driving. "She loved Italy, beautiful cars, windy roads and..."

Charlotte squeezed his arm and bit her lip. She couldn't remember her mother, but she knew that talking about her had always been very hard for her father. She also knew that he thought about her often, usually at times like this, when they were enjoying themselves the most.

It had taken a long time for Charlotte to piece together the story of how her mother had died. In the end she had found a newspaper report on how Sarah Marsh had been killed in a car accident. Charlotte had been less than a year old. It had described how Sarah and Dan, both scientists were doing research into genome sequencing and had just started a new business. What the article did not say was that when the police came to tell Dan the tragic news they had not known that Charlotte should have been with her mother. They had no idea where the baby was.

For half a day, Dan frantically searched for his baby daughter. It was late in the evening when he discovered that Sarah had left Charlotte with a friend while she'd taken a break from her demanding baby daughter and gone to the supermarket alone.

Dan turned to her and smiled apologetically. "Sorry honey, I guess I got overwhelmed by the moment."

Charlotte relaxed back into her seat and listened to the sound of the four litre, straight six growling, spitting and grumbling as Dan negotiated the steep and winding road. She looked out the back window to see if she could see Elizabeth in the red Fiat. There was no sign of her.

"How long have you know Liz, Dad?" she asked.

Dan glanced across at her, then looked back at the road, slowing down slightly.

"I don't know, fifteen or so years, something like that. Why do you ask?"

"Just wondering." she said, shrugging her shoulders and looking out the window. "Did you know her before you started working together?"

"No. In fact she was introduced to me out of the blue by one of those executive head hunting firms. It was a bit strange. I'd got into a bit of a mess with the business and suddenly there she was. If she hadn't turned up when she did I know the company wouldn't be where it is today."

"Why, what sort of mess were you in, and how come I didn't know anything about it?"

Dan frowned. "After the accident I made a conscious decision that you would always be my first priority."

"You probably don't remember, but when you were very small I worked from home. By the time you started school the business had grown and we had offices over at the Uni."

"I remember those." said Charlotte.

"Around that time I was approached by a colleague, a guy called Barry Critchley, who wanted to invest in the firm. He was a really persistent, pushy sort of guy, but with you to think about, eventually I gave in and let Barry buy a forty-nine percent stake in the firm."

"Everything was okay for the first couple of years. The business grew, but Barry started to make moves to take over the company. He tried to stir up resentment among the staff, saying that I was away from the office too much being a single dad and that it wasn't fair on the company. You can guess the kind of crap he spread around."

"What a jerk. He sounds like a real pig. What happened?"

Dan laughed. "The first I knew about it was a group of my employees marched into my office and demanded that I get rid of Barry or they would all walk out the door. The only thing I could do was buy him out. I mortgaged our home, sold the car and borrowed as much as I could."

"I remember when you sold the car. You said it was because cars weren't good for the planet and we had to ride our bikes everywhere. We went vegetarian at the same time, I seem to remember."

"I was that far from going under, financially" said Dan showing her a barely perceptible gap between his thumb and forefinger.

"And that's when Liz turned up?"

"Yup. She was the saviour I didn't know I needed. I wasn't looking to employ anyone, but somehow, despite the fact that she wasn't looking for a job and was a serious contender for the chair of Genetics at her own University, they persuaded her to have a talk to me. We just clicked. The rest is history. She freed me up to complete the designs for the first versions of the ultra rapid gene sequencing machine and with her technical brilliance and managerial savvy the business just took off. We listed on the stock exchange six years later and suddenly I could afford to buy a new car."

Charlotte looked at her father for a long time. She was amazed that she had not realised that any of this had been going on. All she remembered was that her Dad had been there for her nearly every day when she arrived home from school. He had attended every dance recital, every sports day and had helped her blow out the candles on every birthday cake.

"I do remember that Liz used to be out our place a lot for meals. I thought you two were dating, until her husband turned up."

Dan laughed. "Yeah, she was only newly married when she joined the company. Andrew spent half of every year down in Antarctica. He once told me how grateful he was that you and I kept Liz company while he was away."

"I liked Andrew. He was a nice man. How come they got divorced?"

Dan shrugged his shoulders and concentrated on driving. Charlotte watched the sun as it slowly sank into the Mediterranean.

"Im sorry dad." she said suddenly.

Dan looked at her blankly. "What for, kiddo?"

"All the times I was a selfish brat, like the time I ran away just because you tried to make me wear a dress to that birthday party. You must have been frantic with worry."

"Ummm," intoned Dan, frowning. "Having a daughter was hard enough, having a tomboy was just plain confusing. Thank god you had Liz to ask all those womanly questions."

"And fashion advice, Dad, don't forget fashion advice."

Dan rolled his eyes.

They drove on in companionable silence, each lost in their own thoughts. Charlotte eventually broke the silence. "So how is the dig going? Any sign of Alaric yet?"

Dan shook his head. "I'm beginning to worry that the whole story is just a myth."

5. Rome - 24th of Augustus 410 AD

Alaric rested on his haunches, his back against the cold, rough stone of one of the rounded towers of the Salarian Gate, his eyes closed. The night was cold and a thin layer of cloud obscured the moon.

Despite the number and closeness of the men he knew were around him, it was quiet. It was so quiet that he was sure he could hear his own heart thumping in his chest.

He felt a body move against his. "Worried, Alaric?" whispered Ataulf, leaning close to him. "You afraid that you will not be strong enough to carry off your share of the gold?" he chuckled.

"It is not gold that I am seeking in Rome, Ataulf," replied Alaric. "There are more important things in this world than gold."

"I can't imagine what could be more important than a big, fat, pile of Roman solidi!" Ataulf scoffed. "Do you think we are here just because we love to fight? We are here because we have no choice. Pillage and plunder are our only reward for our bitter and brutal lives. This is our chance to walk away with something more than a battered body and a bag of badly silvered coins."

Alaric looked away. Of course Atlauf was right, he thought bitterly. Without land to tend what choice did any of us have but to become mercenaries, dying for people we despise in battles that don't concern us.

"Just as long as the men heed my commands, Atlauf. Unresisting citizens are to be spared and the churches of the apostles must be respected and treated as inviolable sanctuaries."

"Oh, they know what to do," said Atlauf grimly. "Create as much panic as possible, grab what you want and kill anyone who gets in your way. We have all been through sieges before, Alaric."

Alaric grunted. Despite his edicts, he knew that his men would take their frustrations out on the citizenry of Rome. If the Roman defenders could be over powered and the gates opened, many innocents would die, and many who were innocent tonight would not be innocent by morning. He knew that rape and plunder were foremost in the minds of every Goth warrior and nothing he could do or command would stop the despoiling of Rome.

He was about to say something when he thought he heard a muffled noise from beyond the gate. He put a quieting hand on Atlauf's arm. He stood up, wincing at the pain in his knees, and moved quietly towards the heavy wooden gate. His hand rested on the hilt of the heavy iron sword that hung by his side.

He paused, listening, well aware that, if the gate opened, it could be a heavily armed Roman that burst through. He stepped closer to the gate. He could now clearly hear sounds of movement on the other side. He quietly drew his sword, holding it before him, his legs slightly bent, and faced the small postern gate.

He felt a light pressure on his shoulder. Ataulf now stood at his back. Behind him a line of men pressed against the wall, some with swords drawn, some holding short spears. Many of them held oval shaped shields at their sides, or raised, ready to protect their chests.

Silence again descended. No more sounds came from behind the gate. Alaric was beginning to worry that the young men he had sent into the city had been overcome when he heard the scraping sound of large metal bolts being slowly drawn back. Whoever was on the other side was still being careful not to make too much noise. The small gate swung slowly open.

Alaric tightened his grip on his sword and braced himself for the charge. He felt, rather than saw, Ataulf step closer to him, ready to protect his flank.

The point of a short Roman gladius appeared through the gate. It flashed silver as the moonlight glanced off its polished metal surface. Fresh blood was smeared along its blade. Alaric lifted his sword, ready to strike. His hand was suddenly stayed. Ataulf pushed down on Alaric's sword arm and stepped forward. He had recognised the young man who had opened the gate as one of their own. Handsome, clean shaven and dressed in a Roman style tunic, his legs bare, the young Visigoth warrior stepped through the opening out into the dim moonlight.

He nodded at Ataulf and bowed his head as he recognised Alaric. "We have overpowered the guards, my Lord." he said quietly. "The way is clear to enter the city."

Alaric embraced the young man, thanked him and then stood back looking at the open portal. With a nod of his head to Ataulf, he stepped through the postern gate. Other young boys stood waiting inside. He greeted them warmly as he made his way quietly through the short passage that led into the Horti Sallustiani, the gardens that surrounded the Salarian Gate, and which took up much of this area of Rome.

Except for the boys, the Horti Sallustiani was virtually uninhabited, and at this time of night, it was the perfect place to enter the city.

Inside the gates, Alaric, Ataulf and a small group of men secured the area. Others quietly opened the large Salarian gates to let the rest of the Visigoth army into the City.

Quickly and quietly, Alaric and Ataulf, along with their other commanders, gathered the men together into raiding parties.

"It is a good thing so many of us have spent time here, Alaric," said Ataulf, between giving orders to his commanders, "It makes organising raiding parties very easy."

Alaric nodded and then turned to watch as, with torches lit and swords drawn, over ten thousand Visigoth warriors prepared themselves for the rape of Rome.

Alaric raised his arm and barked a command. Suddenly, hundreds of gothic trumpets blasted out a sound that shattered the silence of the Roman night. The men all around him raised their voices, shouting and whooping as they plunged into the city streets. From where he stood Alaric could see the orange flash of burning brands being flung onto roofs and through windows.

Women screamed, weapons clashed and the grunts and groans of men fighting and dying, began to fill the air. Panic flowed through the streets of Rome like a river in flood.

Alaric turned away and walked to where his own men waited patiently for him.

His target was the Roman Forum and the Basilica of Maxentius and Constantine. This would be the meeting and mustering point for his army once they had control of the city. It was to there that his men would bring the treasures of Rome. It was from there that he would begin his search for the blood of the Emperor.

6. Calabria - Present day

Dan settled into one of the comfortable wicker chairs on the verandah and put the three cold beers he had been carrying down on the table beside him, when Charlotte followed him through the door. She was carrying a small package wrapped in brown paper and was turning it over and over, a frown on her face.

"This was in the car when I picked it up." She handed him a parcel. "It was just sitting on the driver's seat. Nobody at the shop knew anything about it. It has your name on it, but no stamp or delivery docket. What do you think it is?" she asked, sitting on the edge of his chair.

"No idea. Let's have a look?" he said, frowning as he started to unwrap the outer covering. Under the first layer of paper, they discovered another layer of wrapping and a piece of notepaper. The second layer was made up of an extraordinary amount of tape. He unfolded the note.

Charlotte tried to read the handwritten page over her father's shoulder.

Absorbed in the note, neither of them noticed Elizabeth when she came out on to the verandah drying her hair with a towel. "Watcha got there?" She threw the towel over the verandah rail and flopped down into a chair on the opposite side of the table.

"A mysterious package that Charlie just delivered," said Dan, holding up the package for Elizabeth to see.

"Who's it from?" she asked.

"Well, it appears to be from some guy called Victor Kachenko," said Charlotte, reading the name from the bottom of the note.

"Victor's dead!" said Elizabeth, sitting up quickly. "We went to his funeral last year!"

"Umm," said Dan frowning, "I'll read you the letter - it is dated January last year - which would be what, a couple of months before he died?" He looked across at Elizabeth, who nodded.

"Hang on. Who's Viktor Kachenko?" asked Charlotte, before Dan could start reading the letter out loud.

"He was a sort of friend of your fathers!" said Elizabeth looking across to Dan. He nodded, so she continued. "Viktor was a huge grizzly bear of a man. He was the sort of larger than life character that, once met, you could never forget. I think he was Ukrainian, certainly from the old Soviet Union, anyway. About seven or eight years ago he tried to buy your dad's business. We had a few meetings with him in the early days, but when your dad had him checked out he found that his background was a bit shady."

"His father, a guy called Alexander Kachenko, had been some sort of big wig in Soviet Intelligence in Stalinist Russia. The rumour was that Victor had followed in his father's footsteps and was ex-KGB. He made his money initially, through trading old Soviet era secrets to the west and then as a black market arms dealer. As a sideline, he had somehow managed to snag himself a couple of privatised businesses on the cheap - mainly research-based businesses, when the Soviet Union imploded. As I remember it he had some pretty hefty government defence contracts."

"Was he really crooked?" asked Charlotte.

"We didn't know for sure, well, not until we had an unexpected visit from a couple of gentlemen spies," said Dan, with a chuckle.

"Seriously?" Charlotte was incredulous.

Dan nodded. "You realise that I will have to kill you if I tell this, but one of the blokes was from our own Australian secret service, ASIS and one was from the Brits' MI6. By the time all this was happening we had expanded the business into the UK and were doing work for their Ministry of Defence. It was pretty sensitive stuff. The spooks intimated that if we sold even part of the business to Kachenko then the Government work would dry up.

"When I did turn down Kachenko's offer he asked me why. I told him straight. He was a seriously scary looking man, especially when he didn't get what he wanted. Like Liz said, he was very big and bearlike. He always had a couple of his "associates" with him. They made Sylvester Stalone look like a bantamweight boxer. They never said much. I'm not sure if they could even speak English. After I had told him my reasons he sat scowling at me for quite a few minutes. We were in the boardroom in Sydney and it was only me and Liz. I was starting to get a bit nervous, then, all of a sudden, he breaks into this huge smile and, in his big gruff voice says, 'Dan, I like you! You are honest man! You are straight! I like straight! We will be friends!'" Dan spoke in his best imitation of a gruff Eastern European accent, but he sounded more like Boris Badenov.

"We shook hands and they left. Every year or so he would turn up in Sydney and we would go out and have a meal. I would talk about what was happening in the world of science. He would feed me interesting bits of gossip about what was happening in Russia. He had some great stories about Putin. He really hated that man for some reason. He never mentioned wanting to buy our business again, but he would always say, when he left, that if ever I needed anything, or if anybody ever gave me trouble, that I should tell him, because that was what friends were for."

"Did you ever ask him for help?" ask Charlotte.

"Christ no!" said Dan vehemently. "I was nervous enough about going out for dinner with him. God knows what would have happened if I had told him about somebody that was giving me trouble. This was real horse-head in the bed stuff!"

"How did he die?" asked Charlotte.

"Well, just like the man himself, it was all a bit mysterious. A bit sinister. The story in the newspapers was that he just got ill and died suddenly. An unexplained illness, they said. The rumour was that the Russian FSS had got him the same way they had supposedly assassinated Alexander Litvinenko, poisoning him with polonium-210[1]."

"And you went to his funeral?" Charlotte asked, genuinely shocked.

"Well his funeral was in Saint Petersburg and we had just been in Oxford, visiting you. It seemed the right thing to do. We weren't the only ones there. Two ex British Prime Ministers were there. Even Putin was there. It was big funeral. He was an extremely well connected, very well known and powerful man. He had a lot of dealings at senior business and government levels throughout Europe."

"Has anyone investigated his death to see if he really was murdered?" asked Charlotte.

"Not as far as I know. He didn't have a family, so there is probably no-one who had a personal interest in finding out what really happened,"

1.   http://en.wikipedia.org/wiki/Polonium

24

said Dan, thoughtfully. "If the FSS was behind it then they certainly wouldn't want it investigated."

"So, enough chit-chat," said Elizabeth, sitting forward and putting the package down in front of Dan. "What does the letter say?"

"Okay," said Dan, adjusting a pair of reading glasses, "He says...

'Dear Dan, I have known of you for many years and I consider you as friend. You have always been straight with me and I treat you as man of honour.

I know that you are a man of science who also has a love of the history so I have chosen for you to receive my greatest treasure. I have sent you something of great value. Guard it with your life.

Perhaps you can unlock its secrets with the resources that you have available.

I will give you its history when I see you next in exchange for what you can find.

I know you like a challenge.

I will see you soon, my friend.

"and then he signs off "Viktor".

"Well, let's open it then," said Elizabeth, now leaning forward, arms on the table, eager to see what the small package contained.

"I'm not sure that I can," said Dan, picking up the package and struggling to find a way through the packing tape that bound it.

"Hang on." said Charlotte, jumping up and heading for the kitchen. She returned with a large bread knife.

Dan cut into the packing and exposed the cardboard box underneath. He tentatively opened the lid. He looked inside and carefully drew out a box that sat nested in a cocoon of white foam packaging pellets.

The box, made of a light coloured wood, had a simple metal clasp and looked careworn and scuffed. He opened it carefully. Inside was yet another box, although the difference between the outer and inner boxes could not have been more marked.

The box, that sat nestled in satin padding, was a stunning piece of craftsmanship. It was made of a lustrous, semi-translucent dark green material, held together at the edges by a strip of ornate, chased gold work. The clasp, with a red jewel set in either end of it, also looked like gold.

Dan lifted the box out of its satin enclosure and placed it on the table. They all leaned in to look at it.

"Is that jade?" asked Elizabeth. Dan and Charlotte shrugged their shoulders.

"That looks like gold around the edges," said Charlotte excitedly.

"And they look like cabochon rubies," said Elizabeth leaning forward to get a better look at the two gemstones in the clasp.

"Do you think this is the treasure - or is there something inside the pretty box?" asked Charlotte, looking first at one Elizabeth and then at Dan.

"Open it up. Let's see," said Elizabeth.

Carefully, Dan moved the clasp and then equally carefully, lifted the hinged lid.

Inside, nested in a cocoon of velvet, was a small opaque glass vial with a long neck and a bulbous base. Red wax covered the neck and top.

"Good God!" said Charlotte, "It's a Roman tear vial."

"A what?" asked Elizabeth.

"You know, a lachrymatory, a tear bottle." Elizabeth looked blankly at Charlotte. "Supposedly, mourners at Roman funerals filled them with their tears and then put them in with their loved ones when they were entombed. They were supposed to have a special seal on the top that allowed the tears to evaporate. When the tears dried up it signified the end of the mourning period. That's the story, although the truth is more likely to be that they were jars for make-up, perfumes and ointments, but a tear vial is a great romantic notion," said Charlotte.

"It's not what I would call a great treasure, though. They are not particularly rare. Even the older ones from Republican Roman times, are reasonably common," she added, thoughtfully.

"I think that the pretty little box might be a different story," said Elizabeth. She had picked up the wooden box that had been ignored once it had been relieved of its more glamorous contents. "If this is the original box that it came in," she said nodding towards the green jade box, "then I think this symbol in the lid means that it was probably made by Carl Fabergé. That little green box could be worth an absolute fortune!"

"I'll get my iPad," said Charlotte, heading back into the apartment.

When she returned she and Elizabeth sat together, poring over the iPad screen.

"Yup, I was right. Look at this, Dan," said Elizabeth, holding up the tablet, to let Dan see an image of the same symbol as the one inside their box. "It's Fabergé all right – unless, of course, it is a forgery. It says here that Fabergé is one of the most forged designers in the world."

Charlotte gave a low whistle. "There was a Fabergé box, a bit like that one, for sale last year. It was made of jade and diamonds and went for close to $250,000."

While the women focused their investigations on the box, Dan had been looking more closely at the small glass vial. He held it up to the light and shook it gently. He then inspected the vial in detail, completing his inspection with the red wax seal that covered the stoppered end.

"So," he said, placing the vial carefully back in its box. "We get a package from a sinister, ex- Soviet, businessman who died under mysterious circumstances, which contains what could be either a fake Fabergé, or a very valuable real Fabergé, jade and gold box. Inside the box is what we think is an ancient Roman tear vial, which is not very valuable and which should be empty, because it was designed to allow the contents to evaporate."

"Don't tell me there is something in the vial?" said Charlotte, reaching for it and holding it up to the light. "It's half full!" she exclaimed.

"If you really want a surprise, have a look at the wax seal on top," said her father, with a slight grin on his face.

Charlotte flipped the vial around to look at the seal. Her expression changed completely. "You're fucking kidding!" she said in an uncharacteristic outburst of swearing.

She passed the tear vial to Elizabeth. She put on her reading glasses and stared at the design that had been pressed into the wax seal.

After a moment's study, she looked up at Dan with the same look of incredulity on her face that Charlotte had. "My God!" she said. "Is that what I think it is?"

Dan nodded. Elizabeth sat, stunned, staring at the stylized image of an eagle, wings outstretched, perched on a laurel wreath. Inside the laurel wreath was a swastika.

7. Calabria - Present day

Dan felt a little bleary eyed as he offered Elizabeth his hand to get down into the trench where they had been digging the previous afternoon.

They had stayed up late into the night discussing the package and its contents.

"So," said Elizabeth as her feet touched the river bed, "what do you think of Victor's gift this morning, in the cold hard light of dawn?"

Dan shook his head. "It's just weird. I still reckon it's some bizarre Russian practical joke that Viktor thought up. But you're right, there is no harm in verifying the authenticity of the box and the vial and getting whatever that stuff is in the vial analysed."

"If Charlie can get that mate of hers at Southeby's to have a look at some photos of the box and the vial, when she goes back to Uni, then that would be a good start." he conceded.

"I think your idea to keep the image on the seal of the vial to ourselves, at least for the moment, is a good one, Dan. I felt a definite chill run up my spine when I saw that."

"I'll take a sample of the stuff in the vial when we get back tonight." said Elizabeth. "Do you think Charlie could drop it off at our Cambridge lab to have it analysed?"

"I am sure she would be more than happy to. I emailed the Sydney office to send me a copy of the last correspondence we had with Viktor." said Dan as he picked up the tools they would be using from a utility box on the edge of the trench. "We can see if the handwriting is the same. At least then we'll know whether it really came from Viktor or not."

Dan handed Elizabeth her tools and they both headed for their allocated dig sites.

****

As Dan got to work he thought about how their moods had changed as their discussion the previous evening had progressed. At the beginning, they had all been excited by the mystery. He had been surprised that, by

29

the end of their deliberations, he had been the one who expressed the need for caution, "...on the off chance that it turns out to be something dangerous."

Perhaps he had gone a bit too far, insisting that they hide the box, and its contents, in the hollowed out centre of a loaf of bread. Charlotte and Elizabeth had made disparaging comments about his sanity as they watched him dig out the soft centre of the loaf, but, despite the scorn they heaped on him, they had both, reluctantly, agreed to help him eat the evidence of his subterfuge before they went to bed.

****

The day was starting to heat up. Dan had been methodically scraping away at the hard clay for a number of hours. He was starting to think about suggesting to Elizabeth that they break for lunch, when the sound and feel of his trowel scraping the ground suddenly changed. He looked down at the path of his blade and saw a narrow band of smooth, yellowish white that his last pass had uncovered. Any thought of stopping for lunch disappeared as he became totally engrossed in the excavation of the artefact he had discovered.

Very carefully, he brushed away the loose debris around the object. He used the point of his trowel to tease away more of the clay that was tightly packed around either side of the object. Gradually, he began to reveal its shape. It soon became obvious that it was a bone of some sort. He called to Elizabeth who came over and knelt beside him. Together they worked at exposing more of the bone. It was long. "Perhaps," Dan whispered excitedly, "it's a human leg bone."

Having uncovered enough of the object to be sure that it was potentially significant, but loath to disturb any more of their find before the experts had looked at it, they agreed to stop working while Dan went to track down Professor Pellegrini.

He found the Professor, on his knees, happily scraping away at his own patch of clay, surrounded by a group of his students. They were all chatting away loudly in Italian and Dan had to shout to get the Professor's attention. As soon as he heard that Dan had something to show him, the Professor was on his feet. He climbed nimbly up the ladder that led out of his trench and followed Dan back to trench eight. An excited gaggle of students trailed behind him.

As they reached the edge of the trench and looked down to where Elizabeth was still brushing dirt away from the bone, the students fell silent.

The Professor scrambled down into the trench and was soon working alongside Elizabeth, brush in hand, examining the find. He suddenly grabbed a trowel and began digging a few inches beyond where the bone lay exposed. Minutes later he gave a shout. He had uncovered another section of bone. This one led off at an acute angle to the one Dan had found.

The Professor looked up to where Dan and the students were perched on the edge of the trench. "It is the bone of a person. This is a magnificent find!" he said excitedly.

"Do any of you remember your Jordanes?" he asked, looking along the line of students. No one was bold enough to answer. The Professor grinned, good-naturedly shook his head in mock despair, then said in a quiet, reverential voice,

"They led a band of captives into the midst of its bed to dig out a place for his grave. In the depths of this pit, they buried Alaric together with many treasures, and then turned the waters back into their channel. And that none might ever know the place, they put to death all the diggers!"

"So Jordanes says in 'De origine actibusque Getarum.' Perhaps this is the skeleton of one of the diggers that was put to death," he said, running his hand gently along the exposed bone.

The unearthing of the skeleton changed the priorities at the dig site. Dan and Elizabeth's trench became the centre of attention with the other trenches temporarily abandoned. Trench eight was now full of people on their knees scraping at the hard dry clay.

By the end of the day fifteen more skeletons had been uncovered. All of them sufficiently complete to be easily recognisable as humans. One, much to the Professor's delight, showed score marks on the neck vertebrae, the unmistakable sign that the person's throat had been cut with a sharp blade.

At dusk, exhausted, happy and excited, Elizabeth and Dan headed back to San Lucido, keen to share the news of their discoveries with Charlotte over dinner.

8. Calabria - Present day

Dan drove off the Lungomare, the road that ran along the sea front at San Lucido, into the driveway of their apartment. Charlotte was sitting on the front steps, waiting for them. It was obvious that something was wrong.

"What's happened?" said Dan as soon as he stepped out of the car.

Charlotte stood up and put her arms around his neck. "I've just had a call from Marco Traverni, at the restoration shop. There has been a fire! The whole place has gone up!"

"Oh no! Are Marco, Maria and the boys okay?" asked Elizabeth.

"Yes. He says that the boys are both fine. Paolo has a few singe marks because he tried to get that Bugatti chassis that was at the back of the shop out into the yard, but it all happened so quickly. They didn't have time to save anything. He said to tell you he was sorry but he couldn't save the Jag."

"Just as long as Marco and the boys are okay," said Dan. "When did it happen? How did it happen?"

"He said it started last night after they had all gone to bed. Marco was woken by the sound of an explosion. Probably the compressor blowing up. He said that he ran across the yard from the house, but by the time he reached the workshop the fire had taken hold."

Dan shook his head. Becoming one of Marco Traverni's clients was like being welcomed into his family. Marco and the boys had always been incredibly welcoming to Dan, Charlotte and Elizabeth. They would flirt outrageously with Elizabeth and Charlotte every time they saw them, at least until Marco's wife, Maria, appeared. Dan had lost count of the number of times the two boys had proposed to Charlotte during their visits to see the progress of restoration on one or other of Dan's expanding car collection.

Dan pulled out his mobile phone and tapped on Marco's name. Elizabeth and Charlotte could heard him answer, "Pronto!"

"Marco" said Dan, "its Dan Marsh. Charlotte just told me what happened. Are you okay?"

"Sì, Signor Dan. We are okay. The shop, she is gone, and your beautiful Jaguar, she too is gone. I am so sorry."

"Never mind, Marco, I will find you something even more special for you to work on, maybe something more Italian eh?"

"Ah, you tease me Senior Dan. I am just glad that Charlotta picked up the Aston Martin yesterday, otherwise the tragedy would have been too much to bear."

"She is beautiful, Marco. You and the boys did an amazing job on her. I should have called you last night to tell you. Do you have any idea what caused the fire?"

"The police have been here all afternoon. They suspect that the fire might have been deliberately lit. They have been asking me if I know anyone who might want to hurt me. I have told them that I get on well with everyone. No one would want to hurt me, Maria, or the boys. I think that it must have been some kids being stupid."

"We will put everything back to rights in a few months, Signor Dan. The boys can go and have a holiday for once and Maria and I can have some quiet time at home while I design a new workshop."

"I will give you a call when we are back in business, Signor Dan. Look after those beautiful girls of yours. Ciao!"

"Ciao Marco."

Dan slipped the phone back into his pocket "You heard?" he asked.

Charlotte and Elizabeth both nodded. Nobody said it, but they were all wondering the same thing as they walked up the steps to the door of the apartment. Did this have anything to do with the package?

****

They decided against going into San Lucido for dinner. Charlotte made a salad and cooked Dan's favourite, puttanesca pasta, while Elizabeth used a syringe with a fine needle to transfer a small amount of the liquid from the vial to a sample bottle.

After dinner Dan got out his laptop. After ten minutes of quietly tapping away on the keyboard, he looked up. "Charlie, I've got you on an early morning direct flight to London from Lamezia Terme Airport."

Before Charlotte could respond he turned to Elizabeth. "Liz, I've booked you on the same flight. I think one of us should go and find out what we have got ourselves involved in as soon as possible. I've emailed Thomas Malm at MI6 to tell him we want to have a chat."

"MI6?" exclaimed Charlotte.

"It's part of the agreement we have with the British Government. We are obliged to tell them about anything that might be a potential security risk. Thomas is our contact point at MI6," said Dan, somewhat dismissively before turning back to Elizabeth. "I told him you will be arriving in London tomorrow morning. I gave him your mobile number. I hope that is okay?" He didn't wait for her response, but went on. "I'll drive you both down to the airport in the morning. The flight leaves at 6.00am so we will need to leave here about 4.30, I'm afraid," said Dan looking suitably apologetic. "I'll drive the Aston up to Rome and meet you in London the day after tomorrow."

Liz made a sound as if she was about to say something. Dan looked at her. Her eyes flashed angrily. She took a deep breath and then looked away.

Dan knew that he had crossed a line. He watched Liz's back as she walked to her bedroom.

"You realise that she is pissed off with you, don't you?" said Charlotte, in a tone that made it clear that she was also not happy.

Dan nodded solemnly. He knew exactly why they were both upset with him, paternalistic prick was an expression that Elizabeth had once used, early in their friendship, when he had crossed a similar line, but he was scared and he wanted them both out of harms way as soon as possible.

9. Calabria - Present day

They left in the dark. There were few cars about as they drove towards Lamezia Terme The Punto was cramped with three tall people and their carry-on luggage but no-one was in the mood to complain. No one was in the mood to talk. The mood was sombre.

Dan waited for them to get on the plane, and then waited another twenty minutes to watch the plane take off.

He did not know if he was being paranoid, but the mysterious appearance of the package from Kachenko and the destruction of Marco Traverni's workshop had really unsettled him.

Watching the plane taxi down the runway he thought about the time, a few years before, when he had been struggling to single handedly bring up his somewhat rebellious teenage girl while running a business with offices all around the world. MI6 had approached him with a plot they had uncovered to abduct Charlotte and hold her for ransom. He had not believed them at first. When Thomas Malm had shown him the evidence he had been totally thrown. He had thought that kidnap plots were just fodder for movies and crime novels.

He had taken Thomas' advice and arranged some training with Charlotte and Elizabeth to help mitigate any future risk, but it had left him with a different, more wary perspective on life.

As the plane lifted into the air he turned away from the big viewing window, feeling more relaxed, satisfied that the two most important people in his life were safely out of harm's way.

He walked to the Avis counter and exchanged the Fiat for a small Renault and arranged to have the Renault picked up from the apartment in San Lucido. He did not know whether they had been followed to the Airport, but if they had, there was a good chance that the simple expedience of changing cars would make it difficult for anyone to continue to follow him.

****

Buckling into her seat next to the window, Charlotte looked across at Elizabeth, who was settling into the seat beside her. She smiled to herself, remembering the first day they had met. She had been waiting for her father to come home to take her to a friend's house. He was late and she had been getting seriously cross. As her father's car pull up in their driveway she had raced out, all prepared to give him a serve of her righteous indignation, when, instead of her dad, this tall, gorgeous, impeccably groomed woman, stepped out of his car.

Charlotte cringed slightly as she remembered her reaction. Her immediate thoughts hadn't been about her father, and what might have happened to him, but self-consciously about how dowdy and boyish she looked in her scruffy jeans and the t-shirt that most annoyed her father, emblazoned with the slogan 'And your point is...?'

Then Liz had smiled her radiant smile and introduced herself with her beautifully, soft, lilting Irish accent. From that moment on they had been mates. When Dan finally got home he found them both cuddled up on the couch chatting happily. For Charlotte it had been like suddenly being given a big sister and, sometimes she thought guiltily, a mum.

Charlotte gently hugged Elizabeth's arm and lay her head on her shoulder. She wondered, sleepily, whether Elizabeth realised how important a part she had played in their family.

****

Elizabeth smiled and kissed the top of Charlotte's head. It amazed her how protective she felt towards this girl. With no children of her own she occasionally wondered if she would have felt any different towards Charlotte if she was her mother. Then again, she thought to herself, she could still remember times, especially when Charlotte was in her early teens, when being able to walk away from her and Dan had felt so unbelievably good.

"You know that your Dad is really worried don't you?" she said quietly to the top of Charlotte's head. She felt her nod in agreement.

"It is like when we got those kidnap threats a few years ago," said Charlotte. "We had to sit through those interminable sessions on what to do if we were kidnapped. Do you remember Schwarzenegger?"

Elizabeth laughed. "His name was Aaron Schwartz. He was just trying to do his job, poor fellow. You spent the entire time baiting and provoking him. You could be such a horrible brat as a teenager! I felt so sorry for him by the time you had chewed him up and spat him out."

"God it was so boring and repetitive - and Dad got so cross," said Charlotte, leaning back into her seat and grinning at the memory.

"Well, he only has you. He doesn't want anything to happen to you," said Elizabeth.

Charlotte sat up and faced her. "Excuse me, He has you as well!" she said, abruptly.

Elizabeth laughed. "We are great friends, your father and I, and I love him dearly, but his first concern will always be you."

Charlotte looked into Elizabeth's eyes, her expression suddenly serious. "Why is it that you and I are being evacuated out of Italy together? How come you and I had to attend the kidnap course together? How come when Dad wanted me to do that self-defence course, you had to come too? Why is it that whenever there is a family crisis, it is you, me and Dad sitting around a table talking it through?"

"We are friends. That's what friends do," said Elizabeth defensively.

"Bollocks!" said Charlotte, thumping back into her seat and staring toward the front of the plane. "He takes as much care of you as he does of me. Why do you think he went all patriarchal last night? That's not dad. He was really worried by what happened at Marco's place. He would be devastated if anything ever happened to you. You are kidding yourself if you think you are just friends. I know married couples who have a more distant relationship than you two!"

Elizabeth sat back in her seat and closed her eyes. She had always had trouble with feelings and emotions when it came to Dan. Had it been anyone else, other than him, who had tried to arrange her life in such a paternalistic and cavalier fashion she would have taken their head off at the knees.

Charlotte was right, though. She did always seem to be part of what was going on in Dan and Charlotte's life, although, she thought, it had been such a gradual thing. When they first met she had been married to Andrew. He was away so often, on trips to Antarctica, or conferences overseas, that in the seven years they had been married they had probably spent less than half of that time actually together. There had been so much to discuss with Dan that she had progressively spent more and more time at his place, when Andrew was away. Eventually she found herself eating there most evenings. It meant that Dan didn't have to worry about a babysitter for Charlotte. Her own place was only ten minutes away so it just seemed... efficient. When Andrew was back in the country he would happily join them. He liked the relaxed, family atmosphere. They all became friends, and still were. It was just the marriage bit that fizzled out.

In all that time Dan had never made a single romantic move towards her, at least not one that she had recognised, she mused. They were business partner and friends. No, not friends, she thought with a slight shock, best friends. It was true, she had fantasied, occasionally, about their relationship being something more than it was, but her track record wasn't great. Two ex-husbands could attest to that. It would be a catastrophe if she somehow destroyed the one male friendship in her life that really worked.

She had been angry at herself for not taking Dan to task last night, and wondered what had made her bite her tongue. Maybe she did have stronger feelings for him than she had thought.

There had been times in the last couple of years, usually when they were working late, when she had thought of telling Dan how she felt, how important he was to her, but she had always stopped herself, worried that he might not feel the same way. Perhaps Charlotte was right. Perhaps the signs were there and she had just not read them properly. Perhaps her relationship with Dan and Charlotte was the reason her relationship with Andrew had fizzled out. Or, she thought ruefully, perhaps Charlotte just wanted them to be together, a young girl's romantic wish for a mother she had never known.

She smiled sadly to herself, opened her eyes and rubbed Charlotte's arm. "Perhaps you are right, sweetheart," she said, smiling. "But whatever happens in the future, just remember that I am your friend too. I will always be around if you need me."

Charlotte smiled and rested her head on Elizabeth's shoulder again. She soon fell asleep.

10. Calabria - Present day

Dan parked the Renault across the road from the apartment and waited. He wasn't sure for what exactly he was waiting, but he was soon glad that he had. Five minutes after he arrived two men walked out of his front door. One, a large man with dark, short, crew cut hair, was shouting into his mobile phone, while the other, a smaller man with blonde lank hair, who was carrying something under his jacket that looked suspiciously like Dan's laptop, was looking around warily as he pulled the door closed behind him.

Dan slunk down in his seat as the two men walked a few metres along the road and got into an old blue Fiat van. They drove it about 500 metres further down the street where they pulled over to the curb and stopped. It looked like they too had decided to wait and see who might turn up.

The loss of his laptop wasn't a big issue. He had lost a few over the years so his hard drive was always encrypted and password protected. All of his files were backed up onto the company's cloud server. Who ever these guys were they were unlikely to be able to access the information on the laptop anytime soon.

He did, however, recognise the need to get Viktor's gift back. He was guessing, given that the only thing the two thugs seemed to be carrying when they came out of the apartment was the laptop, and that they were still hanging around, that they hadn't found it.

Conspicuous though it was, he would also like to get the Aston Martin out of there and safely garaged at his apartment in Rome.

He thought for a while about his next move. His options were limited. He dismissed the idea of fighting it out with the two thugs. Although he kept himself reasonably fit, windsurfing and skiing, he was the first to admit that fist fighting was not one of his talents. Another option was to dash into the apartment, grab the box, jump into the Aston Martin and high tail it of there in cloud of expensive tyre smoke, but he, reluctantly, dismissed that as well. That just left waiting until they went away. So he waited and watched. The Fiat van didn't move and no one else showed any interest in the apartment.

By mid afternoon he was feeling bored and decidedly hungry. He was also starting to worry that he hadn't heard anything from Charlotte or Liz.

11. London – Present day

Walking out of the arrivals gate, chatting happily, arm in arm, Charlotte and Elizabeth didn't immediately see the well dressed man holding a sign with their names on it. They had almost walked passed him when Charlotte noticed.

"Are you looking for us?" she asked.

The man, who had still been looking towards the arrivals gate, looked at the two women and smiled a friendly smile. "If you are Ms Marsh and Ms Garvey, then yes I am," he said pleasantly. "Tommy Malm asked me to pick you up. He is eager to speak with you."

Charlotte looked at Elizabeth, unsure of what to do.

Elizabeth was surprised that Thomas Malm would arrange to send someone to pick them up on the basis of a fairly uninformative email from Dan. As far as she was aware MI6 wasn't in the business of running an airport shuttle service. Something else worried her too, but she was not immediately sure what it was. Nevertheless, she was pleased that they didn't have to get involved in the battle to get a cab into the city and graciously accepted the offer.

The well dressed man held out his hand. "John Smith," he said with a smile.

Elizabeth laughed as she shook his hand. "Really?" she asked, a bemused look on her face.

"Really," he said, smiling back.

After enquiring if they needed to collect any luggage John Smith led them to a sleek black Jaguar. He held the rear door open for them and closed it carefully once they were inside.

As he accelerated away from the terminal, while Charlotte texted her father to tell him that they had arrived safely, Elizabeth leant forward and asked. "John, where will we be meeting Mr Malm?"

"Oh, Tommy has arranged to meet us at an apartment just near Legoland, at St George's Wharf."

"Legoland?" asked Charlotte, looking up from her phone.

"The SIS building, the headquarters of MI6, Ma'am. We call it Legoland because it looks like it is made of lego," said John Smith politely with a pleasant smile.

"Why couldn't we met there?" asked Charlotte. "I would love to see what it is like inside."

"You would have to ask Tommy, ma'am. Today I am just the delivery driver."

Charlotte looked back at her phone. The text had not been sent. Her brows furrowed. Her phone wasn't getting any signal.

Elizabeth who had been sitting quietly listening to this exchange leant forward in her seat and asked, "Would it be okay if we made a quick stop on the way? It won't take long and I would feel much better if we could?"

"I know Tommy is very eager to see you both Ma'am. It would be more than my job is worth to be late."

"I realise that it might be inconvenient, but," Elizabeth paused, looking embarrassed," it's a woman's issue. It would be very much better if we could just make a quick stop. I know there is a Boots Pharmacy just before Harrods. We will be going right past it. It won't take a minute."

A flash of irritation crossed John Smith's face, but he covered it up quickly. "No problem Ma'am," he said over his shoulder.

Charlotte was looking at Elizabeth with a quizzical expression. Elizabeth reached over and squeezed her hand four times. With a shock, Charlotte recognised the signal for "danger" they had agreed on when they had been doing the Schwarzenegger workshops. Elizabeth was worried about something, but for the life of her Charlotte couldn't figure out what could be wrong.

They sat in silence until Elizabeth pointed out the pharmacy to John a little while later. He pulled the car up to the kerb on the opposite side of the road.

Elizabeth grabbed Charlotte's hand and said in a quiet, calm voice, "Come and give me a hand, sweetheart. Leave your bag there. I've got my purse." Then, towing Charlotte with her, she stepped out of the car and quickly headed across the road towards the pharmacy entrance.

The two women walked into the pharmacy, hand in hand. As soon as they were inside Charlotte pulled her hand out of Elizabeth's and turned to face her. 'What is going on? Has something happened that I don't know about?'

"Just keep walking to the counter," said Elizabeth placing her arm around Charlotte and propelling her forward. "That man does not work for Thomas Malm. I very much doubt that he has anything to do with the government at all. If I am wrong then we can apologise to Thomas when we see him. If I am right, then we needed to get out of the car without making our friend John Smith, whoever he is, too suspicious."

As they stood talking an attractive young woman approached them and asked if she could be of assistance.

"Do you have a back door to this shop," asked Elizabeth, glancing quickly over her shoulder. "My ex-husband is following us and I really don't want to confront him. He can be quite..." Elizabeth paused for a moment as if searching for the diplomatic word, and then said nervously, "Aggressive. If you could help us avoid him we would be most grateful."

The girl hesitated for a moment. She excused herself and walked to the back of the shop where she had a whispered conversation with a middle-aged man who had been working behind the counter. The man looked up, smiled at Elizabeth, and nodded to the girl.

The girl came back and spoke quietly. "There is a door at the back of the storeroom that leads to the alley at the back of the building."

"That sounds perfect," said Elizabeth with a conspiratorial smile. "Where does the alley come out?"

"Oh, just behind the coffee shop on the corner, but it is out of sight of anyone coming along Brompton Road," said the girl, getting into the spirit of things.

She led them through the back of the shop to a small storeroom, and then out into a short alley. A large steel gate stood open at the entrance to the alley allowing several motorcycles to park there, along with a row of rubbish bins.

Elizabeth thanked the girl and pressed a ten pound note into her hand. Grasping Charlotte's hand, she led her to the entrance of the alley. She paused for a moment, looked both ways, then, with a smile said,

"Time for coffee, I think." and led Charlotte into the coffee shop on the corner of the street. They settled at a table away from the window, but close enough to still see the roadway outside. It offered a perfect view of John Smith standing beside his sleek black Jaguar and staring, fixedly, at the entrance to the Chemist shop.

Charlotte, who was becoming increasingly frustrated by Elizabeth's behavior, sat down and crossed her arms. "What the hell is going on Liz? This is all way too cloak and dagger for me. I don't understand how we have suddenly found ourselves in the middle of a John le Carré novel. What is going on!"

Elizabeth, with one eye on their erstwhile chauffeur and one eye on Charlotte, said, "That man, whoever he is, doesn't know Thomas Malm. Nobody calls Thomas Malm "Tommy". He doesn't allow it. He is either Thomas, to those that don't know him well, or he is "Swede" to those that do. That was the way he introduced himself when your father and I first met him. His actual words were, "You can call me Thomas if you wish. I don't like Tom and Tommy is a name for children. I prefer my friends to call me Swede." Apparently it was a nickname he was given when he was at boarding school and it stuck, typically British really. Your father has got to know him quite well. I've met him a few times and have only ever heard him called Sir, Mr Malm, Thomas or Swede, never Tom and definitely not Tommy."

"Not only that, but he would never tell someone that my name was Ms Garvey, or for that matter that you where Ms Marsh. He would have told them it was Doctor Garvey and Miss Marsh. Thomas is, in some ways, very old fashioned, very British and very prim and proper. Its just not in his nature to use, what he would call a new fangled feminist term like Ms."

"Now, I might be wrong. The people that work for him might call him Tommy behind his back, I don't know, but I just didn't trust our Mr John Smith."

"Hey!" said Charlotte who had glanced out the window, "He is going across to the chemist."

They watched as John Smith walked across to their side of the road and disappeared into the Chemist's shop. A couple of minutes later he came back through the front doors with the middle aged chemist following him and gesturing in such a way as to suggest that he wasn't welcome in his shop.

John Smith stood looking up and down Brompton Road while the Chemist stood in the doorway of his shop, staring at him, his arms crossed across his chest. At the same time a traffic warden started writing a ticket for the Jaguar, which was illegally parked. Mr Smith ran to the other side of the road, dodging traffic, and began remonstrating with the parking officer.

Two minutes later he was standing by his car, a parking ticket held in his hand, looking angry and frustrated. He hit the top of his car with his fist, threw the parking ticket onto the pavement. Moments later, with a squeal of tires the Jaguar pulled out into the traffic and disappeared from view.

Elizabeth and Charlotte looked at one another. Charlotte had gone very pale. "That didn't look legit. Wouldn't a real MI6 person just show an identity card or something? What have we got ourselves involved in Liz?"

"I don't know Charlie," said Elizabeth, reaching into her bag for her phone, "But I think we had better ring your father. Did you let him know we had landed safely?"

"No, I couldn't get through. For some reason my phone couldn't get a signal. Oh, shit!" said Charlotte, suddenly looking cross, "My phone! My bag! I left them in the car! You told me to leave them in the Car."

"I'm sorry Charlotte. I thought it would be a good way to allay our friend's suspicions. I didn't really think about what you might have had in your bag. I'm sorry," said Elizabeth, genuinely apologetic.

Charlotte thought for a moment. "It was really only my phone and wallet. Nothing that can't be easily replaced."

Elizabeth, who had her phone to her ear, frowned. "I can't get through to your Dad. I keep getting pushed to voice mail. I'll send him a text. He might be driving and not be able to hear the phone. That new car of his is pretty loud."

Elizabeth typed out a short text letting Dan know that they had arrived safely in London and they were expecting a call from him.

"Now, let's see if we have just embarrassed ourselves with the British secret service or managed to avoid being kidnapped," said Elizabeth with a grin as she tapped on the screen of her iPhone and started to compose an email to Thomas Malm.

Twenty minutes later a very worried looking gentlemen, impeccably dressed in a dark grey suit, stepped out of a sleek black Jaguar and strode quickly into the coffee shop.

12. Calabria - Present day

Dan let out a long breath as he watched the Fiat van finally drive off. He waited ten more minutes to make sure they weren't coming back then locked up the Renault and ran across the road to the front door of the apartment.

He stepped through the door and stopped, mouth open, stunned. The apartment looked like a tornado had hit it. Furniture had been smashed, cupboard doors had been ripped from their hinges and drawers had been emptied and their contents scattered all over the floor. Looking at the mess he realised that they hadn't just searched the place, they had intended to send a message as well.

Worried they may have found the box after all, he searched frantically till he found the bread bin. It was empty. The thought went through his head that the thugs may have taken the bread to eat while they watched the apartment. He continued to look, as methodically as he could. Eventually, with a huge sense of relief, he found the bread, still wrapped in paper, under the upturned kitchen table.

He had taken longer than he had wanted to find the box, so he decided not to bother packing anything but the bare essentials.

Clutching an overnight bag he raced down the internal stairs to the garage. The door of the Aston Martin stood open. They had obviously searched the car as well. "Shit." he said to himself as he threw the bag and the bread onto the passenger seat, hit the remote garage door opener, and slid in behind the wheel, hoping that they hadn't disabled the car in some way.

The car started immediately letting out a deep growl that echoed around the small garage as Dan hit the accelerator a little too vigorously in his eagerness to get away. He took a deep breath to calm himself and put the car into reverse. He carefully backed the it out into the street, just as the blue Fiat van pulled up opposite. For a moment Dan looked into the big thug's eyes, then, with great care, not taking his eyes off the man, put the Aston Martin into first gear. With a small smirk he planted his foot to the floor. The car jerked, jumped forward forward, and stalled.

Dan cursed himself for thinking that he was some sort of macho hero. He reached for the starter as the driver's door of the Fiat started to swing open. He turned the key and the engine kicked back into life. The big thug was out of the van and reaching for the passenger side door handle as Dan stamped on the accelerator and lifted his foot smoothly from the clutch. The motor roared as three hundred and fifty horsepower coursed through the drive shaft to the back wheels. The tyres struggled to find grip on the road, spun and then bit into the tarmac. The Aston Martin leapt down the Via Lungomare leaving behind a shower of gravel and a cloud of smoke. Six seconds later he was travelling at over one hundred kilometres and hour and accelerating fast.

Running parallel to the water, the long straight Via Lungomare, stretched out before him. Dan concentrated on putting as much distance, as fast as possible, between him and the Fiat van. He was familiar with this road and knew that the Lungomare joined up with the Autostrada that would take him straight to Rome. It was, normally, a six or seven hour drive. He hoped he could do it in less.

The traffic was light. The noise of the car was tremendous. The sound of the triple weber carburetors sucking in air, the crackle of the exhausts as he changed down gears before overtaking would have, under normal circumstances brought a smile of joy to Dan's face. He wasn't smiling today. He just concentrated on driving and occasionally checking in the rear vision mirror.

As he drove he thought about his current predicament. He knew that the car was not discrete. If the people that were after the box, if that was what they were really after, were more than just local thugs, it was quite probable that they would try to intercept him before he made it to Rome. In hindsight, somewhat shamefacedly, he realised that he should have left the Aston Martin in San Lucido and taken the more inconspicuous Renault to Rome.

Still, he thought to himself with an embarrassed grin, *too late for regrets now, fake Jimmy Bond!*

The road was a good dual carriageway and the driving fast and easy. He flicked his lights at the car in front of him. It immediately changed lanes, moving out of his way. He waved at the driver as he went past.

"Man, you've got to love Italian drivers" he said to himself, as he checked the rear vision mirror again and then looked down at the fuel gauge. "Damn," he said under his breath, surprised at how much petrol he had used. He was just outside Solerno, and not wanting to be caught short, he pulled into the first service station he came to. He was pretty sure that no one would try to accost him in such a public place and it would be a good chance to get something to eat and a coffee to keep him awake.

He stopped in front of a bowser and before he had a chance to get out of the car a small crowd, men and a few boys, had gathered around it. By the time Dan opened the door and got out of the car a spirited conversation had started. One of the onlookers, a solid looking bloke, tall, wearing jeans and a warm looking quilted vest and with a mop of dark curly hair on his head, looked at him and said, smiling *"Che tipo di macchina è questa?"*

Dan's Italian was virtually non existent, but he guessed the big friendly Italian was asking about the car. He replied, "Aston Martin," and then after a pause, "English."

The man looked crestfallen. *"No. Impossibile! Sembra italiana,"* he said, waving his hands about.

Dan smiled, indicated to the man that he should follow him. Dan stepped to the front of the car and pointed to the small Z that sat discreetly under a vent on the front fender. He read the neat lower case letters moulded into the badge, "Zagato. Milano."

A grin slowly formed on the big man's face. "Italiano!" His eyes sparkled as he appreciated the car all over again. "Sono Alberto!" he said holding out his hand.

Dan took the hand and shook. "Dan," he said.

Still looking at the car the man said, "She is both English and Italian, yes?"

Dan nodded.

"She is very beautiful, Dan, like Ferrari, like Maserati," said Alberto. He paused, a concerned look coming on to his face. "Fast?"

Dan nodded again. "Like Ferrari, Alberto!" he said.

Alberto grinned, relieved, and stood back to admire the car again. "You English too, Dan?"

"No. Australian." he answered over his shoulder as he began filling the car with petrol.

Alberto's face lit up. "Ah!, My cousin, she live in Australia. She live in Sydney."

Dan smiled. "I am from Sydney too. Have you ever visited her there?"

Alberto looked sad. "No, It is big expense to get to Sydney. Driving trucks does not pay too much. I would very much like to see her though. I think, maybe, I go in the next year or two."

"Are you heading for Napoli?" asked Alberto conversationally. "Perhaps we could share a meal and talk cars?"

"That would have been nice, but unfortunately I need to get to Rome, as soon as I can," said Dan with obvious regret.

He finished filing the car and by the time he had paid for the petrol, grabbed a sandwich and a coffee, Alberto had gone but there was still a group of admirers standing around the car.

He pushed his way apologetically through the crowd. Once it was clear that he was the owner room was made for him to get into the car. Seated behind the wheel in the comfortable cut-down leather seats he turned the key. The engine let out a throaty roar as he blipped the throttle. The crowd fell back. He gave the throttle another, longer blip. The car burbled and spat. The appreciative crowd gave a cheer.

Feeling very much the boy racer as he put his sunglasses back on, he was sorely tempted to show off. His maturity, for once, got the better of him and he just gave a friendly wave and pulled slowly away.

"It's 106 miles to Chicago, we've got a full tank of gas, half a pack of cigarettes, its dark, and we're wearing sunglasses," he said to himself in a quiet voice, smiling, as he accelerated back out onto the Autostrada.

He checked his rear vision mirror again, but there was no sign of the Fiat van. Feeling confident that he had left the thugs in the Fiat van far behind he started to enjoy the drive, slowing only for the occasional toll booth.

Accelerating around a long sweeping corner he indicated to pass a large, covered semi trailer. As he passed the cab the driver let out a long blast on his horn. An arm appeared waving madly. In his rear vision mirror Dan could see the grinning face of Alberto leaning out the window. He dropped down a gear, double de-clutching to bring the revs up. The car responded with a crackle and burble, slowing enough to allow Alberto's truck to pull along side. With a wave of his hand out the window Dan hit the accelerator. The nose of the car lifted as the car accelerated away. Over the tumultuous roar of the engine Dan heard the fading sound of the continuos blast of an air horn.

With the speedo sitting on a comfortable 85 miles an hour, just above the speed limit, Dan relaxed back into his seat. Now, with time to think, he pulled out his phone. He had been so pre-occupied with getting away from San Lucido he had forgotten to take his phone off silent. He cursed when he saw that he had four missed calls from Elizabeth and a text message.

He accessed the text message and was relieved to see that Liz and Charlotte had made it safely back to London. Distracted as he was, he didn't notice a large black BMW SUV pull into the lane behind him, or the silver Mercedes that slowed and matched speed beside him.

He put his phone on the seat beside him and started looking for an opportunity to pull over so he could ring Elizabeth. A few kilometres further along the Autostrada Dan saw a lay-by. He indicated, slowed and pulled off the highway. The Black BMW pulled in behind him. Suddenly realising how exposed he would be, he thought better of his idea of stopping. He indicated and started to pull back out onto the Autostrada, only to be blocked by the silver Mercedes which pulled into the lay-by along side him. He had to stamp on the brakes hard and only narrowly missed hitting it.

Dan suddenly realised that he was boxed in. He couldn't move forward because of the way the guardrail of the lay-by curved back out towards the highway. He couldn't move back because of the BMW. He couldn't pull out onto the Autostrada because of the Mercedes. In fact, he was so tightly jammed in he couldn't even open the car doors. He was trapped.

He watched in the rear vision mirror as two men got out of the BMW and started walking towards him. Dan surreptitiously checked that the box, still wrapped in its bread-y disguise, was pushed well back under his seat.

13. London - Present day

Thomas Malm strode into the cafe. He was tall and handsome, with a tanned face and short dark hair, greying at the temples. The French cuffs of his white shirt that peeked out from under his suit jacket, were held together with plain gold cuff links. He was the epitome of the Hollywood image of a British secret agent.

Charlotte's first impression was that he looked like a modern day version of David Niven. Based on his dress and erect bearing, she guessed that he was probably ex-military. She and Elizabeth both stood up as he approached their table.

"Elizabeth," he said, looking concerned as he shook her hand, " Are you all right?"

"We are now, thanks Thomas." She turned to Charlotte. "You haven't met Dan's daughter, Charlotte?"

"No," he said, holding out his hand and smiling. Charlotte smiled back and shook his hand.

"I am delighted to meet you at last. Elizabeth and your father have often talked about you."

Even though she had been living in England for years, Charlotte had never met anyone quite so old fashioned and archetypically English before. For some reason she felt herself flush.

At a gesture from Thomas they all sat down at the table and ordered more coffee, but not before Thomas had given an almost imperceptible nod to the two men that had climbed out of the Jaguar after him. One man, dressed in jeans and a casual jacket had seated himself at a table by the side entrance that Charlotte and Elizabeth had used. The other man, dressed in a light grey suit and open neck shirt, had taken a table near the entrance that led out to Brompton Road.

"Now," said Thomas once their coffees had arrived, "What sort of situation have you got yourselves into, and where is my friend Daniel?"

"Dan is driving back to Rome. He should be there this evening," said Elizabeth. "His plan is to get a flight here as soon as he garages his car."

Thomas lifted an eyebrow. "Not the Aston Martin. Don't tell me it is finally finished."

"All done," said Charlotte. "I picked it up and drove it from Milan to Cosenza." She smiled.

"How marvelous," said Thomas turning to look at Charlotte. "I am completely envious. I would kill for that car!" he said with such emotion that Charlotte really believed he would.

"What is it with English spies and Aston Martin's?" asked Elizabeth with a chuckle.

"It is one of the selection criteria for the job, Elizabeth. One can only join the service if one has an appreciation for fine British automobiles," he laughed. "Now," he said becoming serious, "tell me what is going on."

Elizabeth explained about the box that Charlotte had found, the letter from Viktor Kachenko, at the mention of whose name Thomas rolled his eyes, the fire at the Traverni restoration shop and their experience with "John Smith" and subsequent "escape". She also mentioned her feeling that they were being watched when they were working on the archeological dig in the River Busento.

Thomas sat back in his chair. "Viktor Kachenko was ex-KGB and a very wealthy and influential man. His father had been a major player in Stalin's time and Viktor knew how to survive. When the Soviet Union disintegrated, Viktor was one of the winners. We kept an eye on him as a matter of course," he said in a quiet voice. "We knew that he had a relationship with your father, Charlotte, but Viktor was essentially a decent man. 'Cruel but fair', as they say in the classics. Beyond ensuring that our national interest were protected, we didn't interfere, or no more than making sure, with our colonial counterparts in ASIS, that Daniel received the appropriate heads up on who he was dealing with."

"Viktor did a lot of traveling. He was an antiquarian book nut. Perhaps their common interest in history was why he enjoyed your father's company so much. He collected a massive library of books from ancient Greece through to the Cold War. We suspected that he was not averse to bending the rules when acquiring volumes for his library. A number of scrolls from the Villa of the Papyri went missing from an Italian University a few years ago and Interpol flagged Viktor as a possible buyer."

Elizabeth frowned. "The Villa of the Papyri? I've never heard of that."

"It's in Herculaneum, near Naples. You know, the seaside town buried at the same time as Pompeii," said Charlotte. "The excavation of the Villa was started in the 1700s. The story goes that as they tunnelled into the Villa they found bundles of burnt sticks in storage jars and used them to light their way, at least until someone figured out that they were burning papyrus scrolls that had been collected together to evacuate them once the eruption had started. They've excavated thousands of scrolls and there are thousands more still to be excavated."

"What are they about?" asked Elizabeth.

"Most of them are Epicurean Philosophy. Its pretty dry stuff."

"Ah!" said Thomas. "Of course, you are doing your doctorate in history, at Oxford. How exciting," he said, almost wistfully. "I read history there when I was younger. I would love to hear how it is going sometime, when other matters are not so pressing."

"Why are we coming in for all this sudden attention?" asked Elizabeth. "What is so valuable that someone would burn down a car restoration shop and waste time watching us while we dig around in the dirt?"

"I have no idea," said Thomas. "Until the sample you have is analysed we have very little to go on. I have no idea what Viktor was up to, or why he would send Daniel such a package," he said looking out into the street.

"I think it is an excellent idea to get the liquid out of the vial analysed. That is probably the most important clue you have. I would be interested to see the box and the vial, but I fear that, because you have all been handling them, it is unlikely that they would reveal any worthwhile prints or DNA. A scan for DNA might still be worth doing, just in case," he said with a subtle shrug of his shoulders.

"The most disturbing issue, from MI6's perspective, is that Daniel's email appears to have been intercepted on its way to me. That is potentially quite embarrassing. There would seem to be two possibilities. One, that someone had indeed been keeping tabs on you, both physically and digitally, and intercepted Daniel's email on its way out of his computer, or two, that someone has compromised MI6's data security. I will get our boffins to have a look at both possibilities as a matter of urgency."

"So you think this is real? That someone really did just try and kidnap us?" asked Charlotte, going pale.

Thomas looked at them both, a serious expression on his face. "Yes, Charlotte, this is serious and real. I have no idea what is going on, or why someone would try and detain you in the way they have. Perhaps it is about this mysterious box. Perhaps it is about a "simple" kidnap attempt. Perhaps it is something else. Either way I would like to offer you some protection if you would like it. I would be happy to send my two Special Branch friends, Harry and Frank with you, if you would like," he said glancing quickly at each of the men watching the café entrances.

Both women looked shocked. "No really I don't think that is necessary," said Elizabeth.

"Neither do I," said Charlotte. The idea of having a minder trailing her around seemed both bizarre and extreme.

"That is up to you. The offer stands if you change your mind," said Thomas graciously.

"I know we don't have much in the way of information, but do you have any thoughts about who could be behind this?" asked Charlotte.

"If there really were people watching you in Italy I would guess that, given you were in Calabria, there could be some involvement from the 'Ndrangheta, the Calabrian Mafia, or perhaps the Camorra, given your proximity to Naples."

"Seriously?" asked Charlotte, starting to have second thoughts about the need for protection.

"If it's not one of the various brands of Italian mafia then perhaps there is a Russian connection, especially given the involvement of Viktor Kachenko. Perhaps the Russian mafia. They would be potentially harder to identify. They are not family based like the Italians. They tend to be a looser structure. People move in and out of groups more frequently. Or, it could be any number of individuals who want something that you, or

58

someone connected to you, have. At this stage it is all just speculation, I'm afraid."

"The best thing to do now is for each of us to follow up the leads we have. We can pool our knowledge when Daniel arrives. Here is a number on which you can contact me at any time of the day or night," said Thomas, giving them both a nondescript business card with a mobile phone number on it. "Please do not hesitate to call me if you are concerned about anything, anything at all."

"I have arranged for a car to take you to where you want to go," said Thomas nodding towards the window where another black Jaguar had just pulled up behind his own car.

****

As they all stood up to leave Elizabeth felt Thomas put a hand under her arm. He started leading her towards the door, glanced over his shoulder to see that Charlotte was out of earshot and said, in a quiet voice, "I would be grateful if you would call me the moment you hear from Daniel." Elizabeth's step faltered. Thomas, with gently pressure under her arm, kept her moving forward.

"You think he might be in real danger in Italy." she said. The talk of the mafia had worried her more than she wanted to admit and if Thomas was worried... She didn't want to think about what the implications of that were.

"I will be happier when I know he is safe and happier still when he is back in England. Daniel is an important man, a scientist and technologist of world repute and a business man whose activities impact the economies of several Commonwealth countries . More than that, he is a dear friend," he said. "Yes, I am worried. Very worried. I think it was foolish of him to drive to Rome by himself, especially in such an obvious vehicle."

Elizabeth stopped and started into Thomas' grey eyes. They now stood beside the Jaguar. The potential magnitude of what was happening was starting to hit her.

"I will do what I can to make sure he gets to Rome safely and then bring him to London as quickly as I can," said Thomas.

Elizabeth leaned forward and kissed him on the cheek and said quietly, "Thank-you, Swede." before stepping into the backseat of the car. Charlotte slipped in alongside her. Elizabeth took her hand and squeezed it gently in what she hoped was a reassuring way.

14. Calabria - Present day

Dan watched, with a growing sense of dread, as the two men walked toward his car. Both were dressed in black trousers and jackets, one with a black shirt, the other with a black roll neck jumper. Sunglasses masked their eyes. Neither of them looked happy, or friendly.

He looked around, frantically trying to see some way to escape. The Aston Martin was right hand drive. He had pulled into the lay-by and stopped the car close to the guard rail. Not thinking that he might need to get out of the car he had not worried about leaving enough space to open the door. The Mercedes was now stopped close on the other side, slightly in front, with its rear bumper now level with the back edge of his passenger door. If they rolled forward just a bit more he might be able to get the passenger door open and make a run for it, as long as they didn't shoot him, he thought wryly.

Dan jumped. Black roll neck had thumped on his window with his hand and was now indicating, with hand gestures, that Dan should wind the window down. As he leant forward, his jacket fell open revealing a gun in a shoulder holster.

Dan wound the window down a few centimeters and looked up into the man's stoney, expressionless face. "Dottore Marsh, you will give me the package that was put into this car in Milan. If you do not I will make sure that this beautifully restored car is put back into the condition it was a year ago, with you inside it." The man's English was good, with only a hint of an Italian accent.

Dan felt his heart racing. This situation was so far out of his normal experience that his mind seemed to have stopped working. He just stared at the big Italian.

"Did you hear me Dottore?" shouted the Italian, impatiently. "Perhaps you should turn off the car engine." he suggested.

Turning the car off did not seem like a good idea to Dan. He realised it was perhaps irrational, but while the car was still running he felt like he still had some semblance of control over the situation. His mind raced.

"The package, yes! Someone put it in the car when it was picked up, that's right," he said, stalling for thinking time.

If he said that he didn't have it then they would want to know where it was. Presumably they would have searched the apartment in San Lucido again, so they knew it wasn't there. If he said it was with Elizabeth or Charlotte it would put them in danger. He couldn't do that. Inspiration hit. "I don't have the package with me. I posted it to my head office in Australia this morning, from the airport."

The big Italian stared at Dan. Dan stared back, gave an exaggerated shrug of his shoulders and smiled weakly.

"If you are lying to me I will kill you!" shouted the Italian in a tone that made it seem to Dan less a threat and more like a statement of fact. He was under no illusion that this was a man who kept his word. "I will search the car. Turn off the engine and give me the keys, now!" demanded the Italian in an increasingly angry voice.

To accentuate his point, in one swift movement, he pulled the gun from its shoulder holster and smashed the butt of it against the drivers side window. With a bang the window exploded into thousands of pieces. Dan lurched back, but not quickly enough to avoid the massive hand of the Italian that grabbed the front of his shirt and pulled him part way through the window.

"If you do not do as I say I will walk around your beautiful car and kick in every single panel. Then I will do the same to you before I put a bullet in the back of your head. Now, do as I say and turn the car off!" he yelled, pushing Dan back into his seat.

Dan started to reach for the ignition key in the middle of the dashboard when there was the loud sound of air brakes. A semitrailer had pulled into the lay-by not far behind the BMW.

"Merde!" said the big Italian. He turned and walked back towards his own car and the semi-trailer, slipping the gun back under his jacket as he did so. "*Assicurarsi che la testa di cazzo rimane nella sua macchina!*" he shouted angrily to his black shirted partner as he walked past him.

Dan's Italian wasn't good enough to interpret, but it didn't sound friendly.

In the rear vision mirror he watched black roll neck walk past his BMW towards the semitrailer and start to wave his arms around and shout at the driver.

Dan couldn't be sure, and maybe it was just wishful thinking, but he thought that he recognised the big rig. If it was Alberto, maybe he could signal him for help.

The discussion with the semi trailer driver was now getting heated. Black roll neck was gesticulating wildly and shouting up at the driver. The driver, who Dan couldn't see because of the way the sun reflected off the windscreen, was obviously angry as well.

Black roll neck, standing by the door of the truck and looking up towards the driver, started to reach inside his jacket. Suddenly the door of the truck snapped open, catching roll neck full in the face. He hit the ground like a sack of bricks. Black shirt, who had also been watching, started running back towards the truck, reaching into his own jacket. Another man, the driver of the Mercedes, jumped out of his car and he too started running back towards the semitrailer.

The driver of the truck had still not appeared. The door of the truck was abruptly slammed shut. By the time black shirt and the Mercedes driver had covered half the distance to their stricken comrade the semi had started to move.

Dan, still unsure about whether this was just a lucky break or whether his newly found friend Alberto had just given him an opportunity to escape, grabbed the package and started to climb out the smashed driver's side window. A blast on the truck's air-horn stopped him before he got half way.

Now the truck had moved he could clearly see Alberto's face staring at him. The big Italian waved at him to get back into the car as the semitrailer started to roll forward along the lay-by. Dan guessed what Alberto was going to do and scrambled quickly back into the driver's seat.

The big rig accelerated and then, with no discernable checking of its speed, hit the rear end of the Mercedes and shunted it out of the way. The Mercedes cannoned across the road. Cars screeched to a halt. One hit the Mercedes, spinning it sideways.

With one hand on the steering wheel and the other on the gear lever, Dan waited for the rear of the truck to go past. Now, free to go, he planted his foot on the accelerator and the Aston Martin fishtailed out of the lay-by in a spray of gravel. In his rear vision mirror he caught sight of the two men, who had run to roll neck's aide, still helping him to his feet. He grinned to himself as he guessed that his black clad rivals would soon be doing battle against a host of angry Italian motorists.

Dan accelerated away from the lay-by, swerving around Alberto's semi as he did so and narrowly missing the Mercedes. Now, with a clear road ahead and out of immediate danger, Dan noticed that his hand had started to shake. He gripped the wheel more tightly and tried to think what he should do next. If he kept driving to Rome, the people that were after him might well become more desperate and more violent. The Aston Martin had turned out to be a real liability, but he could not just abandon it on the side of the road. He cursed his stupidity. Now he had not only got himself in trouble but he had also involved the good hearted, and brave, Alberto.

On an impulse he slowed down. Travelling at a more normal speed, he constantly checked his rear vision mirror. Before too long Alberto's truck hove into view, moving quickly up behind him. He gestured to him, through the smashed drivers side window, to follow him. With no sign of either the silver Mercedes or the black BMW, Dan sped up again with Alberto following closely behind.

A sign flashed past, indicating that they were approaching the City of Nola. Dan had heard about Nola, although he had never been there. He remembered it was primarily famous for two things. It was the place where the first Roman Emperor, Augustus, died and its population had one of the highest cancer rates in Europe, supposedly because of the way Mafia run businesses treated and disposed of toxic wastes. He immediately discounted the idea of driving into the city itself.

A few minutes later he saw the familiar symbol for service station. Indicating well in advance, he pulled into the crowded Tamoil service station with Alberto's semi trailer close on his heels and drove the car around the back of the main building Dan pulled over and, with a feeling of relief, turned the engine off and rested his head on the steering wheel.

"You look like you have some trouble following you, Mister Dan," said the big Italian as he walked up beside Dan's door.

"And I have you to thank for getting me out of it, Alberto," he said, getting out of the car and holding his hand out to shake Alberto's. "Thank-you. I just hope that you have not made your own life more difficult by helping me."

"It is no problem," said Alberto. "What did those men want of you?"

"I'm not really sure," answered Dan, cautiously, "but I need to get to Rome as quickly as I can and I don't want to risk running into those guys again. I feel a bit safer here in a public place. I really just stopped you because I wanted to thank-you for helping me. I would be honoured if you would let me pay for you and your family to fly out to Australia to see your cousin."

A big grin spread across Alberto's face. "I would like that very much!" he said, "But what are you going to do now?"

"I think that I need to ring the police. After I've talked to them I'll make arrangements to get the car transported to Rome. I'll get a hire car, if I can, and drive through to Rome, or take the train if I have to."

A worried look crossed Alberto's face. "You know that this is not a..." he paused, thinking about the right word to use,"...trustworthy area. The police may not be as helpful as you would like them to be. There are many connections here with the Camorra."

"Even in the police?" asked Dan.

"Very much so," said Alberto looking troubled. "Perhaps," he said hesitantly, "I could help? I am driving to Rome. My truck is half empty. We could put your car in the back and you could ride to Rome with me."

Twenty minutes later Dan was sitting in the cab of the semi trailer. The car was safely stowed in the back of the truck and there was still no sign of the Black BMW or the Silver Mercedes.

After the stress of the first part of the journey, Dan was relishing the opportunity to just sit back, relax and close his eyes. They had been driving for about half an hour. Dan was about to text Charlotte to say he was alright, when he saw a sign showing Naples straight ahead and Rome to the right. As they approached the turnoff, Alberto didn't seem to be slowing down, or indicating.

Dan looked across at Alberto. He was smiling, driving the semi with casual confidence. "There's the turn off to Rome ahead," said Dan.

Alberto turned to him. "We are not going to Rome, Dottore Marsh," he said, no longer smiling. " I need to talk to you about the package you received from Viktor Kachenko."

"You're with them! You bastard!" shouted Dan angrily. Impetuously he lunged across the cab to wrestle the wheel from Alberto.

He didn't even see the big man's fist as it crashed into the side of his head, knocking it hard into the side of the cab. For Dan, everything went black.

15. London – Present day

Thomas Malm was a worried man. He had initially thought that tracking Daniel Marsh would be easy. He had deployed a few of his own people on the main roads between Salerno and Rome. Daniel's car was so distinctive it should have been easy to pick up his trail.

It was now five hours after his meeting with Elizabeth Garvey and Daniel's daughter, and all he had to show for it was a report of a single sighting at a service station near Salerno. After that Daniel and the car seemed to have completely vanished.

He had alerted the Italian secret service, the Agenzia Informazioni e Sicurezza Interna, AISI, but didn't hold out much hope.

He spoke directly to his own contacts at London City, Heathrow, Gatwick, Luton and Stansted airports and sent out an alert to other airports around the country to be on the watch for Daniel.

He was rapidly coming to the conclusion that someone was indeed on Daniel's trail, and that they had succeeded in snatching him. He already knew the why, so the questions now were, who and where to? Angrily he thumped his fist down onto his desk.

16. Cambridge – Present day

Elizabeth sat at her desk staring at the preliminary results of the analysis of the sample she had brought back from Italy and shaking her head. She found what she was looking at deeply confusing.

The first run through the non-destructive testing had produced a list of very peculiar results. She immediately asked for the tests to be rerun as well as arranging for a number of additional tests to be undertaken. She shook her head, threw the results on to her desk, and turned back to the stack of work that remained piled in her in tray.

The afternoon had been busy, catching up on how things had been going. She found it a welcome distraction from worrying about Dan. Now that she had done all the immediate tasks she had set herself, she became conscious that it was well past the time she had expected to hear from him. It was dark outside and most of the staff had gone home. She double-checked her phone. No text messages. No missed calls. No voice mail. No emails. No contact at all from Dan.

She picked up her phone to call Charlotte but stopped when she remembered that Charlotte's phone had been left in the back of John Smith's car. She was just about to look up the number of Sotheby's to see if, on the off chance, she was still there, when Charlotte walked into her office, a worried expression on her face.

"Have you heard anything?" she asked.

Elizabeth shook her head. "You?"

"No. I've got my mobile provider to divert calls from my old number to my new phone" she replied holding up a brand new iPhone. "I suppose Dad could have called before the diversion was put on," she said, sitting down in one of the visitor chairs. "It's not like Dad to stay out of touch. Something must have happened. I'm really scared, Liz." Tears stated to well up in Charlotte's eyes.

"I'm sure he will be OK, Charlie," said Elizabeth. "How about we give Thomas Malm a ring and see what he has found out?"

Charlotte nodded. Elizabeth dialled the number that Thomas had given her. She put the desk phone onto speaker and sat back, waiting for him to answer. After half a dozen rings they heard his cultured tones on the other end of the phone.

"I'm afraid I haven't got much in the way of news for you," said Thomas, sounding apologetic. "There is no sign of Daniel or the Aston Martin. He definitely hasn't flown into any of the airports in the UK. I have even had someone check all the hospitals on the route from San Lucido to Rome, and I can say that he definitely hasn't been in a car accident. The last sighting of him was at a service station near Salerno. Since then, nothing."

"I have put a trace on his mobile phone but it is difficult to get a quick response from the Italian Telcos. Have either of you heard from him?" he asked.

Both women indicated that they hadn't heard a thing.

"How have you two got on with your other investigations?" he asked.

"I talked to my friend at Sotheby's," said Charlotte, leaning forward towards the phone. "The little jade box was definitely made by Faberge. It is incredibly valuable, worth a small fortune. It is made of Siberian green jade and was originally purchased by a wealthy Russian Jew, sometime around 1910. Apparently the family moved to Germany before the First World War and then, unfortunately, got caught up in the holocaust during the Second World War. The whole family was killed."

"The box itself was found in a stash of Nazi loot, soon after the end of the war. Its provenance was not easy to trace. It took quite a few years to determine who the owner was and if they had any living relatives. When it was finally discovered that there were no members of the family to inherit the box, it was auctioned. The proceeds were used to help surviving holocaust victims in accordance with some international treaty."

"My friend at Sotheby's thinks that the glass vial is more than likely of ancient Roman origin, probably dating from the end of the Republican era. Tracing it would be impossible."

"Is there any record of when the box was auctioned and who purchased it?" asked Thomas.

"Oh yes, sorry," said Charlotte. "It was originally auctioned in 1953 and then again in 2001. Kachenko bought it then. He paid nearly £100,000 for it."

"So the box and the vial are both a bit of a dead end. What about you Elizabeth, have you had a chance to get any of the results of your analysis of the liquid back yet."

"Yes I have, but it is a bit weird I'm afraid," she said picking up the sheet of paper she had been making notes on. "Whatever the mixture is it is certainly chemically very complex. There are traces of human cells in it, probably from multiple individuals, plus a whole lot of other chemicals that will take a bit longer to identify."

"It has human cells in it?" asked Thomas, sounding surprised.

"Yes, we could detect the presence of red blood cells as well as other human ones. The boys downstairs reckon that there could be as many as three different individuals who have contributed to it. I have got our guys down in genetics seeing what they can find by examining what is left of the DNA," she said, putting the piece of paper down.

"What do you mean what's left of it?" asked Thomas.

"Well, that is another weird thing. On our first scan we found fragments of DNA in the cells from, what look like, two separate individuals and complete DNA from a third. The degraded DNA may have been degraded by other components in the mixture, or, perhaps, because they are very old. The DNA from the third individual, on the other hand, seems to be more complete."

"What do you mean by "other human cells?" asked Thomas, fascinated.

"Well, just that there are human cells in the mixture. Some are definitely from blood. The others could be from saliva or pieces of skin. I am not really sure yet," said Elizabeth.

"So what do you think this stuff is meant to do?" asked Thomas.

"What do you mean "do"?" asked Elizabeth, surprised by the question.

"Well what would happen if, for instance, someone drank it, or injected it?" asked Thomas.

"I have no idea. Once we have done some more analysis we might be able to make a guess. Do you think that this might be some sort of drug?"

"No!" said Thomas quickly. "Just speculating really."

"I have no idea what this stuff is. At this stage I would say it is someone's idea of a joke. The guys downstairs will work on isolating its ingredients and we will see what we end up with," said Elizabeth.

"Thanks for that," said Thomas, then after a brief pause, "Now we need to figure out what we are going to do about Daniel."

"I have been waiting on an update on his smartphone usage. Let me just check to see if it has come in." There was a short pause while Thomas checked his email. "Ah, here it is. Good. It looks like the last time he used it was to access his text messages in the middle of the afternoon on the Autostrada between Salerno and Naples. Nothing since."

"Thomas," said Charlotte in a quiet voice, "I didn't mention it before, but when we escaped from John Smith I left my bag, with my phone in it, in the car. Would you be able to track that?"

There was silence from the other end of the phone.

"Oh God!" said Elizabeth, putting her hand to her mouth. "I should have told you that back at the cafe!"

"There is no point crying over spilt milk. It may be a bit late, but we can give it a go. Give me the number and I will get some of my people on it straight away," said Thomas.

They could hear him typing quickly on a keyboard as he spoke. Charlotte gave him the number as well as her new number to which her old phone had been diverted.

"Okay, I have organised for your old phone to be traced. It may well be too late. At best we might find the car that John Smith picked you up in abandoned somewhere. You never know, that might give us some leads as to who is behind this. Now, have either of you left any other traceable electronic equipment lying around that you haven't told me about?" asked Thomas with mock severity.

"Well," said Elizabeth, "there is always Dan's laptop. I don't know if he picked it up when he went back to the apartment or not."

"If he did that would only help if the laptop accessed a wireless network. Then we might be able to track it by the IP address," said Thomas dismissively.

"It wouldn't need a wireless network Thomas," said Charlotte suddenly becoming excited. "Dad's laptop has a mobile phone chip in it so he could always access the net."

"Okay," said Thomas, "we need the number for the chip. Do you have it?"

"No," said Charlotte, who had walked around Elizabeth's desk and was in the process of shunting her out of her chair so she could use her computer. "Better than that, Dad and I put a copy of "Prey" on his machine when he first got it."

"What, the antitheft software?" asked Thomas.

"Yep!" said Charlotte. "I have just logged the laptop as stolen and given it Elizabeth's email address. If anyone uses it now it will email the location and a photo of who is using it! We just have to wait for it to activate."

"Well, I can see that you have the situation completely in hand. I am starting to feel a bit redundant," laughed Thomas, then, more seriously. "I am booked on a flight to Rome in about an hour. I will give you a call once I have checked in with our..."

"Naples, not Rome!" said Charlotte interrupting in an excited voice. "Dad's laptop is in Naples!"

"Do you have a picture of who is using it?" asked Thomas.

"No, all I've got is a blurry grey image. I'm guessing the laptop lid is half closed." she replied.

"Send me a copy of the email from Prey and I will change my travel arrangements. This is fantastic. Thank-you both for all your help. I will give you a call from Naples. It will probably be tomorrow morning, so both of you should get some well deserved rest. Charlotte, could you make sure I get copies of all emails you get from that tracking software?"

Charlotte promised to forward the emails. They all said goodbye.

Charlotte and Elizabeth looked at each other. "Do you still have your passport, or was it in your bag?' asked Elizabeth.

Charlotte reached into her back pocket, pulled out her passport and held it up to show Elizabeth.

They grinned at one another.

Elizabeth reached for the phone.

17. Naples - Present day

The darkness lifted slowly. Dan groaned as a stabbing pain lanced through his head.

He opened his eyes slowly. The room was only dimly lit. He could see that he was in a small bedroom. Windows, partially obscured by floor length curtains made up one wall. The others were painted in a nondescript, light colour. A large bookshelf on the wall facing the end of the bed contained an eclectic array of ornaments, including a long legged elephant, a small bust of someone that Dan didn't recognise and a smattering of books. A guitar stood against the wall in the corner. It all looked incredibly normal.

Dan forced himself into a sitting position. The stabbing pains in his head where abating. He reached up and felt an egg shaped lump on the back of his head. His jaw felt stiff and hard to move.

To his left he could see a door, on the same wall as the bed head.

He tried to piece together what had happened. He remembered being in the truck with Alberto and heading, he had thought, towards Rome. He remembered being concerned that Alberto had started heading towards Naples instead of turning off to Rome. After that, nothing.

He wondered for a moment whether they had been in an accident, but dismissed the idea. There was no way this was a hospital room. He gingerly touched his jaw. "Bloody Alberto punched me in the face!" he thought with a shock of realisation.

Did he want to steal the car? Am I being kidnapped? Has this got something to do with the box?" All of these question tumbled through Dan's mind as he turned to sit on the edge of the bed. Then he remembered. Alberto knew about the box and Kachenko. He even knew Dan's surname! He was pretty sure that he hadn't told him.

"First things first," he whispered to himself. "Lets find out where I am." He stood up carefully and walked quietly to the window. He pulled back the curtains and looked out. The peeling yellow paint of the wall of another building blocked his view. Leaning forward he could see a narrow alleyway between the building he was in and its neighbour. Looking to his right and left he could see rows of drab looking, rectangular windows. Chinks of light leaked through some of the curtains that covered the windows. He could see people moving behind other, lighter window coverings. Some of the neighbouring windows had small balconies. Some had flower boxes attached, some had air-conditioners or satellite dishes mounted next to them. He counted three rows of windows below the level he was on, plus the ground floor. That would mean that he was on the fifth floor. The alleyway below seemed dark and, to be honest, Dan thought to himself, fairly forbidding. Climbing through this window and scaling five stories to the ground was not an option.

There was no doubt that he was in a city, perhaps Naples, given that was where Alberto, or whoever he really was, had seemed to want to go.

A quick inspection revealed no way to open the window. It was triple glazed. Banging on it or shouting would be unlikely to attract any attention, at least from outside. He lay carefully back down on the bed with his back against the bed head and closed his eyes. He needed to think through his options.

He must have dozed off because the next thing he was aware of was the smell of food and Alberto standing over him, a bowl in each hand.

"Dottore, you eat, eh?" he said, passing him one of the bowls of spaghetti covered in what looked like a chunky tomato sauce. A piece of bread, torn from a larger loaf, had been put in the bowl as well.

Dan was unsure how to respond. He realised that he hadn't eaten much since the night before and he was starving. On the other hand this was the man who had just kidnapped him and stolen his car. Not a man, he thought ruefully, who he should trust.

He hesitated. Alberto laughed. "Don't worry Dottore, the food he is not poisoned," he said with a laugh. "You choose which one you want, eh?"

Dan hesitated a moment longer and then took the bowl that Alberto had originally offered him. Alberto sat down on the end of the bed and started to eat. Dan decided that he was too hungry to worry about being drugged and started eating as well.

"I am so sorry I had to hit you Dottore," said Alberto through a mouthful of bread. "I hope your head she is not too badly bruised. If you hadn't grabbed the wheel of the truck I would not have punched you in it. I would have explained. You did not give me time. I only just managed to avert an accident with the truck, but I am truly sorry I had to hit you."

Alberto sounded so genuinely contrite and his manner was so friendly and unthreatening that Dan decide to withhold judgement on him, at least until after he had eaten.

"Why have you kidnapped me?" he asked, between mouthfuls of food.

"Ah, it was not my intention to kidnap you, Dottore Marsh. I merely wanted to talk, but I needed to get you to safety first. There are some very bad men who want what you have," said Alberto through a mouthful of food.

Dan laughed. "You mean bad men who want to punch me in the face, knock me unconscious and kidnap me?"

Alberto looked so abashed that Dan relented. "What did you want to talk to me about?" he asked.

"Ah, it is, as they say, complicata Dottore," he said using the last of his bread to wipe up what remained of the tomato sauce in his bowl. Finished eating, he placed his empty bowl carefully on the floor next to the bed and turned to look at Dan. "I need to tell you a story, Dottore. When it is finished, if you wish, you and your beautiful car are free to leave. I will even drive the two of you to Rome, as I promised."

Dan nodded.

"I know that you are a man who knows much about the ancient history, Dottore, but do you know much about the rise and fall of Adolf Hitler?"

Dan was taken aback. This was not what he had expected. "My interest has always been a bit earlier than that. I know a little. As much as most people, I suppose." he said, wondering at the sudden improvement in Alberto's English.

"When I was a child, Dottore, I remember seeing a map showing how much territory Hitler had conquered. By 1942 he controlled pretty well all of Europe. This would have been an astonishing feat for one of

76

your great ancient generals, a Julius Caesar or a Genghis Khan, but they were men who had grown up in an environment where leadership and strategy were to them the mother's milk. They trained all their lives to be warriors and leaders. They knew the art of war like you and I know how to drive a car." Alberto paused for a moment, then said in a quieter voice, "So answer me this Dottore, have you ever wondered how a man, a complete non-entity, a failed artist, a lice ridden vagrant living on the streets of Vienna, a man who could not rise above the rank of lance corporal in the German army, with minimal schooling and no leadership skills, rises from nothing to become the Master of Europe? How did this man achieve the stunning military and political victories that he did? How did this man, literally overnight, become a master strategist, a great orator and an inspiring leader?"

Unwilling to engage too deeply in this conversation, and unsure of where it was heading, Dan said, noncommittally "I am not sure that I would class him as an inspiring leader. But then again, I suppose there were those in Germany who must have seen him that way. Perhaps it was all just circumstances?"

"Perhaps," said Alberto. "Descriptions of Hitler as a young man certainly do not give any hint of his future powers and abilities. Did you know that he was turned down for military service by the Austrian army because he was declared physically and mentally unfit? "

Dan shook his head.

"He did manage to join the German army at the beginning of World War One as a volunteer. Perhaps they were not so choosey. Did you know that he won the iron cross for bravery, twice? The first time was for dragging a wounded officer to safety, while under heavy fire. The second, the one that won him the Iron Cross first class, was for single handedly capturing a group of French soldiers he had come upon huddled in a shell hole. The story goes that Hitler crawled to the edge of their shell hole and shouted out to the men that they were surrounded and had better surrender. The Frenchmen fell for it. He won his highest honour for trickery and deception, not brilliance or bravery."

"Did you know that Hitler never applied for a promotion? asked Alberto. Dan shook his head again. "He could have. You win the Iron

Cross first class and you would be considered a great candidate for promotion. Hitler was never recognised for his leadership potential. That really says something about the man, don't you think, Dottore? In a time when hundreds of thousands of men were being lost on the battlefield, sometimes ten of thousands in a single day, and there was a constant demand for new officers to lead the men, is it not surprising that a man who won the Iron Cross first class was never promoted?"

"So, back to my explanation, eh?" he said with an almost apologetic smile. "Many years ago, when I was a student at University, I became interested in finding out how a man like this could become a great strategist and leader. I was studying psychology at the time. I thought that this would be a good topic for my Masters degree." Dan raised an eyebrow, but Alberto continued without noticing. "As I did my research I became more and more confused. It just didn't make sense to me. There seemed to be four Hitlers, four separate men. The most compelling was the incredibly charismatic leader with hypnotic blue eyes, and an amazing grasp of strategy. A military and political genius who took over first Germany and then the rest of Europe. The second man was the worn out husk whose hands shook, who was prone to massive mood swings and whose violent and aggressive tantrums terrified those around him, the man who had destroyed Germany. The third was the brave and sneaky soldier. Willing to put his life on the line for Germany, who in 1918, when he was lying in a hospital bed recovering from a gas attack, and was told of the German surrender, burst into tears, the brave patriot. The fourth and final one, was the progenitor of all the others, the failure, a vagrant living on the streets of Vienna, unable to get admission into the college of arts.

"You have not mentioned the brutal perpetrator of genocide. Where does he fit in?" asked Dan starting to become interested despite his predicament.

"Ah, I will come back to him!" said Alberto, warming to his topic now that he could see that he had sparked an interest in his audience. "I started, naturally, by looking at what the great psychologists said about this man. Did you know that Carl Jung wrote a personality profile of Hitler for the American Secret Service? Jung was recruited by Allan

Dulles, the man who became the first Director of the American's CIA, to be a secret agent for the Allies during the war. Agent 488 wrote an analysis of Hitler for the Office of Strategic Services. Did you know that he actually predicted that Hitler would ultimately commit suicide?"

Dan shook his head.

"All the analyses I read, including Jung's just seemed," here Alberto paused, searching for the right word, "incomplete. It seemed to me, after tracing his history from his early family life through to his eventual suicide, and reading all I could about him, that there was still something that I was missing. The more I read the more I came to believe that there had to be a better explanation for the profound changes in this man that went beyond him having a violent father, an overly developed love for his mother, repressed sexuality or any of the other theories put forward by psychologists over the years.

Alberto stopped, realising he was getting side tracked.

"I chose to concentrate on the change that occurred at the end of the war. Hitler's apparent psychological and physiological collapse, if you like."

Have you ever heard of a man named Theodor Morell, Dottore Marsh?"

Dan shook his head.

"Dottore Morell was a physician. Some, like Albert Speer, said he was a quack. He was born in the 1880s. He practiced in Germany in the years leading up to the Second World War. He studied under a Nobel Prize winning scientist by the name of Élie Metchnikoff. Metchnikoff shared the 1908 Nobel Prize for Medicine. You would know much more about this than I would, but I understand he won it for the study of something called Phagocytosis."

"It is a type of endocytosis, where cells absorb other molecules, yes," said Dan, still eating.

"Yes, yes," said Alberto, not really interested. "This Dottore Morell, he became Adolf Hitler's personal physician in around 1936. He was there when Hitler was rising to the height of his power and was still around at the very end. He was in Hitler's bunker up until a couple of days before Hitler committed suicide in 1944."

"Hitler had a number of doctors who tended him, but Morell was the main one. One of the others was a Dr Karl Brandt. Under interrogation by the Americans straight after the war, Brandt told them that Hitler had received almost daily injections from Morell, the composition of which Morell refused to reveal. He also told them that Morell kept a notebook with him at all times, in which he documented his treatment of Hitler."

"Morell's notebooks were lost for years. A number of people searched for them without any luck. In 1981 they surfaced, along with a bunch of other medical records, in an American medical intelligence archive. Morell had indeed kept meticulous records, a day-by-day log of the details of the treatments he gave Hitler. Given what the Gestapo would have done to him if anything had gone wrong I think I would have done the same thing," said Alberto with a laugh.

"These documents contained all the treatments that Morell gave to Hitler. There is a lot of information in his notebooks. I am not a medical man, or a scientist like yourself Dottore, but I was interested in what Morell had given Hitler. A feeling was growing in me that, perhaps the explanation for the last change in Hitler was drug induced. It seemed logical. A man under extreme stress seeking relief in drugs."

"It turns out that Dottore Morell did give Hitler an astonishing array of medications. Goering called Morell the 'Reichmaster of Injections'. Apparently Hitler's arms were punctured so frequently that Morell sometimes couldn't find anywhere to insert a needle into his veins.

"Morell would be there in the morning when Hitler woke up. If the Führer was not particularly energetic he would inject him with something out of a little gold wrapped package he called Vitamultin. We have confirmation of what was in it because one of Hitler's SS guards, probably under orders from Himmler, who was becoming increasingly paranoid, stole one of the little gold packages. When it was analysed it turned out that Morell was giving Hitler methamphetamine, to give him a kick start in the morning."

"That might explain Hitler's own paranoia. Doesn't methamphetamine use lead to an increased chance of Parkinson's disease?" asked Dan, becoming more interested.

"Yes, it does. In addition to meth-amphetamine, Morell also prescribed drugs containing a host of what we would now see as very strange ingredients, like belladonna, atropine, caffeine, cocaine, E. Coli, morphine, strychnine, potassium bromide, testosterone and a whole range of vitamins."

"The preparation that most interested me though, was one that he listed in his diary as Vitamultin-forte. Out of all the listings in the diary it is the only one for which there is no documentation. Nowhere is there a list of what it contained, which is very strange. In the diary there is always a letter next to each mention of Vitamultin-forte. The first mention is in late 1941 and there is an "a" written next to it. In the last mention of Vitamultin-forte, in late 1945, there is a "j" next to it."

"So what do you think Morell was doing? Asked Dan "Increasing the dosage of whatever this drug was?"

"Don't know. Perhaps. Maybe they were different variations of the same drug." Said Alberto. "Eventually I discovered that a French reporter had interviewed Morell in the hospital just before he died, a lady by the name of Marion Theuriau. She had first interviewed him soon after he was captured in 1945. She interviewed him again in 1948. She spent a couple of days with him just before he died, but I couldn't find anywhere where she had written a story about him based on that second interview. It took ages to track her down. I eventually found her living alone in a little flat in Paris. She very reluctantly told me her story. Once I heard it I was convinced that there was something much, much stranger going on."

18. Germany - 25th May 1948

Marion sat quietly, legs crossed, in a chair beside the doctor's bed, watching him as he tossed and turned in troubled sleep. She knew that he was in his early sixties, but he looked much older. He was thin, almost emaciated, and his skin, pale and blotchy, seemed to hang off him in folds. He had the look of a fat man who had been deflated. She imagined she could hear the air escaping from him each time he exhaled.

She had followed his trail to Tegernsee and then, eventually, to the makeshift hospital in the old abbey. It was full of refugees and demobbed soldiers. The long room she had found him in was crowded and smelt of carbolic soap and stale bodies. Harried nurses moved quickly from patient to patient, many of whom were lying on the floor because of the lack of beds.

His eyes opened. He looked confused, unsure of where he was. He turned his head and saw her sitting beside him. For a moment he just stared blankly, then she saw a spark of recognition in his eyes. "Hanni?" he said, his voice a dry whisper.

"Hello Doctor Morell, Theodore" she said leaning forward and smiling. "It's Marion, we met a couple of years ago. Do you remember?"

Morell struggled to sit up. Marion stood and helped him into a sitting position. She handed him a glass of water from the small metal bedside table.

He looked at her warily as he drank.

"I met you when you were in Dachau, with the Americans? You told me that you had more to tell me, but when I came back to see you, you'd gone." she prompted. He sat back on the pillows abruptly and his eyes darted around the room, as if he was suddenly frightened.

She gently took the glass from his hand and put it back on the side table, then took his unresisting hand in hers.

"Tell me about Hoffman, the photographer," she asked gently, wary of asking him anything that might scare him into silence.

He looked at her and snorted. "Heinrich Hoffman, the homosexual?" he said, with a sneer.

"Was he?" she asked, innocently.

"He had got himself a nasty dose of gonorrhea from one of his boyfriends. A friend of mine referred him to me."

"When was this?" asked Marion, getting out her notepad.

"It would have been the spring of 1936. Hoffman was in Munich, and I really didn't want to travel all the way from Berlin to see him, but I thought that refusing might not look good." Morell paused and looked furtively around the crowded hospital ward. He leant close to Marion and whispered, "You see, Hoffman was close to the Chancellor. He was his private, official, photographer. He had even published a couple of picture books about Hitler, so I agreed to go. I didn't have a choice, you see?"

"It was a good thing too, because on the day I was to leave there was a knock at my door. These were difficult times in Berlin, and there were lots of rumours flying around about people being taken away from their homes and not coming back, so I always looked out the window before I opened the door to anyone. Just to check."

"Standing on my doorstep was a soldier in a black uniform, and down on the street was a big Mercedes staff car. I didn't know what to do. The solider banged on the door again and as he did he turned and saw me in the window. I remember waving to him and then going to open the door."

"When I opened it he told me that he was there to take me to the airport. The Führer had sent his own private aeroplane to fly me to Munich to see Hoffman."

"But that wasn't the biggest shock." he said leaning forward and lowering his voice. "That evening, when I walked into the dinning room, I couldn't believe my eyes. Adolf Hitler was one of the dinner guests and the only spare seat was the one next to him. Hoffman jumped up and introduced us and then sat me down roght next to the Führer."

Marion raised her eyebrows. "What did you talk about?" she whispered conspiratorially.

Morell seemed pleased by her interest and sat back, looking more confident. "Oh, he had been very concerned about his friend Hoffman and asked me about his treatment. Then he consulted me about the death of his driver Julius Schreck. He knew all the details of the treatment Schreck was given. It sounded to me like he had died of meningitis. I told him that I thought that the treatment had been botched and how it should have been handled."

"To be honest, I was a bit surprised how sad Hitler was about the whole thing. He almost seemed depressed. Apparently he and his chauffeur had known each other for a long time and had been very close."

"I stayed with Hoffman for about four weeks. At the end of that time he was cured. He was so pleased with what I had done that he insisted that I join him on a trip to Venice, as a thank you."

"Did you go?" asked Marion.

"I did, he said. "But, after all that excitement I can tell you that I was glad to finally get back home to Hanni and my practice on the Kurfürstendamm."

"Did the Chancellor go on the trip to Venice?" asked Marion, almost shyly, playing up to the older man.

"No, he didn't, thank God. At that time, before I knew him well, I was terrified of him. I would watch him at dinner at the Hoffman's. He would never say much, at first. He would just pick at the vegetarian meals that were put in front of him. He didn't drink alcohol, but everyone else, of course, did. Often, as the conversations around the table became more animated Hitler would become interested in a topic that one or other of the dinner guests were discussing. He would join in the conversation and then work himself up into a state over some minor issue, almost as if he needed to be angry. He would wave his arms around and shout down anyone who disagreed with him. It was quite a performance."

"After that first time I took to making sure that I was seated well away from him at dinner and only ever spoke to anyone in a whisper."

"Did you ever see Hoffman again?" she asked.

"Yes. It was a bit of surprise really. Hanni and I received an invitation to spend Christmas with Erna and Heinrich." Morell's voice faltered. He looked down at his hands, resting on the grey woollen blanket that covered him. A tear ran down his cheek. Marion reached out and put her hand on his.

"Hanni had been so concerned," he said in a quiet voice. "I can still see the look on her face when she brought the invitation in to me. I was sitting at my desk, finishing up some notes on the patient I had just seen. She was frowning, scared. She told me she really didn't want to go. She said the Nazis terrified her and she was adamant that she didn't want anything to do with them."

"That was the moment," he said sighing. "If I had listened to Hanni, how different our lives would have been. I wish..." he paused again and took a deep breath, "I wish, more than anything in my life, that I hadn't accepted that invitation. I had been so convinced that it was a good career move." he shook his head and fell silent once more.

Marion waited, holding his hand.

"In those days I was always worried about money," he said, after a few minutes. "Being able to provide for Hanni and me as we got older was important. I know people would say we were well off, but, at least in my mind, we weren't wealthy, not wealthy enough."

"I asked her what harm it could possibly do to cultivate contacts at the highest levels of the German government and what opportunities might come our way if we did. She wasn't convinced, but in the end I persuaded her by telling her that we should accept the invitation because it could well be more dangerous to refuse."

"We had gone, of course. Then, one day, the Hoffman's told us we were all going on a trip to the Berghof, Hitler's home in the Obersalzberg."

"I remember how impressed I was with the house. It had its own bowling alley!' he said laughing at the memory and shaking his head. "Hanni and I were watching Eva and Gretl Braun, and the Hoffmans, bowling. We were too old for that sort of stuff so we had found a nice warm spot by the fire. We were sitting there, just enjoying the warmth and each others company, when Hitler walked up. He asked if I could spare him a moment. He was very polite. What could I do?"

Morell closed his eyes. Marion let him rest, wondering if there really was a story in this old man's memories, or if she was just wasting her time. She wondered, as she listened to Morell's laboured breathing, how much time she had to find out,

19. Berghof - December 1936

Morell followed Hitler into the conservatory, where he invited him to sit down. The Führer clearly had something on his mind, but before he could say anything Doctor Brandt, Hitler's doctor, and Martin Bormann, his personal secretary, burst into the room. Hitler jumped to his feet. His face had turned scarlet, enraged by the interruption. Before Brandt or Bormann had a chance to say anything, Hitler was yelling at them to get out. They turned tail and ran. Hitler slammed the door shut after them. Morell sat, unspeaking, stunned by the vehemence of the RiechFührer's rage.

Apologising for the interruption, Hitler settled back comfortably into his chair, almost as if nothing had happened.

" I wanted to talk to you, Morell, on a very personal matter." said Hitler, steepling his fingers. "For some time I have been concerned that my current physician, Doctor Brandt, has been struggling to find a suitable treatment to give me relief from the severe stomach pains that afflict me from time to time. He has also been struggling with this," he said, pulling up his trouser legs. Both legs were wrapped in bandages.

As Hitler unrolled the bandages Morell could see large areas of his flesh that looked red, puffy and angry. Scabs covered areas where Hitler had obviously been scratching and caused his legs to bleed.

"None of my Doctors have been able to do a thing for me," said Hitler angrily. "You seem to have worked wonders on Heinrich. I would like you to see if you can cure me. I don't have time to be sick, Morell!"

Taken aback by the request, Morell hesitated.

Before he had a chance to say anything Hitler said. "I will tell you what Morell. If you can work me a cure I will give you a new house up here in the Obersalzberg."

Stunned by the generosity of the Führer's offer, and prompted by his own greed, Morell nodded his head. "Of course, I would be delighted to see what I can do to help," he said quickly. "Would tomorrow be convenient? I could give you a complete physical examination then.

Hitler nodded. The two men shook hands.

****

"What do we need with a new house! " Hanni hissed angrily, when he told her about his new patient later in the day. "Why do we need to come here of all places? You have got a splendid practice in Berlin and we've got a lovely house. There is no better address than the Kurfürstendamm! We don't need to become part of all this." she had said with a wave of her arm. She had been so angry with him she didn't' talk to him for the rest of the day. She didn't even relent when he had climbed into their freezing cold bed that evening.

20. Germany - 26th May 1948

Morell had seemed pleased to see her when Marion had walked up to his bedside. He seemed to be in better spirits than he had been the previous day and even seemed eager to talk.

When she delicately asked him about becoming Hitler's doctor she noticed his chest puff out and he started to talk, his voice professional and impersonal.

"I first examined Adolf up at the Berghof. He told me all about the lung problems he had as a child. He showed me the scar he had got in the Great War, a deep furrow in the flesh of his thigh, which he said didn't cause him any problem. When I felt the wound I'm sure I felt a solid lump. In my opinion there was still shrapnel in there."

"Hitler talked at length, and in surprising detail, about the regularity of his bowel movements and his frequent bouts of intense abdominal pain. We also discussed, again at length, the eczema that affected much of his body, but particularly his legs."

"Having examined him I told him that I would have him cured within a year, and, true to my word, I did." he said proudly, perhaps, Marion thought, even arrogantly.

"Did being Hitler's doctor change your life?" she asked, trying to appear interested while keeping the rising contempt out of her voice.

"I became one of the kings of the world." he said. "When it got out that I was the Chancellor's doctor my practice in Berlin took off. Suddenly the great and the good of Germany started knocking at my door. Industrialists like Alfried Krupp and August Thyssen, aristocrats like Prince Phillip of Hesse and the Nazi party elite, like Hermann Göring, von Ribbentrop, Albert Speer and Alfred Rosenberg all came to consult me."

He chuckled to himself. "I even treated the British Prime Minister, Mister Neville Chamberlain."

"In those days Adolf and I were inseparable. You should have seen the faces of the Bormanns and the Brandts ,and all the other sycophants that hung around the Führer, when they found out that he regularly just dropped into my house for dinner. They were so jealous. Even Hanni was won over, eventually, trying to please Adolf, going out of her way to make his favourite almond cakes when she knew he was coming for Sunday tea."

Remembering Hanni suddenly deflated the old man. He hung his head and mumbled, in a voice bitter with regret, "They would have torn their own hearts out if they had known how much trust he put in me, if they knew what I knew."

Marion had almost missed the last comment. She stood up and put her hand over his in a manner she hoped was comforting. "What did you know, Theo?"

At first he didn't respond. She thought that he had fallen asleep, but then he said, almost too softly for her to hear. "Secrets... greatest secret .... promised ... never tell... last time I saw him." Then his eyes closed and his breathing became more regular. He had fallen asleep again.

Marion sat back down and waited, her hand still on his, listening to Morell's breathing grow shallower with each breath. Hours later, just when she was nodding off herself, she felt him squeeze her hand.

"I was scared," he said, his voice weak and rasping, "in the Führerbunker, on that last day."

21. Berlin - April 1945

Morell put his hand on the cold concrete wall of the Führerbunker. He could feel the almost continuous vibration caused by the massive Russian bombardment going on in the city above. He shivered.

He looked into the mirror that, miraculously, still managed to cling to the wall. A large man looked back, overweight, balding, with a round head. Round framed, thick, pebble lensed spectacles enhanced the overall look of roundness. He inspected his pallid complexion. "You are a cowardly, stupid, fat and round old man!" he said to himself bitterly.

He looked down at his beautifully tailored uniform. All the officers around the Führer had fancy uniforms so he had this one specially made, to his own design. Now it was grimy and sweat stained and the gold braid was falling off.

He sat down heavily on his bed, casting his gaze around the small, pokey room he had been allocated in the Führerbunker. He put his head in his hands. He wondered, in an increasingly frequent moment of self reflection, how he had ended up in this situation. It did not take much reflection though, he thought. It was obvious. He had ended up here because he was a foolish, greedy, opportunistic man who had not heeded the wise counsel of his beautiful wife, and best friend. Hanni had warned him to stay away from these people. He hadn't listened. He had been seduced by the security and the wealth that he thought being Hitler's physician would give him.

"Money and hubris!" he whispered bitterly to himself. "One I didn't realise I had too much of. The other I always thought I had too little of."

Despite Hanni's counsel, despite the warning signs, he had taken the chance to ride the coat tails of the most powerful and dangerous man in Germany and had held on too long, way too long.

He stood up and straightened his uniform as best he could. Hitler had been sending his staff out of the bunker to safety in Southern Germany for days now. He badly wanted to go too. He checked his pulse. His heart was racing. He knew he was grossly overweight, and that put extra strain on his heart. He promised himself that, if he got out of this mess and back to Hanni, he would go for more walks and stop being such a glutton.

With a deep sigh he stepped towards the door. He was due to give Hitler another injection. This time, he promised himself, he would ask him about leaving.

****

Morell nodded at the guard as the steel door to Hitler's private rooms was opened for him. The Führer, slouched on a sofa, his head hanging down, looked despondent and beaten, a shell of the man he once was. Morell knew that there were those among the high ranking Nazi's who blamed him for the state of Hitler's health. He knew better.

He sat down in front of him and put his black medical bag between them. Hitler lifted his head to look into Morell's eyes. "We didn't find it, did we Theo?" he said. His voice was quiet, flat and resigned.

"No! I failed you my Führer!" said Morell looking down dejectedly at the needles and vials in his bag.

"We didn't even get close, did we? Not even with the electron microscope I got for you?"

"No," said Morell in a quiet voice. "I tried, my Führer. It was just too complex to analyse. If I knew more about where it came from, its history, had a larger sample to work with, perhaps it would have been easier to identify the active ingredients."

Hitler shook his head. "Those few drops were all that was left," he said sadly, hanging his head again. "It gave me such insight. I cannot begin to describe to you how it felt. To be able to see the world through his eyes! I could see the future! All futures! Futures where my Reich lasted for a thousand years! A future where I was remembered as a God!" he said, some of his old fire returning.

"It made me feel like a God! It filled me with such energy, such a sense of power that you wouldn't believe!" he said, becoming more animated. He gripped Morell's hand where it rested on his knee with surprising strength.

"Would you believe that I even saw this future, Morell," he said, his voice becoming calm, almost wistful. "A future where I would be reviled! A conqueror cast upon the scrap heap of history. But the fools do not realise yet what I have created. Germany will rise again, Morell. She will rise like a Phoenix out of the ashes of my achievements, stronger than ever before! Mark my words, Doctor. Germany will rule Europe once again."

Morell shivered. Hitler sat, his hypnotic blue eyes staring at some distant vision. He relaxed. "Perhaps it really was the blood of Constantine the Great. Perhaps I was seeing the world through his eyes. Hess always believed that it was so," he said.

"If it was then it was very unusual blood!" said Morell. "Do you think Hess had any more of it?"

"No. He only had the one vial. I know that he took some of your trials with him when he flew to England, though," said Hitler, his energy fading. His hand was shaking now. He was becoming distressed.

"I will just give you a glucose shot, if you will roll up your sleeve," said Morell, reaching for the Führer's arm.

Hitler suddenly jumped to his feet, his eyes staring wildly and his body shaking with rage, "Do you think I am crazy! I know what you are going to do! You are going to give me Morphine! You are in league with the Generals! I know that they want to take me away from Berlin! I will not go!" he was shouting now. Morell was being sprayed with saliva.

"It is your incompetence that has destroyed me!" shouted Hitler pointing an accusing finger at Morell. "If you had been able to replicate the relic like you promised, we would not be in this place! It is your incompetence, your failure that has brought Germany down! You have destroyed the Third Reich! You have destroyed my great vision through your incompetence!"

Morell fell to the floor at Hitler's feet, terrified. "Please no, my Führer! I tried as hard as I could. I did everything you asked! Please just let me go. Let me out of here. Let me leave Berlin! My heart cannot stand the strain. Please let me go, please!" Sobbing now, Morell felt a pain in his chest. "My heart!" he wailed.

Hitler, still angry, shouted for his adjutant. "Get this pathetic, incompetent quack on the next plane out!" he said in disgust. Morell stood up. He turned to Hitler, to thank him, but the Führer fixed him with a malevolent stare. "Be warned Morell. I have seen your future. If you ever breath a word of my secret to a living soul I will reach out from my grave and tear your beating heart from your chest. Now, get out of that ridiculous vaudeville uniform, put on some plain clothes, and go back to being the pathetic little doctor of the Kurfürstendamm!"

22. Berlin - 2am - 22nd April

Morell, wearing an ill fitting brown suit he had borrowed, watched out the window of the Focke Wulf Condor as the Gatow airfield fell away below. It was 2 am in the morning and it was very dark. The drive to the airport, to the southwest of Berlin, had been a mad dash along back streets and then a terrifying hike through the carcasses of bombed out buildings. Now that they were in the air, Morell could see, for the first time, the extent of the devastation. Berlin was a jagged wasteland of shattered architecture. He stared out the window mesmerised by the sight of the burning city that passed a few hundred metres below the plane.

The plane flew low over the Russian lines. The Russians had already advanced as far as Jüterbog, less than a days walk from Berlin! Everywhere Morell looked he saw burning buildings. Search lights pierced the sky and the flashes of anti aircraft guns were everywhere. Terrified of being shot down, terrified of what the future would hold, Theodor Morell put his head in his hands and cried.

****

In his bunker the Führer lay on his bed, alone. He stared at the concrete ceiling of his room. The sound of the Russian shells was louder than they had been this morning. He knew this was the end. It was only a matter of days now before the Russians overran the Reichstag and the bunker. This was not how it was supposed to end. This was not how he had envisioned his thousand year Reich, not in the beginning.

23. Germany - 26th May 1948

Marion looked down at the cold still body cf Theodore Morell. She thought for a moment about what she had heard. It sounded like the demented ramblings of an old man whose mind had been broken. If they weren't, and if what she had just heard were true, then what good would come of telling this story. Would it help to heal Europe any faster?

She turned towards the door, picking her way carefully between the poor souls scattered around the floor.

A nurse, hurried past, "Did you get a good story Miss?" she asked brightly, with a quick smile.

"No," replied Marion. "It was a dead end, I'm afraid."

24. Naples - Present day

Charlotte and Elizabeth sat in the office of the head of Security at the Naples Airport. They had not been told why they had been taken out of the arrivals queue and were both feeling angry. Despite asking questions in progressively more disjointed but aggressive Italian, none of the uniformed men who had escorted them to the office, or who now stood at the back of the office watching them with impassive faces, had given them any indication of why they were being treated this way.

They had been waiting an hour before the office door opened and Thomas Malm walked in.

Elizabeth was on her feet as soon as she saw him. "Is this your doing Thomas?" she asked angrily. "Have we been arrested? What is going on? How did you even know we were here? Why are we here?"

Thomas smiled his most charming and apologetic smile. He took a step backward and put his arms up in a gesture of submission, as if retreating under the barrage of her anger. "I must apologise. Yes, it was my doing. No, you haven't been arrested. I asked my friends here at the airport to detain you so I could come and talk to you before you got yourselves in real trouble. Daniel would never forgive me if I let anything happen to you!"

Elizabeth calmed down sufficiently to accept Thomas's invitation to resume her seat. He sat down as well.

"I thought," said Thomas, looking serious, "that we had agreed that I would be the one to follow up this lead. Clearly I had not made my position clear enough. You have got yourselves involved in a situation that could turn out to be very dangerous. While we don't know exactly what is going on, we do know that someone has ransacked your San Lucido apartment.

"We suspect that someone followed Daniel when he, foolishly, went back to the apartment to pick up the Aston Martin. Courtesy of our Italian colleagues we have security camera footage from a neighbouring building that shows two men in a van were around the area all morning. They left right after Daniel drove away. The Italian police also now suspect that the fire in the Traverni workshop was deliberately lit. Not only that, but, we found the Jaguar that picked you up at the airport, yesterday. It was still smouldering at the back of a council estate outside London when my people got there. Your bag was still on the back seat, Charlotte. There was nothing salvageable I am afraid." Thomas paused to let the news sink in. "These were professionals, whoever they were. We found the remains of a cell phone jammer in the glove box. This is not a game. It looks like, whatever you have got yourself involved in, involves some extremely unpleasant people. When our systems flagged that you had booked a flight to Naples I had to stop you from doing something that you might later regret. I know you are both concerned about Daniel, but you must let me take charge of this situation."

Neither Charlotte nor Elizabeth looked at Thomas.

They all sat in silence for a few minutes. "I tell you what," said Thomas. "If you give me direct access to Daniel's Prey account, I will arrange for you to come with the team I have put together to retrieve Daniel and his laptop. That way you will know what is going on first hand and I will know that you are not in any danger. I will permit this on one condition, that you agree to do exactly what I tell you, when I tell you, without question."

Reluctantly they agreed to Thomas' proposition. Ten minutes later they were in a black Mercedes heading away from the airport into the city of Naples. Thomas, and two other men, were in another black Mercedes ahead of them.

****

"Save me," said Thomas angrily to no-one in particular, "from the good intentions of fucking amateurs!" He shook his head. Now, he thought to himself, I have to worry about these two bloody tourists on an operation that was already a bit on the edge of legality."

He sighed quietly to himself. It had cost him a lot of favours to get the Italians to turn a blind eye to this little incursion into their territory. If anything went wrong heads would roll, and he knew it would be his head leading the pack.

"Better that than having them blundering around getting in the way, Sir," said the driver. Thomas grunted agreement. Resigned to his lot he reached for his smart phone. At least, he thought to himself, he had control of the access point to Daniel's laptop. That was a big plus.

Checking, once again, the address that the software was showing, he confirmed their destination over his two way radio with the men in the other car. They raced down the wide main thoroughfares of Naples and then plunged into the city's narrow side streets.

****

The car was moving too fast for Elizabeth to see where they were going. She soon lost all sense of direction as the driver, who obviously knew the roads well, steered the car down one narrow side street after another. It was still very early in the morning and there were few cars about, and even fewer people.

The Mercedes stopped, drawing up behind its twin. She saw Thomas jump out of the lead car and walk back to theirs. He gestured for her to wind the window down and then said in a business like manner "Whatever happens, do not get out of the car! Harry here," he said indicating their driver, "Will get you out of here in the unlikely event that any real trouble starts."

As he turned away to talk to his men Elizabeth couldn't help but notice that he now held a small machine gun in his hand. One of his men handed him a solid looking vest that he immediately put on over his shirt. The man who had been sharing the back seat with them also go out of the car and was pulling on a similar vest.

Thomas and his men walked up the street, past the Mercedes. As he passed a van parked a few metres further up the street, Thomas slapped it with the flat of his hand. Almost instantly three men stepped out of it. All carried guns and wore body armour. One of them carried a large, heavy looking steel tube with handles. Moments later they had disappeared around a corner.

The area they had stopped in seemed typical of what both Charlotte and Elizabeth had seen of the backstreets of Naples. The roads were narrow. There was colourful graffiti and layers of peeling posters on the walls and the ubiquitous roller blinds that seemed to cover most of the ground floor openings to the buildings. Cars lined either side of the streets where they could fit between the big wheeled bins that all overflowed with rubbish.

In light of their lack of either body armour or any form of defensive weapon Charlotte and Elizabeth agreed with the driver, Harry, that it was perhaps best if they stayed where they were. With a solid clunk the driver locked the Mercedes' doors. Elizabeth wondered for a moment whether that was to keep them in or others out. Probably both she concluded grimly to herself.

****

Thomas pulled his smart phone from his pocket. Two of the men currently on the other side of the building had done the same. Within a few seconds the software installed on the three smartphones triangulated the location of Daniel's laptop. Thomas quietly forced the entry door. He and the other man from the lead Mercedes moved cautiously into the front hall of the building. It was quiet and dark. The foyer's only decoration was peeling paint and a row of locked mailboxes. A narrow staircase curved upwards. As they moved quietly up the steps the three men from the van fell in behind them.

Thomas pointed upwards and then held up his hand with fingers spread. They were heading for the fifth floor flat. The others nodded. They met no one on the way up the stairs. They paused outside the door to the only apartment on the fifth floor. They knew they would have to be quick. Any hesitation on their part could mean Daniel's life. Two men from the van were pulling pins out of M84 flashbangs. These grenades designed to blind, deafen and disorientate anyone inside would be thrown through the door as soon as it was opened. The third man moved quietly into a position where he could use the Enforcer to open the door. The Enforcer, or the "big key", as it was sometimes jokingly called, could apply a force of over 3 tonnes to a door lock. Assuming the door wasn't reinforced in any way, it was the fastest way to gain entry.

Thomas quickly checked that his Heckler and Koch MP5 submachine gun was ready for action. Satisfied he made eye contact with each of his men. They each nodded. They were ready to go.

Thomas took a deep breadth. He nodded to the man with the Enforcer.

25. Naples - Present day

Dan looked at Alberto. "You don't really believe that Hitler took some sort of magic potion that gave him the power to take over the world do you!? He said scornfully.

Alberto laughed. "Oh I admit I was sceptical at first. I initially thought that it was just Morell making up a story to impress a pretty young reporter, or maybe to make himself seem more mysterious and interesting. Who really understands the motives of these Nazis. They were a strange bunch!"

"Like I said this young reporter, she had interviewed Morell when he was first captured. He told her then about what he had done with Hitler's medical records. Apparently they were taken out of Berlin by one of Hitlers's trusted officers, to supposed safety in southern Germany, to a town called Bad Reichenhall, near Salzburg. Morell had set up some sort of medical institute there run by a Doctor Riedel."

"I found a written deposition made by Riedel that confirmed that two trucks arrived in early April 1945 from Morell's pharmaceutical company Hamma Inc. The trucks were carrying seventy crates of what Morell described as "glandular secretions". These were apparently needed for his pharmaceutical processes, but I believe they were something to do with the work he was doing personally for Hitler. The crates and Morell's diaries and other files were all buried in the courtyard of the institute."

"When the reporter heard about the location of the diaries and files she, quite properly, told the authorities, who happened to be the Americans at that time. A squad of G.I.s raided the place. Doctor Riedel, was happy to give up the location of the buried records in return for being left alone to get on with running his institute."

"The diaries and all the other files were sent to a Military Intelligence Service Centre that had been set up in what had once been the Luftwaffe's notorious Dulag Luft interrogation camp."

"With the records available to them a team set to work interrogating Morell."

"The head of the interrogation team was a former research chemist. That seemed, to me, to be an odd choice. I would have thought that a medical Doctor would have been a more appropriate person to talk to Hitler's physician. That is," said Alberto with a slight pause, "unless the objective was less about investigating Hitler's medical condition, and really about investigating the types of compounds he was being given."

"I couldn't find out much from the American's about how Morell was treated, but his wife, Hanni, made a statement that he had whispered to her, when she had visited him in prison, that the Americans had torn out his toe-nails."

"The official record of interrogation portrays Morell as a bewildered old man with a "shaky" memory. At one point the interrogator's report notes that Morell would recall things that he was later unable to confirm. The whole report, in my mind, was written to discredit Morell as a reliable witness. Then, unbelievably, the Americans let him go!"

"Now, I would imagine that Hitler's Doctor, who had been virtually by his side since 1937, who had been his friend, and no doubt confidante, would be a useful resource for the prosecutors in their preparations for the Nuremberg trials. But no! Morell was never charged with anything! He was never asked to give evidence at Nuremberg, or at any other trial. Not even as a witness! Apparently he was just dumped at a railway station with his discharge papers stuffed in his pocket and left. He was so disoriented that he just stayed at the station. A nurse eventually found him and had him immediately admitted to hospital. He never left. He died a few months later, a confused rambling old man."

"Maybe he really was just an innocent. It sounds like he had been through a lot. Maybe he had just lost it," said Dan.

"Possibly," said Alberto. "Like I said, I find it hard to believe that a man who spent so much time at Hitler's side, wouldn't be called as a witness at the war crimes trials. He must have seen things. He must have heard things! An alternative view would be that he told the American's everything he knew about Hitler and this magical potion and, perhaps, his reward was his freedom. Perhaps they drugged him!"

"What happened to that store of glandular secretions that you mentioned? Did that give any clue to what Morell was doing?" asked Dan.

"There is no record of them that I can find anywhere. They just disappeared," said Alberto.

They sat in silence for some time. Then Dan, always a sucker for a good mystery, reluctantly said, "I'm intrigued, but nowhere near convinced, and I can't imagine you would be. You must have done more research."

"Oh, yes! " said Alberto, "I did. And by doing so opened up a Pandora's box. I actually wish that I had been able to just leave it alone. By pursuing it I came to the notice of certain people who really didn't want someone like me to discover what they had been doing. Once you become involved in this, Dottore, the world becomes a very dangerous, very scary and very different place!"

A sound from beyond the bedroom made Alberto stand up. "Just a moment," he said, a concerned look on his face. He stood up and walked quickly from the room.

26. Naples - Present day

The apartment door shattered under the blow from the Enforcer, taking part of the door jamb with it. Before the door had even fully opened the flash-bangs exploded in the apartment.

Thomas led the way through the door. The apartment was small. A main room leading off a short entrance hall and a bedroom, Kitchen and bathroom leading off the main room. It took only a matter of seconds to check for any occupants. It was empty.

Thomas scanned the room. The laptop sat on the Kitchen counter, its lid half closed. His thoughts raced. With the sudden shock of realisation, he shouted to his men. "The women! Damn it! Its a bloody setup! Back to the cars! Go! Go! Go!"

The men raced for the door and, careless of the amount of noise they now made, stormed down the staircase. Bursting through the front door they raced around the corner to where the Mercedes stood.

The driver's window was smashed. Harry lay sprawled, half in and half out of the car. Blood pooled on the road and in the gutter around him. The rear doors of the car stood open. There was no sign of Elizabeth or Charlotte.

Thomas stood looking at the scene. With an uncharacteristic display of emotion his steel capped boot smashed into the front headlamp of the Mercedes shattering it. "Fuck! Fuck! Fuck!" he said angrily.

Book 2

1. Naples - Present day

Dan got off the bed and followed Alberto into the main room of the apartment. Alberto looked up as he walked in. He had been taking something from the oven in the small Kitchen. The smell of fresh baked cake filled the room.

"Ah! She is not burnt! Thank God!" said Alberto taking a cake from the oven.

"I like to cook," said Alberto almost apologetically when he saw Dan watching him. "My nonna used to make this apple cake for me when I was a boy. I whipped it up while I was waiting for you to uh," Alberto paused, "... to uh, wake up," he said self-consciously, putting the cake down and sliding an espresso pot onto the cooktop and lighting the gas. "I made it as a sort of apology for having to punch you in the head! Again I am sorry for that Dottore."

Dan felt the bruise on his jaw but didn't say anything. He sat down at one of the high stools that stood next to the Kitchen counter. He watched as Alberto carefully removed the steaming cake from the tin it had been baked in and then expertly flipped it over onto a serving plate. In quick movements he sprinkled it with icing sugar and then cut two large slices that he deftly slid onto smaller plates. He placed one in front of Dan then turned, took the coffee pot off the stove and poured its contents into two small coffee cups. He placed one of the coffees next to the cake.

The cake was hot, moist and delicious. The coffee was hot and aromatic. Neither spoke until their plates had been emptied and their cups had been drained.

"Come, sit in a more comfortable chair," said Alberto pointing to two large leather armchairs that, along with a matching settee and a low coffee table, filled most of the living room of the small apartment.

"Is this your place?' asked Dan as he settled himself into one of the armchairs.

"No. It belongs to a," Alberto thought for a moment, "...cousin of mine," he said with a small smile. "She is in America at the moment, studying. She lets me use this place when I come to Napoli."

"So where is your home?" asked Dan, conversationally.

'Originally I come from Calabria," said Alberto. "My family home was in a small town, but I have not been back there in many years. Not since I got involved in this," he said indicating a pile of folders and documents spread out in front of him. "I wouldn't want to involve my family and friends in this business. The people behind all this would not hesitate to use them against me if they knew who they were, or knew who I was."

"But that doesn't include cousins?" asked Dan looking around the apartment.

"Ah," said Alberto, "Elena, she is a very special sort of cousin. More, how do you say in English? A kissing cousin?"

Dan laughed. "I see. So is your real name Alberto?"

"No, Dan, my real name has been hidden for many years. It is the only protection I have for my family. Alberto has become my real name for the time being, perhaps even for the rest of my life," he said sadly.

"So who are these people that are so intent on keeping this magic potion you have stumbled on a secret?" asked Dan.

"That is difficult to say. I have never been able to figure out if there is one person who uses a number of different organisations or several organisations."

"I suspect that people in the American Intelligence agencies knew about it almost straight after the war from Morell. I also know that the Camorra are involved. Whether that is because they know something or just because someone is using them as muscle I don't know. There is also, I suspect, a Russian interest that has arisen. I think, perhaps because they were the first into Hitler's Bunker, that they might have found something, some documents, maybe. They may well have found something there that caused the KGB to become involved. I don't know what the British know, but I suspect that Rudolf Hess could have told the British secret service about the drugs that Morell was trying to make for Hitler."

"How about you continue with your story?" suggested Dan.

"Okay. So, after I tracked down the French lady reporter it looked like I had reached a dead end. Going back over my notes I thought that maybe the Rudolf Hess angle was one that I could follow up. Morell had mentioned something about Hess taking some of the potion he had brewed up to England. It all seemed a bit odd to me."

"Hess, he was the one in Spandau Prison for years and years?" asked Dan.

"Yes," said Alberto. "He died in 1987. They knocked the prison down in the same year, so, at first, I couldn't figure out where to start my search."

"There were plenty of sources that gave me a good background on Hess though. He was a close confidant of Hitler's from the early years. Hitler used to tell a story of how they met during the first world war when Hitler was a runner and Hess was a young officer. After the war, when Hitler was starting to make a name for himself with the national Socialists, as a political agitator, Hess heard him speak at a rally in Munich. Hess must have seen something in Hitler's ravings that impressed him. He joined the party soon after."

"The two young men became close. They became even closer when Hess was injured trying to protect Hitler from a Marxist bomb that exploded during one of their meetings sometime in 1921. After the failure of the famous Beer Hall Putsch in 1923 they both ended up in Landsberg Prison together. By that time Hess had become Hitler's most trusted confidant and there is no doubt that Hess idolised Hitler."

"It was Hess that worked with Hitler on his famous manifesto, Mein Kampf. Have you ever read it?" asked Alberto.

Dan shook his head.

"I don't recommend it!" said Alberto with a laugh. "As far as I can figure it out, Landsberg Prison was where it all changed. Where this new, dynamic Hitler suddenly emerges."

"A few years ago a bundle of papers, including 300 cards filled out by Hitler's visitors, as well as extensive correspondence from the prison management, turned up. Hitler had a lot of visitors. As far as I can tell being in prison didn't restrict his political activities at all."

"When I went through the visitors list there was one name that really stood out for me. Every Wednesday between June and December 1924, Prof. Dr. Karl Haushofer turned up at the prison. Haushofer was one of Hess' old Professors."

"Every Wednesday Haushofer gave his "young eagles," as he liked to call Hess and Hitler, a personalised university course in geopolitics. He had them read historians like Leopold von Ranke and Heinrich Treitschke. Philosophers like Karl Marx and Friedrich Nietzsche. He got them to read the social Darwinist Houston Stewart Chamberlain, the geographer Ratzel, and the the political scientist Kjellén, as well as the writings of Otto von Bismarck, Carl von Clausewitz and Haushofer's own writings on the political situation in Japan. Hitler was a lazy man, so I would guess that Hess read him the books."

"Many of the Nazi's more extreme policies date from this time. The whole idea of "*lebensraum*", the need for more German living space, was an idea that Haushofer had developed and promoted."

"Hitler once described his time in Landsberg Prison as his university education at state expense," said Alberto.

While he had been talking Alberto had been looking through one of the files on the coffee table. He pulled out a single sheet of paper. "Haushofer had ended up a Major General by the end of the first world war, but retired, bitter and disillusioned, convinced that the German Government had stabbed the military in the back by surrendering. After the war he taught at the University in Munich where he took on Hess as an assistant. To give you an idea of how frustrated he was with the way Germany was being run I have a copy of a letter that he wrote to his wife towards the end of the first world war. In it he says, "You see how ready for a Caesar I am, and what kind of a good instrument I would be for a Caesar, if we had one and if he knew how to make use of me.""

"These three men, Hitler, the political agitator, Haushofer, the academic and one of the originators of the discipline of Geopolitics, and Hess all had a common bond through the Great War. They all shared a belief that Germany had been betrayed, not only by the Allies, through the Treaty of Versailles, but by their own government."

"Haushofer vehemently believed that only "real men" fought at the front and that only "real men" had the right to guide the nation's future after the disaster of the first world war. Professor Haushofer had found his future Caesar in Adolf Hitler. All he needed to do was to lead him to the banks of his Rubicon."

"This is all very interesting," said Dan getting restless. "But what has this go to to do with your mysterious potion?"

"Ah well," said Alberto with a smile, "Karl Haushofer had two sons, Albrecht and Heinz. Albrecht often went along to Landsberg prison with his father. Hess had lived with the Professor's family for a time and the young men were about the same age and knew each other well. Albrecht, was initially enamoured with Hitler and the Nazi movement, like Hess and his father, and he too joined the party."

"Through the early years of the Nazi regime both father and son worked in prestigious positions in the Nazi government. Albrecht even took up a position as Hess' assistant. But the Haushofer family was playing a very dangerous game. The Professor's mother, Albrecht's grandmother, was Jewish."

"From what I discovered Albrecht was a very different man to his father. He didn't agree with all of his father's views and he certainly didn't agree with the Nazi views on racial purity. He seemed to have thought, naively as it turns out, that he would be able to work inside the system to curb the excesses of the party. It seems pretty clear to me now that Albrecht Haushofer played a significant role in setting up Hess' strange flight to England."

"I also discovered that ,when the purges started after the famous failed attempt to assassinate Hitler in 1944 in the conference room at the Wolf's lair, Albrecht, without Hess' protection came under suspicion, even though I can't find any evidence that he was directly involved. He escaped to a farm in the mountains, but the SS tracked him down. He was imprisoned and tortured. He almost survived the war. The day the Russians entered Berlin the SS killed him. They took him, and a bunch of other Germans who had resisted the Nazis, out into the street and shot them."

"I'm getting confused. I still don't see where this is heading Alberto! What has this to do with the potion?" asked Dan impatiently.

"I am getting to that Dan. Please bear with me a little longer. Albrecht's brother, Heinz, found his body a couple of weeks after he was killed. Stuffed in his jacket pocket was a sheaf of poems Albrecht had written while he was in prison. They have since been published as the Moabit Sonnets."

"Never heard of them," said Dan.

"You should read them. One of his sonnets was called guilt. I remember it," he said, closing his eyes.

"I am guilty,
But not in the way you think.
I should have earlier recognised my duty;
I should have more sharply called evil;
I reined in my judgment too long.
I did warn,
But not enough, and not clearly enough;
And today I know what I was guilty of."

"Poor bastard!" said Alberto, shaking his head. "Imagine having that much regret! The sonnet that struck me most though, was one called, "The Father." The last stanza says...

But my father broke away the seal.
He did not see the rising breath of evil.
He let the daemon soar into the world."

"Most people read this as meaning that Haushofer gave Hitler the rationale for his later actions. The moment I saw it I knew what it meant. Albrecht was telling us what actually happened in Landsberg Prison. Albrecht was sending us a clue in the only way he could!"

"By now I was pretty sure that somehow Hess was involved in all this and that the time spent in prison with Hitler was significant. I re-doubled my efforts to track down anyone who might have had contact with Hess at Spandau. I followed up every lead I could find. I talked to Americans, French, Russians, whoever I could find, anyone that had been posted there. I talked to each one. Where they had died, I talked to members of their family, if there were any."

"Finally I had a stroke of unbelievable luck. I was talking to the widow of one of the Russian guards when, in the middle of our discussion she suddenly remembered some notebooks that her husband had brought home one day. She had never opened them, and neither apparently had he. They had just been stacked in a shoe box and shoved into the attic."

"I already knew that, when the Russians took their turn at guarding prisoners in Spandau, they confiscated everything from the prisoners. All they left them was their bed and bedding. The Russians had also insisted that each of the notebooks that Hess was given had to be burnt before he got a new one. For some reason, this particular Russian guard had decided to keep them. Perhaps he wanted a memento of his time working at the prison. Perhaps he intended to sell them and kept them as an investment. Either way he had died before he could do anything with them. When I came along it jogged the widow's memory and she suddenly remembered them. Amongst a whole lot of garbage about the deplorable state of the world and over consumption in society, Hess had written the occasional paragraph of reminiscences."

"Some of the notebooks contained pieces about his life as a child in Alexandria, his dictatorial father, and about his time in Landsberg Prison."

Alberto opened one of the files on the table and pulled out a document which he handed to Dan. Dan noticed half a dozen notebooks also sat in the file. "This is all the relevant bits I got out of the notebooks," he said handing the pages to Dan.

2. Bavaria - 1924

Rudolf Hess stood with his back against the prison cell wall, trying to stifle a yawn. They were taking a break from writing Hitler's memoirs. Hitler was going on about the failure of the Beer Hall Pusch, yet again.

"We were stupid, Rudolf! We only had half a plan. If only I had been able to see more clearly what would happen. If only we had stayed put and concentrated on consolidating our power rather than following that buffoon, Ludendorff's suggestion to March to the Defence Ministry!" he said, pacing around the room.

"Next time it must be better planned! Next time there must be no doubt about where we are going. Next time we must have a clearer understanding of the future!"

"When I was a boy in Alexandria," said Hess with a nervous laugh. "I was told by an old man in the Arab bazaar about a relic of Constantine the Great that he said gave Napoleon the gift of foresight. He said it was what made Napoleon such a brilliant strategist. He called it the Blood of the thirteenth Apostle, the blood of Constantine the Great. Perhaps you need some of that!"

Hitler settled into his usual place staring out of the window of the day room in which they worked. He turned and stared at Hess. "What did you say?" he asked, his voice earnest.

"The Blood of Constantine. That was what he called it."

"Really?" said Hitler scornfully, looking back out the window. "It sounds like religious claptrap! Napoleon was brilliant but we know only too well that he didn't always win his battles."

"No, that is true, but I have made a real study of Napoleon. Think about this, Adolf. Napoleon, as a young and ambitious soldier, was sent to Italy by Lazare Carnot and the French Directorate. They saw him as a minor political threat and they wanted to sideline him from French political life. Get him out of the way." Hitler, always interested in political intrigue, sat forward, interested. "He was given responsibility for an army that was too small and badly equipped to do anything significant. His political masters would have been happy if he, and the men he was sent to lead, were destroyed. They were all considered expendable. Then, surprisingly, he has a string of remarkable victories at Lodi, Arcole and Rivoli. He returns to Paris, much to the displeasure of those in charge, a hero of the French people. Now, they can no longer ignore him! Napoleon has, suddenly, become a potential major figure in French politics!"

"With all this going for him why does this obviously ambitious, talented and shrewd man, just at the point where he could become a senior member of the French Government, suddenly leave the centre of the action, Paris, and start a campaign in Egypt? Egypt? Why would this military man suddenly develop an interest in taking an army and a scientific expedition, of all things, across the other side of the Mediterranean, to Egypt?"

"If that is not intriguing enough, why would he then, before the campaign is finished, rush back to Paris? And, most intriguing of all, how did he suddenly become first Consul of France, literally within days of his return!"

"What are you saying Hess, that Napoleon prays before some religious icon, this Blood of Constantine, and suddenly he is successful?"

"He did not pray before it, Adolf. He drank it!" said Hess.

Hitler looked disgusted.

"We know that Napoleon had periods of dynamic brilliance, but towards the end he fell more and more into periods of lassitude, or at least that is how some of his contemporaries, like his Chief of Staff, Alexandre Berthier, described it," said Hess, cautiously. "If the relic of an ancient Emperor made him brilliant, then running out of it may have accounted for the change that people saw in him just before he lost at Waterloo."

Hitler turned away and looked out the window, disinterested.

"I don't know Adolf. Perhaps it is just a story that the old man made up to impress an impressionable boy. Perhaps it is just a story," said Hess quietly. "Constantine was a great leader and became the thirteenth Apostle. Perhaps it really was his blood and it has some mystical power," he said with a shrug. "Perhaps it was a drug that someone made up!"

"I do know, though, that it was something that Napoleon thought a lot about. There is a famous quote of his. I have it here somewhere. " he said searching through a pile of books on the table. "Here it is... *What are we? What is the future? What is the past? What magic fluid envelops us and hides from us the things it is most important for us to know? We are born, we live, and we die in the midst of the marvellous.*"

Hitler turned back towards Hess and stared at him with renewed interest. "Whatever it is it can't be real, it must be a fantasy! Don't you think Rudolf?"

"Why must it be a fantasy?" argued Hess, more strongly. "There have always been mystical talismans. Do you know the story of the Spear of Destiny, the spear that a Roman soldier used to stab into the side of Christ?"

"I have seen the real spear in the Kunsthistorisches Museum in Vienna. It is part of the Reichskleinodien," said Hitler enthusiastically. "I saw it when I lived there before the war. I felt," he paused for a moment."... a connection to it."

He sat thinking for a moment, then, with a smile, said, "It is also mentioned in the opera "Parsifal!" Have you heard it?" Hess nodded his head. "I love the part where Klingsor throws the spear at Parsifal, but it stops in the air, above his head. Then Parsifal takes it and makes the sign of the cross and the castle crumbles to dust!" he said, standing up and acting out the parts as he spoke. Then he stopped and said thoughtfully, "That story talks about the blood of Christ and the holy grail."

"You know then," said Hess "that the spear has been held by some of the greatest rulers of history. Some say that it has a mystical power and that whoever has possession of it will control the destiny of the world! Did you know that Napoleon tried to steal it after the battle of Austerlitz, but someone had smuggled it out of the city before the fighting started?"

Hitler raised an eyebrow and looked thoughtfully at Hess.

"Then there is The Blood of San Gennaro that the people of Naples believe keeps them safe. Every September the nineteenth the dried blood of Saint Gennaro turns back to liquid. When it doesn't they know that something terrible will happen!"

"There are lots of holy relics that are said to have mystical powers!" continued Hess. "But even if it is not mystical, it could be some sort of drug. People have been taking drugs to see the future for thousands of years. The ancient Egyptians used the blue lotus flower to achieve spiritual enlightenment. It apparently produced an ecstatic state and gave them visions!"

"The Greeks and Romans used opium to induce states of mental euphoria, create hallucinations. Perhaps I should become an opium addict." Laughed Hitler.

"The Delphic oracle inhaled some vapours and spoke her divine utterances for more than twelve hundred years! There are historical writers who have even passed on what the prophecies were!" pointed out Hess.

Hitler didn't look convinced. He turned back to gaze out the window. Ten minutes passed then he said in a quiet voice. "You are holding something back from me Hess. Tell me!"

Hess nodded.

3. Alexandria - 1908

The road down to the Arab Bazar, near Fort Napoleon, was hot and dusty. The smell of donkeys and camels and the sweat of people filled the air.

Rudolf knew that his father would be furious with him if he found out that he had come down here. As a prominent merchant in the city he despised the anarchic bazaars that he said "appeared like festering sores all around the city." His father preferred the neater well ordered shops that lined the clean European style streets at the centre of Alexandria.

Rudolf knew his father would not approve of his current mission. He was on a quest to buy some mummy powder. He had been getting stomach cramps again and nothing that his father's doctor had given him made the slightest difference. In looking through an old medical book he had found in his father's library he had come across an entry describing the uses of mummy powder. He had read that mumuia, or ground up mummies, could be used to treat stomach ulcers so he had snuck out of the house and made his way to the Arab bazar to buy some.

The stalls were crowded close together. Flies flew in swarms around the meat stalls where goats heads hung in rows staring blankly out at the passers-by. A fat Arab butcher waved his horsetail whisk lazily over his wares in a vain attempt to keep the flies from landing. Rudolf hurried past. He headed deeper into the bazar, past stalls crammed with leather goods, pottery, pots and pans of brass and tin, and fabrics. Eventually he found the apothecary shop that he had been told about by the family's house maid. It was small and dark. Bottles and canisters lined the walls and bunches of dried herbs hung from the ceiling. The air smelt old and fragrant at the same time. At first he could see no-one in the shop. Slowly his eyes got used to the dim light. A sudden movement in the corner gave away the location of the storekeeper. He was old, with a long beak like nose and more wrinkles than Rudolf could ever remember seeing on anyone.

"What do you want?" the man asked him without moving. His voice was harsh, his accent thick and his manner was aggressive.

Rudolf, hesitantly, explained what he was after. The Apothecary sat for some time without responding, just staring at him. Rudolf knew that the use of mummies for medicine was still common, but he also knew that the establishment of the Egyptian Service of Antiquities had made the finding and using of mummies in this way illegal and therefore more dangerous. Clearly the apothecary was suspicious of him. Eventually, with a grunt, he stood up and shambled to a wall of jars. He took one down and dispensed a small amount of dark brown powder onto a piece of paper. He folded the edges up carefully and then gave them a twist to seal in the powder. He held out his hand "5 millieme!"

Rudolf counted five bronze coins into his hand.

This exchange became a regular occurrence. Every two weeks, when he ran out of mummy powder, Rudolf would sneak out of the house and make his way down to the bazar. Despite now being a regular customer the old Arab remained terse and uncommunicative towards him. That all changed the day Rudolf took a detour to the apothecary on his way home from school. He was carrying a planisphere that he had borrowed from one of his teachers.

As he entered the shop the old Arab's eyes fixed on the Planisphere.

"Let me see that," he commanded.

Rudolph passed it to him, reluctantly. It was valuable and he had promised his teacher that he would take great care of it. The old man held the metal and leather star chart with great reverence, carefully turning it to see the stars that would appear in the night sky in their respective months. As he turned it his brows furrowed, eventually he turned to Rudolf and said in an angry and dismissive voice, "These stars are not correct! This machine does not tell the story of our night sky!"

"No, you don't understand, " stammered Rudolf, suddenly afraid that the old man would damage the star chart. "It was built to work in Germany, not here in Egypt. Our school doesn't have one that shows the stars in the Egyptian sky."

The old man nodded sagely and then held up a finger. From a high shelf he pulled down a leather map case and withdrew a sheet of yellowing parchment. He spread it out on his bench. Rudolf drew in a sharp breath. It was a beautifully ornate, coloured star chart showing the constellations and the phases of the moon. Rudolpf was stunned. The old apothecary and the young man poured over the ancient star chart.

Much later, when Rudolf did finally tear himself away from the apothecary shop he realised that it was late, very late. His father was standing at the front door, watching him as he hurried up the street. He was furious. He confiscated the planisphere as punishment and sent him straight to his room without any dinner.

Despite this minor setback Rudolf began to visit the old Arab on a weekly basis to listen to the old man talk about the stars, astrology and the night sky. He seemed to have a never ending supply of hot sweet tea, maps and old books. Rudolf's need for mummy powder seemed to diminish, but he continued to buy it and take it religiously, if only as an excuse to visit the old man.

****

Approaching his fourteenth birthday, over a year after his first visit to the apothecary, Rudolf's father called him in to his study.

"It is time," his father said sternly, "that we start to think about your future, Rudolph. I have decided that you need to learn about the commercial world, so that you can take over the family business when I retire."

Rudolph was stunned. He had never considered that his future would lie in the family business. "

"Hess and Company is a good solid business. It is important that we keep control of it within the family," continued his father. "I have enrolled you in an excellent boarding school in Bad Godesberg[1]. You will be sailing for Germany in eight days time. What do you think about that?"

Rudolf stared blankly at his father, who was looking at him expectantly. He didn't know what to think, except that he didn't want to go. He was more interested in learning about science and astronomy than numbers in a cash book. His mind was in turmoil. He was scared of his father's reaction if he started to argue with him, and he was afraid that he

---

1.   http://www.wikiwand.com/en/Bad_Godesberg

would burst in to tears if he stayed. He hurriedly thanked his father and walked, as fast as he could, out into the street.

He ran down the hill, away from the house, tears welling up in his eyes, not really thinking about where he was going, but, before long, finding himself among the noise and the clamour of the Arab bazar.

He walked into the apothecary shop and disconsolately looked around. The old man noticed Rudolf's mood.

"What is wrong Efendi? Is there something troubling you" he asked, politely.

Rudolf turned towards apothecary and, before he thought about not doing it, had told him all about his father's plans for his future.

The old man nodded. "The future", he said, is a mysterious thing. The stars can tell us much about how that future will unfold, but it is often hard to interpret." Then he paused and went on in a more conspiratorial tone. "When the great General, Napoleon Bonaparte came to Egypt my great grandfather, Roustam Raza, secured a job with Napoleon himself as his man servant. He stayed in his service for nearly twenty years, sleeping every night on the floor at his door."

He paused, letting the importance of what he had just said to the young man sink in.

"My great grandfather was not Egyptian. He was originally from Tbilisi, in Georgia, born a little over one hundred years ago. When he was a child he was stolen from his poor mother. He was sold in Constantinople at the Slave market to the Mamluks. The Mamluks bought slaves to train as warriors, very much like the Turkish Sultan used to do to create his army of Janissaries."

"At the time Napoleon arrived in Egypt Roustam was with one of the Mamluk chiefs on pilgrimage to Mecca. They arrived back to find that Napoleon had taken over the country. Roustam took off his Mamluk uniform and disguised himself as an ordinary peasant. He walked back into Cairo and, with the help of a wealthy local merchant, got a job with Bonaparte's household. Napoleon had selected two young boys to take back to France with him. Fortunately one of the boys got sick and my great grandfather was selected in his place," said the old man with a roguish smile.

"I think that perhaps young Roustam somehow helped the other boy to become sick!" he said with a rasping laugh.

"Napoleon and my great grandfather developed a strong bond. One evening Napoleon told Roustam that he had to leave immediately to return to France. Something had happened and he needed to return as fast as possible. The trip to France took much longer than normal and Roustam had watched Napoleon become more and more anxious as time dragged on."

"When they finally arrived in France Napoleon took Roustam aside. He told him that he must immediately leave for Paris but that Roustam, in addition to following him with his luggage and a number of the other servants, was to meet a man just outside Aix au Provence. He was to tell no one about this task. Napoleon gave my great grandfather his signet ring and told him to show it to the man who would give him a box. Roustam was to guard that box with his life, as if it where Napoleon himself."

"Soon after he had taken custody of the chest, still outside Aix au Provence, a band of brigands attacked Roustam's party. There were thirty of them, too many to fight, although my great grandfather wanted to. They stole many things, but my great grandfather managed to save the chest by distracting the men with six thousand francs that he carried, on Napoleon's behalf, in his belt. The arguments it caused among them distracted the brigands and gave Roustam and the others an opportunity to escape."

"One man, though would not be distracted. He continued to search even while his comrades fought over the money. In the end my great grandfather put a dagger through his heart," said the old man with a salacious grin.

"When my great grandfather arrived in Paris Napoleon was shocked to hear the news of what had happened. Once he knew his chest was safe, though he laughed at the predicament Roustam had found himself in and praised him for dispatching the thief."

That first evening in Paris Napoleon called Roustam to his private apartment. When he went in to his room the chest stood open on his desk. Napoleon invited Roustam to look at what he had saved from the clutches of the highwaymen."

"Do you know what this is?" he asked him. My Great Grandfather shook his head. Inside the chest was a large rock crystal reliquary. A cylinder of rock crystal bound at either end by gold bands.

"This" said Napoleon "is the greatest treasure in all the world!. This vessel holds the blood of Constantine the Great!"

"My Great Grandfather could see that there was indeed a dried up, reddish brown substance inside the rock crystal container. As a child, before the slave traders had taken him, he had attended church regularly. He knew all about Saint Constantine, the Equal of the Apostles, and how he had brought Christianity to the Roman Empire. Since then he had also read of Constantine the Great, the Roman Emperor who had founded the great city of Constantinople."

"He looked with growing wonder at the dried blood in its crystal container. Napoleon told him to pick it up and turn it over. My Great Grandfather, with great reluctance, did so. He almost dropped the reliquary when the dried up blood suddenly, miraculously, turned back into liquid!"

"Of all my possessions Roustam, this is the one that you must protect above all others." he told my Great Grandfather. He then made Roustam swear that, if anything were to happen to him he would make sure that the container holding the blood of Constantine was taken to Rome and given to His Holiness, the Pope."

"Roustam agreed. From that day on he slept every night at the door of Napoleon's sleeping quarters, guarding his master and the reliquary."

The old man paused to make tea for them. Once they settled down with their drinks he continued his story.

"A few years later, on the morning of the battle of Friedland, Roustam entered Napoleon's tent. He stopped, stunned. He could see that the Crystal Reliquary stood open on Napoleon's desk. Even more shocking was the sight of Napoleon putting a few drops of the blood into a glass of water. He was equally horrified to see that the reliquary was almost empty. There was only a small amount of the Apostles blood left."

"Napoleon turned to my Great Grandfather and seeing the horrified expression on his face, said, "I am not a man of God, Roustam, but I was given this by someone who is. He told me that if I were to drink the blood of Constantine that I would be blessed by visions of the future! That was not quite true, but it was close to the truth. Drinking this allows a man to see the universe anew. It draws the threads of his knowledge into golden pathways that he can choose to follow or not.""

"My Great Grandfather was so shocked that he berated the Emperor for desecrating a holy relic. Napoleon was, apparently, quite taken aback by Roustam's vehemence and a few days later, after he had defeated Count von Bennigsen's Russian army, Napoleon sought out my Great Grandfather and put into his hand a small glass vial."

"He told Roustam that he was giving him charge of this single vial so that he would always know that some of the Apostle's Blood remained. He made him promise though, that should he ever be in desperate need of it, that Roustam would bring it to him. He then said "Roustam, I put the future of France in your hands.""

"My grandfather kept his vial with him always. He also began to watch his master more closely. He watched when Napoleon, before a decisive battle, would take a few drops from his own supply and then sit in a chair and seemingly fall asleep. A little while later he would wake up, invigorated. His eyes, normally grey, would be shining, almost glowing, a blue grey. His decisions and his actions would become even more resolute than normal."

"Roustam would say that at those times Napoleon was like a God. His actions were so decisive, his commands so inspired. These were the times when Napoleon would be victorious. Afterwards, after the celebrations of his victories, he would see the General back in his tent exhausted and washed out, his hands trembling. He would watch over him as he regained his strength, making sure that no one saw him in this debilitated state. Sometimes it would take days for him to return to himself. As time passed the amount of time it would take him to recover become longer and longer. The after effects of drinking the blood of the Apostle became more pronounced. My Great Grandfather became more and more convinced that the blood of Constantine was killing Napoleon."

"Eventually Napoleon's supply of the blood ran out."

"When Napoleon asked for the vial, as Roustam knew he would, he refused to return it. He did it out of respect for Saint Constantine and love for Napoleon. He could see that drinking the blood was not good for Napoleon the man. It was destroying him. So he kept it. Napoleon was furious. When he was exiled to Elba, Roustam wrote Napoleon a letter explaining why he had refused. Napoleon threw the letter on the fire. They never saw each other again."

"My Great Grandfather suspected that he was not the only one given a vial for safe keeping. When he heard about Napoleon's escape from Elba and his return to France, he believed that his suspicions had been confirmed."

"My family has kept the vial for nearly one hundred years. When Napoleon the third came to the throne my grandfather was concerned that he might know something of the vial, and its power, so he left France, returning first to Georgia and then, finding none of his family left there, coming back to Egypt."

"I have no family," said the old man sadly. "I am the last of my line, but I believe that one day there will be a man who is worthy of this gift." He reached into his pocket and drew out a small, leather box.

"I am going to give this to you. Take it back to Europe. You and your children, Rudolf Hess, can be the new custodian of the last remaining vial of the blood of Constantine the Great! If, one day, you, or your descendants, find a man who is truly worthy of it, who has that spark of brilliance that could be fuelled to incandescence by the blood of a saint, then give it to him. Be warned though! Like all great gifts there is a dark side to this. Roustam believed that the blood burnt up Napoleon's soul. If you or your descendants offer this to someone you believe is worthy, be sure to warn them that taking it may cost them more than they gain."

Rudolf Hess opened the box and took out the small, bulbous glass vial that rested within it. As he turned the vial over in his hands he could see a dark liquid move inside it. On the top was a red wax seal. The impression of a bee was moulded into it.

Eight days later, Rudolf Hess left Alexandria for Germany.

4. Bavaria - 1924

Adolf Hitler's pale blue eyes were fixed on Hess. "Where is the vial now?' he asked, obviously intrigued by the story that he had just heard.

"I have it in my safe deposit box at a bank in Neuchâtel. It has been there ever since my father sent me to University."

"Could we send someone to get it?' asked Hitler.

"I could ask Albrecht Haushofer, perhaps. I imagine he would be quite happy to do it for us."

"What can I lose by trying this mystical potion of yours? Arrange it!" ordered Hitler.

It was another week before Hess could ask Albrecht about taking a trip to Switzerland to pick up the small box that contained the vial, and another week for Albrecht to travel by train to Neuchâtel and bring the box back to Germany.

Karl and Albrecht Haushofer walked in to the Landsberg prison day room together. Albrecht had hidden the box in a basket of food that one of Hitler's many admirers had sent to him. The guards, as usual, had not paid much attention to what was brought in, so there was little risk of the basket being searched.

The four men sat around the dayroom table. The small box, wrapped in brown paper and tied with string, sat on the table. When Albrecht had asked what the package was Hitler and Hess had looked at one another, then, after a short pause, Hitler had ordered Hess to recount his story again. They now all sat staring at the box.

"This sounds like a child's bedtime fable!" said Albrecht Haushofer. "For all you know this Egyptian could have filled the vial with anything from camel piss to arsenic!"

Hess didn't say anything. Karl also stayed quiet. Eventually Hitler reached for the box and unwrapped it. The box inside was made of polished brown leather. The faint impression of a stylised N could be seen on the lid. Hitler opened the box and took out the small vial that lay in its velvet lined interior. The vial was glass. An impression of a bee was moulded into the wax that sealed it.

As Hitler held the vial up to the light they could all see a dark, viscous liquid moving slowly backwards and forwards inside it.

"It does look like old blood," said Hitler, fascinated.

"It looks revolting!" Albrecht Haushofer said with obvious disgust.

"That bee symbol is certainly Napoleonic," said Karl Haushofer. "The bee was a symbol of immortality and resurrection. It was always thought that Napoleon chose it as a way of linking his new dynasty to the original French Merovingian dynasty. Bees, or more accurately cicadas, are considered as the oldest emblem of the rulers of France. Given your revelation about this," he said pointing at the vial, "he may have chosen the bee as the symbol of his dynasty for other reasons! Either way, given the symbol on the seal, and the N on the box, these items could certainly have belonged to Napoleon."

They talked for an hour, around in circles, about the merits of trying the liquid in the vial. Karl became more and more convinced that it was worth the risk. Albrecht more and more convinced that it was all a stupid fantasy. Hess stayed quiet, and, as the argument went on, uncharacteristically, so did Hitler. In the end even the father and son ran out of words. Eventually Hitler picked up the vial and placed it back in its velvet nest. He replaced the lid. The discussion was over. No decision was made.

The box, the vial and its contents were not discussed the following Wednesday when Karl Haushofer visited. Instead the two younger men listened to Karl's ideas on the rejuvenation of states through war. "Nations," he told the two young men in his confident, brusque manner, "nations rise and fall through war. The law of the world, is unceasing struggle, not the interminable stagnation of peace! In the last war," he said, his tone suddenly bitter, "the German people were not prepared! They were not prepared for the sacrifices that war requires. For the long suffering and the persevering! Germany should look to Japan to see how a nation becomes stronger. Look to the east and see how they have transformed their economy through war with China and Russia. The Japanese are prepared to sacrifice themselves for honour, for their family, for their country and for Empire! That is the way Germany should be!" he growled, banging his fist on the table!

Each Wednesday for the next few months they discussed the future of Germany, its people, its borders, the nature and structure of government and the ideologies of the countries that surrounded it. During the other days Hess and Hitler would work on Hitler's memoirs. The small leather box stayed on the shelf in Hitler's cell, untouched.

With his own story and that of the National Socialist movement finished, Hitler started to discuss the second volume of his book. After a month though, he had not dictated a single word. He and Hess would sit in the day room, Hess, dutifully sitting in front of the typewriter and Hitler at the window. Hitler would start a chapter and then become confused and angry. His discussions with Karl Haushofer and Hess over the previous months had given him so much food for thought that he seemed mired in too many ideas, confused. He would become increasingly angry with himself, the great orator, the great simplifier of issues, unable to put a logical sentence together. In his frustration he would sit for hours looking out the window, arms tightly crossed over his chest.

One morning, as they sat silently together in the dayroom, to break the monotony more than anything, he said consolingly, "It is just writer's block Adolf. Writers often run out of steam when they are writing."

Hitler turned from the window. "Writers block!" he said angrily, "Writers block! Writers block is for weak minded simpletons! I do not have writers block. I am trying to imagine the creation of a thousand year Reich, Hess! I am trying to plan the future of a greater Germany! I am trying to see how to lead a nation that has been undermined by the Jew and the petty-bourgeois bureaucrats of England, France and America, to a new glory! "

"There are so many things to contemplate, so many ideas to shape into actions that will direct the National Socialists along the path to power. The problem is not writers block it is that there is too much in my head! Too many ideas! Too many possibilities! I need to simplify. The messages need to be clear! The plans need to be straightforward, otherwise the ordinary folk will not understand them. They will get lost in the complexity! The press will misrepresent them! The plan must be clear. It must be easy for people to understand."

He paused for a moment, in thought. "The press is a great power in Germany, Hess. Its importance is immense. It is the press that continues people's education into adulthood. The majority of Germans believe everything they read. They are simple minded. These are the people who have neither been born nor trained to think independently, and who either from incapacity or incompetence, believe, blindly, everything that is set before them. Either that or they are the indolent scum who could perfectly well think for themselves, but from sheer mental laziness seize gratefully on everything that someone else has thought for them."

"These people are not able or willing to examine for themselves what is set before them. As a result their whole attitude toward all the problems of the day can be reduced almost exclusively to the outside influence of others. This is a huge advantage when their enlightenment is provided by a serious and truth-loving party like ours, but it is catastrophic when scoundrels and liars provide it."

"Our messages, our goals and our plans need to be clear and unambiguous. If they are not then the liberal press and international capital, and their Jewish masters, will pervert what we say."

Hitler turned back to look out the window again. Hess waited, not wanting to provoke another tirade. "I will take your holy elixir!" said Hitler in a quiet voice. "When Karl comes tomorrow you and he can be my witnesses. If anything goes wrong there must be witnesses. If I die, or go mad, you must protect my reputation and ensure my legacy is honoured." He turned back and looked Hess in the eye. "Will you promise me that, Rudolf?"

Hess nodded.

****

Karl and Albrecht Haushofer were waiting in the day room when Hitler walked in the next morning. From the look on Max's face Hitler guessed that Hess must have told them his intentions.

"We must do this properly and with a degree of scientific rigour," said Karl once they were all seated around the table. "Albrecht, your task will be to monitor Adolf's breathing and heart rate. If anything goes wrong we will need to call the guards as quickly as possible so that they can get medical assistance. Hess, your job will be to take note of anything that Adolf says, as accurately as possible. I think the most effective way to administer this potion is by drops under the tongue. It will be easily absorbed through the mucous membrane into the body that way. My job will be to administer the potion a drop at a time."

"And my job," said Hitler with a laugh, "is to be the guinea pig!"

Caught in their own thoughts they all stared at the small vial lying in its velvet lined box. After some minutes Karl lifted the vial up and with a penknife cut the wax from around the top of the vial revealing a glass stopper. With a twist of his wrist he pulled the stopper. With an audible "pop" it came free. He put his nose to the opening and then withdrew it, his face not concealing his disgust.

"It smells revolting!" he said. "It will probably taste even worse!"

The vial was passed carefully to Albrecht and Hess, both agreed with Karl. The contents of the vial smelled disgusting, like rotting flesh. Albrecht almost dry retched when he smelt it.

"God!" said Hess when he took his turn, "How you could even consider putting that stuff in your mouth beggars belief. Are you sure you want to do this?"

Hitler impatiently took the vial from Hess. He took a cautious sniff, then another, deeper breath. "I can't smell anything," he said, surprised at the fuss they had all made. "Let's get on with it!"

He passed the vial back to Karl, tilted his head back slightly and opened his mouth. Karl drew a silver toothpick out of his pocket and dipped it into the glass vial. He drew it out. Clinging to its end was a single drop of the vial's reddish brown contents. Holding it above Hitler's open mouth he let the drop of the oily liquid drip onto the soft mucous membrane under his tongue. Hitler closed his mouth and then closed his eyes, tasting the musty flavor of the liquid. He waited.

Five minutes passed. "Anything?" he heard Karl ask. He shook his head.

"Open up," said Karl, bringing the vial up to his mouth again and letting another drop drip under his tongue.

Again, he closed his mouth, shut his eyes and sat back in his chair. Nothing. They went through the process twice more. On the fifth time he started to feel slightly dizzy. He had difficulty maintaining his concentration. Karl started to ask him to open his mouth again. He held up his hand. They all fell silent.

Something was definitely happening inside his head. Ideas started to tumble through his mind, like coloured blocks in a child's toy box. He could move them around, making patterns. He knew instinctively which patterns worked and which didn't. The muscles in his jaw tightened. He furrowed his brow, concentrating hard.

****

Albrecht watched, dispassionately, as whatever Hitler had just swallowed took affect. Suddenly Hitler's eyes snapped open. His normally blue eyes shone startlingly violet. He began to talk, slowly at first then with greater passion.

"I can see many paths forward for the National Socialist Movement. Some lead to disaster. Some lead to ultimate power. They are all so clear in my mind!" said Hitler, a look of wonder on his face.

"I see futures where the Nazi's and Germany become one! An all powerful Germany that leads the world! Russia, France and England, bow down, subservient to a greater Germania!"

"I see a future where the National Socialist bicker and fight among themselves. We fight among ourselves and Germany tears itself apart and becomes a part of a greater Soviet, a Bolshevik state!"

"I see a future where war tears the world apart, and still Germany rises, reborn,out of the ashes, to lead the world!"

"But there!" he said, gesturing with one arm as if they could all see the vision in front of him. "There is the future we must have. A thousand year Reich! Berlin the new Rome! The centre of a Germanic Empire!"

"We will need to be strong! A single party united behind a single leader! We must be the party that is working to smash the chains of the Treaty of Versailles and wipe away the feeble democracy of the Weimar Republic!"

"We will need to wait for a catalyst to drive the German people into our arms. We need to be ready! We need to be organised! We need to become masters of influence, spreading through Germany like blood through water!"

"Germany must change! We must begin that change now! If Germany is to take its rightful place in the world once more, then the character of our people must change! We must create a Volksgemeinschaft, a single nation without classes, bound by blood and by soil!" he said, his upheld hand balling into a fist. "We must put a halt to racial degeneration! We must confront the communist menace before Germany is forced to become the next battlefield for Russian Bolshevism!"

"We must strengthen the German will!"

"Germany must rearm! The pathway to success is through war! First we must take back that which is ours by right! Then we must take what we need for Germany to grow! The prize is there! I can see it! Weltanschauung!"

Hitler was staring manically into the middle distance, his eyes bright, seeing things that the others could not. He sat in this way for an hour, not talking. All the time Albrecht was monitoring his heart rate. It seemed to be beating more quickly and more strongly. His body would occasionally twitch, but most of the time remained rigidly focused on a vision that only he could see.

Hess and Karl were looking on in wonder at the transformation that had come over Hitler. Albrecht felt shaken and sickened.

After another half hour Hitler's eyes closed and, as his heart beat calmed, he fell asleep.

They tried to rouse him but couldn't. They discussed calling a Doctor but in the end decided that they would carry Hitler back to his cell and let him sleep it off.

****

Hess looked up from his book as Hitler walked into the day room. He could see the subtle changes that the previous days experiences had wrought on him. The muscles in his face were firmer. His eyes were more focused, almost hypnotic. His jaw was more set and his whole visage more determined. Making himself comfortable by the window so he could look out at the river, Hitler turned to Hess. "Lets us begin. The next chapter will be entitled Weltanschauung and Party."

During the rest of their stay in Landsberg Prison no mention was made of Constantine's blood or its effects. Hess never saw the vial again.

5. Naples - Present day

"So, if what you are telling me is true, this stuff obviously gives no moral guidance, despite, supposedly being the blood of a Saint?" asked Dan, putting Alberto's notes back down on the table.

"Well, for a start, as I understand it, Constantine was no saint, at least not in his lifetime!" said Alberto. "As far as I can see, if this stuff is real, it gives the user an enhanced clarity of thought and insight based on their own knowledge, views and prejudices. Perhaps it even makes their views more extreme. It doesn't guide them down any particular righteous path. The user still has free will to decide on the direction they want to follow," said Alberto, closing the folders in front of him.

"It is an unbelievable story. You know that don't you?" Dan asked.

"Unbelievable, yes!" said Alberto, "But after all the research I have done I have been forced into believing it! I have more to tell you but," he said standing up and stretching. "Given that the sun appears to be coming up, I think it is time you got in touch with your family to tell them you are OK."

Dan looked out the window and, with a shock, realised that the sky was lightening.

"I wouldn't be surprised if your smart phone was being tracked by the people who want the vial, so I took the liberty of relieving it of your old SIM card and getting you a new one," said Alberto holding out a micro SIM card for Dan.

Dan was annoyed, but took the new card and, using a pin that Alberto also provided, opened the SIM slot and slid the new card into his phone. Once the phone had re-booted he rang Charlotte's number. After four rings the phone answered. He paused, expecting to hear her usually, "Hello Daddy dear!" Then, remembering that he had just changed the SIM card in his phone, so she wouldn't recognise the number, was about to say hello, when a male voice said. "Who is this?" Dan hung up.

"What's wrong?" said Alberto, who had been making another pot of coffee and watching Dan while he made the call.

"I may have dialed the wrong number. A man answered!" said Dan, hesitantly.

"Does your daughter not have men friends? Could it have been one of them?" asked Alberto.

"Of course she does, yes, but she has never let one of them answer the phone when I have rung!" said Dan.

"Don't forget she won't know who is calling because of the new SIM card. Why don't you try again?"

Dan dialed the number again. When the same male voice answered he said, "Oh, excuse me, I was after Charlotte Marsh. This is her number isn't it?"

"She is indisposed at the moment. Who is calling?" demanded the voice.

"Tell her it is her father calling," said Dan, feeling a bit put out.

"Ah, we have been waiting for you to call, Dr Marsh. We have your daughter and your girlfriend. If you want to see either of them again you will give us the box that Victor Kachenko sent to you. You have two hours. I will ring you in one hour, precisely, with instructions for its delivery." The call went dead.

Alberto, who had been standing next to Dan, with a coffee in each hand, had overheard the conversation.

Dan had gone pale and just stared at Alberto.

6. Near Naples - Present day

Elizabeth sat looking out the window, fuming. She doubted whether she had ever been so angry or frightened. Charlotte was lying on an old sofa a few feet from her, thankfully asleep.

She and Charlotte had acquiesced to Thomas Malm's request and stayed in the car while he and his men had gone to retrieve the laptop and, hopefully, rescue Dan. They had been talking quietly in the back of the car when the driver's window exploded. Harry, the driver, had been shot through the head. Blood and brain had sprayed all over them, although at the time they had not realised what had happened. Before they had time to react the passenger side door had been yanked open and a man, dressed in black, and holding a hand gun, had leant into the car and said, in a frighteningly calm voice. "Do not scream. Get out of the car and walk to the van parked behind your vehicle. Do it now or you will also be shot."

She and Charlotte had slid from the car and, without questioning the man's word, walked without a sound to a van that was parked a few metres behind them. Looking back now she realised that they had both been in shock.

Another man, also dressed in black, also holding a gun, had been beside the van. He slid open the side door and gestured that they should get in. They did as they were told.

By the time they had settled themselves into their seats the van was moving. The man who had opened the door for them was sitting with them in the back of the van. The man who had shot Harry and the man that had forced them out of their car, were in the front seat.

"Who are you people and what do you want!" she had demanded once she had regained her composure.

The man in the front passenger seat had turned around with his gun in his hand and said, "The rules are simple, Doctor Garvey. You do not talk. You do not try to escape. You do as you are told. If these things occur and Dr Marsh hands over the box that was given to him then you will be set free. If these things do not happen you will be shot. To me it does not matter. Either way I get paid!"

Elizabeth was about to argue when the man cocked the pistol in his hand. It made an cold, hard, metallic click. He held up his hand. "I will only give you this warning once. Remember, there are two of you and only one box. One of you is, as they say, expendable. Should I remind you of the rules?"

She had shaken her head.

When he had ordered them to give him their bags and your mobile phones they passed them to him, meekly. He searched through them quickly. He had found their phones and switched them off.

The twisting and turning of their route had made it hard for Elizabeth to follow where they were going. After a while she given up trying. It had still been dark and there was little hope of remembering the way they were going. After about an hour they pulled up outside a small cottage and were hustled inside. Outside the window there was nothing but blackness. No lights or signs of life.

When they had first arrived they had been pushed into a rudimentary kitchen. It had a sink, a table with a few mismatched wooden chairs surrounding it and a dusty looking sofa against one wall.

As they were pushed into the room the man who had talked to them in the van, who appeared to be the leader of the group, said in his succinct manner, "Tea and coffee by the sink. There are blankets in the cupboard if you get cold. You will not be disturbed. You may be here for some time. Do not make any noise. Do not try to escape. My men will be outside."

Once the door had been closed on them Elizabeth and Charlotte had talked, very quietly to themselves. It was clear to Elizabeth that Charlotte was so exhausted that, despite their situation, she was almost asleep. After they had done what they could to clean themselves up they agreed that one of them should remain awake, and keep watch, while the other slept. Charlotte had taken the first turn on the sofa. She fell asleep almost immediately.

Sitting alone in the dark, Elizabeth tried to figure out what was going on. Were these the same people who had tried to kidnap them when they arrived in the UK? They were obviously after the vial but they probably didn't know that she had taken a sample of the contents with her to England. How had they known that Dan even had the vial? Or perhaps they were just guessing. If these people didn't have Dan, then where was he? How had these people known that she and Charlotte were in the car? If she and Charlotte were to be exchanged for the vial why had these men not hidden their faces in any way? Did they not care if they could be identified, or, she thought with a shudder, did they not expect there to be anyone left alive to identify them?

Elizabeth put her head in her hands. She listened to Charlotte's gentle breathing. A tear dropped onto the leg of her jeans. In the busy whirl of her life she rarely let her emotions effect her. With a shock she recognised the truth of their situation. There was a high probability that they would be killed, as dispassionately and as cold bloodily as poor Harry. What was more distressing though was the realisation that she was more worried about Charlotte and Dan's safety than her own. Now, confronted with real danger, she knew, without a hesitation of doubt that she would lay down her own life if it could save either of theirs. Head in hands she sobbed quietly to herself, not out of self-pity, but for lost opportunities.

7. Naples - Present day

"Who the fuck are these people?" said Dan angrily.

Alberto shrugged his shoulders. "Like I said to you before, they could be any number of people. What we do know is that they are determined and well resourced, and, I hate to say this, likely to be quite prepared to kill if provoked."

"Fantastic!" said Dan, throwing his arms in the air. "Fucking Victor Kachenko! If it wasn't for that Russian prick I would be happily digging for buried treasure, not here with my daughter's life on the line!" "

"We must determine what you would like to do. Dottore," said Alberto in a calm voice. "We do not have much time."

Dan took a few deep breaths and calmed down. He sat back down on one of the armchairs. "Ok. I think my first priority should be getting back to the UK, there is nothing I can do here. How about, in the mean time, I get in touch with a friend of mine who works for MI6? He should be able to at least give us some advice, perhaps help get them back."

Alberto shook his head. "Dan, we do not know who is behind this. If there was a way to do this without involving others that would be preferable."

"Jesus Alberto!" said Dan angrily, "We have no experience in hostage situations, no weapons, and no backup! I am a scientist and you are a truck driver! How are we meant to do this without getting Liz and my daughter killed?"

"Well," said Alberto, looking at the floor, "You have no experience in these matters, but I do!"

Dan looked at him blankly. "I thought you were a truck driving, mature age student studying psychology at university? Who the fuck are you? What the fuck is going on?" asked Dan getting angry again.

"I have not lied to you Dan. I was studying for my Doctorate when I got involved in this. I was on leave from my other job at the time."

"What was that, a secret agent for the Italian version of MI6?" said Dan sarcastically.

"No, Dan. I was in the police force."

"What, you were a Carabinieri?"

"I was once. I served on peacekeeping missions in Kosovo and in Afghanistan before I left to join the Corpo della Gendarmerie dello Stato della Città del Vaticano. That was who I was working for while I was studying at university."

"Sorry, who were you working for?" asked Dan, confused.

"I was a member of the Vatican police force," said Alberto.

"You mean you were one of the guys in the clown suits that Michelangelo designed? You were a toy soldier in fancy dress!" said Dan, not trying to hide his disdain.

"No! We are a separate group. You're talking about the Swiss Guard who protect the Pope. The Gendarmerie are responsible for public order and investigating crimes within Vatican City. We wore normal police uniforms." explained Alberto, calmly. "And Michelangelo did not design the Swiss guards uniform, and they are not toy soldiers. They are highly trained professionals. The armoury in the Vatican has as many machine guns as it has halberds!"

"Seriously?" questioned Dan, surprised that there would be real weapons in Vatican City. "So, how did you come to have a job like that?"

Alberto took a deep breath. "After Kosovo and Afghanistan I guess I had a bit of a crisis of faith," said Alberto. "The town where I grew up, in Calabria, was small, just a few houses and a church. My family was very religious. Always had been. I was the first one ever to move away from our village to the big city. I joined the Carabinieri and did my tours of duty overseas. What I saw made me question the things I had been taught. I was fairly naive when I left. After Afghanistan I think I probably had a touch of post traumatic stress disorder. When I came back to Italy I thought that I wanted to renew my faith, so again, perhaps naively, I went to work at the Vatican."

"Did that help?" asked Dan.

Alberto shook his head. "What is that saying you have in English, "familiarity breeds contempt"? After a few years all my illusions about the holiness of priests and the mystical nature of the church had been pretty well shattered. Perhaps I will tell you some of the stories one day, but for now we have to plan how we are going to get to England and get your family back."

"Hey!" said Dan suddenly distracted. "When I rang Charlotte there was no international dial tone! She and Elizabeth are supposed to be in London, but they can't be. They must still be in Italy!"

"But didn't you say that you saw them get on the plane?"

Dan nodded. "They must have been brought back to Italy, or came back for some reason. Oh God, if either of them have been harmed..... I don't know what I would do!" Suddenly feeling overwhelmed Dan took a deep breath and tried to calm himself down. He looked at Alberto. "Does your cousin have any weapons, or anything that might be useful to us?"

"No," said Alberto with a grin, "but I have a semitrailer outside that is full of useful stuff! The reality, though, is we can't do anything till they get back to us. Unfortunately we just have to wait."

After sitting in silence for some time, while Alberto busied himself tidying up the small kitchen, Dan said, "You seemed pretty adamant before that I shouldn't ring my friend in MI6. Tell me why."

"Do you know the story of Rudolf Hess' flight to England?" asked Alberto.

"Only what is common knowledge. That Hess was a nut job who flew a plane to England to broker a peace between Germany and England without Hitler's knowledge. Even Hitler said that he had gone mad, didn't he?" asked Dan.

"Yes," said Alberto," that is indeed the story that is common knowledge. Like all good misdirections it has many elements of truth within it. The real story, from what I have been able to piece together, is somewhat different."

8. Berlin - September 1940

Rudolf Hess's steps sounded loud as he walked over the red marble tiles that stretched the length of the very long gallery that led to Hitler's Reich Chancellery office. The Führer rarely used the office. When he did it was usually to intimidate visitors.

He remembered overhearing a conversation between Hitler and his architect, Albert Speer. Hitler had been laughing about the distance that foreign dignitaries would have to walk along this red marble corridor to get to his office and how it would give them a taste of the grandeur of the Third Reich. Speer had been worried about visitors slipping on the highly polished marble. Hitler had slapped him on the back and said that he didn't need to worry because diplomats needed to practice moving on slippery surfaces.

Hitler was right. The gallery was incredibly daunting with its ceiling high windows and austere decoration. Not only did anyone coming to meet Hitler have to do the long walk down the one hundred and fifty metre corridor, but they then had to confront the two, armed, expressionless SS guards in their impeccable black uniforms, who stood on either side of the massive marble portal that framed the entrance to the Führer's office.

Hess saluted the soldiers guarding the entrance with a casual wave of his arm. The soldiers saluted back, their arms rigid and their gazes fixed. They swung their arms down to their sides and, perfectly synchronised, they turned and opened the massive double doors that led into the office.

Hitler stood on the far side of the room, dwarfed by the tall windows, his hands clasped behind his back. As Hess walked across the office, he turned and waved him to the comfortable armchairs that were set around the fireplace, at the opposite end of his office to his massive desk.

Once they were both seated, and had been given a drink by one of his stewards, Hitler said in a loud voice, with a smile, as the attendant left the room, "The war goes well, Hess!"

Hess nodded, watching as the attendant closed the small doors that led into an ante room. They both sat, sipping their drinks for a few moments.

"Did you hear that I visited Napoleon's Tomb when I was in Paris, Hess?" he asked with a smile. " As you know, we have a lot in common, Napoleon and I. I spent a long time just looking down at that great stone sarcophagus. I wish I could have asked him about this experience using the blood of Constantine, where he got it from and who else he had given vials to!" Hitler paused, suddenly deflated. He looked down at the cup he held in his hands.

"I have run out of the potion Rudolf!" he said sadly, a note of desperation in his voice. "It is gone! All but a few drops are left and I have given those to Theo Morell. I have got him to start a program to try and analyse and synthesize it, but I fear that the task will be beyond him."

Hess was shocked. "You haven't told him what it does, have you?"

"No, Rudolf, I haven't," said Hitler, reassuringly. "But that is, in a way, what I want to talk to you about. Events have moved very quickly since our victory in France. The more things change since the last time I took the potion the less sure I am of the path we should follow." He lifted his teacup to his mouth. Hess noticed, for the first time, how his hand shook, ever so slightly, as he held the cup up to his lips.

Hess leaned forward in his seat. "We talked about the possibility that the Catholic's might know about the source of the blood. Now that Eugenio Pacelli is Pope, perhaps we can find out if there is some evidence of where it came from. They might even know if there is any more!"

"I have tried Rudy. Why do you think I spent so much time negotiating the Reichskonkordat with Pacelli when he was Nuncio to Germany, and let the church have so many concessions? It wasn't just to make sure they didn't oppose us from the pulpit!"

"Has he told you, anything? Has he given you any information that might help us?" asked Hess.

Hitler shook his head. "He is playing a game! I know that he knows something, and he knows that I know, but neither of us is willing to give away how much we know."

"I have to treat him with kid gloves, Hess. Imagine what would happen if there is more of the blood and he gives it to Churchill, or worse, to Stalin!" he said, leaning forward to put his teacup on the table in front of him. It rattled as he put it down.

"The Catholics are a pain in the arse Hess!" he said angrily. "We have smashed their political power, shutdown their newspapers and have worked hard to undermine and discredit them. Goebbels tells me that the work he has been doing entrapping and exposing priests and the immorality trials he orchestrated, have been very successful in driving people towards the party, but I have to be careful how much I push the church. I dare not push the new Pope too hard, just in case he does know something!" said Hitler, sitting with his elbows on his knees and his head in his hands.

"I know that the way forward is a series of wars. Each one must follow from the previous one. We must crush the Bolsheviks and then, when that battle is won, the Americans. I need the war with the British to stop, Hess! They are not our true adversaries."

"The time has come to approach the British and seek an agreement, maybe even an alliance, against the Bolsheviks. I want you to approach them as my Deputy."

Hess was stunned. "You want me to take a peace delegation to England! To Churchill? Have you seen that this plan will be successful?"

Hitler shook his head. "No, Rudolf, I have not seen that this plan will be successful. I took the last drops of the potion in 1937. At that time the best course of action was to start the war on Poland in 1938. Unfortunately I was persuaded to accept that idiot Chamberlain's peace proposals. Peace in our time! Bah! That delay of a year may have been the biggest mistake of my life!" He said angrily.

"In 1937 I could see the path clearly laid out before me. By the end of this year we should have secured our control over England. Our Luftwaffe should have undermined their morale and the invasion of England should have been complete. The delay of a year has made me uncertain of the best path. It has given the British RAF time to strengthen their defences and improve their aircraft. It has given the Americans time to make a pact with the British for fifty Destroyers! Now it seems we are at a stalemate. The Luftwaffe have failed to take command of the air! I have had to postpone the invasion of Britain!"

Hess sat back in his chair and stared at Hitler. The implications of what he was saying totally changed his perception of how he thought the war was progressing. "You have cancelled operation Sea Lion?"

Hitler nodded. "Things have become confused. Victory over Britain is no longer certain! In the path I chose the American President Roosevelt is hamstrung by the isolationists in his government. This may still be the case, but I fear that the mood in America may change. I fear that the Jews will persuade the President to become more involved despite his pronouncements about staying out of foreign wars. I need time Rudolf. I need time to either find more of Constantine's Blood or to synthesise it. I need time to focus on crushing the Bolsheviks! I need a treaty with the British before the Americans become aroused. The time for war with the United States is not now. That is one thing that I do know!"

"What would you like me to do Adolf?" asked Hess.

"I have offered the English opportunities to stop this war, several times. Every time I do so my generosity is rebuffed by that madman Churchill. That man is a lunatic! He is an unscrupulous politician who is intent on wrecking whole countries. He is a puppet of Jewry and an unprincipled swine who is drunk eight hours out of every twenty-four. I need you to go to Britain, Hess, and I need you to do it in secret.

We know that the British Foreign Secretary, Viscount Halifax had been in favour of signing a peace treaty. At least he was a few months ago! There is a group of British aristocrats who would not be averse to coming to an arrangement with us. I need you to talk to those people and persuade them that a treaty is not only possible, but the best thing for Britain. We know that there are many people in Churchill's government that would be happy to treat with us."

Hitler let out a sigh. "It is such a shame that the King abdicated! I am certain that through him permanent, friendly relations could have been achieved with Britain. If he had stayed, everything would have been different. His abdication was a severe loss for us, Hess, but there are others who will help. The Duke of Hamilton might be a good starting point. Do you remember him?"

Hess thought for a moment, then nodded, "Good looking man, pilot, was here for the Olympic games? Yes I remember him. He is a good friend of Albrecht Haushofer, Karl Haushofer's son."

"The young Haushofer is still on your staff is he not? That should make an initial arms length approach possible, Yes?" asked Hitler, standing up. "Unfortunately I have a meeting to arrange the details for the signing of the Pact with the Japanese and the Italians, otherwise I would have been happy to talk all evening, Rudolf. It is always good to see a trusted old friend."

Hess stood as well. Clearly the discussion was over. He walked to the entrance of the office. As the doors opened, Hitler, who was once again standing by the one of the large windows, said, "Rudolf, you realise that if this goes wrong I will have to disavow any knowledge of your actions."

"You can say that the strain was too much for me and I had a mental breakdown!" said Hess, laughing.

Hitler laughed, gave a casual Nazi salute, and, as he turned back towards the window, said in a quiet voice that Hess only just caught, "I will keep that in mind, Rudy, I will keep that in mind!'

9. Bavaria - May 10, 1941

Albrecht Haushofer squatted on the wing of the Messerschmitt 110 watching Rudolf Hess settle himself into the cockpit.

"I have done all I can Rudolf, but there is still no word back from Hamilton to confirm the meeting. You are taking a huge risk, with no guarantee of getting a welcome from the Duke when you get to England," said Albrecht.

"I realise that, but there is no choice. It is the Führer's wish that we make the attempt. Heavy bombing of London has been scheduled for tonight. That should keep the focus of the RAF on the south while I fly into Scotland."

"Do you think that they have been able to keep your flight secret from Churchill?"

"I don't know, Albrecht. I am told we have the King on our side. According to our sources, he wants peace, even if Churchill doesn't," said Hess.

"Still, there is a high probability that this is a trap. You do realise that? Despite what Lord Halifax said in Spain."

"I realise that our meetings in Spain and Portugal were "off the record." The whole arrangement has been set up to make any contact between us and the British deniable. I know that this is a very risky strategy, but the Führer is adamant that his vision of the future shows us at peace with Britain before we open the Eastern front."

"Since the failure of both the Portuguese and Finnish Prime Ministers and the Papal Nuncio in Berne to get the British Government to see sense, it is up to me to persuade them!" said Hess, with, Albrecht thought, more than a touch too much arrogance in his voice.

"And if you can't ?" he asked.

"Then I will be abandoned!" said Hess. "I have given a letter to Karl-Heinz Pintsch to take to Hitler at the Berghof. He will formally tell the Führer of my flight and give him the letter that explains why I have flown to England. I have given the Führer my permission to distance himself from my actions and declare me mad if he does not hear anything from either me or the British within a few days."

"If the British for some reason don't believe me, or foolishly decide that they want to continue the war, then I imagine I will be either shot or put in prison."

"On the other hand, if the planets have truly aligned, then I will be returning to Germany at the head of a delegation to discuss a treaty between the two most powerful nations in the world!"

"Is he still taking that revolting concoction that you gave him?" Albrecht asked, as he helped Hess secure his flight harness.

"Unfortunately he has no more left. He has his physician, Morell, trying to replicate it. I have a vial of his latest attempt with me. I thought that it may be useful as a bargaining chip to use with the British," answered Hess.

"Don't you think that taking a copy of it to England is dangerous? How close is Morell to successfully copying it?" asked Albrecht.

"Morell has no idea what it really is or what it is for. Adolf told him that it is a tonic that gives him energy that we stole from the Americans!"

"Admittedly he is a bit suspicious. He spent most of one evening recently quizzing me about Adolf's health. The fat fool couldn't stop himself telling me about the little research project that he was doing personally for Adolf. Interestingly he has been able to identify some of the ingredients and seemed to think that they were potentially dangerous. He was very nervous. He swore me to absolute secrecy and then told me that he suspected that at least some of the ingredients of the tonic were derived from human body fluids. He also let on that some were likely to send a person mad!"

Albrecht bit back a comment that sprang, unbidden, into his mind, but said nothing. Hess looked into the younger man's eyes and then reached out his hand. As they shook hands, Albrecht wished him good luck and then started to climb carefully off the wing. Before he had a chance to jump to the ground, Hess called out to him. "Albrecht! If my mission fails you know that I will not be able to protect either you or your father. If I fail in my mission the SS will come for you."

"I know," said Albrecht as he jumped down onto the ground.

He walked a safe distance from the plane and then turned to watch as Hess began taxiing down the airstrip. He stood at the edge of the runway and watched the Messerschmitt race down the runway and lift effortlessly into the clear spring sky, its twin engines roaring and its double tail fins emblazoned with the Nazi swastika. He watched until the plane disappeared into the distance.

A sense of foreboding overwhelmed him as he climbed into the back seat of Hess' Mercedes staff car. He hesitated before giving the driver his destination. Perhaps now was the time to leave. The driver turned, a questioning look on his face. Albrecht hesitated again, and then, sitting back in his seat told the driver to take him back to Berlin.

10. Germany - May 10, 1941

There were few things that Rudolf Hess loved more than flying. Originally trained as a pilot during the First World War, he was still bitter that the war had ended before he saw active flying duty. He smiled to himself as his eyes swept the gauges in front of him. His life, he thought absentmindedly to himself, has always been charmed. Had he not been in the trenches in the Great War, he wouldn't have been shot through the chest and he would never have applied for a transfer to the Flying Corp. When he moved he could still feel the scar tissue from the bullet wound on his back, rubbing on his shirt a few centimetres from his spine.

He banked the plane slightly and looked down at the silver line of the Rhine River as it meandered its way across Germany. He was heading northwest following the Rhine towards Bonn. His plan was then to continue to follow the river until he reached the West Frisian Islands off the Dutch coast. Once there he would make a dogleg to the right to put some distance between himself and the British radar before coming back to a northwesterly course up the North Sea and then finally, once he had reached the right latitude, turning west until he made landfall on the Northumbrian coast. His ultimate objective was Dungavel House in Scotland, home of the Duke of Hamilton.

The monotonous, unvarying noise of the twin engines rumbled on, hour after hour. Following his flight plan to the letter, well aware that even in this modified Messerschmitt, he was pushing the limits of the plane's range. Hess spotted the Frisian Islands and banked the plane into its turn. Now, flying over the North Sea he began to feel the weight of the responsibility he was carrying. As the plane droned on with the sun sinking towards the horizon and the North Sea stretching out before him, he suddenly began to feel very alone and very exposed.

The sun had still not fully set by the time he sighted the English coast. Checking his fuel gauges Hess realised that it would be a very close run thing. He pushed the control yoke forward and the Messerschmitt responded immediately, diving towards the water. He leveled off at just under three hundred metres. The engines bit into the thicker air and he grinned as the plane roared over the English Coast, the sense of speed enhanced now that he could see solid ground flashing past beneath him.

Checking his location he thought that he should be very close to the Duke of Hamilton's estate, although he couldn't see anything that he could recognise from the descriptions he had been given. Seeing the estuary of a river below him he guessed that he had flown too far and turned the plane back inland, retracing his route.

As the minutes fled by, he watched the terrain below and, with growing anxiety, the fuel gauge located on the dashboard between his legs. He had progressively pumped fuel from each of his reserve tanks and now the warning light was flashing once again. He had no more reserves of fuel. His tanks were almost empty. If he didn't find somewhere to land soon he would have to bail out. With added urgency he searched in the deepening gloom for a place to land.

Still unable to see any landmarks or obvious landing sites, Hess throttled back the Messerschmitt's engines. As he did so the starboard engine coughed once and stopped. Moments later the port side engine did the same. "The decision is made for me!" he said out loud to himself as he reached up to release the cockpit hatch. A rush of cold air hit him. He quickly undid his harness and clambered out of his seat. He pushed himself out of the cockpit and felt a blast of air hit him full in the chest. Pushed backwards along the length of the plane he felt a sharp pain in his ankle. His leg had hit one of the tail fins as he had gone past. The pain was intense. He pulled the rip cord on his parachute. With a jolt it blossomed out above him. A huge sense of relief washed over him as he found himself drifting languidly towards the ground.

He lost sight of his plane for a moment, as his parachute twisted him through the air. Suddenly a plume of orange flame erupted from the ground nearby. The sound of an explosion, like a clap of thunder, rent the still night. Then everything went quiet. For a few moments everything was incredibly peaceful. Hess hung beneath the canopy of his parachute gently swaying from side to side. The sun had gone down and a full moon was bathing the countryside in silver light.

He looked down and suddenly snapped out of his reverie. The ground came towards him with a rush. He tried to land as he had been taught, but realised, as he felt pain erupt in his ankle again, that his inexperience had let him down. He rolled to an awkward stop. He lay on his back. His parachute tugged gently at him as it too fell to earth. He closed his eyes. He had made it to England!

Despite the pain in his ankle he felt triumphant. Looking up at the night sky he wondered how the next day would end. In his mind's eye he could see himself standing beside the King of England, the World's press around them, proclaiming the Pax Germania, or perhaps he would be speaking to the British Parliament, arguing the cause for peace between their two great empires! Either way, he knew that his place in history was assured.

11. Scotland - May 10, 1941

David McLean looked up from where he had been dozing by the fire. He had been listening to the radio and realised he must have nodded off. The rest of the family was in bed. After a long day working on the farm he was thinking of turning in as well.

Then he heard it. The sound of an approaching engine brought him fully awake. "A low flying plane!" he thought to himself "But not one of ours!". Then the engine stopped. He sat listening. There was silence then a muffled explosion.

He sprang from his chair and raced to the door. Looking out into the gathering darkness he could see flames leaping into the air some way off. A plane had crashed into one of his paddocks! He started to run towards it when he caught sight of something above him. He stopped and looked up. A parachute was gently descending towards the ground. Fuck, he thought. A bloody German! It's the invasion!

He ran back to the house. Everyone was still asleep. Desperately he searched for some sort of weapon. His mother called out to him. "What's happened David? What's going on?"

"Plane crash!" he shouted back. "Parachute coming down!"

Outside the front door was the pitchfork he had been using earlier in the day. With nothing better available, he grabbed it and ran towards where he thought the parachute had come to earth.

He cautiously approached the downed airman, his pitchfork held out in front of him. The figure of the pilot was easy to see in the moonlight, still attached to the parachute. The pilot was lying on the ground. At first McLean thought he was dead, but as he walked towards him, the pilot started to struggle awkwardly to his feet. He looked like he had hurt his leg.

"Are you injured? Let me give you a hand!" said David McLean taking hold of the man's arm and helping him stand up. The pilot smiled at him and in accented English said "Thank-you. No, I am not badly injured. Unfortunately I could not find anywhere to land. My name is

Hauptmann Albert Horn. I have an important message for the Duke of Hamilton. Can you take me to him?"

"I can contact the authorities for you, sir," said McLean, respectfully, the pitchfork forgotten as he helped the pilot bundle up his parachute. Together they walked back to the house, the airman resting heavily on his arm.

By the time they walked into the warmth of the cottage's main room, David's mother was out of bed and fussing about putting on the kettle to make a cup of tea.

The pilot bowed, gallantly to Mrs McLean. He apologised politely for the intrusion and the inconvenience he had caused. His mother looked flustered for a moment, but waved him into a seat by the fire.

While Hauptmann Horn settled himself, McLean organised for one of his older children to run to the local policeman's house and tell him that they had captured a German pilot. He then sat back down in his own armchair. His mother offered the pilot a cup of tea, but he graciously refused, saying that he never drank tea, and requested a glass of water instead.

David McLean studied Albert Horn out of the corner of his eye as he sat sipping the cup of tea his mother had given him. There was no doubt, in McLean's mind, that this German was a wealthy and important man. The German was dressed in a very expensive looking leather flying suit. A large gold watch was strapped to his wrist, outside his flying suit. His manner was autocratic. He was claiming to know his lordship, whose estate was about twelve miles away, so he must be well connected. Still, for all that, he was very polite and he had perfect, if maybe even old fashioned, manners. McLean wondered who he was and why he was here.

Twenty minutes later he heard the sound of an engine approaching the cottage. McLean got out of his chair. He met the new comers at the front door. Two members of the local Home Guard had been sent to escort the pilot to the local barracks. They were both keen to pick up the German and get back to their homes. After a few cursory questions and a warning that the police would be around to ask questions in the morning, they took the airman away.

12. Scotland - May 11, 1941

Air Commodore Douglas Hamilton walked into one of the many nondescript offices of Maryhill Barracks. Spread out on the desk were the personal effects of the man called Alfred Horn who had parachuted into Scotland the previous evening.

There was not much to look at, a Leica camera, photographs of a young boy, possibly Alfred Horn or, maybe, his son, some bottles of what were presumably some sort of medicine, and two visiting cards. He picked up the cards and read the names. One was for Dr. Karl Haushofer and the other for a Dr. Albert Haushofer.

"Something interesting, Sir?" asked Flight Lieutenant Benson, the Intelligence Officer that had accompanied him.

"Um?" Hamilton said, lost in thought. "Oh yes. I know this family," he said holding up the card and looking at it. "Albrecht Haushofer is an acquaintance of mine. I met him when I attended the Olympic games in Berlin. Odd that this man should have his calling card."

"Well he has asked specifically to talk to you, Sir," said Benson. "Perhaps we ought to go and have a chat with him?"

"Indeed, Benson. Lead the way," said Hamilton, still distracted.

Hamilton stepped into the cell. The prisoner stood up as he entered and bowed politely. "Herzog von Hamilton, Ich frage mich, ob ich mit Ihnen allein sprechen?" he said in German.

Benson looked irritated. "English please!" he said.

The prisoner bowed his head, acknowledging the request. Turning to Hamilton he said, in heavily accented English, "I wonder if I might speak to you alone?"

Hamilton looked across at Benson and another officer who had joined them for the interrogation. Benson nodded and the two men left the cell, closing the door behind them.

The prisoner gestured towards a seat. Hamilton sat down while the prisoner sat on the edge of the iron cot.

"We have met before, although you probably do not remember it," said Hess. You were a guest in my house for dinner one evening during the Olympic Games."

Hamilton raised an eyebrow, but didn't interrupt.

"My name is Rudolf Hess. I have come to Britain on a mission for mankind. I have come to England, as a good will gesture from the Führer, to demonstrate that he has a genuine desire to discuss peace terms with Britain."

Hamilton's mind raced. Was this really Rudolf Hess? The Deputy Führer? He had only the dimmest recollection of being introduced to the man and had certainly not recognised him when he had entered the cell.

"Why have you come to me? Why would you think I could be of any assistance to you?' asked Hamilton, intrigued.

"It was Albrecht Haushofer who suggested that I should contact you," said Hess. "Albrecht suggested that you might have, " he paused, searching for the right word, "... an understanding, of the thoughts of the Führer."

Again Hamilton raised an eyebrow, but didn't interrupt.

"War is destructive. The British Empire will be much weakened by the continuation of this war, if it survives at all!" said Hess, dramatically. "The Führer has no desire to wage war against Britain. The English are not Germany's enemy. You must see, as the Führer has seen, that the true enemy are the Bolsheviks. It is Russia that we should be fighting, before they become the dominant power in Europe!"

"Does your Führer know you have come here?" asked Hamilton.

Hess laughed. "Oh no! I have come here without his knowledge, absolutely!" he said in an exaggerated tone, still chuckling. "You must recognise that the Führer has seen the future. England is doomed if it does not begin to talk terms, Hamilton. Do you not see that?"

"It is not my place to agree to talk terms for his Majesty's Government, Hess!" replied Hamilton, starting to feel that this situation was slightly surreal. "I am intrigued though. Tell me what Hitler has in mind?"

Hess hesitated. He stared at Hamilton for a moment, his eyes narrowing. Hamilton wondered if he had said something wrong.

"In order to prevent future wars the Führer believes that the main plank of any treaty should include a clear understanding between England and Germany about their respective spheres of interest." Said Hess formally, almost as if he had learnt his lines by rote. "Germany's sphere of interest will be Europe. England's sphere of interest will continue to be her Empire. He believes that Germany's colonies, stolen from her after the war, should be returned."

Hamilton shook his head. "The British Government would never agree to those terms!"

"But what is your alternative? Defeat? Starvation? You must see that German losses in this war have been insignificant," said Hess arrogantly. "We have a huge number of U-boats ready to take to the water. Three quarters of Europe is currently engaged in building more. The Führer's vision of U-boat warfare has not yet been fully realised, and already your convoy system has failed! You, and the Americans, will never be able to produce enough ships to cover your losses! You must be able to see that!"

"Our strength in the air should be enough to give you pause, Hamilton!" he continued, a note of frustration entering his voice. "We are both aviators. Surely, as a pilot, you can appreciate the superiority of the Luftwaffe over your Royal Air Force. You know that our planes and pilots are far superior to yours!"

Hamilton bit the inside of his lip. Hess' arrogance was starting to get to him. He was trying hard not to argue and antagonize him.

Hess pounded his clenched fists on his knees. "You must be able to see that peace with Germany is your only answer. Germany has the strength to destroy your country, but we do not wish to!" Hess paused, took a deep breath and tried a different approach, his tone calmer. "Try to imagine, Hamilton a world where you win this war. Germany would be gone and what would replace it?" He paused briefly and then answered his own question. "Bolshevik Russia. Where would your British Empire be then, Hamilton? You would be overwhelmed by Russia with no Germany to act as a counterweight to Bolshevik expansion!"

"England should ask herself, Hamilton, whether it is worthwhile to try, at such great sacrifice, to defeat the Axis with the certitude that Bolshevik Russia will develop into a much more dangerous opponent in the future!" he said as calmly as he could.

"England's position is hopeless, Hamilton! Can't you see that! What you have seen so far is only a foretaste of what is still to come!"

"You seem so certain of your victory, Hess," said Hamilton, finally letting his frustration spill out, "why do you even need a peace treaty?" He took a deep breath, and then, staring into Hess' eyes said "There is still a lot of fight left in us! England will not be so easily overcome! "

"Ha!" barked Hess derisively. "Your famous British bravado! You have no idea of what you are up against. The Führer knows the future. Without Germany the world will belong to the Bolsheviks and the Capitalists. England will end up a wasteland that the Americans and the Russians squabble over."

Hamilton sat looking at Hess who was breathing heavily. He wondered for a moment whether the man was quite sane.

"Luckily no-one can truly know the future, Hess." Hamilton said in an offhand way, in an effort to placate the German. To his surprise his comment had exactly the opposite affect. Hess looked at him with such intensity that Hamilton was quite taken aback.

"That is where you are wrong Hamilton." hissed Hess. Then, more quietly, almost to himself, "I wish I could make you understand. I wish I could let you see what the Führer has seen. I wish you could see where the world is heading if you persist in stupidly blundering on down your present course."

Hamilton sat watching Hess. He looked old and tired now. His shoulders drooped and his head was bowed. Neither man spoke. Their discussion seemed to be over. Hamilton stood up. Hess stood as well, standing up so quickly that he knocked his chair over. He reached out and grabbed Hamilton's arm. "I wonder if you could do me a favour, Hamilton?' he said, suddenly desperate. Then, in an obvious effort to control his feelings he relaxed his grip and said more calmly. "I would be very grateful if you could bring me the medicine I brought with me. It was confiscated by your men when I arrived."

Hamilton looked into his eyes. Hess looked genuinely desperate. He wondered for a moment whether Hess was some sort of drug addict. It would certainly explain some of his behaviour. "I will pass your request on to the guard," he said calmly as he removed Hess' hand from his arm. He knocked on the Cell door. "I will also pass your thoughts on to my superiors. To be honest, though, I don't think England will ever stoop to negotiating with your Führer."

The cell door opened. He nodded to the guard and walked off to find Flight Lieutenant Benson.

13. London - May 13, 1941

Two days after he had sat in the next-door cell eavesdropping on the conversation between Air Commodore Hamilton and the German who now claimed to be deputy Führer Rudolf Hess, Flight Lieutenant Benson sat pondering the notes in front of him and the report that he needed to finalise.

Following their conversation Hamilton had passed on Hess' request for his medicine to one of the guards who had, without bothering to check with anyone, taken the two bottles of medicine from the unlocked office where they had been left and had given them to Hess. Benson had been furious. Cursing the naivety of pretend soldiers, he had raced to Hess' cell as soon as he had discovered the bungle, expecting the worst.

Crashing through the door he had found Hess, staring blankly at a wall, an open bottle of medicine sitting on the table in front of him.

The Barrack's Doctor, a surly old Scotsman, had been brought in. He could find nothing physically wrong with Hess, nor could he identify the foul smelling medicine that Hess had presumably swallowed. The Doctor didn't take kindly to Bensons's insistence that the prisoner have his stomach pumped, telling him, in no uncertain terms, that when he became medically qualified he would listen to his advice, but not before then.

The Doctor recommended that the patient be laid down on his bed and put under constant observation. He left a telephone number where he could be reached if there was any noticeable change in the patient's condition.

Benson had immediately put in an urgent request for Hess' removal to London and for more expert medical supervision. Then, not trusting anyone else with watching over Hess, he sat down in his cell and waited. Despite the Doctor's assurances, he had been convinced that Hess had poisoned himself and would die at any moment.

Benson had been thinking about getting some food brought in when Hess had started to mutter to himself. He had pulled out his notepad and fountain pen and moved his chair closer to the bed to better catch what Hess was saying.

Over the next three hours he had written down everything that he could understand. A lot of it was in German, which he understood, but some of it sounded like Arabic, which he didn't. Eventually Hess had fallen into a silent, seemingly peaceful, sleep, his breathing strong and regular. When he finally woke up he seemed totally disorientated and confused, but at least, Benson had been relieved to see, he was still alive.

Sitting at his desk, with the knowledge that Hess was securely locked in the Tower of London, Benson went through, for the umpteenth time, the report he had written. He had little doubt that the prisoner was Hess and that Hitler had sanctioned Hess' flight. He was well aware that the Germans had made a number of attempts to start a dialogue with the British government, so it was not surprising that they would try again.

As he read through what he had written he pondered the advisability of Britain allying herself with Russia. He personally had some sympathy for the view that Hess had been pushing with Hamilton, and knew that there were others in the intelligence community who felt the same. Germany was a threat, but nowhere near the threat that was posed by the sleeping giant that was the Soviet Union.

He also knew that his report, along with the transcript of Hess's conversation with Hamilton, and the pages of random words he had captured, would all eventually end up in the hands of both the Americans and the Russians. Such a high profile prisoner could hardly go unnoticed and they could not avoid sharing the intelligence gained from such a high ranking Nazi source.

He felt comfortable that the conversation with Douglas Hamilton, and in particular Hitler's warning regarding Russia, should be the main focus of his report.

He then turned to the short paragraph he had written about his analysis of Hess' garbled mutterings. His notes consisted of pages and pages of what seemed to be just random words, the rantings of a disturbed mind. There was, however, one phrase that kept reoccurring.

His identification of that phrase, assuming he had heard it correctly, was probably something that should be played down. It might turn out to be totally meaningless, but if it did turn out to be the code name for some new weapon, or secret operation, he needed to include his thoughts on it, if only to cover his own backside.

He paused in thought. If it was a clue to a new Nazi super weapon, then perhaps his bosses would think that it would be better for that information to be kept from the Russians, and possibly even the Americans. If it was just an indication that Hess was not quite sane, then that information too should probably be kept from the Allies, at least at this stage. He'd let the higher ups decided. That was their job, after all.

With a few strokes of his fountain pen he scribbled out the section of his report that made reference to his views on Hess' mutterings, and began to type his final draft.

When he had finished his official intelligence report he quickly compiled another, much shorter report based on the repeated mutterings of Rudolf Hess and the potential investigation of a new secret weapon, code name, das Blut von Constantine, the Blood of Constantine.

14. Moscow - 22nd May 1941

Stalin sat at his desk reading a report his intelligence agency, the People's Commissariat for Internal Affairs, the NKVD. It was from their English double agent, Kim Philby.

Stalin found the implications of the report he was reading deeply troubling. He didn't trust Winston Churchill. He was sure that, if it really was Hess who had flown to England, he was probably planning to keep him on ice so that he could use him to broker a peace deal with Hitler later in the war. He could foresee a time when Churchill would ally himself with Hitler against the Soviet Union. He underlined a section of Philby's report that said, '...the time for peace negotiations has not yet arrived, but later in the course of the war Hess could become the centre of intrigues for a compromise peace and would therefore be useful for the peace party and for Hitler.'

He shook his head and picked up a supplementary report that had accompanied the main report on Hess. He scanned it, noting that Hess had mumbled something in his sleep about a new weapon being developed by the Nazis, code named "The Blood of Constantine." He scribbled a quick note on it suggesting that someone in the NKVD be given the task of following it up. He then turned sat back in his chair to ponder the duplicity of Churchill and what he could do about it.

****

Some days later, a new recruit in the NKVD, by the name of Alexander Kachenko, was handed the task of following up yet another rumour about a supposed Nazi super weapon. This one had the code name "Blood of Constantine". He put it in a pile that already included bizarre rumours of a flying bomb, code named cherry- stone, something codenamed Vampire, that could have been some sort of super gun and something called Wotan, that no one had any idea about at all.

15. Naples - Present day

"So you think that Hess ended up taking the elixir that Morell had concocted?" asked Dan.

Alberto nodded. "Hess was a strange character, at the best of times, but his behaviour after his capture became progressively more peculiar. When they put him in Camp Z, down near Aldershot, he made at least two attempts on his own life, throwing himself off a balcony and also stabbing himself in the chest with a knife."

"His behaviour in detention in England was really erratic. He was convinced that the Jews were behind everything, hypnotising people, including himself and his doctors, making him behave in odd ways. He believed that the conspirators who had tried to assassinate Hitler had all been hypnotised by the Jews. He even believed that times when he had been rude to people were times when he had come under the baleful influence of some sort of Jewish mind control. He continually complained of stomach pains, and pasted notes all over the windows of his cell with reminders on them to compensate for his lost memory."

"It sounds like he was the pre-curser of the tin foil hat brigade," laughed Dan.

Alberto smiled, then became serious again. "Personally, I think that he either took Morell's concoction of his own volition or the British secret service forced him to take it, but there is no real way of knowing."

"At the end of the war, when he was taken back to Germany to be tried at Nuremberg, it was reported that he didn't recognise anyone, or pretended not to. Even Karl Haushofer, his old Professor and one of his oldest friends, confronted him. He apparently gave absolutely no sign of recognizing him."

"Herman Goring was convinced that he had lost his memory. So were all the surviving Nazi's that came into contact with him. Bizarrely though, during the trial, he suddenly turns around and says that his memory loss was a tactic, and that his only mental impairment was a reduced ability to concentrate!"

"When von Ribbentrop was told that Hess had been faking it he was stunned. He couldn't believe that he had been taken in."

"I got the report from the prison psychologists. He stated that there was little doubt that Hess was suffering from amnesia, although he did admit, perhaps just to cover his arse, that there may have also been some deliberate suppression of memories."

"It turns out that Hess was his own worst enemy at the Nuremberg Trials. If he had just stayed quiet his sentence would have been more lenient, or he may have been deemed unfit for trial, but as it was he received a life sentence and spent the next forty years at Spandau."

"From all that I read I am convinced that there was something seriously, mentally, wrong with Hess once the British had finished with him."

Dan sat thinking for a moment, then looked across at Alberto. "So your guess is that he drank the potion and that it was a not very good copy of the original."

Alberto nodded. "Morell hadn't perfected the recipe. He didn't have the technology to analyse the remnants of the potion that Hitler had taken, despite the fact that Hitler had gone to immense trouble to arrange for him to get an electron microscope to help with the task. I don't even think Morell had the knowledge or skill to do the job either. He was an odd-ball physician, not an analytical chemist."

Dan shook his head. "I suppose it is possible, but it all sounds incredible! So you also think that Hess told the British about the Blood of Constantine. Maybe he took some to try and convince the Brits it was real?"

Alberto shrugged. "Maybe. I did uncover documentary evidence that both the British and the Russians knew about what was thought to be a German secret weapon codenamed "The Blood of Constantine". The Russian stuff was dated a month or so after Hess parachuted into Scotland."

"So, you think the British Secret Service could be still looking for it? Asked Dan.

Alberto nodded. "I think that they may be one of the groups that are trying to track it down. If it is real, imagine what an advantage it would give to any country that had it," said Alberto.

Dan nodde. The implications were obvious. Whoever controlled this stuff, if it really did what Alberto was suggesting, would have a massive strategic, and possibly commercial advantage over the rest of the world.

"So, if it's true, who can we trust?" Dan said, almost to himself.

At that moment the phone, sitting on the table between them, rang. Dan lifted it to his ear and Alberto moved quietly around the table so he could hear as well.

"Doctor Marsh" said the voice. "Bring the box and its contents to the Piazza del Plebiscito. Stand in the middle of the Piazza at exactly ten o'clock. We will recognise you. Come alone. Do not involve the police. You will give the package to the person we send. When we have it in a place of safety we will release your daughter and your girlfriend. Do not try to follow our courier."

"No!" said Dan "Listen to me you bastard, you do not get the package until I know Charlotte and Elizabeth are safe! Hello, Hello! The bastard hung up on me!" shouted Dan angrily.

"They are very professional, very careful. I do not think we should trust them!" said Alberto.

"You think?" said Dan sarcastically. He then took a deep breath. "You don't think they would harm Charlotte or Liz do you?" asked Dan.

"I will be very straight with you Dottore. I think that, once they have what they want they will dispose of any witnesses. I think that includes you, your daughter and your friend."

"Fuck!" said Dan. "So what are we going to do? We just can't submit to their demands."

"Ah, I have a couple of thoughts that might give us an edge, come with me," said Alberto with a grin.

16. Naples – Present day

Dan stood in the centre of the Piazza del Plebiscito. It was a beautiful blue sky day and the square was filled with locals and tourists enjoying the sights. In front of him was the church of San Francesco di Paola, its dome towering above him. To each side of the church entrance a semicircular colonnade stretched out, embracing the Piazza. To his left and right, as he looked at the church, two statues of men on horseback stood on raised daises, on either side of him. Turning slowly around he could see the Royal Palace behind him and beyond that, on one side of the Royal Palace, he could see the water of the Bay of Naples and Mount Vesuvius beyond. On the other side of the Palace he could see the wrought iron and glass dome of the Galleria Umberto I.

All around him people were walking about, taking photos, eating gelato or just taking in the ambiance. He looked around trying to identify who his contact would be, but no one seemed to be taking an interest in him at all.

He checked his watch. It was exactly ten o'clock. Over the general hubbub of the city he became aware of the sound of an engine. He looked around and saw two people on a motorbike, their helmet visors covering their faces, coming towards him. He had re-wrapped the package in brown paper and he was now holding it in his hands. Suddenly the bike was right in front of him. It stopped. The driver snatched the package from his hands. Before he knew what was happening Dan felt a heavy blow to his chest and a loud bang. Then, before he had hit the ground, another one. He heard the bike accelerate away with a roar and then someone was screaming. "They had a gun! They had a gun! They shot him!"

Dan lay still on the ground. He couldn't breathe. He couldn't suck air into his lungs. He started to panic. Someone knelt down beside him, looking at his face, concerned and said in an American accent, "Are you okay, Mister? I saw them shoot you! Lie still!" Dan calmed himself down. He closed his eyes and let his body relax. He just needed to relax and he would be able to breathe again. He knew this feeling. As a child falling out of trees had been a regular thing. He knew what it felt like to have the wind knocked out of you.

Over the noise of people shouting Dan heard the rattle of another engine. There was a screech of brakes and the crowd parted to reveal an old, blue, Fiat 500. A now familiar voice shouted above the racquet of the little car's engine, "C'mon Dottore! We don't have all day!"

To the astonishment of the crowd, Dan struggled to his feet. He had been able to suck in a couple of lungfuls of air and was almost breathing normally again. Pushing his way through the surprised circle of onlookers, he scrambled into the passenger seat of the car. Alberto thrust an iPad into his hands and said above the rising rattle of the engine as the car accelerated out of the Piazza, "The quadcopter is hovering above the Palace. They headed down the Via San Carlo, towards the Galleria. he said pointing in the direction of the Galleria's spectacular glass and steel dome.

Dan looked at the screen of the iPad and, after twenty minutes practice earlier in the morning, the now familiar controls of the quadcopter. The screen revealed a birds-eye view of the palace and the Piazza. He twisted the iPad around and the image turned. He tilted the iPad forwards and the image started to move across the Palace, across a small park and then he could see the road. He tilted the iPad further forward and the image moved rapidly, the hybrid quadcopters petrol engine moving it forward like a normal radio controlled aeroplane. He could follow the road as if he were in a plane flying above it.

Dan had been amazed when Alberto had taken him down to his semitrailer and unloaded the ungainly looking machine he was now flying above the streets of Naples. The Latitude Engineering Hybrid quadrotor was a combination of a quadrotor platform and a radio controlled airplane. The four helicopter rotors ran on battery power. The larger propeller that faced towards the back of the drone ran on liquid fuel. Alberto had told him that he had installed a 4G chip in the plane and that it could be controlled by a similarly equipped iPad. Luckily it also had its own autopilot so that flying it was simple. Alberto had also fitted the drone with the largest engine he could, and while that reduced its range it meant that, with luck, they would be able to keep up with a moving vehicle.

"I've got them! They have turned right," said Dan as he watched the two helmeted figures on the bike maneuver through the traffic. "Now they are going left, parallel with the waterfront!" He kept up a running commentary as the bike accelerated hard out onto the Via Nuevo Marina.

"They are heading around the Bay. They are really flying! We would never have been able to catch them in this!" shouted Dan above the noise of the little Fiat.

"We don't need to catch them Dottore, we just need to keep an eye on them eh?" Alberto said with a grin, double de-clutching as he changed down gears and accelerated the Fiat through an impossibly small gap in the traffic.

Dan shifted in his seat. He was starting to feel very stiff and sore.

"How are you feeling Dottore? You might feel a bit more comfortable if you loosen off that body armour," said Alberto.

Keeping one eye on the image on the iPad, Dan undid the front clasps on the heavy carbon fibre body vest.

"It's was a good thing that they didn't shoot you in the head, eh?" laughed Alberto.

"Ha!ha! Very funny!" said Dan, again concentrating on flying the quad-copter and keeping the motorbike in sight.

The motorbike was still moving fast thirty minutes later as it started to climb into the hills south of Naples. Dan watched as the bike rider expertly wound his way up the twisting, tree lined road, that would lead, eventually, to the Amalfi Coast. He and Dan were still traveling along the Autostrada, the tiny fiat going flat out, no match for the modern, powerful bike they were trying to follow.

"It looks like they are heading for somewhere around Agerola, perhaps somewhere on the Amalfi Coast," said Alberto glancing across at the image on the tablet. "I hope we don't run out of fuel in the quad-copter before they get to their destination. I hadn't anticipated them being so far out of the city! Now that there are fewer possibilities for them to turn off, try taking the copter up a bit higher. It might save on fuel."

Dan ran his finger gently along the control bar on the screen and the image broadened out as the copter rose higher into the air.

Finally, the bike slowed and turned up a long winding driveway that ended at what he guessed was a farm house.

It came to a stop behind another vehicle, a blue van. Dan recognised it as the one that had been at his apartment the previous day. The two men got off the bike and walked towards the small farm house.

"Got them!" said Dan. "Its a farm house up a long winding driveway! I'll go in a bit and see if I can get a closer look."

"No, get out of there now!" said Alberto with some urgency. "If that drone runs out of fuel or goes out of range and drops out of the sky we are going to lose the advantage of surprise and they may well kill the women!"

"Oh shit!" said Dan, "Its gone! Bugger! I've lost it."

The iPad screen had suddenly gone black. "Fuck!" The iPad's turned itself off! What happens to the drone when that happens?" said Dan, frantically trying to restart the iPad.

"Shit!" said Alberto. "I don't know! If its run out of fuel, or it goes out of range, it is programmed to go into hover mode and lower itself to the ground. Do you think they saw it?" asked Alberto.

"I don't know. Last I saw they were going into the farm house. For all I know the copter could have landed on the roof. I have no way of knowing." replied Dan. "Just make this little bucket of bolts go faster will you!"

The little Fiat 500 wasn't really built for speed, but it cornered well. Alberto concentrated on driving as fast as he could. Dan fretted in the seat beside him as the iPad rebooted and he searched for the entrance to the driveway.

"See if you can see anywhere we can pull off the road," said Alberto

There were no verges on the road. A steep bank came down on one side and a low wall separated it from a steep descent on the other.

"There it is," said Dan.

Alberto drove past the driveway without stopping. A few hundred metres after the entrance they came upon a road maintenance storage depot. Alberto pulled the little car in and tucked it behind a decrepit, rusty old road grader.

With the car out of sight Alberto, with Dan close on his heels, scrambled up the steep bank at the back of the little works depot and headed across country in the direction of the farmhouse.

Picking their way through the trees in silence Dan adjusted the carbon fibre body armour, retightening the straps underneath his jumper. Alberto had put on a similar vest over his shirt. Dan could feel the ache across his ribs with each step he took. There hadn't been much time for him to think about what had happened in the piazza. The shock of being shot, twice, at close range, would no doubt hit him later. For now he knew he needed to concentrate on helping Alberto get Charlotte and Elizabeth back safely.

After fifteen minutes of uphill climbing Alberto held up his hand. He pointed. Just below them, no more than a hundred metres away, was the farmhouse. They could clearly see the motorcycle and the van. There were no signs of movement.

They squatted down and surveyed the area. Dan touched Alberto's shoulder and pointed down the hill. There, caught in the branches of a tree, was the quad-copter.

"With a bit of luck they didn't see it come down," said Alberto in a quiet voice. "Now lets unleash its baby brother!"

Alberto took off his backpack and reached inside, pulling out a small box. Inside was a tiny quad-copter. It fitted easily into the palm of his hand.

"The battery in this thing won't last any more than ten minutes, so we need to be quick. The range is not fantastic either, so lets get a little closer." Alberto said as he started to move further up the bank. Keeping low, they moved as quietly as they could along the line of the slope, keeping well above the farmhouse. Alberto held up his hand, satisfied with their new vantage point. He put the little quad-copter on the ground and pulling out his smartphone he clipped what looked like a battery pack to the back of it and then switched on the miniature quad-copter. Using his finger on the screen of the smartphone he swiped on one of the settings and the little quad-copter's blades jerked into life. An image appeared on the screen of the phone. It was Dan's boot.

"Ok, let's see what is going on in there," said Alberto. The quad-copter lifted off the ground and flew, almost silently, towards the farm house. As it got closer he slowed it down and then let it descend so that it was hovering just above the ground. Manoeuvring the little device carefully he approached the house, under the line of the windows. The quad-copter was now no more than half a metre from the back wall of the farm house. Expertly Alberto brought the copter closer to the wall then, with very delicate adjustments to the angle of his smartphone, allowed the copter to slowly rise up in front of the window.

The inside of the farmhouse was dark. It took a moment for the camera in the quad-copter to adjust for the low light. Alberto, with Dan looking over his shoulder, could see that the room was empty. From the little they could see it was just an empty room with no furniture or fittings.

Alberto grunted. He lowered the quad-copter below the window line again and flew it along the back wall to the only other window on that side of the house. Glancing quickly at his watch Alberto again maneuvered the quad-copter into position below the window. Slowly the little quadcopter ascended in front of the window. The window was covered in dirt but this time they could see shapes of people moving around inside. Light was coming into the room from an open window on the other side of the building, and from the open door at the front of the house.

"If we want to see who is inside we are going to have to go around the other side of the building," Alberto whispered. "I'll land the copter and we can sneak around the hill to that outcrop over there," he said pointing to some rocks that jutted out of the hillside some distance from their current position.

Dan nodded. He watched as Alberto landed the quad-copter on the ground below the window, grabbed his backpack and moved quietly up the hill. Dan followed him.

They settled themselves alongside the rocky outcrop. Alberto was about to activate the quad-copter when a man unexpectedly stepped around the corner of the building. He was smoking a cigarette and did not seem to be particularly on his guard. He was not obviously carrying any weapons.

Dan and Alberto both ducked down out of sight. They watched through the undergrowth as the man strolled nonchalantly along the back of the building, casually looking around as he walked.

Dan held his breath as the man's gaze swept over the area where the big quad-copter hung, suspended in the tree. The man paused. For a moment Dan thought that he had seen the drone. He took one long, last drag on his cigarette dropped it on the ground and then stubbed it out with a twist of his boot.

Something on the ground caught his eye. He walked over to the small quadcopter and picked it up, turning it over in his hand. Alberto and Dan could hear him clearly as he shouted "Hey, Paolo, look what I have found!" The back window opened and a head poked out. "What have you got, Gino?" he said in a patronising voice. Gino held up the little quad-copter. "Its one of those little helicopters. It must be some kids toy that got lost."

"Jesus, Gino!" said Paolo in an exasperated tone of voice. "Chuck it away! Stop worrying about fucking kids junk."

"Fuck you Paolo! I'm taking it home to my sister's kid!" he said, carrying the little quad-copter around the front of the house.

Alberto and Dan stayed glued to the smartphone screen. The image jiggled around as Gino carried it inside and put it on a table.

"There!" said Dan, pointing at the screen. "That was Liz!"

"Damn!" said Alberto. "He's put it on the table facing the wrong way!"

All they could see now was the inside of the window that had been too dirty to see through earlier.

"Lets go to the other side of this outcrop. We should be able to see the front of the building from there," whispered Alberto, getting up and moving further up the hill, keeping the outcrop of rock between himself and the house. Dan followed as Alberto disappeared around the other side of the rock. A moment later he heard sliding gravel and a grunt as Alberto lost his footing on a patch of loose shale and slipped down the hill.

By the time Dan cautiously peered around the corner of the outcrop Alberto was getting to his feet under the watchful eye of Gino, who was now holding a machine pistol and pointing it straight at Alberto.

"Hey, put that gun down. Are you mad! I was just hiking across your land and slipped down the hill! If I am trespassing I'm sorry, but there is no need to get violent!" said Alberto, dusting himself off.

Paolo and another man had now come out of the house and were standing staring at Alberto. "What will we do with him, Luigi?" asked Paolo.

"Search him!" ordered Luigi as he scanned the slopes around the house. Gino motioned with the gun for Alberto to put up his hands. Paolo searched him, taking off his backpack at the same time.

"Body Armour! Since when does a hiker wear body armour?" said Luigi, stepping forward and pushing Alberto in the chest.

"Looks like he was on some sort of hunting expedition!" said Paolo going through Alberto's pack. "There are two pistols here, one with a silencer and three grenades of some sort!"

"Just going for a walk were you?" asked Luigi stepping closer to Alberto.

"I thought I might get in some hunting while I was here!" said Alberto with a disarming grin.

Luigi hit Alberto hard across the face. As Alberto reeled back in shock, Luigi stepped forward and grabbed him by the shoulders then, before Alberto could respond, lifted his knee hard up into his groin.

"No body armour there, I bet!" he said with a nasty laugh as Alberto fell to the ground, doubled up in pain.

Luigi stepped back a pace and looked down at Alberto's prone body. "How many of you are there?" he asked.

Alberto, struggling to stay conscious, didn't answer. Luigi drew back his booted foot and let fly into Alberto's head. Unable to fend off the blow, Alberto's head snapped back. He lay, unmoving, on the ground.

"Lets get out of here now!" ordered Luigi. "This location has been compromised somehow! Paolo, drag him around to the van and keep him covered. Keep an eye out for any friends he might have brought with him! Gino, get the women into the back of the truck and then get Paolo to help you shove this fool in too! Then you two can follow me. I will meet you at that junction just before the tunnel, where the old road to Amalfi doubles back up the hill! I'll take the bike and deliver the package and then meet you there. I know just the spot where we can get rid of these three!"

Dan watched with growing anxiety as first Charlotte, then Liz, and finally Alberto, were bundled into the back of the blue van. He could see that Liz and Charlotte had already had their arms tied behind their backs with cable ties, Alberto, although still unconscious, was now similarly incapacitated. Gino even went the extra mile and cable tied his ankles together as well.

Just as they were closing the van doors, Luigi came out of the house putting his helmet on. He waved to the other two and got on the motorbike. Seconds later he was gone in a swirl of dust and a roar from the high powered bike's engine.

Paolo and Gino watched him go. Once he was out of sight Paolo offered Gino a cigarette. They stood with their backs against the van smoking. They didn't seem to be in a hurry now that Luigi was gone.

Dan was desperately trying to think of what to do. He had no weapons and he knew he would be no good in a straight fight. "Okay," he said to himself, taking a deep breath and trying to calm down. "What resources do I have?" Other than rocks and branches of wood there didn't seem to be a lot of options. Then he saw it, the big quad-copter still hanging from the branch of a tree. He moved as quickly and quietly as he could back around the house. The copter was just within reach. Grabbing on to one of its landing legs he gently pulled it free. It was heavy. He guessed that it probably weighed a good ten or twelve kilos. A quick inspection showed that none of its rotors had been damaged during its unscheduled landing. He opened the fuel tank and saw that there was still a small amount of liquid left. He pulled out the iPad he had stowed in his backpack and touched the quad-copters application icon. The screen filled with the now familiar control panel.

Without a battery pack to start the main petrol engine he would need to start it by hand. While the electric motors that ran the helicopter blades operated almost silently, the copter's aeroplane engine was noisy. In this quiet environment he would need to wait until the van started so that the noise of its motor would cover the sound of the little engine. That meant he needed to be ahead of the van if his plan was going to work.

The driveway wound, switchback style, down the slope out of which it was carved. That meant that Dan could, if he hurried, run straight down the slope and end up well in front of the van. Carrying the drone was awkward but he soon found himself just above the public road. He still couldn't hear the van, but guessed that he was far enough away to attempt to start the petrol motor. He could see from the battery icon on the iPad that there was a reasonable amount of charge in the batteries that supplied the helicopter rotors.

With a flick of the main propeller the motor sprang to life. Over the sound of the idling motor he could now hear the van as it wound its way slowly down the driveway. Making sure he was well hidden from the road Dan touched the iPad screen. The electric motors spun into life and the drone lifted gently into the air, its onboard gyroscope ensuring that it remained stable and level. He maneuvered it out over the driveway. It was now hovering about five feet off the ground facing in the direction of the oncoming van.

****

Alberto could feel that his wrists and his ankles had been tightly bound. He relaxed his body as the two men grunted and groaned, struggling to lift him off the ground enough to drag him around to the front of the house. There was no way that he was going to make it easy on these bastards. They could do the heavy lifting, all by themselves.

They struggled with his dead weight. Eventually they managed to lift him up and dump him, unceremoniously, and none to gently, into the back of the van.

The doors slammed shut behind him. With difficulty he opened one rapidly swelling eye and saw two beautiful women looking down at him with worried expressions, one older, one younger. He grinned at them. In a hoarse whisper he said, "Either I am in heaven or you must be Elizabeth and Charlotte, no?"

"Yes!" said Charlotte, surprised. "Who are you? Are you with Thomas?" she whispered.

"Thomas?" said Alberto, confused. "No, I'm with the Dottore Dan!"

"Dan!" said Elizabeth in surprise. Then realised she had spoken too loudly. "Dan is here?" she asked in a quieter voice.

"Yes," said Alberto, "Although I am not sure what he can do to help us. I was carrying all the weapons."

At that moment the front doors of the van opened and Paolo and Luigi climbed into the front seats.

Alberto lifted himself painfully into a sitting position. At least he would be able to see where they were going now. Catching Charlotte's attention he looked down at this boot. Following his head and eye movements, she too looked down at his boots. They were only a few centimetres from where she was sitting. Not seeing anything she gave him a quizzical look. He moved his head, indicating that she should feel inside the boot. She squirmed aound so that her hands, still tied behind her back, could reach his boot. He could feel her fingers searching inside the boot. They suddenly stopped moving. She had found the narrow pocket that contained the small, sharp ceramic blade that he hid there. Grasping the end of the object, with some difficulty she started to wriggle it free.

As the van started to move down the driveway, Paolo looked around. He saw that Alberto was now sitting up. "So our little hero has woken up eh?" he said with a leer. "Don't worry little hero, it won't be long before you are food of the fish!"

Gino laughed. "The expression is you will be feeding the fishes, not you will be food of the fish, idiot!"

Paolo gave him the finger and they both turned back to look out the front of the van.

Alberto kept an eye on the two thugs as Charlotte withdrew the narrow blade from its pocket in his boot. He remained totally still as she managed to cut through the cable tie that bound his ankles. With his legs free Alberto needed to move into a position from which Charlotte could reach the cable tie around his wrists. Keeping his attention focused on Paolo and Gino he started to move into a more accessible position. Just at that moment, as the truck rounded a bend in the driveway, he caught sight of the drone. It was hovering above the driveway about fifty metres away.

"What the fuck is that!" shouted Paolo, as the drone suddenly tilted forward and started to head, at full power, towards the van.

Alberto, immediately recognising the menacing profile of the drone, guessed what Dan was trying to do. "Down! Now!" he whispered urgently. Alberto threw himself prone on the floor of the van.

Both women tumbled on top of him.

****

Dab concentrated on keeping the drone level. It was now traveling at thirty or forty kilometres an hour. As it smashed into the van's windscreen glass exploded into the cabin. Gino, who had, at the last minute tried to dodge the missile, had turned the wheel hard to the left. Dan watched as the van rode up the steep, dirt bank at the side of the driveway and tipped over. It slammed onto its side and continued skidding down the gravel driveway for a few more metres.

Before the van had stopped, Dan had started running. He reached the back doors of the van and wrenched them open. He dived into the back of the van, amongst the tangle of arms and legs, brandishing a knife. He quickly cut through the cable ties that bound Alberto's wrist. Alberto, as soon as he was released, sprang into the front cabin. He discovered that his quick reaction wasn't necessary. Paolo and Luigi had been knocked unconscious, either by the impact of the drone, or by the subsequent crash. Out of the corner of his eye, Dan saw Alberto retrieve his backpack and liberate the weapons that Gino and Paolo had been carrying.

By the time their erstwhile captors were starting to recover consciousness Dan had freed, and hugged, Charlotte and Elizabeth. Alberto had dragged both men through the smashed window of the van, none too gently, out onto the gravel driveway and used the plastic cable ties he found in the van to tie both men's feet and hands.

Dan, who had one arm around Charlotte and one arm around Elizabeth, saw that Alberto had secured their prisoners. He smiled as the big Italian looked at Dan and said, "May I cut in?" Dan stepped back expecting Alberto to introduce himself to the women. Instead he stepped forward and gave Dan a hug, lifting him off the ground. "Dottore Dan," he said with a smile, "You were magnifico!"

Dan grinned back and said, "I couldn't have done any of it without you, Alberto!" he said, then winced. "Now, my ribs are killing me so if you will put me down carefully I will introduce you to my family!" Alberto lowered him to the ground. Dan turned to Elizabeth and Charlotte and introduced them to Alberto.

"Liz, Charlotte, this is my new mate, Alberto. In our brief, but torrid friendship he has punched me in the face, knocked me unconscious and managed to got me shot!"

"Twice!" said Alberto proudly.

"Twice! In the chest!" said Dan grinning now as well.

Elizabeth looked shocked. "Both of you look pretty much the worse for wear," she said with real concern.

"We will be Ok, eh Dottore?" said Alberto, dismissively. "Now if you will excuse me, I need to have a brief chat with our two friends over here," he said in a voice that was louder than necessary. As he walked towards them, he nonchalantly cocked one of the machine pistols he had taken from the front of the van.

"Now my pretty boys, I am a man without much patience. My face is hurting where your friend kicked it and my balls still ache. You will tell me who you work for and where your nasty friend with the steel capped boots was taking the package that you stole from my friend Dottore Marsh!"

Neither man spoke.

"If you do not do so," said Alberto nonchalantly, "I will put a bullet in each of your feet, then another three inches above that, then another three inches above that until I reach your kneecaps. If you still haven't told me what I want to know I will continue up your legs at three inch intervals until I blow your balls off. After that I will work my way up your body puncturing your intestines and then your stomach. If you are still conscious after that I will assume you do not know anything and you are free to leave."

Gino and Paolo looked terrified. Paolo started talking in a rush. "We work for Luigi! He has always been our boss. He gets work for us. We were to meet him on the road to Amalfi, near the tunnel. We do not know who we are working for. Luigi just calls him the "old man". I think he lives on a boat in Amalfi. I am not sure. I think that is where Luigi has taken your package. That is all I know. Please do not shoot us!"

"He is right," said Gino. "That is all we know!"

Alberto put the gun down. He spat on the ground in front of the two men and turned back to Dan, Elizabeth and Charlotte.

"I think we should get out of here before this Luigi fellow comes back! Follow me," said Alberto as he grabbed his backpack. He led them down the driveway. As soon as they were out of sight of Gino and Paolo, he led them off the road and into the trees.

"I thought it best to not let them know the direction we were taking. Just in case," said Alberto as they made their way through the scrubby undergrowth back down the slope to where he and Dan had left the car.

Fifteen minutes later they were all standing beside the Fiat. During the walk they had started to catch each other up on what had been happening. Elizabeth and Charlotte had insisted on stopping and seeing the damage the two gun shots had done to Dan. They were horrified. Even Dan was stunned by the amount of bruising that had now spread across his chest and stomach.

They were still catching up as they headed down the road towards the coast, crammed together in the tiny Fiat.

Alberto had been concerned when he heard about the involvement of Thomas Malm and MI6 but stunned when he heard that Elizabeth had taken a sample of the liquid and already had some preliminary results.

"That is fantastico!" he said. "I was thinking that we had to get the package back, but we don't! All we need to know now is who has it!"

At that moment a motorbike roared passed them heading back towards Agerola.

"Hey!" said Dan, recognising the clothes of the rider, "That looked like Luigi!"

"I think it was," said Alberto. "The sooner we get to a place where there are lots of people the safer we will be."

"That didn't help Dad in Naples!" said Charlotte, glancing at her father with a frown.

The little Fiat turned a corner, and, suddenly, there, laid out before them, was the beautiful blue expanse of the Mediterranean. The narrow road now ran along the coast. Low stone walls on one side, protected them from falling off the edge of the cliff. Steep banks or houses ran along the other side of the road. Terraced gardens cascaded down the side of the hills towards the rocky coast below them. Alberto expertly navigated the little car down the winding road. Coming out of a tunnel they suddenly saw the town of Amalfi before them, nestled in its little coastal valley. Its houses, rising up the walls of the valley, were stacked one on top of another, facing out onto the Mediterranean.

Alberto squeezed the car into a non-existent car space in the centre of town, close to one of the stone breakwaters that jutted out into the Bay. There were people and buses all around them.

"We need to talk to the police," said Charlotte.

"I don't think so!" said Dan. "I think from what we have heard I don't want to involve anyone in this that I don't trust implicitly, and at the moment, that would only include the four of us, and I'm still not a hundred percent sure about him." He said with a grin and a nod towards Alberto.

"Someone, somehow, has been one step ahead of us all the time and I can't figure out who or how." continued Dan. "Before yesterday I would have thought that I could have trusted Thomas with my life, but now I am not so sure. Who was it, for instance, that told Luigi and his henchmen where you guys were so you could be kidnapped? Thomas was one of the few people who even knew you were in Italy. It could have been someone in the Italian security service, or police that was working with Thomas. Either way, I think we are in this on our own for the moment."

"I'm not sure," said Elizabeth. "I don't know enough about how the police operate here, but if I was at home I wouldn't hesitate to contact them."

"Most of the police here are, how do you say, very straight?" said Alberto. "But there is more going on here than a normal crime. I think we need to talk more about this situation. I have more information that I must share with you before you talk with anyone else."

"So what shold we do about Thomas Malm?" asked Charlotte.

"I need to tell him we are safe," said Elizabeth, "but given what Dan has said I don't want to tell him where we are. I still have his card in my pocket. Dan lend me your phone and I'll give him a quick ring."

Somewhat reluctantly Dan handed over his phone. He watched while she dialed the number. It went straight to voicemail. She hung up. "I'll try again later."

"We need to keep a low profile. This place is too crowded for anyone to try anything on the spur of the moment, but as a basic precaution none of us should wander off alone!" said Alberto.

"Okay," said Dan, "how about we find somewhere to hole up for a while? I would feel a lot safer if we were off the streets!"

"Me too!" said Elizabeth. I need to get some food and I need a stiff drink! as well!"

"I'd die for a cold beer!" said Dan.

"I'd die for a cold beer and a panino!" said Alberto. "And some aspirin." he added as an afterthought.

"I'll see what I can do about getting a hotel room if you lend me your phone," said Elizabeth to Dan.

While Elizabeth and Charlotte looked for a hotel using Dan's smartphone, Dan and Alberto sat looking out at the yachts in the bay. "So, you really think we shouldn't get the local police involved now. Elizabeth may be right. We have been the victims of two kidnappings, one attempted murder, a serious assault and a robbery. We would seem to have cause."

Alberto looked at Dan. "I would advise not, but I am not here to tell you what to do Dottore. I have been on the trail of this relic for the last five years, putting together little bits of information here and collecting scraps of evidence there. This is the first time I have ever come close to putting some major pieces of this puzzle together."

He turned back towards the water before he continued. "There are three things that are important to me in this investigation, Dottore. Number one is the science. This leads us to the question about what this stuff is made from and what it does to someone who uses it. Number two is the history. I want to know where this stuff comes from and who has used it in the past. The third area is the most important of all. It is an issue of the future. Who is after this potion now and what do they want it for?"

"I am convinced that Hitler used it. I am pretty sure Napoleon used it and I have some suspicions about some others. If the person that is searching for it now is prepared to kill to get it then I think they have to be stopped. Until now I have been searching for answers alone. I have never been able to trust anyone enough to confide in them, until now," he said turning to Dan and clasping his shoulder. "So, do I think we should involve the police? No I don't, at least not yet. I will get in touch with a couple of my own friends in the Swiss Guard and see if they would like to come for a little holiday in Amalfi. I think we would all feel more comfortable if we had a little extra protection. What I would really like to do, though, is share with you and your family what I know. After that you can decide what needs to be done."

Dan smiled. He liked this man and he felt strongly that he was a man that he could trust, with his life if necessary. At that moment Charlotte leant forward and put her hand on her father's shoulder. "We have got a couple of rooms in a hotel overlooking the marina," she said, looking around a little nervously.

"Fantastic!" said Dan. "Where is it?"

She looked out the car window, back the way they had come and up. Dan followed her gaze. He saw a long white building, half way up the cliff that faced the sea.

"How do we get up there?" he asked.

"Back to the tunnel we came through, park the car opposite the entrance and then up to the top by elevator," she said, looking at the iPhone screen.

"That's great," said Dan. "We'll be safely out of the way, have a couple of body guards for protection and still be able to keep an eye out for our friends, if they turn up!"

17. Amalfi - Present day

Despite their own somewhat disheveled appearance, Elizabeth and Charlotte had registered at Reception while Dan and Alberto had kept out of the way. Alberto's swollen and bruised face was getting to a stage where it was scaring small children so they all decided that it would be best if they kept him hidden, at least untill after they had booked in.

While they waited for lunch to be delivered they all stood on the terrace of their suite at the Grand Hotel Convento Di Amalfi, overlooking the town and the marina, and made a detailed inspection of the boats below them. There were six large super-yachts in the Marina. Two were moored in the marina and four more were moored a little way off shore, too large to tie up to the breakwater in the harbour itself.

"That could be the boat of someone who is into blackmail, kidnapping and corruption!" said Charlotte, standing close to Dan and pointing down into the marina. "The big one with the black hull and superstructure. It looks sinister enough to be the boat of a baddie out of a James Bond film. Very graceful, very beautiful and very forbidding!"

"Or it could be the one next to it, the one with the blue hull and the grey superstructure," said Dan admiring the lines and modern design of the super yacht moored stern on to the breakwater. "Expensive, but subtle!"

"Only if those two thugs told us the truth!" said Elizabeth, coming up behind them. "It could be neither of them!"

"It should be easy enough to check. We just keep an eye on the Marina and see if anyone we recognise turns up to visit one of those boats," said Charlotte, with a sweep of her arm, which encompassed the marina in front of them as well as the larger boats, moored out beyond the breakwater.

After lunch, with Alberto's binoculars in one hand and a glass of wine in the other, Dan could easily keep an eye on what was going on in the town below them. They had decided to take it in turns keeping watch so that they would all get a chance to relax. Dan was intermittently scanning the bay with the binoculars. Elizabeth, Charlotte and Alberto were all relaxing on lounges enjoying the warmth of the late afternoon sun.

"Alberto," said Elizabeth, "I get the fact that you were with the Vatican police force and doing your Master degree in Psychology on the side, and all that, but who gave you the job of hunting down this relic and who funds you?" she asked bluntly.

Dan and Charlotte both looked around. It was an obvious question, but one that neither of them had yet thought to ask.

Alberto grinned in his good natured way. "I will have to tell you a story to explain. I guess this is as good a time as any."

"When I first joined Corpo della Gendarmeria dello Stato della Città del Vaticano my commander gave me the job of investigating a growing list of reliquaries that had gone missing from churches."

"Reliquaries?" asked Elizabeth, "Like bits of saints you mean?"

"Well yes, but it can be any sacred treasure, really. Many relics are housed in ornate and very valuable containers. There are three classes of relics," said Alberto.

"What, like a football league table!" scoffed Elizabeth.

"In a way!" laughed Alberto. "At the top, in the Division One, are the relics that come from Christ himself, or one of the saint's bodies. The second division, are the clothes or objects that have been touched by a saint, or the instrument of martyrdom of a martyr."

"And who gets relegated to third division?" laughed Elizabeth.

"That would be the relics that have been touched by a first class relic," said Alberto.

"These devotional objects like the bones, blood or clothes of a saint, first started to appear some time after about the third century. They became increasingly common during the medieval period. It may even have been the establishment of the new Imperial capital in Constantinople that started the whole reliquary thing."

"Constantinople? Why? "What has that got to do with anything?" asked Elizabeth.

"The original city of Byzantium hadn't been a significant part of the early history of the church. When Constantine the Great established his new capital there in 330AD, it had no religious history to speak of."

"Constantinople, as you no doubt know, became the centre of not only the empire, but also of the Christian Church, so it needed to have some iconic relics for people to worship. It couldn't lay claim to have any saints buried there or of having its church founded by one of the Apostles like Antioch, Alexandria, Jerusalem or Rome. So, perhaps to get pilgrims there, or perhaps to increase the status of the City, or to give it some Christian cred, it could be argued that Constantine started the trend of going out and acquiring relics, including parts of the saints that other churches throughout the empire already had," said Alberto.

"Wasn't it Constantine's mother, Helena, that did most of the heavy lifting?" asked Charlotte.

"Yes," said Alberto. "I suppose that is true. She was appointed as Augusta Imperatrix, by her son, and given unlimited access to the Imperial treasury to go and find holy relics. The story goes that she travelled all over the holy land and is said to have brought back the true cross, Jesus' tunic and the nails used in the crucifixion. It is even said that she brought back earth from Golgotha and spread it on the gardens of the Vatican."

"So do these relics often get stolen?" asked Elizabeth.

"Oh yes! There is a long history of relics being stolen. One of the biggest relic heists of all time was in 1204 during the fourth crusade, when the Venetians and western Europeans sacked Constantinople. At that time the Church of the Apostle housed one of the greatest collection of relics in Christendom, including bones of the Apostles Saint Andrew, Saint Luke and Saint Timothy, as well as a host of other saints and Martyrs. It also housed the remains of most of the Emperors that had ruled the Empire from Constantinople, so it was pretty rich pickings for the guys that got to it first!"

"The real treasures though, relics like the holy lance, part of the true cross, the Holy Mandylion, the right arm of John the Baptist, the crown of thorns and many, many others, were all in the Church of the Virgin of Pharos, the royal chapel. They were protected during the sacking but got distributed all around Europe afterwards.

"It's actually a bit problematic in a way, given that some of the stolen relics, and some of those that got gifted by the Latin Emporers, ended up in the Vatican and other catholic churches all across Western Europe," he said.

"I can sort of understand, in those days, why there might be a healthy trafficking of relics, but does it still happen much today?" asked Elizabeth.

"More and more, surprisingly.' said Alberto. "There was the famous theft, for example, in the early eighties from a church in Calcata, just north of Rome, of what the church had once believed was Christ's foreskin."

Charlotte looked at Alberto in amazement. "You are kidding! Really!"

"Yes, seriously! It was in a beautiful crystal reliquary and there was documented evidence that it had been in the church since at least the late 1500s. It was the cause of a great argument sometime in the nineteenth century. Another church, in France I think, claimed that they had the holy foreskin some time in the 1800s. It caused such a fuss that it actually became an excommunicate-able offence to talk about the holy foreskin." Alberto said, his expression serious.

Dan looked at him to see if he was pulling their legs. "You are kidding us!" he said.

"No! No! I am not the kidding type!" said Alberto, holding up his hands and protesting his innocence. "The Holy Prepuce of Calcata caused a huge ruckus. In the 1950s the penalty for talking about Jesus' foreskin was given an even worse punishment, excommunication vitandi."

"Good God! That sounds gruesome. What is it?" asked Dan.

"It means that the person is to not only to be cast out from the church, but also shunned, even on secular matters," said Alberto.

"Like being sent to Coventry?" asked Dan.

"I do not know that expression, but it was a very serious penalty," said Alberto. "Personally I liked the way that the Vatican librarian, Leo Allatius, dealt with the foreskin issue in the 1700s. He is said to have written a discussion of the foreskin of Our Lord Jesus Christ in which he proposed that the foreskin couldn't exist on earth because it would have physically ascended into heaven, just as Jesus had done. He even suggested that the foreskin turned into the rings of Saturn!" Now Alberto was smiling.

Elizabeth was frowning. "I still don't get it. Why do people steal them? Do they believe that they have some magical power or is it just because they are valuable or are there other reasons?"

"In a way that was what I was asked to investigate. If it was just theft and resale, that would be bad, but at least understandable. There was a fear, in some parts of the Church, that the relics might be being used for other, darker purposes."

"What, like black magic!" asked Elizabeth, incredulous.

Alberto shrugged his shoulders. "I keep an open mind. Anyway, as part of my duties I investigate these thefts, like the theft of the heart of Saint Laurence O'Toole which was stolen from Dublin Cathedral a few years ago," he said. "The thieves went to all the trouble of breaking open an iron cage to get to the reliquary that contained the heart of the Saint but left a whole lot of other, more easily accessible and valuable stuff behind."

"That's a bit weird, isn't it?!" asked Charlotte.

"I discovered that many of the thefts were not reported to the police and have never become public knowledge. Those that have, like the relics stolen from Saint Petersburg Cathedral relatively recently, the theft of Saint Laurence's heart and a bunch of robberies of churches in Mexico, just seem like random thefts. On the other hand, I got to see all the thefts that were occurring. I do know that many of them were just robberies for monetary gain, but some of them made me wonder. At times I thought I could see an underlying pattern, at least for some of the thefts."

"Still, putting that aside, my job was in two parts. I was given responsibility for any current cases of stolen relics and also given the slightly more sensitive job of trying to hunt down relics that had been stolen by the Nazis during the Second World War."

"Given my state of mind at the time it was the ideal job for me. I was studying psychology in my spare time and doing detective work during the day! It was my ideal job."

"What it also did, which was a fantastic bonus, was give me unprecedented, pretty well unrestricted, access to the Vatican library and archives."

"Really?" said Charlotte, her preconceived ideas about Alberto as a rough and tough cop suddenly flying out the window. "You have access to the Archivum Secretum Apostolicum Vaticanum?"

"The what?" asked Elizabeth.

"She is talking about the Vatican's secret archives," said Dan, also interested.

"Why do they call it the secret archive? Is it really secret?" Elizabeth asked Alberto.

"Well they were pretty well secret up until the late 1800's when the Pope, one of the Leos, I forget which number, opened them up to scholarly research," he said. "They are the Pope's personal papers, so the meaning of secret is more like private, rather than confidential."

"And they are pretty selective about who they will let in!" said Charlotte. "A number of my colleagues have requested access and not been give it!" She paused, thinking, then said, "But hang on! You are investigating the second world war stuff, right?" Alberto nodded. "But the Vatican still hasn't released anything dated after 1939! Are you saying you have access to unreleased documents as well?"

"It was necessary for me to do my job properly! I was given access to the Pope's private library. All the material that has never been released!" said Alberto. "I had access to all these documents, so when I started to do my Masters I couldn't help but do a bit of personal research about Hitler on the side. That is when I found it."

"Found what?" they all asked.

"Proof that the Blood of Constantine is real," he said. " I found a letter from Pope Pius VI to his successor that had never been opened. It explained why Pius VI gave the Blood of Constantine to Napoleon Bonaparte!"

18. Rome - 1797

"We have no choice, your eminence!" said Cardinal Giuseppe Doria Pamphili, the Cardinal Secretary of State. "The French will invade unless we negotiate with them."

Pope Pius VI put his head in his hands. He was weary. "Why does God try me so, Giuseppe!? Was it not trial enough to deal with the Hapsburg's and see the Lord's Church in Germany devastated by Joseph the second's misguided policies? Seven Hundred monasteries closed! Forty thousand nuns and monks expelled! Marriage made a civil contract! How can the man claim to be the Holy Roman Emperor?"

"Now I am confronted by these French regicides! This radical government that puts nuns and monks to the guillotine! Madmen who confiscate the property of the church and turn the Lord's places of worship into warehouses and factories! Madmen who continually try to re-write history."

"Robespierre!" he said, exasperated. "That lunatic Robespierre and his pursuit of his cult of the supreme being or this latest nonsense, Theophilanthropy! Such a cynical creation, so transparently designed to manipulate the population. Pretending to bring to God those very people whom they drive away from Him by estranging them from the true faith. The world is going mad, Giuseppe! I weep for the future of France. I weep for my Church!"

Cardinal Pamphili put a hand gently on the Popes shoulder.

"Tell me about this man Bonaparte and what he is likely to want. Tell me what I have to do to keep our lands, bring back the church to France and end all this madness!" said the Pope.

"He is Corsican, your Eminence. I understand his family comes from a line of minor Italian noblemen. He is only a young man, not yet thirty. He trained at the Military College at Briennne, and then the Ecole Miltaire in Paris. He did well in his studies. He had a brief dalliance with the Corsican resistance, but he had a falling out with its leader, Pasquale Paoli. The French must have had a good opinion of him because he was excepted readily back into the French army despite having fought against them in Corsica."

"If you wanted to get a sense of how he thinks you could read a pamphlet he wrote called, entertainingly, "Le souper de Beaucaire" where he fabricates a discussion between a number of merchants and himself. It is just the sort of document you would write if you were an ambitious young man seeking to ingratiate yourself with that republican rabble that has taken over France."

"I have been told he is a gifted soldier, but all that means is that he will, no doubt, lose his head to the guillotine as so many other French Generals have!"

"When he first arrived in Italy I would have said that he would not last long. But to my amazement he has taken charge of that run down, demoralised crowd that the French call the army of Italy, and driven the Austrians back."

"I have heard rumours that he was sent to Italy to get him out of the way, perhaps killed, but I hear, from my sources in Paris, that his successes have caught them off guard."

"Do you know if he supports the Church, or is he one of these atheists that the French find so fashionable these days?" asked the Pope, with undisguised bitterness.

"From the little I can glean he may be, at worst, agnostic," said the Cardinal.

"Can we use him?" asked the Pope.

"Use him, your eminence, in what way?"

"Use him to bring the church back to France, Giuseppe," said the Pope.

"I don't know, your eminence. I don't know what we could offer such a man. He is the sort of man who seems to be motivated by success on the battlefield. He may be able to be bribed, if we knew what it was that he values."

They Pope rested his hands in his lap and closed his eyes. The world, he thought, was changing rapidly. Too rapidly. He felt the weight of responsibility for a church beset on all sides weighing on him heavily.

Pamphili looked across at the old man. He bowed his head and prayed for guidance on how to lift some of the burdens from the Holy Father. Times had not been good for the church and the Pope seemed beaten down and care worn. The dark shadows and folds of flesh under his eyes attested to the fact that he no longer slept well.

After a few minutes Pamphili was surprised to hear a gentle snore. He looked up at the old man. Pope Pius VI had fallen asleep. Pamphili was amazed to see a look of contentment on the Pope's face and on his lips the smallest of smiles.

He bowed his head and thanked God for answering his prayers so quickly. He left the old man sleeping peacefully in his chair.

****

Pope Pius had slept for little more than an hour, but when he awoke he felt refreshed. He now sat with an ancient looking wooden box and an empty rock crystal reliquary in front of him.

He sat for a long time, with his head bowed, seeking guidance on what he was about to do. Eventually, with a trembling hand, he opened the lid of the box and looked down on a magnificently jewelled casket, nestled in a lining of faded and crumbling material.

The casket was gold with elaborate inlays of turquoise, carnelian and lapis lazuli creating a fantastical scene of bulls and stags and, in the centre, an astonishing beast with the head of a bearded man and the body of a winged lion.

Pope Pius ran his hand over the surface of the box and shivered. He could almost feel the spirits inside this box calling out to him. Carefully he lifted the lid. Inside, the box was divided into compartments. At the back was a scroll. In front of the scroll were a series of small compartments that held even smaller glass bottles, each holding varying amounts of a different coloured powder. At the very front was an even smaller bottle, not glass, but gold. The Pope withdrew it and unscrewed

193

its lid. Very carefully he spilled its contents onto a piece of parchment he had laid on the table for that purpose.

The gold vial was far from full, and the powder which poured from it, made only a small pile. The Pope, daring not even to breath, divided the small pile in half, using a small gold knife. He moved one of the piles to the opposite side of the parchment, then, with a single stroke, cut the parchment in two. He used the parchment, folding it carefully, to pour the smaller amount of powder into the opening of the rock crystal reliquary.

With the same knife he cut a small incision deeply into the index finger of his left hand. Blood welled up. He quickly put his finger over the reliquary to catch the blood as it dripped out of his finger.

As he sat, blood slowly dripping into the reliquary, he contemplated the remaining pile of powder. Then, quietly to himself he said, "Forgive me father!" lifted the parchment up and blew the small pile of dust into the air. The tiny grains floated in the air for a moment, glinting in the light from his small lantern, and then a draft caught them, and they were gone.

19.Tolentino - February 16, 1797

Napoleon sat at his desk. He was tired. It had been an exhausting few months. They had finally broken the siege of Mantua and he had accepted the surrender of the Austrian, von Wurmser. Now he controlled nearly all of Northern Italy. The next target was the Papal States, then Rome. He should have been focusing on the discussions with the Holy See, but he couldn't concentrate. He looked down at the letter he had just written.

Dearest Josephine,

You are sad, you are sick, you write to me no longer, you wish to return to Paris! Do you no longer love your friend? This thought makes me very unhappy. My dear friend, life is intolerable to me, since I have heard of your sadness.

I send you at once Moscati to take care of you. My health is somewhat feeble; my cold hangs on. I pray you spare yourself, and love me as much as I love you, and do write every day. My restlessness is horrible.

I have given orders to Moscati to accompany you to Ancona, if you will come. I will write to you and let you know where I am.

I may perhaps make peace with the Pope, and then will soon be with you; it is the most intense desire of my life.

I send a hundred kisses. Think not that any thing can equal my love, unless it be my solicitude for you. Write to me every day yourself, my dearly-beloved one!

He folded the letter and as he finished putting his seal on the back of the envelope. He heard a knock at the door. He turned and nodded at his friend and brother in law, Joachim Murat, as he stepped into the room.

Joachim stopped and looked at Napoleon sitting dejectedly at his desk. 'She has still not written, my friend?" he asked, solicitously.

He shook his head. "I have not heard from her. Perhaps she was too angry with me for leaving Paris for Italy only two days after we married. I know she has a good life in Paris, but surely it was not unreasonable that she should want to be with her husband?"

Napoleon banged his fist on his desk. "For months I begged her to come to Italy, but all I got were excuses. I have to admit, Joachim , I was beginning to think that she was just making excuses and she really did not want to be with me."

Joachim didn't respond.

"Finally out of desperation I send you to Paris to bring her back. You bring me the news that she is with child, but no Josephine." He paused and sat moodily looking at the ground.

"Then, when she had finally acquiesces to my pleading, and actually comes to Italy, she brings that damnable Hussar, Hippolyte Charles, with her! Are they lovers, Joachim? Is she sleeping with that buffoon? Is everyone laughing at me behind my back?" he asked angrily.

He knew that she had many lovers in the past, but surely being married should have put an end to her old way of life. It made him so wild to think of her with other men.

"Now that she is here in Italy this campaign has become so demanding that we have only been able to spend a few brief days together. The least she could do is write a few simple lines, a few lines of affectionate prose. How difficult can that be?"

He sat looking at Joachim, who was still standing by the door. He shook his head, as if to clear. "Sorry my friend. I shouldn't burden you with my woes. What is it that you want, is everything alright with my sister?"

"Caroline is well, Napoleon. I came to tell you that you have a visitor. Francois Cacault, the French Directorate's Ambassador to the Holy See has arrived. Do you wish to see him now?" he asked.

Napoleon nodded as Joachim left, closing the door behind him. He stood up and straightened his jacket. A few moments later the door opened again and the Ambassador stepped in to the room and held out his hand. Napoleon shook it and waved him to a comfortable chair.

"So Cacault, are we ready to sign?" he asked, glad of the distraction and a chance to concentrate on something other than his infuriating wife.

"We are, Bonaparte! The terms have been agreed. The Papal States will pay us fifteen million lire. This added to the twenty one million lire that was agreed at the armistice signed at Bologna, makes a total of thirty six million! They have also agreed that the Comtat and the City of Avignon will be formally ceded back to France, as will the Romagna region of the Papal States. Everything from the Apennines to the Adriatic and from the Reno River in the north to the Sillaro River in the west."

"We, in our turn, have agreed to withdraw from Umbria, Perugia and Camerino, as soon as his Holiness pays up in full! We have also agreed to get out of Macerata, as soon as the first five million is paid."

Napoleon nodded, pleased.

"The Pope has also agreed that all the harbours in the Papal States will remain open at all times to our ships and remain closed to those we declare as our enemies."

"And the works of art?" asked Napoleon.

"Yes. They have agreed, as you specified in the Armistice of Bologna, that they will surrender 100 objects of art and 500 manuscripts from the Vatican. I have left the details to be fixed by a commission of our experts. They will be transported to the Louvre, as you have requested."

"I had a note the other day from Jean-Francois Rewbell." Napoleon said reaching for a letter that lay on his desk. "He is writing on behalf of the Directorate. He makes no secret of his desire to destroy the church of Rome! He asks me to tell him the best way to achieve that outcome. He says here that he gives me permission to find the best way to,...*destroy the Papal government, placing Rome under another power, or establishing a form of national government that would render odious and contemptible the government of the priests, and the Pope and the Sacred College could have no hope of residing in Rome and would be obliged to seek a residence elsewhere...*" As he finished reading he looked up at Cacault.

Cacault had raised an eyebrow. "He wants you to de-throne the Pope? And you intend to do that? Have you no fear?"

Napoleon thought for a moment. "Why would I fear that madman. Will the Pope's curse make the muskets fall from my soldiers hands? No! It makes no difference to me. I would happily see Rome ruled by a revolutionary Council rather than a Sacred one!"

Cacault laughed. "There is one more thing you should know. The Pope has asked for a private audience with you before we sign the treaty. Are you happy to do that?"

"Of course!" said Napoleon. "It is not like he can influence me or change my mind. I am not one of the superstitious sheep of his flock!"

20. Tolentino - February 19, 1797

Pope Pius VI sat alone, waiting for Napoleon. The door at the other end of the room opened and he watched the young man stride confidently towards him. He was not as tall as he had imagined and looked younger than he had been led to believe. He walked with the self-assured stride of someone who believed he knew his place in the world. He was dressed in a plain dark dress coat with a red sash around his waist. A sword hung at his side and occasionally slapped against his long black leather boots.

Napoleon stopped in front of the Pope and tilted his head slightly, saying, politely, "Your Holiness!"

Pius lifted his right hand so the young General could kiss the Papal ring. Napoleon held the hand for a moment, then let it go.

The Pope saw how things would be and rose stiffly to his feet. He stood taller than the young man. He indicated that they should walk. He knew that there was a door out to a private garden at the far side of the room. He walked to it. He paused at the door allowing Napoleon to show him the courtesy of opening it for him, younger man for older. Napoleon nodded and opened the door, allowing the Pope to walk out into the cool morning air.

Walking side by side down the narrow garden path the Pope learned towards his companion and said in his calm, quiet voice, "I understand that you have no love for my Church, General Bonaparte and I am aware that there are those in your new French Government that would prefer to see it stripped of its treasures and wiped from the face of the earth to be replace by some vague spirituality, a religion without dogmas, miracles, priesthood or sacraments." he paused to see if the Frenchman would disagree.

"It is true," he said curtly.`

"And you?" asked the Pope.

"If I felt the need to choose a religion, then I would choose the sun, the universal giver of life, as my god." replied Napoleon without hesitation.

The Pope sighed. He took a different tack. "You are a talented commander General Bonaparte. I hear much of your successes and your personal courage. Your bravery at the battle of Arcole, standing in the open holding a flag while under heavy fire sounds," he paused, "... inspirational, and, dare I say it, somewhat foolhardy. It was a miracle you were not killed," he said, a small smile on his face.

"Perhaps!" said Napoleon, not rising to the bait, "I am sometimes impetuous, it is true. But I cannot imagine that you asked for this conversation because you wanted to spend your time flattering me or giving me fatherly advice!"

"No, that is true, General." The Pontiff paused, as if looking for the right words. "France is a troubled nation. Even those who would appear to have its best interest at heart can fall foul of its rapidly changing political climate. You were, I am told, well acquainted with the younger Robespierre before he and his brother Maximilien were sent to the guillotine?"

"I knew Augustine," said Napoleon, curtly.

"The fate of the two Robespierres is an example of how, without the right insights, one can fall, very quickly, from the highest of highs," said the Pope, watching Napoleon out of the corner of his eye as they continued their slow walk down the long garden path.

"Perhaps if Maximilien had seen more clearly the effect of the Terror he unleashed on the people around him, he might have survived. From all reports he was scrupulously honest, a gentleman, a learned man, a man of culture who thought deeply about his decisions and worked long and hard all his life. I have to say I admired his stand on the rights of man. And yet, with all those noble virtues, without the natural justice or common decency of a trial, he ended up with his neck under the unforgiving blade of the guillotine!"

Napoleon made a noise, but did not speak. The Pope paused, giving the General time to reflect on the fate of Maximilien and Augustine and the cloud of suspicion that had subsequently fallen over him. He knew knew it had been a difficult time for Bonaparte who had spent a month languishing in prison, the threat of the guillotine hanging over his own head!

"Robespierre did not have the natural instinct of a great statesman. He was not gifted with flashes of insight," said the Pope.

"It is true. Imagination rules the world!" said Napoleon. "The man of ability takes advantage of everything and neglects nothing that can give him a chance of success! Less able men sometimes lose everything by neglecting a single one of those opportunities."

"What if there was a way that a man could be given such insight, such breadth of vision that he would be able to see every one of those chances!" asked the Pope quietly.

Napoleon stopped and turned to the Pope. "There is nothing more difficult, or more precious, than to be able to make a good decision, decisively, if possible. If there were a way to make decisions clearer, to have such insight, then a man who was able to see with such perfect clarity would no longer be a man. He would be a God!"

The Pope pondered Napoleon's answer for a moment, before asking, "And what would a man of ambition do for such power, do you think?"

"A man of ambition would give his life to take hold of such a power! It is what a wise man of ambition strives for! Perfect knowledge! Perfect insight!" said Napoleon.

The Pope stared at Napoleon, trying to see into his soul. Grey eyes stared back, fixed and unblinking.

"I can grant you this power, General!" said the Pope, bluntly.

Napoleon's expression didn't change. "How can you grant me such a power?" he asked, a note of derision entering his voice. "Your God is famous for not working in such a direct manner!"

"There are many miraculous things in this world, General. Many that God has not seen fit to let us fully understand. I have in my possession such an object. It is a relic that Constantine the Great bequeathed to the Church, which, when taken, produces such a change in the mind of the user that, it is said, they have all possible futures revealed to them."

Napoleon stood staring at Pope Pius. The Pope smiled. He could see the doubt in the young man's face. Perhaps he was even wondering if the Pontiff had lost his mind. Finally, he asked, "What is this relic made of?"

"I am told it is the actual blood of Constantine," said the Pope.

"And you have drunk this blood?" Napoleon asked, incredulous.

The Pope smiled again. He reached out and touched Napoleon's arm. "No. I do not have the courage to do so! The potion tampers with the mind. Some who have taken it have died. Some have gone mad. It is only the rare, the exceptional, to whom it delivers the gift of insight."

The Pope could see that Napoleon was far from convinced. He, nevertheless, kept quiet, giving the young General time to think.

"Who has taken this elixir of yours and survived, then, for they must stand above mere mortal men like a colossus?"

"Do you know the story of the Holy Ampulla, General?" The Pope asked.

Napoleon blinked, clearly, taken aback by the apparent change of subject. He nodded. "All the kings of France are anointed with it, or should I say, were anointed with it. Philippe Rüh destroyed it at the direction of the Convention a few years ago. He smashed it to pieces."

"Did you know what the Sainte Ampoule actually was?" asked the Pope. Napoleon shook his head again.

"It was said to be the oil that Saint Remigius, the Bishop who converted King Clovis to Christianity, used to baptise Clovis," said the Pope.

"I have, of course, heard of Clovis. He conquered the Romans and the Visigoth. He was the founder of the Merovingian dynasty, the one who brought the Frankish tribes together and became their King. The first King of France!" said Napoleon.

"That is right," said the Pope. "Clovis was, in addition to being a talented leader, a pagan, although his wife, a woman by the name of Clotilde, was a Christian. At that time the Arian heresy was running rampant, and there were many more Arians in Europe than those that followed the true Catholic faith."

"Arian?" asked Napoleon.

"God, Jesus and the Holy Spirit are three persons of one being. Arians believed, wrongly, that Jesus was a separate being, subordinate to and created by God," said the Pope almost dismissively, then continued, "Clotilde must have been a formidable woman. She had her first son baptised, in secret, and against Clovis' express wishes. The child died soon after. Clotilde did the same with their second son, who,

202

fortuitously, didn't die, but became very ill straight after the baptism. You can imagine Clovis' attitude to the Church after losing one son and nearly losing a second immediately after they were baptised!"

"Despite their loss, Clotilde still managed to convince Clovis to be baptised himself. A remarkable feat!"

Napoleon grunted, but did not speak.

"Legend has it, that, on Christmas Day 496, the Holy Ampulla was brought by a dove, the Holy Spirit incarnate, and given to Saint Remigius, to be used in the baptism of Clovis."

"Do you believe that?" asked Napoleon.

"No, I don't," said the Pope. "What I know is that Remigius received a vial of the Blood of Constantine. It was in a small Roman glass ampule and it came directly from the newly elevated Pope Anastasius II."

"At the time we are talking about, the Catholic Church was in crisis. Not only was the Arian heresy wide spread, but the Church was also deeply embroiled in trying to resolve the Acacian schism with the Eastern Church. Anastasius believed that he could resolve both issues by supporting the union of the Frankish tribes and aligning the Church with, what would then be a formidable new western power. Clovis was the key. If he could bring him into the true faith then both the Arian heresy and the threat from the East would be diminished and he would, literally overnight, have a more powerful bargaining position with the Eastern Roman Empire."

"Pope Anastasius sent an ampule of the Blood of Constantine to Remigius to be used as a bribe to bring Clovis into the faith."

"If this potion of yours is so powerful, then why didn't Anastasius just take the potion himself, and see his way through his own difficulties?" said Napoleon, somewhat sarcastically.

"I believe that he did," replied the Pope. "Two years later, just when the issues for the church were at their most vexing he did take the potion."

"Did it work? Did he see the future?" asked Napoleon.

"No," said the Pope sadly, "He took the risk and died. For his trouble the church vilified him. He is one of only two popes in the church's first five hundred years who never attained Sainthood."

"So you know, from documents in the Vatican, that the Blood of Constantine actually came from Constantine the Great, the founder of Constantinople?" asked Napoleon directly. The Pope nodded. "And you have documents in your possession, that you could show me, that Clovis was given the Blood of Constantine by Pope Anastasius, who later took it himself and died?" The Pope nodded.

Napoleon walked a few more steps then stopped and turned to the Pope. "So what happened to the Blood of Constantine that Clovis had?"

"I believe that Saint Remigius took it with him to his grave, literally," replied the Pope. "When the Saints sarcophagus was opened some four hundred years later, the ampule was found, still clasped in his hand!"

"How could that be? His body would have turned to dust," said Napoleon, dismissively.

The Pope shook his head, and said defensively, "When Archbishop Hincmar opened the coffin, the body was found to be incorrupt!"

They walked in silence for a few minutes, each lost in their own thoughts, then the Pope said, "A reliquary was made for the ampoule. It was encrusted with jewels and in the centre, representing the Holy Spirit, was a white enamelled dove. The Holy Ampulla itself formed the body of the dove."

"From that time the Abbot of the Abbey of Saint-Remi has traditionally worn it around his neck on a heavy gold chain."

"During the coronation of a King of France, the monarch is required to remove his outer clothes and open up his shirt, revealing his chest, upper back and arms. The Archbishop uses a gold stylus to extract some of the oil from the Holy Ampoule and mixes it on a gold paten with chrism. The Archbishop then anoints the king. He marks a cross on the top of his head, on his chest, between his shoulders and on the joints of both arms," said the Pope.

"If this potion does what you say, then it clearly has not worked for the Kings of France!" said Napoleon.

"The potion is meant to be taken internally, not put on the skin. It is not surprising that it had no appreciable effect," said the Pope.

"So, a king took your potion what, thirteen hundred years ago? It is a bit far fetched." The general paused. "Suppose I believed you? Who else has taken the potion that you know of?" asked Napoleon.

The Pope looked at him. He had finally realised what he was being offered.

"I have done much research into this potion and there is one other, besides some of my predecessors who I have evidence of being given the potion. Pope Adrian the first gave the potion to the King of the Franks in return for his protection," said the Pope.

"What year was this?" Napoleon asked.

"I believe it was around the time Adrian ascended to the throne of Saint Peter, around the early 770's."

Napoleon stared at the Pope, astounded. "Charlemagne! Are you telling me that Charlemagne, the father of Europe, used this potion?" he asked, incredulously.

"I am saying that it is possible. I have a letter that intimates that Adrian gave the Blood of Constantine to Charlemagne as a gift. The two men had a, surprisingly, close relationship over a long time. There is an epitaph, written by Charlemagne himself, that was taken from Pope Adrian's tomb and placed in the portico of Saint Peters. If you read it you feel that their relationship was a very strong one. It ends with '*O most illustrious, I unite our two names and titles, Adrian and Charles, the king and the father.*' recited the Pope from memory.

"That says nothing about a magic potion!" said Napoleon.

"No, but think for a moment about the extraordinary shared vision that those two men had. Their relationship lasted over twenty five years and during that time they brought the whole of Europe to heel, both temporal and secular," said the Pope.

"That is hardly a convincing argument. Charlemagne was a great man. A visionary. There is nothing to suggest that he took some magical elixir that gave him superhuman powers!"

"I will not lie to you General. I can not show you any definite proof that Charlemagne took the potion, but I have a strong suspicion that he did."

"And you are offering me this potion. You are offering me the same bargain that you say Clovis and Charlemagne had? In return for the potion I give you the hearts of the people of France and the protection of its Armies!" said the General.

The Pope nodded. "And, in return, I can give you its future General Bonaparte!"

He looked into Napoleon's eyes, wondering whether this young man would grasp this opportunity. The important thing was that Napoleon took the elixir. If it killed him, or sent him mad, that would be God's will. He would then possibly have the benefit of contending with a less formidable General. If the potion really did affect the mind as he had read, then the future would be in this man's hands, and he, and the Church, would have placed it there. For that power he knew he could ask the highest of prices.

21. Amalfi - Present day

Elizabeth nodded as Alberto introduced his two friends as Sabastiano and Martinus. She was relieved to see they had brought with them an armful of packages that they had picked up in Naples. She and Charlotte had done some quick online clothes shopping, for themselves and for Dan and Alberto, when they had heard the two young men were driving through the city.

They were both clean cut and solid looking young men. After a brief discussion with Alberto their two new bodyguards started to head for the door. "I will just have a walk around with the boys," said Alberto turning to follow them.

"Hold on Alberto!" said Elizabeth holding up a hand while staring through the binoculars at the Marina. "Here they come!"

Alberto waved the two young men on, indicating that he would catch up to them later. Dan and Charlotte were standing beside Elizabeth, looking down at the Marina, when he joined them.

"Oh dear!" said Dan with a laugh. "They look a little worse for wear!"

The Fiat van was making its way along the road into Amalfi. It then turned and started to come back towards them, along the road that ran along the waterfront. Through the binoculars Elizabeth could see that the van was badly battered, with scrapes and dents along one side, and no front windscreen. It stopped on the waterfront and three men got out.

They all continued to watch as the men opened up the back and unloaded the motorbike that Luigi had been riding.

"They don't look happy!" said Charlotte, who had taken the binoculars from Elizabeth. "They seem to be doing a lot of looking around. Do you think they expect us to be watching them?"

"I guess so," said Dan. "But its not like they can do a lot about it. They would have to have binoculars to see us up here and Amalfi is a busy town. From their perspective we could be anywhere!"

They continued to watch from the safety of their vantage point as the three men walked to a nearby outside cafe and seated themselves at one of the outside tables. A few minutes later, a fourth man walked up and joined them. He sat down at the table. He was elegantly dressed in a white linen suit and wore a hat that, unfortunately, shielded his face.

"Damn!" said Charlotte. "I can't see his face at all!"

Alberto rang Martinus and gave him a quick update on what was happeneing.

Dan took the binoculars from Charlotte. "He doesn't look happy though!" said Dan peering through the binoculars. "Oh ho! He has just slapped Luigi in the face! He really is pissed off! I would love to be a fly on the wall down there!"

The man in the hat continued to gesticulate aggressively towards Luigi. Eventually he stopped, stood up and walked away, his back towards Dan.

Luigi sat still for a few minutes watching the retreating back of the man who they all agreed had to be Luigi's mysterious employer. Luigi then turned around and waved his arms at Gino and Paolo. They sat for some time finishing their drinks. All three men then got up and headed off in separate directions. Dan lost sight of them as they blended with the crowds of tourists who were starting to promenade along the waterfront.

As they all resumed their seats Dan sat down to do another stint as lookout. Rather than moving to Dan's seat Elizabeth stayed where she was. Dan sat down next to her with a smile. She put her hand on his shoulder and then rested her cheek on her hand.

She closed her eyes for a moment and when she opened them she saw that Charlotte was watching her smiling. She turned away and started to sort through the packages of clothing as soon as she realised Elizabeth was looking at her. After a moment she stopped and turned to Alberto. "So, Alberto, if we suspect that Napoleon took the potion, is there any more evidence of Napoleon dealing with Pope Pius?"

"Ah, yes!" said Alberto with a note of sadness in his voice. "Some of it I understand and other parts I don't, but I will tell you what my researches uncovered."

"Napoleon did not immediately ask for the Blood of Constantine. He found an excuse for taking the Pope prisoner, which he did, almost exactly a year later."

"Napoleon was using the strategy of fomenting unrest in Rome to destabilise the Pontiff's rule. A riot was started involving some French Revolutionaries that, unfortunately, led to the death of one of Napoleon's Generals, Léonard Duphot. Duphot was shot by Papal troops. This gave Napoleon an excuse to send his armies back into Rome. The Pope was arrested on the 10th of February 1798."

"He then tried to force the Pope to give him the Blood of Constantine and to renunciate his temporal powers. The Pope was an old man. He was over eighty and had been Pope for longer than any other man up till that time, some twenty four years."

"From what I gleaned from letters sent between Napoleon and the Spaniard Pedro Labrador, the Marquis of Labrador, who was charged with accompanying the Pope, Napoleon was putting pressure on this guy, Pedro Labrador, to force Pius to hand over the Blood of Constantine."

"Pedro Labrador was a man who moved in exalted circles, but he was not a high flyer. I read somewhere one of his contemporaries describing him as mediocre and haughty. One modern historian describes him as '...a caricature Spaniard who specialised in frantic rages, haughty silences and maladroit demarches.' In fact, the Duke of Wellington said he was the most stupid man he had ever come across," Alberto said with a laugh, before continuing.

"It was probably not surprising that Napoleon used this man to try and force the head of the catholic church to hand over the reliquary, effectively keeping his involvement at arms length. The Pope died in August 1799, a little over a year from when he was taken captive. Whether it was from old age or an overzealous Marquis of Labrador, we will never really know."

"Did he give up the Blood of Constantine?" asked Elizabeth, engrossed in the story.

"I think so. Perhaps he made an arrangement to send Napoleon the relic just before he died. Pius VII, the next Pope, was the beneficiary of the deal though," said Alberto.

"The Concordant of 1801!" said Charlotte, excitedly.

"The what?" asked Elizabeth.

"The Concordant. It was an agreement between Napoleon and the new Pope Pius VII. It was the agreement that made the Roman Catholic Church the majority Church of France and restored, at least some, of the Papacy's powers. So that means that, if this is all true, that Napoleon had the Blood of Constantine by 1801, possibly as early as 1799." said Charlotte.

"Which ties in with the story that Rudolf Hess told. That means that Napoleon received the Blood of Constantine some time soon after his return from Egypt," said Dan.

"It still leaves a lot of unanswered question, though," said Charlotte. "Why did he rush off to Egypt with a scientific expedition in the first place? He took over one hundred and sixty scientists and scholars with him! Why? Why would he take a bunch of engineers, artists, mathematicians, chemists, physicists and botanists to Egypt? It wasn't like these were just scholars that happened to be in the army. These were people who were at the cutting edge of their disciplines. One of his geologists, Dolomieu is the man that dolomite is named after! Berthollet, one of his chemists, was the first person to demonstrate the bleaching action of chlorine gas, and discovered sodium hypochlorite's use as a modern bleaching agent. He took Joseph Fourier with him - the creator of Fourier's Law! What was he looking for in Egypt? What is the connection?"

"Perhaps", said Elizabeth, "now that he knew about the Blood of Constantine, he was chasing up an alternate source of it. Perhaps there was some clue that led him to Egypt!"

"Yes, that is a possibility," said Alberto, as his phone vibrated. He looked at the text message that had just arrived. "According to Martinus, our man in the white suit went back to that very expensive looking blue and black yacht."

They all got up and looked down at the marina.

"I would have given any money to bet the person behind this would have been on that big one with the black hull and superstructure." said Charlotte, sounding slightly disappointed.

They all stared at the elegant blue hulled yacht tied up at the marina beside its more sinister looking berth mate. Dan promised to keep an eye on it as they all resumed their seats.

"So, Alberto, back to Napoleon," said Charlotte settling back on her sun lounge.

Alberto smiled at her enthusiasm. "We know that Napoleon had mixed success in Egypt. He was defeated at sea by the British, by the famous Admiral Horatio Nelson. He had some victories and some defeats on land, and then in August 1799 he sneaks out of Egypt and rushes back to France without telling anyone!"

"Really?" asked Elizabeth. "He snuck back to France?"

"Yes. He initially only shared the secret that he was leaving with a few of his closest companions. He made up a story that he was going for a voyage in the Nile Delta, but in reality boarded the frigate Muiron and, with three other ships escorting her, sailed back to France. His departure was only announced to the army once he had left," said Alberto.

"Maybe he rushed back because he wanted to get his hands on the Blood of Constantine as soon as he could. Perhaps he discovered what he was looking for wasn't in Egypt!" said Dan. "Or perhaps the death of Pius VI caused him to rush back. Perhaps he had a deadline to pick up the potion?

"Those things may be true, or they may not, but why the sudden change of heart?" Asked Alberto. "Something significant must have happened to him when he was in Egypt to make him change his mind about taking the potion. He knew he would be risking his life if he did."

Charlotte, who had been typing on the iPad, said, suddenly excited, "I think I know! I did a paper a few years ago on Napoleon. I remember a story about the English intercepting a letter he wrote while he was in Cairo, to his brother Joseph. The British published it in the London Morning Chronicle to embarrass him. Hang on, I am just getting it on the screen, here we go! It was published on the 24 November 1798. This is what it said. *The veil is torn...It is sad when one and the same heart is torn by such conflicting feelings for one person... Make arrangements for a country place to be ready for my return, either near Paris or in Burgundy. I expect to shut myself away there for the winter. I need to be alone. I am tired of grandeur; all my feelings have dried up. I no longer care about my glory. At twenty-nine I have exhausted everything. There is nothing now left for me but to become selfish"*

Alberto looked confused. "What is he talking about?"

"He wrote this after he was finally convinced that the rumours about Josephine's affair with the Hussar, Hippolyte Charles were actually true. From that time on he has a complete change of heart about love. So much so, that in 1804, just before he becomes Emperor he wrote, hang on, I'll just find it. Here we are... *I am not a man like others and moral laws or the laws that govern conventional behaviour do not apply to me. My mistresses do not in the least engage my feelings. Power is my mistress,"* said Charlotte, looking up from her tablet. "So if you want a reason why he suddenly had a change of heart about taking the Blood of Constantine, then I guess it was that his heart had been shattered. He no longer cared about anything but power."

"Wow!," said Alberto, with a big grin on his face. "That is brilliant! A broken heart!"

"Hang on. Let me get this straight," said Elizabeth, leaning forward, elbows on her knees. "Pius VI offers Napoleon a deal which he doesn't immediately accept. Napoleon goes on an unprecedented military and scientific expedition to Egypt. We now think that he is possibly searching for another source of the Blood of Constantine. Do we know if the expedition to Egypt was planned before the signing of the treaty with the Pope in Tolentino?"

"The signing of the treaty was in February. Napoleon proposed the idea of the Egyptian expedition in August," said Alberto.

"Okay," continued Elizabeth, trying to get the timeline sorted out in her head. "Then the Pope gets taken prisoner. When was that?"

"In February 1798." answered Alberto.

"So when did Napoleon leave for Egypt?" she asked.

"In May." replied Alberto.

"So, there is still no deal in May, and he was holding Pius VI prisoner by then. Sometime towards the end of the year he is gutted when he finds out about Josephine. How successful was the Egyptian campaign?"

"It was OK," said Alberto. "But the siege of Acre was a disaster! So I suppose he wouldn't count it among his best campaigns!"

"A single loss doesn't seem too bad!" said Elizabeth

"No, perhaps not, but put in context. Napoleon only lost nine battles in his whole career. Three of them, including Acre, were before 1799. The rest, except for one, were all after 1812," said Alberto.

"Nine. That seems like quite a lot. How many did he actually fight?" she asked.

"I am not sure of the exact number. It is more than sixty though." replied Alberto.

"Oh!" said Elizabeth, amazed. "So in Napoleon's terms the Egyptian campaign wasn't great. In fact it was a disaster! He gets back to France in 1799. Is that before or after Pius VI dies?"

"Napoleon leaves Egypt in August, 1799, the same month the Pope dies. He doesn't get back to France until October."

"So he could have got a message that the Pope was on his last legs and wanted to get back to seal the deal?" asked Elizabeth.

"It is possible," said Alberto. "But I would guess that the deal was already agreed if what I learned from Rudolf Hess' account of Roustam Raza's experiences is correct. I would imagine that the Pope organised someone to deliver the Blood of Constantine to Napoleon before he died."

"So he got the Blood of Constantine pretty well as soon as he got back to Paris?"

Alberto nodded.

"Did anything happen soon after that? Is there any event that might be an indication that he actually took the Blood?" asked Elizabeth.

"Would outwitting the entire French Government and all the Generals of the Army to be made First Consul of France within three weeks of arriving back in Paris be a possibility?" asked Charlotte.

"Yup!" said Elizabeth. "That would probably do it! Are there any other indications that he might have used this stuff?"

"Given what we have already found out there are certainly some possibilities," said Charlotte.

"Like what," said Elizabeth.

"Well, Napoleon's loss at Waterloo has always been somewhat controversial. There is some documented evidence that he might have been ill that morning. Some say that he was suffering from a bad case of thrombosed hemorrhoids, and wasn't able to get around the battle field as well as he should have. Others have concluded that he had ongoing kidney trouble, or stomach cancer. There was no doubt though that Waterloo was an aberration. Napoleon was very lethargic on the morning of the battle, to the point of falling asleep before the fighting started and delaying the start of it till the middle of the morning."

"So, if we assume that this drug is what gave him the edge in his battles, then he got it from the Pope Pius VI, became Emperor and then, by the time he attacked Russia he had run out of the stuff. He gets exiled to Elba. Then what?" asked Elizabeth.

Well," said Charlotte, "after Elba he starts the hundred days. If we believe all this stuff, then he must have got hold of another vial of the stuff, used it to become Emperor again, displaying his legendary brilliance, and then runs out just before the battle of Waterloo. It does make sense in a weird sort of way. It actually explains his career really well."

"So we can deduce from this," said Alberto, "that Napoleon decanted a number of vials of the potion and gave them to people he trusted. We now know why he was so angry at poor Raustum Raza when he wouldn't go to Elba. He was really angry because he wouldn't give him the vial back!"

"Given what eventually happened to it perhaps it would have been better if he had just forgotten about it altogether!" said Elizabeth.

"You may be right! But we have to assume that at least one other person had a vial of this stuff. Perhaps more than one. There could still be others somewhere out there," said Dan.

"I could do a check to see who visited him on the island and see if there were any likely suspects," said Charlotte thoughtfully. She then said in a quiet voice. "I wonder if that story of Roustam Raza's about being held up by Highwaymen is significant? Do you think it is possible that someone else knew that the blood of Constantine was being given to Napoleon?"

Elizabeth was about to ask her own question when Dan, who had been keeping an eye on the movements on the boats, suddenly sat up. "Hey someone is getting off that blue yacht!" They all watched as two figures stepped off the boat and began to walk along the breakwater towards the town.

Dan looked at the others. "Its a man and a woman. It looks like they are on their way out to dinner. They are all dressed up. Do you think we could follow them?"

Alberto shook his head. "We would never catch them. By the time we ran down the hill from here they would be gone. We might be able to see from up here which restaurant they go to, as long as we don't lose them in the crowd, or they don't take a car somewhere."

Dan continued to watch through the binoculars as the elegant couple turned the corner towards the town. They stopped at the first building past the breakwater and went inside.

"There is a stroke of luck!" said Dan. "They have gone into that restaurant just by the marina. My stomach is rumbling. Given that we've got some clean clothes now, and can make ourselves moderately presentable, perhaps we could kill two birds with one stone. If we went for dinner at that restaurant then we could maybe get a better look at this guy and see if he is likely to be our baddy, and we could get a meal at the same time. I'm sure that Martinus and Sabastino could do with something to eat as well."

"Do you think it would be safe?" asked Elizabeth, concerned.

"I think so," said Alberto. "No one is likely to try anything in such a crowded place and we have the boys to keep an eye on things."

"I think, now that they have the vial, there is probably no need for them to try and get to us. Yes, we did see the thugs faces, but if they have contact with crooked cops who could get them out of trouble, then why would they worry about us?" asked Dan.

Alberto nodded agreement, and then said with a grin, " That restaurant, Lo Smeraldino would certainly be a good choice for dinner. By a touch of luck I think I have a cousin working there! I will give her a ring and see if we can get a table!"

They all waited as Alberto spoke into his mobile. He asked to talk to someone called Silvia. There was a bit of friendly banter when Silvia came to the phone and a few moments of waiting and then Alberto turned to them. "It is very crowded this evening, but my cousin says she has found us a table if we go in the next half hour."

22. Amalfi - Present day

Having done the best they could to make themselves presentable, they walked into Lo Smeraldino twenty minutes later. It was crowded with people obviously enjoying their meals. As soon as they entered a beautiful young woman with lustrous dark hair tied in a long ponytail, approached Alberto, gave him a long and appraising look, frowning, but, at least as far as Charlotte could tell, not surprised at the sight of his bruises. Satisfied, despite his somewhat disheveled appearance, she gave him a coquettish smile and a peck on each cheek. Her mood changed instantly as Elizabeth and Charlotte suddenly appeared behind him. Her eyes flashed darkly back to Alberto's bruised and swollen face.

"Scusie Silvia," he said looking contrite, "These are friends of mine. Dottore Dan and his daughter Charlotte, and their friend Elizabeth."

Silvia looked Charlotte and Elizabeth up and down. Elizabeth put her hand on Dan's arm in a proprietorial way, and stretched her own out. Silvia shook it as they introduced themselves. Charlotte, realising that her relationship with Alberto was still potentially ambiguous, took Dan's free arm and also reached out and shook Silvia's hand. With a pleasant smile Silvia led them through the restaurant out to the terrace that overlooked the Marina. She sat them at a table by the rail, resting her hand on Alberto's shoulder as she explained the menu and took their drink orders.

A few minutes later, as Silvia put their drinks down on the table Alberto leant over and asked her in a quiet voice, "Silvia, the couple over in the corner, the man in the dark suit and open neck shirt and the woman in the grey gown, do you know who they are?"

Silvia followed Alberto's eyes. "His name is Andris Dragas. He is, I think, Hungarian, maybe Russian. He has a big yacht here in the Marina. It is the blue one over there with the grey top," she said pointing out into the marina. "The woman, she is Italian. She is a model. Julia DiMartino. She often appears in Vogue magazine. Do you want me to take a message to them."

"Oh God no!" said Alberto. "We don't even want them to notice us! I was just interested," said Alberto, somewhat lamely Charlotte thought.

Silvia gave him another suspicious look. She told him that she was just going to arrange some food for his "nice young friends' and then would be back to get their orders.

"So!" said Dan, leaning forward and talking in a quiet voice, "Where are we with all of this? We've lost the box and the vial, but we have the sample being tested. We have jus randomly followed a man we now know is called Andris Dragas, who I suspect none of us have ever heard of, and who may, or may not be, the one who has been chasing us and now has the vial. What next?"

"I am still waiting on the analysis to be completed," volunteered Elizabeth.

"Despite how incredible this all sounds, I am beginning to think that this whole story may actually have some truth in it. All of the history just fits so well. It's bizarre." Charlotte said, noticing that her father was getting his concerned parent expression on.

"I am wondering if we should continue to be involved," said Dan, looking very serious. "We got into this whole thing by accident. Whatever it is all about it is obviously dangerous. We have all been very lucky to have come through this, so far, without being too badly hurt," he said, his hand rubbing the bruises on his chest. "We have to seriously consider whether we should pursue this any further!"

Everyone was quiet. It was Alberto who eventually broke the silence. "I understand your concerns, Dottore." He looked around the table. "I am very grateful to you all for what you have done. I have been alone in this quest for so many years, not knowing who to trust. Not knowing who to talk to. If nothing else I would appreciate being able to converse with you all once more, for I am unclear too, about what I should do next."

"I never expected to actually find one of the vials and have it analysed. But the vial that we have, had," he corrected himself and glanced over his shoulder at Dragas," is not, how do you say in English, "the real deal". It may have a small part of the original, but it is really the mixture made by Morell based on his, inadequate analysis of the original. To have an unadulterated example seems not to be possible."

"You said before that part of your job was to hunt down stolen treasures for the church. Couldn't you do some sort of search to see if any other reliquaries containing the Blood of Constantine exist?" asked Charlotte.

"It is funny that you should say that, because that is exactly what I originally thought too."

"Did you find any clues to follow up?" asked Elizabeth.

"No. Which surprised me greatly," said Alberto. "What surprised me more though was that it had all been done before!"

"What! Someone else had searched for Constantine's Blood?" asked Elizabeth.

"Yes and No," said Alberto. "I can't be sure that they were looking for the same relic as I was, but starting in the late 1400s there were some really big efforts to collect Holy relics. Prince Frederick the Wise, Elector of Saxony, started an unbelievable collection of relics, which, by the time he stopped collecting, numbered in excess of nineteen thousand."

"Wow! That is a lot of bits of Saints!" said Elizabeth. "That sounds like a great place to start. Where are they now?"

"Well, that is part of the problem. Bizarrely, when Frederick died, the gold and silver reliquaries went to the local mint to be melted down. The relics themselves were mostly destroyed."

"How did he get so many?" asked Charlotte.

"Well, following the paper trail in the Vatican Library it looks like the Pope, it was Julius the Second by then , sent out a Papal brief asking every Bishop and prelate in the Empire to share relics with the Elector Frederick."

"What year was that?" asked Dan.

"1507." replied Alberto. "There was something odd going on at the time. Pope Julius was elected after a Pope that only lasted 26 days, Pius III."

"Do you think that Pius the third took the Blood of Constantine and died?" asked Elizabeth.

Alberto nodded. "There were certainly rumours around at the time that he was poisoned, which could suggest that he took the Blood and it did not work for him."

"Why would Pius risk taking the Blood of Constantine?" asked Elizabeth.

"Well it could have been because he thought that the church had suffered so badly at the hands of the previous Pope," said Alberto.

"Who was the Pope before Pius the third?" asked Elizabeth.

"Pope Alexander the sixth," said Alberto.

Charlotte groaned. Elizabeth looked at her. "Better known as Rodrigo Borgia, the father of Lucrezia and Cesare Borgia!" she said, picking up her iPhone.

"Was he bad?" asked Elizabeth.

"The worst! He was famous for it!" said Charlotte tapping on her screen. "Let me tell you what Pope Julius said on the day of his inauguration," she said, reading from her phone. "*I will not live in the same rooms as the Borgias lived. He desecrated the Holy Church as none before. He usurped the papal power by the devil's aid, and I forbid under the pain of excommunication anyone to speak or think of Borgia again. His name and memory must be forgotten. It must be crossed out of every document and memorial. His reign must be obliterated. All paintings made of the Borgias or for them must be covered over with black crepe. All the tombs of the Borgias must be opened and their bodies sent back to where they belong – to Spain.*" He had Alexander's apartments sealed, and they weren't opened again until the nineteenth century!"

"Holy smoke! What did Alexander do that was so bad?" asked Elizabeth, fascinated.

"Edward Gibbon said that he presided over more orgies than masses," said Charlotte.

"He was pretty bad," said Alberto. "They say he had a lusty and adventurous sex life. He had numerous children. He even had an affair with Guilia Farnese, Guilia la bella, the most beautiful woman in all of Italy! He supposedly hosted orgies in the Papal palace!"

"My guess is that Alexander, at some stage in his papacy, took the blood of Constantine which led him to the excesses for which he became famous. After Pope Pius died, probably from drinking it as well, Pope Julius decided that the Blood of Constantine was the work of the devil and decided to make sure there was no more of it about, and that should have been the end of the story," said Alberto. "At least that's what I thought at first."

"Was tsomeone else looking for it?" asked Dan.

"The more I looked into it the more I began to see little indications that there was another influence at work. I could never pin it down precisely, but every time I found a new lead there was always something that gave me the impression that someone else had been there before me, often many many years before. It was weird. I started to put together evidence that, since the late 1400s, someone has been systematically searching for the relics of Constantine."

"What, for over 500 years!" exclaimed Dan.

"Certainly through the time of Napoleon, and even in the research I did on Hitler and Hess. I admit," said Alberto holding up his hands, "it sounds incredible, I know. It sounded incredible to me, too. Then, while I was still working at the Vatican, some things happened that convinced me that it might not be so far from the truth. I had a couple of near misses over a couple of weeks. An out of control car just missed me when I was walking home one night. A couple of weeks later a mugger pulled a knife and tried to slash my throat."

"That could be just coincidence, surely!" said Elizabeth. "Rome is a big city and accidents do happen. Muggings happen."

"That's what I thought, so I didn't take any particular precautions. I certainly didn't tie it to the research I was doing in the Vatican library!" Then one evening, as I opened the door to my apartment a grenade smashed through my front window and landed right in front of me," said Alberto.

"Shit! You were lucky it didn't go off!" said Dan.

"It did," said Alberto. He lifted up his shirt, revealing a mass of scar tissue. "I was in hospital for several months. The only lucky part was that my front door was still open, so I got blasted back through the door and down a flight of stairs. A lot of the blast hit the wall around the door, rather than me."

"The Investigators came. They decided that it must have had something to do with my old job. Maybe some type of revenge attack for work I had done while I was in the Carabinieri. The police decided that I needed to go into a witness protection program. My mother had passed away by then, but I had a brother and a sister, so it was reported that I died in the explosion. A body was provided for them to bury back home, just in case anyone checked. After a few months in hospital, I disappeared," said Alberto. "Since then I have been working under cover. Mostly on my own."

"Oh my God Alberto!" said Charlotte. "That's awful!"

Alberto just bowed his head, then, after a few moments, said, "The events of the last few days, with the sudden appearance of Hitler's Vial, have just confirmed the fact that someone is still actively looking for the relics."

"And you don't think it is the Church?" asked Dan

Alberto shook his head.

They all concentrated on their food for a few minutes, then Dan asked, looking around the table, "So what do you guys think? Should we give all this stuff to the police and leave Alberto to continue his work, or what?"

"I think we see this thing through as far as we can!" said Elizabeth. "Now that we know we have to be careful we can be even more cautious. Besides, whoever these people are have the vial now. Why would they take any more interest in us? They don't know that we took a sample of it."

"I agree with Liz!" said Charlotte. "I think we should help Alberto as much as we can," she said, smiling at him. "I could help Alberto do some of the background historical research.

"And we need to complete the analysis of the sample we took from the Hitler vial," said Elizabeth.

Dan looked at his daughter and his friend, then at Alberto.

"It looks like we are sticking together, for the moment at least, Alberto," said Dan. "Are you OK with that?"

Alberto nodded. "It will be a great relief for me to work with people I know I can trust. Yes, I would be very grateful if we could continue to work together for a while longer," he said seriously.

"While you guys are doing your research perhaps I can find out what I can about Andris Dragas," said Dan glancing over his shoulder in the direction of the handsome man and his beautiful companion.

Almost as if he had heard his name mentioned, Charlotte saw Dragas stand up and start coming towards their table. She kicked her father under the table and whispered, "He's coming over!"

Moments later he was standing behind Dan. He coughed, politely. Dan turned around and looked up. Dan stood up. Charlotte thought that the two men were roughly the same height. He was very well dressed in a tailored suit. His hair was cut short. He wore a neatly trimmed goatee and his skin was tanned.

"Andris Dragas, Doctor Marsh," he said politely offering his hand to her father. "We have not met but I have attended a number of the talks you have given over the last few years. I have also invested in the public offerings of some of your companies. Much to my financial benefit I am pleased to say. And," he said turning to Elizabeth," Doctor Garvey, I presume? A pleasure to meet you, finally. I particularly enjoyed the TED talk you did last year in San Francisco on epigenetics."

"Thank you, Mr Dragas," said Elizabeth.

"No, please, you must both call me Andris!" he said smiling pleasantly.

"And this young lady must be Charlotte?" he asked politely, nodding his head towards her. Charlotte started to get up, but he waved her down and looked expectantly at Alberto. Alberto just smiled and gave a cursory wave."I look forward to hearing more about your good works in the future, Dan." He said smiling pleasantly. "Now, if you will excuse me, I must be off. I have a busy day tomorrow. Goodnight!" said Dragas, bowing slightly.

Dan sat down as they all watched Dragas and his companion walk from the restaurant.

"Seems like a nice man," said Dan, sitting back down.

"Looks like the Master from Doctor Who!" said Charlotte. "Handsome but creepy!" she said with an exaggerated shiver. "He was worse than the daleks!"

Dan laughed. "I seem to remember you spent a lot of time hiding behind the couch when Doctor Who came on!" Dan yawned, looked at his watch and said, "It's getting late, I suppose it is time that we went back to the Hotel. Can we get the bill, Alberto?"

"Do not worry about it Dottore. I will have a talk to my cousin and it will be all fixed up. I think too that I will have a visit with my cousin who I haven't seen for a some time," said Alberto. "I will see you back at the hotel in the morning," he said, standing up and waving to his cousin who came over to their table.

Dan reached for his wallet, but Silvia put her hand on his shoulder and shook her head. "Let the meal be on me," she said with a small smile. "It is the least I can do for someone who is the friend of my," she paused, just for a moment, and then said, "cousin."

****

Elizabeth, Charlotte and Dan took their leave. Dan looked back and saw that Alberto was sitting at their table talking earnestly with Sylvia. He wondered briefly what their relationship really was. He certainly did seem to have a few attractive female cousins.

As they were walking out of the restaurant Dan thought he saw someone step into the shadows on the other side of the road. Without wanting to worry Elizabeth or Charlotte, he suggested that they walk back the long way, through the town, even though this meant initially walking in the opposite direction to their hotel, along the waterfront of Amalfi.

They both agreed. It was a warm evening and the lights in the trees and on the buildings made for a magical scene. Charlotte, as was her want, slipped her arm into his, something she had done since she was a teenager and something that didn't cease to delight him.

Elizabeth, walking on his other side, suddenly slipped her arm into his as well, something that she had never done before. Dan felt a wave of happiness wash over him. He wondered for a moment what Sarah would have thought, but the thought slipped away before it had time to take hold.

Walking arm in arm in arm, the three of them looked into the shop windows and the restaurants and bars as they strolled along the Lungomare towards the centre of town. Once they reached the roundabout that was the junction between the Lungomare and the road back up to the hotel, they decided to continue their walk and took the junction that led to the Duomo. They bought a gelato each and sat on the steps of the cathedral watching the world go by. Dan could see no sign of Sabastiano or Martinus, nor for that matter could he see Luigi or his two assistants.

"So Charlotte Mary," said Dan "tell me something interesting about where we are!" This was a game that he and Charlotte had often played, virtually since she had first learned to read. It had been Dan's way of getting her interested in the places he had to go for business. He would buy her a book about their next stop and then, when they had some time alone, ask her the same question. Charlotte, who had always loved to read, and loved to surprise her father, would look for the most esoteric facts that she could. Dan credited the game with giving her a passion for history and a passion for research.

"Ah, Amalfi!" she said, obviously stalling for thinking time. "Amalfi is famous for its lemons and the production of that delicious lemon liquor, limoncello!"

Dan shook his head. "I knew that," he said, feigning disappointment.

Charlotte pouted. They both knew that she always started with the obvious and progressed to the more bizarre. It was always a low build up. That was part of the fun.

"At its height, at the end of the first millennium, Amalfi had a population of over seventy thousand!"

Dan shook his head, but Elizabeth, who had been the occasional onlooker of this game in the past, said, "Really, that is incredible. Seventy thousand people crammed into this little place."

Charlotte looked pleased that she had elicited a good response so early in the game, even though it wasn't from her father.

"What about the big bronze doors, do you know about those?" Charlotte asked, turning to Dan.

He shook his head.

"Cast in Constantinople sometime around 1000 AD. The earliest example of bronze doors in post Imperial Italy. Pretty impressive," she said. "Given to Amalfi by a rich merchant, one Pantaleone of Amalfi."

"Umm, thousand year old doors. Good, but not amazingly amazing," said her father.

Charlotte's brow furrowed.

"Oh, give her a break Dan!" Elizabeth said with a laugh. "That is amazing!"

"Ah!" said Charlotte, with a grin, "After all that talk about reliquaries, do you know about the one in here?" she said indicating the church behind them.

"Something to do with Saint Andrew?" asked Dan, guessing.

"Which one was he?" asked Elizabeth.

"He was Jesus' first disciple. He was Peter's brother, but tended to be overshadowed by his more extroverted brother," said Dan.

"That's right," said Charlotte, "but did you know that some of the relics of Saint Andrew, his actual bones, are in the Cathedral right here, as well as in Patras, in Greece, where they say he was crucified, and in Scotland, where he is the Patron Saint, and in Poland?"

"No!" said Dan. "Boy, he has certainly racked up the frequent flyer points since he died! Now It's getting interesting, but it is still not amazing!"

"Ah well," said Charlotte with obvious enthusiasm, "Did you know that Saint Andrew's bones produce a clear oily liquid that the church calls *manna* and that they have done since his death in around 60AD?"

"What is manna?" asked Elizabeth.

"Manna is either liquid or dust that miraculously accumulates in a saint's crypt. In medieval times it became quite a business. There is a stained glass window in York Minster, in England, that shows taps attached to the sarcophagus of Saint William for drawing off the manna."

"The manna from Saint Andrew, which is supposed to be the oldest known source of it, started to flow on the anniversary of his death. It was initially recorded as a perfumed oil, but sometimes it is written about as a powder that collected in his tomb. It was so abundant that there were times when it flowed out of his tomb and down the aisles of the church in Patras."

"Sometime around the mid three hundreds the relics of Saint Andrew were taken to Constantinople, probably as part of that whole thing to make the city a more important religious centre. The manna continued to flow and at the time of the fourth Crusade in around 1200 AD, an Italian Cardinal brought back the relics to Amalfi. A hundred years or so later a worshipper discovered a white powder building up in his Tomb."

"What did they do with all the stuff? Did Saint Andrew's manna have any amazing magical powers?" asked Elizabeth.

"Well there is a story from Amalfi about it being used to miraculously heal someone that was blind. It was often distributed to other churches as a holy relic, or in some instances, became a bit of a business opportunity and was sold to pilgrims. That's why I think it is entirely possible that there are still vials of Constantine's blood around. The trade in relics was a pretty significant business."

"So what happened here?' asked Dan, finally giving in and declaring his interest.

"Got you!" said Charlotte, pointing a finger at him. He grinned back. "Ok. This is pretty interesting stuff, especially given our other little project! You've got me!"

"The bones had a couple of periods where they were lost. I guess as time passed they got forgotten. The history is that they were re-discovered by a stone mason working on the Church who unearthed an inscribed marble slab. They were then re-interred with a whole bunch of town bigwigs watching as witnesses, with a document describing what they were."

"The tomb was forgotten about again until the mid 1800's. The church was undergoing restorations. The stone masons were working slowly and carefully because they had heard a legend that there was a great treasure buried in the church. They were removing stones from one of the walls when they found the marble slab and the urn containing the relics. The next day the Archbishop opened up the urn and found the notarised document. To save them from being lost again the relics were moved to the main altar, and that's where they are to this very day," said Charlotte with a triumphant wave of her hand.

"Wow!" said Elizabeth. "Do the bones still produce the manna?"

"Yep, every 28th of January, on the anniversary of their re-discovery, and on the main religious holidays. In fact there was a Bishop in the early part of last century who started a logbook, to record the manna that was siphoned off. Apparently it varies a lot. Sometimes there is a little and sometimes a lot."

"Has it ever been analysed, this stuff, to see what it really is?" asked Elizabeth, ever the scientist.

"Not that I have seen, but I haven't really done the research. I have always been more into the history than the chemical composition."

"It is a good object lesson though, on how relics can get lost and forgotten," said Dan thoughtfully. "Ok! I am satisfied that was truly amazing!. Shall we get back to the hotel?" he asked, standing up.

The two women stood up and grabbed an arm each for the walk back up the road to the Hotel Entrance set in the cliff face. Dan kept an eye out for anyone following them, but saw no-one.

The stroll up the hill to the hotel was pleasant. They chatted about inconsequential things, enjoying each others company. When they arrived at the hotel they decided to convene in Dan's suite for a nightcap.

As Dan entered the room he saw a piece of paper had been slipped under the door. He picked it up and read it. Charlotte and Elizabeth both looked at him expectantly. Dan burst out laughing. "Its from Alberto," he said. "Apparently Luigi was following us when we left the restaurant, but had an accident."

"What sort of accident?" asked Elizabeth, not sure whether to be pleased or show some concern.

"He says, unfortunately Luigi was not watching where he was going and was hit a glancing blow by a careless couple on a motorino. He fell into a restaurant! Then he says, have a good night!"

"Do you think Silvia had a motorino?" laughed Charlotte.

Chuckling to herself Elizabeth ordered them drinks. Within a few minutes room service had delivered a whisky for Dan and two limoncellos. They sat on the terrace, sipping their drinks, enjoying the mild evening and looking out over the beautiful lights of Amalfi.

Charlotte finished her drink quickly. She kissed her father goodnight and said happily, "Since Alberto has gone off to visit his cousin, I'll take the opportunity to have a room to myself! I'll take the spare room next door if that is OK with you two?"

Dan nodded his agreement, but reminded her, using his serious, no nonsense father voice, to make sure her door was locked, just in case.

Charlotte patted him on the head with a smile and said, dutifully, "Yes father," as she walked out of the room.

Left alone Elizabeth and Dan sat in silence. Eventually Dan reached across and touched Elizabeth gently on the arm. "Are you OK?" he said in a quiet, concerned voice.

He couldn't see her expression clearly in the dim lights, but felt her hand on top of his. "Its been quite a day, but I think I am!" she said quietly.

"Will you be okay, on your own tonight?' said Dan hesitantly.

Elizabeth didn't respond immediately and Dan suddenly realised that what he had just asked could be seriously misinterpreted.

"I'm a bit surprised I am still holding it all together, but," she said hesitating, I ..."

He interrupted her. "It's OK Liz, I only wanted to make sure you felt safe, I didn't mean ..." he said stumbling nervously over his words.

"Dan," she said, interrupting him and squeezing his hand, "I would feel much better if I could spend the night with you!"

Dan felt a huge sense of relief flow through him. He stood up, taking her hand and drawing her to him. He felt her arms encircle his body. For a long time they just stood there, holding each other, feeling each other's warmth, feeling the pleasure of physical contact.

"You have no idea how long I have wanted to just do this!" said Dan in a quiet voice, kissing the top of her head.

"Not as long as me," she said in a voice he could hardly hear as she hugged him tighter. He could feel wet tears on his neck.

****

Dan and Elizabeth, dressed in hotel robes, and with towels over their shoulders, walked hand in hand past the tables on the long terrace towards the pool. It was early and there were few people about.

Dan threw his towel onto one of the sun lounges and turned towards the pool. Charlotte, floating at the far end, stared back at him. He hadn't noticed her as they had approached. She was smiling at him. "Good morning you two." She said brightly and started to swim towards them.

"Oh!" exclaimed Dan. "There you are. We were just going to go for a swim. It looks like you beat us to it!"

Charlotte lifted herself out of the pool and walked across to where she had left her towel. "I was just finishing," she said with a smile. "See you for breakfast on the terrace in half an hour?" she asked, innocently.

As she walked off, back towards her room, Dan looked at Elizabeth. "Do you think she saw?" he asked apprehensively.

"What, us holding hands? I am sure she did!" said Elizabeth, giving Dan a quick peck on the cheek before turning and diving into the pool.

****

Charlotte was waiting for them on the terrace. Sabastinio and Martinus were at a table further along the terrace. It was a beautiful morning. The sky was blue and cloudless and there was a gentle, warm breeze blowing. She stood up as they approached and gave Elizabeth a hug. She then hugged her father, whispering in his ear, "Its about time!" and sat back down.

Dan looked across at his daughter as she poured orange juice for them all. "Is it that obvious?" he asked.

"Yes, Father." Charlotte said with a smile. "I think it is wonderful. You don't know how long I have wanted you two to be together. You are perfect for one another. I can't believe it has taken you this long to recognise it."

Dan turned to Elizabeth. "I've known it for a long time. I was just," he paused, "afraid, I guess. Afraid that I would do something stupid and end up loosing my best friend." Dan paused, and said more quietly, "And I didn't want you to think I was replacing your mother."

Tears welled up in Elizabeth's eyes. "That's how I felt too!" she said. "I didn't want you think I was trying to take Sarah's place. I think of you as my family! I couldn't bear the thought of losing either of you!"

Charlotte reached out and took hold of Dan and Elizabeth's hands and said, with mock solemnity "Now that you two are finally in a relationship you have to make sure you stay together, for the child's sake!". Dan and Elizabeth, with equal seriousness, promised that they would do everything they could to keep their family together.

They were all chatting happily when Alberto strolled up. "Good morning!" he said in an exuberant manner. "May I join you for coffee?"

Charlotte pulled out a chair and Alberto sat down next to her. "How was your cousin?" she asked with a smirk.

Alberto looked at her, slightly taken aback by the personal nature of her question. "We had a lot of ... family news to catch up on!" he said somewhat defensively. "It has been a number of years since we have seen one another."

Charlotte nodded, with mock seriousness.

"Anyway," said Alberto clearly wanting to change subject, "we need to decide what we do now." As he said this a waiter coughed quietly behind him.

"Excuse, I have a note for Dottore Marsh?"

Dan reached out and took the note. His name, beautifully handwritten, was on the front of the expensively embossed envelope. He picked up a table knife and slit it open. He quickly read the handwritten note and then looked up. "It is an invitation!" he said, "from Andris Dragas!"

"What does he say?" asked Charlotte.

"*Dear Doctor Marsh,*" read Dan,"*It was a pleasure to meet you last night at the restaurant. I have followed your career for many years with great interest and would be delighted if you, Ms Garvey and your daughter would join me for dinner on my yacht this evening at 8:30.*

If you are able to join me, please let the reception desk at your hotel know.

Yours,

Andris Dragas"

"That is so creepy!" said Charlotte. "It makes him sound like some sort of stalker! I don't want to go! I don't think it is safe!"

Dan thought for a moment, then said, "I think that, at least, I should go. It is not as if he can just kidnap me!" said Dan. "And anyway, we don't know if he is actually involved in all this stuff."

"What, like he probably didn't have Liz and me kidnapped? I bet he is behind it." said Charlotte. "But I agree that you and Elizabeth should go. You should be safe enough if we know where you are going and you tell the hotel where you are going as well."

"As Mister Dragas does not think me worthy of an invitation to dinner, I think that I should go to Rome," said Alberto, with a touch of mock petulance. Then, more seriously, "I can leave the boys here to watch over you. I need to see if I can arrange to have a talk to a few people at the Vatican. I would also like to follow up a few things in the Vatican library."

"Oh!" said Charlotte, her eyes opening wide. "Could I come? I have always wanted to see the secret archives, please?" she pleaded, putting her hand on Alberto's arm.

Alberto looked concerned. "It would be up to your father, to give his permission!" he said turning to Dan.

Dan laughed. "I haven't given her permission to do anything in years Alberto. Australian girls do what they want, not what their fathers let them do! I think that, if it were okay with you, I would feel much safer if Charlie was with you than staying here," said Dan.

Charlotte smiled at he father's response.

Alberto agreed. "Charlotte and I will go to Rome."

"I've got an apartment there that you could use as a base," said Dan. "and it would be a good chance to get the Aston Martin out of your truck.

232

"That's a great idea," said Charlotte, "but you have to promise me Dad, that you will text me as soon as you get back here from dinner with Dragas!"

Dan smiled. He nodded.

"How about we drive them to Naples, Dan?" said Elizabeth. "You wanted to buy a new laptop to replace the stolen one and we both need some posh clothes if they were going to have dinner with Andris Dragas."

Having decided on the day's activities they all set about enjoying their breakfasts. While they were sitting sipping coffee, Elizabeth borrowed Dan's smartphone to check her emails. He watched her as she scrolled through them. Something must have caught her attention as her brows furrowed.

"Stranger and stranger!" she said. "The guys at the lab have just sent the next lot of test results through!"

Dan, Alberto and Charlotte all leaned in closer to listen.

"They have found traces of levodopa, and a whole range of nootropics, including huperzine A and Choline."

"Hold on" said Alberto, interrupting, "You lost me at "They have found...". What are nootropics and what were those names you reeled off?"

"Nootropics are a class of drug that the tabloid media now call smart drugs or cognitive enhancers. They purport to enhance people's memory and intelligence. A significant number of the chemicals that they found in this mixture appear to be nootropics. It is a relatively new classification, but it includes drugs like huperzine A and Choline. They also found traces of L-Dopa, or, more formally, L-3,4-dihydroxyphenylalanine. It is used to treat, among other things Parkinson's disease. It promotes the production of dopamine in the brain."

"Wow! Anything else?" asked Dan.

"They found traces of what they think is atropine, which is an hallucinogenic and Pseudo ephedrine, as well as a whole bunch of things they are still trying to identify."

"So what do you think this stuff would do if you took it?" asked Charlotte.

Elizabeth shook her head. "I would guess if you took it orally it would probably blow your head off! Given some of the ingredients in this I'm not sure I would even want to put it on topically. At this stage I would say this concoction was put together by a complete nut job, who had no idea what he was doing. It certainly wouldn't get FDA approval!

"If I didn't know the provenance of this stuff I would say that it was someone's idea of a joke and chuck it in the bin! Knowing that this is probably Morell's best guess at copying whatever the blood of Constantine was, I would have to say that he got it wrong, big time. The guys say they will keep isolating the ingredients and follow up on the human cells and see what we end up with. They say they could have some more results late this afternoon."

"But if these nootropics you talked about are in this mixture, then it is possible that it could be based on a drug that somehow enhances the strategic abilities of people who take it?" asked Alberto.

"I can tell you for certain Alberto, that this stuff that we are analysing would not do what the Blood of Constantine is reported to have done. It would be more likely to kill you! Having said that, some of the compounds in it could well be consistent with a drug that impacts on brain function."

They all sat back and thought about the implications of the report as they finished their coffees.

23. Naples - Present day

Dan carefully backed the Aston Martin out of the semitrailer onto the narrow Naples street.

"There you go Charlie," he said tossing her the keys. "I've got my gear out of the boot."

Alberto finished closing up the back of his truck and walked over to where they were all standing.

Charlotte gave Dan and Elizabeth a hug and climbed into the driver's seat of the Aston Martin. Alberto, looked at Dan. 'Do you not think I should drive?" he said, sounding concerned.

Dan laughed. "I think Charlotte will do just fine. " he said. He then grabbed Alberto by the arm, and, leaning towards him whispered, "But put your seat belt on, tight. Real tight."

Alberto expression went from concerned to worried. Dan patted him on the back. He waved to Charlotte, "Drive safely, kiddo!"

Alberto, obviously unaware of the family history did not know that Dan, paranoid about car accidents, had made sure that Charlotte could drive, but more than that, had been with her on defensive and advanced driving courses, so that now he knew she could handle a car as well as any professional driver, maybe better than most, she had lapped the Nürburgring in his Ferrari Dino in under ten minutes and she had a real love of cars.

Elizabeth and Dan watched them drive off and then got into their rented Fiat for the drive back to Amalfi. They stopped at an Apple reseller to buy a couple of new laptops on the way.

Dan took the highway to Salerno and then turned off when they reached Vietra Sul Mare. The Strada Statale Almafiana stretched before them, a beautifully made, but narrow, road that twists its way along the gloriously picturesque Amalfi Coast, sometimes weaving inland to follow the line of a valley, sometimes running almost along the cliff top. The views were spectacular, out over an impossibly blue Mediterranean Sea.

They stopped at the little town of Minori, with its palm tree lined waterfront, and bought the makings of a picnic, beautiful plump red tomatoes, prosciutto, a couple of different types of Italian Cheese, an avocado some mushrooms, a filone and two bottles of Nastro Azzurro.

With their purchases in a bag they walked, hand in hand, over to the waterfront and sat in the sun, sharing their picnic.

"You know that Charlotte is thrilled that we have become... closer?" Elizabeth said, suddenly unsure of how to describe their new status.

"Did she say something to you?" asked Dan taking a swig from his bottle of beer.

"Yes. While we were shopping for clothes in Naples," she said.

"She's not the only one that is thrilled!" said Dan, putting his arm around her shoulder, and drawing her close.

They sat in companionable silence looking down on the rows of deck chairs and sun umbrellas stretching, in their orderly lines, along the beach.

24. Amalfi – Present Day

Sitting on the terrace of their suite at the Convento di Amalfi, both with their heads down configuring their new laptops, trying to remember passwords and usernames, Elizabeth let out a cry. "Yes!" she shouted, "Finally! The guys have finished the report on the analysis of the sample."

Dan put his own laptop down and looked across expectantly.

"They have done an analysis on the complete strands of DNA and, guess what? It is Hitler's! They compared it with that job we did for that documentary company a few years ago. You know the one where we tested the 47 relatives of Hitler. There is a 98% chance that it is Hitler's DNA!"

"They say that the other, incomplete sections of DNA, the older ones, are not really identifiable, other than to say that the DNA probably comes from someone from the Mediterranean basin, probably northern Italy. Oh, and the DNA comes from a male or males. They can't be sure."

"Their best guess is that the older strands of DNA could actually be from at least two different people! Probably from two different eras."

"Have they dated any of the shorter DNA strands?" asked Dan.

"It looks like they are still working on it. Best guess at the moment is that one is much older than the other. " said Elizabeth scanning the rest of the report, "by several hundred years."

"Where was Pope Pius the sixth born?" asked Dan

Elizabeth typed in a Google search. "Mister Google says he was born in Cesena."

"Where's that?" asked Dan coming over and sitting on the bed next to her, so he could see the laptop screen.

"Northern Italy!" she said pointing at the map. "So it really could be part of the blood of Constantine that Alberto described, mixed with the Blood of a Pope!" she said.

"Umm," she said, suddenly closing her laptop. "I think its time we started getting ready for our dinner date," she said decisively.

Dan looked at the bedside clock. "Its only six o'clock! We don't have to even leave till after eight!" He said, surprised.

"That's, true, but you are forgetting that you now have a woman to help get ready!" she said, getting off the bed. "And she needs her back scrubbed in the bath!"

A smile spread across Dan's face as Elizabeth stood up, pulled her t-shirt over her head and threw it at him as she walked towards the bathroom.

25. Amalfi - Present day

Leaning on the terrace rail Dan was dressed in a pair of tailored black trousers and a black shirt. He had always found it easier to dress in black, much to Charlotte's displeasure. It saved him from having to try and coordinate colours, something he found frustrating. He turned at the sound of a heel hitting the tiles of the terrace.

He barely recognised the woman silhouetted in the light of their room. Elizabeth stood in the doorway. A sheer white dress clung to the curves of her body, suspended by the thinnest of straps from her shoulders. A single pearl hung from a silver chain around her long neck. Her hair was caught up behind her head, with only a wisp of it falling down past her ears, hinting at its true length. She looked taller, and as Dan took in this vision, she stepped towards him, revealing a split in the skirt that went all the way up her leg. He realised that she was wearing stilettos. He had never seen Elizabeth dressed quite like this. They had been to many formal dinners together, but they had always been work related. She had always dressed appropriately for a senior executive. This would definitely not have been considered appropriate for a senior executive of any organization he knew.

"Wow!" said Dan, slightly breathless. "You scrub up well!" he said, unable to think of anything more eloquent.

Elizabeth smiled. "Your daughter chose it for me this morning. She said if I wore the black dress I liked we would look like we were going to a funeral. Do you like it!" she pirouetting on the ball of one foot.

"You look absolutely fantastic! Stunning! I'm not sure that I want to go out for dinner anymore. Do you think we could stay in and have a meal?" he asked.

"Come on you. Let's get going or we will be late!" she said wrapping her arms around his neck and giving him a quick kiss on the cheek.

Dan, enveloped in the warmth and smell of her, found it incredibly intoxicating. She unwound herself and started to walk towards the doors "No really" he said desperately, "we could just say we forgot, or got lost, couldn't find the boat..." his voice trailed off and he, reluctantly followed her off the terrace.

26. Amalfi - Present day

Arm in arm, Elizabeth and Dan walked along the breakwater towards Andris Dragas' yacht. It was moored so that its stern abutted the concrete walkway. As they approached Dragas himself walked out onto the rear deck and waved to them.

Dan and Elizabeth both took of their shoes, as yacht etiquette required, before they stepped on to the polished teak of the yachts aft deck.

"Welcome to my home away from home!" Dragas said shaking Dan's hand and kissing Elizabeth on both cheeks.

"Now can I get you a drink?" he asked, holding up his Champagne flute. "I am having some of this rather excellent Champagne, from, of all places, an Island off the bottom of Australia. You may have been there. Tasmania?"

Dan smiled."Yes, I have a holiday house there. It is a beautiful place, so different from Europe. Peaceful. Clean. Natural." Dan noticed the large M on the label of the wine bottle. "Ah! Milton! That's not far from my place on the east coast!" he said with a smile. "Although I don't think the French let us call it Champagne anymore!"

"Goodness! We wouldn't want to upset the French," he said, theatrically rolling his eyes. "Can I offer you a glass of this excellent sparkling wine that tastes a lot like Champagne? said Dragas with a slight, conspiratorial smile. He led them through to a palatially decorated lounge and sat them down on a leather couch, one of three that surrounded a beautiful wooden coffee table that took up the centre of the cabin. A beautiful silk, Persian rug covered almost all of a highly polished teak floor.

Elizabeth looked through the large picture windows at the lights of Amalfi. "This must be a lovely way to live, being able to move from one exotic location to another in such comfort," she said. "Never having to pack and unpack your luggage!"

Dragas smiled at her, with, what Dan thought was a sad smile. "Yes, it is a lovely way to live, but it is not a real home. When I am here I feel a bit like a gypsy."

At that moment the beautiful woman who had accompanied Dragas to dinner the previous evening walked through the companionway. She was as tall as Elizabeth but had much paler skin. Her hair, in contrast to Elizabeth's lustrous red brown curls was as long, but straight and almost white.

"Ah, Julia!" said Dragas, grabbing a champagne flute from the bar and quickly filling it. "Let me introduce you to our guests. This gentleman is Doctor Daniel Marsh, geneticist and entrepreneur, and his beautiful companion is Doctor Elizabeth Garvey, businesswoman and research scientist extraordinaire. She is a pioneer in the area of epigenetic research!"

Dan and Elizabeth both smiled politely at Dragas' effusive introduction. Julia said hello to Dan and, smiling, kissed him quickly on both cheeks. She then turned and did the same to Elizabeth, although, Dan thought, she did so with a slightly more lingering kiss, and the way she seemed to caress Elizabeth's arm as she stepped away from her gave Dan an uncharacteristic twinge of jealousy. He immediately dismissed the thought, telling himself that he was being overly sensitive. Julia invited them all to sit down again.

"Epigenetics? I have never heard of it. All my studies have been in the arts I am afraid, not the sciences. Is it possible to explain this epigenetics in simple terms that a mere arts graduate could understand?" asked Julia as they settled comfortably back into their seats.

"I can try," said Elizabeth. "But it is fairly dry stuff! If it gets too boring please just stop me."

Julia smiled back.

"You have no doubt heard about the nature versus nurture argument?" Elizabeth asked.

Julia nodded. "Whether it is our genes that determine who we are or our environment?"

"That's right." confirmed Elizabeth. "The reality is that it is not an either or argument. Both have an impact on who we are. There have been many studies of identical twins over the years and we know that things like your intelligence are more affected by genetics and things like our, say, political leanings are more affected by our environment."

"These same studies of identical twins also revealed that there are some things that just can't be explained by either nature or nurture. Identical twins that grew up together, in the same house, aren't the same. One twin could, for example, have asthma and the other won't. One twin would have early onset bipolar disorder and the other wouldn't. It turns out that there are, in fact, three types of impact that make us who we are - nature, nurture and epigenetics."

"Do you know much about DNA and what it does?" she asked Julia, who shook her head.

"Okay. Every cell in our body, all fifty or so trillion of them, contain about two metres of DNA."

"What! Two metres?" said Julia stretching out her arms. "In a tiny little cell?"

"Amazing but true!" said Elizabeth with a laugh. "The DNA holds the code of who we are. Every cell in our body has exactly the same DNA. Its like a barcode on something you buy, a really long barcode. Now, to just stuff that two metres of barcode into a single cell would be pretty difficult. The cell though has a nifty trick to pack all that information into such a tiny space. The DNA is wrapped around a thing called a histone - a sort of biological cotton reel. There are about thirty million of these tiny cotton reels in each of your cells."

"Thirty million, two metre long barcodes in one cell?" said Julia, fascinated.

"Yup!" said Elizabeth. "But this solution causes its own problem. If the cell wants to access the DNA, to read it, so it can reproduce, then it can't because the DNA is all tightly wound around its cotton reel. This is where epigenetics comes in. Epigenetic markers, little chemical markers, tell the DNA to either wind up tightly, because they don't need to be read, or unwind to be accessible to the cell. It is these markers that tell the cell which bit to read so that it has the pattern to be able to become a brain cell or a muscle cell or whatever type of cell is needed."

Julia, who was leaning forward listening with rapt attention, asked, "So where do these markers come from?"

"Most of the markers are put in place when an embryo is growing inside its mothers uterus. All sorts of things can affect them, for example, the food that the mother eats, or the stresses that she is under, or whether she smokes. These things can all influence the epigenetic markers. In fact, it might not even be the mother's environment that has the most profound influence. It might be the stresses or the food that the mother's mother ate, or the mother's father." explained Elizabeth.

"There was a long term study done of boys who over ate and started smoking before they reached puberty. It turned out that the children and grandchildren of those boys had significantly shorter lives than those whose grandparents didn't smoke or over eat. It showed that the lifestyle decisions we make directly impact on the health and well being of not just one but potentially many future generations. The epigenetic markers were most likely laid down as a consequence of these sort of lifestyle decisions."

Andris, who was also listening intently, said. "But epigenetic markers can also be laid down after someone is born, can't they?"

"Absolutely!" said Elizabeth. "Especially in the areas that continue to grow throughout our lives such as our brains. There is a particular receptor in the body called a glucocorticoid receptor. In a certain part of our brain, this particular receptor helps us deal with stress. There have been studies with rats that suggest that it is the way a mother rat treats her babies that determines the amount of this receptor that is produced. When a rat baby is born the gene that affects the Glucocorticoid receptor production is effectively turned off by the epigenetic markers that surround it. But, and here is the amazing thing, if a rat mother takes good care of her babies, licking them and grooming them, the epigenetic markers that switched off the receptor gene can be removed. So the receptor gene gets turned back on. The rat baby then has the benefit of increased Glucocorticoid receptors in their brain and can handle stress much more effectively."

"The big thing to note is that epigenetic marks are reversible. That is part of the work that we are doing. Trying to find out what chemicals impact on which epigenetic marker."

"There are, for instance, genes which protect cells from becoming cancerous. If the right mix of chemicals can be found to turn those genes on when they have effectively been switched off, then we can remind the cells in the body what they are there to do and potentially stop cancers in their tracks, or cure diabetes, asthma or Parkinson's disease."

"Wow!" said Julia, looking impressed. "That is truly amazing! Could I change these markers in my own body?"

"Sure," said Elizabeth. "If you eat well, for instance, then that can impact on the markers. Or, if we knew what they were, there could be drugs that could change those markers."

Julia looked warily at her half finished glass of champagne.

Elizabeth laughed. "I don't think you have to worry about one glass of champagne," she said draining her glass. "or two!" she said holding out her glass to Dragas who dutifully refilled it.

While Elizabeth had been talking Dan had been looking around the yacht's saloon. "These are beautiful pieces of mosaic you have here," he said, standing up and looking closely at an exquisitely wrought section of mosaic showing the head of a woman picked out in the most delicate coloured tessera.

"Yes. They are beautiful. They are all part of my family's collection. Heirlooms," said Dragas indicating the other similarly displayed pieces of mosaic around the saloon.

Dan was staring at a large round section of mosaic. "Is this the story of the Minotaur?"

Dragas came over a stood beside Dan. "Yes! It is one of my most prized possessions. It once graced the floor of the villa of the Roman Proconsul Sergius Paulus at Paphos."

Dan moved to the next mosaic. Gold tiles reflected back the light of the ships saloon.

"I have seen similar mosaics in Ravenna and in Istanbul, I think. Are they Byzantine?" asked Elizabeth.

Dragas smiled. "Yes, indeed! These are a little later, towards the end of the Empire though. The quality of the workmanship, the dynamism of the images themselves, and the subtlety of colour is a feature of the later Imperial period," he said with real enthusiasm. "Did you enjoy Istanbul?"

"I have been a couple of times. It is an overwhelming city, so busy. To be honest I found the bazaars too much for me, too aggressive, too noisy," said Elizabeth. "Hagia Sofia on the other hand I found so moving. It is a magnificent building. To be able to touch stones that have seen sixteen hundred years of history is such a privilege!"

"Have either of you been to the Chora?" he asked.

Both Dan and Elizabeth shook their heads.

"To see the pinnacle of Byzantine Art you must see the Church of the Chora. Both the mosaics and the frescoes are absolutely stunning," said Dragas.

"You seem to have a strong connection with the Byzantine era. Is it an area of interest for you?" asked Dan.

"More like an obsession!" said Julia with a laugh. "Andris has strong family connections with the old empire."

Dan, who had been looking at Dragas as Julia was speaking saw a flash of irritation cross his face, replaced almost instantly by a smile.

"Do you mean the Byzantine Empire?" asked Elizabeth.

"Ah! An interesting question!" said Dragas. "There are in fact no people on earth who have ever said that they are part of a Byzantine Empire. It is a name made up by historians from the west, who wanted to believe that the Roman Empire fell in the middle of the first millennium. The reality is that the people who lived in Constantinople up until the middle 1400's thought of themselves as Romans! Part of the same Empire that Augustus Caesar founded two thousand years ago, and which lasted until Mehmed II broke down the walls and sacked the City."

"It is like the myth of the "Dark ages"." A note of anger had entered his voice. "It was only dark for a few countries in western Europe. The rest of the world, China, the middle east, southeast Asia, the Roman Empire, were getting on with things."

246

"I think we had better go through to dinner, now!" said Julia, interrupting Dragas, taking Elizabeth by the arm and starting to lead her through to the dinning room. "Once you get Andris started on western historians and their Europe centric bias against the east, we will be here all night!" she whispered in Elizabeth's ear.

"No, I find it fascinating!" said Elizabeth. "I love history. Dan and have been helping out on an archeological dig, looking for the tomb of a Gothic King."

"Really. That sounds terribly exciting. Have you found any treasure?" asked Julia.

Elizabeth sat down at a beautifully laid table. "No, but just before we left we helped uncover a few skeletons that we are hoping will turn out to be the remains of one of the Romans who actually dug Alaric's tomb."

She turned to Dan. "We must give the Professor running the dig a call, Dan, to see what else they have uncovered."

Dan nodded as he and Dragas seated themselves at the table. A white jacketed waiter served them wine and placed their entrees, a row of neatly arranged scallops covered in a creamy sauce and topped with a generous serving of black caviar, in front of them.

Dan was about to pick up his fork when Dragas and Julia bowed their heads.

"Our Father, Who art in heaven, hallowed be thy Name. Thy Kingdom come. Thy will be done, on earth as it is in heaven. Give us this day our daily bread; and forgive us our trespasses, as we forgive those who trespass against us; and lead us not into temptation, but deliver us from evil. Glory to the Father, and to the Son, and to the Holy Spirit, now and ever and unto ages of ages. Amen. Lord, have mercy! Lord, have mercy! Lord, have mercy! O Christ God, bless the food and drink of Thy servants, for Thou art holy, always, now and ever and unto ages of ages. Amen." he intoned quietly, then looking up said with a smile, "I hope you like seafood."

Dragas caught the look that Dan had given Elizabeth as he had finished saying grace. "I detect, Doctor Marsh, that you are, perhaps, not a believer?"

Dan, a passionate atheist, had often found himself in arguments with people who held strong religious beliefs. He knew that he often offended people with his views, and was loathe to start an argument over dinner. "I am a scientist. I am afraid I do not believe in any form of god, pagan, christian, muslim or jedi."

Dragas stared at Dan, looking directly into his eyes. "I feel sorry for you," he said. "Religion has always been a passion for my family." He took a mouthful of scallop and then continued. "Are you a fundamentalist atheist, like Richard Dawkins or a self proclaimed antithesis, like Christopher Hitchens or perhaps a Daniel Dennett a seeker of scientific verification?"

"I would say that I am pretty much a fundamentalist atheist," said Dan. "But two people arguing about religion from opposite ends of the spectrum is not the most enjoyable conversation to have over such beautiful food. It would be much more pleasant to talk about something of mutual interest."

Dragas nodded, smiling pleasantly. "Indeed. I understand that you have financed a number of archeological digs over the years, Doctor. I would be fascinated to hear about one of those. You financed one in Istanbul I understand?"

"Yes, but that was many years ago. We only contributed some money to the research done on the artefacts that were found when the old Ottoman Prison near Sultanahmet Park was being converted into a Four Seasons Hotel. I actually don't know much about the Eastern Roman Empire. It seems to be a passion of yours, though. Does your family have a connection with Istanbul?" asked Dan.

"No, not with Istanbul. My family's connection was with Constantinople," said Dragas. "No member of my family has been back to the City since the invasion of the Saracen."

"If that is the case then I imagine your ancestors would not recognise the city these days. There is not much of the old Christian City left now, unfortunately."

"That is something that we can both agree on," said Dagras. "By all accounts the old city was a beautiful place."

"Yes, I was quite surprised when I first went there. I was expecting it to be more like Rome. I hadn't realised that the Ottoman's had wiped away so much of the old city. The current Turkish Government seems more intent on ensuring Istanbul is seen as a modern, progressive city than preserving its history. Such is progress, I suppose," said Dan with a shrug.

"Do you know much about the last days of the Romans in Constantinople?" asked Dragas, obviously keen to retell the story.

"Only the basics, that the Ottoman Turks broke down the walls and invaded and that the Emperor was killed. I would be interested to know more," said Dan, always happy to learn more of the history of the world and, in this instance, to avoid an argument about religion.

"It is a fascinating and tragic story," said Dragas.

27. Constantinople – 1452

Constantine, absent mindedly stroking his beard, looked at the signature on the document he had just signed. Constantine XI, Emperor and Autokrator of the Romans and then the date, January sixth. He had been Emperor for three years. He glanced across to where his friend and confidant, George Sphrantzes was reading.

"It is hard to imagine, George," he said, "how far the great empire of the Romans has fallen. In Constantine the Great's time, the empire stretched from one end of the world to the other. Now what am I left with? This run down City and a few scattered provinces."

His hand tightened on the quill he was holding. Bitterness welled up inside him. He hadn't wanted to be Emperor. He hadn't wanted any of this. The quill broke. He threw it on the table.

"I know we have to live in the world that God has given us, but if I could have one prayer answered it would be that we never allowed the Latins into our city. They are at the heart of all our troubles." He had often pondered how the Empire had been betrayed by the Europeans. How the now infamous fourth Crusade had finally revealed the true intentions of the Latins, showing that they cared less about stopping the advance of Islam than they did about lining their own pockets with the wealth of the City.

"You know it is not that simple, my Lord," said George, quietly and reasonably. They had been friends since they were children and George would always speak his mind. "The Latin's were here a long time before the Fourth Crusade, as merchants and as mercenaries fighting to defend our borders. We needed them then and we still need them."

"I know," said Constantine. "But I can never forgive them for what they did to my City. Each time I go to Venice I see our beautiful golden horses from the hippodrome, that they stole and put on the roof of their basilica. I still remember the day I first saw them there. I stood looking up at my heritage and cried, George. I stood there with tears streaming down my face. They belong here, in Constantinople, not in Venice."

"The City that my family won back from them is a pale shadow of the city that was lost. For sixty years they looted and plundered our churches and palaces, stripped the city of its grandeur, and why? Because the Venetians and the Italians were greedy and jealous of what we had," he said answering his own question.

"Our Empire used to be the bulwark of Europe. We held the infidels back. Now, look at us. We are surrounded on all sides by lands controlled by the Sultan. What is left for us to defend except a crumbling ruin and our own people, or at least the few that remain?" he added despondently.

He slowly shook his head, thinking about how so many of his people had left. Who could blame them them for heading west to safety, away from the oncoming storm. So many of the scholars and the nobles had left that parts of the city were totally uninhabited now, overgrown and falling into ruin. Even the great Theodosian walls were finally crumbling, after standing for a thousand years. Even the lifeblood of the city, trade, seemed to be drying up.

"Constantinople is dying, George, and I don't know if I have the strength to save it."

"We will find a way, my Lord," said George. "The City has survived many trials and tribulations. She will survive these."

Constantine sighed and put his hands on his head. "All I need to do is find a way to persuade the Europeans to send us men and arms to help us defend the city against the Turks, without giving them the opportunity to take over the City again. To do that all I have to convince the Pope to support us, which he won't do until our orthodox church and his catholic church are once again united. To unite the churches all I have to do is convince our own people to bow down and accept that the Latin Pope in Rome has spiritual authority over our church, and accept the heresy of the inclusion of the Filioque in the Nicene Creed." He rolled his eyes. "All of that might have been a bit easier if God hadn't taken the Patriarch of our church from us two days after signing the agreement with the Pope at the Ecumenical Council in Florence."

"Poor old Patriarch Joseph was a good man," said George shaking his head slowly. "you are right. Things might have been different if he had lived. Now there are those in the city that are saying that God struck him down."

They both sat, lost in their own thoughts, then Constantine said, his voice tightly controlled, "I was there, George, when my brother came home from the Council of Florence. His own people shouted and spat at him as he entered the city. John didn't deserve that. Not straight after the death of his wife. No one deserves to be treated like that, let alone an Emperor who is trying to save his people."

"Your brother was a fine man and a good Emperor, Constantine. He tried his best to do what he thought was the right thing." said George quietly.

"I know George, but mark my words, this issue will be the death of us all if we can't find a solution," said Constantine, putting his head in his hands again. Why was it all so difficult? He understood the arguments of those that opposed the Union. In truth, he actually agreed with them, but, try as he might he could not get them to see that without acceptance of the agreement to unification, Constantinople would never get the men and arms for m the West it needed to defend itself against the Ottomans.

"If that isn't problem enough," he said, "my treasury is empty and whatever I try to do to refill it seems to put me in a worse situation. I tried to raise taxes. Those that could afford to pay, the Venetians and the other traders, squealed like piglets. The Venetians threatened to close down their operations and move their trade elsewhere. They threatened to move to a port already under Ottoman control, making it clear that they think it is only a matter of time before the Sultan rules my City. What choice did I have but to back down?" he said, exasperated.

"And now, this new young Sultan, Mehmed, who everyone assured me was just an immature and ineffectual youth who could be easily cajoled, flattered and outwitted, has started to build a new fort on the European side of the Bosporus. A matching pair to the one his grandfather built on the Asian side. When it's finished he will control all access to the Black Sea. He could starve Constantinople, both economically and literally, from both land and sea. The Turks call the fort Rumeli Hisar, the European castle. Do you know what my men call it? Laimokopia, the throat cutter." He paused for a few moments. "At least," he said grimly, "things can't get any worse!"

****

George Sphrantzes hesitated at the door to the Emperor's private apartment. Constantine was sitting with his head in his hands, his broad shoulders slumped. Papers were strewn across the desk in front of him. To George he looked like a man burdened by the weight of the world. The words that he had said a few months earlier, that things couldn't get any worse, still rung in his ears. He knew that the news that he had brought would not make his friend's life any easier.

George gave a polite cough and Constantine looked up. Seeing George he smiled and pointed to a chair.

"Was there ever an Emperor, George, who was beset by so many trials at one time?" he said waving his hand at the papers in front of him.

"I am afraid, my Lord that I have yet another burden to lay upon you," said George, hesitantly. "We have had a report that the Turks at the new fort have just slaughtered forty of your people at the village of Epibatai!"

The blood drained from Constantine's face. "Tell me what happened!" he said, his voice flat and expressionless.

"As you know, your Majesty, it is getting close to harvest time. The villagers had gone out to check their crops, and, much to their dismay, they discovered that the Turks building the new fort had turned their horses and pack animals into their fields. What had not been eaten had been despoiled, trampled into the dirt. A delegation of villagers went up to the fort and made their feelings known. As you can imagine, they were none to gentle in the words they used. The next day the Sultan sent his troops to the village. They slaughtered all the villagers they could find, men women and children."

Constantine sat in silence. "I guess I was wrong George when I said things couldn't get any worse for us," he said quietly, looking down at his desk. He sat like that for some time. When he looked up his expression was stern. "Give the order to close the gates of the city. Have every Turk that can be found arrested."

George was shocked. "But, my Lord! That is tantamount to declaring war on the Ottoman Empire! What if they retaliate! We will be crushed!" said George passionately.

Constantine looked at him, his eyes hard and his jaw set. "I have no choice George. I will not ignore the murder of my own people. What sort of Emperor would I be If I did nothing when our enemy kills our women and our children. These infidels press around us on all sides. It is only a matter of time before they come for us! It is time to make a stand!"

He took a deep breath. "We are the last bastion of Christianity in the East, George. Send messengers to Venice, to the King of Naples and to the Pope in Rome. Tell them all that the final judgement is coming. If they do not send support to us now, then the great City of Constantinople will fall!" he said.

"Tell the heralds to let it be known throughout the City that we will soon be at war. Give my blessing to any that wish to leave and seek sanctuary in the West. Give my thanks to those that decide to stay and fight." He paused, and then continued, "Give orders to begin rebuilding those sections of the city walls that need it. Talk to our agents and have them buy as much food as they can to stockpile and have the great cisterns under the city checked to make sure we have sufficient water. It will be a long siege."

George could feel his heart swelling in his chest. Constantine had been his friend for a long time, almost all their lives. They had fought side by side in Greece against the old Sultan. He had watched him grow into one of the finest and most noble and most principled men he knew. Now, in a moment of great peril, seeing the fire in his eyes, the compassion in his heart and the strength of his resolve to fight to the bitter end, under overwhelming odds, he could not but wonder what a great Emperor this man would have been in earlier times, when the Empire was more than just a tired old City.

****

George strode towards the Emperor's audience chamber, brushing the dust from his clothes as he walked and regretting his decision to walk up the hill to the Blachernae Palace. It was turning into a long hot summer and rain was long over due.

As he walked into the cooler air of the Audience Chamber Constantine turned to him, waving a piece of parchment in the air. "Months we wait for replies from our so called allies, and when they finally come they are full of platitudes." Constantine threw the papers on to the floor. He took a deep breath to calm himself. "Our plea to the Venetian's has drawn sympathy but little else, I am afraid. The Doge has made it very clear that they have other priorities. He has, however, sent us some gunpowder and armour and a promise that, if the other western powers send men, they will do the same."

"They do not believe that the City can be saved!" said George angrily. "They do not want to risk damaging their relationship with the Sultan! They care more about the weight of their purses than they do about helping us! What about the Pope of Rome, does he offer us anything?"

"More platitudes and promises. The reply from Pope Nicholas is no more encouraging." said Constantine bitterly. "He continues to take the hard line that support from the West will only come with the re-unification of our churches. He has told me he is sending a legate, Cardinal Isidore of Kiev, to confirm and celebrate the union of the churches in a ceremony at the Church of the Holy Wisdom. After that is done he will consider my request for support."

"Another who does not believe the City can be saved. He believes unification will save our people's souls, but cares little for their lives," said George scathingly. "He cares little for the fact that our people will be in open revolt if the unification ceremony in Hagia Sofia goes ahead!"

"Perhaps we can persuade this Cardinal Isidore that there is a compromise solution. Perhaps we can persuade him of the seriousness of the threat to the City. Hopefully he will be a reasonable man." said Constantine.

****

Constantine made his way out of the Blachernae Palace and onto the streets of the City. He had found, since his mother had died a year after he had become Emperor, that there were few people he could truly trust. She had been such a store of wisdom and unbiased advice that her loss had been a devastating blow. He missed her. Now he relied more on George than ever before, and to a lesser extent, the guidance and experience of the old Grand Duke, Loukas Notaras.

They all knew that he walked a political and religious tightrope and, as the weather had started to get cooler in the City, Cardinal Isidore had arrived. His arrival seemed to be the spark that set alight a slow burning fuse. Now Constantine wanted to find out for himself the mood of the people in the City. Dressed in a heavy cloak, with a hood hiding his face, he walked down to the forum to listen to what the leaders of those that spoke against the re-unification of the churches had to say.

He pushed his way through the crowd. The noise around him started to increase as John Eugenikos, one of the most fervent anti-unionists, sprang on to the plinth at the base of Constantine's Column, the huge porphyry column, surmounted with a giant cross, that towered above the forum.

"This column," shouted John Eugenikos, holding up his hands to quiet the crowd, "built by the first Christian Roman Emperor, Constantine the Great, equal of the Apostles, stands witness to the strength of our faith. A wonderful statue of Constantine the Great once stood atop this column, but it was toppled by a great gale. Emperor Manual Komnenos repaired it. This cross was raised in place of the statue," he said pointing upwards. "When the Latin's invaded our city they stole the many beautiful bronze wreaths that surrounded the column, but still it stands, stripped now of its ornamentation, but still testament to the power of the one true orthodox church! This column has stood for over one thousand years! It has stood despite the vagaries of nature and the greed and venality of men."

"We must be like this column. We too must stand firm against the heresies of the Latin Church. It is Constantinople, not Rome, that lies at the heart of Christianity. It is Constantinople, not Rome that is the centre of God's empire on earth."

"This union is evil! Our church is in disarray as a result of the turmoil and confusion brought upon us by the Emperor's brother and predecessor John Palaiologos! He was misled. This union is an affront to God and is the source of all our misfortune. God has taken the life of the Patriarch who signed the agreement and the Emperor who commanded it. What more proof do you need that God himself is against it!"

"These are dangerous times! We have an Emperor without a crown! We have a government that puts ships, money and soldiers from the West above the purity of our true faith. They set human fear above the fear of God! Let it be known that we will never, never bow down to the Bishop of Rome!" He shouted.

The crowd roared their agreement.

Constantine turned his back and walked away. Yes, he thought, as he threaded his way through the crowd, out of the forum, he's right. I am an Emperor without a crown. It was tradition that the Patriarch of Constantinople place the crown on the head of the new Emperor but, given the popular feeling against the new, pro unionist Patriarch, Gregory, who John had appointed just before he died, he had decided not to be crowned by him. It would have been political suicide. He hoped that, once this issue was behind them he could arrange a proper Imperial coronation in Hagia Sofia. At the moment it wasn't important. What was important was finding a way to re-unite his people.

****

The Emporer sat on a stone bench, just below the ruin of the Great Palace, staring out at the Sea of Marmara. He watched the ships as they plied their way back and forth. It was an unusual, and rare, moment of solitude in which he was taking particular delight. It was coming up to Christmas, the sun was shining. It was cold, but the skies were blue and there was a gentle breeze blowing. In his hand he held a small glass vial, encased in an intricately wrought design of gold.

When his brother, John, had given it to him he had told him that the vial contained the blood of Constantine the Great, the equal of the Apostles, Saint Constantine. They had been young then. Their father had

257

been Emperor and life had been much simpler. It had been the evening of his fifteenth birthday. John had crept into his bedroom and, with only the light of the moon to see by, had told his impressionable younger brother the legend of the blood of Constantine the Great.

John had said that he and some friends had crept into the crypt of the Church of the Apostles and stolen the reliquary from the sarcophagus of Constantine the Great himself! The legend, he said, was that the blood of the Saint bestowed, on the rightful heir to the throne of Constantine's city, the power of augury, the ability to see the golden path, the path that would lead the Empire to its ultimate salvation. Then he had told him, in a very solemn voice, that If the one who drank it was not the true heir, then he would die a hideous and painful death!

"Keep this safe." John had said, pressing the vial into his hand. "If ever the City is in peril I will call on you, and you must bring me the vial!"

Constantine smiled as he looked at the object in his hand. He had worn it around his neck ever since that evening. He occasionally wondered where his bother had really got it from, and what the dark liquid inside it really was. He held it to his lips and kissed the vial, not because he believed his brother's story, but because it was a reminder of the brother he loved and of a fondly remembered kindness, a memory of more innocent, happier times.

Now John was gone and he was the one facing the loss of the City to the Saracen. Time was running out. Hope was running out. He sat staring at the liquid that moved sluggishly inside the reliquary, and wished that it truly did have some mystical power that would save the city.

His reverie was broken by the distant sound of thunder. Looking up, confused, he scanned the sky. There was not a cloud in sight. Unable to determine the source of the noise, and still distracted by his own thoughts, he decided that he must have imagined the sound.

He was still sitting in the same spot when, some time later George Sphrantzes hurried down to him. "My Lord, they have sunk a Venetian trader!" he said, breathless and excited.

Constantine looked up. "Who has?" he asked.

"The Turks. They have fired their guns from Rumeli Hisar!" said George breathing heavily. "They have sunk a Venetian trader who would not stop and pay their toll. A single shot sunk the vessel!"

By the time that Constantine and George had walked through the old Palace Gardens and up the hill to the Blachernae Palace, a small but noisy group of nobles had gathered in the Emperor's audience chamber. Notable among the crowd was the Venetian Bailo, the most senior Venetian noble in the City, Girolamo Minotto.

As Constantine strode into the chamber the men in the room fell silent. He acknowledged each of them and then said, "The time has come for a decision gentleman! Either you leave our City or you stay and help defend her against the oncoming Turk. There is no doubt in my mind, given this latest atrocity, that it will only be a short time before the Sultan brings his army to our gates. There is a chance, given the work that has been done by so many hardworking souls, that our walls will, once again protect us, just as they have in the past."

He paused. Yes, he thought to himself as he looked at the worried faces staring back at him, now is the time to find out who will stand with us. "Given our dire predicament I need to ask each of you your intentions. Will you stay, or will you go?" He looked first at the Venetian Bailo, the most important representative of the most important colony in the City. He was not only the leader of the Venetians in the City but also controlled a small naval contingent of twelve ships that currently rested safely in the harbour of the Golden Horn. His response to the Emperor's question would influence many in the room.

Girolamo Minotto paused before answering. Constantine could feel his heart pounding in his chest. If the Bailo quit the City, then all hope of support from the West was lost, he thought to himself. A messenger appeared and walked quietly up to the Grand Duke Loukas Notaras and whispered in his ear. Notaras' face fell. He turned and looked at the messenger in disbelief. The messenger nodded reassurance that his message had been confirmed.

"Excuse me, your highness," said Notaras respectfully. Constantine and the others turned to look at him. "I have just learnt that there has been a tragic development. The Venetians that managed to make it ashore from their stricken vessel my Lord, have all been slain by the Turkish garrison."

An angry murmur ran around the room. Constantine's head fell in silent prayer for the souls of the murdered men. He then looked again at the Bailo. "My heart grieves for these men and their families, Girolamo. I will send my condolences to their families. They were not part of this dispute. They did not deserve to die in this way. Please feel free to take your leave. I understand that, at this time, being with your people is important. We can reconvene at a less distressing time."

"Your Imperial Majesty," Girolamo began formally, obviously trying hard to control his emotions "for many years I have called this great City home. Other than my own city of Venice there is not a place in this world that holds a larger place in my heart. While you and I have not always seen eye to eye in matters of commerce, our purpose has always, I believe, been the same, the continuation of this most noble of cities under the benevolent rule of your family." He paused.

"This latest tragedy only reinforces my own personal resolve. I, for one, with your Majesty's permission, wish to stay and assist in the defence of our City." He paused again and looked across at his son, who was standing close by. His son nodded. "My son also wishes to stay and fight in the defence, your Majesty."

"Once this meeting is adjourned I will call an emergency meeting of the Venetian Council of the City to ascertain who among my countrymen are prepared to join us. I will also propose that all Venetian ships currently in the harbour remain here to help in the defence. This may not be in accord with the wishes of our Doge, but he is not here. I will immediately write to him and implore him for his support in the strongest terms. These decisions I take upon my self."

A wave of relief and gratitude washed over Constantine. He knew that the bond between this man and the city was strong, but it was as nothing compared to the bond between this man and his son. To have them both standing side by side helping defend his city was more than he could have expected.

Constantine held out his hand to Girolamo who took it in his own strong grasp. He then took his son's hand and shook that as well. Turning to the other men in the room he asked, "Who else will join with us?"

A chorus of support filled the room.

28. Constantinople – January 1453

As Constantine was inspecting the repairs to the fortifications along the sea wall that looked down onto the Golden Horn he noticed a number of ships sailing into the harbour, all flying the red and white pennant of Genoa. From where he was standing he watched in amazement as a young man leapt from one of the ships, followed by a host of armed men who, under this young man's direction, began unloading equipment and stores.

Eager to see for himself what was going on Constantine called for his horse. Trailed by his small contingent of soldiers, he made his way down to the dock.

By the time he reached the port the ships were almost unloaded. He dismounted. The young man he had seen previously broke away from his tasks and walked towards Constantine. He stopped before the Emperor and knelt down on one knee.

"Your majesty," he said respectfully "Captain Giovanni Giustiniani Longo, and seven hundred fighting men, at your service, and the service of your great City."

"You are very welcome Captain," said Constantine with a smile. He guessed that Giustiniani was a good ten years younger than he was, perhaps in his mid thirties. "Where do you come from and on who's orders?"

"The Island of Chios, Your Majesty, on my own orders. I heard of your plight from a Venetian merchant and put together this fine band of men, all keen to help in the defence of your mighty City."

"Your family is well known to us Giovanni," said Constantine who knew the rulers of the Genoese colony that had once been a part of his own family's empire. "You have come at a time of great need. We are very grateful for your offer of service, which we humbly accept."

Constantine's eyes scanned the men who were now crowded around, watching their Captain kneeling before the Emperor. Constantine reached down and grasped Giovanni's arm. He lifted him to his feet. The two men now stood eye to eye, Giovanni grinned in a boyish way.

Constantine smiled at the sparkling eyes and infectious smile of the handsome, self assured young man standing before him.

"Once you have your men housed, come to the Palace. I have called a meeting of those that will be in charge of the defence of the City. I would like you to be among them." He looked up at the men that crowded the dock and said in a louder voice. "Thank you for coming to our aide. You are most welcome in our city. We will do all that we can to ensure you are made comfortable." Mounting his horse, and with his retinue in tow, he turned and headed back up the hill to continue his inspection of the sea wall.

29. Amalfi - Present day

"So that was the trigger, the sinking of a venetian ship?" asked Dan as the empty plates were taken from the table.

"Not really," said Dragas. "Sultan Mehmed had always wanted to conquer the City. His grandfather had tried. His father had tried. Both had failed. Mehmed was determined to succeed or die trying."

"Did many people leave the City before the siege?" asked Elizabeth.

Dragas nodded. "Many, many people left the City and they took with them many books and much knowledge that had been, up until that time, lost to the West. It is said that the fall of Constantinople and the Empire, first to the Latins and then to the Turk, was one of the foundations for the renaissance in Europe."

"So how many people were left to defend the City, then?" asked Elizabeth.

"It was said that Constantine had no more than seven or eight thousand men at arms. Sultan Mehmed had around eighty to one hundred thousand!"

"But the Sultan still had to get through the walls!" said Elizabeth.

"Yes, but in that regard the Sultan had help," said Dragas. "A young Hungarian engineer by the name of Orban arrived in Constantinople in around 1450. He was a master gunsmith and he offered his services to the Emperor. Unfortunately the building of guns was expensive and Constantine had neither the money to pay Orban more than a small stipend, nor the wherewithal to purchase the brass needed to actually build any guns."

"Orban, frustrated with hanging around Constantinople and kicking his heels and no doubt open to an opportunity, went to see Sultan Mehmed. The young Sultan was only too happy to listen to the young engineer and his vision for these amazing new weapons of war. According to the legend Mehmed asked him if he was familiar with the walls of Constantinople and whether he could build a gun to breach them. Orban is said to have told the Sultan that he was extremely familiar with the walls of Constantinople, having spent a few months in the City taking careful note of their construction, and that he could build a gun that could shatter to dust, not only the walls of Constantinople, but the very walls of Babylon itself!"

"Cocky young man! Did he?" asked Elizabeth fascinated.

"The gun he built was said to be twenty seven feet long with a barrel diameter big enough for a man to crawl into on his hands and knees. Its barrel was solid bronze eight inches thick. When they test fired it, it was said that it threw a boulder, weighing more than half a ton, over a mile before it buried itself six feet into the earth."

"It took sixty oxen to pull it the one hundred and forty miles from where it was cast in Adrianople to Constantinople, moving at the amazing speed of two and a half miles a day!"

"Not only did Orban build this massive gun for the Sultan, he also built a host of smaller ones that were designed to be set up in batteries along the walls so they could continually pound them into dust!" said Dragas.

"Who was actually in charge of the defence of the city? Was that something Constantine did? Did he have any experience in defending a city?" asked Dan, caught up in the story.

"Constantine was a very experienced Commander. Have you ever heard of the Hexamilion wall?" Dan and Elizabeth both shook their heads.

Dragas, clearly enjoyed his role as lecturer. He continued, "The Hexamilion wall was the defensive wall built at the Isthmus of Corinth. Originally, it had been built by the Emperor Theodosius. In fact, there are some historians who believe that it was your friend, Alaric the Goth, Elizabeth, whose activities prompted its construction. The wall was built in the first half of the fifth century. It runs parallel to the modern day Corinth Canal, but a bit further south. You can, in fact, still see sections of it."

"Constantine rebuilt the wall in around 1444 to protect the Peloponnese against the Turks."

"What was he doing in Greece?" asked Elizabeth.

"The Peloponnese, or the Morea as it was called at the time, was the only other major area of land where the old Empire still ruled. The city of Mystras was their capital. Mystras was close to where the city of Sparta was in ancient times."

"Once Constantine had rebuilt the wall he started to make incursions into Attica, the Greek mainland, with the intentions of expanding the Empire's presence. He had quite some success, taking control of both Athens and Thebes, which were at the time under the control of the Turks. In the process of his conquests, Constantine also managed to infuriate the Venetians by usurping one of their commercial colonies and evicting their governor."

"His actions also irritated the Duke of Athens. In fact, he was so annoyed at having to pay homage to this young upstart, that he trotted off to the old Sultan, Sultan Murad, his previous lord and master, and asked for some help to put things back the way they were!"

"Murad, who had just decimated an Hungarian army, killing their King and around ten thousand Hungarian soldiers, decided that he would go and deal with the situation himself, while he was in the area!"

"Constantine and one of his brothers, Thomas, rather than take on the whole Ottoman army, retreated from the mainland and took their stand at their newly refurbished Hexamilion wall. After some pretty fierce fighting Constantine decided discretion was the better part of valour, especially given the fact that the Sultan had brought some sixty thousand men with him, and sent a messenger to the Sultan proposing peace terms."

"Murad was a bit annoyed by this stage, and threw Constantine's messenger in prison and demanded that the wall be dismantled. Constantine refused. The Sultan gave Constantine a few days to think about it.

"Under normal circumstances, Constantine should have been able to rely on his defensive wall, but this was a time of changing technology. The Sultan, with the wealth of the Ottoman Empire behind him, had brought his latest weapons, cannons, to the fight. He deployed them along the seven or eight kilometre length of the wall, along with his more old fashioned siege engines and scaling ladders."

"With no sign that Constantine was going to change his mind, the sultan opened fire on the walls. The reports from the time indicated that the barrage was so constant that none of the defenders dared show their heads above the battlements. After five days, with the wall pretty well in ruins, the trumpets sounded and the best of the Sultans troops, the Janissaries, launched themselves over the wall. Constantine and his brother barely escaped.

The Sultan then ravaged the countryside, took some sixty thousand Christians from the Peloponnese as prisoners to sell in the slave markets. The only reason he didn't attack Mystras was because it was coming to winter and it would have been too difficult to cross the mountains with his army. Constantine and Thomas had to accept their defeat and agree to pay a yearly tribute to the Sultan. They also had to agree to never rebuild the hexamilion wall."

"So Constantine knew all about Turkish tactics. He learnt one other important lesson at that time. The Western powers might praise him for blooding the nose of the Saracen, but in the end it would always be their own self interest that would come before sending him any assistance. The Venetians had ships and men nearby and could have helped but they were angry with Constantine for taking over one of their colonies, which, in the end, was lost back to the Turks and the Venetians. Business before heroics, or maybe business before principles, seems to have been a Venetian philosophy at the time."

"You mentioned the Janissaries like they were the elite troops of the Sultan?" queried Elizabeth.

"Janissaries were, as you say, the elite troops. They were the Sultan's bodyguard. Their role was to protect the throne. Every five years or so the Ottoman administrators would tour the Christian areas of the Empire looking for the strongest, fittest and healthiest boys. They placed the boys with Turkish families to learn the language and to be indoctrinated into Islam. After that they entered the education system. They were subject to severe discipline, were not allowed to grow a beard or take up any other skill other than that of war, nor where they allowed to marry."

"They were very much like the Christian military orders, like the Knights Hospitaller in some ways. The Egyptians used the same sort of system with the Mamluks. The expectation was that they would remain celibate and see the Janissary corps as their family with the Sultan as their father."

"They were very innovative, at least initially. They were one of the first groups of soldiers to wear a uniform and they were one of the first military units to start using firearms anywhere in the world, probably around the time of the siege of Constantinople. Traditionally they fought with a Kilij, a curved sword like a sabre. That sword over on the bulkhead there is a Kiliji from around the time of the siege," said Dragas, pointing to a curved sword hanging in a frame on the wall."

"So, said Elizabeth, "poor old Constantine was cut off from outside help. He was abandoned by the western powers. His enemy had an army likely to be ten times larger than the one who could muster. He was going to be facing the latest medieval super weapons, giant mega cannons. He probably only had bows and arrows. His own people were rioting in the streets, upset about the Roman Catholics trying to take over their church. She checked each of her points off on her fingers. "I am guessing that it is not going to be a happy ending for Constantine?"

Dragas waited while dessert was placed in front of them. "You put the situation very succinctly," he laughed. "but I don't think I will answer your question, I wouldn't want to spoil the suspense!"

30. Constantinople - 2nd April, 1453

It was early. The sun was rising above the horizon into a clear blue sky. Constantine had decided to walk the walls of his city with Giustiniani, without the distraction of courtiers, to see for what condition the walls were in and check on the disposition of the men.

They started their inspection near the Imperial palace, in the Northern corner of the City, mounting the wall near the gate of Kaligaria where a single wall had been strengthened by the fortifications built for the Blachernae Palace itself.

"This is the area that I think is one of the most vulnerable. Mehmed is most likely to concentrate some of his forces here," said Constantine gesturing towards the single wall. "That is why I have put you and the Grand Duke in charge of this section of the wall. Your compatriot, Maurizio Cattaneo, will take charge of the next section of the wall with the men he brought from Genoa."

The two men walked south, away from the Golden Horn, passing over a small postern gate, the Kerkoporta. Constantine stopped and looked at the small gate set into the wall. "We could send out raiding parties to harass the Sultans army through there,it's small and easily defensible," he said indicating the Kerkoporta.

Giustiniani nodded.

Constantine turned and looked back towards the Golden Horn. From here, high on the wall, he could see the full length of the inlet, all the way to the town of Pera on its other side. The Galata Tower, with its high conical roof, stood out brightly in the early morning light. His eyes scanned the scene and came to rest on the building just below where they were standing, the Palace of the Porphyrogenitus.

They continued walking, passing a long stone staircase that led down from the top of the inner wall to the City itself, then along the parapet until they came to another stone staircase. This one led from the walkway they were on to the top of one the inner wall's towers. Constantine leapt up the stairs, two steps at a time, closely followed by Giustiniani.

Constantine grinned to himself as he reached the last step and walked over to lean on the stone parapet surrounding the top of the big, square stone tower. The view was wonderful.

Feeling the solid stonework under his hands he leant forward and looked down at the gap between the inner and outer walls, the peribolos, which separated the inner and outer walls by around twelve metres and stretched its whole length. The tower on which he was standing was about twenty metres above the peribolos and about six or seven metres higher than the path that topped the walls themselves.

Beyond the peribolos was the outer wall. That too was studded with towers, albeit much smaller in both height and width. The smaller towers were about fifty to a hundred metres apart and constructed so that they occurred in the spaces between the larger towers of the inner wall.

"It is unfortunate that we don't have enough men to man both walls, Giustiniani," said Constantine still looking down into the peribolos.

"Yes, my Lord, but focusing our energies on the outer walls is a plan that has proven its worth in the past. Is it not true that, when the Sultan's father, Murad, laid siege to the City only the outer walls were manned?"

"Yes, that is true, and the walls were not breached then," agreed Constantine.

"And we still have the protection of the foss, even before they get to the wall itself," said Giustiniani, confidently.

Constantine looked out beyond the walls to the long, eighteen metre wide moat that ran the length of the mighty land walls. Known as the foss, this barrier, or at least parts of it, could be flooded with water, if necessary. Beyond the foss was open country. Open country, he mused, that would soon be occupied by who knew how many Turks and their allies.

They both turned to walk back down the stairs and Constantine stopped. From this vantage point he could see the City spread out below him. It was like a park. Trees and gardens were everywhere, many now, sadly, overgrown. He could see the towering dome of the magnificent Hagia Sophia and beyond the church the remains of the Hippodrome. Behind the Hippodrome he could see the Great Palace. He could see the dome of the Million, the mile marker that was the starting place for the measurement of all roads that led to the City, another sad reminder, he thought to himself, of how we had once stood at the centre of a vast Empire. He could also see Constantine's Column standing out above the trees.

If he didn't look too closely the City looked a pleasant and refreshing place, the grandeur of its palaces and churches still able to inspire awe. Too close an inspection revealed deserted houses, dilapidated palaces and crumbling churches.

"My Lord?" said Giustiniani from the bottom of the steps.

Constantine snapped out of his reverie. "Yes, coming Giustiniani," he said as he walked down the stairs of the tower to continue their inspection.

They passed over the Charisian Gate which was positioned at the top of a ridge looking down into the valley that had been formed by the River Lycus. The River passed under the walls into the city itself. Near the river, at the bottom of the valley, was the military gate of Saint Kyriake. Ahead, about one kilometre, they could see the Gate of Romanus on the top of the other side of the valley.

"This section of the wall, Giustiniani, that spans this valley, is the single most vulnerable point in all our defences, said Constantine, leaning over the wall and looking down towards the River Lycus. "I will take personal responsibility for it, but may well need to call on you for support."

Giustiniani nodded and the kept walking, passing over the Gate of Saint Romanus and four more gates before they came to the Pegae Gate. They could see men working on repairs to both the inner and outer walls. Standing down in the peribolos, directing the work was his cousin, Theo Palaeologus. Theo was responsible for this section of the wall. He waved up to Constantine and Giustiniani and then went back to his task.

They walked the final few hundred metres to the Golden Gate, the traditional, ceremonial entrance to the City. Constantine stood looking out at the Sea of Marmara while Giustiniani talked to the Genoese soldiers who were stationed there.

Finally they reached the tower that stood at the point where the solid double walls met the sea. Here the wall turned and ran along the waters edge. So far they had walked about six and half kilometres, the full length of the wall that protected the city from any landward invasion. The sun was now climbing higher into the sky and both men took a moment to rest against the stone parapet, enjoying the beauty of the shimmering blue Sea of Marmara that stretched out in front of them.

"The Golden Gate, my Lord, why is it walled up and no longer used?" asked Giustiniani.

Constantine looked at the younger man for a moment. "It was walled up well before my time. The last time it was used, I believe, was when the Emperor Michael Palaiologos entered the City after he won it back. That would have been in 1261. Before that it was used when Emperors returned to the City after great victories and I am afraid there have been few of those of late." he said with a wry smile.

Constantine turned and started to walk along the sea wall. This single wall was the second side of the triangle that made up the Theodosian walls. He looked over the edge. The waves broke gently on the base of the wall, some fifteen metres below. There was less activity along this wall. The two small fortified harbours that pierced the walls on this side of the city were really only for small boats to shelter when they found themselves beating into the prevailing wind and unable to make it around the point into the safety of the Golden Horn.

Constantine and Giustiniani crossed over what Constantine knew to be an old, abandoned harbour, the harbour of Eleutherius, or Portus Theodosianus as it was sometimes called. The River Lycas made its exit from the city here and the silt it carried had always made keeping this little harbour dredged more trouble than it was worth.

Walking on he felt comfortable that the currents that swirled around the base of the walls, the shoals and reefs that lurked just under the water and the protrusions in the wall itself would be sufficient deterrent for the Turks to allow him the luxury of only manning these walls lightly.

"The Greek monks have agreed to man this wall," said Constantine, as they strode along.

"You expect your monks to fight?" asked Giustiniani, taken aback.

"No," said Constantine with a laugh, "I don't expect them to fight, but they have agreed to watch and call in reinforcements in the unlikely event that these walls are attacked. I have arranged for Prince Şehzade Orkan to protect this section of the sea wall as well. He has a small band of Turkish soldiers with him and can come to the Monks aide if necessary."

Giustiniani stopped walking so suddenly that Constantine was some distance away when he realised that the young Captain was no longer with him. He looked back.

"You have an Ottoman Prince helping you defend the City?" he asked dumbfounded.

"Yes," said Constantine walking back towards Giustiniani. "He is living here under my protection He is a grandson of Sultan Bayezid. Other than Mehmed, we believe he is the only known male member of the Ottoman ruling house. We keep him here, and he doesn't become a focal point for rebellion among the Turks."

"And you trust him?" the younger man asked.

"The Prince knows that his life would not be worth living if he stepped outside the Gates of the City. He is as eager to keep Mehmed out of Constantinople as we are."

Giustiniani, shaking his head, followed Constantine along the wall as it followed the Marmara shore.

Constantine could now see the old Imperial Palace laid out above him, with the hippodrome behind it. His stomach growled at him as he came close to Acropolis Point, just past the Gate of Saint Barbara, which, like the Golden Gate, was flanked by two large towers. These towers were clad in white marble and glowed beautifully in the mid morning sunshine. Constantine stopped at the apex of the wall. To his right was the Sea of Marmara. To his left lay the Golden Horn. Straight ahead he could see the long channel of the Bosporus. He marvelled at the foresight of the first Constantine, building his City here. His hand went unconsciously to the reliquary that hung around his neck.

On the Northern shore of the Golden Horn the Tower of Galata now stood out starkly, towering above the little walled town of Pera. He could also see the great chain that stretched from the walls below him across to the walls of Pera on the other side of the Golden Horn.

Attached to the chain where ten ships placed strategically along its length.

"The chain should stop the Sultan's fleet from being able to attack the sea walls along this side of the City." said Giustiniani.

Constantine nodded. "We should be able to man these walls less heavily than those on the landward side as long as the chain remain unbroken." he said. "But there are no guarantees, the Venetians broke through it in 1204. We will have to be prepared to divert men down to the ships moored to the chain if the Sultan makes a concerted effort to enter the inlet."

Constantine continued to lead the way along the wall. Below him, between the wall and the shore was a jumble of warehouse. Everywhere he looked people were bustling about, working on protecting their own possessions or on preparations for the siege that they all knew was coming.

As they walked the last part of the wall, in sight once again of the Blachernae Palace, Constantine turned to Giustiniani. "Have you ever fought against massed cannon, Giovanni?"

Giustiniani shook his head. "I have seen one or two used in battle, but I have never seen them used in a siege. From what I have seen they would not be powerful enough to do much damage to walls as thick as these."

Constantine nodded thoughtfully. He had seen, first hand, in Corinth what a large number of cannon were capable ofdoing. A shiver ran through him despite the warmth of the day.

Having walked the walls of the city he was now content that all that could be done was being done. He had a feeling that their preparations would soon be tested. Almost as the thought passed through his mind he heard shouting.

"They are here! The Turks have come! The Turks have come!"

He and Giustiniani ran to the wall of his palace and up the stone steps of the first of the great towers. Others had beaten him to it, and were standing in awed silence.

Across the whole landscape, that a few hours ago had been open fields, now was arrayed a seemingly never-ending mass of people and in the middle of the multitude an enormous cannon the size of which no one had ever seen.

31. Constantinople - 20th April 1453

Constantine stood on top of the seawall with Megas, Doux Lucas Notaras, inspecting the damage caused by the last attack of the Turkish fleet. He looked down at the great chain that stretched across the entrance to the Golden Horn and then up at the old Duke. He looked old and tired.

"It is lucky that the design of the Venetian and Genoese ships that we had moored to it are so much taller than the Turkish galleys," said the old man looking down on their ships where the areas of burnt, scorched and splintered wood were still clearly visible.

"The height advantage certainly allowed us to keep the Turks at bay, even though they outnumbered us," agreed Constantine.

He, and the citizens of Constantinople, had been stunned by the strength of the Sultan's fleet, when, at the end of March, under the command of Suleiman Baltoghlu, it had paraded past the City. Six two masted triremes, had rowed past first, followed by ten, single masted biremes, slightly smaller but no less deadly. Fifteen galleys, their single bank of oars moving in synchronised rhythm, then led a host, perhaps nearly eighty, smaller, faster boats called fustae. Bringing up the rear of the fleet had been twenty parandaria, the heavy sailing barges used for transporting men and equipment. Around the fleet had flitted small sloops and cutters carrying messages.

They were now based a short distance up the Bosporus, at a place called the Double Columns.

A few days earlier, under the command of Admiral Baltoghlu, they had attempted to break the chain. Constantine and the old Duke had watched as the Turkish boats had swarmed in. Their aim had clearly been to either board and destroy the defender's ships, or, to cut their anchor ropes, giving them access to the chain itself. Constantine had guessed that Baltoghlu knew the story of the 1203 siege when the Venetians had used one of their large ships to ram and break the chain. With the chain broken the Venetians had taken control of the Golden Horn and then attacked the less well fortified sea walls, gaining entrance to the City

276

The attack, with arrow, cannon and flaming brands, had been bravely fought off by the sailors with the support of Notaras and his men. The mortar bombardment that followed the attack had inflicted more damage and, unfortunately, lost them one ship, but, despite the loss it had been a victory, albeit a small one, but one that had buoyed the spirits of those in the city.

As Constantine and Notaras stood talking they were interrupted by a shout from further around the wall.

A messenger ran up, bowed and said, pointing out across the sea of Marmara towards the Dardanelles. "Your Majesty, ships have been spotted heading towards the City."

Constantine glanced at Notaras. Neither of them had expected any help from the west. He wondered fleetingly if this could be a relief convoy?

They followed the soldier around the wall. In the distance they could see the tiny specks of sails. The breeze was from the South, pushing the ships directly towards them. As they watched the sails grew noticeably bigger.

"Do you think they are ours?" asked Constantine, struggling to make out the shape of the sails. he thought he could see three distinct shapes.

As they watched more and more people came up and stood on the walls. Women and children stood in silence beside their men folk. They all watched, hoping, that they were allies, not more Turkish ships.

Constantine looked around and was surprised to see even more people standing up on the walls of the old, ruined hippodrome and the broken walls of the great Palace. It seemed that the whole population of the city had come out to watch. They all stood in silence, staring out to see.

A sharp-eyed boy standing not far away from Constantine suddenly shouted. "Look, there are three galleys and they are unfurling their pennants!"

Sure enough, the three small ships had unfurled long pennants from the tops of their masts. It seemed to Constantine that the crowd held their breath as the pennants flapped, hiding their colours, and then a shout went up. "They're red and white. They are Genoese!" And then another voice shouted, "And look, behind them, an imperial transport!"

Out from behind the fast moving galleys, their triangular sails hiding the larger vessel, appeared a grain ship, its red and yellow imperial pennants now unfurled and flapping in the strong breeze."

A deafening cheer went up. All around him people began to talk excitedly.

Then there was another shout. "The Turks have seen them." A hush fell over the crowd.

Constantine looked up the Bosporus and sure enough, heading out into the channel, was the Turkish fleet. Their oars pushed them relentlessly into the strong head wind. The crowd watched the fleet speed past them, heading straight for the oncoming ships.

As the Turks rowed past the City, they were close enough for Constantine to make out the sweating faces of the rowers and the determined expressions of the soldiers standing on their decks, only partially hidden behind the shields and bucklers that had been strapped to the gunwales of the biremes and triremes for protection. Some of the ships clearly had cannons newly mounted on their decks.

Vastly outnumbered by the Turkish fleet heading towards them, the four ships ploughed on, apparently undaunted by the intimidating reception committee that awaited them.

Notaras put his hand on Constantine's arm. Constantine turned to him. "I think the Sultan may be taking an active interest in this," he said nodding towards Pera. Just outside the walls of Pera Constantine could see a host of people on the shore. He could just make out the figure of the Sultan astride a white horse.

Constantine turned his attention back to the ships. His hand went unconsciously to the reliquary at his neck. The Turkish armada was now approaching the small relief fleet, but they didn't slow down. They kept sailing their course, straight for the Golden Horn.

There was a sudden arc of yellow light. A cloud of black smoke surrounded a Turkish bireme. The Imperial transport had unleashed a stream of flaming Greek fire on their attackers. A cheer went up from the crowd around him. The ships were getting close enough now to be able to make out the shapes of individuals on their decks. The citizens of the City watched, mesmerised as, time after time, Turkish vessels attacked the Imperial transport or the Genoese galleys. Soldiers from the Turkish boats swarmed up their sides only to be beaten back. Time after time, they watched as axes swung down onto arms, heads and shoulders as Turkish soldiers tried to board the Imperial vessels. Arrows rained down on the Turks from the high sides and even higher poops, prows and crows nests, of the Imperial ships.

Finally the ships reached Acropolis point. Constantine could see below him that preparations were being made to drop the great chain and let the ships into the safety of the Golden Horn. The ships of the relief fleet were just about to round the point for the last reach into the Golden Horn when disaster struck. The breeze, that had been so constant, pushing the ships towards their safe harbour, died. The ships slowed, the sound of their now useless sails flapping in the fickle breeze.

Unable to use their oars because of the press of Turkish boats around them, the relief fleet was now at the mercy of the Bosporus current. The ships, almost within touching distance of the City walls were now being dragged, inexorably, towards the Pera shore and Sultan Mehmed.

Constantine could see that Admiral Baltoghlu was positioning his fleet around his prey. Clearly wary of the damage that the Greek fire had already done to some of his ships, he maneuvered his larger vessels into position around the small relief fleet at a safe distance. The crowd in the city watched in horror as the Turks began to fire round after round of cannon balls into the ships. Flaming lances and arrows also flew through the air, hurled by the soldiers on the decks of the Turkish galleys.

The scene being played out before them was heart wrenching. The men on the relief ships worked valiantly, deafened by the noise of cannon, choking in the acrid smoke, dodging missiles and working tirelessly to dampen the fires the flaming brands started.

"They are getting in their own way!" said Notaras watching as a Turkish trireme tried to get close to the side of the Imperial Transport, only to have its oars tangled in a bireme that was trying to do the same thing.

The battle went on into the afternoon. For every Turkish vessel that was damaged or sunk, another would be standing ready to take its place. From every new vessel came a new wave of soldiers trying to scale the sides of the relief fleet's ships, but the Imperial and Genoese sailors fought on tirelessly.

As the fleet drew closer to the Pera shore the figure on the white horse became ever more agitated. Constantine could hear Mehmed screaming at the men on the Turkish ships, riding his horse back and forth along the shore and gesticulating wildly. At times he rode right into the water, as if he was trying to ride out to join the fight.

The relief fleet had somehow managed to raft up together. Now all four ships, like a floating island, were at the centre of the melee, surrounded by a swarm of Turkish vessels.

The crowd shouted themselves hoarse trying to encourage, by sheer force of will, the sailors and soldiers of the relief fleet to keep on fighting. The citizens of Constantinople, desperate to help, hurled rocks at any Turkish boats that came too close to the walls. Even Constantine joined in, whooping with joy as a Turkish ship was damaged and forced to withdraw from the battle, crying out warnings when he could see a new vessels preparing to attack and throwing spears and stones down on those Turks that came within range.

Now the sun was beginning to go down and the ships were all moving further away. Despite their valiant efforts it seemed that the relief fleet would be lost, overwhelmed by the sheer weight of numbers.

Feeling powerless to help Constantine could only watch as the fight went on. Holding his reliquary tightly in his hand he prayed to Saint Constantine to save the fleet. He had almost resigned himself to its loss when he felt a breath of wind on his face. He looked through the gathering gloom and thought he could see the tell tale rippling of wind on the water that flowed down the Bosporus. At first he wasn't sure. He saw the sails of one of the Genoese galleys sanp and begin to billow. Others had seen it as well! A shout went up. What was left of the big imperial transport's sails also began to fill. The ships began to move. As they moved they pushed the smaller craft that surrounded them out of the way.

Caught unawares, Admiral Baltoghlu, tried, in vain, to reorganise his fleet. He tried desperately to place boats between the relief fleet and the great chain. With, no doubt, a sense of impending doom, he must have realised that the heavier ships of his enemy were forcing their way inexorably towards the Golden Horn and safety.

As night fell the chain was lowered. The relief fleet sailed into the safe anchorage of the Golden Horn while, to confuse the Turkish fleet, three Venetian galleys rowed out with trumpets blaring, as if they were the vanguard of a counter attack. The people of the City cheered and hollered as the Turkish fleet withdrew. A number of the bolder residents stood on the walls and shouted abuse at the Sultan and his entourage on the far shore.

****

Sitting over a meal with Notaras, Giovanni, and the senior officers of the relief fleet, that evening, Constantine thanked God and Saint Constantine for their safe delivery. The Imperial transport had brought much needed grain to the city and the three Genoese galleys had been stocked with arms and provisions purchased by the Pope.

"Perhaps" said Giovanni, always the optimist, 'this is the turning point! I tell you one thing though, I wouldn't like to be in the shoes of the Admiral commanding the Sultan's fleet tonight!"

"You should have heard the Sultan screaming from the shore!" said Captain Phlatanelas, the commander of the Imperial transport. " He was almost apoplectic with rage! I don't think the Admiral will be worrying too much about filling his shoes, it's his turban that he might find hard to fill!"

They all laughed, enjoying what they knew might well be their last victory celebration before the final battle.

Constantine laughed along with the others, but in the back of his mind he suspected that the humiliation that had been inflicted on Sultan Mehmed today could well come back to bite them all tomorrow. The bombardment of the land walls had not ceased and the walls of his city were slowly crumbling to dust around him.

32. Constantinople - 22nd April 1453

Two days after their celebration of the arrival of the relief ships, Constantine and Giovanni Guitanaili were supervising repairs to a section of the land wall when Megas Doux Notaras approached them.

His face was ashen. "Your Majesty," he said' "I am not sure that I believe it , though I have seen it with my own eyes. The Turks have sailed across land to the Golden Horn!"

Constantine would have laughed had his Grand Duke not looked so completely shaken. "What do you mean, Notaras? How can he have sailed into the Golden Horn? Is the chain still in place?"

Notaras nodded. "As we stand here his fleet is sailing down the hill, past Pera, into the inlet. I counted thirty ships and still they come!"

The three men, Constantine in the lead headed around the wall above the Imperial Palace and made their way to where they could get a good view.

"Good God!" said Constantine coming to a halt. It took him a moment to understand what he was actually seeing. There, stretched out in the Golden Horn was a fleet of Turkish ships! There were triremes, biremes and the heavier cargo hauling parandaria. Down the hill, on the opposite shore, sailing past the walls of Pera, where even more ships, their oars moving in time and their sails flapping in the light breeze blowing from the South.

Giovani was the first to speak. "Look, they have the boats on carriages!"

Sure enough, now that Constantine was over the initial shock, he could see that the boats were being led on wheeled carriages down the hill and into the water.

The Ventian Bailo, Girolamo Minotto, and three men Constantine recognised as Captains of Venetian ships, hurried to where Constantine was standing. "Your Majesty. You have seen this disaster?" said Moinotto.

Constantine nodded, still unable to believe his eyes. "How did they think to do this?" he asked no-one in particular. "Who can imagine such a preposterous scheme as to sail boats over land?"

Giovani said with a glance at Minotto, "I understand that the Venetians did something similar a few years ago, taking ships across land to Lake Garda in their fight with the Lombards! Didn't the mercenary Gattamelata rely on a similar trick in besting the Visconti?"

"Yes, that is true," said Minotto. "Perhaps that is where the Sultan got the idea. But that was over flat land, an impressive but not impossible task. This! This is ..." Minotto couldn't find a word to fit.

"A disaster." said Giovanni. "We must do something immediately, before they can begin to bombard these walls as well. They are already setting up additional gun emplacements in the Valley of the Springs. If we lose control of the Golden Horn then we are lost! Do you think we could convince the Geonese in Pera to attack the fleet?"

Constantine's hand went instinctively to the reliquary hanging around his neck. He shook his head. "The Genoese of Pera have shown a decided reluctance to do anything that might compromise their neutrality," he said that last word in such a way as to leave little doubt among those listening how he felt about the actions of the citizens of the small town, despite the clandestine assistance that they had provided since the beginning of the siege.

"We could land a small force of men on the other shore, take their gun emplacements and then use their guns to bombard their own fleet," said Giovanni.

"We do not have the men!" said Loukas Nortoras in a disapproving and dismissive tone. His resentment of the dashing and energetic Giovanni was obvious. "We could not risk the few men we have on such a foolhardy excursion!"

Giacomo Coco, the captain of a galley from the Black Sea port of Trebizond, coughed. Constantine turned to look at him. Coco took this as an opportunity to speak. "With your indulgence your majesty, I have a thought which may be worth considering." Constantine nodded for him to continue. "I would be happy to lead an assault against the Turkish fleet. I believe that an attack, under the cover of darkness, using some large ships for cover and a couple of small galleys armed with firebrands could do much damage. We could easily sneak throughout the fleet cutting their anchor chains and setting light to them. They would not be able to escape!"

"You would be prepared to lead such an attack?" asked Constantine.

"I would my lord, if you could give me say, two large transports for cover and two small fustae for the attack itself."

Minotto, who had been listening carefully, looked at Constantine. "We would be happy to provide the ships your Majesty. Secrecy would of course be vital. Should word of this attack leak out there would be no chance of success. I suggest that we keep the knowledge of this attack restricted to a very small group."

Constantine looked first at Giovanni and then at Notaras. They both nodded their agreement. Notaras somewhat reluctantly, it seemed to Constantine.

"So be it!" he said and gave Coco leave to begin to make the preparations while he and Giovanni went back to the never-ending task of supervising the repair of the land wall. Loukas Notaras started giving orders to have additional men from his reserves deployed along the sea walls in case the Sultan decided to open another front along this side of the City.

****

Coco immediately set to work. Two large transport galleys were brought close to shore and bales of wool and cotton attached to their sides to reduce the impact of cannon fire. Much to Coco's growing frustration, it took three days to make the ships ready.

Coco was sitting with his men, talking through the strategy for the attack that night, when the Emperor himself appeared on the dock. Coco jumped up and hurried to him.

He politely greeted Constantine and the other noble gentlemen that stood around him. "I am grateful that you have come to wish us well in our venture your majesty," he said bowing his head.

"'I wish that I were, Captain," said Constantine, his voice sounding strained. "It seems that the Genoese of Pera have caught wind of our little venture and have insisted that they be involved. They have offered us one of their ships."

"That is good news, your Majesty. It matters not to us whose ships we use," said Coco, unsure of why the Emperor would see this as a problem.

"Their ship will not, unfortunately be ready for another few days, Captain. It has been agreed to hold off until it is ready!" said Constantine.

Coco could feel his anger rising. He looked at the Emperor, ready to lash out but stopped. He could see that the Emperor was as frustrated and angry as he was, and more than that, the Emperor looked completely exhausted. Dark rings surrounded his eyes. This was not the time to argue with a man who was giving his all to save his city. Coco realised that Constantine knew better than he did the risks of a further delay, but clearly there was more at stake here than just the timing of his assault. He bowed his head and, as respectfully as he could, agreed to wait.

****

Constantine watched the young Captain walk back to his men. He turned back towards the city before he had to witness their disappointment as well as his. Pera was riddled with people who were sympathetic to the Sultan, or actively on his payroll. He had argued long and hard with the Genoese. They were angry that they had been excluded from the plan and argued that the Venetians were trying to take all the glory for themselves. In the end the only way that Constantine could ensure the assault would happen, without being undermined, was to agree to the inclusion of the Genoese ship and the subsequent delay.

Everything was becoming overly complicated. He was continually trying to balance the politics of the relationships between the various factions in the city, especially the Venetians and the Genoese. He sighed. He was having to think of the needs of the people of the city, most of whom were terrified of what would happen if the Turks entered the city. He had to concern himself with the practical day-to-day needs of the defence of the city as well as trying to plan how they might all come out of this situation alive. As well as all those issues he had the intrigues within his own court to keep an eye on. He had suspicions that the Megas Doux Notaras was being less than open with him. He knew that he had, long ago, sent his wealth out of the city to Venice. Surprisingly, he thought to himself, other than George Sphrantzes, the only other person he trusted whole-heartedly was young Giovanni. His leadership, wisdom and unflagging energy repairing the walls had been a godsend. Without him the City may well have fallen already.

He reached for the reliquary and wished, not for the first time, that it really did have the power to show him how to save his city and its people.

33. The Golden Horn - 28th April 1453

Giacomo Coco stood just outside the sea wall of Pera looking at the waters of the Golden Horn. In the early morning darkness he could barely make out the two large transports, the bales of wool and cotton lashed to their sides, resting at anchor out in the walled harbour. He was eager to get his mission underway and was impatiently waiting for the commanders of the other vessels to appear.

He heard the creaking of the postern gate and looked around. A man appeared out of the gloom. He was alone. "I have come to wish you good luck, Captain Coco," said the Emperor.

Surprised Coco went down on one knee. "Your majesty, forgive me. I did not realise it was you!"

"Stand up," said Constantine in a gentle voice. "At this time of the morning, when we are alone and when you are about to risk your life for my City, I think that we can forego the formalities."

"Thank-you, Your Majesty," he said standing up. "I am honoured that you would think to come and wish us luck."

"I find it hard to sleep these days, Captain!" he said in a subdued tone. "So many people are doing so many brave things on my behalf. The least I can do is be there to thank them."

The gate creaked again. Other men started to arrive and move quietly to where Coco and Constantine where standing. Coco watched as the Emperor shook hands with each man as he arrived. He had never seen anything like this before in his life. Most of the men did not know how to respond, but stood there dumbfounded. All the while the Emperor walked among them shaking their hands, thanking them for what they were about to do.

An hour later, with dawn still two hours away, the two big transporters ghosted silently out from beneath the protective walls of Pera into the waters of the Golden Horn. Two galleys followed them. Coco led a group of three fast fustae, narrow, lightweight, shallow drafted galleys. Each fustae was manned by seventy two oarsmen, as compared to only forty on the larger, more ponderous Venetian galleys that were ahead of them.

Coco looked back along the line of his fustae. A small boat carrying the flammable materials bobbed obediently behind each one. As his eyes swept the boats behind him he saw a flash of light from one of the towers of Pera. He wondered for a moment whether they had been betrayed, or whether it was just someone unable to sleep lighting an oil lamp to keep themselves company in the cold hours before dawn. He turned back to look in the direction of the Turkish fleet. He saw no answering light. All seemed quiet as the boats glided down the still waters of the estuary.

The big transport ships moved too slowly for Coco. He turned to his men and indicated that they should pick up the pace. He felt the boat surge forward. He grinned to himself as he imagined the looks on the faces of the Venetian and Genoese Captains of the larger, slower galleys as his nimble craft sped past. They could play politics all they wanted. He was a simple fighting man. Now was the time for action!

Coco's fustae sped through the gap between the two big transports and out into the clear water beyond. Before him, in the light of the waning moon, he could see a multitude of Turkish ships riding at anchor.

He looked over his shoulder. His fustae was moving fast through the water now. They had left the other ships well behind. He grinned at his men who where as eager as he was to put their plan into action. Coco turned back towards the Turkish fleet and saw, out of the corner of his eye another flash of light from the Pera shore. A moment later he heard the sound of a cannon, and a moment after that the splash as a cannon ball landed in the water near him.

"The bastards have betrayed us!" he yelled. At that moment a cannon ball struck his fustae amidships. The last thing that Coco felt was a shard of splintered wood pierce his body and the cold water of the Golden Horn swallow him.

****

Constantine had watched the whole disaster unfold from the top of the sea wall. He had seen the first flash of cannon fire and the eruption of flares. They had been betrayed. Someone in Pera had warned the Sultan. The fight had still gone on for nearly two hours. Now he sat, alone, in the audience chamber of the Blachernae Palace waiting for the Venetian Bailo, Girolamo Minotto to join him.

He didn't have to wait for long. The Bailo, along with the commander of the Venetian gallies, Gabriele Trevisano, were led into the chamber.

Trevisano looked angry as he and the Bailo seated themselves at the Emperor's invitation.

The Bailo described the battle, the impetuous actions of young Giacomo Coco the loss of one of Trevisano's galleys and the counter attack by the Turkish fleet that the raiding party had only barely been able to fend off.

"We were betrayed by the Genoese Your Majesty!" Trevisano blurted out, unable to control his anger any longer.

The Emperor nodded.

"We lost a lot of good men and ships because of those traitorous dogs!" Trevisano continued, his voice hoarse with emotion. The Bailo put his hand on Trevisano's arm to quieten him. The Emperor shook his head. The Bailo removed his hand. "We have lost about fifty of our best men, God save their souls, and forty more are now in the hands of the Sultan." he continued. He paused his eyes looking first at the Bailo and then at the Emperor and said. "We will have to ransom them!" Minotto and Constantine both nodded in agreement.

"Yes, we will. Fortunately, we have many more than forty Turks in our prisons. I am sure we can come to an agreement with the Sultan to get our men back. You go and get some rest Trevisano," he said kindly, dismissing both the Bailo and the Captain. As they walked towards the door the Emperor asked, "And what of the fate of the impetuous young Coco, did he make it back?"

Trevisano looked back at the Emperor and shook his head. Constantine's hand went to the reliquary around his neck and closed his eyes and prayed for the men they had lost. He felt totally bereft.

****

Needing distraction from the disaster, unable to sleep and dogged by a black mood, Constantine threw himself back into the job of organising the defence of the city with redoubled energy. He was discussing with Giovanni how it seemed that the earth and rubble repairs to the walls were fairing far better than those made of wood or stone as they resisted the pounding of the stone cannonballs more easily, when a soldier ran up. "Your Majesty, there is movement on the Pera shore. Megas Doux Notaras has sent me to ask that you come as soon as you can," he said bowing his head.

The Grand Duke nodded as Constantine and Giovanni walked up to where he was watching the activity on the opposite shore. At first they were not sure what was happening. It appeared that the men who had ended up on the Pera shore earlier in the day, after the disastrous attack on the Sultan's fleet, were being paraded in front of them. As they watched a pile of wooden poles was brought to the shore. The men were stripped naked.

Further up the bank, seated on his white horse, and surrounded by a corps of Janissaries, the Sultan watched unmoving.

The crowd on the sea wall watched in growing horror as they realised what was about to happen. The men were forced to their knees. Ropes were tied around their ankles and their legs were pulled apart, forcing them to lie flat on their stomachs. The sharpened poles were then placed on the ground between their legs. Many of the men were screaming in terror at what they knew was about to happen. Soldiers, carrying large sledgehammers positioned themselves at the other end of the poles.

The sultan nodded and the soldiers lifted their hammers on to their shoulders. He nodded again and as one, the soldiers hit the end of the poles, ramming them into the men's groins. At each blow of the hammers screams rent the air. Women, standing on the sea wall watching, fainted. Men fell to their knees and vomited.

The soldiers did not stop until the poles had punched their way out of the men's backs. Soldiers then lifted the staked bodies up and placed the poles, none too gently into holes that had been dug along the shore.

The screams of the men carried clearly across the water. They begged for their lives. They called out to God! They called out to their families! Some just screamed in agony. The luckiest were already dead.

The Emperor turned to Notaras. "Bring me the Turkish prisoners," he ordered in a chillingly calm voice.

Notaras looked at him. He had never seen a look of such anger and hatred on Constantine's face. Seeing the rage and the pain in his eyes, he asked "How many my Lord?"

"All of them Notaras. Bring me them all!" he said in a voice made more frightening by its quiet determination.

Constantine forced himself to continue to watch. Eventually he was distracted by the arrival of the Turkish prisoners. Two hundred and sixty men were lined up on top of the sea wall. Constantine ordered that they be made to stand at the edge of the parapet. Behind each prisoner stood a defender of the City. Each held in his hand his sword. Each had watched, along with their Emperor, the appalling scene on the opposite shore.

Constantine could see that the Sultan had seen the prisoners now arrayed along the wall. He had moved his horse closer to the water's edge. He was obviously agitated. Constantine nodded. Without hesitating each soldier sliced through the neck of his prisoner, letting his body fall forward, over the wall. A red stain started to spill out into the Golden Horn.

Constantine still stood on the sea wall as night fell. The screaming of the impaled men had finally stopped and the citizens of Constantinople, shaken by what they had seen, had gone home. His hand gripped the reliquary that hung around his neck so tightly that it had cut his hand. Blood ran down his wrist and dripped onto the stones of the sea wall.

34. Constantinople- 29th May 1453

The service for Matins ended. Constantine knelt in prayer, the chanting of the Doxastikon still echoing around the beautiful church of Saint Sophia. As he lifted his head he could see the golden glow of sunrise start to filter into the great dome above him. The light seemed to Constantine to be made almost solid as it caught the rising smoke from the beautiful golden incense burners. The dome floated above him.

An overwhelming wave of sadness washed over him. He wondered if this would be the last day. He rose stiffly to his feet and led a small procession out of the Church, saddened too by the small numbers of worshippers who now attended services. In hindsight none of it had been worth it, he thought. His brother's attempts to placate the Pope of the Latin Church by agreeing to the union of the churches had not brought any significant help from the west. All that it had done was to cause division and dissension among his own people at a time when they most needed to support one another.

Disconsolately he mounted his Arabian stallion and, with George Sphrantez and a few others, he set out in the early morning light on their daily ritual of checking the walls. They were soon joined by Gionvanni Gustianni, and the Megas Doux Loukas Notaras.

Reaching the Roman Gate, Constantine dismounted and walked up to the top of the inner wall. He stood for some time looking at the camps of the Turks, stretching out in a huge crescent before the walls of his City.

Over the last few weeks they had all become accustomed to the noise of their enemy, the booming of their cannon, the incessant beating of their drums and the blowing of fifes and trumpets as they worked night and day pouring ever more debris into the foss. The light of their fires had been so bright at times he had thought that the Turkish camp was on fire.

This morning was different. This morning the world was ominously silent. The fires had all burnt out and smoke now lay heavily all around the Sultan's encampment. Not even a breath of wind disturbed the eerie silence.

For a long time Constantine stood looking out at the Turkish camp. "The day has come," he said finally. "The Turks are preparing themselves for the final battle. We stand on the eve of Armageddon!"

****

While the others continued to stare out at the Turkish Camp, Giovanni turned and looked into the face of the Emperor. In the last few weeks he had, almost unconsciously, begun to think of him as "his" Emperor. He admired this man more than any other he had ever met. He was inspired by his bravery and by his dogged determination to do his duty in the face of insurmountable odds. He marveled at his compassion for the people he served. Now, watching Constantine as he looked out on the overwhelming forces that assailed him, Giovanni saw a tear roll down the Emperors cheek. He was nearly overcome with pity. He turned away wishing that he had known this man in better times.

****

Constantine eventually turned away from the Turkish Camp and back towards his City. "We have much to do," he said as he turned and started walking back along the battlement.

Loukas Notaras, not moving said "I am told that the servants of the altar have seen unmistakable signs that it is God's will that the city must fall." Constantine stopped to look at him. Loukas continued. "While it might be His divine will that the City falls, your Majesty, it doesn't mean the Empire should fall! While we must all bow to the decree of the Almighty, we should hope that his mercy will return to our people as it returned to Israel in olden times!" He paused, and then looked into Constantine's eyes. "If the Imperial City cannot be saved, let the Emperor be saved, for it is in his person that are centred all the hopes of his people!"

"Your Majesty," said Constantine's cousin, Theophilus, stepping forward "The Megas Doux is right. There is still time for you to save yourself. The Empire will not end with the fall of a city, but with the death of the Emperor! If you escape now you can seek help from the West. Given more time I am sure that you could gather support to re-take the City, just as your ancestors did."

Giovanni listened to both men and nodded his agreement. "Take my ship, your Majesty. Go to Chios, my family would be honoured to provide you with sanctuary for as long as you need it!"

Constantine looked around at the men who had now drawn in close around him. They were all nodding, encouraging him to leave the City.

Constantine smiled. He put his hand to the reliquary hanging around his neck, a gesture they had all seen him do many times. "My friends," he said. "if it is God's will that our city falls, then we must accept His judgement. How many Emperors, great and glorious before me, have had to suffer and to die for their people and their Empires? I would do no less. I will not flee from my duty. I will stay and, if it is God's will, die here, but I will die knowing that I have done everything I can to protect this city and its people who have put their faith in me. I can not ask less of myself than I do of all of you!" Constantine turned and headed down the steps back to the City.

****

As the day wore on it was clear that the Sultan was preparing for the final assault. The eerie quiet of the Turkish camp had now fallen over the City.

Late in the afternoon the Emperor stood before a gathering of the people of Constantinople. All around him were anxious faces. He looked at them and was shocked by how few people there were left in the City.

"My nobles, my brothers, my sons, my people," said Constantine in a strong, resolute voice. Then, his eyes fell on the faces of the terrified women and children. In a no less strong, but more compassionate tone, he continued "My most loyal and honest citizens." He paused. He knew that those close to him could see he was struggling to control his emotions. He took an intake of breath. "The hour of our final battle is approaching. We stand here, together, our resolve firmer than ever. The fate and the eternal reputation of Christendom is in our hands."

"After fifty two days of siege, I pass to you, who have always fought with glory against the enemies of Christ, the defence of this the most glorious and noble of cities, Our Mother and our protector.

"Do not be afraid. The walls that protect us may have been worn down by the enemy's battering, but our true strength lies in the protection of our God."

"Fight like the brave souls that you are, as you have done from the beginning up to this day, against the enemy of our faith."

"Men of Genoa," he said turning towards Giovanni who was standing together with his men, "you are renowned for your courage and your victories over the Turk. You have fought many battles to protect this great City. We can ask no more of you than to do as you have done before and give your strength to our city."

"Men of Venice!" he said, turning toward the Baillo and his son who also stood surrounded by their countrymen. "You have shown your spirit times without number! Your swords have shed Turkish blood and your fleets have sent so many Turkish vessels to the bottom of our sea that the number is lost!! You have adorned this city, as if it were your own, with fine and noble men. Now, let your lofty spirits be exalted in preparation for the contest to come!"

"Men of my Empire," he said, letting his eyes sweep over the silent crowd and letting them fall on George Sphrantzes, Loukas Natoras and his own men, "I can only thank-you for your loyalty and obedience! It has been an honour to fight beside you in the past and it will be a greater honour still to do so in defence of our home."

He let his eyes sweep over the crowd once again. "The infidel will strike the walls. They will strike our breastplates and our shields. They will assault our ears with the sounds of their trumpets, but we will not be intimidated like the Romans of old who ran terrified from the the fearsome sight and sound of elephants!"

"In this battle we will stand firm . We will have no fear! We will have no thought of flight! With each blow against us we will be inspired to resist with ever more Herculean strength! Animals may run away from animals, but we are men, men of stout heart, men of noble spirit, men of courage! We will hold at bay these dumb brutes!"

"With thrusting spears and swords we will let them know that they are fighting not against their own kind but against the masters of brutes!"

Constantine's voice rose. "This impious infidel has disturbed the peace!" he shouted. A few in the crowd shouted back their agreement. "This wretched Sultan has violated the oath and the treaty that he made with us!" More people in the crowd shouted their agreement. "He has slaughtered our farmers at harvest time! " the crowd, shouted back, defiant. "He has held us to ransom with his stone fortresses!" The crowd shouted their disapproval. "He has encircled Galata under a pretence of peace!" Angry shouts came from the crowd.

"Now he threatens to capture the city of Constantine the Great, our fatherland! The place of sanctuary for all Christians! The guardian City of all Greeks! He plans to profane its holy shrines by turning them into stables for his horses and camels!"

The crowd was restless now, the pent up emotions of the last fifty days spilling over. Constantine raised his hands. The crowd quieted. "My lords, my brothers, my children, the everlasting honour of Christianity is in your hands!"

"My comrades in arms, my countrymen, obey the commands of your leaders in the knowledge that this is the day of our glory! This is the day that, if you shed but a single drop of blood, you will win for yourselves crowns of martyrdom and eternal fame. Be ready tomorrow to show your mettle. With God's help we will be victorious!"

The crowd shouted and cheered for their Emperor. Constantine the Eleventh stood proudly before his people, ready to face, with them, the end of the world.

****

The tree-lined streets were deserted as Constantine rode back towards his Palace. Darkness had finally begun to fall over the city as the day ended. He stopped to take one last look at the great church of Saint Sophia. He was surprised to see a red light suddenly appear at the base of the great cupola. The light wavered and then crept slowly up and around the great dome. The light reached the golden cross that towered above it, where it lingered for a few moments. Then the ruddy glow grew pale and paler, trembled for a few moments and then faded away as the sun sank below the horizon.

It was, he thought, as though the sun, lingering awhile in the west, had looked back from behind the dark curtain of night to glance, with one last loving look, on the most glorious Christian temple the world had ever seen. Constantine shivered. With a gentle tap of his heel, he urged his horse forward, up the hill towards his palace.

****

The battle had raged all day. Constantine, his face streaked with blood and dust, looked down at Giovanni's face. His skin had turned grey and his eyes were tightly closed as a wave of pain wracked his body. His breastplate had been removed and blood now soaked the heavy woollen vest he wore under his armour. The blood had started to stain the stones where he was lying. Constantine laid his hand on the man's shoulder. "Thank you Giovanni. Without you we would have not kept the Turks from the City for so long. You have been my inspiration, my dear friend!" Constantine started to get stiffly to his feet when he felt Giovanni's hand grasp his arm. He knelt down again next to him. Giovanni, looked up at the Emperor. "My Lord, it has been an honour to serve by your side. I would never have imagined that I would find, in these times where men think more of money than honour and more of self than others, a man as noble as you. If I could stand, my Emperor, I would fight on, if for no other reason than to honour you."

Constantine looked down at Giustiniani's ashen face and smiled. "No-one could have asked any more of you than you have given. You have achieved the impossible! It is up to us now! Be well, my friend!" Constantine turned to Giustiniani's men and, knowing how well they loved their commander and what effect this brave warrior's departure would have on them ordered them to take him down to his ship.

Finally, turning to face the tower above the Kerkoporta, Constantine saw for himself the flag of the Turks flapping in the breeze where only minutes before the Imperial double headed Eagle had been flying. He mounted his horse. He paused for a moment, his hand going to the reliquary around his neck. His eyes closed in a silent prayer, then, with a new resolve he shouted to those around him, "Whoever wishes to escape, let him save himself if he can! Whoever is ready to face death, let him follow me!" Sword drawn, without looking back to see if anyone was following, Constantine spurred his horse into action, heading back toward the Lycus Valley, his men close behind him.

The rumour that Giustiniani had been carried from the field had spread along the wall and disheartened the men protecting the gate. Constantine dismounted from his horse. Around him lay Greeks, Italians and Turks dead or dying. The carnage and the noise was appalling. The Greeks and the Italians were trying to get back through the gate to safety. The Turks pressed hard behind them.

Constantine glanced at his companions. His cousin, Theo, put his hand on the Emperor's arm. "My Lord there is still time to get to the safety of the harbour. You should go with Giustiniani!"

Constantine threw off the imperial insignia and his cloak and shook his head. "If the City falls, Theo, then I fall with it!" In a louder voice he shouted, "Whoever is ready to face death, follow me!"

Theophilus ran forward, sword raised, a wild look in his eyes, shouting, "I would rather die than live!" and plunged into the melee that filled a breech in the wall. Constantine followed him, sword held high.

A wave of Janissaries fell on the defenders. For a few minutes, with their Emperor leading them, the defenders forced the Janissaires back. Constantine felt invigorated, renewed by the freedom of his anonymity and the knowledge that this was, finally, the time of reckoning! Out of the corner of his eye he saw Theo fall to the blade of a snarling Janissary. With a mighty two handed swing of his sword Constantine took pleasure in relieving the Janissary of his head. Before he had a chance to raise his sword again, two Turks knocked him from his feet, pushing him backward over the bodies that now littered the ground. The same bodies that had tripped Constantine also impeded his attackers, both of whom stumbled in their efforts to reach him. Constantine lifted the body that he had fallen on and pushed it towards his attackers, using it as a shield. With a direct thrust he stabbed his sword into the stomach of one of his attackers while pushing his improvised shield into the other.

He put his foot on the chest of the writhing body and withdrew his gore-smeared sword. He turned just as a huge Turk smashed his sword hilt into Constantine's' face. The blow rocked him and his half raised sword fell to the ground. A second blow to the side of the head knocked him senseless. He fell to the ground, his body immediately covered by the blood and bodies of the last of the defenders. The Janissaries surged through the crumbling walls into the city, trampling him beneath their feet.

Unheard by the man who had been Emperor a cry went up in the streets beyond the wall that the City was lost. Women and children screamed in terror as the gates of the city burst open and the Turkish conquers swept into the city.

Book 3

1. Amalfi - Present day

"So, did Constantine survive or not?" asked Elizabeth.

"There are certainly a number of accounts from those that were in Constantinople at the time that suggest that the severed head of the Emperor was paraded around the city on a pike." replied Dragas.

"There was a gentleman by the name of Ubertino Pusculo from Brescia, in Italy, who was studying in the city. He was taken prisoner after the walls fell. A Florentine merchant eventually agreed to pay his ransom and Ubertino, much relieved, started on his way back to Italy. Unfortunately pirates captured him on his way home. Poor old Ubertino did, eventually, get back to Rome where he wrote a poem about the fall of Constantinople. In it he declares that the Emperor's head was severed from its body by a Janissary and then taken to the Sultan."

"Another story, from a Venetian writing in the year following the siege said that three heads were taken to the Sultan. One was the Emperors, one was a Turkish man who had fought alongside the defenders of the city and the third was that of Cardinal Isidore, the papal legate. Now we know this can't be true because we know that Isidore escaped."

"Most of the accounts at the time suggest that the Emperor's body was found and beheaded and the Sultan consolidated his victory by having the head paraded about."

"On the other hand," said Dragas, a smile coming to his lips, "Nicolo Barbaro, a Venetian who escaped from the city after the siege, wrote in his diary that no one knew whether the emperor was alive or dead. There were a number of people who reported that Constantine escaped. One was a Greek Bishop called Samuel who was also captured by the Turks, had his ransom paid then fled to Transylvania. Then there was an Armenian poet named Abraham. Both these gentlemen stated that Constantine, and some others, escaped in a boat."

"Would that have even been possible?" asked Dan.

"Oh yes!" said Dragas. "A number of people in ships escaped from the Golden Horn once the sack of the city had begun. The invaders were so intent on getting their part of the spoils that they didn't really care to either secure the harbour or chase down any escapees."

"It is quite plausible that Constantine escaped on a ship. If he did, though, there is no record of him turning up in Mystras or anywhere else for that matter. If he was alive he stayed out of sight for the rest of his life," said Dragas. He then paused. "Well, that is not quite true. There is, of course, the legend of the Marble Emperor to consider."

"That sounds mysterious. What is the legend of the Marble Emperor?" asked Elizabeth.

"Soon after the Turks took over the City a rumour started that Constantine, as he was about to be slain by the Turks, was taken up by an angel, his body turned into marble and placed in a cavern, beneath the Golden Gate, the ceremonial entrance to the City. The legend says that the Marble Emperor will awaken, take up the sword he had in battle, and drive the Turks from the City, reclaiming it for Christendom."

"Ah, but there are lots of legends like that one," said Dan. "From memory Merlin in the Arthurian legend was imprisoned in an oak tree, and King Arthur himself was taken back to Avalon, so he could return when the English are in dire need."

"Yes," agreed Dragas. "There are a lot of legends that make reference to a sleeping King. Interestingly enough, the Turks were so superstitious that it was they who walled up the Golden Gate, just in case the legend were true. It is still walled up to this day."

"So Constantine doesn't have a tomb, there is no grave for him?" asked Elizabeth.

"No, nothing. There is a statue of him in Athens, but no grave for him, or most of the other Emperors for that matter. When the Latin's invaded the city in 1204 the imperial tombs were all plundered for their gold and jewels. When the Ottomans took the city, it is said that a group of fanatical Dervishes broke into the Church of the Holy Apostles, where many of the Emperors had been buried, and over fourteen hours they smashed the sarcophagi and other relics to pieces with iron bars. What remained inside them was apparently thrown into a lime kiln."

Dan wondered at the bitterness in Dragas's voice as he said this. Noticing the time, he looked quickly at Elizabeth who, from her expression, would be happy to call an end to the evening.

"That was a wonderful meal, and a most fascinating history lesson," said Dan. "But it is getting late and I think that Elizabeth and I should be going."

Dragas nodded politely, bowing his head in acknowledgement of the compliment. "I fear I may have spoken for too long. I am sorry, I tend to get carried away if no one stops me. I am passionate about many things, but the late Roman Empire is perhaps my greatest passion."

"Would you like me to have a car take you to your hotel?" Dragas asked politely.

"Dan smiled. "That is very kind of you, but it is such a beautiful night I think we might walk," he said. Elizabeth nodded in agreement.

2. Amalfi - Present day

Elizabeth and Dan walked slowly up the road that led to the Hotel, hand in hand. Martinus was walking up the same path some distance behind. There was no sign of Sabastiano.

"What did you think of our host?" asked Dan.

"Knowledgeable. Erudite. Very intelligent. Handsome, in a sleazy Hollywood kind of way. Clearly very wealthy. Wouldn't trust him as far as I could spit a rat!" said Elizabeth.

"I would like to know more about him. Do you think he has the vial?" asked Dan.

"No doubt about it at all!" said Elizabeth. "The problem would be proving it!"

"I wonder what his motivation is for all this. I might ring Thomas Malm tomorrow and have a talk with him. He must know who Dragas is. What do you think?"

"Oh, my God!" said Elizabeth, stopping dead and covering her mouth with her hands. "I haven't told Thomas we are safe. Oh God, he has probably got half the British army out searching for us all by now! I will ring him as soon as we get back to our room. It's late, but, at the very least, I can leave him a message.

They walked quickly the last kilometre up the hill to the hotel and were both breathing heavily when they went past reception on the way to the elevator that would take them up to the hotel proper.

"Did you see the look the guy on reception gave us as we walked passed? God knows what they think we are up to," said Dan as they stepped into their room.

"Two old codgers all worked up for a dalliance, I except!" said Elizabeth with a laugh.

"Enough of the old, thank you very much." replied Dan grabbing her by the arm and swinging her into his arms and giving her a passionate kiss.

"He would have been right then!" Elizabeth said when their embrace finally ended.

"You will just have to wait and see," said Dan opening up the minibar and taking out a couple of bottles of cold water. "Frizzante or flat?"

"Oh frizzante - the more frizz the better. Ah, I have Thomas's number here somewhere," she said, searching through her online address book.

Dan put the bottle of water down next to Elizabeth and went out onto the verandah. He picked up Alberto's binoculars that had been left on the table and focused them on Dragas's yacht. There were people moving about on the aft deck, moving in and out of the light. Dan took a closer look. There was something familiar about one of the people. He sat down, resting the binoculars on the veranda rail to steady them. He could hear the tick tick of Elizabeth's smart phone as she dialed Thomas's number. In the quiet of the evening he could hear it ringing. He watched as the man standing on Dragas yacht pulled a mobile out of his pocket and put it up to his ear. He could hear, across the room from where Liz was holding her own phone to her ear, the voice of Thomas Malm answering his phone.

Dan ran inside, madly indicating, by slicing his finger across his throat, that she should cut the call. "I think Thomas is on Dragas yacht!" he said in a frantic whisper.

"What is going on?" she asked, as soon as she had terminated the call.

"Shit! Sorry!" said Dan. "I didn't mean you to hang up. But hang on let me see if the guy on the boat is still on his phone. Elizabeth followed him out to the verandah. Through the binoculars Dan could see the man on the back of the boat looking at his phone and tapping at the screen.

"Quick, ring him back. Pretend that your call just dropped out. Don't tell him anything except that we are OK! Tell him we will meet him as soon as we can either in Amalfi or Rome!" said Dan.

Elizabeth tapped re-dial. Down on the yacht the man once again lifted his phone to his ear.

"Thomas! It's Elizabeth Garvey! Thank God I've got you! I am so sorry. Dan and Charlotte and I are all safe. I meant to ring you yesterday but to be honest it totally slipped my mind!"

"Are you Okay?" asked Thomas in his cultivated, unflappable way. "What happened? The last thing I knew you were in my car. When we came out of the building we found Henry dead and you gone. There was blood all over the pavement! We have half the Italian police force out looking for you!"

"We were kidnapped, but Dan and..." Dan touched her arm to get her attention. He shook his head. "Lets not tell him about Alberto eh?" he said in an urgent whisper.

They could hear Thomas saying "Hello, Hello, Elizabeth? Are you still there?"

"Sorry Thomas. This phone is acting up I'm afraid. Where did I get to?" she asked.

"You were telling me about your escape," said Thomas.

"OK, yeah. Dan tracked us down and got us away from the kidnappers. We can give you a full report when we see you next. Are you still in Italy? We are in a hotel in Amalfi."

"Oh, lovely!' said Thomas. I am still in Naples. I can be in Amalfi first thing. How about we meet for breakfast? What hotel are you staying at?"

"We are at the Convento on the hill. How about we see you at nine for breakfast on the terrace. Would that be too early for you to get here from Naples?" asked Elizabeth.

"No, see you then. I am very glad that you and Daniel are safe. I will let the Italian authorities know. I look forward to hearing all about your adventures tomorrow morning. Good night, Elizabeth."

Elizabeth said goodnight and hung up the phone. Dan was still watching through the binoculars as the man on the Dragas yacht put his phone back in his pocket and looked up to where Dan was sitting before he stepped back into the yacht's saloon.

"Shit!" said Dan. "Bloody Thomas is in league with Dragas! I guess there is no question now that Dragas is behind all this."

Elizabeth shook her head.

"We need to understand who Dragas is and what his likely tie in is with Thomas. Is he acting alone, or on behalf of Her Majesty's Government? Thomas may not even be still working for MI6," said Dan, starting to feel nervous about their breakfast meeting in the morning.

"How about you start working on who Dragas is and I will see what I can find out about his business dealings. It is nearly midnight now. The guys in the office in Sydney should be just about back from lunch. I'll get them doing some background as well," said Dan reaching for his phone.

Dan, sat at the table on the veranda, and Elizabeth worked at the writing desk inside. They worked diligently on their assigned tasks, interrogating data bases, making calls and arranging access to information, until, two hours later, Dan walked through the door and threw himself on the bed.

"I think I have got all I am going to get today. The guys in business analysis have been working their butts off in Sydney and come up with some interesting stuff. Can you take a break or do you want to keep on going?" he asked Elizabeth.

"No, I am just about done here as well. I am not sure you are going to be impressed by what I have got though!" said Elizabeth looking at the notepad in her hand and shaking her head.

"Ok, how about I go first. Lets see who has found out the most amazing stuff!" Dan said with a laugh, sitting up on the edge of the bed.

"Dragas's name does not appear on any known shareholders register anywhere, in any country, nor does he hold any formal positions in any company about which we could access records. The yacht he is on is listed in the super-yacht registry but the owner is listed as unknown. It only lists a foundation registered in Liechtenstein. Not only that, but for a man of such obvious wealth, unless of course he is some sort of confidence trickster, he doesn't appear in the Dun and Bradstreet database or the Forbes data base of the worlds richest people or on any of the other lists we could access.

"Well who does?" said Elizabeth flippantly. Dan looked away, feeling his face go red. "No! Are you really on the Forbes list?" said Elizabeth in amazement.

"Only this year," said Dan, "and only because I bought a whole lot of Apple stock in 2001 when they were less than ten dollars. When we first floated the company I didn't know what to do with the money, and I certainly didn't need it, so I bought shares in company's I liked. Apple was one of them."

"I'm glad I learnt about this now, not a few days ago, otherwise you would have thought I was a gold digger!" she said laughing. "So he is

307

a man who has hidden his wealth behind shelf companies, trusts and foundations. Do you think he gets his money from illegal sources?"

"It is impossible to tell. I have asked the guys in Sydney to keep digging, but I don't hold out much hope," said Dan shutting his laptop.

"So you don't win the amazing game! How about this," said Elizabeth looking through her notes. "The most likely origin of the name Dragas is Serbia. Serbia still has the highest concentration of people with that surname."

"Um, that's a bit light weight. What else have you got?" asked Dan playfully.

"All right. How about Constantine the eleventh, the guy that Dragas spent most of the evening talking about, was the son of Manuel Palaiologos and Helena Dragas!" Dan raised an eyebrow. "And," continued Elizabeth, "Constantine Palaiologos added his mother's name to his own dynastic one when he ascended to the Imperial throne."

"Um, an interesting twist. I wonder if Dragas is our man's real name? Got anything else?"

"Nope!" said Elizabeth shutting her own laptop. "But I did send an email to Charlotte asking her to use her research skills to see if she could track down any sort of history on the Dragas family that might link to Andris Dragas."

"It does make you wonder though doesn't it, what really happened to poor old Constantine the eleventh," said Dan thoughtfully.

"Ummm," said Elizabeth, rolling across the bed and snuggling into Dan's arms, where she promptly fell asleep.

****

Dan came awake slowly. He was lying on his back and Elizabeth was sprawled on the bed beside him. They were both still fully dressed. It took a moment for Dan to realise what had woken him. His phone vibrated on the bedside table. A quick look at the screen showed him that someone had tried several times in the last ten minutes to contact him.

He got carefully off the bed and walked quietly out on to the terrace.

"Dottore Marsh? Dan? Is that you?" said an excited voice.

"Speaking." replied Dan. "Professor Pellegrini?"

"Si, Dan. I have wonderful news. We have found him!"

Dan still half asleep and not sure what the Professor was talking about asked, "Who Professor?"

"King Alaric. Dan. We have found the tomb of Alaric the Goth. It was in your trench. It is amazing! We have almost uncovered the tomb itself. You must come here as quickly as you can. You must be here for the opening of the tomb!"

"That is fantastic Professor," said Dan coming fully awake. "It's amazing. We are in Amalfi at the moment. It shouldn't take us more than three or four hours to get there. It will probably take us an hour to pack up, so we should see you about...," he looked at the time on his phone. It was seven thirty. "around lunch time. See you soon!"

Dan put the phone in his pocket. Before he had a chance to turn around two arms slipped around him and Elizabeth rested her head on his back. "What's going on?" she asked sleepily. "Anything exciting?"

Dan turned around, holding her arms around him. "They have found Alaric's Tomb!' he said triumphantly. "It was right where you and I were digging!"

Elizabeth came immediately awake. She stepped backwards so should could more easily focus on Dan's face. "No! You're kidding me!"

Dan shook his head, grinning! "The Professor wants us there as soon as possible."

"Have they opened it yet?" asked Elizabeth excitedly.

"No! They are waiting for us before they do! You grab a shower while I do some packing, and ring Charlotte and Alberto." he said, suddenly business like.

Elizabeth watched him for a moment wondering if she should suggest that it would be faster if they showered together, but, turning towards the bathroom with a smile, she knew it simply wasn't true.

Fifty minutes later they were driving along the Amalfi coast road towards Salerno. They had thanked Martinus and Sabastiano before they had left, but even without their bodyguards, they felt much safer now that they were driving away from Amalfi.

Three and a quarter-hours later they were parking their Fiat next to the River Busento in Cosenza.

****

At nine o'clock, when he arrived for their breakfast meeting, Thomas Malm was surprised to find that Daniel and Elizabeth had checked out. He had been given a hastly scribbled note from Dan, apologizing for not being able to keep their appointment. Its tone was formal and almost dismissive. It offered no clue as to why he and Elizabeth had left so suddenly. He stood for a moment, on the hotel's terrace, staring at the marina below him. Dragas' yacht was clearly visible. A flash of irritation crossed his face as he turned away from the view.

3. Calabria - Present day

The dig site in the riverbed looked totally different from the way they had last seen it only a few days before. A large marquee now covered the trench that they had been working in and a wire mesh fence had been erected around the entire site. Police, holding lethal looking machine guns, stood around the perimetre of the site, sometimes singularly, sometimes in groups. The crowd of spectators had grown and there was almost a carnival atmosphere along the banks of the river, with food and bric-a-brac stalls set up along the roadside.

Dan and Elizabeth made their way through the crowds and past a mass of reporters and television crews waiting at the gate of the newly built compound. They told the guards at the gate who they were and one of them strolled off to find the Professor.

Dan looked at a text message he had just received. It was from Thomas Malm. He showed Elizabeth and then ignored it. Ten minutes later the Professor rushed up looking agitated and cross.

He talked quickly, in Italian, to the guard who opened the gate for them. Once inside the Professor shook Dan's hand and kissed Elizabeth on each cheek.

"Welcome, welcome! I am so sorry that you were made to wait!" he said as he led them towards the tent opening.

"You must come and see. It is amazing! I have never been so excited in all my life!" he said.

They stepped into the tent and stopped. Dumbfounded. The trench that they had been digging in was now transformed. Half buried skeletons of people seemed to be everywhere. Dan did a quick count of those that he could see from the doorway. He got to forty-five before he gave up.

"Good god!" he said. "There must be a hundred bodies here!"

"Yes, Yes!" said the Professor, drawing them further into the tent. "We have counted over six hundred so far, in this and a couple of the other trenches. Clearly the legend is true. The Goths slaughtered the slaves in the riverbed! But come, come. There is something more important for you to see!"

It was then that they saw it. A huge, rough hewn block of stone.

"Is that the tomb?" asked Elizabeth.

"We think so," said the Professor. "As far as we can tell these poor devils, " he said indicating the skeletons, "were forced to dig out the rock of the river bed to make the tomb. We had to chip away a thick layer of opus caementicium to uncover the tomb itself. The covering is made of two large marble slabs. We are drilling a small hole between the slabs . We will then push an optic fibre probe in to see if there is anything inside."

They could now see a couple of men working on the stone slab. The sound of a drill working its way into the rock could be heard above the general hubbub in the tent.

"Come. We have set up a command centre over here!" The Professor led them to a bank of large screen monitors, all displaying a rotating image of the seal of the University of Pisa.

Elizabeth leant towards Dan and whispered into his ear, "Opus what-ya-ma-call-it?"

"Roman Cement" he said with a smile

One of the men working on the top of the tomb nodded to the Professor who turned and pressed a key on a keyboard in front of the monitors. The screens changed. As one of the technicians picked up, what looked to Dan, like an endoscope and pointed it at the other technicians face. The image on the screen moved around, finally resolving itself into the grinning face of the technician.

Other people started to gather around, watching the screen that had now gone completely black. Dan and Elizabeth watched as the thin cable was fed into the newly made hole in the top of the tomb.

The Professor tapped another key and the screen lightened. He nodded at the technicians who locked the endoscope in position and stepped away from the grave. He picked up a joystick and began slowly moving it around. The blurry image on the screen moved. He made a few more adjustments and a pattern came into sharp relief. Whatever they were looking at was black and seemed to have some sort of intricate pattern on it. In a voice overcome with emotion he said, "It's a sarcophagus, an incredibly ornate sarcophagus!Look! Look!"

The Professor studied the image for a few minutes. He moved the endoscope again. This time a blurry face flashed onto the screen. The Professor adjusted the controls and the face came into sharp focus. It was a face of such calm beauty that there was an audible intake of breath from the onlookers. A black crown rested on the figure's head. The Professor turned, grinning, to Dan and Elizabeth.

"We have found it! We have found the tomb of Alaric the Great!" Then, so that others could hear, he repeated in a louder voice. "We have found it. We have found Alaric's Tomb!"

A cheer went up from all those inside the tent. Someone at the back must have shouted to the crowd on the banks of the river, because an even louder cheer went up a few minutes later from the spectators outside.

Champagne seemed to appear from nowhere. Suddenly there was a party going on inside the tent. Everyone was congratulating the Professor, who couldn't stop grinning.

Eventually, still with a smile on his face he escaped the throng and came over to where Dan and Elizabeth had been enjoying watching the party.

"I would like to thank you so much, Dan, for supporting this dig. I guarantee that the next few days will be the most amazing of all our lives! Tonight they are bringing in the equipment and tomorrow we will lift the stone slab."

"What is the process after that?" asked Elizabeth.

"First, we will lift these slabs. Inside, as we have just seen, is the stone sarcophagus. Around the sarcophagus we hope will be all those treasures looted from Rome that were too big to put inside the sarcophagus, with the body. They will all have to be carefully excavated first. Inside the sarcophagus there will probably be a lead coffin. Inside that should be the body of Alaric."

"Was that Alaric's face that we saw?" asked Elizabeth.

"'I don't think so, my dear," said the Professor. "I suspect that what we saw was an image of Christ looted from one of the churches of Rome.

It may even have been one of the gifts that Constantine the Great gave to the Church in Rome. We are in for such an exciting time," he said rubbing his hands together with glee.

"Now, I took the liberty of having a booking made for you at the Hotel Centrale, just up the hill. I booked two rooms for you. I hope that is OK?" he said, with a raised eyebrow.

Dan and Elizabeth thanked him. They agreed to meet the Professor outside the Hotel foyer at eight the next morning. The Professor disappeared into the crowd and Elizabeth and Dan slipped out of the tent and made their way to their hotel, where they cancelled one of the rooms, much to the delight of the hotel receptionist who, given the excitement the dig had created, could have sold the room a hundred times over.

****

The Professor, Dan and Elizabeth arrived at the site soon after half past eight the next morning. There was a palpable sense of excitement in the air as Dan and Elizabeth found a good spot, out of the way, to observe the opening of the tomb.

The Professor seemed to be everywhere at once. He rushed from place to place to ensure that everything was ready for the great moment. The University had sold the media rights to an Italian news agency. They had four camera crews on site, all jostling for a good position. National Geographic, who had sponsored the dig along with Dan, had two camera crews setting up. The machinery they had brought in to lift the giant slabs was still being moved into position. The men who operated the lifting equipment were all shouting at one another and waving their arms about. To Dan and Elizabeth it looked like chaos, but as the minutes ticked past, under the guidance of the indefatigable Professor, a sense of order imposed itself. After an hour the shouting had died down, people stopped moving around and a sense of calm gradually descended on the dig site.

The Professor walked to a spot just in front of the stone slab and, putting his hand up to his mouth, coughed quietly. He nodded to the camera crews whose lenses where now focused directly on him.

"Ladies and Gentlemen," he began solemnly, "This is a momentous occasion. For millennia scholars and amateur treasure hunters alike have wondered if the story of the burial of Alaric the Visigoth were true.

"Our first hint of this unusual event can be found in a book written, probably in Constantinople, some one hundred and fifty years after Alaric's death. Jordanes' Getica is the earliest surviving history of the Gothic peoples. Jordanes was himself a Goth who, according to his own admission, once borrowed for three days a copy of a longer history of the Goths by the statesmen and writer Flavius Magnus Aurelius Cassiodorus Senator, who had been asked by Theodoric the Great, King of the Ostrogoths to write a history of his people.

"The words of Jordanes were simple and straightforward," he said, picking up a book from the top of the tomb and starting to read, "*Alaric was cast down by his reverse and, while deliberating what he should do, was suddenly overtaken by an untimely death and departed from human cares. His people mourned for him with the utmost affection. Then turning from its course the river Busentus near the city of Consentia—for this stream flows with its wholesome waters from the foot of a mountain near that city—they led a band of captives into the midst of its bed to dig out a place for his grave. In the depths of this pit they buried Alaric, together with many treasures, and then turned the waters back into their channel. And that none might ever know the place, they put to death all the diggers.*"

"From these few words, from a man who freely admitted that he could not recall the exact words he had read but believed he could remember the sense and the deeds that Cassiodorus related, we set about our search."

"A few days ago we started to uncover the bones of people. We then found a sealed tomb. Behind me is what could very well be the tomb of King Alaric, the King of the Visigoths."

"Alaric is most famous for the sack of Rome in the year 410, but that event should not define the life of this man." he said kneeling down and resting his hand on the the marble slab. "Alaric instead should be

315

remembered as a noble leader whose ambition was to find a homeland and security for his people. He neither set out, nor ever intended to conquer Rome. He had grown up in a Roman world and had adopted many Roman customs and values."

"If this is truly the tomb of King Alaric then it may well be one of the few examples of a high status Visigoth burial that have ever been discovered."

"If it is the tomb of King Alaric, then it might contain treasures that have touched the hands of the great, the good and the infamous of Rome. We may find treasures that touched the hands of the likes of Julius Caesar, Augustus, Caligula, Vespasian, Trajan, Caracalla, Tacticus, Constantine and Valens. It could contain the treasure of a hundred different ancient cultures that Rome conquered over the eight hundred years that it had remained inviolate, from the Carthaginians to the people of Judea.

"On the other hand," he said with a grin, standing up, "it could contain nothing but dust."

"This is a unique event. Like Howard Carter opening the Tomb of the boy King Tutankhamen, we are on the verge of a momentous moment in history - the opening of a window into a world that no longer exists. A time capsule of ancient Rome." An excited murmur ran around the tent, but the Professor hadn't finished.

"Before we proceed let us take a moment to remember the poor souls whose remains are scattered all around us. The poor slaves who gave their lives to hide the location of the King's tomb." He bowed his head. The crowded tent fell into silent prayer.

After a few minutes the Professor stepped away from the tomb and nodded to his site manager. The sounds of engines filled the room and the slow process of gently lifting the slab began.

****

Everyone in the tent was staring at the giant monitors that now revealed the inside of the tomb. The plain marble slabs that had sealed the tomb had been lifted aside, and now lay, ignored, beside the open pit.

316

The cameraman panned around the tomb slowly. The tomb itself was square. It measured a little over three metres on each side. Around its walls Dan counted fourteen seated men and several angels, half buried in dried earth. They all seemed to be staring at an exquisitely carved sarcophagus, raised on a stone dais that rested in the centre of the tomb. The sarcophagus, about two metres long and about a metre wide, was covered in, what looked to Dan, like scenes from army life in ancient Rome. Men, women, horses and chariots were all visible on the side and end he could see.

Scattered around the floor of the tomb were intriguing shapes, presumably offerings made to the dead King. At some time, Dan guessed, mud must have somehow leaked into the tomb, half filling it. The offerings on the floor, as well as the lower halves of the statues that stood around the edge of the tomb, were now blanketed in a layer of thick, dried mud.

Looking across at the Professor, Dan could see the excitement on his face as he stood in rapturous awe of his discovery. He had found the tomb of Alaric the first, King of the Visigoth! He had found part of the treasure taken from ancient Rome. The Professor's life would never be the same. He would go down in History as the twenty first century Howard Carter.

The Professor seemed overwhelmed. He walked over to Dan in a daze. "My dear friend Dan," he said opening his arms wide and embracing him, "Thank you. Without your support we would never have been able to do this! We have found him! We have found him! It is amazing!"

Dan hugged the Professor back. "I only provide money Professor. It is you that have found him. It is your perseverance that has made this possible!"

"You are too kind, Daniel!" said the Professor still holding Dan's arms, but drawing back so he could look up into Dan's face. "This is a great triumph but we must be careful now," he said in a quieter voice. "We do not know what treasures we will find and who we may upset when we find them. History, politics and religion are issues that can

317

excite the passions of powerful people. Not to mention priceless treasures!"

"I am sure that you will manage the sensitivities. Please let me know if I can help in any way, even if you only need a sounding board. Now, I think from the look on the faces of that group of anxious journalists, you are needed over there!" said Dan pointing towards a crowd near the entrance of the marquee. "

The Professor took a deep breath, gave Dan another hug and then walked over to the waiting journalists.

4. Calabria - Present day

Dan and Elizabeth sat cuddled together on the couch in their hotel room watching the news coverage on the BBC of the opening of the tomb. Once it finished Dan flicked from channel to channel. It seemed that every channel in the world was covering the event.

"Wow! It certainly is big news!" said Elizabeth. "I am guessing that the Professor won't have any problems getting funding for the next phase of the dig!"

"I guess not," said Dan. "He told me just before we left that he has been offered the use of some sort of brand new portable CT scanner to see inside the sarcophagus. He is so excited. He has already arranged for it to be flown in from Germany."

"It is so incredible." said Elizabeth. "What do you think they will find?"

"I don't know." said Dan as his phone signaled that he had received a text message. He looked down at the name on the screen. "Thomas Malm is trying again."

"Just ignore him. The less we have to do with that scumbag, the better," said Elizabeth dismissively.

"Did I tell you that the Professor has invited us to be on the crew that starts clearing the floor of the tomb? Only if you are interested, of course," said Dan with a grin.

"Oh, I'm not really sure. I was going to get my hair done. I'm not sure I want to waste my time digging in the mud of a sixteen hundred year old King's tomb, possibly filled with some of the most precious artefacts from ancient Rome!" Elizabeth dug her elbow into Dan's stomach, and then hit him in the face with a well-aimed cushion she had grabbed from beside her on the couch. "Of course I want to be in the dig team, who wouldn't! This is potentially the best treasure find in the history of," she paused searching for the right word, "well, ...history!"

5. Calabria - Present day

Next morning, after passing through a newly setup security cordon, Elizabeth and Dan walked into the tent that covered the dig site. They were both amazed at how much seemed to have happened since the previous afternoon. A metal frame had been built over the tomb itself to allow access to its floor without having to walk on it. A new lab area for handling and cleaning artefacts, housed in what looked like a shipping container, had been placed in the back of the tent.

The Professor was in the middle of directing a flurry of activity as the final preparations were being made to start the retrieval of the artefacts. He looked up from his tablet computer as Dan and Elizabeth approached. With a smile he welcomed them both and, with his arm around Elizabeth's waist led them over to the large screens that had been used the day before.

"Come, have a look at what we have been doing," he said stopping in front of the screens. With a swipe of his finger across his iPad an image suddenly appeared on the screen. It was a wire frame image of the tomb in three-dimensional space. "We have scanned the site and mapped it on our computer system," he said, manipulating the image by rotating and pinching the surface of his tablet. "I have allocated you two this area to work in," he said pinching in on a section of the floor that had some intriguing shapes protruding from it. "We have set up the steel frame with cameras on the underside so that we will be able to record and monitor every step of the excavation."

"Fantastic!" said Elizabeth. "When can we start?"

The Professor chuckled at her eagerness. 'Right now, my dear," he said extending his arm out towards the gantry that led to the framework suspended above the tomb.

The work was tiring as they lay, prostrate, on the frame reaching down to the floor of the tomb, but Dan and Elizabeth, working side by side, would not have wished to be anywhere else in the world. About eight people could comfortably work on the platform. From time to time one of the archaeologists would get excited as they uncovered a recognisable object. By mid afternoon the silver heads of three signa militaria had been uncovered, the military ensigns of the Roman Legions. The first one found was an eagle resting on an arch. The second one was an eagle with its talons grasping a sphere and the latest one found was a hand. All of them were black, encrusted in a layer of silver sulphide. None of them had been lifted from the tomb, but still lay where they had been unearthed while their exact position and orientation was methodically recorded.

Each time someone revealed a new find work stopped while all the diggers, and all those working in the surrounding area, came to look.

"I've got something here!" said Dan excitedly, as he continued to brush and scrape the dried and crumbling dirt away from what looked like the nose of an animal. Elizabeth shuffled across next to Dan and looked at the area he had been working on. Excitedly she began to work on an adjoining part of the find. As they worked it became more obvious that it was the face of an animal, cast in some sort of metal.

"Do you think it's a mask? Perhaps it's part of one of those ceremonial helmets like the one that sold in the UK a few years ago for over two million pounds!" said Elizabeth excitedly.

"You mean the Crosby Garret helmet?" asked Dan, carefully scrapping away the dirt from around a beautifully sculptured ear. "That would be fantastic."

They continued to work until Dan said, "I don't think this is a mask Liz. I've got right around the back of the head. I think this is a full size statue!"

"It looks like the face of a dog," said Elizabeth, kneeling up and stretching. Dan knelt as well. "Or maybe not..." he said with a thoughtful expression on his face. "I think it is about time we called the Professor over.

With a shout and a wave of his arm Dan called to the Professor who carefully made his way over the recumbent bodies lying on the raised platform.

"What have you got for me Dan? It had better be good to take me away from the beautiful golden bowl that..." The Professor stopped in mid sentence. He stared at the face of the animal that stared out of the floor of the tomb, his Jaw, literally dropped.

"Mamma Mia!" he said lifting a hand to his mouth. "Is incredible! Look what you have found!" He fell to his knees and learnt forward and gently caressed the animals nose, almost as if it were alive.

"Oh, she is beautiful!" he said.

"What do you think it is?" asked Elizabeth, taken aback by the Professors reaction.

The Professor stood up, unable to take his eyes off the face. "She is Rome!" he said in an awestruck whisper, tears in his eyes. "She could be the original Lupa Capataliona." The other archeologist had all stopped work and were crowding around to see what had been found.

"The what?" asked Elizabeth.

"The Capitoline wolf! She stood in the forum! She was described by Pliny the Elder. She was described by Marcus Tullius Cicero. Oh, what a treasure! She was one of the most sacred objects in all of Rome! It would be such a statement to bury her with the King! Oh! This is so much more than amazing!"

Around them all work had stopped. Excited voices filled the tent as more and more people heard what had been uncovered.

Elizabeth leaned across to Dan and said in a very quiet whisper, "Didn't we see the Capitoline Wolf in the Capitoline Museum a couple of years ago, big wolf, small children underneath?"

"We did, yeah," replied Dan in an equally quiet voice. "They used to think it was the original, but they discovered a couple of years ago that it was made sometime in the twelfth or thirteenth century and that the two little figures of Romulus and Remus where added sometime in the 15th century. It was widely known that the twins were a later addition, but it had been thought that the wolf herself was cast around four or five hundred BC. It was devastating to the Museum, and to the people of Rome. It is such an iconic image. You see her everywhere, on advertising, in souvenir shops, on websites. It looks like we might have just hit the jackpot and found the original!"

The big monitors now focused on the wolf, and, as they worked, Dan and Elizabeth had the strange experience of seeing their hands, and every

322

movement they made, enlarged to twenty times their usual size on the big screens.

As they carefully pared away the dirt around the wolf they discovered that it was a little larger than life size. Gradually Elizabeth and Dan revealed the whole side of the wolf. "She is definitely a she!" said Elizabeth, who was working on the bottom edge of the statue. "I've just uncovered a nipple!"

Work stopped again as the Professor came over to inspect the new revelation. As he inspected the work he looked further up the flank of the she wolf, his attention caught by a darker, rough area. "Dan, could you brush away the dirt on that top area, please?" he asked pointing to the place on the back of the wolf that had caught his eye.

Dan brushed the area clean. "It looks a bit like a weld mark! Its like the metal has been melted at some time after the body was cast," he said.

The Professor changed places with Dan and spent a long time looking at the mark. He took a jewelers eyeglass out of his pocket and leant as close as he could. "Oh my god!" said the Professor as he stood up. "It looks like it could be damage from the strike of a lightening bolt! This is so exciting! It is as it was written. The she wolf, she was struck by lightening in the year 65 BC. This must be her! Oh il mio dio! What a thing to find!"

For the rest of the day and long into the night Elizabeth and Dan worked diligently at uncovering their sculpture, causing yet another wave of excitement to wash through the tent when Elizabeth uncovered a small hand reaching out of the dirt just below one of the nipples. By the time they were too exhausted to continue the tent was largely in darkness. Nearly everyone but the Professor had gone home.

"Come, my children, sit with me and have a glass of vino! You deserve a reward for all your hard work!" said the Professor, handing them each a glass of red wine. "What an amazing day! I have never in my life been so overcome. Such finds! Your wolf she is so beautiful!"

"What else has been uncovered? We have been so focused on digging the wolf that we have no idea what anyone else has found," said Dan.

The Professor swung around in his chair and tapped the keyboard. The big screens came to life. With a few clicks of the mouse the screen filled with the image of a golden helmet, still half buried. "It is beautiful, No?" asked the Professor. Perhaps the helmet of an Emperor?" he said. 'Then there is this!" The screen flickered and an image of a section of what could have been a cuirass appeared on the screen. "This is odd," said the Professor, frowning. "It does not appear to be Roman at all. Roman breastplates are more fitted. It was on the other side of the tomb to the helmet."

"It is beautiful though!" said Elizabeth. "Are those fittings gold?"

"We think so, said the Professor. One of my students thinks it may be Greek. Then there is this!" he said as the image changed to a large gold coloured bowl, also still half buried. It was slightly bent out of shape but it seemed to come alive with images of men fighting around it.

"And this!" said the Professor, as the image flicked again to reveal the rim of another bowl, this one obviously containing smaller objects that could have been jewellery.

"Stop! Stop!" said Dan with a laugh. "It is all too much to take in! How are you going with the sarcophagus?" he asked.

"Ah! Our aim is to clear the area around it, and under it, so that we can install the CT scanner as soon as possible. We have had a stroke of luck there. It looks like the sarcophagus itself is resting on two large stones, one at either end, so that the C shaped arm of the scanner will be able to rotate completely around the sarcophagus. Most of it will be mounted on the gantry on a moving rail. We are having some problems with the power supply but the German engineers don't seem to think it is anything they can't deal with. We should be able to start scanning early next week," said the Professor.

"Fantastic! I can't wait to see what is in there!" said Elizabeth yawning. "I think it is time we went back to our hotel Doctor Marsh. I won't be able to keep my eyes open much longer I am afraid."

Dan agreed and after wishing the Professor good night walked back through the security cordon, said good night to the police standing at the entrance and drove the short distance back to their hotel where they Skyped Charlotte to tell her of the day's events while they waited for room service to bring them their dinner.

"You don't need to tell me what you have been doing!" she said with a laugh when they got through to her. "I've been watching the two of you all day. You do realise you have been on every news channel and there has been a live stream of you on the internet all day, don't you?"

****

Five days later, after running the security cordon, which seemed to get tighter each time they went through it, Elizabeth and Dan got back to work uncovering the last of the she wolf and the small child that was resting its hand on one of her nipples.

The day proved every bit as exciting as the previous ones, with new discoveries being unearthed throughout the day. They rested from time to time to see the progress with the installation of the CT Scanner, which now hung underneath the gantry. Priority had been given to making a space around the sarcophagus and a trench, with gently curving sides, now revealed its full extent, and a good sized space between its base and the rock floor of the tomb itself. Every now and then the scanner arm would rotate as they tested it.

Elizabeth and Dan concentrated on their find until, late in the afternoon, the Professor came over and tapped them on the shoulders. "Dan, Elizabeth, come with me," he said in a quiet, almost conspiratorial voice. They followed him off the grid and over to where the German technicians had been working with the CT scanner.

"I thought you would like to see this, Johannes is just about to image the results," he said pointing to his young technical officer, tapping rapidly on a keyboard in front of a monitor.

The Professor, Elizabeth and Dan stood behind Johannes, staring at the screen. The young man looked up at the Professor, who nodded. Johannes tapped the return key and an image started to resolve itself on the screen.

"This preliminary scan should show us the size of the lead coffin inside the sarcophagus," said the Professor excitedly, "and perhaps some ...." His voice trailed off as the image of a skull appeared on the screen. Around it was what seemed to be a band of some sort of metal. The neck bones could be clearly seen. There appeared to be some sort of cuirass, on top of which lay a sword and what looked like skeletal hands gripping it. The bones of the thighs could be seen but the lower legs appeared to be covered in something that could have been a pair of grieves. The whole process of resolving the image took about ten minutes. Around the body could be seen small shapes, circles and crosses of various types.

Throughout the whole process the Professor, Elizabeth and Dan had stood in silent awe.

"That is amazing!" said Dan. "There is no lead coffin. When do you think you will open the sarcophagus Professor?"

"I am not in a hurry." he said thoughtfully. "I would like to clear the rest of the floor of the tomb first. That will probably take another week at least. Once the floor is cleared we will have easier access and not risk damaging any of the other artefacts."

"Could I get a copy of this image?" asked Dan pointing to the screen. "I know that Charlotte would love to see it. I think she is a bit miffed that she has not been here for all this excitement!"

"Of course!" said the Professor with a smile. "But we will keep it under our hats for the time being I think. It would not be good to have these images appear in the media before we are ready!"

Dan laughed. "Always the consummate media manipulator! Of course Professor, I will make it clear to her that they are for her eyes only! In fact, I have a few work things to attend to that I could more easily do in our Rome office. We could deliver the file to her in person, what do you think Liz?"

Elizabeth smiled. "That would be great," she said. "I think we have done enough here for the time being. I am sure there are others who would like the opportunity to use the space we have been taking up on the platform and I am not sure my back and neck can take another full day of hanging over our wolf."

Dan arranged with Johannes to give him the CT scan image on a USB stick that he put carefully in his pocket before going back with Elizabeth to do some more work on the she wolf.

By knockoff time that evening the little figure underneath the wolf had been completely uncovered. Its small, angelic face a picture of bliss as it reached up to suckle on the she wolf's teat. The she wolf had not given up all her surprises though. Careful cleaning around the she wolf's nipples had revealed a small hand moulded onto the nipple itself. A ragged edge at the wrist suggested that there had once been another twin that had been broken from the statue.

After saying goodbye to the Professor, Dan and Elizabeth made their way to their hotel, tired but happy. They Skyped Charlotte and Alberto and after updating them on the day's discoveries, Dan offhandedly mentioned the CT scan and told her they would bring it to Rome with them. Charlotte was so excited she begged Dan to send it straight away. In the end he agreed to send it through the company's secure cloud server.

"Alberto and I will be working at the Vatican library again tomorrow. How about I book a table at Flavio al Velavevodetto for tomorrow night?" Dan nodded. He could see how excited she was. He guessed that her researches had thrown up something interesting, but as always with his daughter, he realised he would have to wait until she was ready to reveal what she had discovered. He said goodnight, and trying to stifle a yawn, closed his laptop.

Two hours later, just as he and Elizabeth were dropping off to sleep, the telephone on his bedside table buzzed.

"Dad!" Charlotte said, the excitement in her voice obvious.

"Charlotte! What's wrong? What's happened?" he asked, suddenly wide-awake.

"Nothing's happened. Have you looked at this CT scan?" she asked.

"Not really. It was only done late this afternoon. Why?"

"I think you had better, Dad. If what I have just seen is real, then opening that sarcophagus will change everything! I need you to have a look without any preconceived ideas. Alberto and I agree on what I found, but another couple of fresh perspectives would confirm it."

"Ok, we will have a look and call you back." Charlotte hung up. Dan loaded the CT scan image on to his laptop. While he was waiting for it to load across from the memory stick Elizabeth made two cups of coffee.

They both sat down in front of the screen, the image from the CT scan displayed in front of them. The image had been generated as slices along the whole length of the body, as if someone had sliced the sarcophagus like a very thinly sliced loaf of bread. The images were then put together to create a 3D model of the sarcophagus and the body inside it.

They let the image run through. What they saw still amazed them. They could see the shape of the sarcophagus itself and then a human skeleton, easily recognisable. They could see a breastplate and, resting on the top of it, a long metal sword that ran down the length of the coffin. They could see rings around the fingers of the skeletal hands and an ornate circlet around the skull. While what they were looking at was amazing, it was clearly not what had excited Charlotte.

Dan's smart phone made a noise. He picked it up. "Its a text from Charlotte. She wants to know if we have seen it yet!"

"Tell her we are still looking. Our eyes are older than hers!" said Elizabeth, adjusting her reading glasses on the end of her nose.

Dan typed in his reply and sat down again. They worked for an hour going over the image in minute detail, and still they almost missed it. "Oh my God!" said Elizabeth, "Are you seeing what I am seeing?"

Dan nodded. Gripped in the skeletal hand of the dead king was the misty image of a glass vial!

"And look!" said Elizabeth, zooming in on the vial, and then through its translucent walls. "There is something still inside it!"

Dan grabbed his phone and texted. "Another one?"

Charlotte sent back an emoticon of a smiley face, followed by twenty-seven exclamation marks.

6. Cosenza to Rome - Present day

After the excitement of the previous evening Dan and Elizabeth slept late and indulged in a long, leisurely breakfast, before setting off to Rome.

The drive from Cosenza to Rome was pleasant but uneventful.

Both Elizabeth and Dan kept on eye out for anyone following them, but the traffic was fairly heavy and it was hard to keep track of individual cars. In the end they gave up and just enjoyed their time together.

As they were passing the town of Cassino, with Monte Cassino rising up behind it, Dan, instead of mentioning the fact that Hannibal passed through this area, near the old Roman town of Casinum, which was his first thought when he realised where they were, he finally broached a subject that had been troubling him. "Liz, would you like to move in with me? When we get back home I mean." and then quickly added, "If you don't want to that would be okay. I just wondered if it, you know, might work, even on a sort of trial basis, to see if you would like it?" he asked in a nervous rush.

"That's a big step!" I'm not sure that I'm ready for that kind of commitment!" she said with a laugh, and then saw the expression on Dan's face. He looked suddenly so dejected she realised that her attempt at humour had missed the mark. She cursed herself. She should have known that, with Dan, joking about some things, especially important emotional issues, did not go down well.

"Of course I will!" she said quickly, squeezing his leg with the hand that had been resting on it and then, because she wanted him to realise how committed she was, she added, "How about I sell my place on the North Shore, when we get back?"

Dan glanced over at her then, with a smile on his face said, "Did you know that Hannibal passed through this area during the second Punic war?"

Elizabeth rolled her eyes.

7. Rome - Present day

The dining room of Flavio al Velavevodetto was crowded but Dan, Elizabeth, Alberto and Charlotte had managed to get a table right under one of the large arched windows that revealed the mountain of ancient, broken amphora that was Monte dei Cocci.

As they settled down with their drinks, Dan looked across at Charlotte who was looking happy and excited, clearly desperate to discuss the results of her researches.

"So, how were the famous secret archives of the Vatican?" Dan asked. "Did you have to swear on a stack of bibles to get in?"

"No." she laughed. "The archives are truly amazing, though! I don't know what sort of pull this man has," she said touching Alberto on the arm, "but as soon as he turned up doors just opened, wherever we went! On our first day I got a personalised grand tour. One of the archivists told me that there are more than 84 kilometres of shelving! The people that work there were really lovely. They showed me all the flashy documents, the records of Galileo's trial before the Inquisition, a letter signed by Abraham Lincoln to the Pope during the American Civil War, a letter from an American Indian chief written on a strip of bark that called the pope the "Grand Master of Prayers", and a letter signed by Michelangelo himself complaining that he had been stiffed on his payment for the Sistine Chapel. It was really mind blowing stuff," she said, finally taking a breath, before continuing.

"But that was nothing compared to the next day! Alberto took me into the Pope's private library! I had to sign a confidentiality agreement to even be allowed to walk through the door! I saw the letters between the Pope Pius-es and Napoleon. It is all true! Napoleon really was drinking a relic that he believed was made from the Blood of Constantine! Once we knew where to look it was all there!"

"So I can categorically confirm that Napoleon was given the potion by Pope Pius the sixth. Pius also wrote a record of what he did and why he did it. He says in one document that Napoleon was putting pressure on him to reveal the source of the relic that he had agreed to give him.

Bonaparte could see himself eventually running out of it and wanted to find out where it came from. Pius wouldn't give the information to him and so Napoleon had him taken prisoner. The excuse they used at the time was that the Pope wouldn't renounce his claim over the Vatican states, which was a load of rubbish really because Napoleon didn't need the Pope's approval to take over the Vatican states. He just took them in 1809 anyway and set up a Roman republic."

"And I found out something else interesting as well. As the Archivist was taking me around I occasionally caught a glimpse of numbers on the documents that didn't seem to fit. When I asked him what they were he told me that, in 1810 Napoleon took the Archivum Secretum Apostolicum Vaticanum, the entire secret archive, to Paris! In fact, about one quarter of the documents never made it back from Paris. My guess is that Napoleon was searching for information about the Blood of Constantine and he thought that the secret archives would be the most likely place to find it."

"But," said Elizabeth, fascinated, "we know that he didn't find any more, because he obviously didn't have enough of it to see him through to the Battle of Waterloo!"

"That is right, and from the research I've done it looks like he had so many visitors on Elba that literally anyone could have passed a vial of the Blood of Constantine to him," said Charlotte. She stopped for a moment to take a sip from her glass of wine, then lent forward in a decidedly conspiratorial way. "But, after last night's discovery, Alberto and I spent today doing a little more digging around the date of our friend's death. You will not believe what we discovered!"

"Something about Alaric?" asked Dan quietly.

She shook her head. "Not directly. Alberto and I had been looking through all the material, which, to be honest, wasn't much, around the time of Alaric. We didn't find anything, so we went for a walk around Saint Peter's Basilica. The only time I had been in there was on our first trip to Rome. Do you remember Dad? It was freezing cold and I was being a bratty teenager. All I wanted to do was go shopping!"

"I remember it all too well!" said Dan shaking his head. "Hours and hours spent in shoe shops. It was torture!"

"Well, anyway," said Charlotte quickly changing the subject, "Bert was showing me the Basilica and we came upon the relief of Attila the Hun."

"What, in the Vatican?" said Elizabeth in surprise.

"That's what I said when he showed it to me!" said Charlotte, nodding to Alberto to continue the story.

"It is true, Elizabeth. Attila is depicted in a marble relief, carved in the 1600s by Alessandro Algardi. The relief shows the famous confrontation between Pope Leo the First and the "Scourge of God" himself, Attila the Hun."

"My God! I have never heard this story," said Elizabeth leaning forward.

"It was in the year 452, forty years after Alaric had sacked Roma. Attila had arrived in northern Italy, just near the city of Mantua on the Northern side of the Po River. He had begun his advance towards Rome."

"Ah!" said Charlotte, but remember that Rome wasn't the capital of the Empire then. The Imperial court had been moved to Ravenna."

"That's right," said Alberto, "but Rome was still an important city, with much wealth, even after the sacking of the city by Alaric. Rome was still a major prize, but it wasn't Rome that Attila was after, or so we found out today. After looking at the relief, Charlie had a brain swell. So we went back and looked at the papers in the Pope's Library from the time of Leo the first, and Bingo! We found the key to the whole puzzle."

"What key?" asked Dan.

"The key that unlocks the whole puzzle about where the Blood of Constantine came from! Haven't you been listening Dad?" said Charlotte with a grin.

8. Northern Italy - 452 AD

It had been a year since the battle fought on the Catalaunian Plains. The bitter taste of defeat at the hands of the Roman General Flavius Aetius still burned in Attila's gut. Now, sitting astride his pony with over a hundred thousand warriors at his back, he could almost taste the sweetness of his revenge. Rome, weakened by famine, lay but a few days ride to the south like some fat courtesan waiting to be taken. He imagined that even from this distance he could hear the great city murmuring to itself like a demented, pox ridden, old maid, her empty belly rumbling.

He watched the sun set and then gently guided his pony away from the promontory back towards the yurt that had been erected for him. As he swung himself from the saddle one of his men stepped up to take the pony. He let his hand run fondly down its flank as it was walked away. He continued to watch as the pony was lost among the yurts and tents of the camp. He knew his mount would be well looked after but sometimes he yearned for the quiet pleasure of brushing his own horse after a day in the saddle. Simple pleasures were often denied the ruler of an empire, especially one so far from home. He smiled sadly to himself, alone in the dark, before lifting the heavy rug that hung over the entrance to his home.

Kreka looked up as he stepped into his living quarters. He nodded and she started to serve his evening meal.

Seated around the fire, warming themselves, were two of his sons, Ellac and Dengizich, as well as two of his most trusted Generals, Uldiz and Karatun. He grinned at them as he too sat down by the fire.

Dengizich looked at his father, his expression serious. "So father, do we take Rome or do we scurry back to the Steppe?" he asked, his tone coldly contemptuous.

Attila raised an eyebrow, and looked more closely at the faces of the men seated around the fire. They all looked angry. Clearly he had come in half way through an argument.

"I counsel that we negotiate for gold and head home before the winter sets in," said Karatun before anyone else could respond. "Sacking Rome will bring us no good. Remember how Alaric the Goth died after sacking Rome! The place is bewitched, an evil, festering stinking sewer." He spat on the ground in disgust.

"We should consider our own position father," said Ellac. "Our food supplies are getting low and there has been nothing worth taking of any note for the last few days. It won't be long before the men feel the pangs of hunger. I agree with Karatum. Negotiate with the Roman scum for their gold and then let us head for home while we are still well fed."

"And you Uldiz, do you sit there without an opinion to share?" asked Dengizich angrily. "Are you for trotting back home with my brother for fear of a little rumble in your tummy, or are you afraid that if we violate the fat bitch Rome she will curse us all and leave us to die?"

Uldiz looked at each of the men that sat around the fire. His eyes ended up focusing on Dengizich. "There has never been a man of this earth, so favoured by the gods, so brilliant a warrior, who has been able to conquer as much territory as your father, Dengizich. There has never been a man of this earth who has so terrified the great empires of Rome, both East and West, that they will pay wagon loads of gold for him to live peacefully at home. There has never been a man who I would willingly follow across the breadth of the world except your father. I am for following your father's wishes Dengizich. When he decides what is best for the Hun I will follow his orders, when he is ready to give them. Now, I am going to let him eat his meal in peace." Uldiz, finished speaking, looked each of them in the eye in turn then stood up. He nodded to Attila and walked out of the tent.

Chastened, Dengizich stood, bowed to his father and he too left. The others followed. As the last of the men left Kreka knelt beside her husband and handed him a wooden bowl filled with soup.

****

"And you, my love, what do you think we should do? Take Rome and become rulers of the great Roman Empire?

In the flickering light of the fire Kreka looked at Attila, his short powerful body sitting comfortably on the thick woollen rugs that carpeted the floor of the yurt. She took his now empty bowl from his hand and knelt down beside him. As his most favoured wife he shared many confidences with her that he did not share with even his Generals or his sons. Despite that she knew she could easily incur his disfavour. Her position, and the position of her own three sons, depended on Attila's trust in her. Since they had been children she had always been honest with him, even if that honesty could disadvantage her. She was one of the few people, perhaps the only person, who, in the privacy of their tent, could challenge his thinking and listen to his doubts.

"There are other ways of conquering an Empire, my Lord," She said humbly, her eyes looking down at her hands. "Do you not have in your possession an offer of marriage and an engagement gift from the sister of the Emperor Valentinian."

"I do. Is that not why we are here? I am but a wronged suitor, heartbroken, come to claim my dowry, protest the innocence of my future wife, Honoria, and seek her release from her unjust imprisonment in a nunnery?" Attila tried to put on the face of a saddened and aggrieved husband, unsuccessfully.

Kreka laughed. "My husband, I worry that you sell yourself short. You are offered the hand of the Emperor's sister, a woman who has recently tried to kill her own brother! All you ask in return for taking this burden from the Emperor is a reasonable dowry, half the Western Roman Empire. I can not see how Emperor Valentinian will not approve of such an arrangement. Who would not want to be rid of such a woman for such a trifling cost!"

"And yet Valentinian has already written to me repudiating the marriage proposal. He will not honour it," said Attila with feigned sadness. "But how does any of this help me with making a decision about attacking the Roman City?"

"There is the gift, my lord," said Kreka, almost shyly.

"There is," said Attila, after long pause. He reached under his tunic and withdrew an ornate glass vial attached to a chain.

The vial was clearly designed to be worn around the neck. It was made of glass but was covered in a fine net of gold. Small, exquisitely detailed lions claws held the chain in place. Attila held the vial so that it caught the light of the fire. A small amount of oily liquid moved back and forth as he turned it to catch the flicker of the flames.

"Do you think it is true?" asked Kreka as they both watched the resinous liquid inside the vial move slowly back and forth.

"What? That this is the blood of the great Emperor Constantine, and it has some mystical power?" That if I were to drink it I would become greater than I am and have the ability to conquer the whole world?" he said scornfully.

"I have conquered much of it already without the need for magic potions. I have brought the warriors of the great steppe together! We have swept across the world, pushing all before us! The great Roman Emperors of both East and West have showered me with gold to keep me from destroying their cities. The world trembles when it hears my name. Am I not the 'Scourge of God'? Why would I need a magic potion when I am already Attila of the Hun?

"And yet, my Lord," said Kreka, her voice faltering, almost whispering, " We were driven back by Aëtius and the Visigoth, Theodoric."

A silence closed around Attila and Kreka. She kept her head bowed, afraid that she had gone too far, been too honest.

****

Attila sat, staring at the vial. Kreka was right. Things had become less easy over the last few years. Their defeat at the hands of the Roman Visigoth alliance had been a shock. It had been fortuitous that Theodoric had been slain in battle. If his son had not rushed off to secure the newly vacant throne, that Roman demon Aëtius might have pursued his advantage. That could have been disastrous. The fact that a Roman had been able to create an alliance with Visigoth, Alans and Burgundians was still an accomplishment that made Attila wake in the middle of the night in a cold sweat.

The situation was becoming more complicated. There was now a new Emperor in the East, Marcian who had refused to pay tribute. Not only that, but he had been receiving messages for the last few weeks that a Roman army had left Constantinople and was heading towards the Hun home settlements in the north.

To be considered too, was the rumour that Rome was not the prize that it once was. It was said that Alaric the Visigoth had taken much of its wealth away with him.

To help him decide if Rome were worth the effort he had sought out the old men who had fought with the Goth King. He had listened to their stories of the sack of Rome and the mountains of gold that had been taken away. That was when he had first heard the strange and garbled stories about the Gothic King seeking out the daughter of the dead Emperor, Theodosius, and making a pact with the devil.

He had listened to the stories of the sudden death of the Great Gothic King soon after the sacking of Rome. More intriguing, though, was the story that Alaric had been poisoned by drinking the blood of an Emperor.

Attila snapped out of his brief revere. "Is this then a potion I should drink to make me Emperor of the whole world? Is this a potion that makes the drinker invincible? No. I think that this is one of Honoria's pathetic little plots by a conniving woman to gain back favour with her brother. Honoria believes me to be such a gullible, barbarian fool as to taste her magic elixir and die. I think Honoria is a scheming, manipulative woman desperate to ingratiate herself with her brother and keep her head attached to the rest of her body. If I was Valentinian I would have had her put down long ago."

The Hunnic way was ruthless and unforgiving, and Attila knew that he had to be the most ruthless and unforgiving of all. He had no doubt that if one of his own wives had done the things that his informers had told him that Honoria had done, her life would have ended long ago. Valentinian was soft and lazy, like most of his royal court in Ravenna, and the Western Empire he ruled.

"My informers have told me many stories of Honoria's appetite for men. It is well known that she seduced Eugenius, her brother's royal chamberlain, and then plotted to murder Valentinian and take his Empire for themselves. The plot failed. Eugenius lost his head. Her brother, persuaded by his mother pleas to her daughter's life had Honoria shipped to a nunnery in Constantinople."

"From what I hear, my Lord, the nunnery she is in may be more a punishment than death for Honoria," said Kreka with a chuckle.

Attila dropped the vial into the palm of his hand, slipped it back under his tunic and let out a loud laugh. He grabbed Kreka and rolled them both playfully onto his sleeping mat.

Later, lying awake next to the gently breathing Kreka, he wondered what the truth about the vial really was. The letter that had come with it from Honoria had been a simple plea for help to rescue her from the predicament in which she found herself. The gift, she had intimated, was a talisman of great power and great value.

He would have ignored it as a mere trinket had the box in which it came not contained a second letter. At first it had appeared to be just a meaningless jumble of letters, but something about it had jogged a childhood memory.

When he was a boy Attila had met a young Roman about his own age, Aëtius. The same Aëtius who had recently commanded the army that stood against them on the Catalaunian Plains. He had been sent as a hostage to the court of the Hun warlord Rugila.

The two boys had often spent time together, riding out on the steppe. Aëtius, was not a good horseman, but he was very competitive. Unable to best Attila on horseback he had looked for other ways to prove himself. One day he had boasted how he knew the secret of the code that Julius Caesar himself had invented to send messages that others could not read. He had written Atilla's name, and a message, in the secret code and given it to him. He had laughed, mockingly, at Atilla when he had not been able to read it.

It had taken Attila many nights to work out the code, with only the knowledge that his name was somewhere in the message. The trick, he discovered eventually was to shuffle the letters of the alphabet along a few places to disguise the words.

Looking at the letter in the box had reminded him of the note that Aëtius had written. Again, it had taken Attila many nights, working, unobserved in the flickering fire light of his yurt, to untangle the letters. When he had finished he realised that the coded letter had not been written by Honoria at all. It had been written by Emporer Constantine himself!

He had shared the contents of the letter only with Kreka. He could trust no other person on earth with its contents, because, as improbable as it sounded, the story the letter told might just be true.

9. Rome - Present day

"As Attila's hordes approached Rome, the Western Emperor, Valentinian sent a delegation of three men to persuade him not to attack Rome. The Emperor of the West sent Pope Leo as the leader of that delegation," said Alberto.

"The Western Emperor? You are talking about the Roman Emperor?" asked Elizabeth.

Charlotte, leaning forward in her seat, revelling in the telling of the story smiled eagerly, this was her area of expertise after all. "The Roman Empire was often, administratively, spilt in two parts, with two, sometimes even more, Emperors. It was Diocletian, in the late 200's who originally divided up the empire, and then of course there were periods when it was brought back together under the control of a single Emperor, like Constantine the Great. The Eastern Empire, the one people often now call the Byzantine Empire, continued on for a lot longer than the Western Empire. There is an argument that Gibbon's 'Rise and Fall of the Roman Empire" is a biased, Western hemisphere centric view of the world. The people who lived in Constantinople, the capital of the Eastern Empire, considered themselves to be Roman. They would have been gob smacked by Gibbons' view that the Roman Empire finished up sometime in the in the 600s. In their view the Roman Empire didn't end until the fall of Constantinople to the Ottoman Turks in 1453." Charlotte looked over at Alberto, who nodded.

"Oh, I've heard all about this already," said Elizabeth. "Our host, Mister Dragas got very cross about how the history of the Eastern Roman Empire has been portrayed in the West!"

"Well, he actually has got a point," said Alberto. Then he went on. "In Algardi's sculpture in Saint Peter's, the figures of Leo and Attila are both looking up towards Saint Peter and Saint Paul who appear to be descending on the barbarian with swords raised, ready to strike him down. There are others around them but the story goes that it was only Leo and Attila that could see the Apostles. Everyone else around them is going about their business oblivious to the drama that is occurring."

"The actual, documented evidence of the event says that there was no-one present at the meeting except Leo and Attila. Up until recently the belief was that no-one knew what was said or what arguments Leo had used. The only thing known for certain was that he convinced Attila to turn away from Rome and go home."

"The official, Church history says that Leo, unarmed, with no army to support him, just his faith, turned away the Hun horde. Attila was, apparently, so impressed by the power of Leo's conviction that he gave up his march into Italy. It is also said, as the sculpture depicts, that Attila saw the presence of Peter and Paul standing behind Leo, and was afraid to go any further."

"Well that all sounds a little bit like Church spin to me! said Elizabeth scornfully. "Now tell us what really happened!"

"Ah! You are very much the pragmatist Elizabeth," said Alberto with a laugh. "Yes, it does seem a bit of a stretch for the non-believer that a notoriously aggressive barbarian King, an unbeliever, a pagan, who has just led his barbarian horde of savage warriors across half of Europe intent on sacking Rome suddenly turns around because he is confronted by the Bishop of Rome holding a cross."

"While historians have argued over the reasons for Attila's decision, within the Vatican, there has never been any argument or doubt. This is simply one of the many demonstrations of the power that God gives to the successor of the Prince of the Apostles[1], as his representative on earth. As our Lord said, "You are Peter, and upon this Rock, I will build my Church and the gates of Hell[2] shall not prevail against it," said Alberto.

"The truth, as we discovered over the last few days, was somewhat different, and a lot stranger," said Charlotte.

---

1.   http://en.wikipedia.org/wiki/Prince_of_the_Apostles

2.   http://en.wikipedia.org/wiki/Hell

10. Northern Italy - 452 AD

Leo and Attila sat in chairs that had been set up, at Attila's insistence, under cover some distance from the other members of their delegations. The two men sat sizing each other up. Leo had heard much about this barbarian King, "the scourge of God". Looking at him now it seemed hard to believe that the man that sat before him was the devil incarnate. He sat relaxed on his chair, his legs encased in long trousers and his soft, leather, riding boots stretched out in front of him. A loose fitting long sleeved shirt covered his broad chest. Leo would not judge him a handsome man, at least not in the classical Greek or Roman tradition, but he was not as hideous to look at as some of the stories about him had suggested. He had a twinkle in his eye when he spoke that Leo found quite engaging.

Other things did not fit with the stories told about him. Far from being a vicious, uncouth barbarian, Leo had found Attila to be a modest, reserved, perhaps even conservative, man. While Leo had been served refreshments in the most beautiful and ornate bowls and cups, Attila had drunk out of a plain wooden cup. Nor did he wear any of the regalia of a King, but instead, the plain, simple, loose fitting attire of a nomad horseman.

"I noticed that you have brought a number of chests with you." Attila said. "I presume that they are full of gold to buy me off?"

Leo looked into Attila's face and once again saw the twinkle of humour in his eye. He guessed that the barbarian quite liked this game. "There is no doubt, my Lord, that the Emperor would be pleased if you were to leave his lands and his people to their peaceful existence. He finds the idea of another battle between our two peoples distasteful. He found the tragic death of Theodoric the Visigoth, on the Catalaunian Plains, most disturbing."

"As you have noticed, he has sent a number of chests of gold, not as a bribe you understand, but as a token of his esteem for the Lord of the Northern Steppe, knowing that it is but a trifle, given the great wealth of the Hun Kingdom."

Leo paused and furrowed his brow. "The Emperor is also concerned that you may still hold a desire to pursue the offer of marriage sent to you by his poor sister Honoria. He wanted you to know that his sister has had bouts of illness that leave her .... confused ... and prone to actions that are not always ... rational."

Leo watched as Attila lifted his wooden goblet to his lips and drank. As he lifted his arm, his shirt opened exposing a glass pendant, ornately decorated in fine gold filigree that hung, on a golden chain, around his neck. With a shock Leo recognised the object.

He must have given himself away. Attila put his goblet down and took hold of the pendant, holding it up to be admired. "A beautiful gift. Did you know that Honoria sent it to me with the proposal of marriage. I am not one for normally wearing jewels, but I find this pendant particularly captivating."

Leo was almost unable to speak. How could this treasure of the Empire, of the church, above all others, have got into the hands of this man. Did Honoria know what she had done? Had she done it on purpose? She was both devious and clever, but would she knowingly take such a risk?

"An unusual object," said Leo, frantically trying to think how to cope with this development. Trying to keep his voice as calm as possible he asked, "Do you know anything about it? It is certainly an odd choice for a gift for someone who is not a Christian."

"I am told it is Roman in origin. A relic of the Emperor Constantine! I am told that there may be a certain... powers attached to it," said Attila, still admiring the vial, not looking at Leo. "I am told that Alaric the Goth came to Rome seeking this relic."

Leo's heart sank. How did he find out? How much does he know?

Before he could reply Attila, said, as if he was changing the direction of the conversation, "I enjoy story telling. It is something that we Hun do on the long, long winter nights on the Steppe. A tradition. Perhaps you will tell me a story, perhaps the dstory of this relic and its miraculous contents. If I like your story, perhaps I will leave your country, along with the gifts your Emperor has sent."

Leo thought for a while. It seemed to him the damage was done. He would trust in God and tell the story, or at least as much of the story as necessary.

Leo smiled. "You are holding in your hand a vial that contains the blood of Constantine the Great. You are quite right. It is the reason why King Alaric came to Rome, and the reason he died," said Leo.

11. Rome - Present day

Dan looked at Charlotte and Alberto. "So you are saying that the vial in Alaric's sarcophagus really could be the Blood of Constantine. The real thing!"

"That's what we think," said Charlotte. "If we assume that Alaric found the relic in Rome somewhere, and then soon after drank some of it, it could very well be what killed him."

"If that is the case where did Alaric get it from and how did he even find out about it? Asked Elizabeth.

12. Rome – 25th of Augustus 410 AD

Alaric stood in the grey dawn looking at the temple of Apollo, the now looted treasury of Rome. By turning his head to the left he could see the beautiful two-story colonnade of marble arches that graced the front of the law courts, the Basilica Julia.

He drew in a breath. The air around him was tainted with the acrid smell of smoke. Bodies of dead Romans, men women and children were littered around the forum. Alaric shook his head. All he had wanted was land for his people to live in peace and safety. The intransigence and stupidity of the Emperor had led to this.

Still, he thought grimly to himself as he hefted two large sacks gold solidus on to his shoulder, there are compensations, I suppose. He turned towards the rising sun and began walking, trailing after his men, towards the Basilica Maxentius and Constantine.

Passing under the ornate portico of the basilica, Alaric paused for a moment and looked up at the massive barrel vaulted concrete ceiling above him. His eyes adjusted to the early morning gloom. He walked across the marble floor to the already large pile of looted treasure and placed his bags of gold next to a large chest which stood, its lid open, exposing a horde of silver miliarense.

He stood for a while, watching his men bring in more and more treasure. Two men struggled to carry in large, gold candelabra, with seven curving arms and a two-tiered base. They sat it down heavily next to a roll of purple cloth and a small box of gold and silver jewelry.

The men had started a number of separate piles of looted weapons. One pile was for swords, another for spears and pikes, and another for armour. He could see, as his countrymen walked in, adding their finds to the piles, that they had already upgraded their own gear. Many of the men had silver and gold chains around their necks and silver, gold and iron rings on their fingers. He gave only a fleeting thought to whether the rings, the symbols of Roman citizenship, had been taken from living or dead Romans.

As the morning wore on, Alaric continued to look through the ever growing piles of loot. Occasionally one or other of his sub commanders would interrupt him to give him an update on what was happening in the area of the city for which they had been made responsible, but the length of the siege appeared to have made the population basically compliant, and there were only a few pockets of resistance.

Towards midday one of his men approached him.

"My Lord Alaric", he said, nervously." My captain has found a horde of treasure the size of which you would not believe" he paused for a moment, taking in the now enormous pile of treasure that stood in the basilica, his eyes almost popping out of his head. He rushed on with his message, " but there is a young woman who stands over it and has said that they are consecrated vessels belonging to Saint Peter."

Alaric looked down at the man kneeling before him. " Is she defending this horde of treasure with a cohort of soldiers?'

"No my lord" said the soldier. "She is alone. She took us straight to it and offered it to us."

"So what is the problem?" asked Alaric, starting to become irritated.

"My Lord, she told the Captain that if we touched the treasure, that such a sacrilegious act would remain on our consciences forever. She is such a saintly woman, so calm and so determined, that we did not know what to do. My captain sent me to you for direction, my Lord."

Alaric shook his head. He told the messenger to return to his Captain and to tell him that all the consecrated plate and ornaments should be transported, without damage or delay, to the church of the apostle on the Vatican Hill.

The messenger nodded, took one more wide-eyed look at the pile of treasure that had grown even larger since his arrival and quickly walked off to deliver Alaric's instructions.

Later in the afternoon Ataulf arrived at the basilica. He sauntered in, adjusting his belt and sheathing his sword as he sought some shade from the hot sun.

Alaric watched him as he scanned the room and then walked toward him, grinning. "My brother," he said gesturing at the mountain of treasure that now dominated the room, "I have never seen anything like this in my life. Such wealth in one place!"

Alaric looked at the pile of plunder again and then turned to Ataulf. "There are greater treasures in Rome than these trinkets, my brother, if we can only find them. I want you to come with me to look at what else of value we can dig up in this city."

He signaled to four of his royal guard. They fell in behind him as he and Ataulf walked out into the forum. The sun was starting to go down and the smoke in the air had turned it into an angry red eye that watched them as they strode across the marble paving.

The small group walked in the direction of the setting sun, towards the Campus Martius. The streets were quiet now and largely deserted. They wound their way through the Campus, passing the temples, public buildings, circuses, theatres, porticoes, baths, monuments, columns, and obelisks.

Turning a corner, to Alaric's surprise, they came upon a procession. It was heading out of the city led by a detachment of his own men and a striking looking young Roman noble woman. The procession was of Roman citizens, many holding above their heads plates and vessels of gold and silver. Alaric and Ataulf watched in amazement as even more Roman citizens spilled from the surrounding buildings and joined the procession.

As Alaric's small band stood watching a Goth captain presented himself to Alaric. "I am not sure that this is what you intended my Lord, but I have followed your orders."

'My orders?" said Alaric, taken aback by the Captain's assertion.

"Yes my lord, you sent word that the consecrated items should be moved to the Church of Saint Peter. When we started to move the items a host of these Romans came from their rat holes to help. Now they all think it is some sort of religious procession. What should I do my Lord?"

Alaric looked bemused. He had to admire these Romans for their gall! They were taking the opportunity to get across the Tiber to the sanctuary of the Basilica of Saint Peter. Clearly the young woman leading them was a woman of great resource!

Shaking his head he let out a laugh and told the Captain to make sure that the young woman and her treasures made it safely to Saint Peter's.

As the Captain was walking away Alaric stopped him with a shout. He raised his voice loud enough for those in the procession to hear. "If any of these pious Romans show their heads outside the doors of the basilica, once they have delivered their burdens, I trust that you will cut them off!"

The Captain, grinning, nodded, put his hand on his sword, and strode after the column.

Those Romans Alaric could see started to look, if it were possible, even more pious.

"A striking woman!" said Ataulf, looking after the woman leading the procession.

Alaric nodded thoughtfully. "I think we may have just found one of the true treasures of the Roman Empire!" he said. "It might be interesting to follow the procession."

Alaric, Ataulf and their small squad of warriors trailled after the procession across the Tiber and up the Vatican Hill to the Basilica of Saint Peter.

Alaric stood before the steps that led up to the basilica's gatehouse. To his left he could see the ruins of Caligula's circus. The obelisk the mad Emperor had taken from Egypt still stood where it had been raised on the spina of the circus, to mark its central point. Alaric had read the works of Tacticus and knew that many, many Christians, including perhaps Saint Peter himself, had been martyred in Caligula's circus.

He turned back towards the basilica and started up the steps. He led Ataulf and his men through the gate house into a large open area surrounded by a colonnade. A covered fountain stood at the centre of this atrium. They followed the last of the procession through a porch and passed through the central doorway, one of five, that led into the main building.

Alaric, Ataulf and his men all stopped and marveled at the size of the basilica.

In front of them was a long central hall. A murky light made its way into the massive space through a row of high windows just below the wooden beamed roof. On either side of the central hall were two aisles each delineated by rows of columns. The walls above the colonnade, on either side below the windows, were resplendent with beautifully coloured images. Alaric recognized the creation stories that he had known all his life, captured forever in tesserae. The life of Christ and the martyrdom of Peter were all beautifully captured in the mosaics as well.

Entranced, he started to walk towards the far end of the basilica. He marvelled at the artistry of the craftsmen and the power of the images on the walls. As he approached the end of the main part of the church, he looked up. Inscribed on the arch that separated the nave from the transept were the words, 'Since under Thy leadership the Empire rose once again triumphant to the stars, Constantine the victor founded this hall church in thine honour.'

He started to walk across the transept towards the altar, intrigued by the unusual structure arching over it with its twisted, Solomonic columns, when his eyes glanced upwards. At that moment a beam of sunlight struck the end wall of the basilica. There, larger than life, floating in a golden aura, was Christ enthroned in Heaven, looking down at him. Saint Peter and Saint Paul stood at his side. Alaric fell to his knees and bowed his head in prayer. Ataulf and his men knelt as well.

When he opened his eyes and looked up he saw the young woman that had led the procession staring at him. She was tall with a regal bearing. Dark hair framed an angelic face. Large brown eyes showed no sign of fear. Standing next to her was an old man, balding with a white beard.

As Alaric rose to his feet the old man stepped forward. "I am Innocent, father of this congregation," he said with a wave of his arm.

Alaric stared at him for a moment. "I am Alaric, conqueror of your city!" he said with a smile.

Innocent bowed his head. "What is it you seek in this house of worship, my lord?"

"I seek that which the Emperor Constantine left with your church in trust," he replied, watching for the old man's reaction.

Despite his attempt to disguise his expression, Alaric saw the look of fear momentarily caught in Innocent's eyes. Stilicho had been right!

"I will make you a promise, Innocent," said Alaric staring into the old man's eyes. "The moment that you bring me the relic of Constantine I will leave your city."

The old man blanched. He put his hand out and rested it on the woman's arm to steady himself. "How do you know of the relic? Who told you that it was here?"

Alaric smiled a humourless smile. "Do you remember a General by the name of Flavius Stilicho?" he asked.

Innocent nodded, but this time it was the woman's reaction that caught Alaric's attention. At the mention of Stilicho's name her body had involuntarily stiffened.

"General Stilicho was a man I respected. He and I negotiated a treaty that your Emperor, Honorius, did not honour. A treaty that would have meant that all this," he said waving his arm in the direction of the city, "would not have been necessary!"

"It was the Emperor Theodosius himself, your Emperor's father, that told Stilicho the story of the relic when he appointed Stilicho guardian of his son. It is a pity that Honorius has not grown up to be even a tenth of the man his father was." spat Alaric. "It was Stilicho that told me the story of the relic. I have occasionally wondered if it was that knowledge that was the real reason that Honrorius had him killed?"

"I can not do what you ask," said Innocent, desperately. "The church was given a sacred trust by the Emperor Constantine himself. I can not be the one to break that trust!"

"And yet you can watch as our men defile your women and enslave your congregation!?" Ataulf said with disdain, shaking his head.

"I will stand by my promise, Innocent. Bring me the relic and you will save many lives. Refuse me and Rome will run with rivers of blood." Alaric turned and led his men back out into the city.

****

Ataulf and Alaric were sitting alone on the steps of a temple in the forum. The city was quiet. A few fires still burned and the smell of smoke still hung heavily in the air. It was dusk.

"What is this relic you seek, brother? Why is it so important to you?" Ataulf asked in a quiet voice.

Alaric looked around to make sure that no one was nearby. "Stilicho told me a story, Ataulf, many years ago. He said that a great alchemist, whose name has been lost to us, created a potion that gave the person who drank it the power to see the future. It was this potion that gave the Emperor Constantine the power to rebuild the Empire. If I can find it, I believe that this potion will finally show me how to provide a homeland for our people."

"Why did Stilicho tell you about it? How did you know where to look?" asked Ataulf, intrigued.

"Do you remember, a few years ago, when we negotiated that treaty with Stilicho? I was to be given a command within the Roman army and enough gold to compensate us for our service to Rome. In return we would swear allegiance to the Emperor."

Ataulf nodded.

"Stilicho wanted to celebrate our agreement, so he and I had started drinking. The treaty had not won living space for our people, but it offered a stepping-stone to a homeland and it paid us for some of what we had lost in the service of the Emperor. I didn't feel much like drinking, but felt obliged to sit with him. He had perhaps had too much to drink and had started to become boastful. He taunted me about the times he had beaten us in battle. Typically Roman, he was goading me for his own entertainment."

"When I didn't rise to the bait, he became more boastful and indiscreet. He told me of his plans to become Emperor. It was then that he told me the story."

"He said that Constantine, the great Emperor, had a son, Crispus, to a woman by the name of Minerva. Minerva died and Crispus and Constantine became very close. He took him with him on campaigns. He had him taught by the best tutors in the world. When he was old enough he appointed him commander of Gaul."

"Crispus was, by all accounts, a talented leader. He married and had a son of his own. Constantine was a proud father and now an even prouder grandfather."

"When Crispus and Constantine visited Rome together the crowds feted young Crispus. His success against the people that the Romans call barbarians, in Gaul, had made him very popular."

"A few years later he had a great victory commanding Constantine's fleet in a battle against the Eastern Augusts, Licinius. He also fought alongside his father in the final battle that gave Constantine control of all the lands of the Roman Empire, both East and West.

"He sounds like a son to be thankful for. How come I have never heard of him?" asked Ataulf.

"Because his father had him executed along with his own wife, Fausta, the mother of his six other children." Alaric said. "Crispus, his wife Helena, and their infant son all suffered damnatio memoriae. Their names were never again spoken at court and all mention of them was expunged from the Imperial records."

"Ah!" said Ataulf with a knowing nod, "The wife of Constantine and the son had become lovers and were conspiring to take over the Empire!"

"Not according to Stilicho," said Alaric, shaking his head. "The story he heard was that, when young Crispus had come of age, his father had shared a great secret with him. He had given him a few drops of this magic elixir, but Crispus became greedy for it. He wanted it for himself and his own son."

"Stilicho told me that the father and son argued. Fausta overheard them shouting at one another. She decided that her own children should be given the elixir. She began to demand that Constantine give her children the same opportunity that he had given Crispus."

"Constantine's family, his dynasty, was starting to split apart. According to Stilicho, Constantine, with the power of the elixir to see the future, saw the fall of the Roman Empire, ripped apart by civil war between Crispus, and his offspring, and Fausta and hers. To save his Empire he had Crispus and his family wiped from the face of the earth. His own wife he had suffocated while she was bathing."

"It was then that Constantine saw the need to put the elixir somewhere safe, well away from the Imperial court and its intrigues. He gave it, in trust, to the Bishop of Rome, Sylvester."

"Do you think that this Innocent, this Bishop of Rome, still has the relic?" asked Ataulf.

"Oh, I know that he has it. I saw it in his eyes. The question is how long will he allow us to continue to rape and plunder his city before he gives it to me!"

"But what if he doesn't? Will you take it from him?"

"There will be no need," said Alaric. "There will come a time when the people of the city will begin to wonder why the wealth of the churches is not among our trophies and the priests are not among our slaves. If the Bishop of Rome does not make a decision soon the people of Rome will turn against their church. He will bring the treasures of the church to me!"

13. Rome - 26th of Augustus 410 AD

Alaric and Ataulf walked across the Campus Martius, following the path they had followed the previous day. Alaric stopped in front of two tall, pink stone obelisks that stood in front of a large circular building. Ataulf looked up. The roof had cyprus trees growing from it. It towered above them. At the apex of the roof stood a statue of a man in a toga, looking out across the city.

"What is this place Alaric?" asked Ataulf.

"This, my dear brother, is the tomb of the Caesars. It was built by the Emperor Augustus. Here, by the door, see these copper plates? They tell of the achievements of the first Emperor of the Romans."

"Here it says," said Alaric reading slowly from one of the copper panels that was affixed either side of the great entrance door to the mausoleum, following the inscribed letters with his finger, "*In my sixth and seventh consulships, when I had extinguished the flames of civil war, after receiving by universal consent the absolute control of affairs, I transferred the republic from my own control to the will of the Senate and the Roman people. For this service on my part I was given the title of Augustus by decree of the Senate, and the doorposts of my house were covered with laurels by public act, and a civic crown was fixed above my door, and a golden shield was placed in the Curia Julia whose inscription testified that the Senate and the Roman people gave me this in recognition of my valour, my clemency, my justice, and my piety.*"

Ataulf looked unimpressed. Alaric shrugged his shoulders and pulled open the heavy doors. A waft of cool air enveloped them as they walked into the darkened interior. Dim light shone through the doorway and an arched window above the entrance.

The two men walked down a corridor that led from the entrance. As their eyes became accustomed to the tenebrous interior, they began to make out the shapes of ornate marble steles.

Alaric could see the names of famous, and infamous, Romans all around him. Names he recognised from stories he had been told about Rome, names like Tiberius, Caligula, Britannicus and Claudius.

Everywhere there were gold and silver urns mounted on marble bases, with inscriptions extolling the virtues of these mighty Roman Emperors and their families.

Ataulf looked around. "So what are we looking for Alaric? Why have we come to this place? There are places in this city that have more gold, more silver, more silk, more wine, more people who are alive, than this place. Why are we here?"

Alaric turned to look at him. In the half light of the tomb Ataulf could see that his king was in a serious mood. "Have you ever contemplated the greatness and the madness of the Emperors of the great Roman Empire?"

"Look around you" he said, moving his arm to embrace the tombs of the Caesars, "There is a mystery here that it is hard to explain. Rome, once a republic, had such a fear of dictators that it would elect new leaders every year. Not one, but two people, two consuls, to rule, so that no single individual would ever have too much power. Rome had been this way since the time of Lucius Junius Brutus, who slew the last of the Roman kings, Lucius Tarquinius Superbus."

"Under the republic Rome rose to become the greatest power in the world. Then these Caesars appear. Overnight Rome has an Emperor. First the great General Julius Caesar, then his son, Augustus," he said putting his hand on the urn that held Augustus remains.

"But then what happens? After them, so many madmen! Tiberius! Caligula! Nero! All of them bewitched! I thought that perhaps I would find some clue to their greatness or their depravity here."

Alaric walked around the mausoleum, reading the inscriptions, while Ataulf, taking the opportunity to relax, sat down, to enjoy the cool and the quiet. He watched as Alaric wandered from one urn to another, completing a whole circuit of the Mausoleum.

"You have not found what you want brother?" asked Ataulf as he stood up and walked over to join Alaric standing in front of the urn of Augustus. "There is only one place you have not looked," he said. He pulled the top from the urn and upended it in one smooth movement.

"See," said Ataulf with a smirk, "just dead Roman." Grey powder flowed from the jar onto the marble floor.

They spent the rest of the afternoon upending the urns that filled the niches in the mausoleum. By the time they were done the air was full of floating ash and they had a pile of gold and silver funerary urns stacked near the entrance. They had found nothing else.

14. Rome - 27th of Augustus 410 AD

It had been a long day and Alaric was sitting with his back against a marble column, resting. A shadow fell across his face. He looked up to see who had approached him. It was the young woman from the Basilica.

"Lord Alaric, I have come to give you what you have asked for," she said, holding out a jeweled box.

Alaric looked around to see if any one had accompanied her. "And the Holy Father? Did he not come with you?" asked Alaric.

"The Holy Father does not know I have come," she said. "You are a Christian, my lord. You of all people should understand the power of a promise made under the eyes of God! Father Innocent will not break a vow made on behalf of the Church."

"As I stand here he is praying for guidance. He has aged many years since you placed this burden so unfairly upon him."

Alaric took the box and looked inside. A small glass vial rested in a bed of silk. 'How do you know about things like this?" he asked her.

"My name is Galla Placidia, my Lord. I am the daughter of the Emperor Theodosius and the sister of the Emperor Honorius. Like you, I knew Stilicho well. I lived for a number of years in his house, and under his protection, after my father died."

Alaric stood up and bowed his head slightly in acknowledgement of her status. A thought came into his head. "How do I know that you have not concocted a poison for me to drink?"

Galla Placidia smiled. "My Lord, I anticipated you might ask. I am prepared to be taken as hostage, should you wish. If the potion is poison then I am sure your brothers will see that my life is forfeit. Now, you must honour your promise and leave the city."

Alaric looked into her eyes. She stared back, challenging him. He laughed. "So be it! I will give the order for my men to take what they have and leave the city."

15. Italy - 410AD

They had been riding south for a few days. Ataulf looked over his shoulder. Behind him in a long line came warriors on horseback, women, children and slaves. Their supply wagons groaned under the weight of the plunder that they had taken from Rome.

Many of the men behind him were dressed in the armour and clothes that they had looted. Some where even wearing the jewels and chains that they had taken. Ataulf could hear the men still bickering and squabbling over their spoils.

For three days they had looted the city, raping, stealing and killing. In an orgy of greed and blood lust they had even started to kill each other over the trinkets of Roman matrons and the purses of Roman peasants. In the end Alaric had what he wanted and called a halt.

In the caravan behind him were thousands of Romans, many from noble families, who were now slaves. Some would be ransomed, some would be kept as playthings and slaves and some would be sold on to Syrian slave traders. Those that were too old or too feeble to march along with their captors were dispatched with a swift sword thrust, their bodies left to rot beside the Appian Way.

Ataulf glanced across to where Alaric was riding. He looked deep in thought, troubled. Ataulf kicked his heels into his horse's flank, bringing the horse alongside Alaric's.

"Alaric, you seem unhappy. You should be smiling. We have bested the Romans. We have plenty of food for once and we are heading out of Italy to Africa, and yet you still frown. What troubles you?"

"I was thinking about what we should do next. Sailing across the sea to Africa, taking control of the lands that provide the food for Rome does seem to be a good option. We could settle there and never again have to wander aimlessly from place to place. We will no longer have to sell our souls to the Romans. They will give us respect and our people will be safe," he said.

"So," said Ataulf with a grin, "all is well then. Why are you worried?"

"Because, my brother, that is not the only option. We could, for instance, go to Gaul or across to Iberia. They might be better places for our people to grow and prosper. How can I know which path is the best? I pray for guidance but receive no answer. This is a critical decision for our people," he said.

"Look at the result of my decision to sack Rome," he said thoughtfully. "On the one hand we now have gold, silver and food falling off our wagons. There are a host of slaves trailing along with us. We have more than enough for our needs long into the future, but in gaining that our own people, consumed by greed, have started to turn on one another!"

"I walk through the camp at night now and instead of the singing, the story telling and the joking of the past I hear arguing, brawling and sullen silences."

"I have made us an enemy of the Emperor Honorius in Ravennna and the Pretorian Prefect, Flavius Anthemius in Constantinople."

Ataulf nodded. "That is true, but I hear that Anthemius is consumed building new walls around his city while he waits for the young Emperor Theodosius to grow to manhood and Honorius is too scared to move out of Ravenna. It would have been more of a problem if Stilicho had not had his head separated from his body by the honourable Honorius. He would have been a formidable enemy," said Ataulf.

"That is true," said Alaric thoughtfully, "But there is another example of what I am struggling with. From that one event, the killing of Stilicho, a chain of events occurred that led us directly to where we are now. If Stilicho had been a Roman all his machinations in the Emperor's courts would have meant nothing to the normal Roman in the street."

"Because he was half Vandal, the Roman citizens suddenly decided that they couldn't trust him. Driven by that irrational fear of outsiders the Romans turned their hatred on anyone born north of the Danube. They took out their anger on the wives and children of our brethren, killing the poor innocents whose menfolk had fought and died in the service of their Emperor. They slaughtered the Foederati, the wives and children of the very men who the Romans had permitted to settle within the borders of the Empire to help them protect it."

"Fought against us!" said Ataulf with a laugh.

"Yes, that's true, but all we wanted was land within the borders of the Empire as well," said Alaric. "The Foederati came to me seeking sanctuary from Roman persecution. It was the addition of the nearly thirty thousand trained fighting men that, when added to our own ranks, made it possible for us to lay siege to Rome, and here we are!"

"But you could not know that Stilicho would try to place his own son on the throne in Constantinople or that the Roman people would turn on the wives and children of the Foederati!" said Ataulf.

"No, maybe that is true," said Alaric reaching for the vial now hanging around his neck. " But I wonder if the Constantine's potion would have let me see such a turn of events."

"You are talking sorcery, my brother!" said Ataulf angrily. "If God had meant us to know the future he would send us a sign, a sign that would show us that what we are doing is either right or wrong."

"That is easy for you to say brother, but these people," he said waving his arm behind him, "are not your responsibility. They are mine. There is a burden in Kingship that you will never know. The future of our people is at stake! There are so many pathways that we could follow. Some will take us to safety and some will take us to extinction! As much as I rely on the advice and wisdom of others, like yourself, the decision, and the responsibility, is ultimately mine. That is why I am King!"

"So you want to take a potion, about which you have heard only rumours, handed to you by the sister of a devious, untrustworthy Emperor. For all you know it could have been concocted by some witch or warlock, or even the devil himself. How can you even think of putting your trust in that?" argued Ataulf, pointing to the vial.

"Or it could have been passed down from God!" said Alaric. "Just as he created Jesus to walk among us, he could have created this potion to help us better understand the future!"

Ataulf stared at him, belligerently.

"The ways of God are mysterious to us, Ataulf. God knows the future. It seems logical to me that God might give, to one such as Constantine Isapostolos, a way to make his faith the faith of the world!"

"Is it not possible then that God might give into the hands of those he would wish to guide, a way of illuminating their path, just as he gives us water and grain to sustain us in our journey of life?" asked Alaric passionately.

"Perhaps you are right Alaric. Perhaps the contents of that vial of yours will let you see the future, but at what cost. Madness? Death? Is it really worth your life?" asked Ataulf.

"If it means the survival of our people, yes! I am still hoping that God will give me some direction, some sign!" said Alaric. "I just wish I knew that I was doing the right thing for my people."

16. Calabria - 410AD

Ataulf looked down at Alaric's body. It rested on a bed of animal skins in an ornate marble sarcophagus. His arms were crossed on his chest. His right hand still gripped the vial. They had tried to take it from his hand. They could not, even in death, release the grip he had upon it. At least, Ataulf thought, he now looks at peace, and that accursed vial will be buried with him.

The days after the storm, after the loss of so many lives, when their ships had been forced back to Italy, had been difficult for Alaric. He had decided that God had finally given him the sign that he had prayed for. Africa was not to be the homeland that God would grant his people.

He had called the nobles together. They had argued about what they should do next. Some had been in favour of returning to Rome. Some had argued for heading back to Greece and settling in the Peloponnese. Good arguments had been made in favour of moving to Gaul, some in moving even as far as the Iberian peninsular. A few had even suggested moving back over the Danube to their ancestral lands. There had been good arguments for all the options put forward, but there had been no agreement. No consensus. No decision.

Alaric had sat pondering the issue for days. The disastrous attempt to get to Africa seemed to have sapped his confidence. Food was running short again, but still Alaric could not make a decision. He sat staring at the glass vial for hours, as if willing it to give him the answers he needed.

Eventually he had called Ataulf to his tent. He had told him that he had decided to drink the contents of the vial. He demanded that Ataulf promise him three things. First, that he would stay with him until the ordeal was over, one way or the other. Second, that, should he go mad, Ataulf would kill him quickly. Finally, he had made him promise that, if he died, whether by Ataulf's hand or not, that Ataulf would take on the burden of Kingship.

He had, reluctantly agreed. He had watched as Alaric had broken the seal on the top of the vial and swallowed a good part of its contents, then recapped the vial and lain back on his couch, eyes staring into the distance, waiting.

For several hours nothing had happened. Then, while Ataulf was half dozing in the warmth of the late afternoon, he heard Alaric groan. He looked across to see the King's face covered in sweat. His tunic was soaked and his face was flushed. As the night descended the King's skin seemed to grow hotter and hotter. It was as if he was burning up, a fire raging inside him. He tossed and turned, occasionally shouting out words that Ataulf did not understand.

Throughout the next day the situation got worse. Nothing they could do seemed to help. Only once did Alaric regain any lucidity. It was on his last day, just before he finally died. Ataulf had, as he had promised his King, sat by his bedside throughout his illness. Ataulf had been almost asleep when Alaric had grabbed his arm. He woke with a start and turned to Alaric who was staring at him with an intensity that Ataulf had never seen in a man's eyes before. "Ataulf," said Alaric, his voice hoarse and brittle, "My brother! I was wrong! Our path lies not to Africa or to the lands around us now, but to Gaul and Iberia! Rome is too strong, even in her enfeebled state! For our people to survive we must become more Roman, not less. Galla Placidia has not poisoned me. Stilicho was right. I have seen the future, many futures. Trust Galla Placidia. Take her as your wife. Through her bind our people's fate to that of Rome. Promise me!"

Ataulf looked at his brother in law, unsure if he was still delirious, gone mad or was passing on a message from God.

Alaric continued to stare at him so Ataulf nodded his head and said, "I will do as you wish brother."

Alaric, still staring said in a desperate voice. "Swear it brother!"

"I swear it, my Lord," said Ataulf. As soon as the words had passed his lips Ataulf saw Alaric's eyes glaze over. His head fell back onto the bed. He took one last convulsive breath and was gone.

Looking down at him now Ataulf thought Alaric finally looked at peace. Having been acclaimed King it was now his task to see to the funeral of his brother. In a land full of their enemies Ataulf had struck upon the idea of burying Alaric in the bed of a river.

Under the guidance of a young Roman engineer the Romans whom they had enslaved had been forced to build a dam and a diversion channel. It had given him a perverse pleasure to see Roman citizens, stripped of their finery, arrogance and conceit, toil in the mud of the river. It had not been an easy task. Many slaves had perished when their first attempt failed and the dam wall collapsed.

The burial site had eventually been carved out of the solid rock of the river bed and an ornate sarcophagus, looted from the tomb of a wealthy Roman, placed in its centre. Around the walls of the tomb were reliefs beaten out of silver panels that had been taken from a church they had passed as they had left Rome. The images were of Christ, the disciples and angels. They would watch over his departed brother.

His people filed past the sarcophagus, each taking a moment to say their goodbyes. It was a strange scene. Ataulf wondered at the gold and silver items that people left in the tomb. Never before in the history of his people had they had so much wealth, but that very fact, in a strange way, made the offerings to their departed King meaningless.

Ataulf had chosen his own offering to place in the tomb. He looked at the bronze wolf standing beside the sarcophagus. He smiled, touched Alarics cheek gently and said, in a whisper "I give you Rome, my brother. Let her be buried with you!"

By the time that they were ready to move the giant stone slab into place the tomb was resplendent with treasures, but it barely made a dent in the horde they still carried with them.

Ataulf watched as the stone slab slid into place. Concrete, was poured around the tomb so that water would not leak into it once the river was put back into its course.

He continued to watch, as the work was being completed, well aware that all these Romans, including the young engineer who had been so helpful, would be spending eternity in the bed of the river with Alaric. He had already given the order . Once the river stones were placed back over the tomb, all the slaves would be slain. Once they were dead the dam could be breached and the accumulated mud and water released to finally bury both slaves and tomb, for eternity.

17. Rome - Present day

"So, the vial in Alaric's hand, that we saw in the CT scan, has to be the real blood of Constantine, or whatever the stuff is," said Dan enthusiastically.

Charlotte nodded.

"But it still doesn't explain where this stuff came from, or whether it really is the actual Blood of Constantine." said Elizabeth, frowning. "In fact, if the story that Stilicho so indiscreetly told Alaric was true, that this stuff was the reason Constantine killed his own son, doesn't that mean..."

"That this stuff could predate Constantine!" said Dan excitedly, interrupting Elizabeth's train of thought.

"Unless there was something about Constantine's actual blood....No, that is actually impossible..."said Elizabeth shaking her head. "If this stuff really works then there is no way that it can be naturally occurring."

Charlotte nodded, grinning. "...and Attila guessed that too. According to Pope Leo's writings, Attila put the hard word on Pope Leo and the wily old Pope used his knowledge about the potion as a bargaining chip to save Rome."

18. Italy - 452 AD

"So, Alaric died to find the wisdom to lead his own people to a new homeland. A very noble act!" said Attila with admiration. "But there are questions that still remain unanswered. Where did my future wife, the remarkable and beautiful Honoria, get this vial?" asked Attila, holding the vial up and letting the light that filtered into the tent catch the movement within it. "And, if this was a secret shared by Constantine with his son, then does that mean that Constantine had taken the potion? If that were true, then it can't be his blood, for how would drinking your own blood give you the insight that you say this gives? He must have got it from somewhere else."

Leo's shoulders slumped. This man was perhaps too shrewd to be so easily deceived. "The answers to some of those questions require me to tell you yet another story," he said reluctantly. "For me to tell you such a secret I will need your solemn oath that you will leave Rome unmolested!"

"You ask a lot in trade for a few words!" said Attila. Leo remained silent. Attila stared at him. Leo stared back. Eventually, with an exaggerated sigh he smiled. "Very well. Tell your story! If I am pleased with it, then I shall take my men and return home for this year. If I decide you are lying to me I will raze Rome to the ground!"

"If I tell you this story, you will leave Rome and never return!" said Leo sharply.

Attila laughed. "You believe that this story is of such value! It must be a momentous truth for you to ask so much!" He paused, thinking to himself that Ravenna and Constantinople would be much greater prizes than Rome would ever be. "Alright, I will agree to your terms, on the condition that you hold nothing back! If I suspect that you are lying to me, even by omission, I will personally put a blade through each of your eyes and cut your tongue from your mouth!"

Leo looked into Attila's eyes. They were hard and cold. He had no doubt that this barbarian would deliver on his promises. To save Rome he would have to break a sacred oath and give away one of the Church's greatest secrets. He took a deep breath and put his trust in God.

"More than one hundred years ago, during the reign of Constantine the first, the Emperor gave the Pope of the time, Sylvester, a sacred trust. He told him that he would pass on to him a relic containing the blood of the Emperor. This sacred relic was to be handed on from one Pope to the next. The box in which the relic was brought from Constantinople, was not to be opened, unless there was an emergency of such magnitude that it threatened the very existence of the Empire, at which time it was to be given to the reigning Emperor himself. As the relic contained the blood of the Emperor it has become known as the Blood of Constantine." Leo paused.

"The story of the relic was written by Constantine himself, near the end of his life, and brought to Rome after he died."

19. Prima Porta - 27th October 312

Flavius Valerius Aurelius Constantius walked slowly out of his tent into the morning sunshine. He was tired. His right arm still ached, every time he moved it, from the blow he had received in their last fight with Maxentius' troops at Verona, even though the bruising and swelling had disappeared.

After the submission of Ravenna, he had led his men on a slow march down the Via Flaminia in the hope that they would benefit from the more relaxed pace, a chance to rest and recuperate. It seemed that it had not worked. As they had drawn closer to Rome his men had become more quarrelsome with each other, more edgy.

They all knew that Rome was the final prize, the final battle, the final confrontation. If they defeated Maxentius and his legions then the Western Empire was theirs. If they lost there would be no mercy. Death, or worse, awaited them all.

He walked through the orderly lines of tents. He could feel the eyes of his men watching him, looking for an indication of what the future might hold. They trusted him. Many of these same men had acclaimed him Augustus of the West in Britainnia after his father had died. They had been angry when the Emperor Galerius had only elevated him to the level of deputy Emperor, or Caesar of the West, subordinate to the Emperor or Augustus of the West, Severus.

Constantine, while not happy, accepted the Emperor's decision. It was, after all, his own father, Constantius who had promoted Severus to the position of Caesar of the West. It was, in a way, a fair decision, when Constantine's father died, to promote Severus to senior Emperor, and Constantine to junior Emperor. All would have been well, had not Maxentius usurped the throne and installed himself as Augustus.

The tetrarchy, that the Emperor Diocletian had established, was, to Constantine's mind, a good strategy to pull the empire out of the political and economic setbacks of the time. It was not, however the way he would run the Empire.

Constantine knew that he was a beneficiary of Diocletian's reforms. His father had, after all, been promoted, initially to the role of Pretorian Prefect in Gaul, then to the role of Caesar, and finally to the position of Augustus of the West on the back of those very reforms. While his father's success had meant that Constantine had effectively been held hostage at the court of Diocletian, to ensure his father's loyalty, his captivity had not been onerous.

He smiled to himself. He had enjoyed his time at Diocletian's Palace in Nicomedia. The Imperial court had been a fascinating place for an ambitious young man. He was tutored by some of the greatest minds of the day and had been permitted to actively participate in the running of the Empire. He had fought under Diocletian in Syria, against the Persians, and under Galerius, the Caesar of the East, in Mesopotamia, as well as fighting with him against the barbarians on the Danube border. He had watched, listened and learned. He had been the model of the loyal noble.

When Diocletian "retired", under duress from Galerius, Constantine found himself in a difficult position. While the reorganisation of the tetrarchy that Gallerius initiated had promoted his own father to Emperor of the West, he had been overlooked completely for promotion. He had been angry. Unfortunately, his feelings had become known to the new Emperor.

Constantine had always considered Galerius a duplicitous bastard and he knew that Gallerius saw him as a threat. Constantine's father knew of his son's predicament. In an effort to help him, he made a formal request to Gallerius, asking that Constantine be permitted to join him in his fight against the Picts in Britannia.

After an evening of over indulgence, Constantine took the opportunity to ask Galerius about his father's request. Galerius, with wine soaked magnanimity, agreed. He gave Constantine permission to leave the Imperial court. He even gave him his imperial seal, his sigillum, to facilitate his progress across the Empire.

Constantine did not wait. Before Galerius had even taken to his bed that evening, before the sun had risen, Constantine had taken his leave.

Knowing that Galerius, sober, would more than likely rescind his decision, Constantine had ridden away from Nicomedia like death itself was chasing him. He had literally flown across Europe, stopping every few miles to change horses at the imperial post houses along his route. So sure was he that Galerius would send his agents after him, that he hamstrung or killed any horses left behind at the post houses. He even went to the extreme of riding over the Alps, rather than take the more expected, and much easier route through the north of Italy.

He smiled to himself at the memory. He could still feel his relief when he had finally embraced his father at the Port of Bononia on the Gallic coast, and his even greater relief as he watched the Gallic cost recede as they made their way across the water to Britannia.

A shout interrupted Constantine's reverie and he turned to see one of his General's, Marcellus Agrippa approaching him. Another man he did not recognise, dressed in a simple tunic and bearing no obvious signs of rank, walked beside him.

"Greetings Caesar" said the General, bowing his head.

"Greetings Marcellus. You have brought someone to see me?" said Constantine acknowledging the presence of the civilian.

"This is Quintus Varius. He is one of the informers that we sent into the City. I thought you might like to hear what is happening behind the walls of Rome," said the General.

"Very thoughtful of you Marcellus." he replied with a friendly smile. Then, turning to the informer he asked, "So, Quintus Varius, what is the mood of the city?"

"My lord," said the informer respectfully, "Emperor Maxentius is holding games to celebrate the sixth anniversary of his accession to Augustus, but the people are unhappy. Maxentius is not popular and the people have begun to jeer him when he appears in public. The closer you, and your army have come to Rome, the more disrespect they show the Emperor! There is little love lost between the City and Maxentius, my Lord!"

"And what of the Legions, Quintus? How do they fare?" asked Constantine.

"They are more loyal than the people of the City, my Lord," said Quintus, nervously. "The victories they had against the Emperor Severus and then against the Emperor Galerius, made them loyal. Maxentius' success in getting the North African provinces back under his control, have made them even more so. Now that the City's grain stores are full to over flowing there is bread for all. Maxentius also pays the legions well, my Lord, taxing the people of Rome heavily for the privilege." The last comment was made with an obvious degree of bitterness.

"The Pretorian Guard are particularly devoted to Maxentius. They are like pampered dogs! They would likely fight to the death using the children of Rome as shields, to save their Emperor!" Quintus spat.

"And the strength of the legions, Quintus?" asked Constantine.

"With the Pretorians and the men camped on the Campus Martius, there would be more than seventy-five thousand men under arms in and around the City. Perhaps even as many as one hundred and twenty thousand. It is hard to tell precisely. Many of the men have been working outside the city, dismantling the bridges across the Tiber to frustrate your approach."

"Thank-you Quintus. You have been most helpful. Please, find yourself some food and drink before you leave the camp," said Constantine with a grateful smile.

"There is one other thing, my Lord," said Quintus in a rush, before he was dismissed.

Constantine indicated that he should continue with a nod of his head.

"I have heard that the Emperor has announced to the Senate that he will visit the temple of Apollo Patrous, my lord, and consult the Sibylline Books!"

Constantine raised an eyebrow. "He must be feeling more worried than I had imagined!' said Constantine, thoughtfully. "Thank-you again, Quintus. You have been most helpful!"

Qunitus bowed and, after a short exchange with Marcellus Agrippa, disappeared between the rows of tents. Constantine waited until Marcellus returned and then the two men walked back along the path that Constantine had originally been following.

"It is as we had feared, Marcellus. Maxentius is well provisioned. He has many more men than we do and has the walls of Rome to protect him. If we attack we could be in for a long siege and suffer the same fate as both Severus and Galerius."

"If I were Maxentius I certainly wouldn't be in any hurry to fight," said Marcellus.

"Neither would I Marcellus. Neither would I!" said Constantine. "And yet, Maxentius is to consult the Sibylline Books! I will need to think on this issue. In the mean time, Marcellus, see if you can have one of your informers find out what the books have foretold. Maxentius has always been superstitious. It might be useful if we knew what the prophecy said and an interpretation of what the gods intended!"

The General nodded, bowed and walked back the way they had come. After a few minutes reflection Constantine changed his direction and headed towards the yard where his horse waited patiently for him.

****

Constantine rode away from the camp at Prima Porta towards the River Tiber. It was not far, and he wanted to find a quiet place to think and clear his head. Two of his personal guards rode with him, but kept their distance.

Once the small group had reached the Via Flamina, Constantine turned under the arch of an aqueduct that crossed the road and then, letting his horse find its own path, sank into a revere. They passed a small shrine and then turned up a footpath that led towards the top of the hill. Stone walls, in a state of disrepair, rose up on either side of the overgrown path. The footpath itself seemed well constructed. Large paving stones were evident in places, where the path wasn't littered with debris.

A flock of black and brown hens, startled by Constantine's appearance, scattered as he emerged from the head of the path. He stopped and looked back over his shoulder. To the south he could see the Alban Hills and a stunning view down the Tiber Valley to Rome itself. Below him he could see the junction of the Via Flaminia and the Via

Tiberina. He sat contemplating the view down the river while his two companions caught up to him.

With a gentle nudge Constantine urged his horse down a small path that, to his surprise, led to a large Villa. The villa, like the footpath, looked neglected and abandoned.

Dismounting and passing the reins of his horse to one of his guards, Constantine walked through the entrance. To his left, through a large portico he could see a huge garden, once, presumably well cared for, but now a virtually impenetrable tangle of trees and vines.

He walked cautiously into the Villa's atrium. The impluvium, the sunken pool in the middle of the atrium, was clogged with debris that partially covered the black and white tiles of a mosaic. Towards the back of the Atrium, in front of a beautifully painted fresco, standing on a marble base, was the statue of a man in Roman armour, its faded colours hinting at its age. The man was barefoot, a cupid, riding a dolphin seemed to be reaching up towards him from the base of the statue. The man's cuirass was covered with figures of people and animals. In the centre of the chest he could make out two horses pulling a chariot. The man's right hand was outstretched as if he had been caught in the moment of addressing a crowd.

Constantine stood, stunned. He recognised the face. The statue was of a young Augustus. A thought suddenly struck him. He had read, during his studies in Niccomedia, something about a Villa Caesarum, near the Via Flaminia. Perhaps, he thought, this was it.

With his curiosity aroused he began to explore more carefully. He walked from room to room admiring the beautiful, but old fashioned, frescoes that seemed to adorn every wall. He eventually made his way through to the peristyle. A large portico, supported by red and white columns surrounded the large open space. Statues, some with heads broken off, others with vines growing over them, stood dotted around the courtyard. At its centre was a large pool.

Constantine sat down, his back against a pillar, and let the rays of the westering autumn sun warm him. His mind wandered. After a while, the answer he had been seeking floated into his mind. It was Pliny, in the Natural Histories, who had written about a villa near the ninth milestone of the Via Flaminia! But the story wasn't about Augustus or any of the Julian Emperors, it was about Livia, Augustus' wife. This was her Villa. It was called, his brows creased as he tried to visualise the name, then it came to him, *ad gallinus*, the House of the Chickens!

Constantine shook his head, realising that he was getting confused. He had read this same story somewhere else.

Pliny had written about an eagle dropping a white chicken with a sprig of laurel clasped in its beak into Livia's lap as she was being driven along in a carriage. He had described how the chicken had become the matriarch of a huge flock of white chickens, and how Livia had planted the laurel twig which had grown into a great plantation. When any of the Caesars were to celebrate a triumph they would come here and pick the laurel to make a wreath that they would wear around their head.

His brow furrowed again. Suetonius! Suetonius had written about this place in his "Life of Galba". It was Suetonius that had called it the house of chickens, and he had also written that it was the habit of the Emperors, when they picked their laurel, to plant another tree. He had also written that, just before the death of an Emperor their tree would wither and die.

When Nero, the last of the Julian line had died, Suetonius had written that the whole grove had withered and all the white chickens died.

He wondered whether it were true. He had seen no laurel trees outside and none in either of the gardens he had found inside the Villa's walls. There certainly were a lot of chickens around, but they were every colour but white. Of course, he thought to himself, with no one to tend them the white chickens would stand out to birds of prey and be picked off pretty quickly. The laurels could well have died naturally from a lack of water.

He closed his eyes and relaxed, safe in the knowledge that his men were on guard outside the Villa. He pondered the cleverness of whoever had invented the legend that both Pliny and Suetonius had re-told. The Julian family had obviously used it to enhance their hold on power. The linking of the strength of the Roman eagle with the living laurel and its amazing ability to regrow from a broken branch, symbolising the perpetual rebirth of their dynastic line. It was all very clever. He wondered about the meaning of the white chicken. Perhaps it represented fertility, perhaps purity or perhaps there was some other meaning, after all, chickens were used by the augurs for determining the will of the Gods. Linking the whole story to a place, especially one that you owned, added even more weight to the legend. He smiled to himself. It was a good lesson. The use of stories, either fiction or true, was certainly a powerful way to influence people.

He must have fallen asleep, because he awoke with a start. The sun was still shining on him, but it was much lower in the sky. His eyes swept the tangled vegetation of the garden. With a shock he realised that he was no longer alone. A woman stood looking at him, from the shade of the peristyle.

The woman's face was lined and wrinkled by age but her posture was erect and her smile was warm and friendly. She was dressed in a way that Constantine thought of as old fashioned. Her dress was long and covered her arms and legs. She wore a veil that was deep yellow, almost orange in colour.

Constantine scrambled to his feet and bowed his head instinctively, in respect to her, without really thinking why.

She closed her eyes and bowed her head to him in reply. Then, looking at him with her startlingly clear blue eyes, said, "Flavius Valerius Aurelius Constantinus, welcome to the house of Julia Augusta. I am the priestess of the divine Julia Augusta. I have been waiting for you for some time."

"Julia Augusta?" asked Constantine, unsure of the name.

"Julia Augusta, the wife of Emperor Augustus, Livia Drusilla," said the women quietly and reverently.

"So this really is the Villa of the Caesars, ad gallinus!" he exclaimed, pleased that he had identified it.

"It is, Caesar," she said, using his formal title and bowing her head once again, in recognition of his position and his insight.

"You said you have been waiting for me. How could you possibly have been waiting for me? How did you know I would come here?" he asked, then as the thought struck him, "and how did you get past my guards?"

The woman smiled, "Your guards are children!" she said not unkindly. "Distracting children is not hard and there are many entrances to this Villa. Some are obvious, others are not," she said and then paused. "Yes I have been waiting for you, just as my predecessors waited."

"What do you mean? How could you have waited for me when even I didn't know I was coming here?" asked Constantine.

"I have foreseen your coming, just as I have seen the changes that are coming to our world. The old ways are giving way to the new. New beliefs are making themselves felt. The old ways of doing things no longer work as well as they once did. We call ourselves Roman's, but Rome is no longer at the heart of the Empire. The imperial court is split into many parts. Disunity and division rule our world! Every year that passes sees threats from outside our borders grow. More barbarians demand land within our borders each year because they are pressed upon by ever more dangerous threats that bear down upon them. If we continue along this path there will be nothing but anarchy in our future, an age of darkness and suffering. Our civilisation, our art and literature will all be forgotten. Everything we have accomplished will fall into ruin and be lost."

"So you are a seer? I have to tell you that I do not believe in magic! Nor do I believe in your gods! They are all just stories used to manipulate the gullible and ignorant. This Villa, and the legends that surround it, is a perfect example of how people use stories to distort the truth to influence others. The Emperor Augustus was not a god. He was a shrewd politician. His wife was not a goddess, just a very intelligent woman who knew how to protect herself and ensure her family stayed in power."

The woman looked at Constantine with her unsettling blue eyes, a knowing smile on her face. "You are truly a modern man, Constantine, but there are still mysteries in this world, that to some, would seem like magic.

Constantine stood staring at the woman. She gestured towards a clear space on the edge of the peristyle pool. "I am an old woman, Constantine, who gets tired standing for long periods. Come, sit with me and let me tell you a story."

377

Constantine stood unmoving for a moment and then, as the old lady stood waiting patiently, nodded and, taking her arm, helped her walk to the edge of the pool where they both sat bathed in the warm autumn sun.

"The story I have to tell started with the Emperor Augustus. Augustus was given a beautiful box by his uncle. The box contained a scroll and the ingredients to make a powerful medicine. This medicine was for the mind, not the body. Just like wine makes some people bold this medicine gives some people the power to see into the future."

Constantine started to interrupt, but the woman held up her hand. "This medicine is not magic. It works in the same way that physical exercise works on your body, making you stronger, faster, more agile. This medicine gives you better control over your mind. It helps you build a clearer picture from all the things you have observed in your life and the beliefs that you hold. It gives your mind the agility to recall every event of your life, every experience. It helps to makes connections between those events and allows you to see things that you missed when you first saw them. It organises your mind in a way that allows you to focus more clearly. It allows you to see the consequences of the actions you might take."

"It sounds like you know this potion well. Have you drunk of it yourself!" interrupted Constantine.

The woman nodded. "To become the priestess of Julia Augusta and the guardian of this treasure it is necessary to drink the potion. It is how I knew of your coming."

Constantine looked at her questioningly, but stayed silent. The woman looked Constantine in the eyes again, nodded approval, and continued.

"Along with the box comes a warning from the Emperor Augustus himself. This medicine is dangerous. It will only work for some people. Some it will kill. Others it will turn mad. For some, madness will come straight away, others will become addicted to its use and madness will come later. It was for this reason that, when Augustus died he bequeathed the box to his most trusted companion, Livia Drussila and not to his adopted son Tiberius."

"It was Livia Drusilla who controlled the use of the potion." The priestess smiled. "The Augusta was a very," she paused for a moment, searching for the most appropriate word, "... determined woman. She wanted to see her family line prosper. Unfortunately, while Augustus was able to use the potion sparingly with no apparent ill effects, the same was not true of her own bloodline.

"Livia gave Tiberius the drug when he ascended to the Principate. For him, for some reason, it did not work. It made him unsure of himself and sometimes vague. It progressively made him more and more paranoid, although how much of his paranoia was caused by the drug and how much the events of his life, one can never really know. Perhaps the drug just exacerbated what was already there."

"Livia Drusilla was shocked by the effect of the drug on her own son. She worked hard to support him so that the Senate, and the people of Rome did not lose faith in him. She refused to give him any more of the drug and Tiberius became more and more bitter towards his mother. Eventually his resentment of her led to his retiring to the island of Capri. You have no doubt read the stories of his paranoia and his moral depravity."

Constantine nodded. As a young boy, he and his friends had giggled over the descriptions in Suetonius of the salacious activities of the Emperor Tiberius on Capri.

"Livia told her great grandson, Gaius about the potion when he was living with her, after his mother and brother had been banished, for treason, by Tiberius. She promised to leave him a phial of the medicine, to be given to him when he became Emperor."

"Gaius?" asked Constantine.

"The son of Germanicus. Gaius is better known now by his nickname, Caligula," said the priestess.

Constantine's eyes widened. "So it was the drug that created that monster?"

"Initially Gaius was hailed as the saviour of the Empire. He was much loved by the people, as much for being the son of a much loved father, Germanicus, as for not being the much hated Tiberius. His first six months as Emperor where characterised by great generosity and magnanimity. He overturned many of the laws that had made Tiberius unpopular. He stopped the treason trials that Tiberius had instigated, recalled people from exile, published the accounts of the Empire for all to see, just as Augustus had and put on lavish and elaborate games for the people."

"So what went wrong? From what I have read Caligula was a monster," said Constantine.

"Gaius' life had not been easy. Growing up in army camps, his adored father dying under what were unusual circumstances, with Tiberius implicated in his death. Tiberius had Gaius' mother imprisoned and beaten so mercilessly that she lost an eye and eventually, despite being force fed, starved herself to death. He then had to suffer the indignity of watching the Senate declare her birthday a date of bad omen. One way or another Tiberius had both Gaius' brothers, Nero and Drusus, killed. Imagine what it did to the poor boy's mind. He then had to suffer six years of living with the man who had murdered his family. Living with Tiberius on Capri must have been a living hell for him."

"Some six months after he became Emperor the Augusta's directions were carried out and a phial of the drug was delivered to Gaius. He drank some and immediately fell seriously ill. He eventually recovered, but his personality had changed."

"His behaviour became increasingly erratic. He came to believe that he was a god! He had an annex built onto the Imperial residence in Rome that linked it directly to the temple of Castor and Pollux. He rededicated the temple to himself. Anyone unlucky enough to be present in the temple when he walked in had to bow down and worship him."

"If you were in a market selling this magic medicine of yours, I tell you now that I wouldn't be buying it!" said Constantine laughing. "The possibility of becoming the next Caligula is not an appealing one!"

"I tell you these things first because I want you to know what could happen if this medicine is abused," said the priestess looking into Constantine's' eyes. Convinced that he understood the dangers she looked down and grasped his hand. "There is another side to this medicine, Caesar, that may interest you. It is a story that, for the last two hundred years has been passed from each of my predecessors to the next. In all that time it has not been shared with anyone else."

She paused and seeing that Constantine was prepared to listen began her story. "Livia received the box from her husband Augustus. Augustus had used the medicine on a very few occasions. He knew that the potion, taken too many times would cause the mind to deteriorate. He knew this because he had seen first hand the effect the medicine could have on the physical body. He had seen the way it had affected his uncle, Julius Caesar."

Constantine turned to look at the priestess, who nodded affirmation of the statement she had just made. "Caesar discovered the box when he was a quaestor in Spain. He had used the potion throughout his remarkable rise to power, but it had taken its toll on him. It was Caesars' warning that made Augustus cautious."

A thought struck Constantine. "If Caesar found the box, who had it before him?

The priestess smiled. "That was the question that Augustus asked, but for a different reason," she said, wanting to tell the story in her own way. "The box contained a number of vials of ingredients. Most of the ingredients could be found relatively easily, especially for a man who ruled most of the known world, but one ingredient was more problematic. To determine what that ingredient was, Augustus needed to know who had made the original potion!"

"And who was that?" asked Constantine bluntly.

"I don't know. I am merely the keeper of the box. I don't know all its secrets," she said apologetically. "I do know that whoever had possession of the box in Spain, was a Carthaginian."

Constantine looked at the priestess, clearly shocked. "But Rome destroyed Carthage! Razed the city to the ground and had salt sown into the land!"

She nodded. "All I know is that the box originally came from the Iberian Peninsular. When Julius Caesar first opened the box he found a letter from a man called Hamilcar.

"What did the letter say?" asked Constantine, intrigued.

"I do not know Constantine," said the priestess. "All I know is that the box was hidden in Spain and that is where Caesar found it."

"Does the letter tell where the box came from?" asked Constantine.

"I do not know. Perhaps you will be able to read it when I give you the box," said the priestess.

Constantine looked at her in silence for some time and then asked, "Why are you giving it to me?"

The priestess put her hands in her lap and bowed her head. "I am not giving you the box Constantine. I am passing the responsibility to you. Rome is dying. In my mind I have seen it overrun by barbarians. I have seen it fall into ruin. You have proven yourself in battle. I have been told that you are an honourable man who is prepared to rule for all the people of the empire. I have seen what will happen if a man like you were to become Augustus. I have seen the creation of a new Rome, a Rome that will last for a thousand years. I have also seen that the time of cults is ending. Few people remember Livia, and fewer still care that she existed. I am the last of the priestesses of Julia Augusta."

"And if I don't accept it, or don't take this magic potion of yours?" he asked.

She looked at him again with her incredibly blue eyes. "You are facing a turning point in your life Constantine. It is also a turning point for our world! Maxentius is a good administrator but he has no vision! He can not inspire people! You can!"

"You are facing a long cold winter, Constantine! Maxentius has many more men than you. The walls of the greatest city in the world protect him. He has enough grain to last him easily through the longest of winters. He knows he can wear you down just by sitting in his Palace on the Palatine Hill."

"I know. I rode up here to get some peace and to think what my next move should be. I do not appear to have many choices," said Constantine with a sigh.

The priestess squeezed Constantine's hand. He felt the warmth of the gesture. "I don't know what effect this drug will have on you. Nobody does until they take it. All I can tell you is that, when I took it, for a single moment I saw the world with incredible clarity. The futures laid themselves out before me like a series of pathways paved in light. I could see what was important and what were mere distractions. I have been waiting for a long time for a man like you to appear. Take the potion. Take the risk, Constantine! Save Rome! Save our Empire!"

She stood up. As she did so he saw, sitting on the edge of the empty pool, next to where she had been sitting, a box. It was wrapped in a beige coloured material and bound with a strip of red cloth. The priestess rested her hand on it, stroking it gently. "This is yours now Constantine. Guard it well!" and then she turned and started to walk away.

Before she was lost in the trees of the overgrown garden she stopped and turned back towards him with a smile. "It may be of interest to you to know what the Sibylline oracles have told Maxentius."

Constantine raised an eyebrow.

The priestess laughed. "It is no secret. Maxentius has sent his agents into the streets of Rome telling all those that will listen. The oracles have prophesied that tomorrow an enemy of Rome will die."

Constantine watched as she disappeared among the tangle of trees.

20. Rome - 27th October 312AD

"This should be a time of celebration! I should be lauded for my six years of achievements, not heckled by a bunch of ungrateful scum!" shouted the Emperor Maxentius to anyone who was not too scared to be in the same room with him.

Memory of the heckling he had received at the chariot race had set him off. "Once I have dealt with Constantine I can deal with the situation here in Rome. Give this rabble a few more days holiday, a decent chariot race and a bit of blood in the arena and they will be cheering me again soon enough. For those that don't, there is always the sword!" he said, sitting heavily down on a couch.

"Tell me, where is my dear brother-in-law and what is he doing?" he asked. No one answered. "I said, tell me what Constantine is doing! Where is my Pretorian Prefect? Where is Ruricius Pompeianus?" shouted Maxentius, his face flushing red.

His Generals looked at one another, avoiding Maxentius' eyes. A young pretorian guard, braver than most, said in a quiet voice. "Ruricius Pompeianus died in Verona, Augustus, fighting Constantine. You have not yet appointed a new Pretorian Prefect for Rome."

Maxentius stared at the young man, who, wisely, kept his eyes averted.

"Have the gods deserted me?" said Maxentius, angrily, almost to himself. "This man takes my sister, my father and now the best of my Generals!"

Maxentius sat brooding for a few minutes then stood up. In a loud voice he announced, "Constantine will *not* take Rome from me! The Sybiline Books have prophesied that tomorrow *he* will die!"

"Rufius Volusianus," he said, turning to his most trusted adviser, "the auguries are good. We will do battle with Constantine tomorrow. Have the army prepared!"

"My lord!" exclaimed Volusianus, "Would it not be more prudent to wait. Let Constantine waste his time sitting outside the walls of Rome. A siege will not hurt us, but will weaken his resolve."

"No! Fools!" shouted Maxentius, his face red. "Tomorrow is the anniversary of my ascension to the Imperial throne. There will never be a more auspicious day for battle. The Sibylline oracle has stated that Constantine will die on the 28th of October. Tomorrow we have to take the battle to him."

21. Prima Porta - 27th October 312AD

He sat alone in his tent looking at the box. Outside the noise of the camp had quieted. Constantine had felt a sense of expectation and apprehension in the air as he walked through the camp earlier that evening. His men, experienced veterans, knew that the night before a possible battle was a time to prepare yourself, and leave others to do the same.

He ran his hand over its surface, wondering if he should believe what the woman in the villa had told him. It had crossed his mind that this may be an elaborate ruse invented by Maxentius. There was no doubt that Maxentius was both clever and shrewd. He had, after all, reached the exalted position of Augustus and managed to keep control of Rome for six years. But Maxentius was a bureaucrat, not a warrior. He preffered to send others, like the Pretorian Prefect Ruricius Pompeianus, to fight his battles for him. In Constantine's' eyes, that made him unworthy of ruling even a small part of the great Roman Empire. It also made it more plausible that he would stoop to such an ignoble deception to bring down a rival. How convenient it would be for Maxentius if the man about to lay siege to Rome was found dead in his tent, a phial of poison clasped in his hand.

Despite his nagging doubts, Constantine picked up the package and carefully unwound the strip of red material, which he then cast aside. He unwound the rough linen wrapping. He involuntarily gasped as the box was revealed. It was beautiful. It was not large, perhaps the length of his two hands outstretched, half as wide, and about half that length again in depth. It was made of gold with elaborate inlays creating a scene of bulls, stags and a powerful animal with the head of a man and the body of a winged lion. He had seen such a beast before. It was a shedu.

Constantine carefully opened the lid. Inside, neatly slotted into separate compartments, were a series of twelve small glass containers. Each had an ornate silver stopper. Taking one out, and holding it up to the light of the oil lamp, he could see something inside. He shook the

386

small bottle revealing the contents to be a fine powder. He opened the lid. It smelt faintly of pine.

Looking more closely he saw that there was one bottle with a gold stopper in the shape of a Lion's head. When he withdrew that bottle he discovered, unlike the others, this one was not glass but gold. A serpent design wrapped around it. Lifting up a small sheet of papyrus he noticed that the box also contained a scroll that fitted neatly within the width of the box. There were also three slots for another set of small containers. Two of the slots were empty, but the third was not. He withdrew the container, a small glass tear vial with a glass stopper covered in sealing wax. He could see a dark, viscous liquid moving sluggishly within the phial. He placed the container carefully back into the hole designed for it and turned his attention to the piece of papyrus.

The papyrus was covered with writing that Constantine did not immediately recognise. Holding it closer to his lamp he suddenly realised that the writing was Punic, the language of the ancient Phoenicians. He knew a few words of the language. In his travels in the east, while serving under the Emporer Diocletian, he had often heard it spoken, but rarely seen it written. He couldn't read it. He doubted whether anyone in the camp would be able to. He put the document aside and lifted the scroll out of the box.

The Scroll was tightly wound. He could tell by the feel and smell, as he gently unrolled it, that it was made of leather. It was beginning to show signs of considerable age. Holding it close to his lamp he could see that it was written in Latin. He recognised it immediately. It was the Song of Ilium, Homer's great epic poem describing the siege of Troy, sometimes called the Iliad. Constantine was very familiar with the poem. This version was beautifully written. He started to carefully rewind the scroll. He smiled to himself, anticipating the pleasure of re-reading the poem when time permitted.

He picked up the Punic papyrus. Another piece of papyrus, that he had not noticed earlier, was stuck to it. He carefully pulled the two pieces apart. The second document was written in Latin.

Holding it up to the light he could see that it was a letter written to someone called Gaius. The letter described the box's contents and indicated that the silver and gold stoppered containers were the ingredients of the potion and that the glass vial contained the made up mixture, which should be taken only in small drops. It also referred to another letter that was part of the writer's will, lodged with the vestal virgins. Presumably, Constantine thought to himself, the letter with the will would have described what this magic potion actually did. He came to the end of the letter and stared at the ragged edge of the torn papyrus. Part of the signature was gone, but a single name remained, Julius.

22. Rome - Present day

Elizabeth held up her hands. "Hang on a minute you guys. You are really starting to befuddle me now. You history nerds might be familiar with all these people and ideas but you have to take things slow for me. Who was this person, Livia or Julia or whatever you called her, who had some sort of priestess named after her?"

"Do you mean Livia Drusilla?" asked Charlotte.

"I guess so," answered Elizabeth, "but you rattled off a bunch of other names names for her as well. Is it all the same person?"

"Her original name, the one her family gave her was Livia Drusilla. When her husband, the first Emperor, Augustus died, he stated in his will that she should be adopted into his family, the Julian family, and be given the title of Augusta, so she is also known as Julia Augusta."

"And they made her a God? Is that what having a cult means?"

Charlotte nodded. "She was deified by the Senate in the time of the Emperor Claudius, in the year 41or 42 AD. In her time she was the most powerful woman in Rome. After her death and deification there is evidence that she was worshipped right across the Empire. It is quite possible that a priestess of her cult survived through until the time of Constantine."

"And this Julian family, this is the family of Julius Caesar, the Julius Caesar that got stabbed in the back?" asked Elizabeth.

Charlotte nodded again. "Giaus Julius Caesar is *the* Julius Caesar, big Julie. He adopted his nephew, Giaus Octavius, who is usually known, before his adoption, as Octavian. After he was adopted he became Giaus Julius Caesar Octavianus, but everyone would have just called him Caesar. Then, after big Julie was turned into a God, Octavian, or Caesar, became Gaius Julius Caesar Divi Filius, meaning that he was Gaius Julius Caesar son of the Divine. Then, he changed his own name to Imperator Caesar Divi Filius. Then, after he defeated Mark Antony and Cleopatra, he became Imperator Caesar Divi Filius Augustus. So now we just call him Augustus. Perhaps his mates just called him Gus, we don't know."

Charlotte smiled at Elizabeth who had put her head in her hands and was shaking it from side to side.

"Okay, okay. I give in. So in simple terms, we now think that Livia was given the potion by Augustus, Gus, who got it from big Julie?"

"That's right," said Alberto, laughing at their irreverent turn of phrase. "According to the writings of Pope Leo, Constantine also had some things to say about what happened in the time of Julius Caesar. We don't know how he would have known these things, but so many historical records that would have been available to Constantine are now lost. It is quite possible that he had access to information about the contents of Caesar's will, maybe even the letter he wrote to Octavian."

"So you think you know the story from big Julie's perspective?" asked Dan.

23. Rome - 14th of March 44BCE

Julius Caesar sat in the dark, only a small oil lamp on the desk before him. His slaves had long since gone off to their sleeping places and his wife, Calpurnia, to hers. The night was cold and he pulled his blanket more tightly around his shoulders.

He reached for the goblet of wine that sat on the desk and stopped. He sat looking at his hand caught in the flickering lantern light. It shook noticeably now. Try as he might he could not stop it. The falling fits, too, had started to become more frequent. He wondered, if he had known the consequences of taking the potion when he was young and ambitious and desperate for success, whether he would have thought it worth it. Would he have done it? Would he trade all the power he now held in this trembling hand for a steady hand and a few more years of life? Would he trade those moments of absolute clarity when he could see the future laid out before him as clearly as a map on a piece of parchment? Would he trade those glorious moments standing at the rostrum in the forum before a crowd of his countrymen, when he felt the power of influence swell within him, rising up through his chest and then bursting out over his audience, washing any doubts they might have had away and sweeping them up in his will? Would he trade a single one of those magical battlefield moments when he saw the path to victory so clearly in his mind?

No! He knew that he could not give up a single one.

He had made a vow when he was thirty, to the gods and before the bust of Alexander the Great, that he would not waste the rest of his life. He knew, here at the end, that he could now look the gods, and Alexander, squarely in the eye, confident that his name would be remembered alongside theirs. He, Gaius Julius Caesar had made Rome ruler of the world, just as Alexander had done for Macedon.

He knew that his life was fast running out. Over the last few months he had begun to sense that his body and mind were starting to burn up. Like the oil in the lamp on his desk his vital spirit had almost run dry. He watched, a sad smile on his face, as the little oil lamp guttered

- flaring brightly and then dimming to almost nothing. That was him. He only had a short time left. His most fervent desire was that he not be remembered as a burnt out shell, spittle dribbling down the front of his toga, in some forgotten corner, unable to feed himself or remember his own name.

It was time to give the future to the next generation. He looked down at the letter he had just written to Octavius. He would have a slave take it, and the box, to the House of the Vestal Virgins in the morning where they would both be lodged with his will. It was Octavius who would stand on his shoulders and rule the world for the family Julii.

Wearily he reached out to the two scrolls resting beside the beautifully ornate box that sat on his desk. He put the one that he had arranged to give his father-in-law, Lucius to one side, along with the note he had written earlier. He opened the box and slipped the other scroll into the place that was made for it. He looked down at the small glass vial that lay nestled in its own slot in the box, wrapped in a piece of silk. He picked it up, holding it so that the flickering light of the lantern caught the oily movement of the liquid inside it. Turning it over he checked to see that the wax seal, impressed with the Roman eagle, the aquila, had not been tampered with. "Well my friend," he said in a whisper to the glass vial, "this will be the last time that you and I journey together. We have had a merry ride these last few years. I just hope that we have the strength to do what must be done today and that you will treat young Gaius a little more kindly than you did me."

Caesar broke the seal and pulled the stopper from the vial. With one movement he drank its contents and then threw the vial across the room where it shattered against the ornately painted wall. Shards of glass rained onto the tiled floor. He sat heavily back in his chair and closed his eyes, a tired old man.

Outside the sky lightened as the sun rose on the Ides of March.

24. Rome - 15th of March 44BC

Calpurnia had slept badly. She had been having nightmares and had only managed a fitful sleep. She had awoken with a feeling of dread.

Getting out of bed she wrapped a blanket around her shoulders and walked to the doorway of her room.

She could see Caesar sitting on a bench in the peristylium, deep in thought. She walked over to him and put her hand gently on his shoulder.

He reached up and covered her hand with his. It felt warm, but she could feel the tremor that he tried so hard to hide. She still marvelled at the fact that she was still married to the first man of Rome. She loved him deeply, despite Cleopatra, his philandering and his political manoeuvring. She was proud to be the wife of Julius Caesar, Imperator of Rome.

Tears started to roll down her cheeks.

Caesar looked up at her. Seeing her tears he gently sat her down beside him. Her hands were in her lap with his still covering them.

"What is troubling you?" he asked, his voice rich, soft and caring.

"I have dreamed terrible things," she said in a quiet voice, not looking up. "I dreamed that the pediment of this house collapsed, falling into the street. I dreamed that the door to my bedroom was flung open and yet no-one was there. Worst of all I dreamt that you were stabbed while I held you in my arms. Blood streamed from your wounds and I could not stop it."

She said the last with a heartfelt wail and fell onto his shoulder, crying with loud sobs, unable to hold back the fears that plagued her.

Caesar put his arms around her and drew her close. He sat quietly holding her, protecting her against the chill of the cold March morning.

"...and there was the warnings of that soothsayer, Spurinna, about the Ides of March. Could you not stay at home today?" she asked once she had regained her composure. "I could send word to the Senate that you are ill and need to rest. No-one would question it."

393

Caesar lifted her chin and looked her in the eyes. "I am Caesar," he said. A thrill ran though her as she involuntarily responded to his voice and the force of his personality. "Caesar will not lie to the Senate of Rome."

"I will though, to calm your fears, seek guidance. Why don't you have someone go and ask the priests to take a reading of the will of the gods. Let us see what the fates say about the future of Caesar."

Calpurnia and Caesar both stood up. He leant down, brushed her cheek tenderly with his hand and kissed her lightly on the lips. She smiled weakly and then went to find one of the household slaves to take Caesar's instructions to the Augurs.

****

While Caesar waited for the priest, people started to appear at his door, clients come to accompany him to the Senate house. One of the last to arrive was Decimus Junius Brutus Albinus who, as he walked into the atrium of the house, looked surprised to see Caesar seated and dealing with clients.

Not long after a priest entered. He walked to where Caesar sat and greeted him. "Ave Caesar, Ave!". Caesar nodded. The priest looked at the ground. "The sacrifice has been made, Caesar, and the omens are, inauspicious!" he said nervously.

"What signs were there that you should make such a prediction?' asked Caesar, feeling irritated and not trying to hide it.

"The sacrifice had no heart, Caesar," said the priest still looking at the ground. "This is a portent of death."

"A portent of death!" said Caesar in a loud voice. "I have had these before! When I was in Spain fighting the great Pompey the portents told of death."

"That is true," the priest said hesitantly. "That was, no doubt, a time of great danger for you Caesar. The portents confirmed it. The signs now foretell of a much more serious danger."

"Ha!" said Caesar with a raucous laugh. "Go and sacrifice again, and bring me back portents that are more auspicious." The priest frowned, nodded and walked back across the atrium.

The general hubbub of conversation, which had died with the entrance of the priest, started up again. Caesar went back to greeting and dealing with his clients. He caught sight of Decimus Junius Brutus Albinus watching Caesar and talking to no-one.

As he paused to take a sip of wine before dealing with his next client, Decimus Albinus took advantage of the opportunity and approached him. "Ave Caesar, Ave!" He leaned forward and kissed Caesar lightly on the cheek.

Caesar smiled, acknowledging the greeting. "Decimus, it is good to see you again."

He had a long history with his cousin Decimus. They had fought together in the Gallic wars and in the Civil war. He had been impressed by the way Decimus had so ably commanded fleet operations for him. He was a man he knew he could trust to work diligently to achieve a goal.

"Caesar, I came to accompany you to the Senate but you seem to be in no hurry to leave home. Has something happened of which I am not aware?" asked Decimus.

"The signs are not auspicious for me to attend the Senate today, Decimus. My wife has had terrifying dreams and the Augurs cannot get a good sacrifice. I have, just this minute, sent word to Antonius that I will not be coming."

Decimus looked stunned. "Caesar, you can't let the rantings of a distressed woman and the babbling of soothsayers dictate your actions. The Roman Senate has been in session since early this morning. You summoned them! They await your arrival. Will you not rise above this superstitious nonsense and honour them with your presence?"

Caesar looked directly into Decimus' eyes. He held them until Decimus looked away. "Yes!" said Caesar, making up his mind and standing up, "Let us get this over with. It is time we put an end to this game." He adjusted his toga and strode from the atrium, his clients hurrying to fall in around him.

****

In the quiet of a suddenly empty house, Calpurnia, who had been watching the events of the morning from her own apartment, fell to her knees, loud sobs wracking her body.

25. Rome - 15th of March 44BC

Caesar approached the Theatre of Pompey surrounded by his clients. The street was busy as he stepped out of his litter onto the cobbled street. As he did so he saw the familiar figure of Spurinna the soothsayer standing nearby. He called to him, with a slightly mocking tone, remembering their last encounter, "Spurrina! The ides of March are upon us and Caesar still lives!"

"Aye Caesar." Spurrina called back "But they have not yet left us!" With that he turned away and was lost in the crowd.

Caesar smiled. He enjoyed repartee with those who were quick witted. He walked into the the Theatre of Pompey, enjoying the grandeur of its enclosed courtyard, and walked towards the Curia of Pompey, the small building at the opposite end of the courtyard to the area where performances were normally staged.

The Senate had been sitting at the Theatre since the Senate House in the forum had been burnt down several years earlier. Caesar mounted the steps that led into the Curia and made his way to the gilded chair at the head of the chamber.

As was customary, once he was seated, senators began to approach him with petitions. At the head of the queue was Lucius Tilius Cimber. "Ah, my friend Cimber!" said Caesar with a smile. "What boon can I grant you?"

"It is my brother, Caesar. I have here a petition requesting his return from exile." Caesar frowned. "Why do you ask me this? We have spoken of this before and you have heard my answer! Why do you persist in this futile course of action?" he said, his undisguised irritation obvious in his voice and in his expression.

"But Caesar, reconsider!" said a voice from close behind him. Caesar had to stand to see who had addressed him. He rose, recognising Publius Servilius Casca, as the one who had spoken. There were many senators crowding around him now. It was at that moment that he knew that his time had finally come.

He felt a sudden, excruciating pain in his shoulder as Casca thrust a knife into him. His anger flared, he grabbed Casca's arm and, with teeth clenched, he brought the only weapon he had to hand, his writing stylus, to bear, stabbing it hard into the flesh of Casca's arm. The man screamed. Caesar braced himself for what he knew was coming. He felt the second thrust, the third the fourth the fifth, but then as he began to lose consciousness and as his legs gave way, he lost count. Determined not to cry out he kept his teeth clenched. As he fell he pulled his toga over his head to prevent anyone seeing his face as he died.

He was still breathing, barely conscious, when the last blade was withdrawn from his body. He heard them walk away, leaving him lying on the cold marble floor. He could actually feel his life blood flowing away. Under the toga a faint smile touched his lips as he saw in his mind's eye how the future would now unfold. "You greedy, self interested fools!" he whispered to himself. "It is not me you have killed it is the Republic!"

26. Rome - Present day

"So Caesar died to advance his own plan for the creation of a Roman Empire!" said Dan, shocked. "And the Emperor Augustus took advantage of the potion as well?"

Alberto nodded. "He did. Unlike his uncle he did so with great moderation, but then Octavian was a politician, not a warrior. He had others do his fighting for him. His great talent was his political acumen,"

"Julius Caesar's story, though tells of the detrimental effect of this drug on the mental faculties of someone who takes it. It is well documented that Caesar's fits and his shaking were becoming more and more frequent leading up to his death," said Charlotte.

"Ah, but the Emperor Augustus lived to a ripe old age!" stated Dan.

"Yes, that is true!" said Charlotte with a nod. "But from what we read, I think that Augustus only used the potion a few times in his life. I would suggest that the same couldn't be said of others in his family. The interesting thing, and perhaps it is significant, is that the Emperors immediately after Augustus were not of the same family. They were descendants of the adopted family of Augustus, of his wife Livia. Perhaps this potion is somehow coded to a particular pattern of DNA."

"After the Julian Dynasty died out with Nero, we believe that the potion was lost, or forgotten, at least by those who held the Imperial sceptre," said Alberto.

"But not by the cult of Livia, it seems," said Elizabeth.

"No." said Charlotte. "Which brings us back to Constantine's story."

27. Prima Porta - 27th October 312AD

Constantine held the letter in has hand for a long time. If this was a trick perpetrated by Maxentius than it was an incredibly elaborate one. Eventually he put the letter down and picked up the glass vial that contained the potion. He broke the wax seal and withdrew the glass stopper. Tentatively he sniffed the contents. It didn't seem to have a smell.

Knowing that he faced a vastly superior force as well as the likelihood of a prolonged siege, Constantine still had not resolved, in his own mind, how he should proceed. He sat staring at the glass vial in his hand. After some time he placed it carefully back in the box, closed the lid and lay down to sleep.

He slept fitfully. Visions haunted his sleep. He saw himself being dragged in golden chains behind Maxentius' chariot at the head of a triumph. He saw his head being paraded through the streets of Rome on a pike. He saw his men chained together in long lines, being sold at the slave markets. He woke sweating, tangled in his sodden bed clothes.

He fell back into troubled sleep. Maxentius and his commanders now stood around his bed laughing at his lifeless body, the open glass vial, drained of its contents, still held loosely in his dead hand.

He awoke with a feeling of dread. Sitting up , he saw that it was still dark outside. He looked across at the box. He opened it and withdrew the phial. After a moments hesitation, he withdrew the stopper and dripped two drops of the reddish brown liquid into a goblet of watered down wine that stood on a small table beside his bed.

After replacing the phial in the box and closing its lid he drank the wine in a single swallow.

At first nothing happened. He shrugged his shoulders and, disappointed, lay back down, laughing at himself for his own foolishness and his gullibility in believing such a ridiculous story.

He tried to relax. Almost imperceptivity at first, his heart started to beat more strongly in his chest. He moved his hand across his bedclothes, and as he did so he suddenly realized that he could feel the detail of the sheet beneath his hand, the warp and weft of its silken threads. He felt his mind separate from his body and rise into the air above his tent, where it floated.

From this unique vantage point he could see the tents of his camp laid out in ordered lines below him. He could sense his men sleeping inside their tents. Beyond the camp he could see forests, open fields, roads and the river. His mind followed the river Tiber as it moved, like a sinuous snake, towards Rome.

As his mind approached Rome he could feel its people. Hundreds of thousands of them crammed into their insulae. He could see the seven hills enclosed within the Aurelian walls.

His mind paused, stopping above the Palatine Hill, the palaces of the Roman elite below him. Then then image in his mind began to expand. He could see the countryside to the south of Rome, the mountains to the North, which he had so recently crossed, and the lands to the east. He saw Athens, with its beautiful Acropolis glowing gold in the light of the rising sun.

The image grew larger still. He could see the coast of Britannia, its white cliffs still in darkness. He could see the farthest reaches of the Empire to the north. The Danube wound its way through dark forests beneath him. To the east he could see the lands of the Persians. Alexandria came into view with its magnificent lighthouse bathed in morning light, and beyond that the great pyramids standing out starkly against the Giza plateau. He followed the mighty Nile River back to its source in the great lakes of Africa.

Constantine marveled at the size and variety of the world, its beauty and its drama. Then his mind changed focus. Across this vast Empire he began to feel the mood of its people. He could sense the fear and the disunity and how conflict was tearing the Roman world apart.

His mind began to focus. He could see the things that had weakened the Empire, the devastating plagues, the infighting of claimants to the Imperial throne, the continuous battle to defend the empire's borders, the undermining of the imperial coinage and the aspirations of those who sought power for it own sake. So many complex issues all working against the Empire.

He could see clearly, in his mind, how each of these complex issues impacted on the others. For one moment he saw his world as a single giant, complex machine, far too complex for any one person to control.

Looking closely at the inner workings of the great machine he saw that parts of it were broken, or worn out. The Roman pantheon of gods was failing. Deifying Emperors, with all their obvious human frailties, had undermined the people's faith in their Gods. The rituals, the common threads that had held the Empire together for so long, were becoming meaningless. Sol Invictus, the unconquerable sun, was taking a more prominent role in the lives of the people of the Empire now. People needed something clear, unambiguous and well defined, to believe in.

As Constantine studied the intricacies of the machine, he could see, at its heart, the worn out and rundown city of Rome. The eternal city had not been the centre of the Empire for years, but still its influence, and the influence of its decadent noble families, dragged the Empire down.

He awoke with a start. He felt invigorated, wide awake and full of energy. It was as if his mind and his senses had been switched on for the first time.

He rose from his sleeping palette and washed his face, noticing, as if for the first time the way the flow of water dribbled from his hands. He slipped a clean tunic over his head, delighting in the fineness of the fabric. He put his boots on, spending a moment marveling at the rich texture of the leather and then walked to the entrance of his tent, nodded to the guards and stepped out into the cold morning light. The hustle and bustle of the camp was all around him, people waking up, some preparing meals, others preparing their weapons. As he walked through the camp he revelled in the flood of sights, sounds and smells that assailed him.

Smoke, from the many cooking fires hung over the camp. As he walked the disparate origins of his men was brought home to him once again. Each individual maintained their own identity through their dress, their weapon choice or the manner in which they wore their hair, but within that individuality each man also maintained his ethnic identity as well. An Allen dressed like an Allen, a Celt, like a Celt and a Roman like a Roman. He, like other Roman commanders before him, had often used that diversity to their advantage, playing one group's strength off against another's.

Walking down the long straight rows of tents, Constantine suddenly realised how unusual his situation was. He was leading a Roman army to attack Rome itself! He was leading an army, with a large contingent of barbarians, into the heart of the Empire! He would be fighting an army of Romans led by the self-professed Augustus, Maxentius. His men would, no doubt, believe that they were fighting to protect Rome. What were his men fighting for?

His mind raced as he continued to walk past tents and cooking fires. He heard someone shout his name. He turned and saw Marcellus Agrippa hurrying towards him. He watched as the old General lumbered up.

Marcellus was frowning. "Maxentius is coming Constantine!" he said breathlessly. "He is leading his men up the Via Flaminia as we stand here talking!" Marcellus paused. "Our informers are saying that the oracles have told him that today is the day that you will die! Maxentius has had his spies spreading the news throughout our camp. It is starting to unsettle the men!"

Constantine stood for a moment, processing this information. Interestingly, he thought to himself, I have seen this possibility, but had not known it would happen. He turned to Marcellus. "If the gates are open now then they will be at the river crossing by the middle of the morning," he said. "It is only four leagues to Rome. We do not have much time."

"I want you to do something for me. I want you to arrange for all the men to paint this symbol on their shields," he said drawing his dagger from his belt and squatting down to draw a symbol in the dust. The symbol resembled a P with an X crossing through it.

"What does it mean?" asked Marcellus.

"It means a lot of things Marcellus. It is called the Chi-Rho." said Constantine. "Greek scribes used it to mark a particularly brilliant passage in the scrolls they were writing. It is a short way of writing chreston, which means good! It can also stand for Chronos, the god of time, or sometimes it is used to denote the word chresterion, the gift of an oracle. It could even represent the new Christian saviour Christos!" he said with a smile.

Marcellus gave him a sceptical look. "What will I tell the men?"

"Tell them that I have had a dream. Today we will have a glorious victory and that this symbol that will protect them!"

****

Constantine sat astride his horse. In front of him his Gaulish cavalry, to either side of them, his infantry. Emblazoned on each shield, hastily painted, was the Chi-Rho. He took a deep breath. "Men of the Empire, you and I have fought together from the shores of Britannia to the doorstep of Rome. Today, for the first time, we will fight together under a new symbol!"

"Last night I had a vision! I saw us all, whether we be Roman, Gaul, Allan, Goth, whatever tribe we have come from, whatever country we call home, all of us fighting, united, under a single banner. Under the protection of this symbol," he pointed to a banner, emblazoned with the Chi Rho, held aloft by one of his aquilifer, "we will conquer!" he shouted.

"Today we will do battle for the future of Rome! Not the old city, or the privileged families who live their, behind its walls, but the Empire of Rome! The Empire that stretches from one end of the earth to the other. We fight for an Empire no longer riven by civil wars! We fight for an Empire which is united! We fight for an Empire that is strong!"

He could see nods of approval as his words were passed through the assembled men. He paused for a few moments, then shouted "We have fought many battles together and in all of them we have been victorious!"

There were more nods this time, as he paused again for his words to be spread through the assembled ranks of men.

"I have heard what the Sibylline Oracle has told the usurper Maxentius. They have told him that today an enemy of Rome will die! Look into your hearts. Are we enemies of Rome?" he shouted.

Constantine paused and heard the rumblings of the men as they responded to his question.

"Are we enemies of Rome?" he shouted more loudly.

A resounding "No!" was shouted back at him.

"This symbol under which we will fight can mean many things. Today let it be the acknowledgement of the gift of the Sibylline oracle. Today their prophecy will come true. Today the enemy of Rome will die! Today we fight to release Rome from the tyranny of that enemy, the usurper, Maxentius!"

The men cheered.

"Today we free Rome!" he shouted, then, pulling on his horse's rein, he turned and headed, without looking back, towards the River Tiber and the road to Rome.

28. Rome - 28th October 312

Surrounded on either side and behind by the equites singulares Augusti, the cavalry arm of his Praetorian Guard, Maxentius felt safe. Unlike his elite cavalry unit who wore flexible, utilitarian scale armour, the lorica squamata, and carried a hexagonal shield emblazoned with the images of 4 scorpions, Maxentius wore a beautifully wrought cuirass that was shaped in the form of a heavily muscled warrior and was patterned with scenes from Greek mythology. From his shoulders a long purple cloak swept back over his horse's haunches. At his waist he wore a long gladius, about the length of one of his arms. It too, was ornate, its scabbard lavishly covered with designs in gold. He did not carry a shield. It was not, after all, his intention to fight, only to lead his men to the field of battle.

Directly behind his Pretorian cavalry came the Pretorian Guard itself, marching in formation, their curved shields with their distinctive star and moon design held unwaveringly before them. Further back still came the other legions. Some had fought for his father, Maximian.

With almost one hundred thousand men behind him, Maxentius sat tall in his saddle. Resplendent in his parade armour. He felt truly Imperial.

As they approached the Milvian Bridge, he could see that the preparations that had been discussed with his officers had been made. The stone bridge had been partially demolished to prevent Constantine's army from crossing. A wooden pontoon bridge had now been strung between the banks of the Tiber, slightly downriver from the old stone bridge. Iron pins had been used to secure the rope that joined each of the pontoons to its neighbour. The pins had been arranged so they could be easily withdrawn, releasing the pontoons to the current and cutting the river crossing completely, should that be required.

Maxentius' horse baulked slightly as it stepped out onto the dirt covered wooden bridge that had been consructed atop the pontoons. He thrust his heels into the horses flank and, with the press of other horses around it, the horse reluctantly continued out onto to the makeshift bridge. Looking ahead Maxentius could see the Via Flaminia heading north. He urged his horse forward. The horse walked nervously across the bridge, but settled as it stepped onto firm ground on the western side of the river. At that moment Maxentius heard a shout and saw, to his horror, a squad of cavalry, still some distance away but heading at a gallop towards him. Caught at the head of the column of his own cavalry he tried to turn his horse around, to get back over the bridge, but the press of horses on either side made it impossible. He was caught in the vanguard of his own army. The one place he most wanted not to be!

Maxentius turned to Rufius Volusianus, his most able and trusted adviser, who was riding alongside him. "Take a turma of cavalry up there to engage with Constantine's cavalry," he said pointing up the hill. "That will give us time to cross the river."

Rufius, looking over his shoulder and seeing how their army had been caught straddling the bottleneck created by the bridge, nodded agreement and, with a few shouted commands, spurred his horse into a gallop. A stream of mounted horsemen flowed around Maxentius while he sat, unmoving, on his horse. As the last of the cavalrymen passed him Maxentius shouted orders to his other commanders, commanding them to move his infantry into a defensive wall as quickly as they could.

Men passed him at a run. Two hundred metres in advance of his position, they spread out at right angles to the Via Flaminia. The first row of men knelt down, placing the bottoms of their shields on the ground forming a defensive wall. Their javelins protruded through the wall like the spikes on a sea urchin.

To his right and left the remainder of his cavalry was spreading out to protect the infantry from attack. Archers formed up behind the wall of infantry and, as more men crossed the bridge, they too continued to form up behind the defensive wall. Maxentius, now able to move more freely wheeled his horse back, closer to the bridge, although he realised, with the continual flow of men crossing it, he would be unable to retreat across to the other side anytime soon. Despite his exposed position, Maxentius was starting to feel more safe and confident. Almost a third of his men had now crossed the bridge and were organised into a defensive formation between Constantine and himself. Behind him, still crossing the river, was an almost limitless supply of reserves. He smiled to himself, urging his horse still closer to the bridge, comfortable in the knowledge that the oracles had promised that it was his enemy that would die this day.

29. Italy - 28th October 312AD

Constantine led his men across country toward the Milvian Bridge. He could see, even without the insight provided by the potion, that the river crossing would be the key. His aim was to get to the crossing before Maxentius, but, as the bridge came in sight, he could see that Maxentius had already crossed. They were too late. He reined his horse in and sat looking towards the river. Marcellus rode up beside him. "It looks like they have beaten us to it, Constantine. Should I have the men get into battle formation?"

Constantine considered his options. Even at this stage it looked like Maxentius had more troops on this side of the river than he had in his whole army. There was no doubt they were outnumbered. A set piece battle would undoubtably lead to his own army being overwhelmed as Maxentius' army continued to grow in size as more troops poured across the river.

A cavalry troop suddenly broke away from the head of Maxentius' column and men moved rapidly into the traditional defensive formation in front of the advancing army. While he watched more cavalry started to spread out on either side of the bridge to protect Maxentius' flanks.

Constantine stared at the scene being played out in front of him. Options and opportunities started to race through his mind. He had never experienced anything like this before. As quickly as an idea presented itself his mind evaluated it. To his amazement, after only a few moments, he had resolved his options and decided on a course of action.

He turned to Marcellus. "We need to keep Maxentius boxed in around the bridge head. Establish a fighting line across the path of the Via Flaminia. Make it look like a normal battle formation, but make sure the wings are stronger than the centre. Take half the cavalry and engage that group of cavalry heading towards us, but before you go get me five of your best men. I have a special job for them. Your priority Marcellus will be to hold the wings at all costs. Maxentius' army must not to be allowed to spread out."

Marcellus nodded. "And you my Lord?" he asked.

"After I give your men their instructions I will lead the rest of the cavalry to support the centre. Be ready for a signal from me, and be prepared to follow my lead," said Constantine.

A few minutes later five burly legionnaires approached Constantine. He swung down off his horse and looked at them. They were all young men. By the look of them they came from wealthy families that could afford to equip their sons in the best armour. They were all from the equestrian rank, smart, educated and, no doubt, ambitious. Each man saluted and introduced himself. One man, Lucius Festus, who had introduced himself first, was slightly older and brawnier than the others. He was standing slightly ahead of them. The other four men continually glanced in his direction before acting. He was clearly the leader of the small group.

"I have a task for you men," said Constantine in a quiet voice. "It is likely to be extremely dangerous but vital if we are to win this battle today. Can you swim?" All but the youngest of the group nodded. Constantine continued. "As you can see, Maxentius has destroyed part of the old stone bridge to stop us crossing. My informers tell me that the pontoon bridge he has built is securely tied together, but that iron pins have been used to allow for their quick release should Maxentius need to retreat back over the bridge. I want four of you to enter the Tiber, beyond that bend above the bridge and then, using whatever flotsam you can find for cover, float down the river. Once you hit the pontoon bridge I want you to release the pins holding the bridge. If this is not possible I want you to cut the ropes that hold the pontoons together. As soon as you have done so I want you Lucius Festus to use this mirror to signal young Quintus Servilius here," Constantine put his hand on the shoulder of the young man who had said he could not swim, a youth no more than sixteen years old, " who will be standing on that rise over there," he said pointing at a high point not far from where they sat. Constantine handed Lucius a highly polished silver mirror.

"Once you see the signal, Quintus, you will immediately have the horn-blower sound four short blasts on his lituus. That will be the signal for us to attack! Have you got that?" Qunitus nodded, overawed by Constantine's familiarity.

"Lucius, do you have any questions?" Lucius thought for a moment. "What should we do once the pontoons are released, Caesar?" he asked.

Constantine gave him a friendly smile. "If you can achieve this Lucius, then I would be happy for you to float all the way down the Tiber to Rome so that you can open the gates for us when we arrive!"

Lucius laughed. Constantine stood up and wished the men good luck. He mounted his horse and watched as they mounted theirs and headed north towards a bend in the river. He nodded to young Quintus and rode off towards where his own cavalry troop waited.

****

Lucius led his men around the bend in the river. When they could no longer see the bridge they dismounted and secured their horses. They all stood for a moment looking at the river. Recent rains in the mountains had left the river swollen, angry and aggressive. Patches of white water broke its surface. Logs and branches occasionally floated past, but more often snagged on the trees that over hung the banks.

They stripped off their armour and strapped it to their horses. Wearing only their tunics and a wide leather belt strapped around their waists, they each chose a couple of daggers to slide into their belts. Once they were ready they gathered some branches to use as cover. They had resolved to travel down the river in pairs. Lucius and his companion, Gaius Procula waited for the other two men to float off down the river before they entered the water.

Lucius could feel the freezing water chilling his body as he and Gaius pushed the branch they had chosen to use as cover out into the middle of the river. The bank fell away quickly as they moved out into the middle of the channel.

The first obstacle was the old bridge. The recent rains had sent a lot of debris down the river, and while this was useful in terms of cover, it made navigating past the old stone bridge difficult. Despite the other two men leaving earlier, Lucius and Gaius passed them at the stone bridge. They had become tangled in the debris under one of the arches and were desperately trying to remain under cover while, at the same time, free

411

themselves for the short down stream journey between the stone and pontoon bridges.

Lucius and Gaius passed under the stone arch of the bridge without trouble. The Pontoon Bridge was made up of a number of small boats that floated in line with the current. Over the boats a wooden deck had been laid. Wooden railings ran along each side of the temporary roadway.

Both Gaius and Lucius were familiar with this type of structure as their own legion had often used this technique to cross rivers in Britannia and Gaul. They had both experienced the struggle of fighting against a swift moving current to get the small boats into position, so they could be lashed together.

The pontoon bridge in front of them was a slow moving mass of men pushing from the east bank to the west. "Constantine's plan is working, Lucius!" said Gaius in a low whisper. "He has put a cork in the bottle!"

Lucius looked across to the western bank. Maxentius' legions were certainly crowded around the bridge head. Looking back along the bridge he could see that the slow pace of the army, unfortunately, gave the men on the bridge time to look around, heightening the chance that they might be spotted.

The current was pushing them towards the western bank. They struggled to keep their branch in the middle of the River, but it was a losing battle. "Gaius!" said Lucius in a hoarse whisper, as the sound of the river and of the clatter of Maxentius army grew louder, "We are going to have to swim for it! On my word dive deep and stay under for as long as you can. See if you can make it into the shadows between the pontoons somewhere near the middle of the bridge!" Gaius nodded. The bridge and the western bank drew closer. They were about two thirds of the way across the river when Lucius said "Now!"

****

Gaius took a deep breath and pushed on the branch, forcing himself under the water. Once below the surface he swam hard towards the bottom of the river. He could feel the cold penetrate his skin as he dove as deeper. It was dark, visibility was non-existent, and there was a sudden and terrible pain in his ears.

Gaius knew what would happen if he was spotted by the men on the bridge. He would be an easy target for an archer or a legionnaires javelin. The fear kept him moving forward. His lungs burnt. With each stroke of his arms he could feel them becoming weaker. He could go no further. He stopped swimming and let his body rise slowly towards the surface. A dark shadow appeared above him. He hoped that it was the pontoon bridge and not merely a mass of debris floating down the river. He broke the surface. He looked up, gasping for breath and found himself staring straight into the eyes of a startled looking legionnaire standing guard on the stern of a pontoon.

Before Gaius had time to react the legionnaire, who was holding his pilum in his hand, thrust down at Gaius. Gaius instinctively tried to dodge, but was not quick enough. The iron spear tip stabbed into his eye. Pain exploded in his head. Gaius began to struggle as the Legionnaire put his full weight behind the spear and thrust again, forcing Gaius' back under the water and into blackness.

****

Lucius watched as the legionnaire pulled hard on his pilum. It came free of the water, washed clean of its contact with Gaius whose unmoving body now floated under the pontoon bridge. It was soon lost to sight. The death of Gaius had taken only moments.

The Legionnaire started shouting "The enemy is in the water! The enemy is in the water!" Men all around him turned to scan the river. Another shout went up. "Over there, near the bridge!" The other two would be saboteurs had been spotted as they still struggled to free themselves from their entanglement under the half demolished stone bridge.

Arrows started to fly through the air. The two men were struck again and again.

Lucius watched his comrades die with a growing feeling of rage. He had come to the surface in a tangle of brushwood between two pontoons. He was now hanging on to one of them. He was freezing cold and his hands were beginning to lose feeling. His one consolation was that he was, at least for the moment, well hidden.

In the dim light under the bridge he could see that the ropes that tied the pontoons to one another, rather than being continuous, ended in loops of rope through which iron bars had been passed. By withdrawing the bar the pontoon could be detached from its neighbour. While the wooden roadway laid across the pontoons might hold it together initially, the force of the river would soon push the pontoons apart. The steel bars looked like they protruded through the roadway so they could only be accessed from above.

For a moment Lucius thought of just letting go of the pontoon and drifting off down the river. He could easily disappear. No one would ever know that he was still alive. He could have been killed along with his comrades, whose bodies, even now, were drifting down the river towards Rome. The moment passed. He looked up at the bars above him. Hoping that no-one on the walk way above him would notice, he wrapped a hand around the first of the iron bars and pulled. The bar would not move. Lucius grabbed hold of the rope on either side of the bar and hauled himself up so he could look through the gap where the bar went through the road way. From this position he could easily see why pulling down on the bar had little effect. The bar on the other side terminated in a ring to make it easier to pull it out. There was no way that he would be able to withdraw the bars from underneath.

The ropes that bound the pontoons together were as thick as his wrist. They were stretched taught by the force of the river pushing on the pontoons. There was no alternative. The only solution would be to try and cut through the ropes. He reached up and grabbed hold of a rope with his left hand. Drawing his dagger from his belt he began to saw at it. His blade was sharp. He worked the dagger backwards and forwards. It sliced through strand after strand of the rope. His left arm started to ache. To relieve the strain he changed arms, grabbing the rope above his head with his right hand and using the dagger with his left. Finally only a few strands, perhaps the thickness of his small finger remained uncut.

414

He paused for a few minutes and then carefully moved back towards the pontoon, taking hold of its wooden gunwale and moving carefully into a position where he could grab the next rope.

By the time he was halfway through the third rope his arms felt like lead. He could barely feel his fingers and he had lost feeling in his legs. To add to his woes his dagger was now blunt. He slipped it into his belt and reached across his body to grasp the handle of his second dagger. It would not initially come clear of his belt. It was tangled in the wet cloth of his tunic. He tugged at it, harder and harder. Suddenly it came loose. As it arced up out of the water the razor sharp blade sliced through the muscle of his other arm.

Lucius involuntarily gasped and almost lost his grip on the rope. Blood poured from the wound, down his chest and into the water.

Gritting his teeth, Lucius set to work sawing through the remainder of the third rope. Once again he stopped short of cutting the rope completely. The cold and the loss of blood were starting to take their toll. He did not think that he would be able to maintain his grip on the last rope long enough to cut through it.

Cautiously he moved into position. Cutting through the rope was difficult. He was feeling faint and began to doubt whether he would be able to hold on long enough to cut all the way through it. An idea suddenly struck him. Hanging on to the rope by his right arm, the dagger in his mouth, he used his injured arm to release the wide leather belt he wore around his waist. Then, with the last of his strength, he wrapped the belt around the rope and buckled it up, capturing his injured arm.

He let himself rest for a few minutes, floating under the bridge with his injured arm through the belt. Slowly he started to saw through the rope, cutting backwards and forwards, thinking about nothing but the movement of the blade. He lost all sense of time as he drifted nearer and nearer to unconsciousness. Finally his knife cut through the last rope completely. The dagger fell from his hands.

He did not know how long he remained hanging under the bridge, suspended from the belt, but he knew that he had one last task to complete. He just could not remember what it was. It has something to do with meeting Caesar in Rome! The thought of Constantine brought it back to him.

All I have to do, he thought as he unbuckled his belt, is float out from under this bridge, under the gaze of half of Maxentius' legions, and signal young Quintus. Simple! He was about to drop down into the river and swim from under the bridge when he caught sight of the body of a dead cow. It had been washed down the river and was currently trapped in a pile of branches that was about to float into the gap between the pontoons where he was resting.

Lucius waited for the bloated black and white body to float under the bridge. Taking a deep breath just before it reached him he dropped into the water, grabbed the cow and, floating on his back, aligned himself beneath it. The cow was floating on its side, with its legs protruding out towards the west bank.

Lucius saw the light change as he and the cow floated free of the shadow of the bridge. He held his breath for as long as he could and then carefully let his face break the surface. He took a deep breath and gagged as the smell of rotting flesh almost overwhelmed him.

As quickly as he could he reached under his tunic and withdraw the silver mirror that he had placed around his neck. Using the cow as cover he made a guess as to where Quintus would be, lined up the sun and moved the mirror backwards and forwards.

Lucius heard a shout from someone on the bridge. He had been spotted. Someone on the bridge had seen his signal. He hoped that Quintus had seen it as well. He heard a splash. He hoped for a moment that it was a fish, but looking up he could see a flight of arrows coming towards him. He drew himself closer underneath the cow. It would at least offer some protection from the rain of arrows.

In the distance he heard four horn blasts. Quintus had seen his signal!

At that moment an arrow pieced the cow's bloated belly. A cheer went up on the bridge as the cow exploded in a fountain of pink mist. Legionaries on the up river side of the bridge suddenly shifted position to try and see what had just happened. The bridge creaked and groaned.

Underneath the wooden roadway one of the remaining ropes snapped.

****

Time was passing. Constantine began to wonder whether Lucius and his men had managed to achieve their goal. Time was running out. Maxentius men were still marching over the bridge and taking up position across the Via Flaminia.

As each cohort crossed on to the western side of the bridge the likelihood of Constantine's forces prevailing reduced. In his mind he could see the balance starting to tip in favour of Maxentius. With no viable options available to him except retreat.

He was still considering his tactics when he heard four high pitched blasts of the lituus. Constantine shouted to Marcellus Agrippa, who had also heard the signal, and was in the process of breaking away from the fight in which he was engaged.

Constantine positioned his horse behind the line that his legionaries had made directly facing Maxentius' army. Partially hidden, it took only a few minutes for the rest of the available cavalry to draw up behind him.

Looking over his shoulder he could see a wall of mounted men, javelins in hand, forming into a broadly wedge shaped formation.

Constantine waved to the cornicen, the horn-blower who stood on a raised hillock nearby. The cornicen gave the signal and Constantine urged his horse into a trot. Behind him several hundred cavalrymen were doing the same.

As they approached their own line of infantry, on a command from their officers, they fell back to either side. The line opened like water parting before the prow of a ship.

Constantine urged his horse on. He was now galloping across a stretch of level ground. Four hundred metres away was Maxentius' front line. Behind a wall of shields bristling with javelins were five or six rows of men. Behind them, a disorganised rabble of soldiers who did not have space to move into position. Behind them a stream of soldiers were still trying to force their way over the bridge.

With three hundred metres to go the wall of shields in front of him looked solid and impenetrable. Constantine leaned into the neck of his horse, kicked his heels and held his javelin tightly to his side. The wind in his face made his eyes stream. The pounding of horse's hooves reverberated in his ears like the roar of a giant waterfall. His heart pounded. He had never felt so alive!

With two hundred metres to go he felt like he was flying! The shields in front of him were starting to move as the soldiers holding them realised that the charging cavalry were not going to stop!

With one hundred metres to go Constantine lifted the tip of his lance into position and gave his horse one last kick. The soldiers in Maxentius front line started to panic. They let their shields drop, some of them turned away from the oncoming storm.

Constantine's flying wedge smashed into Maxentius' legionnaires like a battering ram. Had Maxentius' men stayed in formation, spears raised, they would have inflicted massive causalities on Constantine's cavalry. As it was, Constantine had guessed correctly. The men, in a large part not enamoured with Maxentius as an Emperor, and confronted with a dramatic and overwhelming attack, did not hold their position.

As the wave of cavalry struck, the flow of men and equipment coming across the bridge suddenly tried to reverse. Constantine caught sight of Maxentius. He stood out clearly in the bright afternoon sun in his purple cloak and gold parade armour. Surrounded by a group of Praetorian guards, they were trying to force their way back across the bridge. At that moment the final finger of rope snapped and the roadway fell apart as the pontoons broke away.

Maxentius screamed. His horse, with no solid footing on which to stand, reared up, throwing the Emperor backwards into the water. He struggled desperately for a few seconds to keep his head above water but the weight of his heavy armour dragged him down.

The bridge, which only moments before had been covered in a teeming mass of men, was now floating away in pieces, down the River Tiber. Men and horses screamed and tumbled into the water. Some of the men managed to clamber onto bits of broken bridge. Others, fighting against the weight of their own armour, like Maxentius, sank out of sight.

Most of Maxentius army, seeing that their Emperor was gone, simply stopped fighting. They had no reason to fight now that Maxentius was dead. The Praetorian guardsmen that were still on the western bank, however, would not surrender. They fought on viciously, but even they were soon overwhelmed by Constantine's forces.

By the middle of the afternoon Constantine's troops had rebuilt the river crossing and he was leading them down the Via Flaminia to Rome.

****

Lucius Festus sat, his back against the solid stone wall of Rome. He was not quite sure what had happened, but when he had regained consciousness he had found himself, covered in cow and tangled in a tree branch floating down the river. He had navigated his way to the Eastern bank and, scrambled ashore.

It only took a moment to figure out where he was. He could see the walls of Rome a short distance away. He was in an area outside the City walls. The streets and buildings around him all seemed desolate and deserted.

His arm ached. The bleeding had not quite stopped so Lucius pulled his tunic over his head and carefully ripped a strip of material from its hem. He bound his arm tightly and then wrung the water out of the tunic.

The afternoon had become warm so he sat, naked, on the bank of the River revelling in the warmth of the late autumn sun and picking small pieces of rancid meat out of his hair and beard.

He watched the river flow past and wondered whether his efforts had been in vain. He did not have to wonder for long. Parts of the wooden pontoon bridge soon started to drift past. Once his tunic was dry he pulled it on and walked the short distance up a deserted street, to the semi circular brick towers of the Porta Flaminia.

The gate was closed so he sat down beside it and waited. A voice from above disturbed his reverie. "Where are you from, stranger, and what are you doing here?"

Lucius looked up. A Praetorian guardsman was looking down at him.

"I am the advance guard for your new Emperor's army!' he shouted back.

"We have no need of new Emperor. The old one is good enough for us!" shouted the guardsman.

"You Praetorians might be happy with him, but I hear tell that the rest of Rome would like to see his head on a spit!" shouted Lucius.

"You are a madman!" said the guard, dismissively. "You wouldn't know an Emperor if you tripped over one! The oracle has prophesied that Constantine will be dead by the end of this day, if he is not already!"

Lucius grunted dismissively, closed his eyes and rested his head on the stone wall.

Late in the afternoon he was woken by the sound of approaching trumpets and of men shouting. From where he sat he could see a standard emblazoned with a crude version of the chi-rho leading a column of men towards the gate.

"Hey, guard! You still there?" he shouted. The Praetorian Guard looked down at him from his watchtower. "I think it might be time for you to open the gate! I wouldn't want to be the man who stopped the Emperor from entering his city!"

As the army drew closer Lucius could see that Constantine, riding in a quadriga, a four horse chariot, was leading the way.

As the column drew close to the gate Lucius stood up. Constantine, who had been looking up at the watch tower, glanced across to where Lucius was now standing. "Lucius Festus! It is good to see you again! Where are the others?" said Constantine with a broad smile, looking around for Lucius' men.

Lucius looked down at the ground. "Dead, Caesar. I am sorry!"

Constantine looked at the man in front of him, bedraggled, obviously exhausted and said kindly. "Lucius, you have nothing to be sorry for. You and your men have made our victory possible. I thank you for all you have done for us! I would like to repay you for what you have achieved today. Come and see me tomorrow, once you are rested."

Lucius nodded.

"Now, said Constantine in a loud voice, "perhaps you would open the gate for me, so that I may enter my City!"

Lucius walked up to the city gate and shouted, "Guardsman! Flavius Valerius Aurelius Constantinus", he paused briefly, and then added, "Augustus, wishes to enter his City!"

The gates opened and Constantine urged his horses forward, entering Rome, its new Master.

Book 4

1. Rome - Present day

"So we have to assume the Blood of Constantine predates Constantine the first, and even predates Julius Caesar!" said Dan, flabbergasted. "That means that this stuff, whatever it is, is definitely not just blood and is definitely not just the blood of Constantine the Great. In fact it comes from a time before Constantine, from the time of the Caesars! When Constantine said it contained the blood of the Emperor, he must have meant the Emperor Augustus, not himself," said Dan thoughtfully. "Pope Leo was taking a hell of a risk telling Attila that story."

"It certainly was a gamble! If Attila had taken it and survived then, he might have become totally invincible. We might all be speaking Hunnish now!" said Charlotte.

"So what did happen to Attila?" asked Elizabeth.

"He died soon after he got back to his homeland. On his wedding night in fact. There has always been a lot of controversy about how he died. It is said that he died of a haemorrhage, drowning in his own blood while he slept off the excesses of the wedding feast. I guess we now know the truth! He decided to take the gamble and lost," said Alberto.

"But hang on!" said Dan, still assimilating all the information that he and Elizabeth had just heard. "I get that Pope Leo had all this information from Constantine the Great, but how did Pope Leo find out about what happened to Alaric?"

Charlotte thought for a moment. "It had to have been someone who was there at the time. Ataulf would probably have known, but he didn't have long on the throne did he?"

"No, it couldn't have been him," said Dan. "Ataulf died in around 415AD. He was only King for about seven years."

"When was Pope Leo Pope? When was he born?" Elizabeth asked.

"Ah, good question!" said Charlotte. "He was born in 400 and died when he was sixty one years old. He was Pope for twenty one years."

"So, Dan's right, there is no way it could have been Ataulf who told him. Leo would have only been about, what? fifteen years old by then?

and hardly in a position to be taken into the confidences of a Visigoth King. Did Ataulf have a wife or a child?" asked Elizabeth.

"Oh yes!" said Dan suddenly, interrupting, "The famous Galla Placidia!"

"It had to have been Galla Placidia!" said Charlotte.

Elizabeth turned to look at Dan, "How? I thought she was taken prisoner by the Goths?"

"She was! But she ended up marrying Ataulf," said Dan.

Elizabeth looked confused. "I don't get it. I'm getting lost again. Why is this Galla Placidia likely to be the link? I get the fact that she was a prisoner of the Goths after the sack of Rome and you are telling me now that she married the Visigoth king, but why would she be the one to have talked to Pope Leo?"

"Because," said Charlotte with a smile, "she was an amazingly gutsy woman! After Ataulf died, another Goth, Sigeric, won the throne by force. He only lasted seven days before they murdered him. In that time, though, he had all of Ataulf's children slaughtered. According to the documented history he treated Galla Placidia with 'cruel and wanton insult'. She was, among other depravations, forced to walk barefoot for twelve miles in front of Sigeric and his horse. He was a real bastard. It was partly because of the way Galla was treated that Sigeric was assassinated."

"Wow! The Goths must have thought she was something special then?" said Elizabeth.

"Yeah, I guess so. The new King, a guy by the name of Wallia, eventually traded her back to her brother, the Emperor Honorius. That wasn't the end of her story though. Honorius forced Galla Placidia to marry the bloke who had been doing all the heavy lifting in defending the Empire for him, Constantius. Constantius was the General who booted Ataulf out of Italy after Alaric died."

"Galla Placidia and Constantius had two children, a boy and a girl. They had been married for about three years when Honorius appointed Constantius co-Emperor and Galla Placidia was given the tittle of Augusta. Unfortunately for Galla Placidia, Constantius died seven months later."

"Within a year or so Ravenna was bursting with scandalous rumours about an incestuous relationship between Honorius and his beautiful sister, Galla Placidia. The Goths, who still held her in great esteem, started to get excited, and in the end she fled, with her kids, to Constantinople, to the Eastern Empire."

"Honorius died a couple of years later and eventually, after a bit of fighting and bit more Palace intrigue, guess who arrives back in Ravenna?"

"Galla Placidia," answered Elizabeth uncertainly.

"Yup!" said Charlotte with a laugh. "The incredible, amazing Galla Placidia arrived back in Ravenna as Regent for her five year old son, Valentinian. She then effectively ran the Western Empire for about twelve years! She died only one year before Attila arrived in Italy."

"Wow! A woman running the Empire! That is fantastic! What an incredible lady! Is there any evidence that she actually knew the Pope?" asked Elizabeth.

"Absolutely!" said Charlotte. "There is a fifth century mosaic in the Basilica of Saint Paul Outside the Wall, here in Rome, that has an inscription that says that Leo and Galla Placidia paid for the restoration of the church. She was very involved in the church and its politics."

"So Galla Placidia told Leo about what had happened to Alaric. The story is more than likely true then!"

Charlotte nodded. "But that's not all! Do you remember how Alberto mentioned about Attila getting the vial with the potion in it from a woman called Honoria?"

Elizabeth nodded.

"Honoria was Galla Placidia's daughter!" said Charlotte.

"So Honoria probably heard about the potion from her own mother?" asked Elizabeth.

Charlotte nodded.

"Honoria probably knew that she was playing a very dangerous game with Attila by sending him the vial. Either she would be responsible for killing the scourge of God, and saving the Empire from the Hun menace, or creating the Roman world's worst nightmare!"

Charlotte nodded again. "But Honoria probably thought she would win either way. Either Attila is dead or she is the wife of the potential ruler of the world."

The remnants of their meal lay scattered all around them. They were the only ones left in the restaurant. Dan paid the bill and they all caught a taxi back to the apartment.

2. Rome - Present day

Charlotte poured them all a night cap when they got back to the apartment. They settled into comfortable chairs, in the large living room, and sat looking at one another.

Dan finally broke the silence. "Well, what do we do now?"

They all started talking at once. Dan held up his hand. "One at a time, one at a time! Liz, you first, what do you think?"

"We have to get our hands on that vial in Alaric's coffin. That's vital! If we can get a sample out of it, then we should be able to finally figure out what this stuff really is!" she said enthusiastically.

"We need to find out where Julius Caesar got this stuff from!" said Charlotte, sitting forward in her seat. "If we can figure out where it came from then it might help with understanding what it is really meant for!"

Dan looked at Alberto who was frowning into his drink. "Alberto?" he asked.

"I do not want to be the one that puts a damp towel on your enthusiasm," he said, seriously, "but we have just made a series of discoveries that have put us all in extreme danger. The knowledge that we now have is knowledge that someone out there," he said with a sweep of his arm, "has spent years, possibly hundreds of years, looking for."

They all sat quietly, waiting for him to continue. "More worse than that, is the fact that we know that they are quite prepared to kill for the knowledge that we all now possess. I think that we should remember this as we plan our next moves."

The mood turned sombre.

"I have a question to ask you all, that has been worrying me," said Dan. "Let us say, for a moment, that we do manage to get the vial, that we do find out its genesis and manage to stay alive during that process. What do we do then? Have any of you thought about that?" He looked around the room. "Can you imagine what this stuff, this blood, this drug, potion, magic elixir, whatever it is, might really be able to do? We are talking about something that could potentially push the human mind to an entirely new level! Think about what that means! Think of the things

427

that would be possible if there were one thousand Einsteins, all alive at the same time, working across all the sciences. The advances that could be made, would be incredible!" he said excitedly, getting out of his seat. "We could cure cancer, reverse climate change..."

They all watched him as he started to pace around the apartment. Dan looked up, suddenly conscious that he was standing up and beginning to rant. He sat back down. "I was just saying..." he said lamely.

"We know Dad!" said Charlotte reaching across and patting him on the arm and laughing. "Clearly not everybody needs the Blood of Constantine to make them see possible futures!"

"I agree with you Dottore Dan! This could be a great step forward for mankind. It has been kept secret and hidden too long! It is because it was kept a secret that people like Hitler and Napoleon, Charlemagne and Julius Caesar have all become powerful at the expense of others. This knowledge should be shared. Given to everyone!"

"Hear, hear!" said Elizabeth holding up her glass.

Charlotte was looking at Alberto, a smile on her face. "I agree too!" she said, raising her glass. "Here's to freedom of knowledge!"

"Okay!" said Dan raising his glass too! "Now, what do you think about Liz and I going back to the tomb site and seeing if we can get hold of the vial, without raising any suspicion?"

"Sounds perfect," said Elizabeth. "But I am not going back to that apartment in San Lucido. Can we find somewhere else to stay?"

"I'm sure we'll be able to find some where to your liking madam!" said Dan. "What about you two?" he said turning to Charlotte and Alberto.

"I think we should go back to the Vatican," said Charlotte. "We need to see if we can find the original documents and the box that came from Constantine. That could hold the clues that we need to track down where it came from. What do you think Bert?"

"Well, now we know that the Blood of Constantine is probably a made up mixture, then we have to assume that the original recipe for it, or at least some of the ingredients must be hidden somewhere in the Vatican."

"Hidden well enough," said Charlotte, "so that Napoleon Bonaparte couldn't t find it, even after taking a huge part of the Secret Archive from the Vatican back to Paris and, presumably having his clerks scour through it."

"That's right," said Elizabeth. "We also know, or at least think we do, that the potion pre-dates Constantine by hundreds of years. The potion really has nothing to do with Constantine's blood. He was just a beneficiary like Napoleon and Hitler, as were possibly, Charlemagne, Augustus and Julius Caesar."

"We also know that it was used by a bunch of people for whom things didn't work out so well. At the moment our guesses of people it possibly killed, or sent mad, were probably all the Julian Emperors after Augustus, Alaric the Goth and possibly Attila the Hun."

"Which brings us neatly back to the key questions. Where did this stuff come from? Who made it? What were the magic ingredients? and Why does it only work for some people?" asked Dan.

"Let me just work through some logic," said Charlotte. "Admittedly most of our evidence is circumstantial, but, bearing that in mind, we can make the following deductions. First," she said holding a finger up, "whoever made it lived before Julius Caesar and was in Spain sometime before say 70 BC."

They all nodded. "Makes sense ," said Dan.

"Ok!" said Charlotte. "Number two. We have to assume that whoever made the potion had to be an important figure in history."

"Why?" asked Elizabeth.

"Because the potion must have worked," said Charlotte. "If the potion had been a dud, or had been used by some minor league player, then how would it attract the attention of someone like Julius Caesar and convince him to the swallow the story, so to speak?"

"Maybe Caesar made it up!" said Alberto.

"Possibly, but that brings me to my third big assumption. This potion is complex. Morell had trouble piecing together how it works and he had access to some reasonably modern scientific equipment. We have access to much more sophisticated equipment and analyzing Hitler's version it is still proving problematic."

"Whoever put this together would have had to have been brilliant! and I don't mean just brilliant,brilliant, I mean like Da Vinci brilliant, or Einstein brilliant. Whoever put this together would have had to have spent a lifetime studying the natural world and have an encyclopaedic knowledge of medicine and plants and the human body."

"So we are looking for a brilliant strategist who was also one of the most brilliant scientific minds in human history! Sounds like a bit of a stretch!" said Elizabeth.

"Archimedes!" said Dan suddenly. "Archimedes was brilliant. He was a world-class brain and was the strategist behind keeping the Romans out of Syracuse. He died during the second Punic war!"

"He was also alive during the first Punic war, so if the papyrus that Constantine the Great found in the box was real, and that was written in Punic, then he could be our man!!"

"Did he ever go to Spain?" asked Alberto.

"As far as we know he spent most of his time on his home island of Syracuse. There is some pretty flimsy evidence that he might have gone to Spain. Something to do with an Archimedes' screw and getting water out of mines, but I can't quite remember where I saw it," said Charlotte.

"Well that could put him at around the right time and, potentially, in the right sort of place to hide the potion" said Elizabeth.

"And there is possibly an Egyptian connection as well. It is believed, although there is no real evidence for it, that Archimedes studied in Alexandria," said Charlotte excitedly. "Which might explain why Napoleon went to Egypt."

"Ah, but Archimedes was a mathematician and a physicist!" said Dan, pouring cold water on his own idea. "Brilliant yes, but as far as we know he didn't work in the natural sciences at all!"

"Which brings me to my next big question. What if we are not looking for one person? What if the potion was made by a different person to the one who used it?"

"What, now we're looking for two people?" asked Dan in a disappointed voice. "I'm afraid my head is starting to spin and I am too tired to think straight anymore. I'm off to bed, I 'm afraid." He looked across at Elizabeth.

"Me too!" she said and accepted Dan's hand when he offered to help her out of her chair.

Ten minutes later Dan and Elizabeth were lying in each others arms. "Have you noticed anything about Charlie and Alberto?" he asked Elizabeth.

"What do you mean?" she said, lifting her self up and looking him in the eye. "Like the fact that he calls her Charlie and she has suddenly started calling him Bert? Or how she keeps watching him and smiling? or that he is trying very hard not to look at her all the time and keeps checking to see that you haven't noticed him looking at her? No, haven't noticed a thing. Why?" she asked innocently, flopping back down onto the bed. "And anyway, it is none of our business!" she said rolling over to face him. "This, on the other hand," she said giving him a gentle kiss on the lips, "...is our business."

3. Calabria - Present day

As Dan and Elizabeth were driving back to Cosenza the next day, Dan received a phone call from Professor Pelegrinni asking them if they would be available next day for the unveiling of their wolf to the media. Dan said they would be delighted to attend and arranged to be at the dig site at midday. They arrived back in Cosenza late in the evening. They had booked into an apartment they had found through AirBnB. It was large, quirky and well appointed and was only a short walk away from the River and the Dig site.

Alberto had approved of their choice, agreeing that the apartment would be safer than a hotel.

In the morning they took a leisurely walk, exploring the alleys around the apartment, and slowly making their way down the hill to the river. From there it was an easy walk to the dig site.

Professor Pellegrini saw them as they walked, hand in hand, into the huge tent that covered the area around the sarcophagus. His face lit up with a merry grin and he held his arms out to embrace them both. "Welcome back! This is fantastic. You are just in time!"

The Professor led them across to the media centre that had been set up beside the main control booth. On a table in the middle of the area, surrounded by television crews and photographers, stood an object covered in a black cloth. Behind it the big computer monitors had been moved to provide a backdrop. The logo of the Professor's University floated lazily around the screens.

The Professor pushed his way through the crowd and stood in front of the shrouded object. He waited patiently while the assembled media noticed him and stopped talking. Once all was quiet around him he took a couple of steps forward. He waited for a full minute before he began to speak.

Dan and Elizabeth listened as the Professor re-told the story of Romulus and Remus and the she-wolf. He then showed a series of images of the she-wolf. The first one was on a Roman coin dating back to the Republican era of Rome from around 260 BCE, then virtually the same image on a coin from the time of the Emperor Vespasian, around seventy five AD and then one from the time of Constantine the Great, nearly six hundred years later. He showed similar images on a first century ring stone and on a beautiful mosaic on the floor of the cathedral of Sienna, created in the late 1300s. Finally he showed pictures of a range of she-wolf souvenirs that could be purchased all around Italy. Some were on teaspoons, others key fobs and the last one, much to the amusement of the crowd, was inside a snow globe.

"This image of the she wolf is iconic," he said. "As we have just seen, it has been associated with Rome for thousands of years. This image is Rome! And yet, we now know that the she wolf in the Capitoline museum in Rome is, sadly, not the original. The discovery that it is a mediaeval copy, not the wolf that watched over Julius Caesar, Pompey the Great, Scipio Africanus and their contemporaries, was a great blow to many of us who had believed, for so long, that, through her, we had a tangible connection with the glories of our ancient past."

"The original she wolf was lost. No-one knew where she was or when she was taken, until now!" said the Professor, theatrically pulling the sheet from the statue and revealing the she wolf to the waiting media. Cameras flashed and all at once a barrage of questions was being fired at the Professor.

Dan and Elizabeth grinned at each other, enjoying the show. Then suddenly, the media pack turned on them. They could see the Professor laughing and pointing as he told the assembled crowd who had initially uncovered the she wolf. They were then hustled through the crowd to have their pictures taken along with the Professor and their discovery.

Some hours later, with the reporters and television crews temporarily sated, the Professor, Dan and Elizabeth were sitting down having a break.

"When will you be lifting the lid on the sarcophagus Professor?" asked Elizabeth, as she put down her empty coffee cup.

"I think two days from now." he replied. "As you can see the floor of the tomb is now clear, so we can work around it quite easily. Will you be here for the grand opening?"

"We wouldn't miss it for the world!" said Dan. "But I think we would prefer it if we didn't get to be part of the sideshow next time!" he said seriously.

"I am sorry about that Daniel. I am afraid I got a bit carried away. When the young reporter asked me who found the wolf, and I saw you and Elizabeth sitting there at the back of the room, I just pointed. I am sorry if I have caused you any embarrassment."

"I don't think there has been any permanent harm done," said Elizabeth with a laugh. She glanced at Dan, who clearly was not thrilled with the idea of having his face on the front of every newspaper and on every television news bulletin in Italy, if not the world. She put her hand over his. "Our Daniel is a little camera shy, I am afraid, Professor. He does like to keep himself out of the limelight!"

"I am truly sorry Daniel. If there is anything I can do to make things better please let me know," said the Professor sincerely.

"Well," said Dan thoughtfully, "Would it be possible for us to be there when the sarcophagus is opened and the body is unwrapped from its shroud?"

"Why of course!" said the Professor. "I thought we would have a media event for the lifting of the lid of the sarcophagus," said the Professor. "At which your presence will not be mentioned." he quickly added. "Then we will close down the site for visitors and set up a clean room to remove the body from the sarcophagus and unwrap and catalogue it. I would be delighted if you would join us in the clean room!"

"That sounds fantastic," said Dan with a smile. "Is there anything that we can do between now and then?" he asked.

"No, not really. We are only doing clean up tasks, getting ready for the opening of the sarcophagus itself. But I do have something that I wanted to show you that I think you might find interesting. Come with me."

The Professor led them towards an area that was surrounded by a steel mesh fence, past an armed guard standing at the gate of the secure area and into a shipping container that the Professor called the treasury. The shipping container was fitted out like a modern, highly functional, laboratory. Spread all around the shelves and benches of the cramped space were the artefacts that had been unearthed in the tomb. They were in varies stages of the preservation process. Some pieces where soaking in containers of liquid, some just sitting on a bench and some stacked in wire trays on the shelves that ran down one side of the re-purposed container. The Professor led them to its furthest end. On a bench were several large objects. One was the beautiful, large gold bowl that they had seen during the dig. The Professor walked straight past it and stood in front of the breastplate that they had last seen partially uncovered in the bottom of the tomb. The breast plate looked to be of iron with heavy gold ornamentation over the shoulders and around the body. It had been cleaned and now the shape of a muscled, male torso could be easily made out.

"Is it not beautiful? "asked the Professor, with obvious pride.

"It is fantastic!" said Dan. "But haven't I seen something similar to this, somewhere else." he thought for a moment. "I know, from the tombs at Vergina! This is like a more elaborate version of the armour that is supposed to be Phillip the Second's."

"Ah Dan! You should have been an archeologist, not a scientist!" said the Professor with an indulgent smile. "You are right! The cuirass is Greek, from around the same time as the armour that was found at Vergina. We date this armour to sometime around the mid fourth century BCE. "

"What is Greek armour doing in the tomb of a Visigoth King?" asked Elizabeth, then, before anyone could answer, said, "In fact, assuming it was part of the plunder that the Goth's took from Rome, what was Greek armour doing in Rome, eight hundred years after it was made?"

"Those, my dear Elizabeth, are exactly the questions to ask! There is another way of asking this question that may be more enlightening. What is so important about this cuirass that would lead to its preservation for eight hundred years and be considered exceptional enough, given the treasure that they had just looted from Rome, to be put into the tomb of a Visigoth King?" asked the Professor with a roguish smile.

Elizabeth shook her head.

The Professor looked at Dan. Dan was just staring at the Cuirass, transfixed. He reached out and touched it lightly, reverentially, resting his palm on the chest.

The Professor put his hand on Dan's shoulder. "I think you have had the same thought that I did, Daniel," he said quietly.

"What is going on?" asked Elizabeth. She had never seen Dan so awestruck.

The Professor moved closer to Elizabeth, and in a whisper, so as not to disturb Dan, he said, " Let me read you something, he said, picking up an iPad from a nearby table and tapping on its screen for a few seconds. "Here we go!" he said, "This is from the historian Suetonius, writing in the early second century, talking about the Emperor Caligula. The Professor adjusted his glasses and began to read,

"In the fashion of his clothes, shoes, and all the rest of his dress, he did not wear what was either national, or properly civic, or peculiar to the male sex, or appropriate to mere mortals. He often appeared abroad in a short coat of stout cloth, richly embroidered and blazing with jewels, in a tunic with sleeves, and with bracelets upon his arms; sometimes all in silks and habited like a woman; at other times in the crepidae ..."

"... sort of sandal," he said when he saw Elizabeth's confusion,

"... or buskins;"

"...knee high boots ..."

"... sometimes in the sort of shoes used by the light-armed soldiers, or in the sock used by women, and commonly with a golden beard fixed to his chin, holding in his hand a thunderbolt, a trident, or a caduceus,"

"...a winged staff with two snakes wrapped around "

"... marks of distinction belonging to the gods only. Sometimes, too, he appeared in the habit of Venus. He wore very commonly the triumphal ornaments, even before his expedition, and sometimes the breast-plate of Alexander the Great, taken out of his coffin."

Elizabeth stared at the Professor, then turned to stare at the breastplate. After a minute she turned back to the Professor. "The breast plate of *the* Alexander the Great?"

The Professor nodded. "Certainly the style is of the right period. Iron and gold would be materials that few people of the time could afford. There are traces of linen still on the inside of the breast plate, so we are having them carbon dated, to see if our dating is correct, and this is not a later copy. But it is possible that this is the armour of Alexander the Great," he said with a grin.

Dan finally stepped away from the breastplate and turned to Elizabeth and the Professor. "What an amazing discovery!"

"If it is true!" said the Professor. "We have a lot of work to do before we can establish if it really is Alexander's breastplate."

"Well please keep us in the loop. We would love to know how you progress with your investigations," said Dan.

"I will. I am arranging to work with a small documentary team to follow our progress," said the Professor self-consciously.

Dan laughed. "Always open to the main chance Professor! If I am a loss to the world of archaeology, then you are a similarly significant loss to the world of Public Relations!"

The Professor laughed. "Maybe so, Daniel, but this work is expensive. As you well know this dig doesn't end with the recovery of these artefacts. There is years of work that needs to be done to preserve and document these finds. We can't always rely on finding benefactors like yourself to help, especially with the more mundane work."

"Now come, that is enough seriousness for one evening. I would be honoured if you would join me for dinner. I have discovered the best restaurant in Cosenza, and I would like to share it with you!"

4. Rome - Present day

Charlotte sat on the couch with her feet resting on the coffee table in front of her. Her laptop was on her knees and she was reviewing the images of the documents that they had worked through during the last couple of days. In the background she could hear Alberto working in the kitchen. She felt a bit guilty that he continually insisted on cooking, pushing her out of the kitchen every time she ventured into it, but she thought to herself, what the heck, if the big stud muffin wants to cook, then so be it, I'm not big enough to stop him! Then she checked herself. *Stud muffin*! Where did that come from!

She shook her head and got back to work. Then it struck her. She slapped her palm against her forehead. "Duh! Hey Bert!" she shouted.

"What's up?" he said from somewhere below the kitchen bench where he was taking a vegetarian lasagne out of the oven.

"We have been looking in the wrong place! The box that the potion came in can't be hidden in the Vatican!"

"What?" said Alberto walking over to the couch. Charlie smiled. Seeing him in an apron, albeit one of her father's aprons, made her smile every time.

"Do you remember the letter that Pius the sixth wrote about how he had mixed up the potion for Napoleon?" Alberto nodded. "We assumed that he had been sitting in his apartment in the Vatican?" Alberto nodded again. "What year do we think that was?"

"About seventeen ninety something I think. Ninety-seven was it?" he replied, not sure where she was heading.

"And where did the pope live in 1797?" she asked looking up at him.

"In the Papal Apartments on the top floor of the Palazzo Apostolico," he said without hesitation. He then stopped and hit his own forehead with the palm of his hand. "Or it could have been the Pope's summer residence, Castel Gandolfo! What time of year are we talking about?"

"I don't know. I hadn't thought of the Castel Gondolfo, but that is a possibility. I was thinking about the Quirinal Palace. It was the official residence of the Popes from the end of the sixteenth century until 1870."

"Ah, Crap. So you think we should go and search the official residence of the President of the Italian Republic!" he said with a laugh.

"No, not really, I suppose," she said putting her laptop down on the couch. "This is a bit hopeless, isn't it. That box could be anywhere, or nowhere. The Quirinal Palace would have been totally remodelled when it was taken over by the King in 1870, and then again by the various Presidents of Italy. I can't even think of where to start looking to even get a clue to its location!"

"Perhaps Berlusconi found it! Alberto said with a laugh.

"It's not Viagra we are looking for!" said Charlotte standing up and stretching.

Alberto smiled. "Come, have some dinner. Things always look better on a full stomach!" he said as he headed back to the kitchen. She followed him, taking up a position on one of the high stools that stood beside the island bench that was the demarcation between kitchen and living room. She opened a bottle of red wine and poured two glasses and sat sipping hers while Alberto tossed a salad in a bowl.

"These last few days, having such free access to the Vatican's records, and the Pope's private library, has been amazing," said Charlotte.

Alberto smiled at her as he slid a large slice of lasagna on to a plate and placed it in front of her. "It was incredible to have that insight of yours to look at the documents of Pope Leo. My problem is that I have never known exactly where to look and my Latin is nowhere near good enough to read half of the stuff we found. With so much information to chose from I could have been searching for years without finding anything useful!" He slid a second plate across the bench and came and sat down next to her.

"How does someone get the sort of access you get to Church records? I have never heard of anyone who has the freedom that you do," she said, finally asking the question that had been nagging at her for the last few days.

Alberto put salad on his plate and took a sip of wine. "A few years ago there was a theft of another reliquary. This one contained the blood of Pope John Paul II," said Alberto, a tinge of sadness appearing around his eyes. "The reliquary was in in the form of a copy of the Gospels. A young priest was taking it, in his backpack on a train to a Cathedral here in Rome when it was stolen. It was recovered by the local police shortly after, but it got me thinking. Before the Pope died his personal physician had saved some of his blood in case he ever needed a transfusion. While he was still alive they were held at the Vatican's Bambino Gesu Hospital, here in Rome.

Fortunately for the Pope they weren't ever needed. After his the death, two of the vials went to the pope's personal secretary in Poland, and the other two remained in the custody of the Daughters of Charity of St Vincent de Paul at the hospital."

"After the theft of the reliquary I had the four vials secured. It took me weeks of arguing. Even my own boss didn't think it was important enough to follow up. In the end I had to go over his head. I asked the Holy Father to intervene. Two days after the blood had been properly secured there were simultanious break-ins at both the hospital here in Rome and the one in Poland. If I had not been so pushy all of the Pope's blood would have been stolen."

"Wow! And you were rewarded with access to his library!" said Charlotte.

"No, not then. It was a little while later. Do you remember when Pope John Paul II was shot in 1981?"

"Sure. Some Turkish guy shot him, didn't he?"

"Yes, his name was Mehmed Ali Agca. A reliquary, with a small piece of blood soaked cloth from the cassock he was wearing when he was shot, was stolen a couple of years ago. When the police found the reliquary it had been smashed and the blood soaked cloth was gone. The cloth was found a few days later. The story that was put out was that the thieves didn't know what they had. Once the relic was returned I had it examined. I asked the Carabinieri forensics people to have a look at it. I already had a digital record of it so it didn't take them long to establish that there were a few threads missing."

"That is weird!" said Charlotte.

"I reported my findings to my boss and a couple of days later was asked to go and see his Holiness. That was when he asked me to resign from the Corpo della Gendarmeria dello Stato della Città del Vaticano."

"Why? You hadn't done anything wrong!" said Charlotte, a feeling of righteous indignation welling up inside her.

"It wasn't because I had done anything wrong. He wanted to give me a special commission. He wanted me to track down who was behind the thefts. For some reason he had become convinced that some group of people, or an organisation, perhaps even inside the Vatican itself, was behind both the attempt to steal the Pope's blood and the blood soaked threads. He believed that, whoever it was, had their sights set on the destruction of the Church," said Alberto.

"Did he have any evidence other than the theft of the relics and the attempted theft of the blood," asked Charlotte.

"Well he had the words that Pope John Paul spoke to a nurse straight after he had been shot," said Alberto.

"Why, what did he say?" asked Charlotte.

"He said, "How could they do it?" said Alberto.

"*They*? Who didi he mean? Did Mehmed Ali Agca ever say anything to implicate anyone else?"

"He said a lot of things while he was in prison, mostly contradictory. There are number of people who have suggested that it was a KGB backed plot. The unsubstantiated rumour was that the KGB had asked the Bulgarian and East German secret services to kill the Pope," said Alberto.

"I guess that would be understandable if you were sitting in the Soviet Union and watching the rise of Solidarity in Poland. Especially given the Pope's involvement and support. I am sure there were people in the USSR who saw the threat," said Charlotte, taking a sip from her wine glass.

"On the other hand," said Alberto "there were those that felt that the whole Bulgarian connection was a load of rubbish. Ağca made no mention of Bulgarian involvement until after he had been visited by a couple of blokes from Italian Military Intelligence. So maybe he just made it up, or perhaps they suggested it to him."

"Man, I love a good conspiracy theory," said Charlotte.

"There is one other weird connection with the story, though. The date the Pope was shot was the 13th May, the feast day of Our Lady of Fatima. The Pope took this date as auspicious and claimed that the attempted assassination was the fulfillment of the Third Secret of Fatima." Charlotte looked blank, "You know the visions of the three little girls in Spain, that supposedly predicted the Second World War."

"Vaguely," said Charlotte, distracted by her own train of thought. "So," said Charlotte thinking back over what Alberto had just told her, "You are telling me that you are working privately for the Pope?"

Alberto nodded. "Yes and no. I was given a task by a Pope that I have been asked to do outside the auspices of the Church. I was given certain resources to pursue that task and told only to report back if and when I believed it was necessary. I have a papal letter that explains what I have been asked to do. I can present it to whoever the Pope is when I need to. As for the access to the library, the cover story is that I am undertaking a security review. This gives me access wherever and whenever I need it. Having worked there, and being known by most of the Swiss Guard and the Police makes it easier." He paused for a moment. "I have told no-one else this. I would prefer if it remained between you and me. I would prefer if you kept it even from your father and Elizabeth. Will you do that?"

Charlotte nodded. "Do you mean that you haven't even told any of your cousins?" she asked with a grin.

"My cousins are no business of yours Charlotte Marsh!" he said, laughing. "How about we go for a walk! I've spent enough time inside the last couple of days. It would be good to replace the dust in our lungs with some fresh air."

"In Rome!" she said with a wry smile."Sure. I'll just get a coat."

They walked across to the Piazza Navona and then on to the church of Saint Maria della Pace, where Alberto showed her his favourite paintings, the beautiful Sybil frescoes that Raphael had painted in 1514.

After finding a cafe and standing at the counter to drink their coffees, they walked back across the Piazza where Charlotte had stopped to read the Hieroglyphs on the Egyptian Obelisk, while Alberto went off to find a gelato for the walk back to the apartment. As Charlotte stood, absorbed in her task, one of the many handsome young men, who used the area to scam tourists, approached her.

He offered, in heavily accented English, to weave a good-luck bracelet on her wrist to welcome her to Rome. Charlotte declined in English. The man continued to badger her. She tried to ignore him, but in the end turned and let him have it, both barrels, in perfect Italian invective. The man's face first registered shock and then turned nasty. He was just about to harangue her when he noticed her eyes move to the right of his shoulder.

He turned to see what she was looking at. Alberto was standing, a gelato in each of his massive hands, scowling. The young man looked back at Charlotte, who nodded. The young man ran.

Charlotte burst out laughing. "Do you always have that affect on young men?" she asked as he handed her a gelato. "You will make a wonderful father one day!"

Charlotte was still giggling as she led Alberto up the stairs to the apartment half an hour later. She was reaching into her pocket for her key when Alberto put his hand on her arm. He raised a finger to his lips. Charlotte stepped back from the door and let Alberto move past her. He pushed gently on the door. It swung open. He indicated that she should stay where she was while he entered the apartment. She watched him slip quietly through the door.

A few minutes later he called out. "Its OK! There is no one here!"

Charlotte entered the main room and looked around. It all looked as they left it, until she looked for her laptop. It was gone. "Shit, they've taken my laptop!" she said.

"That's OK. We can replace the stuff from the Vatican library that was on it," said Alberto, continuing to look around to see if he could see anything else missing.

"I know, but the scan of Alaric's sarcophagus was on there, with a screenshot of the vial in his hand!"

"Shit!" said Alberto. "We had better warn your father that he might get some unwanted visitors!"

5. Calabria - Present day

Dan was reading when his mobile phone rang. He smiled when Charlotte's picture came up on the screen. "Ciao, Bella, what's up?"

"Hi, Dad! I've got some bad news. We have just been robbed," said Charlotte.

"Shit! Are you and Alberto OK," he asked sitting up in his chair. Elizabeth, who had been working on her laptop on the other side of the room, looked up.

"Yes. We are fine. They broke into the apartment while we were out having a walk. They took my laptop, but worse than that, I still had a downloaded copy of the Alaric scan on it." she said, obviously distressed.

"Oh, crap!" said Dan, twisting the phone so that Elizabeth, who was now sitting on the arm of his chair, could hear.

"Dad, Alberto reckons that whoever took the CT scan, might go after the vial."

"Assuming they see it in the scan. It was pretty hard to spot. Even when you told me there was something there, and I knew I had to keep looking, I almost missed it," said Dan.

"I think we have to assume that they will find it. , I took a screenshot that clearly shows the vial in his hand. I'm really sorry Dad. I should have taken more care of it."

"No point crying over spilled milk, honey. First thing in the morning I will go and have a talk to the Professor. I'll tell him what has happened and see if I can persuade him to increase the security around the site," Dan said.

"What are you going to tell him? You can't tell him about the vial," said Charlotte.

"No. We'll think of something. How have you two been getting on with your researches?" he asked, changing the subject.

"Not brilliantly," she said and then explained her thoughts on the many possible locations of the box that Pope Pius VI had mentioned in his letter. Dan commiserated, then said, "Will you be staying in the apartment?"

"No. We have booked a couple of rooms for the night at the Hotel Raphael, just down the road. Apparently it is run by one of Bert's cousins!" she said rolling her eyes. "Tomorrow, while I go back to the Vatican, he is going to re-do the security at the apartment for us,"

Dan promised to ring Charlotte straight after they talked to the Professor in the morning and then hung up. He looked at Elizabeth. "Do you think we were just unlucky that the apartment was robbed, or do you think there is more to it?"

"I don't know," she said in a concerned voice, "But I am sure glad that Alberto is keeping an eye on Charlotte."

****

The next morning, after a quick breakfast, Dan and Elizabeth walked down to the dig site and were surprised to see the Professor standing at the gate arguing with two large men in suits. A small crowd of his staff stood nearby watching.

They walked over to the group. Dan saw Johannes, the Professor's young technical guru. "What's going on?" he asked.

"We don't know!" said Johannes. "We arrived this morning and these guys were stopping anyone from going inside. The Prof has been arguing with them for the last half hour, but he is not getting anywhere."

"Who are they?" asked Elizabeth.

Johanne shrugged his shoulders. "We don't know. They were just here when we arrived. The police who were here yesterday seem to have been replaced."

Just then the Professor turned away from the gate, and spotting Dan walked towards him. He was clearly very upset and angry. He stopped in front of the small crowd of people and said, "I am sorry everyone, but we appear to have some sort of mix up. Apparently we do not have the correct permits to work on the site. It will take me some time to sort this out, so please, have a day off. Go and enjoy yourselves. I will see you back here tomorrow." He then turned towards Dan and Elizabeth. "I need a cup of coffee. Will you join me?" They nodded. He led them out of the riverbed, and into the town.

A few minutes later, seated at a table at the back of a small cafe, with one coffee inside him and another one on the way, the Professor finally settled down enough to speak. "It is unbelievable! It is just complete stupidity. We have all the permits we needed, and suddenly this! They take over the site. It is just unbelievable."

"Who has taken over the site?" asked Elizabeth. "What happened to the police and who are the men there now?"

"I do not know who they are. They say they are from a private security firm, but will not tell me who has hired them! I can't understand what is going on. I will have to go and see the President of Calabria to sort this out. That means driving all the way to Reggio Calabria. Such a waste of time!"

"Professor" said Dan, "I think there might be more to this than just a mix up over permits."

The Professor looked at him. "What do you mean Daniel. What else could have happened?"

"You remember you gave me a copy of the CT scan?" the Professor nodded. "We gave a copy to Charlotte. My apartment in Rome was broken into last night. Charlotte's laptop was stolen. There was a copy of the scan on it. That was all they took. We think that, somehow, they knew that we had a copy and knew where it was."

The Professor looked dumbfounded. "So you think that whatever is going on here it has to do with the sarcophagus?"

"My guess is that there is something in the sarcophagus that someone wants, and they must have a fair bit of clout to be able to just take over the dig site like they did," said Dan.

"What could they want?" said the Professor, more to himself than to Elizabeth or Dan. "Nothing I have seen on the scan is any more valuable or amazing than what we have already found. This doesn't make sense!"

"Professor is there anyway we can see what is going on inside the complex. To see what these people might be doing?" asked Dan.

"I don't know," said the Professor. "But young Johannes would! He set up all the technical stuff!" He thought for a moment. "I see where you are going with this. Okay, see if you can find out what is going on inside the compound while I go and do battle with the authorities."

Four hours later, in Dan and Elizabeth's apartment, Johannes punched the air with his fist. "Yes! We have contact!" Elizabeth and Dan came over to where he was working and looked at the laptop screen in front of him. They could see multiple views of the inside of the dig enclosure.

"Lucky these bastards didn't know about the enclosures surveillance systems, hey?" said Elizabeth with a smirk.

The problem had not been getting access to the wireless cameras, given that it was Johannes own systems they were accessing, it was extending the small wireless network from the enclosure to a safe location. In the end it had been relatively simple. They parked a car, with a wireless range extender, connected to a power inverter connected to the cars battery, near the riverbank, just above the site. Then, after a bit of negotiation with 5 different apartment owners, simply bounced the wireless signal up the hill to Dan and Elizabeth's apartment. Simple, crude, but effective.

On the screen they could see that people were working around the sarcophagus. They had manoeuvred the lifting equipment that had been used to remove the lid of the tomb itself into position, obviously in preparation for lifting the ornate marble lid of the sarcophagus.

"How many men have they got in there?" asked Dan.

"I count four," said Johannes. "Hang on. Let me look at the other cameras." Different views of the enclosure flashed up on the screen. "No, it looks like there are only these guys."

"Let's get all this recorded Johannes." Dan said looking closely at what was going on. "If these goons lift the lid then I want to see what they are up to and what they take out of the coffin."

Johannes nodded and set the video stream to record.

****

"At least they seem to be doing all this with a bit of care," said Elizabeth a few hours later. "I was a bit worried that they would just slide the lid off and dump it on the ground."

"No, they actually seem very professional. Which is a bit of a surprise," said Dan from the couch where he was lying. They had been taking it in turns to watch the screen. Johannes had gone to make sure the battery in the car was not going to run flat.

"Hey! Here we go! They are lifting the lid!" Dan jumped up and watched over Elizabeth's shoulder. He could see the men working the lifting gear and the lid of the sarcophagus slowly rising up into the air.

They both watched, enthralled, as the lid was swung aside and the contents were revealed for the first time in over sixteen hundred years. They couldn't see much, just the dark outline of a nondescript shape.

"It is such a shame that the Professor didn't get a chance to do this," said Elizabeth still staring at the screen. "This would have been such a thrill for him."

"I'm sure he would have stage managed it beautifully," said Dan.

The lid was gently lowered to the ground. As soon as it touched down the men crowded around the coffin. No-one touched what lay inside. After a few minutes all four men moved away from the coffin and out of the camera's view.

Dan reached past Elizabeth and tapped the keyboard. He cycled through the different cameras to see what was going on. He just caught sight of the last man as he walked away from the area covered by the cameras and into the enclosure's small refectory.

"There are no cameras in there," he said, "But it looks like they have done their job and are waiting for something."

"Or someone, more likely." said Elizabeth. "Perhaps they are waiting for their boss to arrive, after all, if it really is about the vial, I can't imagine that whoever is behind all this would tell anyone about the relic unless they had to."

"You are probably right," said Dan walking over to a window. It was starting to get dark outside and he could see Johannes walking back up the hill towards him. "You know what I am thinking?"

Elizabeth looked across at him. "Ummm, let me guess," said Elizabeth turning to look at him. "Given some of your more impetuous actions over the years, I would guess it is not sitting here and waiting for the big boss to arrive and take the reliquary."

Dan shook his head.

"Would it involve a pair of bolt cutters and some dark clothing?" she asked, her tone cautious.

"Look, all we would have to do is sneak up to the back of the enclosure, snip through a couple of the wires, creep in, grab the vial and sneak out again. If we took a phone with us we could log into the network and we could see if any of the men left the refectory. We'd have plenty of time to hide."

Elizabeth sat thinking for a few minutes about all the things that could go wrong. She had always been the more cautious one in their business relationship.

"This is probably our only chance to get hold of the vial!" Dan said trying to convince her.

"Okay," she said as Johannes walked into the room. "I agree. There is really no other option is there? If we don't get it soon, whoever is behind all this will take it and that will be it. Game over!"

Johannes just looked at them, one to the other, not sure what was going on. Dan put his hand on his shoulder. "Johannes, we need to get into the enclosure, and then into the sarcophagus. Can you disable the security system so we can get in without letting the goons inside know?"

Johannes grinned. "Sure can. When do you want to go?"

Dan looked at Elizabeth. "As soon as it gets properly dark," she said.

****

It was a little past half past five when Dan and Elizabeth drove their rental car, a little Fiat 500, down to the river. They sat for some time watching the site to see if there were any guards patrolling. Other than the two who guarded the single entrance gate, it looked like there were no more.

They got out of the car and slipped over the stone wall that ran along the river bank. The river had been diverted around the dig site almost a year before and in that time a host of weeds and small bushes had grown up providing plenty of cover as they moved, unseen, to the back fence of the compound.

Elizabeth texted Johannes. Two minutes later she received a reply saying that the security system had been disarmed and all the men inside the enclosure where still in the refectory.

She slipped her phone back into her pocket and nodded to Dan. He quickly cut through a dozen strands of the mesh fencing with a large pair of bolt cutters creating a small doorway which he bent outwards. He passed the bolt cutters to Elizabeth, took out a blade and sliced through the tough plastic sheeting that had been hung on the inside of the fence. He gave Elizabeth a quick peck on the lips. "Wish me luck!" he whispered. He slithered through the small opening. Elizabeth watched his feet disappear into the darkness.

Dan squatted on the ground, inside the enclosure's fence, orientating himself. He had entered the enclosure at the back. He could dimly make out the command centre to his left, the lights of the electronic equipment, still on standby, glowed in the dark like a swarm of fireflies. In front of him was the edge of trench eight, his trench. In the middle of the trench a darker area defined the tomb itself. He couldn't see the sarcophagus. Trying to see into the darkness he wished that he had talked about this whole adventure with Alberto. If he were here he would have had night vision goggles for sure, he thought to himself. He moved cautiously forward on his hands and knees, feeling his way with his hands. He reached the edge of the trench and worked his way along it until he came to one of the ladders that led down into it.

Looking to his left he could see the slight illumination that was coming from around the door that led to the refectory. With the traffic noise of Cosenza blocked out he could also hear the low mumble of voices coming from that direction.

Dan moved carefully onto the ladder and slipped down into the trench. Just as his foot touched the ground the door to the refectory opened casting light across the whole tomb excavation. Dan, caught out in the open, dived to his left and the comparative safety of the deeper darkness of the tomb itself. He landed awkwardly in the bottom of the tomb, banging his right knee hard on the ground. He fell backwards cracking the back of his head on the base of the sarcophagus. He saw stars.

451

Still dazed he pulled himself up behind the sarcophagus, out of sight of whoever had opened the door. The voices were getting louder. Something was happening. They were talking about someone having arrived, but it wasn't with any sense of urgency in their voices. It didn't seem as though they knew he was there. Someone they were expecting had arrived, and they were all heading to the entrance of the enclosure to meet whoever it was.

It's now or never, Dan thought to himself. He stood up and reached into the sarcophagus. Under his questing hand, he felt the hard round mass of Alaric's skull. Layers of material fell apart as he felt his way down the body. Leaning further forward he felt the jawbone and then the hard edge of the cuirass that hey had seen in the CT scan. He pictured in his mind how the vial had been lying. He moved his hand down to the right. He could feel the hand resting on the breastplate. He tried to feel inside the hand but he was becoming tangled in the decaying material that covered the corpse. He gave a gentle tug, and, as if he had just turned on a switch, the lights of the enclosure flickered into life.

With his hand still in the sarcophagus Dan was suddenly caught in the stark white glare of the neon lights that hung from the roof of the enclosure. Standing near the entrance, surrounded by the four men who had taken the lid from the sarcophagus and the two men who had been guarding the door, was Andris Dragas.

He gave another yank at the material that had covered the vial. The material gave way and the skeletal hand, hopefully with the vial inside, came with it. Clasping his prize in his hand he ran for the ladder that led out of the tomb. He scrambled up it and ran for the ladder that led out of the back of the trench. Just as he reached it a shot rang out. Mud and dirt showered over him as the bullet hit the side of the trench. He stopped and put his arms above his head.

"Lovely to see you again, Doctor Marsh!" said Dragas in his usual polite manner. "I see that you have been doing a bit of grave robbing. I would appreciate it if you would give me what you have stolen. Perhaps you would be kind enough to come up here and bring it with you!"

Dan turned around to face Dragas. He was standing in the middle of the group of men, all of whom now had guns, of various types, trained on him. He was out of options. He climbed slowly up the steps out of the trench, using the same ladder that he had used to climb down into it. He turned to walk along the back of the trench, past the hole that he had cut in the back wall. He looked down to see if his handiwork was visible, worried that Liz might now be in danger too. He couldn't see anything that might suggest that was the way he had entered.

He reached the corner of the trench and had just turned to walk along its edge when everything went black. For a moment Dan stood still, wondering what was going on. Either Johannes or Liz must have switched the lights off. He fell to the ground and rolled to the back wall. He felt along it, feeling for the hole he had made.

Around him he could hear Dragas shouting at his men to find him. He knew that they would be coming around either side of the trench, thinking that they could box him in. It wouldn't take a smart man like Dragas long to figure out that he must have come through the back wall and send someone outside to cover the back of the enclosure.

He could hear the men coming closer from both directions. They were already past the sides of the trench and now working their way along the back edge. If he didn't find the hole soon he would be trapped. At that moment his hand slid behind the sheeting and almost at once he felt someone grab him and pull him hard. He almost flew through the hole landing on top of Elizabeth. "Run!" She said in a loud whisper, scrambling to her feet.

Dan didn't need telling twice. He got to his feet and followed her. "To the car?" he said as he caught up with her. She nodded, and the two of them raced as fast as they could through the scrubby undergrowth to the riverbank wall. They were climbing up the stone steps when they saw the first of Dragas' men appear outside the compound.

There was shout. They had been spotted, silhouetted against the lights of Cosenza, just as they topped the wall. Dragas' men started running towards them.

The little Fiat was only a few metres away. Dan flung open the driver's side door, threw the wad of decaying material with the hand wrapped up inside it onto the back seat and started the car.

Elizabeth slammed her door as Dan let the clutch out. The little Fiat accelerated away from the curb and along the road that ran parallel with the river. Men emerged from another set of stairs that led from the river bed just as the little Fiat tore past. "Oh crap!" said Dan. "Now they know what sort of car we've got."

"They don't look happy!" said Elizabeth looking back over her shoulder.

"Where to?" asked Dan, concentrating hard on getting the most out of the little Fiat's turbocharged engine. "Back to the apartment? Rome? A police station?"

Elizabeth thought for a moment, looked back over her shoulder and then said. "I know it sounds risky but I think Rome is our only real option. The apartment here might be compromised and given the relationship that Dragas must have with the police to be able to have them replaced so quickly, I think going to the authorities around here might be way too risky."

"Rome it is, then!" said Dan "But before we do anything else, give Johannes a ring and tell him to make himself scarce. If the apartment has been compromised then we don't want him to get involved with these guys."

"He is already long gone!" said Elizabeth. "It was Johannes that warned me that you were in trouble and shut the lights down. He was out of the building as soon as he pulled the plug on those guys, with our laptops and whatever other gear he could carry."

Dan, who had been following the road beside the river, suddenly jammed on the brakes. "Fuck!" he said putting the car into reverse. "It's a dead end, I missed the turnoff!"

The Fiat accelerated backwards one block. Dan swung the wheel hard, put the car in gear and accelerated up a road at right angles to the river.

Elizabeth saw a blue and white street sign flash past. "Dan, senso unico! This is one way, and not the way we're going!"

Dan drifted the car around a corner and started accelerating along the road parallel with the river again, but, this time, one street back.

They passed under an overpass. "That's the road to Rome up there!" said Elizabeth.

Dan kept driving fast. The road rapidly deteriorated and the car bounced and crashed on its firm suspension as he hit pothole after pothole. He slammed on the brakes. He had reached a one-lane bridge and another car was coming slowly across it. Dan waited impatiently, his eyes flicking up to the rear view mirror every few seconds. Headlights suddenly appeared, coming rapidly closer. "Shit, here they come!" he said as he planted his foot and ducked behind the slow moving car the moment it cleared the bridge.

The road they were on suddenly started heading up hill. The little car roared up the steep, narrow road. A guardrail was barely visible through the undergrowth on one side, a stone wall flashed past on the other.

Elizabeth had been tapping on her phone. As Dan approached the fork in the road she suddenly said, "Hard left! The other ways a dead end!"

Dan stomped his foot on the brake pedal, double de-clutched and slammed the little car into second gear. He turned the wheel hard. The Fiat struggled for grip on loose gravel, threatened to plough straight ahead, and then found its footing and spun around. As Dan planted his foot on the accelerator the little car's wheels struggled again for a moment to find grip and then shot up the hill.

"When we get to the top there will be a stop sign. You need to turn up the hill, hard right!" said Elizabeth looking at the map on her phone.

Dan couldn't see the stop sign but could see the lights of cars coming down a hill in front of him. In his rear vision mirror he could see the lights of the car he thought was following them. They were closer than before.

As the Fiat reached the crest of the hill, where the two roads met, Dan slammed on the brakes again. The Fiat stopped, just in time to miss a car coming down the hill. The car's horn blared as the driver reacted to the near miss.

Dan glanced at Elizabeth who, white faced was holding tightly onto her seat belt. Dan planted his foot on the accelerator again and the Fiat shot out onto the new road. He headed up the hill.

"Oh shit!" said Elizabeth staring at the screen of her phone a few minutes later. We've just gone over the top of the Autostrada to Rome. I thought that there would be an intersection, but it was a tunnel! I'm sorry!"

"So, can we get back to it any way?" asked Dan.

"If we keep following this road it eventually comes out on the Autostrada that goes to the coast. That road joins the highway we normally take to Rome. It intersects with it just north of San Lucido. The other alternative is to turn around and head back towards Cosenza and join the autostrada we were on the other day, when we drove down from Rome," said Elizabeth. Or, we could go south to Lamezia Terme airport and get a flight to Rome from there. Its a one hour drive and a one hour flight as against a six hour drive."

"When's the next flight?"

Elizabeth tapped on the screen of her phone. "Eight forty five. Its six thirty now, so we would have to hang around for an hour or so."

"We should be safe enough in an airport terminal, don't you think? Let's just keep driving on this road. Its what, half an hour or so to the autostrada?"

'According to Mister Google twenty-eight minutes from here. At this speed though it is probably more like twenty!"

Dan glanced into the rear vision mirror. He couldn't see any lights. Whatever car Dragas' men were driving it wasn't as well suited to the narrow winding road as the Fiat was. "Ok. We get to the autostrada and then turn south, double back on them and head to the airport. As long as you can get us on that eight forty five flight."

"I'm on it Boss!" said Elizabeth.

While she purchased two tickets to Rome, Dan concentrated on putting as much distance as possible between them and the car behind.

There were few vehicles on the road. The first half of the trip had been through built up areas, but as they got closer to the intersection to the autostrada the distances between inhabited areas became greater. Only the occasional light now punctuated long dark stretches of road. While the little Fiat was great on the winding roads, Dan had seen that the road straightened out as they got closer to the intersection. If, as he suspected, Dragas had a larger, more powerful car, then the advantage that they currently had was only temporary.

As if on cue, as the road straightened out Dan caught site of headlights coming up fast behind them. "Shit! Here they come!" he said.

"And that must be the Autostrada!" said Elizabeth pointing to a well-lit bridge crossing a valley off to their right. "The junction can't be more than a few kilometres ahead!"

"I was hoping that we would have had more distance between them and us when we turned off, but it looks like they are going to be right on top of us!" he said glancing in the mirror. The lights were now only a few metres behind them.

"What the fuck are they doing!" said Dan, as the car behind them suddenly lunged at them. Dan felt the impact. The little car started to slide. Dan spun the wheel, trying desperately to correct the spin, but the front wheels wouldn't grip the road. In a flash of illumination he saw a guardrail spin past them and then, for a brief moment nothing, as the little car flew over the edge of the road. With a jolt the Fiat landed on its side and started tumbling down a steep bank. It rolled over and over until it came to rest at the bottom of the steep slope, five hundred metres below the road.

6. Calabria - Present day

Andris Dragas stood impassively at the edge of the road looking down into the darkness. Two men stood beside him. "Go and get what they stole from the sarcophagus," he said to them. "It should be a small glass vial, possibly with a chain attached to it. If the woman is still alive bring her too. If the man is alive, kill him!"

The two men, torches in hand, slid and scrabbled their way towards the bottom of the slope. They could hear the ticking of the hot metal of the car, but, in the darkness, they couldn't see it. As they approached the bottom of the valley, one of the men shouted that he had found it, highlighting it with the beam from his torch. The smell of petrol was strong.

The Fiat rested on its roof. It was crushed and dented almost beyond recognition. As the two men approached they could see that Elizabeth was still in the car, suspended by her seat belt and surrounded by the ghostly white shapes of deflated air bags. The driver's side door had been ripped from its hinges when it had tumbled down the hill. The driver was nowhere to be seen.

One of the men felt for a pulse on Elizabeth's neck. "She's alive. It looks like the airbags saved her. There doesn't seem to be any blood around. Give us a hand to get her out of here."

The other man walked to the passenger side of the car. They wrenched open the door and then gently lifted Elizabeth's limp and unresisting body free. As they put her on the ground one of the men heard a crunch under his boot. He stooped down and picked up a bundle of rags that had fallen onto the ground beside the car. He opened up the wad of decaying and dusty material. Pieces of broken glass tinkled to the ground. "Fuck!" he said, looking at the shards of glass that remained. "I've just trodden on that glass thing Dragas wanted!"

****

Half an hour later, after an unproductive search for Dan's body, with a still unconscious Elizabeth strapped into the back of his BMW, Andris Dragas looked down at the shards of glass, all that remained of the reliquary. He could see a brownish residue on many of them. He smiled to himself.

7. Amalfi - Present day

Elizabeth slowly came awake. The first thing she noticed was that she had a splitting headache and was lying on a bed in a darkened room. The second thing she noticed was that a man was sitting in a chair watching her. She couldn't see his face.

"Dan?" she asked in a hoarse whisper.

"No, Elizabeth," said Andris Dragas. "Unfortunately Dan is dead. He died in the car crash. You on the other hand were luckier. You have a slight concussion and what looks like a broken shoulder, and the odd bruise, but other than that you are fine."

Elizabeth collapsed back onto the bed. Grief and anger flowed through her. "Why are you doing this?"

"My family has never looked kindly on those that get in our way. We have invested too many years and too much effort in our objectives to let amateur meddlers like you and Dan Marsh interfere."

She felt like she was in a James Bond novel, talking to some ridiculous, egotistical Bond villain. Disgusted by the man's calmness and lack of humanity, she asked, "Who the hell are you?"

"I am Andris Palaiologos Vasilivich Dragas," he said with obvious pride. "I am a direct descendant of Manuel Palaiologos, Emperor of the Romans. I am also a descendant of Ivan Vasilyevich, Grand Prince of all Rus. My family has been working towards the re-instatement of our city, our religion and our honour for more years than someone like you could imagine."

"The only reason that you are alive now is that you are, regrettably, one of the few people who can unlock a mystery that has been haunting my family since the fall of our City to the Saracen. Since you already know some parts of the story it seems opportune for us to take advantage of your knowledge to finally solve that mystery."

"What mystery is that?" said Elizabeth.

"This mystery!" said Dragas, leaning forward and turning on a light. He was holding a small plastic bottle that contained the remnants of the vial that Dan had taken from the sarcophagus a few hours before.

"A number of these vials were stolen from the Church of the Apostles in Constantinople when the Latins invaded the City in 1204. Fortuitously, one was taken before the siege by a member of my own family for safe keeping. The others were spread throughout Europe, taken by those that desecrated our City, along with the many other treasures they had no right to remove."

"My family has spent hundreds of years searching for what was stolen from us. We believed that we had recovered all of the vials. Then we started to hear persistent rumours that there was another source of the blood of Constantine."

"Over the centuries we followed those rumours. One, as yet unresolved mystery occurred in the late eighteenth century. A predecessor of mine thought he had discovered the source. Unfortunately, before he could pass on his suspicions, his body was found lying in a ditch beside a road in southern France, near Aix-en-Provence. After that the rumours seemed to dry up. Whispers started again, briefly, during the reign of Napoleon the Third, but nothing came of it. Everything remained quiet, until rumours started about the Hitler vial a few years ago."

"Over the centuries we have learnt much about the blood of Constantine. We know, for instance, that not everyone can use it. We know that some who take have gone mad. Some die."

"Are you really so gullible as to believe that it is the blood of a Saint?" asked Elizabeth mockingly. You do know that it is not really blood, don't you?"

She could feel Dragas' hesitation.

"Until this sample is analysed we will not know the truth," he replied, a note of irritation in his voice. "Theodor Morell was a fool, working for a madman! I have no reason to believe that the concoction he put together resembles, in any way, the true blood of Constantine!"

"You really do believe it is the blood of saint?" asked Elizabeth, incredulous.

"We keep an open mind!" he replied angrily. "Over the years we have tested the idea that the blood of particularly pious individuals may have unique qualities."

"And how did that work out for you?" she mocked.

He ignored her question.

"You will analyse this sample for me. I have a well-equipped laboratory available. If you do this task well I will see that you are treated well and then released."

Elizabeth stared into his eyes. They were hard and unforgiving.

"How do you even know this stuff works? The whole thing could just be some hocus pocus made up by medieval morons."

"Because I have used it. It is the tradition in our family that the heir apparent drinks two drops of the blood of Constantine on his fourteenth birthday. If he survives, on the death of the patriarch of the family, he takes over. It has been the way it has been since Constantine Palaiologos."

"Clearly being a psychopath doesn't stop you getting the job, then!" spat Elizabeth. She saw Dragas' hand ball into a fist. She realised that, if she was to get out of this situation alive, she needed to be less abrasive.

"So Constantine really did survive the fall of Constantinople?" she asked more pleasantly.

Dragas looked at her for some time before he answered, trying to decide if she was genuinely interested. "Yes. He survived. It was Constantine who laid the foundation for the family's future."

8. Constantinople - 30th May 1453

Constantine came slowly back to consciousness. His head ached. It was like no other headache he had ever experienced. He tried to open his eyes. He wasn't sure if they were open or not. Everything was black. He couldn't move his arms or his legs. He pushed downward. His hands sunk into something wet and slippery. He stopped trying. He was struggling to get enough air. He felt a panic rising within him. Had he been buried alive? Was this hell? Panicking, he struggled. Pain lanced through his shoulder every time he tried to move.

He managed to get his right arm free. He found a gap through which he could force it. He could feel something soft beneath his hand. He felt around it, feeling a sharp jagged edge and then the shape of a nose. He felt vomit surge up into his mouth. He gagged.

He moved his hand away from the smashed skull and felt the reassuringly solid metal of a cuirass. He pulled himself forward. He realised that his inability to move was caused by the weight of bodies lying on top of him.

Still unable to see anything, and starting to think that he might have been struck blind, he pulled his way over one body after another, always working his way up towards what he hoped would be fresh air.

He paused frequently. He realised that if this wasn't hell then he was trapped under a pile of bodies, probably thrown into a mass grave, perhaps into the foss. He moved cautiously. Assuming he could get out before he suffocated, his sudden appearance could lose him his head.

For what seemed like hours he inched his way over one dead body after another. Occasionally he would put his hand on something living. It would squeal and squirm away from him. Several times he put his hand on the sharp edge of a sword or dagger.

Finally, just as he was starting to believe that he was condemned to eternal damnation in a pit of dead bodies, his hand broke free. He felt a cool breeze caress it. He drew it back quickly and waited, listening to see if he could hear anything that might indicate that someone had seen him. Nothing.

With infinite care he pushed the body, that now lay directly on top of him, out of the way. Relief washed over him as he realised he wasn't blind but almost immediately a sense of panic overwhelmed him again. He looked out into a dark sky full of the red glow and the roiling smoke of fires. All around him, lay devastation. Bodies lay in massive piles. Small animals flitted from corpse to corpse. Dogs, half starved during the long siege tore at the bodies of their dead masters. Rats seemed to be everywhere, carpeting the ground. He had been cast into the pits of hell. Hell on earth.

Tears filled his eyes as he lay still, half buried in the dead bodies of his comrades, and watched his city burn. The Empire was gone. The City was gone, and yet he had survived. He didn't understand. Why had God allowed him to live when everything that he had cared about in his life, both his beautiful wives, his mother, his city, his empire, had all been taken from him. What possible reason could there be for forcing him to survive?

Unable to look upon the burning city any longer, Constantine dragged himself free of the pile of bodies. He slithered on his belly, heading away from the walls, out into the darkness.

Once free of the pit he took off what remained of his armour. It was difficult. He guessed that his left arm was broken. He had a long sword wound running down his thigh which had, thankfully stopped bleeding. Dressed only in his linen underclothes and woollen stockings he made his way cautiously down towards the Golden Horn, past the Adrianople Gate and then down past the walls of his own palace. Eventually he reached the water's edge.

In the distance he could see people boarding a Venetian cargo ship. He made his way carefully along the foreshore. When he was about one hundred metres from the ship one of the passengers leaning on the rail saw him and started waving and shouting at him, urging him to hurry.

A large Venetian seaman grabbed him as he approached the edge of the dock, took one look at the blood and mud that covered him and hurried him on board, half lifting him onto the ship's deck. "Get down and stay out of sight if you know what's good for you," he said in a terse whisper. "If they catch us with any soldiers on board we are all dead, understand?!"

Constantine nodded. "Why are they letting you go?" he asked, surprised that any ships, let alone a Venetian trading galley, would be allowed to leave the Golden Horn.

"They're all too busy thieving and butchering," he said bitterly. "If we're quick we might be able to get away. There is still a chance that they will send ships after us as soon as those murderous scum realise we have escaped. Heaven help anyone left in the City now!" said the sailor as he turned to help get the ship ready for departure.

Constantine found a space on deck between a woman clutching a baby tightly to her chest and an old man clutching several large books to his. Neither bothered to give him more than a cursory glance.

Constantine, exhausted, dispirited and feeling ashamed that he was still alive, sat staring at the burning city.

9. Venice - June 1453

Two weeks after escaping the Golden Horn the galley arrived in Venice. Constantine had introduced himself on the boat as Manuel Dragas, a distant cousin of the Palaiologos family, just in case anyone thought they recognised a similarity between the Emperor and himself. His face was still swollen and bruised, his nose had been broken and his clothes were torn and dirty. No one had recognised him. No one had even given him a second glance.

During the voyage he had given a great deal of thought to what he should do once he arrived in Venice. He decided that it would be best for him to get as far away as possible from anyone that might recognise him. That meant getting to the mainland and heading north or northeast into his mother's country. Perhaps going further north to Hungary or the Kingdom of Poland. Staying in Venice was not an option, given the number of refugees that were streaming into the city from Constantinople and its surrounding areas. Moving further West was not an option either. The family still controlled Morea and he was certainly well known across many parts of Greece. Further west was Italy. He didn't have the stomach to go there or further west into the Kingdom of the Francs.

He had left Venice almost immediately and headed North. Now he sat, his back to the crumbling stone wall of a deserted cottage he had stumbled across, with the late afternoon sun warming him. Set well back from the road, the cottage offered him sanctuary and seclusion as well as a modicum of protection for the weather. He had avoided people on his trek north and survived by scavenging and hunting. It was a long way from the Court of Constantinople. He smiled to himself. He had to admit that he was happier now than he had been for a long time, perhaps since even before Maddalena had died.

It had been a long time, he thought sadly, since he had given himself permission to think of his beautiful, gentle, first wife. He and Maddalena had only been given a year together. It had been a year like none he had ever known, before or since. Of all his memories, the memories of that time were the ones he held most dear, and of those, the one he cherished most, the one he avoided, was that glorious spring afternoon, with the scent of the wildflowers everywhere, when she had told him that she was pregnant. They had sat for hours together, their backs against the warm stone wall of the palace in Mystras, and talked about their future and the family they would have together. Tears streamed down his face as he finally let himself remember the day that she and his daughter had died. He had held Maddalena's hand, comforted her as best he could, and prayed. God had forsaken him then, as now, he thought bitterly.

He had been devastated by Maddalena's death. It had taken him a long time to recover. Eventually, bowing to the demands of his family to marry again, he had agreed to marry Caterina. Twelve years after Maddalena died he had taken his new wife only to have her fall ill, miscarry and die.

He stared at the small glass and gold reliquary that contained the blood of Constantine. He knew well the story of how his namesake had seen a vision just before the battle of the Milvian Bridge. A sign from God had given him direction and shown him how to proceed. God, he thought bitterly, did not forsake you Constantine the Great. Perhaps after eleven Constantine's wearing the imperial purple God has got tired of us!

Perhaps, he wondered, it was not God's wish for the churches of the west and east to be re-united. Perhaps the Latin Church truly had become heretical and strayed from our Lord's path! Perhaps it was us who had forsaken the true path. Perhaps we should have trusted in God, instead of in the Italians. Perhaps losing our faith had lost us our City!

He and his brother John had both worked hard to convince the Pope in Rome to support their cause. They had believed that the price they had been asked to pay for that support was not too high. Clearly God did not agree. In spite of having paid the price, no help had come from the west.

"We were deceived!" he thought to himself angrily. "They wanted to undermine the true faith! They wanted our city to fall! What other explanation can there be for the way they have acted! They were jealous of the purity of our church and the nobility of our City!"

An idea started to form in Constantine's mind. "There must be a way to put this right," he said to himself. "Christianity must be brought back to Orthodoxy. The City must be restored. It must become, once again, the centre of the true faith!" He looked down at the small gold reliquary that he had gripped so tightly in his closed fist that the pattern on its surface had transferred itself to his skin.

He held the vial up to the last of the day's light. He could see the liquid inside moving sluggishly backwards and forwards.

Going down on his knees he bowed his head. "Heavenly King, Comforter, the Spirit of Truth, present in all places and filling all things, Treasury of Goodness and Giver of life." he prayed out loud, "Come and abide in us. Cleanse us from every stain of sin and save our soul, O Gracious Lord. Guide me as you guided my namesake Constantine the Great, Equal of the Apostles. If during this day we have sinned in word, deed or thought forgive us in Your goodness and love. Grant us peaceful sleep; protect us from all evil and awake us in the morning that we may glorify You, Your Son and Your Holy Spirit now and forever and ever. Amen."

Constantine broke the top off the reliquary and then broke the seal on the vial within it. "With the partaking of this precious blood I give myself and my descendants to the purification of your church and the restoration of Your City. I vow, on behalf of my unborn children to do all I can to bring about the downfall of the heretical church of the west and the infidel, wherever we may find them. Amen" he prayed. He brought the vial to his lips and swallowed the contents.

10. Amalfi - Present day

"We know that the blood of Constantine gives the user insight into the future. The Codex Palaiologos, started by Constantine himself, has guided and recorded the actions of my family for six hundred years. My family has documented the power of the relic, its amazing effects on the mind, as well as its equally terrible effects on those who were not deemed worthy."

"Now science has developed to the point where it may be able to unlock the mysteries that up until now God alone has understood. That, obviously, is where you come in."

"Like I said, Dragas, that stuff is not blood. Not only is it not blood, it doesn't even originate with Constantine the Great!"

"What?" exclaimed Dragas, clearly shocked by Elizabeth's statement. "What have your researches uncovered? Tell me what you have discovered!" he demanded.

"I wouldn't tell you the way to the toilet, you worthless piece of shit!" spat Elizabeth.

"I realise you are upset, by the death of your...partner. I will excuse your vulgarity in this instance," said Dragas icily. "But I warn you that I do not accept that sort of disrespectful behaviour from anyone, especially women."

"Fuck you!" said Elizabeth angrily under her breath.

Dragas leaned forward and, before Elizabeth knew what was going on, slapped her so hard across the face that she was knocked backwards, hitting her head on the wall behind her with an audible thud. She stayed where she lay, stunned, just staring angrily at Dragas.

"I do not tell people things twice!" he said. He sat back back in his seat and steepled his hands in front of him. He tapped them gently on his bottom lip. "I need you to understand, Elizabeth, that you have become involved in something that may be well beyond your comprehension. Certainly well beyond your experience."

"My family has been working tirelessly for six hundred years to restore the rightful order to the world. It has done this through the accumulation of wealth and influence and an unrelenting focus on our goal. You would be amazed at what can be achieved with that level of single minded purpose!"

"So, what are your goals, world domination with you as Emperor?" said Elizabeth with as much sarcasm as her rapidly swelling lip would allow.

"Ha! Nothing so prosaic or ignoble. If we had wanted power we could have had that centuries ago. No. We have been working to undo what was done to us. We will restore Constantinople to its rightful place at the centre of the Christian world, rid the world of the heresies of the West and at the same time take our revenge on the Saracen."

"You're a complete nut job!" said Elizabeth.

Dragas' hand balled into a fist, again. He took a deep breath and then relaxed it. "You have no faith. Godless people like you could never understand the importance of what we must do!"

"Well you haven't been very successful. In six hundred years what have you achieved? The Roman Catholic Church has become the biggest religion in the world, challenged only by the growth of Islam. The Pope is as popular as ever. Most of the world has forgotten that Constantinople ever existed and the Eastern Orthodox Church has been relegated to a position of minor player in the world's religions. Hagia Sophia has even gone back to being a mosque. Good job on your long term plan!" said Elizabeth with a bitter laugh.

"You display a level of ignorance about what really happens in the world that I find laughable. The Western church is destroying itself from within. The Roman Curia has the Pope so constrained that he is becoming more of a media star than a religious leader. Islam is becoming the target of the secular superpowers because of its radical fundamentalist elements and the Eastern Orthodox has never compromised its beliefs.

"Just semantics! You haven't contributed to any of those things happening!" said Elizabeth.

"Haven't we?" said Dragas with the slightest of smiles. "My family has been working diligently away at destroying the Latin Church for hundreds of years. Thomas Cromwell was a protege of my family. My

470

ancestor recognised his intelligence and talent and schooled him in religion and the art of political survival. He was a bit of a ruffian when he first joined the cause, but by the time we sent him back to England he was formidable!"

"You are claiming credit for the Reformation in England?" asked Elizabeth, incredulous.

"No," said Dragas quietly. "We just took advantage of the situation that Henry the eighth had got himself into. It was people like Luther, Zwingli and Calvin who instigated the reformation, not us. My family merely helped it along. Cromwell was a facilitator. We helped by giving him guidance and by investing in new technologies, like the printing press, to help spread the word. We have done the same thing for hundreds of years. We invest in the political careers of individuals with potential, and new technologies to help spread the word. It was printing presses in the fifteenth and sixteenth centuries, radio and film in the early twentieth century, television in the fifties and internet companies at the end of the twentieth century."

"You might be surprised at how easy it is to create scandals that undermine a church, especially when they make themselves so vulnerable by thinking that they can do things like run their own bank, for instance. A suggestion in the right ear at the right time...."

"I suppose you are going to take credit for all the sex scandals as well," sneered Elizabeth.

Dragas laughed. "No, that is their own stupidity! Perhaps we help them along by encouraging certain friendships, making the right introductions, and pointing ambitious young journalists in the right direction."

"So you waste your time trying to embarrass the church. Big deal! The world will survive a few scandals in the Roman Catholic Church. You haven't been able to damage the Muslims like that. " said Elizabeth scornfully.

"Why do you think we financed 9/11?" said Dragas quietly.

"Bullshit! That was al-Qaeda!" said Elizabeth.

"Osama and I moved in the same circles for a while. It is amazing how the right idea at the right time can lead to a mutually beneficial outcome!" said Dragas.

"So you are trying to tell me that you were behind the destruction of the World Trade Centres!" said Elizabeth scornfully.

"Not only the World Trade Centres. There have been many points in history where we have intervened to ensure that our objectives are advanced. The destabilising of the Austrian -Hungarian Empire was important. Our investments in armaments manufacture and banking were greatly enhanced through the early part of the last century."

"In fact we almost managed to get Constantinople back in 1915 with the agreement between the British, the French and Tsar Nicholas. If that buffoon Churchill hadn't bungled the Gallipoli campaign Constantinople would already be a Christian city again."

"Hang on. Are you now saying that you caused the First World War!" said Elizabeth in total disbelief.

"No!" said Dragas with a laugh. "That would be absurd. We did arrange the death of the Crown Prince Rudolf at Mayerling and we provided support to the Black Hand in their activities in Bosnia. We may have had someone even suggest that they target the Arch Duke Franz Ferdinand, but no, we didn't cause the First World War. At the very most we hurried along the inevitable," said Dragas.

"So you are trying to tell me that you were involved in starting the First World War and that you were somehow involved in the Gallipoli campaign, one of the most defining events in my adopted country's history?"

Dragas nodded. "Yes, we influenced the timing of the First World War and yes, we put a lot of time, effort and money into getting the attack at Gallipoli to happen. You have to understand that it was a unique opportunity. The Ottoman Empire was dying. The Ottomans had finally run out of energy. There was civil unrest and political instability all over the Empire."

"We convinced Churchill to renege on the delivery of a couple of warships that the Ottomans had bought from the British knowing that the German's would step in by providing a couple of their own. We knew that would annoy the British. It was easy enough to push that buffoon Kaiser Wilhelm into entering into a treaty, but the real problem was that, despite his Ministers signing the treaty the Sultan wouldn't be persuaded. We got around the problem by convincing the religious leaders of their Empire to declare a Jihad on behalf of the Ottoman Government against the Allies," he chuckled.

"Once the war had started we persuaded the French that an attack on the Dardanelles would be a strategically good decision. The British weren't initially keen but once we got Churchill to come around to our way of thinking things finally started to take off. Admittedly we had to fabricate a few slightly misleading reports on troop numbers that tipped the balance in our favour. We did the same thing, in a slightly more contemporary way, to get the West to stir up trouble in the Middle East, weapons of mass destruction, rather than troop numbers, but basically the same strategy. It amazing how often the same tactics work over and over again!" he laughed.

"But the whole Gallipoli expedition was a fiasco. It failed miserably. You killed thousands of men and you lost!" said Elizabeth.

"Yes, but that's life! That is what happens when there are so many unpredictable elements to consider. That is why we have needed the blood of Constantine," he said holding up the bottle that contained the remaining pieces of Alaric's vial.

"The world is too complex! We can't control every aspect of it. The Gallipoli campaign is a case in point. You are correct. We did lose the opportunity. Our ally in the British Government at the time, Mister Churchill, got demoted! The Bolsheviks took over in Russia! We did briefly hold the City at the end of the war, from 1918 till 1923 but by then Mustafa Kemal had led the Turks to independence, snatching away any likelihood of Constantinople permanently falling back into our control any time soon. But it was just another step in nearly five hundred years of continual prodding and pushing the major powers, especially Russia, towards regaining Constantinople for Christianity. We've been working at it since we helped stir up the Russo-Turkish war in the middle of the sixteenth Century."

"But it was not a total loss. Turkey, under Ataturk, became a secular nation. To us that was a step forward. Admittedly it was only a small one. It did lead to the achievement of one of our most cherished dreams, though. Hagia Sofia stopped being used as a mosque! I admit that we have had a set back there, but one day it will be a Christian place of worship again. Small steps Elizabeth, small steps!"

"You really are delusional! You are trying to make yourself out as some sort of grand master of the Illuminati! You're as mad as all those deluded idiots who believe all that paranoid, conspiracy drivel."

Dragas let out a laugh. "For your information it was one of my ancestors that established the Illuminati, but I imagine that you are as ignorant of the true history of that group as most people."

"The real Illuminati was set up in 1776 by a group of enlightened gentlemen, including my ancestor. You should be thanking me. One of their goals was to support women's education and gender equality. They also worked to oppose superstition, prejudice, abuses of state power, and, more importantly, the influence of the Roman Catholic Church over government, philosophy and science."

"Unfortunately the Roman Catholic Church persuaded the Elector of Bavaria to outlaw the Illuminati. By 1785 it no longer existed."

"Another failure of one of your grand schemes?" said Elizabeth with a note of sarcasm in her voice.

"Maybe," said Dragas. "We did learn a salutary lesson from the experience, though. The idea of a group like the Illuminati, as a force for secretly influencing and manipulating the world, appealed to people. The idea seemed to take on a life of its own. The uneducated and ignorant believed it. We recognized that it was a great idea for deflecting and discrediting any suspicions regarding our own activities. It is especially so these days with the internet being such a good vehicle for disinformation. There is no reason why we shouldn't take advantage of those paranoid conspiracy idiots you mentioned!"

"Now, Elizabeth, I have been very open with you, very patient. Now it is your turn. Tell me what you know about the history of this phial!" said Dragas in a pleasant, but insistent voice.

"Why should I?" she asked. "You are a madman. You have murdered Dan! You have kidnapped me! You have punched me in the face! You can take that phial and stick it as far up your arse as you can!"

"You are disrespectful and have a foul mouthed woman, Elizabeth, no wonder your marriages continually fail. As to why you should help us. Let me see. Do you remember the scholarship you won to further your study into genetics and allow you to finish your Phd?"

"Yes," said Elizabeth hesitantly.

"That was us! We paid for you to pursue what we thought, and what has subsequently proven to be, a very useful area of research."

"Bullshit. That scholarship has been awarded since the 1920s. You are just making this up."

Dragas shook his head. "We set up that fund after we saw how successful the Rhodes trust was. It is a perfect way to keep tabs on the brightest and the best in the areas in which we are interested. They come to us, just as you did. We don't have to chase them. We maintain some control over who gets the funds. That's how we knew about you and your work."

"You couldn't have known that I would end up working with Dan though, and it is primarily through the links with his work that I was able to progress my research so quickly. I know that he didn't win a scholarship, so you wouldn't have known about him at all!" said Elizabeth.

"You continually underestimate us," said Dragas, shaking his head. "Do you remember how you got the job with Dan's company?" he asked.

"Yes, I was approached by a head hunting firm. Dan was looking for someone to help him run the company after he had a parting of the ways with his business partner."

"Yes, Barry was a bit of a failure, I have to admit. We had thought that he and Dan would make a good team. Better than his wife, anyway. She was a bit pedestrian and would have held him back if we hadn't done something about it. Anyway, the headhunting firm is one of our ventures. A useful way to get the right people in the right place."

Elizabeth stared at Dragas. She could feel the blood drain from her face. "No, you didn't? You didn't kill Dan's wife?" she said, horrified.

"Automobile accidents happen all the time! Sometimes you just have to create the right opportunities," said Dragas with a shrug.

"Now, as I said, I have been exceedingly patient with you. I want you to tell me what you currently know about the composition of Hitler's version of the Relic and what you and your friends have found out from their researches in the Vatican library!"

"As I am hoping you are becoming aware, while it would be regrettable, I will have no compunction in having you tortured if you waste any more of my time! You must realise that you do not have a choice. I will give you one hour to regain your composure and think about what I have told you. When I return I want your full cooperation." Dragas stood up and started to walk from the room. As he got to the door he stopped and turned back towards her. "If you have any thoughts of escape, please don't bother. Should you escape, Doctor Marsh's daughter, whom I have people watching in Rome, will suffer in the most painful way, until you are found. Then she will be killed in front of you."

Elizabeth felt paralysed with fear as she watched the door close behind Dragas.

11. Calabria - Present day

Dan was lying in thick underbrush. He could feel pinpricks of pain all over his body where he had been scratched as thorns from the bushes he had been thrown into had torn at his skin. He tried to move, but with every attempt the sharp spikes dug more deeply into his flesh. He stopped struggling.

He heard voices. Twisting around carefully he could see the lights of two torches as they passed him and headed further down the slope. One of the men shouted that Elizabeth was still alive. A few minutes later someone shouted that they had found the vial.

Suddenly, without warning, the Fiat exploded. Dan, visions of Elizabeth caught in the conflagration, struggled, desperately to get free of the thorns. They ripped more deeply into his flesh every time he moved. He paused, letting the pain subside, steeling himself for another effort, when he heard voices again. The two men, dragging Elizabeth between them, struggled past, back up the slope, grumbling about the loose rocks and shale that made the slope so difficult to climb.

A few minutes later Dan saw the two torches moving back down the slope. The methodical way they were covering the ground suggested that they were searching for him. Although one of the men came close to where he was trapped, Dan's dark clothing and the thickness of the thicket he had become entangled in, effectively camouflaged him. After half an hour they gave up. He heard a car drive off. Then everything was quiet, except for the sounds made by the still smouldering Fiat.

It took Dan until the morning to extricate himself from the bushes he had fallen into. Finally standing free of them he took stock of his injuries. His hands and face were covered in scratches. Some of them quite deep. Other than that, and a soreness around his ribs, he thought he had survived pretty well. The dreadful thorn bush had, bizarrely, saved him from more serious injury, cushioning his impact when he had been thrown from the car.

He walked down to where the burnt out shell of the Fiat rested, ticking occasionally as the burned metal cooled in the chill of the morning. Nothing was salvageable. He sat on a rock and stared at the wreck. The morning sun hit him, warming him slightly. He was just about to start up the slope when something sparkled on the ground near the car. He walked across to where he had seen the flash of light and knelt down. He recognised the small pieces of rotting material that he had ripped from the sarcophagus. Pieces of white bone were scattered around and there, among the debris, was a single shard of glass. Dan leant down to examine it more closely. Clinging to the glass shard was a reddish brown lump. Dan searched through the rubbish that was lying all around the bottom of the deep gully. Eventually he found a small plastic bag. He cleaned it as best he could and then used it to, very carefully, pick up and wrap the little glass shard. He stuffed it carefully into his pocket and started up the slope to the road.

12. Rome - Present day

Dan arrived at his apartment in Rome with a real sense of relief. He had flagged down a car when he had reached the Autostrada. The driver, initially reticent to do anything but drive him to the nearest town, eventually warmed to Dan and, realising he wasn't an axe murderer, despite his blooded and bruised appearance, offered him a ride all the way to Rome.

He put his key into the lock, but it wouldn't open. He knocked on the door and after a couple of minutes he heard a muffled exclamation from inside. The door was yanked open and Charlotte stood, eyes wide and hand over her mouth. "God Dad! What's happened to you?!" Then, looking past him, "Where's Liz?"

Alberto appeared. The two of them half led and half carried him to a large sofa and sat him down. He told them about the events of the previous evening. When he was finished Charlotte ordered him to go and have a hot shower, put some antiseptic on the worst of his scratches and get into some fresh clothes. Alberto volunteered to make a late lunch.

Sitting around the dining table Dan looked at Alberto. "I think that we ought to call in the police. You must know someone who we can trust," he said, finally breaking the silence as he put down his fork and pushed the half finished plate of fettuccine into the middle of the table.

"It is too great a risk," said Alberto, pushing his own unfinished meal away from him.

"That only leaves one possible course of action then," said Charlotte. "We have to go after her ourselves!"

"We don't even know where she is!" said Dan, in an exasperated voice.

"But we do know where Dragas is. We can check to see if she was taken to his boat." said Charlotte jumping up out of her seat. "There is one of those tourist webcams that looks down at the marina. I saw it the other day. We can have a look to see if they store a back history of images!"

They crowded around her computer. "Look, they do, every five minutes for the last twenty four hours!" Charlotte clicked through the images searching for anything that might give a hint that Elizabeth was taken on board Dragas' yacht.

"That could be her!" said Alberto. The image was dark, but they could clearly see two men carrying something the size of a person onto the yacht.

"OK!" said Dan sitting down on the sofa, "Lets assume that was her. Dragas knows that we know about his boat, so he is unlikely to drop his guard and just let us on board to rescue her. He will probably have a permanent guard watching out in case we do something."

"Let me check!" said Charlotte, turning back to her laptop. "Yep, I can just make out someone on the back of the boat. Looking back through these images I can see someone on guard since they took her onboard. We can't approach the boat by land. What about by water? Could we get some scuba gear and approach the boat underwater?"

"Can either of you scuba dive?" asked Alberto.

"Yes," said Dan. "We have both got hundreds of hours diving, both daytime and night diving, but I don't think that will help us. The only way onto that boat is over the rear transom. If it is our intention to get one of us on board then it won't be while they are moored in a Marina. They will always have a guard watching, on the boat, and no doubt on the land approaches as well."

"Hang on," said Alberto. "What would you do if you did get on board? I am guessing that pretty well everyone on that yacht will be armed and quite happy to shoot anyone they find who shouldn't be there. I've got some training that might help me survive a stunt like the one your talking about, but neither of you have!"

"Could we gas them? Put them all to sleep somehow?" asked Charlotte.

"Not without risking killing someone, perhaps even Elizabeth. The only weaponised incapacitating agent I know about is the one they used a few years ago in the Moscow Theatre incident, when Chechen Rebels took a whole lot of people hostage. The gas that they used was some

480

sort of derivative of fentanyl. It killed about 15% of the hostages," said Alberto.

"In that case I don't think we should be trying to mount a rescue mission on the boat at all! Attacking them on their own ground isn't wise, anyway. We need to draw them off the boat. If we could disable the boat so that they had to take Elizabeth somewhere else, then we might open up more opportunities to snatch her back!" said Charlotte.

"Okay, so our objective is first, to disable the yacht so it can't leave the marina, and then to force Dragas to abandon the yacht and take Elizabeth to a less secure location?" asked Alberto seeking agreement.

"Without putting any of us in danger!" said Charlotte.

"And without tipping Dragas off that we are mounting a rescue mission!" said Alberto.

"How do we do that?" asked Dan.

"Simple!" said Alberto. "We suspect that Dragas is having us watched, no?"

Dan nodded.

"Then after we have disabled his yacht we take Dan for a visit to the local police station! If Dragas thinks that Dan is getting the local Carabinieri involved then, even if he does have half the Italian police force in his pocket, he will probably want to move Elizabeth so he doesn't have to answer any difficult questions," said Alberto.

"So how do we disable his boat so it can't move? asked Dan.

"How about we go with something simple. Wrap something around the yachts propeller!" said Charlotte. "If we did it properly he wouldn't be able to move far from the Marina before his boat broke."

"We could approach the yacht from underwater, tie something around the prop and sneak off. No-one would know we were even there," said Dan.

"Perfecto!" said Alberto. "We have a plan!"

"Oh no we don't!" said Charlotte who had been keeping an eye on Dragas yacht through the webcam. "There is a big fuel tanker pulling up to the end of the marina. I think he could be getting ready to leave Amalfi!"

"Shit!" said Dan. "We have to stop him! We will just have to disable the boat when it is out at sea. That would force Dragas to take people off! We'll need a small fast speedboat to get us within a reasonable distance of them."

"We would still need a way to approach the yacht undetected. If they know it was anything other than an accident then we would have lost any sense of surprise that we might have had," said Alberto.

"What could we use to snare her props?" asked Dan.

"How about a long length of floating, high strength rope, like they use for fishing?" suggested Charlotte.

"No, the props would probably have rope cutters to protect them. But we could use something like a drift net. That would definitely foul the propellers," said Dan. "That would mean we would have to drop the net just in front her so that she went over the top of it."

"She probably has a top speed of about twenty to twenty-five knots," he continued, "so we would have to be going well in excess of that to catch her, get in front of her and then deploy the net so she runs over it."

"The real problem is how to get close enough to her without being seen?" asked Alberto.

"It will take two of us, but I can think of one way we could do it. What is the weather forecast for the next few days Charlie?"

Charlotte checked the weather on her iPhone. "Clear, cool, breezes gusting to thirty knots, why?"

"I was thinking maybe we could use windsurfers," said Dan with an embarrassed laugh.

" Really?" said Alberto sceptically.

"No," said Dan, thinking about what he had just said, 'it was just a silly suggestion. There must be a way though."

"Hang on a minute Dad!" said Charlotte, excitedly. "It's not such a daft notion. Just think about it. You and I have both been clocked at over thirty knots at home in decent breezes. We'd be easily fast enough. It might just work."

Dan looked thoughtful. "If we got a couple of windsurfers, with clear mylar sails, or maybe even black sails, if we could find them, they would be virtually undetectable if we make our move once the sun went down.

The libeccio is usually pretty consistent at this time of year. It might get a bit rough, but we should be able to handle it."

"The libeccio, what's that?" asked Alberto.

"It's the breeze that comes in from the west. Those white caps that we were looking at the other day in Amalfi - that was the libeccio."

"Dad, why don't we use hydrofoils? They would leave less wake and there wouldn't be a risk of them hearing the thump of the board hitting waves if it does cut up rough. They would be a lot faster." said Charlotte excitedly.

"Great idea!" said Dan.

"This sounds crazy," said Alberto. "Even if you two could get close enough how do you intend to get the yacht to run over a drift net?"

"Simple enough. We tie the drift net up with strands of PVA string that dissolves when it gets wet. It's the sort of thing fisherman use. We then take one end of the net each and drop it in front of yacht. The PVA dissolves, the drift net floats free, the yacht goes over it, catches it in its propellers and bingo, yacht stopped! Once she goes past we get out of there as fast as we can and follow them when they take Liz off," said Dan.

"What if there is no wind?" Alberto asked still looking sceptical.

"Then we just follow the yacht to its next destination in the speedboat and hope we get another chance," he said.

"Given our objectives, and our limited options, then that sounds like a plan," said Alberto somewhat reluctantly. "I will leave you two to get the windsurfers and the right sort of drift net. I'll go back to Amalfi and find us a small fast boat and keep an eye on the yacht. Hopefully he won't leave before we can get organised."

13. Amalfi - Present day

Charlotte was negotiating their hire car, with the two new windsurfers strapped to the roof, down the road to Amalfi when Dan's phone rang.

"They are getting ready to move. How far away are you?" asked Alberto.

"We are just coming into Amalfi," said Dan, shielding his eyes from the westering sun.

"Come straight down to the Marina. I've got our boat at the far end, as far away from Dragas' yacht as I could get it. Just be careful that they don't see you," said Alberto.

A few minutes later, Dan and Charlotte, both wearing dark glasses and hats and carrying windsurfer masts and sails, appeared next to a large sleek speedboat.

"Very nice!' said Dan, appreciatively, as Alberto reached down to take one of the masts. "How fast?"

"According to the charter company she will do thirty two knots. That should be fast enough to keep up with Dragas. She is all fuelled up and I got in some food and drink as well. How did you go?"

"Great. It was a bit of a rush but we got two AFS-1 Hydrofoil windsurfers. We bought some fast drying matt black paint, so if we get time, we can spray paint the boards and sails. Hopefully that should make them almost impossible to see!" said Dan, hoisting his gear bag onto the speedboats deck.

Twenty minutes later, with Dan at the helm and keeping an eye on Dragas' yacht, Alberto was looking quizzically at the small windsurfer boards that Charlotte had just finished spray painting.

The two windsurfers had long fins projecting from the bottom of each board. At the end of the fin was what looked like a very streamlined stylised aeroplane with long wings at the front. The tips of the wings were turned up, like the winglets at the end of the wings of a modern day commercial jet. Smaller wings, with their ends turned down, protruded from the back of the little aeroplane's fuselage. The boards themselves looked like normal windsurfer boards, except that there was a large hole right through the front of the board, near the nose.

"So how does this work?" asked Alberto looking confused.

"When you start moving through the water the board rises up," said Charlotte. "This bit, the hydrofoil," she said putting her hand on the aeroplane shaped contraption, "literally starts flying underwater. It lifts the board up and out of the water. The hole in the front of the board is shaped to help balance the board as it floats through the air. When you're riding it, it looks like the board is suspended on top of this!" she said running her hand down the long, narrow fin that connected the board to the hydrofoil. "It is amazing to watch, but even more amazing to ride. Once it is up on the foil the board can go up to three times the speed of the wind."

A shout from the deck above interrupted their conversation "Hey you guys!" shouted Dan, "Dragas is changing direction!"

Alberto and Charlotte poked their heads through the companionway hatch. They all watched as Dragas' yacht turned south.

"Where do you think he is going?" asked Alberto.

"Hard to say. He could be heading to Sicily, or maybe the North African coast."

"I reckon he's heading for the Strait of Messina," said Charlotte looking into the radar screen.

"If that is the case we could hit him somewhere around Stromboli or Salina. There are a few small islands around there. It might just add a bit of incentive to get off the boat if there is a chance of running aground!" said Alberto with a laugh.

They waited patiently, their speedboat continuing on a steady westerly course, watching as both the sun and Dragas' yacht began to disappear over the horizon. When they were all comfortable that there was sufficient distance between them and Dragas, they too turned south.

As the boat sliced through a light chop, Dan studied the chart in the light from the cabin. "If we continue at about twenty knots, and it is about 280 kilometres from here to where we hit him, then we would be going over the side in about eight hours. That would mean about two or three in the morning. That has the added advantage of being the time when people are least observant. OK. That's it then. Charlie, how about you and I try and get some sleep. Alberto, will you be OK on your own?"

"No problem Dottore. As you Aussies say, she'll be right mate!"

"Do you think we'll be OK for fuel?" asked Dan concerned.

"They told me with full tanks she has a cruising range of 800 kilometres. We should be OK," said Alberto. "You two go and get some rest and stop worrying. I'll give you a call if anything happens."

Much to his surprise Dan fell asleep almost immediately.

****

The first thing Dan was aware of was the smell of freshly percolated coffee. He woke up slowly, wondering where he was, and why everything was moving around.

"Coffee Dad?" asked Charlotte from the speedboat's small galley.

"Yeah thanks.' he said, still half asleep.

With a cup of coffee in his hand he came back to full consciousness. "What time is it?" he asked, yawning.

"Its one thirty five. We should be getting ready to go. You ought to have a look outside. We are quite near Stromboli. You can see the glow from her eruptions. It looks fantastic and should help us keep orientated!" said Charlotte with enthusiasm.

They spent the next twenty minutes getting ready. Both put on thick black wetsuits. Dan checked the drift net, tied with short pieces of PVA string. It would be heavy to carry, because they had erred on the side of caution and got the longest net they could.

Alberto had got as close to Dragas' yacht as he thought wise and slowed the speedboat almost to a stop. The wind was gusting around twenty-five knots.

Charlotte and Dan dragged their masts and sails out onto the deck. The wind whipped the sails around. They both struggled to rig their sails onto their windsurfers wishbones. Finally, with a last pull on the outhaul to ensure his sail was stretched as tightly as it could be, Dan nodded to Charlotte.

"Alberto, see if you can keep the boat side on to the wind while we drop the boards into the water," said Dan. Alberto carefully manoeuvred the speedboat so that it gave them some protection from the wind that was now starting to strip spray from the tops of the choppy sea around them.

Dan dropped his board into the water beside the speedboat. He carefully positioned his sail so that the wind didn't catch it and tear it out of his hand. In one swift movement he slid from the boat, holding tightly onto the sail and dropped into the water. He surfaced and, with a few strokes of his arm, grabbed onto the board. He was already drifting rapidly away from the boat.

With his eyes already accustomed to the dark, an almost full moon and a clear sky to help, he watched as Charlotte slipped from the boat with her windsurfer. He watched her manoeuvre the sail into position for a water start. He did the same. As Charlotte's sail lifted out of the water he lifted his own sail to let the wind slip under it. In a single movement, his body was wrenched out of the water as the full force of the wind hit his sail.

He struggled to balance the pressure on his sail and the continually moving board under his feet. The windsurfer was starting to accelerate as he leaned back, letting the sail support him. He tried to keep Charlotte in view as he concentrated on putting his feet into the board's foot-straps.

Once he felt secure he looked up to where Charlotte should have been. He couldn't see her. He gritted his teeth and pulled the sail back towards his chest to let the rope attached to the windsurfer's boom fall into the hook on the harness he was wearing. Now, safely locked into the board. he could lean back, letting the sail support his body, and concentrate on finding his daughter. He caught two quick flashes of blue light out of the corner of his eye. Alberto's suggestion to put small flashing LED lights from a pushbike onto the wishbone of the windsurfer had been a good one. Charlotte was a hundred metres or so downwind of him. He could barely see her sail. He let his arm relax, and tilted the mast slightly forward, the board carved a small turn and accelerated downwind, rising up out of the water as it did so. In a matter of seconds he had caught up to Charlotte, who had been feathering her own sail while she had been scanning the water for him. He pulled alongside, feathering his own sail and letting the board lower back down onto the surface of the water.

"Okay, lets go!" he shouted above the wind. and the noise of their flapping sails.

They both leant back, leaning into the wind. The wind pushed hard against the surface of their sails and the windsurfers started to accelerate. Moments later they lifted clear of the water. All Dan could hear now was the hiss of the blade of the hydrofoil as it sliced through the water. He looked back. The only thing he could see was the thin line of phosphorescence the blade of the hydrofoil made. It looked like a white scar, that quickly healed over.

It was an amazing feeling. Dan, locked into the board with his foot-straps, and the sail with his harness, felt the acceleration and then the sensation of flying as the board flew above the choppy Mediterranean, moving up and down slightly as he adjusted his speed with the sail.

Charlotte's board was just to leeward of his. He caught the occasional flash of her LEDs but other than that could hardly see her at all, even up close. They had done a good job with their impromptu stealth coating.

Dan settled back, concentrating on heading for the running lights of Dragas yacht in the distance. They had estimated that Dragas was cruising at about fifteen knots. The windspeed was in excess of 25 knots. Alberto had got to within a kilometre of Dragas before he had stopped. They had figured it shouldn't take more than half an hour to overhaul the yacht. Dan guessed, feeling the pressure of the wind on his sail, it was going to take a lot less than that.

Judging their speed by how quickly they were catching up to Dragas's yacht, Dan estimated that they must be doing close to thirty knots, around fifty kilometres an hour.

As they got closer they moved into position to be able to pass down the windward side of the yacht. The risk of being spotted was minimal as the ship was only displaying her running lights. The saloon and other cabins were all in darkness. Dan could just make out a faint glow coming from the wheelhouse as he flew past.

They stayed on the same course, getting well ahead of the yacht. The idea was to get far enough ahead for Dan to have time to throw one end of the line, attached to the drift net, to Charlotte. She would then sail downwind, across the path of the oncoming yacht. With luck the PVA strings would dissolve, the yacht would run over the floating net and the net would twist around her propellers, stopping her dead in the water.

When he felt they were far enough ahead, Dan let his sail feather and his board sank back down into the water. He dropped the sail. He could see Charlotte had done the same and was kneeling on her board some ten metres away.

In preparation for this moment they had tied a tennis ball onto a light line, attached at the other end to the drift net. Dan pulled the ball from his spray jacket pocket and threw it towards Charlotte's board. The ball went over her head. She grabbed at the line, but missed it.

Dan swore to himself. He could see the lights of the yacht getting closer. He pulled on the line, dragging it back toward him, being as careful as he could not to tangle it. The yellow tennis ball appeared. He grabbed it and took a deep breath to calm himself.

He took aim and threw the ball again. This time it splashed a few metres from Charlotte's board. He saw her dive into the water and swim to it. He felt a tug on the line as she swam back to her board. He checked on the yacht. It was getting close. They were running out of time. Charlotte needed to move now if she was going to make it across the bow of the oncoming yacht safely.

He could see that she was preparing to start off. The wind was still strong and he would need to be quick if he was to feed out the drift net without pulling her off her board.

He took off his backpack and removed the drift net just as a gust of wind lifted Charlotte out of the water. He saw her overbalance. The sail slammed into the water, throwing her through the air into the path of the oncoming yacht!

Dan didn't know what to do. Feeling helpless he watched as she swam back towards her board. He turned to look at Dragas' yacht. It was even closer now. He could clearly see the head of someone on watch on the bridge.

He looked back to where he thought Charlotte was. He saw a flash of moonlight on the wet sail as it lifted her clear of the water. He crossed his fingers. A moment later he saw the telltail scar of phosphorescence as her board accelerated away, carving a perfect arc twenty metres in front of the yacht. The line snatched at his fingers. He watched as the drift net, carefully layered on the deck of his board, was dragged behind her. His daughter disappeared into the darkness.

Too concerned with Charlotte's safety Dan had not noticed that his end of the drift net had fallen off his board and floated up around his leg.

The first he knew of it was when the yacht passed over the net and he was suddenly yanked from his board and dragged under water.

Disorientated, surrounded by blackness, rushing water, and the noise of the yacht's engines, an image of the rapidly spinning propellers flashed into his mind. Dan struggled to free his leg. He could feel the drift net tightening around his calf. He grabbed at it, desperately trying to extricate himself. The thin netting cut into his hands. His lungs were burning. He knew that he couldn't last much longer. He was starting to loose consciousness when he heard a muffled boom.

Dan burst through the surface of the water, his lungs aching as he gulped in air. It took a moment for him to orientate himself. Now that he wasn't being pulled through the water he easily unwound the net from his leg.

Turning in the water he saw Stromboli glowing red off to his left. Turning to the right he could see Dragas's yacht close by. She was all lit up now, stopped dead in the water. He turned further to the right hoping to catch sight of the intermittent flash of the blue light emitting diodes on Charlotte's windsurfer boom or the green lights they had fitted to his own.

He started to panic, afraid that she had been tangled in the drift net as well and pulled under the yacht.

The flashes of the LEDs were set to be twenty seconds apart. He counted to twenty. Nothing. He turned further to the right and counted again. Nothing. He turned further around, now facing away from

Dragas' yacht. He counted to fifteen and saw a brief green flash. He started to breaststroke in the direction of his board.

He was half way to it when he heard the crackle of gunfire. He stopped swimming and turned back towards the yacht. There was movement on the aft deck. Two men were standing on the platform at the stern of the yacht looking out into the night. One was clearly holding a gun and pointing out into the darkness. Dan kept watching. Had they seen Charlotte? Had they seen her windsurfer? He looked in the direction the man was pointing. The bright lights of the yacht were destroying his night vision. If her board was close to the yacht he wouldn't be able to see the blue flash of the LEDs. He needed to find a better angle. He decided that if he moved closer to the yacht, and then looked back, he might be able to see better.

Dan tried to keep his feelings of rising panic in check as he reached his board and swung it around so that it was at right angles to the breeze and the head of the sail was pointing into the wind. He rested a foot on the back of the board and pushed the sail upwards. The wind caught it. Dan moved his foot towards the rear foot-strap, and missed it. Before he had time to correct the wind had caught the sail and he was being lifted up and over the front of the board. He hit the water hard. Winded, he struggled to the surface. He cursed himself for his ineptitude and quickly looked back towards the yacht. There was only one guard on the back of the boat now and he was looking directly at Dan. Clearly he thought he had heard or seen something.

Dan stayed floating next to the board. Eventually the guard looked away, his attention caught by something in the water on the other side of the yacht. Dan scanned the area where the guard was looking. Then he saw it. A flash of blue! He guessed that the guard had seen it as well. The guard shouted to someone and the lights on the boat suddenly went dark. Dan focused on the area where he had last seen the tiny flash of light. He counted to twenty. Nothing. Perhaps it had been his imagination, or perhaps the swell was getting in the way. If Charlottes' windsurfer boom was lying flat in the water it was quite possible that he wouldn't be able to see it from water level.

There was a sudden flash of light from the stern of the yacht, then the sound of gunfire. The guard clearly thought he had seen something and was firing out into the darkness, in the direction that Dan thought he had seen the LED flash.

If Charlotte was out there he had to stop this bastard from shooting at her!

Dan gritted his teeth and duck dived under his windsurfer. He moved the sail and board into position. He cleared his mind. Concentrating, he pushed the boom so that the corner of the sail lifted above the surface of the water. As the wind swept under the sail it lifted it off the water. Dan, with one foot braced on the edge of the board at the back and the other closer to the mast step, let the sail lift him clear of the water. He pushed his left foot into the rear foot-strap and then leant back into the sail. The board accelerated, rising clear of the water.

The guard had stopped shooting and was staring out into the blackness again. Dan pulled back on the sail and the windsurfer accelerated towards the yacht. His intention was to pass close to the stern of the yacht to distract the guard. Hopefully he would then be able to hit the water on the leeward side of the yacht and be in a better position to see where Charlotte was.

Suddenly a beam of light stabbed out into the darkness. Someone had got a high-powered torch. Dan followed the beam and saw, at the same time as the guards, Charlotte bobbing next to her windsurfer, her blonde hair shining in the light of the torch.

Dan could see the guard lifting his gun to eye level. The second guard, right beside the first on the stern of the boat, held the torch steady.

Dan, without thinking, pushed down with his back foot, pulled the sail hard towards his body and, in one long carving turn headed straight for the stern of the yacht. The board, now travelling at around twenty five knots and riding at the full height of the hydrofoil's fin, smashed into the back of the boat. The board, floating above the height of the yacht's transom, sliced into the legs of the two guards, closely followed by the sail, boom and Dan. Dan felt the sail give as he hit it, breaking the speed of his impact. His progress was further softened as he landed heavily on top of the two guards. Dan lay in a tangle of splintered fibreglass, bent aluminium, sailcloth and bodies. He started to move. He felt a sharp pain in his shoulder. He groaned. He lay back in the debris. Dragas was looking down at him, from the deck above, with a sardonic grin.

"And I thought you were an intelligent man!" he said shaking his head. "Put him with the woman and then get rid of this mess!" he said as he walked away.

He felt a hand on his injured shoulder. He looked up to see Luigi grinning at him. Without any change of expression Luigi pulled him to his feet and twisted his injured arm around behind his back. The pain was excruciating. Dan stumbled, almost fainted. Another twist of his arm brought him back to full consciousness. Luigi let go of his arm and said in a low voice. "It is going to be such fun having you as a guest Dottore Marsh!" and then pushed him in the small of the back, up the steps towards the main saloon.

14. Mediterranean - Present day

Elizabeth was lying on the bed in the dark, resting when the door burst open and Dan was pushed into the cabin. "Have fun you two! While you can!," said Luigi in a threatening voice as he slammed the door behind him.

Elizabeth turned on the cabin light.

"Dan?" she asked in stunned amazement. She sprang from the bed and came around to where Dan was kneeling, his head resting on the bed and his wetsuit leaking water onto the carpeted floor. She put her arms around him. Tears coursing down her cheeks she held him as tightly as she could. "That bastard told me you were dead! I thought you were dead!" she sobbed.

Dan held her as tightly as she was holding him. "Not dead, just battered!" he said, feeling the intense pain in his shoulder. He gently untangled himself from Elizabeth's embrace.

He explained what had happened after the car accident as Elizabeth tried to help him off with his wetsuit. Dan winced as she pulled the wetsuit away from his shoulder. She could see that it was already starting to swell. She dried him off with a towel from the small ensuite and then ripped up one of the sheets from the double bed to bind the injured arm to his body.

Finally, when they were both sitting on the bed, Dan wrapped in a blanket, he hung his head and sighed. "I think Dragas was right, you know. This wasn't a particularly intelligent thing to do! I don't know what I was thinking, putting Charlotte, and you, at risk!"

"Perhaps it wasn't," said Elizabeth gently hugging him and resting her head on his good shoulder, "but it was very brave! I never expected you to turn into my knight in shining armour!"

Dan chuckled, and then grimaced at the pain from his shoulder.

"What now Sir Galahad? How do we get out of this one?" asked Elizabeth.

"I don't know. Is there a gun or a couple of hand grenades in the cupboard that we could use?" asked Dan with a wan smile.

"No, the only things I have found are the normal things you find in a hotel bathroom, a few toiletries and grooming stuff, like hairdryers and electric razors. Perhaps we could threaten them with dental hygiene products or threaten to give them all a Brazilian if they don't let us go! Oh, there is a packet of condoms in the bedside table along with a copy of the Bible, a pen and paper and a couple of magazines. Two vogues and a Time I think. The door is locked and guarded and the porthole doesn't open, I'm afraid."

Dan sat looking down at his hands.

"Worried about your girl?" she asked in a quiet voice.

"Yeah!" said Dan in a subdued tone. "Both of them!" he said putting his hand on top of hers.

****

Charlotte floated in the water a little way from her windsurfer. She guessed that the goon on the back of the yacht had spotted the LED on her windsurfer boom. She had swum away from it when the guard had started shooting. Bullets had whistled past her and she worried that he might hit her by dumb luck when she had seen her father's windsurfer suddenly appear out of nowhere and smash into the back of the yacht, taking out the two guards.

After her initial relief at seeing him alive, she had continued to watch in dismay as he was roughly manhandled into the yacht. A light had come on in one of the cabins soon after. From the deck layouts they had studied on the Internet, she guessed that her father had been put in one of the lower deck staterooms. The porthole that now glowed with a yellow light was large and oval, and close to the waterline of the yacht.

She swam back to her board. She swore under her breath when she saw, even in this dim light, that her sail had suffered a number of direct hits, as had her board. She hoped that none of the damage would be sufficient to stop her sailing it. Her father's board, which she had seen unceremoniously kicked off the back of the yacht, now floated, in several large pieces, around the stern of the immobilised yacht.

She released her mast from the board and let it drift away. Sliding on top of the board she paddled slowly towards the yacht. There was no-one on deck. She worked her way up the leeward side of the yacht to where light spilled out of the porthole she identified earlier. Kneeling on the board, she peeped in. To her immense relief she could see her father and Elizabeth sitting on the bed. Using her fingernail she tapped on the glass of the porthole.

Elizabeth saw her first, said something to Dan, who looked up. Dan looked up and grinned. She could see that he was injured. Dan said something to Elizabeth who grabbed a pen and paper from the bedside table drawer. She held it up the note she had written to the window. "Are you OK" it said.

Charlotte could easily read the note written on thin paper, backlit by the light from the cabin. She gave a thumbs up and then pointed at Dan and Elizabeth. Elizabeth gave a thumbs up and then pointed at Dan and rocked her hand from side to side, then grabbed her own shoulder and then pointed at Dan again.

****

"It seems to me" said Dan to Elizabeth, "that we have two options. Either we stay on the boat and get taken to wherever Dragas is going, and hope that Charlotte and Alberto can find an opportunity to rescue us, or we go for broke and get away now. Which do you prefer?"

"I can't see how we can get away now. We are locked in a cabin in a yacht in the middle of the Mediterranean!"

"Give me a minute," said Dan going to the small ensuite bathroom.

Elizabeth heard him opening drawers and cupboards. A minute later he returned. "If I could get us off the boat then Alberto could pick us up!" said Dan. "Should we risk it?"

"If you can get us off the boat, and Alberto can pick us up before we drown, get shot or get eaten by sharks, then I go with that plan. Staying here is only going to lead to a whole lot of pain for both of us. Dragas and his men are not beyond torture," she said looking away from Dan. "I would prefer to avoid any more pain if I can," she said in a quiet voice.

Dan's jaw tightened. "OK. So, all we have to do is bust out of this cabin, get to Alberto, and get away!"

"You have a plan? she asked.

"Yup. Tell Charlie to get well away from the boat, say a hundred yards or so, and get her to signal Alberto to come and pick us up!"

****

Charlotte read the note that Elizabeth held it up to the porthole. She held up both hands wanting more information. Elizabeth gave a shrug of her shoulders and pointed at Dan.

Charlotte, knowing her father's mind, lay back down on the board and quietly paddled out into the darkness. When she felt she was far enough away from the yacht she sat up on the board, checked her direction and used a small LED torch to give Alberto the signal to pick her up. A single flash of white light in the far distance assured her that he had seen her signal.

She then turned towards the yacht and crossed her fingers.

****

"Let's get this mattress up against the door. We need to keep them out for as long as we can," said Dan.

Together, with Elizabeth doing most of the heavy lifting, they slid the mattress off the cabin's double bed and jammed it up against the door.

Dan then started throwing everything he could find into a pile on the cabin floor. He moved into the ensuite and was soon throwing more stuff through the door into the pile.

With everything in a pile he sat on the exposed wooden slats of the bed and stared at his eclectic collection.

"Ok" he said. "I think we have enough here to blow out the porthole and make enough of a distraction to give us time to get away. You up for it!"

Elizabeth just nodded, having no idea what he was doing.

"Right!" said Dan, "You are going to have to do this because I can barely move my arm. First we are going to make a hand grenade, just in case they get into the cabin before we get out. What we are going to do is strip down the razor and take out the lithium ion batteries. I need you to take them apart. They will be our detonator. We'll use a condom full of water as our trigger and our explosive will be one of the tins of spray-on deodorant. Our bomb housing will be two of those glass tumblers tied together with dental floss."

"So the condom breaks, water spills onto the battery and short circuits it, it heats up and ignites the spray can. That is brilliant!" said Elizabeth with enthusiasm.

"Thank-you!" said Dan with a bow. "The product of a misspent and sometimes overly lonely youth I am afraid!"

"How about I put some of that perfume in there as well. That should add a bit of pizzaz to the explosion, given that it is almost pure alcohol!" said Elizabeth.

"I like the way you are thinking. If nothing else it should encourage them to keep out of the cabin while we get away," said Dan who was using his good arm to rip the light fitting at the head of the bed out of the wall.

"We can use the other two aerosol cans wrapped up tightly in those magazines, with the other lithium ion battery, wired directly to this switch. If we jam one end of the rolled magazines up against the porthole and the other end is covered by the top of that bedside table, and the whole lot is jammed up against the porthole and braced by these wooden slats from the bed then it should blow that little sucker right out!"

Ten minutes later the cabin looked like a tornado had hit it. Dan had continued his destructive rampage breaking up the base of the double bed and one of the small wooden bedside tables. To hold their cabin door closed they had replaced the mattress with a slat from the bed, jamming it under the door handle. Elizabeth had set up their homemade hand grenade so that it would fall to the floor if the cabin door was forced open.

The mattress now protected them from their improvised explosive charge. Holding the wire and switch he had pulled from the wall, Dan sat hunched down behind it with Elizabeth.

"Ready?" he asked. She nodded. He clicked the switch and they both put their fingers in their ears. Inside the rolled up magazines the short circuited battery began to smoke and then burst into flame. The two aerosol cans of deodorant exploded. The force of the explosion blew the porthole out into the night.

Dan and Elizabeth scrambled for the porthole. They could hear the sound of running feet. Gallantly Dan stood aside as Elizabeth slipped through the newly made opening and dropped down into the water. Loud bangs were now coming from the cabin door as Dragas' men tried to break it down. Dan saw Liz's homemade grenade start to fall. He dived through the opening in the side of the yacht just as it hit the floor. A sheet of flame erupted from the porthole. Dan hit the water hard. Pain shot through his shoulder.

He struggled to the surface. Moments later Elizabeth was beside him. With only one arm, Dan side stroked away from the yacht. Elizabeth swam beside him. They had swum no more than fifty yards when a light stabbed out from rear deck of the yacht. Silhouetted in the light of the main cabin they could see two figures. One had a rifle at his shoulder. Dan, seeing that they were an easy target, started to shout a warning to Elizabeth.

Before the words came out of his mouth there was a muffled explosion and a burst of flame illuminated the water all around them.

Smoke was now belching from the main cabin of Dragas' yacht.

Dan, supported by Elizabeth continued to move away from the yacht as fast as they could. A few minutes later they heard a voice calling quietly out of the darkness.

"What is it they say, the couple that plays together stays together!" said Charlotte with a chuckle. "Come on you two, we can't hang around here all day." Charlotte slipped off her windsurfer board and graciously allowed her father, with some difficulty, to struggle on to it.

With Dan lying prone on the board Elizabeth and Charlotte guided it away from the smoking yacht. A few minutes latter they heard the low rumble of a motorboat. Alberto guided the power boat alongside the board and carefully helped lift Dan on board, followed immediately by Charlotte and Elizabeth.

"Welcome back!" he said with a grin. "Not a bad job, for amateurs!"

15. Rome - Present day

"So do you think we are safe Bert?" asked Charlotte.

Alberto passed her a slice of apple cake and slid a cup of coffee across the counter to her. "Well, we're safe enough here in your apartment, especially after I rigged up a proper security system. From Dragas' point of view, he has a sample of the relic, and I am guessing, even though he now knows Dan is alive, he has no real reason to come after him. He doesn't know that Dan has a sample as well," he said, looking across at Dan. Dan still looked like he had been in the mother of all catfights, but the scratches were beginning to heal. His arm was still strapped to his chest to protect his injured shoulder.

"I agree!" said Dan through a mouthful of cake. "He might be a bit pissed off that we blew the side out of his lovely boat, but I can't see why he would bother coming after us now. Unless he wanted revenge, of course! I suppose he could be a vindictive prick?"

"Okay, guys. I think I am ready to go through this now," said Elizabeth who had been sitting on the couch working on her laptop.

It had been almost a week since their escape from Dragas' yacht and since that time they had all been busy.

Elizabeth had been able to arrange the use of an appropriately equipped laboratory in Rome to analyse the tiny sample that Dan had retrieved from the car wreck. Dan, after dropping Elizabeth off at the lab each day, had been spending his time doing research to support Elizabeth's work as well as trying to find out who Dragas really was. He returned most days, frustrated and cursing European bureaucracies.

Alberto had been taking Charlotte to the Vatican each day where she had been continuing her research in the library. He had continued to make Dan's apartment more secure.

Elizabeth put her laptop on the kitchen counter. Alberto slid cake and coffee across to her and then came and sat down as well.

Charlotte, Dan and Alberto all looked expectantly at her.

"Ok, first up, I have to tell you that Morell had some stuff right. The sample that we had of the Hitler potion was pretty close in some respects.

The Hitler analysis showed us that there were a fair number of drugs that we would now define as nootropics in the mixture."

"So it is a mixture, it really isn't someone's blood?" asked Alberto.

"Well, that is one of the interesting things. It does have human blood in it. But I will come back to that," said Elizabeth.

"Just like Morell, I found huperzine A and Choline and traces of L-Dopa, atropine and Pseudo-ephedrine."

"So the potion would promote the production of dopamine," said Dan. "That might account for the increased ability to think strategically and process large amounts of information. That would be potentially brilliant if you are in a battle, and it might explain the problem of taking it too often, diminishing the brain's own ability to produce dopamine, and causing the Parkinson's disease like effects that we know Julius Caesar and Hitler both had."

"Not only that, said Elizabeth, "but abnormally high amounts of dopamine cause, amongst other things, psychosis and schizophrenia, which would be consistent with some of the historical evidence we have."

"But hang on a minute!" said Charlotte looking at her father and Elizabeth. "Do you two realise what you are saying? You are talking about a drug that would be a wonder of today's cutting edge science, not a drug that was developed over what? Two thousand years ago!"

"Well, it is not so far-fetched," said Dan. "Let's imagine that we are back in Ancient Rome. What resources would we have had available?" he asked. "You could use something like velvet beans. They have been shown to increase dopamine levels in rats. They grow in places like Africa and India, so they would have been available to someone in Rome at that time. Joint Pine grows throughout the Mediterranean area, and that can be distilled to make methamphetamine. It contains both ephedrine and pseudo-ephedrine. Atropine can be extracted from the deadly nightshade plant, so that's easy to get. Huperzine is a naturally occurring nootropic that comes from a plant called firmmoss."

"I don't think that it is impossible for this to have been developed in ancient Rome, but it does confirm your idea about whoever put this thing together originally must have had an absolutely encyclopedic knowledge of plants and medicine."

"What about the DNA in the Hitler sample?" asked Charlotte. "Is that replicated in the Alaric potion?"

"Yes, I did find strands of DNA in the new sample. But this is where it starts getting weird," said Elizabeth.

"Starts getting weird!" exclaimed Charlotte. "You must have the highest weirdness threshold on the planet if you think what we have got this far and it it is only just starting to get weird!" she laughed.

"Ok, more weirder then!" said Elizabeth with a laugh. "The human cells that I found in the Alaric sample contain stem cells!"

"You are kidding me!" said Charlotte. "How would someone even know about stem cells, let alone put them into a magic potion, two thousand years ago?"

"Hang on a minute!" said Alberto holding up a hand. You are getting into stuff I don't understand. I often hear this term 'Stem Cells' especially to do with babies. What are they?" he asked.

"Stems cells are basically human cells, that are capable of renewing themselves through cell division, that have not yet decided what sort of cell they are going to be," said Dan. "Embryonic stem cells are stem cells that are taken from an embryo. Somatic stem cells are taken from an adult."

"But what are they?" asked Alberto.

"Imagine a three day old embryo," said Dan. "At that age the embryo, or blastocyst, is no more than a little bunch of cells. The cells of the embryo have to reproduce in such a way as to create all of the specialised cells that make up a human body. Heart cells are different from skin cells, which are different from lung cells, which are different from brain cells. Each type of cell in your body is different because it has a different job to do. The thing about stem cells is that they can become, with the right stimulus, any type of cell you want them to be."

"The promise of stem cells is that they could solve a whole range of medical problems. You could repair the spinal cords of paraplegics, the dopamine producing cells of sufferers of Parkinson's disease, the damaged brains of stroke victims. But there are, as you are no doubt aware, ethical considerations when using embryos to generate stem cells. More recently the science community has found ways of harvesting adult stem cells. Adult stem cells, Somatic stem cells, don't create the same ethical problems."

"But could stem cells survive for hundreds, or even thousands of years and still work?" asked Alberto

"I don't know. It seems hard to imagine, although I am aware that scientists in Israel have freeze dried stem cells, stored them at room temperature and that they have maintained their clonogenicity upon rehydration."

Alberto just stared at Dan.

"Sorry," said Dan with a self-effacing smile. "They still worked afterwards."

"So whoever made this potion took some human cells and mixed them in. Why?" asked Alberto.

"I suppose it is possible," said Elizabeth, "that the stem cells would start reproducing and either repair damage or increase the natural capabilities of the individual. Perhaps, increase their mental capacity. I just don't know. Whoever thought this up must have been an absolute genius."

"Not only that," she continued, "but, if we go with Charlie's hypothesis that the maker of the potion and the taker were two different people, then the individual from whom they got the stem cells must have been a truly exceptional person to warrant the effort of putting this potion together!"

"In modern terms, this potion is a targeted, DNA sequence specific drug that promotes the replication of specific attributes. Because of that it may well only work for some individuals. There is work being done currently on personalised drugs for cancer therapy. So we know that it is possible to tailor drugs to specific individuals."

"But how would someone get stem cells in ancient Rome?" asked Charlotte.

"One easy source would have been the placenta of a child. A study in 2009 in the United States proved that it was viable to harvest stem cells from the placenta. In fact they found that there were quite a lot of them, more than in umbilical cord blood," said Elizabeth.

"I did a bit of research into the historical attitude to placenta.," said Dan. "Listen to this, he said tapping on his laptop. This is from and old Chinese medicine book. "*The placenta should be stowed away in a felicitous spot under the salutary influences of the sky and the moon, deep in the ground with the earth piled over it carefully in order that the child may be ensured long life. If it is devoured by a swine or a dog, the child loses its intellect. If insects or ants eat it, the child becomes scrofulous. If crows or magpies swallow it, the child will have an abrupt or violent death. If it is cast into fire, the child incurs running sores.*"

"It is also recorded that in Styria, in Austria, and in parts of Italy, powdered, dried placenta was a remedy for epilepsy. Up until the mid 1800s the dried placenta of a child was still sold by pharmacists to cure epilepsy."

"There are lots of cultures where the placenta is honoured and saved. The Egyptians even gave placenta a hieroglyph of its own!" he said. "It is even eaten in some cultures. In fact there are people today who advocate the eating of placentas as part of recovering from having a baby. It's very nutritious and apparently contains vitamins, minerals and hormones that help a new mother's body recover from the pregnancy. It is not a big stretch to think that the placenta of an ancient baby might have been kept," said Dan.

"I'll put it on the shopping list!" said Charlotte sarcastically.

Elizabeth laughed. "So, the stem cells were a surprise, but they weren't the weird thing. The first weird thing was that I found a virus inside the stem cells."

"What sort of virus? asked Charlotte.

"Well, I am no expert, but it looked to me like a variant of HIV, a Lentivirus" she said.

"What?" asked Charlotte, looking from Dan to Elizabeth.

"A Lentivirus is a type of virus used in gene therapy. The virus is used like a bullet to get inside the cell. It carries a payload, the DNA sequence that you want to insert into the cell. Once it is in the cell it splices into the actual DNA of the cell. Lentiviruses have a really unique ability in that they can infect non-dividing cells," said Dan.

"You are right!" said Charlotte. "This is really getting weird."

505

"The second weird thing," said Elizabeth, "is that I found two strands of DNA from the same person, but separated by thirty or forty years. When I compared them I could see significant changes to the epigenetic markers between the two DNA samples. I think that this stuff might actually be able to modify the DNA of whoever uses it."

"How the hell can someone have done all this two thousand, or more, years ago?" asked Charlotte, shaking her head.

"I'm not sure they did," said Elizabeth. "At least not intentionally. All of the other stuff, the nootropics and the stem cells, I can understand. There is a certain logic to it and there is a probable link with ancient historical practices. The virus thing though, is a bit too much of a stretch. My guess would be that this part of it was purely serendipitous."

"Serendipitous?" asked Alberto, eyebrows raised.

"Happened by chance. A lucky fluke!" said Charlotte with a smile.

"So what is your view about the potion? What does it do? In simple terms," asked Alberto.

"Best guess? It stimulates the production of neurones in the brain, increases the capacity of the brain and feeds it the chemicals it needs to enhance the connection between the neurones. Basically it supercharges the brain!"

"But why the reports of people mixing it with their own blood. What is that all about?" asked Charlotte.

"Well, it could have been just the way the original instructions were put together. Maybe it's necessary to re-activate the potion, I haven't really thought about that. Maybe it has something to do with the stem cells, after all blood does have stem cells. In fact, in the present day blood stem cells are the only type of adult stem cell regularly used for medical treatments," said Elizabeth.

"Bottom line though, however this stuff works, it does work, but it is potentially lethal. The crucial ingredient though, appears to be this virus, that facilitates the whole process," she said.

"So is this stuff easy to reproduce?" asked Charlotte.

Elizabeth shook her head. "There is a lot of work to do to investigate it further. The virus in the Alaric sample is dead. Getting a sample of the

506

live virus would be critical for a proper analysis. I have barely scratched the surface, really."

"Would you take it?" Charlotte asked.

"No way!" said Elizabeth vehemently. "I wouldn't take this stuff, or even a modern equivalent of it, if you paid me! Introducing somebody else's DNA into your brain? Never going to happen!"

They all sat thinking about the implications of what Elizabeth had discovered. Finally Dan turned to Charlotte. "How did you go kid? Did you find out anything interesting?"

Charlotte looked at Alberto, and then opened up her laptop. "Sure did! Not weird like Liz, but interesting. One of the things I did was go back through Pope Leo the First's writings. It was a bit of a hard slog because my training is in classical Latin. Medieval Latin is a bit different, but I got the gist of it. We know that he saw the original container that the relic came in. Do you remember that there was the bit in there about a bit of papyrus in Punic script?"

They all nodded.

"Well, I started to think about that piece of information. What if the papyrus and the box had been separated after it arrived in Rome. So, on the off chance I had the archivists do a search of all the papyrus in the Vatican library, just in case the papyrus and the box had become separated, and guess, what? I think I found it! I realise it is out of context, so I can't be one hundred percent sure, but it could well be the one that Constantine handled. It is dated from around two hundred BCE. It is only short and it is quite damaged. The bits that can be read say, "*To my eldest son. For the destructions of the Romans. Keep hidden...*" and then there is a two part name. The first part, which in English, translates to Brother of Melqart is clear. The second part less so, but it looks like the word for thunderbolt."

They all looked at Charlotte blankly.

She rolled her eyes. "Sorry! Brother of Melqart was a pretty common name in Carthage. Its Punic pronunciation, Anglicised, would be something like Hamilcar. The second name would sound something like Baraq."

Dan just stared at her. She was grinning. Elizabeth and Alberto looked from father to daughter. From the looks on their faces it looked like Charlotte had just won the grand final of the amazing game with a last second goal.

Finally, Elizabeth broke the silence. "Ok history nerds, what is going on? Who is Hamilcar Baraq?"

"Hamilcar Baraq, or Barca was a Carthaginian General. You might have heard of his son, Hannibal?"

"You mean the man with the elephants?" asked Alberto.

Charlotte nodded.

"So, tell us non-history buffs about Hannibal. I know he did the elephant thing but there must be more to him than that!" said Elizabeth.

"Well," said Charlotte, smiling happily, "once upon a time there was a city called Carthage. It was in modern day Tunisia, in North Africa. Carthage was, by all accounts a wondrous city. It had a huge enclosed circular marina for its warships, a massive commercial trading fleet and had apartment buildings six stories high. It had a population of, probably, around half a million or more!"

"When was this? What year are we talking about?" asked Alberto.

"This would have been around 250 BCE."

"Really! Wow!' exclaimed Elizabeth, making herself comfortable on the couch.

Charlotte continued. "One of the noble families was the Barca family. It is thought that they originally came from the city of Cyrene, which is in modern day Libya, getting close to the Egyptian border."

"At the time there were two big cities in the Mediterranean world. One was Carthage and the other one was Rome. The Romans were mostly land based. The Carthaginians came from a seafaring tradition, and were primarily merchants and sailors. It was thought that their ships at this time were traveling to places as far away as Britain, and maybe even the Azores."

"It was almost inevitable that these two great cities would come head to head. They fought what we call the first Punic War. Hamilcar was a General in that war, which Carthage eventually lost, The Roman Senate exacted some pretty stiff terms. It was bit like the Allies after the First World War when they tried to cripple Germany by imposing really harsh terms on them. The Romans wanted significant reparations. From memory it was something like fifty-six tons of silver, restrictions on where the Carthaginian fleet could sail, ransom had to be paid for all Carthaginian prisoners, while all Roman prisoners had to be freed, that sort of thing."

"Hamilcar, Hannibal's dad, probably not unlike many German Generals in the first world War, was angry with the way the war ended. Eventually he took his young family to Spain. He actually had three sons, the 'lion's brood' they were called. There was Mago, he was the youngest, then there was Hasdrubal. The oldest, and most brilliant, was Hannibal."

"Hannibal was born in Carthage, but he grew up in Spain. When he attacked the Romans by leading his army on that impossibly unlikely march over the Alps, he was actually coming from New Carthage in Spain," said Charlotte excitedly.

"Hannibal and his brother grew up as warriors and they grew up passionately hating Rome. Between Hannibal, the other two brothers and their father they pretty well conquered all of the Iberian peninsular. It is said that Barcelona was founded by Hamilcar and named after the Barca family."

"Hannibal did his thing with the elephants and the Alps and then spent the next decade beating up the Romans. I read somewhere that after three fighting seasons he had actually killed one fifth of all Roman males over seventeen. There was no doubt that he kept winning battles," said Charlotte.

"What happened to him in the end?" asked Elizabeth.

"I am not sure of the details, but I do know he never attacked Rome itself," said Charlotte.

"Why not? That would seem the logical thing to do if you wanted to smash your enemy," asked Elizabeth.

"I don't really know why he didn't take Rome. Eventually he left Italy and returned to Carthage. He fought a battle with his great nemesis, the Roman General, Scipio Aficanus, and lost. Another peace treaty was drawn up, creating more bitterness, and things went, sort of, back to normal."

"The Romans, not surprisingly really, wanted to get Hannibal. They spent the next decade or so chasing him down. I think, in the end, he died somewhere in Turkey, in a country called Bithynia, which, from memory, bordered on the Bosporus and the Black sea."

"The problem is," said Charlotte, "that we will never really know the true story. We are just going too far back in time."

16. Nicomedia - 180 BCE

Hannibal pulled a woollen shawl around his shoulders. It was cold here at night in Bithynia, in Autumn, but it was, at least at the moment, safe from Roman domination. King Prusias had been kind, allowing him to live in a beautiful villa in the village of Libyssa, not far from the capital, Nicomedia. He had, so far, been able to keep a low profile. The King had been at pains to assure him that he would not be advertising his presence to anyone so it came as a surprise when he heard a troop of horsemen approaching late one evening.

For years now Hannibal had managed to be one step ahead of the Romans. He knew with certainty that they sought him, intent on dragging him back to their infernal city to be bound in chains and dragged through its streets as the centre of some ambitious Roman's triumph. That was never going to happen. He was over sixty years old now. Dying held no fear. Around his finger he wore a ring that contained a small amount of a very toxic poison that would allow him to escape the Roman's should they ever come for him.

He toyed with that ring now, twisting it around his finger. If he heard the sounds of Roman soldiers forcing their way into his home, he would take the poison without a moments hesitation. He waited, listening.

A few minutes later one of his house slaves came in looking flustered. "It is the King my Lord!" he said. "He wishes to speak to you."

Hannibal let his hand drop from the ring and stood up. "Well ask him to come in man!" said Hannibal, both relived that he could live a little longer, but intrigued that King Prusias would arrive unannounced.

As the King entered he looked Hannibal up and down. "I am pleased to see that you are keeping well Hannibal."

"Thank you Your Majesty. Your generous hospitality and protection has given an old man time to regain some of his strength."

"I am glad to hear it," smiled the King. He paused. "Hannibal I know that you are my guest, but I would like to ask you a favour, not as your host, or as a King, but as a friend."

Hannibal nodded.

"The war with Pergamon is not going well for me. King Eumenens has inflicted upon us some serious setbacks. As a client of Rome, Pergamum has access to technology and resources that we do not. With Rome's help they will eventually beat us down. Hannibal, I need your help." he held up his hand as Hannibal was about to say something. "I know that the Romans still seek you! I know that there is a risk to you in helping us, but we are one of the few countries that have been able to resist the Romans. Every year it is becoming harder to keep them at bay. I beseech you, without your help it is inevitable that we will become just another part of the Roman Empire!"

Hannibal stayed silent for a long time. "Your Highness," he said eventually. "I am as you know an old man. My life has been lived to honour the promise I made before my father and my god Melqart, that I would never be a friend to Rome. You have given me sanctuary. You have given me friendship. In return I can do no more than give you help when you ask it!"

"Then you will help us fight?" said the King, surprised that the old man had acquiesced so easily.

"Your Majesty, I will not just help you fight, I will help you put the fear of Melqart into these lovers of Rome!"

****

It had taken many months to prepare for this battle, but now Hannibal stood on the deck of a Bithynian war galley as it slid through the waters of the Aegean Sea, moving into a position that would allow it to command the rest of the fleet.

Below decks the rowers were primed and ready, well drilled in the new manoeuvres he had taught them. A supply of the new Bithynian secret weapon lay stacked in clay pots on the decks of each of the ships, along with a small catapult that had been mounted on the prow of each ship.

On the horizon he could now see the Pergamine fleet. He looked around at the armoured soldiers as they too watched the enemy fleet grow larger. The wind was light and the sea was glassy. Neither fleet had set sails. The rhythmic beat of the drummer could be heard as Hannibal's flagship plied gently through the water, surging forward with each stroke of its many oars.

Hannibal knew his fleet was outnumbered. If the fighting was at close quarters they would surely be overwhelmed. The Romans and their allies no longer used the corvus, the heavy bridge that they deployed to trap, hold and board enemy ships. Despite this, the aim of naval warfare was still to either ram or board. If the Pergamines managed to get their grapples onto the Bythnian ships, then all would be lost.

The fleets drew closer. As they did so, the speed of the drum beats rose. Hannibal could now see the shape of the men on the decks of the opposing fleet. He turned to his Captain. "Build to ramming speed!"

The men on deck, hearing the command, began to check their gear. Some started to slap their shields with their swords in time with the beat of the drums. The drums beat faster.

"Prepare the catapults!" yelled Hannibal above the rising noise of the drums and the sound of sword on shield.

The catapult on his ship was swung into position and a big clay jar placed in it, ready to fire. The other ships in the fleet did the same.

Hannibal breathed in the salty spray as the big trireme surged forward. Its deadly bronze ram sliced through the swell, eager to find its enemy. He grinned to himself, adrenaline pumped through his body. It's like being young again, he thought to himself.

He could now see the faces of the Pergamine soldiers staring at him from the decks of their galleys. He raised his arm. "Fire!"

The clay jar shot from the catapult. It fell just short of the leading Pergamine ship.

"Again!" he cried, but his men, drilled for weeks, didn't need telling. They had already loaded another of the clay jars into the catapult.

They fired. Hannibal watched as the clay jar arced through he air and smashed onto the enemy's deck. The enemy trireme was now only a few hundred metres away. Another jar smashed on the deck, then another and another.

Looking across the fleet, Hannibal could see that all of his ships had started to send their own jars smashing into the enemy.

At first nothing happened. As they surged closer flying pottery filled the air. Jar after jar smashed on the decks of the enemy. Confusion started to erupt on the enemy ships.

More jars smashed on the deck of the Pergamine galley directly in front of him. Suddenly the oars lost their rhythm. Some dug into the water. The Pergamine vessel started to slew sideways, offering its broadside to Hannibal's ram.

The captain shouted "Brace!" Hannibal and the men on deck grabbed for the nearest solid part of their ship. The big boat slammed into the hull of the other ship with a thunderous noise of splintering wood and screaming, terrified men.

Normally, once a ship was rammed, both sides would try to grapple and then board the enemy ship. Hannibal's secret weapon called for a different strategy. It didn't involve getting on the enemy's ship at all.

While Hannibal regained his position he heard the Captain's voice again. "Back oar!" The big ship, having come to a complete halt, now reversed away from its impaled victim. Hannibal looked across at the deck of the other ship. The men were in absolute panic. None of them were attempting to grapple the Bithynian ship. Among the screaming, terrified men, he could make out the contents of the jars. Hundreds of poisonous snakes slithered across its decks.

As his ship backed away from his now mortally wounded enemy, his men took aim at another enemy ship and loaded more jars of snakes into the waiting catapult.

****

King Prusias met Hannibal as he walked down the gangplank to the shore. Even before Hannibal had a chance to greet him formally the King embraced him.

"Their fleet is destroyed!" he said excitedly. "Those ships that haven't been rammed have been deserted by their crews. Most of them drowned trying to escape the snakes. What a brilliant strategy! You are a true genius, Hannibal Barca! It is no wonder the Roman's fear you!"

Hannibal acknowledged the compliment and bowed his head. "It is a privilege to serve Your Majesty. But it wasn't strategy. It was a cheap trick, played on gullible men."

"Well if you can rout an entire navy with a cheap trick I would like to hear what we could do when you really put your mind to it!" said the King with a laugh.

"No you wouldn't, your majesty," he said sombrely as he turned away.

****

Hannibal sat by a fire in his garden, a woollen shawl pulled tightly around his neck. The fighting season had ended. The chill of winter had started to creep across the land again. Staring into the flames he did not notice one of his slaves enter and stand silently beside him until he gave a quiet cough.

"Master, there is a man at the door. He wishes to speak to you," said the slave nervously.

"And what is this man's name?" he asked.

The slave hesitated. "He will not say your lordship, but he is a Roman. He asked for you by name."

Hannibal's hand went straight to the ring on on his hand. "Is he alone?' he asked calmly.

"Yes my lord," said the slave.

"You had better send him in then," said Hannibal, standing up and dropping the shawl onto the seat on which he had been sitting. The man entered, his head covered by the hood of his travelling cloak. He reached his hand out towards Hannibal, and at the same time pulled back the hood. He was solidly built man, bald and clean shaven. A smile came to his lips as he saw the shock on Hannibal's' face.

"Scipio!" said Hannibal, reaching his own hand out to clasp that of his erstwhile adversary.

"To say that this is a surprise would be a considerable understatement! Have you come to take me back to Rome?"

"No, Hannibal. I have come to warn you. I still have some friends left in the Roman Senate. They let me know that King Prusias' envoys have given you away. I am not sure that they knew that your location was supposed to be a state secret, so do not blame them, or the King. Rome is on its way, as we speak, to demand that King Prusias hand you over. There was no-one I could trust to bring this warning to you, so I decided that I would come, myself."

Hannibal looked at the man who had treated him, and Carthage with so much respect when he had beaten them at the battle of Zama. They were not friends, but they knew each other better than most., More importantly, they trusted one another to act honourably. They were moulded from the same substance. They were warriors, strategists and Generals.

Hannibal also had friends that told him what was happening in the Senate houses of both Carthage and Rome. He had been sad to hear that Scipio had been treated so badly by the politicians of Rome once the first glow of his victories in Africa had waned. He had heard that there were members of the Senate, influential members, who had been undermining Scipio and his family. He knew that Scipio himself had been accused of having taken a bribe from the city of Antiochus. It had only been by reminding people of his victories in Africa, that he had deflected the accusations.

The chief among his detractors was Marcus Porcius Cato. Cato was the same man that would not let the enmity that some Romans had for Carthage die. He was a mean and vindictive little man who would repeat, again and again, every chance he got, "Ceterum censeo Carthaginem esse delendam" - "Moreover, I advise that Carthage must be destroyed."

Hannibal gestured for Scipio to take a seat by the fire while he organised some wine. Seated comfortably in front of the fire the two men stared into its flames while they sipped their drinks.

"I hear you have started using wild animals to defeat your enemies again! Snakes no less!" said Scipio with a chuckle.

"Well, I couldn't get the elephants into the catapults!" said Hannibal with a laugh.

Scipio let out a loud guffaw. "You certainly would have needed a lot fewer of them!"

They both settled back to watching the flames. "I don't think that I will run this time!" said Hannibal.

"You mean to be taken back to Rome?!" asked Scipio, shocked.

"No. I think my time has come. I have felt for sometime Melqart calling to me," said Hannibal quietly. "I have nothing left to do here."

"I too feel that my time is coming to an end. I believe that Mars would welcome me now," said Scipio not looking up from the flames.

"It seems that we have both fulfilled the destinies that our Gods have set us!" said Hannibal softly, and then, with a note of hesitation in his usually strong voice, he said. "Scipio, I have a need to tell someone my story. Someone I can trust. Someone who has no desire for conquest or personal gain. Someone who will take my story with them to the grave."

Scipio looked across at Hannibal. He could see his face illuminated by the light of the fire and saw a man living under a great burden. "Hannibal, I would be honoured to bear witness to whatever you wish to tell me."

Hannibal reached for the wine decanter and proffered it to Scipio. After they had both refilled their goblets Hannibal, leaning forward, again looking into the flames, started to talk in a quiet voice.

"When I was young, and we had been living in Iberia for a number of years, my father took me to the temple of Melqart. It was a dark place and I was a little afraid. He took my hand and placed it on the offering that lay on the altar and he had me swear that I would be the enemy of Rome forever."

"I have heard that story," said Scipio.

"What you haven't heard, because I have never told anyone, is what he also made me swear. While he still held my hand on the offering he took a glass vial out from underneath his tunic. He told me he had stolen it from a great warrior. He said that if I put a few drops of the liquid on my tongue it would give me the strength to achieve victory when none was possible. He made me swear that I should use this elixir only when I could not fathom for myself how to overcome my enemies, and no other option was available."

"He gave me a box containing the recipe and the ingredients of the potion. I hid it well. I hope it is still where I left it and hope that it will never be found."

He paused. "I swore to him that I would do as he said. I had forgotten about the vial until the day we confronted the army of Rome at Cannae."

"Crossing the Alps had taken a heavy toll on my men. I had lost some thirty thousand infantry, and three thousand cavalry as well as most of our supplies. When we finally staggered out of the alpine passes there would have only been about twenty thousand foot and six thousand cavalry and thirty seven elephants left. We were exhausted, half starved and many of us had toes and fingers that were turning black, eaten by the cold."

"We hardly had any time to recover when we stumbled on an army commanded by your father, Scipio. Our first encounter was at Ticinus."

"I was there." said Scipio, smiling at the memory. "It was my first command. I would have been only sixteen. My father had wanted to see the strength of your forces. He put me in command of a turma. They were all veterans. All experienced cavalrymen."

"I remember that you had your cavalry charge us before our infantry had formed up. Your Namibian cavalry came around behind us and we were forced to fight in small groups. My father and a number of others dismounted and were fighting hand to hand. I saw my father fall. We were still mounted. I remember calling on my men to follow. By this time my father was on the ground, surrounded by a host of your cavalry. My men must have seen this impetuous youth driving his mount into the melee and thought I was crazy. I think I probably embarrassed them into action. Thank the gods they charged after me and cleared the way for me to get my father off the battle field," said Scipio.

"Imagine how much trouble I could have saved myself if the Scipio's had died that day!" said Hannibal with a chuckle. "I heard they offered you a Corona Civica that day, but you rejected it. It is not like a Roman to reject such an honour!"

"It was my father, Hannibal. Would you have not done the same, if your father fell in battle and you still had strength in your limbs to

518

help him?" he asked, not really expecting an answer. "You do not accept honours for taking an action for which you have no choice. He was my father."

"I too saw my father fall in battle. We were fighting the Vettoni in Iberia. The Oretani had offered to help us but traitorously broke their word and turned on us, hitching burning wagons to oxen and driving them at us. The last I saw of my father was his body falling under an overturning cart. He was consumed by the flames. I would have done anything to save him, if I could."

Hannibal sat without talking, looking at the flames. Scipio waited.

"At Cannea we were confronted by such overwhelming odds it didn't seem to me possible that we could prevail. The evening before the battle I took a few drops of the elixir for the first time. The effect was incredible. My mind became so clear. I seemed to be able to think up new strategies without effort. I thought up and discarded ideas so quickly. When I thought of the envelopment strategy it was obvious that it was the best opportunity that we would have. I knew that there were weaknesses in it. I knew things could go wrong, but I also knew it was the best chance out of all possible options."

"You had nearly double our strength. We could put to the field about fifty thousand men. You brought nearly ninety thousand to the field. We shouldn't have stood a chance!" said Hannibal.

"It was a tragic day for Rome," said Scipio sadly. "To have fifty thousand soldiers slain in a single day was a catastrophe."

"It is a day that has haunted me for every day that I have been alive. I discovered that day that this marvellous potion, which gave me the power to think so clearly, gave me the power to hate as I have never known hate. The potion is a poison that makes you think so fast, see things so clearly, and amplifies all your feelings. The hate that I felt for Rome, the vow I had made to my father, became all consuming. I had no control. I had no sense of perspective!"

"I remember walking across the battlefield as evening started to fall. All around me my men were slaying your countrymen. There were piles of bodies, some still writhing in pain, trapped under the weight of their comrades. The ground had turned to mud, not from rain but from the blood of Roman soldiers."

"I have seen much carnage in my life but to know that it was my hatred for Rome that had caused this! I had always considered myself an honourable man but that evening I realised that, under the influence of this poison, I was a monster, an animal. I was ashamed of what I had done. I should have taken your legions hostage, not slaughtered them.

"My aim," said Hannibal, "was to so dishearten your people so that we would be able to negotiate a permanent peace between our two countries. As time went on, I could see that Rome would never bend. I had killed so many Romans by that time that there was not a person in Rome who did not know someone, family or friend, whom we had slain. It was no wonder that the Senate would not talk peace terms with me!"

"Reluctant as I was to use the potion again, I eventually decided that I needed to do something to end the war. I decided that I would take it and put my mind to what strategy I should follow, not in the heat of battle, but at a time of repose. By that time I had been in Italy for nearly eight years. I knew your people. My informers told me what was happening in Rome. I knew your allies. Some of them had even become my allies."

"So, one evening I sat down in my tent and drank some of the potion. My mind raced through option after option, but to my horror the outcome was always the same. Carthage would be destroyed. Rome would prevail. There was something about the Roman State that made its dominance inevitable. It was almost like Rome was an unstoppable force of nature. It had already passed the point at which individual actions by mere men could stop it. All I could hope to do was nudge it off course for a while."

"I saw that the oath I had made to my father and my God were nothing but spiteful vengeance. I could no more crush Rome than I could jump to the moon."

"After taking the potion I slept. I awoke the next day in the middle of the morning. I sat for a long time going over in my mind my options. The first thing I did was crush the vial under my boot. No man should have his purpose taken away from him so cruelly. My life seemed suddenly empty and meaningless."

"I continued to do the best I could. In the end I fought not only Rome, but the reluctance of my own people."

"When my brother Hasdrubal was killed at a battle at the Metaurus River I knew that it was only a matter of time. I was effectively stranded. There was no chance of reinforcements."

"When I heard that you were leading a campaign to Africa itself, my worst fears were realised. I had to leave Italy and return to do what I could to help protect Carthage itself."

"The rest of the story you know."

They sat in silence, both staring into the flames.

"So what now, Hannibal?" asked Scipio eventually.

"Now I enjoy the time I have left until Rome comes knocking at my door," said Hannibal with half a smile. "I have had a warrior's life for which I thank Melqart. I have unburdened myself to a man I trust and am ready to face the future. That I couldn't do more to save Carthage I regret. I don't know whether either my men or I will be remembered, but I am at peace knowing that we fought, for the most part, with honour."

Scipio stood up and held out his hand. Hannibal stood as well, grasping the hand that was offered to him. The two old generals looked into each others eyes and saw themselves reflected back.

Scipio took his leave, his hood pulled up over his head.

****

Several months passed. Hannibal was again sitting in his garden. The evenings were getting warmer. He enjoyed the tranquility of the garden and the flickering light of the fire. He had been warned, by his informers at King Prusias' palace, that a Roman delegation had arrived a few days earlier. He was under no illusion about what they wanted. As good a friend as King Prusias was, Hannibal knew that he could not afford to make a stand against Rome for long. He would have to give Hannibal up or risk the wrath of Rome.

He smiled as he rested his pen down on the piece of papyrus, being careful not to smear the still wet ink. As he leaned back in his chair he heard the sound of horses outside, then the banging of a sword pommel on his stout wooden door.

Calmly he flicked the catch the opened the secret compartment in the lid of the ring on his finger. Two small pilules fell into his hand. He had acquired the Aconite tablets many years ago. Without hesitation he swallowed them. Almost immediately he started to feel his fingers tingling. He felt his heart starting to pound, then a sharp pain stabbed through his chest. He slumped forward and then slowly fell from his chair onto the ground.

He didn't hear the stamping of heavy Roman hobnail boots on the beautiful mosaic floors. He didn't hear the oath of the Roman commander as he entered the garden and saw the lifeless body of Rome's greatest enemy lying prone on the ground. He didn't hear the commander swear again as he read the last words of Hannibal the Carthaginian.

"Let us relieve the Romans from the anxiety they have so long experienced, since they think it tries their patience too much to wait for an old man's death."

He had escaped them one last time.

17. Rome - Present day

"So, it was Hanibal who hid the box originally in Spain." said Alberto as he put a fresh pot of coffee down on the bench.

"It fits with what we know. Julius Caesar found it in Spain a hundred or so years later and started, albeit a bit late, on his stellar career. Hannibal's father grew up somewhere near Egypt, so the whole Egyptian connection is still there," said Charlotte.

"But that still leaves us with the question of who made this stuff up in the first palce! Perhaps it was an unknown Carthaginian polymath!" said Elizabeth. "But that doesn't fit, because the DNA from the Alaric sample is from around Greece, not northern Africa or the Eastern Mediterranean."

"What!" said Charlotte, shocked. "When did you find this out?"

"Didn't I mention it before? Sorry. I thought I had. The DNA results show that one of the DNA strands is definitely Greek, the other from perhaps somewhere north of Greece, but it is less easily identifiable."

"Brilliant! That means we can narrow down the search to something manageable. I have been looking for links to all this and I think I might have an idea that is worth talking through. Let me ask you who was the most brilliant polymath in the ancient Greek world?" asked Charlotte.

"I don't know. Plato? Socrates? Zeno? Archimedes? Epicurus? Aristotle? Parmenides?" said Dan. "They were all brilliant, but so little remains of their work it is sometimes hard to judge how brilliant."

"But how about if one of them is known to have written books on physics, biology, zoology, metaphysics, logic, ethics, aesthetics, poetry, politics and government, among other things? What if I was to tell you that the same person wrote the first systematic and comprehensive study of animals that was so sophisticated that nothing rivalled it until the Renaissance?"

"Really?" said Elizabeth surprised.

"Let me read you something," said Charlotte, typing on her computer keyboard. 'here we go...Hence if the eyes of swallows, while still young, be put out, they recover their sight again, for the birds are still developing, not yet developed, when the injury is inflicted, so that the eyes grow and sprout afresh. What does that sound like to you?" she said, turning to Elizabeth.

"Well," said Elizabeth cautiously, "It could be talking about the action of embryonic stem cells in a developing embryo. When was it written?"

"About two and half thousand years ago!" she said.

"No! That can't be true. You must be taking it out of context!" said Elizabeth.

"The man who wrote it also wrote an accurate, and I mean properly accurate, in modern terms, treaties on the development of chicken embryos," said Charlotte.

"Really?" said Elizabeth.

"And, to cap it all off, he also wrote two books on the regeneration of limbs, based around the observable regeneration of lizards tails!" said Charlotte.

"My God! He sounds amazing! Who was this genius?" asked Elizabeth, obviously intrigued.

"Hang on!" she said holding up her hand. "He also compiled an amazing list of detailed descriptions of in excess of five hundred creatures, some of them described in such perfect detail that some of his observations were not reported again until after the invention of the microscope in the 17th century!"

"I know that this is starting to sound like one of those quiz shows where you are given more and more clues, but I think it is important to get an idea of this man's range of achievements. His initial training was in medicine. He established, in the one place that attracted the greatest thinkers of his time, the first full on research institute in the history of the world, setting up a place where scholars worked collaboratively together on issues. Not only that, he was probably the first person ever to create a research library to be used by others and to be kept for posterity!"

"Okay, so we've got a genius who collaborates with other genius and has set up some sort of ancient Manhattan project," said Dan. "Is he Greek?"

"He sure is! As Greek as anything!" replied Charlotte.

"Ah, but did this person ever have any contact with anyone who became a world famous strategist?" asked Alberto.

"How about the known and documented fact that he was the teacher, mentor and friend of the greatest conquerer of the ancient world?" said Charlotte.

"Holy fuck!" said Dan jumping out of his seat. "Of course! Now that you say that, it is so obvious! Even the Egyptian connection fits perfectly!"

Elizabeth started at him in amazement. "It ain't obvious to me, brother! Who the hell are you guys talking about."

"Unbelievable!" said Dan putting both hands on top of his head as if to stop it exploding. 'Holy shit!" he said as he walked around the room. "This is mind blowing! She is talking about Aristotle and Alexander the fucking Great!"

18. Pella - Macedonia - 343 BCE

Aristotle rubbed his beard as a he watched the young boy striding up the pathway that ran beside the river. He was surrounded by his friends, but even from this distance you could see who was the leader of this small group. The furtive glances each boy made to see if Alexander approved of what they had done or said, and the way in which they showed him objects upon which they stumbled first, before the others.

He was thirteen years old, more a young man than a boy. His mane of blonde hair, his perfectly formed physique would have made him stand out among any group of boys, but there was such confidence and grace in his every movement that he seemed so well formed as to be almost perfect.

Aristotle smiled to himself, wondering if the young man would measure up to his own definition of perfection. Certainly, physically, the young prince was as perfect an example of a young man as could be imagined. He could see no aspect of his physique or form that could be improved upon, but the real questions were what sort of mind lay within that noble head? What values drove his actions? What potential lay within that perfect body and would this young prince be able to attain that potential?

A few days before, on the day he had arrived in Pella, Aristotle had found himself resting under a gnarled old olive tree, tired after the long journey from Athens. He was watching a young boy on a very large horse practicing rapidly changing direction. It was the sort of manoeuvre cavalry officers needed to perfect to be able to successfully negotiate a battlefield. The boy practiced the same action over and over again.

As he watched he felt a presence beside him. He looked up to see King Philip standing beside him. Aristotle started to rise but Philip rested his hand lightly on his shoulder to indicate that he should stay where he was and then sat down beside him.

"I see that you are becoming aquatinted with my son?" He said with a smile.

Aristotle looked at the King. "I'm sorry my Lord, I wasn't aware that this young lad was Prince Alexander. I was merely admiring the boy's dedication to his task, and his obvious understanding of the need to continually practice a skill in which he wants to achieve excellence. It is a real life example of one of the principles upon which I base my teaching."

"Yes." responded Philip, "He is a very determined young man. Do you see his horse? Bucephalus, he calls him. You can of course see why."

Aristotle nodded. Bucephalus was a massive animal, with a coat as black as midnight and a white star prominent on its forehead. Despite it's size the horse's head was even more massive and almost looked out of proportion to its body. "Ox head" was a fitting name for such an animal.

"Do you know the story of this horse and my son, Master Aristotle?"

Aristotle shook his head.

"Three or four years ago, when the boy was about ten years old, I was offered a horse by Philonicus the Thessalian horse dealer. It was a beautiful beast, despite its overly large head. The Thessolonians are well regarded for the breeding of noble and elegant horses."

"I had always judged Philonicus to be an honest man, but when he brought this horse before me I began to have my doubts. It seemed to me to be a vicious and undisciplined animal, kicking and fighting my most able horse breakers. The horse had a true, unbroken, wild spirit. We had all agreed that he was untameable. I was about to have stern words with Philonicus when Alexander suddenly appeared before me. He must have been watching from somewhere in the crowd that had gathered around. The young pup looked me in the eye and told me that I should let him try to master the horse."

"I tell you Aristotle I could feel my heart grow in my chest when he said that. A mere strip of a boy wanting to take on a wild animal that had just thrown my best horseman and broken the arm of one of my grooms."

"My inclination was to say no. The Gods themselves would not have been able to protect me from his mother if I let any harm come to the boy. But, by the powers, that lad has a will of iron. He argued with me in front of that crowd of grown men, but not like a child. He argued logically and boldly. He offered to pay for the horse himself. In the end I could not find an argument to dissuade him. Reluctantly I let him try, knowing the risk I took , but convincing myself that it might prove to be a valuable lesson in humility for him, if nothing else."

"Ah, Aristotle you should have seen the boy. No taller than the distance between the ground and my belt buckle and as thin as a newly planted olive tree. He strode out into the middle of the arena, flicking his cloak from his shoulder as he went. He didn't falter or hesitate. He took the reigns from the groom that was holding them and he gently turned the horse around. I could see him talking to the hose and patting its muzzle as he did so. Then as quick as lighting, he leapt from the ground to the horses back. I think the horse was more shocked than we were! I can tell you my heart was in my mouth. The horse reared up but Alexander leaned into its neck and then they were off! The horse sprang forward with a mighty leap the like of which I have never seen before or since. The two of them became like a single beast, moving faster and faster around the arena until it could no longer contain them and then I swear, they flew over the crowd and disappeared down the road."

"The whole crowd just cheered. They were hooting and hollering so impressed were they with what they had just seen."

"In that moment, Master Aristotle, I realised that my son had the potential to be someone truly great. Beating within that young breast is a heart so strong that nothing will be able to contain it. I swear to you now that my kingdom of Macedon will be nowhere big enough for him once he is grown to manhood."

Aristotle looked with growing interest at the young man still working his horse in the arena.

"The day I heard of his birth the very same messenger that brought me that welcome news also brought news of Parmenio's great victory over the Illyrian's and the victory of my horse at the Olympic games. I can not remember a more portentous moment in my life," said Phillip.

"I too have heard stories of his birth from members of your court," said Aristotle. "I hear tell that the great temple of Diana at Ephesus burnt to the ground on the day he was born! They say that the soothsayers ran about Ephesus, beating their faces, and crying, that this day had brought forth something that would prove fatal and destructive to all Asia."

Philip's expression became suddenly dark and hard. "The conquering of Asia is a task that has fallen on my shoulders. I will be the one to crush the Persians. Alexander will need to find other, more distant, realms to conquer."

Aristotle watched Philip's expression soften.

"I too have heard those stories," he said, almost dismissively. "People are so willing to believe all types of nonsense, Aristotle. Just you make sure that my son becomes both wise and virtuous and can tell the truth from superstitious nonsense."

"I have not had time to devote to the raising of my son but I would charge you with the responsibility of ensuring that he grows to manhood without having to make the mistakes that I have made in my life. Teach him to lead a better, more virtuous life than mine."

Philip stood with a slight groan, bid Aristotle good afternoon, and strode off, back towards his Palace.

It was a few days after this discussion that Alexander and a number of his close friends departed with him for the village of Mieza where Aristotle had agreed to set up his school.

19. Mieza - Macedonia - 343 BCE

Aristotle had located his school in Mieza in the grounds of the temple of the Nymphs. It was an idyllic spot. The school building was built around three small caves. Beautifully proportioned Ionic columns elegantly supported the rest of the structure. Stone seats were set all around the area.

Springs bubbled from the earth filling the many streams that ran through the gardens with sweet clear water and making the grounds around it cool and leafy. A multitude of pathways wound their way through the grounds.

Aristotle shook his head as one of the young boys, Hephaestion, a page in King Philip's court, came running up to him. "Have you heard the news Master Aristotle, King Phillip is to march against King Cersobleptes of Thrace. Our army will crush him into the ground!" he said with boyish enthusiasm.

Alexander had come up behind Hephaestion. On hearing his friend's enthusiastic support for the Macedonian army, and Philip's plans, Aristotle saw a flicker of some dark emotion move across Alexander's face. It was only fleeting and was swiftly replaced by his engaging smile that charmed those around him so easily.

Aristotle recognised that darker emotion. He had seen it before. Philip had revealed the same emotions when they had talked some weeks ago. There is a dangerous competitiveness between a great father and his unproven son. Here were the makings of a great tragedy, he thought to himself.

It didn't take long for Aristotle to discover that the young Alexander had a prodigious intelligence and a capacity for thinking that often astounded him. He absorbed information like no other young man he had met. His ability to argue logically, from a basis of fact, was extraordinary.

As he began to know him better Aristotle began to observe Alexander's reaction to his father's achievements more keenly. He observed a number of times how Alexander's mood would change when he received reports of his father's success. He would become more introspective, occasionally melancholic.

Walking with the young prince, late one afternoon, Aristotle noticed that Alexander seemed pensive and distracted. They strolled in silence for some time. Aristotle, well aware that Alexander wanted to talk about something that had been troubling him, waited patiently for the boy to break his silence. Eventually Alexander asked, "Is it a good thing, Master, to be ambitious?"

Aristotle smiled at the young prince. "Ambition and lack of ambition are the extremes of a nameless virtue which is related to high-mindedness in the same way that generosity is related to magnificence," he said.

"Ambition can be described as desiring honour in the right amount, in the right manner, for the right reason, and at the right time. The ambitious man strives for more honour in any particular area than he is entitled to. The unambitious man tries to avoid honour, even for noble achievements."

"Why do you ask about ambition?" asked Aristotle after they had walked a little further in silence.

"I would like to try and understand myself. I have this feeling that I am destined for great things, but King Philip is conquering the world, while I remain here at school," he said. A note of bitterness and frustration had entered his voice. "Every time there is news of another of his victories I feel angry. Should I feel proud of his achievements? Does my ambition make me ignoble? Does it make me less virtuous?"

"There are two kinds of virtue, Alexander —intellectual and moral. Intellectual virtue is the result of learning. That is why you and I are here. Moral virtue, on the other hand, comes about as the result of habit and practice. Man is not born either moral or immoral, but he has the capacity to develop moral virtue and this capacity can only be developed through habit."

Aristotle thought for a moment. "The development of moral excellence is not comparable to the development of other human capabilities. All men are endowed with certain faculties by nature. The ability to use these faculties is acquired before they are actually used.

Man has the ability to see before he sees. He has the ability to hear before he hears."

"The moral virtues, though, are acquired only by exercising them, just as skill in the arts and crafts is acquired only through use. For instance, it is only by playing the harp that a man becomes either a good or bad harpist. If this were not so, there would be no need for teachers and everyone would be born either a good or a bad musician. Likewise, it is only by action, and by dealing with other men, that one is able to become either just or unjust, brave or cowardly, noble or ignoble, temperate or intemperate."

"If it is greatness that you desire, then you should cultivate the virtue of high mindedness. High mindedness is the virtue that falls midway between vanity and pettiness. It presupposes possession of all the other virtues. High-mindedness is the quality of those who think they deserve great things and actually do deserve them."

"High-mindedness is knowing that to which you are entitled and insisting on it, but it also involves maintaining high standards in all things and setting an example for the community. A man, who falsely claims honour, and other great things, is vain. A man who underestimates his own value is small-minded and petty."

Alexander, uncharacteristically, looked nervously, almost shyly across to Aristotle. " I have always thought to myself that I should aspire to be like the great Achilles, after all, I am his direct descendant on my mother's side."

"Ah, so I have heard. Your mother is, I am told, a grand daughter of Achilles." Aristotle paused. "Achilles, the best of Greeks!" he mused. "That," said Aristotle with a smile, " is an aspiration fit for a great warrior. Your mother's family has given you the potential for greatness! What qualities do you think you have gained from your father's side of the family?"

Alexander's brow furrowed. "I think, probably, justice and mercy."

Aristotle started in surprise. "Oh, I would have thought that the characteristics that have led to your father's success in battle would be something that you might aspire to?

Alexander looked at Aristotle quizzically. "My father's battles are not anything I would aspire to! Perhaps," said Alexander with a chuckle, "the ability to hurl thunderbolts might be useful, but then again, where would the challenge be if we had such overwhelming power?"

Aristotle stopped on the path, suddenly realising that he had misunderstood what the boy had been talking about. Alexander walked on several strides before he realised the philosopher had stopped and looked back at him.

"You look shocked Aristotle, have I said something to offend you?"

"No, no, Alexander," said Aristotle shaking his head. "I would just like to sit for a while and think. You go on. I will see you tomorrow."

As Aristotle watched the young man stride away, his cloak billowing behind him, he wondered what the implications were for a prince who did not acknowledge the King as his father, but believed that he was the son of Zeus, father of the Gods!

Like all Greeks, Aristotle was familiar with the whole pantheon of Gods that supposedly ruled their daily lives. He had grown up with the knowledge of which of the great Greek heroes was descended from which of the Gods. What he had not experienced before was a rational, sane individual who believed so obviously, and so completely, that he had one of those Gods as a parent, and not just any god, but Zeus himself.

Aristotle's own views on the Gods were problematic. He had serious doubts about the existence of the Olympian Gods. He felt sure that there was some divine influence behind the world, but found the almost day to day involvement of the Gods in the lives of mere mortals less than convincing, if not slightly ridiculous.

Sitting in the shaded glade by the stream in the warmth of the late afternoon he thought about the situation of his young pupil.

He had heard stories, whispered around court, that Philip had been wary of sleeping with Alexander's mother, Olympias, because of her reputed penchant for sleeping with snakes. It was this bizarre habit that, according to palace rumour, had given Zeus an opportunity to father her child.

He had been told, in very hushed tones, by one of the Queen's attendants, that the night before the consummation of the royal marriage

Olympias dreamed that a thunderbolt fell upon her womb and a great fire was kindled.

He had also heard court gossip that, after the marriage, Philip had dreamed that he put a seal upon his wife's womb, the device of which was the figure of a lion.

Aristotle, pragmatically, saw in these stories evidence of the bolstering of Alexander's position in the succession. Someone within the royal court was clearly trying to ensure that Alexander was not challenged as the heir to the throne. The obvious candidate for spreading these rumours was his mother, Olympias.

Alexander was the second eldest of Philip's male children. Arrhidaeus, son of Philip's second wife, was first in line for the throne, but Arrhidaeus was a weak child with little ambition and, in Aristotle's view, from their first meeting, little intellect.

It had been whispered to him that Olympias had been systematically poisoning Arrhidaes since he was a small child to ensure that he would never became King.

While Olympias was the first among Philip's wives her position, and therefore the position of her son, was not as secure as it might be. Olympias was not Macedonian, or even Greek. Olympias was from Epirus, the land to the east of Greece, between the Pindus Mountains and the Ionian Sea. She was the daughter of King Neoptolemus.

Olympias certainly seemed to be ambitious enough for herself and her son to spread gossip and rumours that would strengthen Alexander's position but was she ambitious enough to convince her son that he was the son of a God? mused Aristotle, and what would that do to the boys mind?

Aristotle put his head in his hands and sighed. Alexander had so much potential. Probably more than any man he had ever known. He was physically perfect, well muscled, perhaps a little short, but perfectly proportioned. He was intelligent, precociously so. He would have made a good, perhaps even a great philosopher. He could be a good and wise king of Macedon, and perhaps a great leader for the Greeks. But to believe you are the son of a god! What would that do to a man? What mortal man could carry the burden of being convinced that he is the son of Zeus? What sort of expectations do you then have for yourself? No matter how brilliant you are how do you act when you believe your half brothers are the likes of Heracles the hero, Lakedaimon the father of the Spartans and Perseus the slayer of the Medusa!

Getting slowly to his feet Aristotle looked in the direction that Alexander had gone and shook his head. No wonder the boy is always angry when he hears of Philip's victories. He thought to himself. Not only does he believe Philip is not his true father, but he thinks that there will be no great deeds left for him to do by the time he becomes King. How will he ever be able to live up to his own expectations?

20. Mieza - Macedonia - 342 BCE

Alexander walked beside Aristotle through the gardens. He thought to himself how much he had enjoyed his time at Mieza. Despite the nagging feeling that he wanted to be on campaign, sharing victories with King Philip, Aristotle was a great teacher who continually challenged him, and who, he liked to believe, was now a friend.

He and his companions had sat through the normal lessons on poetry, rhetoric, geometry, astronomy, and eristics but it was the discussions about politics and morals with Aristotle that really engaged him and, much to Alexander's own surprise, the lessons he took with Aristotle on medicine.

Aristotle's knowledge of the human body, of plants and animals, astounded Alexander. There were times when he was convinced that Aristotle knew everything there was to know.

It was times like these, though, when it was just the two of them, that he liked best. He relished the opportunity to discuss issues which he had been mulling over, without the others boys around to overhear.

"You said Master, when we spoke the other day, that you felt that animals grow not only in size in their mother's wombs, but also in complexity. How did you come by this conclusion?"

Aristotle smiled. "I am pleased that you have asked the question the way you have. Most of your peers would have challenged my conclusion. You first seek to understand how I came to that conclusion. The gathering of information, knowledge and facts is vital if we are to better understand the world."

"I have spent a number of years studying how animals develop. A few years ago I studied the way that chicken's developed within an egg. When you crack open a newly fertilised egg, along with the yolk and the white, you can observe a small red dot. Over a number of days that red spot grows and spreads out over the yolk, spreading out a network of fine red lines, almost like a spider in shape.

"Within a few days you can see a creature developing, but it is not like a baby chicken that just grows bigger. It is a tiny, unformed thing.

Over the next few days it starts to form a recognisable shape. Somehow an eye develops and then legs and wings, all naked without feathers."

"A few more days and it is a recognisable baby chicken that then starts to grow bigger until it hatches through its shell."

"It took many eggs to follow the progression through, but I have seen the same sort of development in other animals, not hatched from eggs, that are born too early. There is something inside an egg, or a mother's womb, that guides the form of an animal. Like the chicken, it shapes us from a mere spot of life, through the growing of all the parts that makes us what we are."

"But how does it happen? What makes one chicken white and the other black? What makes one person strong of mind and another weak?" asked Alexander.

"I don't have an answer for you", replied Aristotle, "but I have thought about it and can see a number of possibilities. It could be, as many would say, something supernatural, an intervention of the Gods. It could be that there is some essence in the beginnings of life that show a person or an animal the way to develop. Perhaps it is something that comes from the mother or father, or perhaps something that comes from them both."

"How then, asked Alexander, "do we get cripples and people who are born deformed at birth?"

"Perhaps sometimes there is a mistake in the pattern passed from the parents. I have observed though, that the children of deformed parents, either one or both, do not always have the deformity of their parents."

I too have noticed that," said Alexander thoughtfully.

They walked in silence, enjoying the warm wind that blew on their faces, both lost in their own thoughts.

"Would it be possible to make someone better than they are?" asked Alexander suddenly.

"By practice and repetition, one can become better at many things, but I think you are asking more than that?" asked Aristotle.

"Yes, I know I can become a better horseman by riding each day, or better at argument by listening to the way others argue and then trying

537

the tricks that they use. I mean, is there a way that a person can go beyond the boundaries of what is possible for a normal human."

Alexander thought for a moment. "A cat can wake from sleep and leap on to a wall many times its own height. The best athletes I know can, proportionally for their size, come nowhere near being able to leap as far as a cat can, and yet they both have muscles that seem to be the same."

Aristotle smiled, "You want to be able to win the Olympic games by having the agility of a cat?"

"No" replied Alexander in all seriousness. "I want to conquer the world by having a mind that can see every possibility. Like a God!"

21. Mieza - Macedonia - 340 BCE

Aristotle could see Alexander sitting under a tree with his friend, Hephaestion. The two young men were deep in conversation. Aristotle coughed quietly to get their attention.

"I wonder Alexander, whether you would walk with me for a while. I have some issues to discuss with you."

Hephaestion picked up on the cue and bid his tutor and friend, politely, goodbye.

"He is a good friend?" asked Aristotle as they started to walk down to the path that led along the river.

"We have always been friends. There is nothing that I do or think that Hephaestion does not know," said Alexander.

"It is a rare thing that sort of friendship. One soul abiding in two bodies!" said Aristotle thoughtfully.

"You need to discuss something with me Master?" asked Alexander after they had been walking in silence for a few minutes.

"I have had word from your father, Alexander. He wishes you to return to Pella and assume the role of regent while he prepares for the Persian war."

Alexander had learnt to mask his feelings well over the last few years as he had grown in maturity, but Aristotle could see the subtle changes that indicated that he was not happy.

"Two years ago," Aristotle went on without acknowledging Alexander's change of mood, "you asked me whether a man could reach beyond the potential of ordinary men. I think you used the analogy of a cat?"

"I remember the conversation Master, and I am embarrassed by my naivety. I now realise that there is no magic that can make a man better than he is. It is only by hard work that we improve."

"That may be true, Alexander, but I have been giving much thought to the question you asked. It reflected an aspect of my researches upon which I have struggled for many years. I have always believed that there was a way that a man can enhance his mental abilities, albeit temporarily, through the use of certain herbs. What started me down this path was thinking about the power of the Delphic Oracle, whose visions have assisted my own people avert tragedy a number of times. As you know she inhales the vapours that seep through the rocks at Delphi and speaks a prophecy. It may be, as is generally believed, that Apollo speaks through her, or it may be, as I suspect, that the vapours enhance her ability to see possible futures."

Alexander stopped and looked at Aristotle. "Are you saying that you have found a way for me to see the future?"

"No Alexander," said Aristotle, shaking his head. "But I may have found a way to enhance your own, inherent, natural abilities, which are already, without any assistance from me, prodigious. There is no magic here, but there may be a way to make your intellect more vibrant, and allow you to become more aware of possibilities that exists. There is, however, a danger with doing this. I have struggled with my own conscience, unsure of whether to discuss what I have done with you. There is great danger in what I am about to tell you, for both you and for me."

Aristotle paused and took a deep breath. "As you know a truly healthy body is in balance between the four humours, earth, air, fire and water. They need to be in balance. As I have taught you, these translate in our bodies to the black bile, the blood, the yellow bile and water. Your body is already in natural balance. To enhance your thinking it is necessary to disrupt that balance. To do this I have created a mixture of herbs, mandrake root, Joint Fir, velvet beans, belladonna and other ingredients mixed with your own essence."

"What do you mean you mixed it with my own essence?"

"I have obtained, by deception, I am afraid," he said, letting his eyes fall from Alexander's, "some of the placenta and membranes that surrounded you when you were inside your mother's womb."

"What?" asked Alexander, astonished.

"This must be our secret Alexander," said Aristotle. "Your mother would be most angry if she discovered that I had obtained even the smallest amount of it. Your mother believes it has power. She keeps it in a casket in her chambers. Many cultures bury the afterbirth with great ceremony, believing that it remains linked to the person it protected in the womb. I believe that it contains the essence, the pattern, of who we are, as, within its embrace, we are formed as human beings."

"Now, remember this Alexander, for it is of the greatest importance, if you use this potion too often, in too great a quantity, it will permanently upset the balance of your body. If it doesn't kill you, it will certainly affect you in unpleasant ways. It may make you go mad. You must decide if what you are trying to achieve is worth the risk of using the potion. You must use it sparingly, and remember, it will only enhance the abilities that already exist within you, not create new ones."

Aristotle reached under his tunic and pulled out a small glass vial. He hesitated as Alexander reached for it. "This mixture is extremely dangerous Alexander. I can not impress on you enough the need for care in its use."

"When you take it you will likely feel your heart beat faster. You may see visions and feel disorientated for a time. The more you take the more profound will be the effect on your body and mind. Using it in times of great peril, may give you insights that may lead you to victory, but every time you use it you will risk unbalancing the humours, risk madness and possibly shorten your life."

"I would rather live a short life of glory than a long one of obscurity! It is better to burn out than fade away!" said Alexander with a vehemence that would come back to haunt Aristotle in years to come.

Hesitantly he said,"I have one other gift for you. It is a copy of the Iliad that I have corrected myself." Aristotle passed the scroll, that he had been holding in his left hand, to Alexander. Alexander took the scroll with a look of genuine delight on his face.

It was beautifully crafted, with ornate knurled knobs. The scroll itself felt smooth and soft to the touch.

"Being a descendant of Achilles, I know," said Aristotle, "that this poem is important to you. This copy holds two secrets of importance beyond the words of Homer. I have woven into the text the formula for the potion that you hold in your other hand. I will show you the secret of how to read it, but only you will know that it is there. I have also had the scroll modified so that the vial you hold in your hand slips inside it. Keep it close to you Alexander."

Alexander looked at the scroll and twisted the ornate knob on the scroll. It turned easily but did not unscrew. He looked up into Aristotle's eyes. Aristotle smiled. "I have designed a mechanism that will ensure that the secret chamber can not be opened accidentally. You need to push down on the knob to engage the thread. Then turn it."

Alexander pushed down and then found that he could unscrew the ornate knob easily. He slipped the vial into the recess that was revealed and then screwed the top back on.

"Thank you, Master," said Alexander, humbly.'I will keep this, greatest of treasures, close by me so that I can protect it."

Aristotle smiled and started to continue their walk. Alexander strode along beside him. They walked in silence for some time, each lost in their own thoughts. Alexander was the first to break the silence.

"What would happen if someone else were to drink from the vial?"

Aristotle walked a few more steps and then stopped. He lifted his hand to rub his chin. "I don't know. I think perhaps that a mighty battle would occur inside them. Your essence would attack theirs and they perhaps would die or go mad straight away. Perhaps if they were of your family the effect on them would be similar to the effect on you. I am afraid I just don't know."

The rest of their walk was undertaken in silence.

The next day Alexander set off for Pella to take up the role of regent while his father prepared for war with the Persian Empire.

22. Pella - Macedonia - 337 BCE

"Master Aristotle!" Alexander called as he walked down the steps of the Royal Palace. "It is so good to see you again after all this time, Master. Are you well?"

"Yes, Alexander." replied Aristotle, clasping his former pupil by the arm. "I am well. I hear that you have been busy, putting down rebellions and founding your own city! Alexandropolis no less!"

"Ah, yes." Alexander looked somewhat embarrassed." More a tribal skirmish and the establishment of a military compound than a rebellion and a city," he said with a laugh. He smiled, roguishly. "But I have high hopes for it!" he said conspiratorially. "Perhaps Alexandropolis will become a great city one day!"

"Perhaps it will, Alexander. Now, I have not had an opportunity to congratulate your father and Kleopatra on their marriage. Will you be kind enough to lead me to him? We can talk on the way."

Alexander led Aristotle across a large courtyard to the Palace entrance.

"Tell me young man, how have you found the medicine that I made for you last time we met? asked Aristotle as they wound their way through the corridors of the Palace.

"I have not yet taken it!" he said. "I am still considering the cost of doing so, nor have I yet found a need to take it. Admittedly it is never far from my thoughts. I now keep your copy of the Iliad under my pillow at night, along with my knife."

Aristotle looked thoughtful as they continued towards the hall where the wedding feast was to be held. After a short time he asked conversationally, "Tell me about the wedding Alexander?"

Alexander's face grew hard. "The King takes yet another wife. It is his habit to marry a new one every time he undertakes a new campaign. What else is there to say?"

Aristotle didn't respond, but kept on walking.

"She is the niece of one of his generals, Attalus."

Aristotle nodded. "A Macedonian?" he asked innocently, watching Alexander out of the corner of his eye. The frown on Alexander's face was answer enough.

After paying his respects to the King, Aristotle found his way to the back of the hall. He preferred the Athenian practice of symposia, where drinking was in moderation and partaken after the meal. These Macedonians drank and celebrated in a much more boisterous way. Aristotle was happy to find a quiet spot out of the way of the carousing nobles.

His vantage point gave him a clear view of Alexander. He was interested, and a bit surprised, to see how much he had matured over the last few years. Although they corresponded frequently it had been some time since he had seen the young Prince. He was still as handsome a young man as ever, but his face had become stronger and leaner, accentuating his fine facial bone structure. His movements also seemed as athletic as always but his body, especially around his broad shoulders, looked more heavily muscled.

Alexander was reclining on a couch with his young friend Hephaestion. A number of other young men of his close inner circle reclined on the nearby couches. Aristotle recognised Ptolemy Lagides, Perdiccas, Craterus, Nicanor, Coenus and Amyntas. For the most part they appeared to be enjoying the festivities, but to Aristotle's keen eye he could sense that Alexander was not comfortable. Alexander was, however, trying hard to project an appropriately enthusiastic demeanor to those around him. In unguarded moments Aristotle observed a darkness in Alexander's mood that lurked just below the surface of his apparent amiability.

As always Alexander was drinking sparingly while those around him become progressively more loud and rowdy as the wine flowed freely. His father, Philip, in contrast, lying on a couch next to his new bride, Kleopatra, was, as was his habit, drinking prodigious amounts of wine and becoming progressively more effusive in manner.

Aristotle took the opportunity to study the two men. Philip, older and bearded, was outgoing and aggressive in his manner. The loss of his right eye at the siege of Methoni was a visible sign of his courage and tenacity. Aristotle wondered if it still gave him pain. Perhaps it was the reason for his quickness of temper. Alexander, clean shaven and, Aristotle smiled to himself, beautiful, was more restrained in manner than his father.

There was no doubt in Aristotle's mind that Alexander was Philip's son. While he had more of the features passed down from his mother, there were certainly physical aspects of him that reflected his father.

Looking more closely at Alexander, he observed, not for the first time, that Alexander held his head in an odd way. He wondered whether Alexander was as perfect a specimen of the human body as he had at first thought. He recalled reading some of the work of the great Hippocrates about the way the bones of the spine work and how, in some people a curvature of the spine can occur, a scoliosis. Perhaps the way Alexander held his head, was a result of a mild deformity of his spine.

Aristotle was brought out of his reverie by the bride's uncle, Attalus getting to his feet. He held a goblet of wine out in front of him and called loudly for silence. "Drink to the bride and groom!" he shouted. "To our noble king, Philip and my beautiful niece, Kleopatra! Let their union by blessed by the Gods and bring forth a lawful successor to the throne of Macedon and the..." Attalus did not get to finish his toast. Alexander sprang from his couch and hurled, with unerring accuracy, his own goblet at Attalus.

"You mongrel!" Alexander shouted angrily. "You pray for a legitimate heir to the Macedonian Throne? What am I then, a bastard?!"

Philip sprang from his own couch. He was clearly very angry and deeply offended by Alexander's outburst. Drawing his dagger he started to move towards his son. Alexander put his hand on the pommel of his own dagger, but before he had time to draw it from its sheath his father stumbled. Alexander watched, a look of disgust on his face, as his father sprawled on the floor. Philip's dagger fell from his grip and skidded across the floor. Alexander stopped it with his sandalled foot.

He looked down at his father with a look of total disdain. "Here is the man who is making ready to cross from Europe to Asia, and who cannot even cross from one seat to another without falling flat on his face!" he spat, deliberately and contemptuously kicking Philip's dagger back across the room.

Aristotle watched as Alexander strode from the hall. He noted how quickly, and unbidden, his friends followed him.

Attalus and several others helped Philip to his feet. The King angrily pushed them aside, staring after his son.

By the time that Aristotle left Pella the next morning, to return to Athens, Alexander and his mother were gone. The rumour in the Palace was that they were heading west, out of Macedon, to the sanctuary of Olympias' brother's court in Epirus.

23. Aigai - Macedonia - 336 BCE

Hephaestion looked into Alexander's eyes. They were still not focusing. He had entered Alexander's Chamber some time before hoping to be, if nothing else, a shoulder for Alexander to lean on in this time of great sorrow and turmoil. The murder of his father earlier in the day had created a power vacuum that was already seeing the major players vie for position. While Alexander was the heir apparent, he was not a full blood Macedonian, and there were those in Philip's court who would see him usurped if they could. Despite Alexander being acclaimed King at the theatre straight after it was realised Philip was dead, if Alexander did not move quickly, and decisively, he could still lose the throne.

When Hephaestion had entered the room he had found Alexander lying on a couch with a distant and unfocussed look in his eyes. Cold sweat glazed his face. A glass of wine lay spilled across the table that stood beside his couch. Alexander's copy of the Iliad rested in his lap.

Hephaestion's immediate reaction was that Alexander had been poisoned. He had checked his vital signs. His breathing was regular. His heartbeat was fast, but steady, as if he had been exercising. He was clearly not in pain. The last thing he wanted to do was start a panic that would give others in the palace an advantage in ascending to the throne.

He had decided that the best thing to do was wait. He tried to talk to Alexander, but received no response. Now he was getting really worried. It had been several hours. Alexander's condition had not changed.

Sitting on the floor, with his back resting on the end of the couch, Hephaestion remembered how pleased he had been when Alexander had finally been welcomed back to his father's house. It had been a difficult six months for those of his friends who had remained at court. Thankfully the King had, eventually, persuaded Alexander to return for his sisters' wedding. As an added inducement he had offered him command of the Companions, the elite Macedonian cavalry, in the forthcoming invasion of Persia. At the height of the wedding celebrations tragedy had struck. Philip had been assassinated.

Hephaestion, starting to panic because Alexander was still not showing any signs of waking, finally decided to seek help. He was lifting himself up off the ground when he felt Alexander's hand grab his arm. He looked across into Alexander's eyes. Far from being unfocussed they were now as hard and precise as he had ever seen them. It looked almost as if they were glowing. Alexander's one blue eye seemed to glow violet, his brown eye almost like burnished copper.

"It was the traitor Attalus, Demosthenes the Athenian and the Persian Darius who killed my father," said Alexander, sitting up and putting his copy of the Iliad carefully beside him.

"No", said Hephaestion, thinking that Alexander must be confused in his grief. "Attalus is in Asia. Pausanias killed your father."

Hephaestion knew the background to the story of Pausanias well. He had been the subject of court gossip and the butt of ribald jokes for years. Pausanias had been a member of the king's somatophylakes, his personal bodyguard. He had also been Philip's lover for a time. The affair had ended and Philip had taken a new lover, coincidently also called Pausanias, who was a very good friend of General Attalus.

The old lover had, out of spite, purposely embarrassed the king's new lover in public. When the opportunity arose to prove his worthiness during a battle with the Illyrians, the new lover recklessly threw himself in front of the King as he was about to be impaled on a spear. Philip's new lover had died on the battlefield.

Attalus had blamed Pausanias for his friend's death and, one evening, had enacted his revenge. He got the unsuspecting Pausanias drunk and then had him set upon and raped by a pack of stable boys.

Pausanias, humiliated and degraded, had sought Philip's support against Attalus and his relatives, who he believed to be behind the attack. Philip had done nothing to bring to justice those who Pausanias believed had connived to have him raped. Philip had, instead, perhaps out of a remaining affection for Pausanias, promoted him to membership of his somatophylakes.

These events had taken place some eight years before, and it was the consensus of the Palace gossips that Pausanias had been nursing a grudge against Philip ever since. He saw an opportunity to get his revenge and stabbed Philip as he entered the Theatre.

"We all know his reputation was in tatters. It was the spontaneous act of a jilted lover!" said Hephaestion.

"No," said Alexander with a confidence that brooked no disagreement. "Do you think it just coincidence that this plot occurs a few days after the King's new wife gave birth to a son?"

"The King's assassination was a Persian inspired plot that would see Kleopatra's son, Caranus, pronounced King. I was meant to have been slain today, along with Philip. If the King had not wanted to enter the theatre by himself, and sent me on ahead, I would have been standing alongside him when Pausanias attacked."

"How can you possibly say that Alexander?" asked Hephaestion. "What proof do you have?"

"I have no proof but logic. Think for a moment about what we already know. The timing is not coincidental. Macedon has an army perched on the edge of Asia ready to attack Darius and his mighty Persian empire. A pure blood heir to the Macedonian throne has just been born. Athens, seeking affirmation of her past glories and struggling to remain relevant in changed times, flirts with Darius. Do you remember how the Athenian, Demosthenes described my father as a 'pestilent knave from Macedonia, whence it was never yet possible to buy a decent slave.' He hates us so much, and thirsts so much for the lost glories of Athens that he is even prepared to crawl into bed with the Persian King."

Alexander took a breath and continued. "There were a number of horses tied up waiting to take more than one person away, therefore there was more than one assassin and more than one intended victim."

"Waiting horses also implies that the assassins must have had somewhere to go. They must have known that they would not be safe anywhere in Greece. Where could they go? Only Persia would offer them a safe haven. In Persia, with Darius' protection, they could find refuge, safety and a grateful and generous king to give them shelter."

"The only conclusion you can draw is that this was not a spontaneous act. This was a planned, well thought out, pre-meditated, conspiracy."

"Somebody persuaded Pausanias to kill the King. I agree that he might well have had a grudge against Philip and yes, Pausanias' reputation was in tatters after the affair with the stable boys, but committing regicide is no way to restore your reputation or recover your honour. No, Pausanias was just a scapegoat in a much bigger game!"

"The fact that I am not a pure bred Macedonian rankles with many of the older nobles. There is no doubt in my mind that there are those that would prefer to see Caranus named as King, even though he is but a few days old. He is the legitimate heir that Attalus wished for."

"A regent would have to be appointed then," said Hephaestion.

"That's right," said Alexander with a smile. "And who do you imagine would be regent for young Caranus?"

Hephaestion looked aghast. "Attalus!"

Alexander nodded.

"But why would Pausanias help Attalus? I know for a fact," said Hephaestion, "that Pausanias believed it was Attalus that had him raped. He has told me so himself! And why would Attalus have anything to do with Pausanias when he believed that it was Pausanias who caused his friends death?"

"Have you heard the reports of what happened after Pausanias killed the King today?" asked Alexander.

Hephaestion nodded. "Yes, Perdiccas, Leonnatus and young Attalus chased after him. He almost got away, and would have if he hadn't tripped over as he tried to reach his horse. "

Alexander smiled. "It is not yet clear who ran him through with a spear out of those three, but ask yourself, why would you spear a man who is sprawled on the ground defenseless?"

"I expect you could do it out of enthusiasm to revenge the King," said Hephaestion thoughtfully, "but perhaps you would also do it if you did not want the man to be questioned.".

"As to why Pausanias would be involved with Attalus, the simple fact is he didn't know he was being used. Why would Attalus choose Pausanias as his weapon? Because he knew that the man would be killed and forever reviled if he succeeded."

Hephaestion looked at his friend and new King, Alexander the third of Macedon. He could not believe the transformation that had occurred since he had first entered his room. Alexander now seemed to be burning with an inner fire. His eyes flashed and his skin glowed. He watched as Alexander strode across the room, picked up his cloak and swung it around his shoulders.

"Time to get to work Hephaestion!" he said heading towards the door. "I have seen the future! It starts with making it clear to the world who is the new master of the Greeks!"

24. Rome - Present day

"Now hang on a minute," said Elizabeth. "It could be Alexander and Aristotle, but have you found any corroborating evidence?"

"Let me read you a passage from Cassius Dio's Roman History," said Charlotte quickly tapping on the keyboard of her laptop "*The speech in which he proclaimed to them his pardon he delivered in Greek, so that they might understand him. After this he viewed the body of Alexander and actually touched it, whereupon, it is said, a piece of the nose was broken off*"

"Who are we talking about, who broke off Alexander's nose?" asked Dan.

"Cassius Dio is writing about events that occurred after the Emperor Augustus defeated Anthony and Cleopatra. Augustus broke off Alexander's nose!" said Charlotte.

"...and if it was Alexander's DNA in the potion, and the DNA came from the beginning and end of his life, that would explain where the old DNA came from!" said Elizabeth. "Are there any other mentions of Alexander in that history?"

"No, there aren't. There are however several mentions of Alexander the Great in Suetonius, which could be significant. The first is the one where Julius Caesar confronts the statute of Alexander in Spain," said Charlotte, typing on her laptop." Here it is...*While he was Quaestor it fell to him by lot to serve in farther Spain. While there, as he rode his circuit of the assize towns to hold court under order of the Praetor, he came to Gades, where he noticed a statue of Alexander the Great in the temple of Hercules. At the sight of it he drew a deep sigh, as one displeased with his own shortcomings, in that he had as yet performed no memorable act, whereas at his age Alexander had already conquered the whole world. He soon after made earnest suit for his discharge, in order to seize the first opportunity to compass greater enterprises at home within the city. The following night he was much disquieted by a dream in which he imagined he had carnal company with his own mother. But hopes of most glorious achievement were kindled in him by the soothsayers, who interpreted the dream to mean that he was destined to have sovereignty over all the world, his mother whom he*

552

saw under him signifying none other than the earth, which is counted the mother of all things."

"Certainly his successes seemed to stem from that sort of time," said Dan. "It could mean that he found the potion around then. What else have you got?"

"Well, there is this bit in the life of Augustus which perhaps shows an unusual fixation with Alexander, *"In passports, dispatches, and private letters he used as his seal at first a sphinx, later an image of Alexander the Great, and finally his own, carved by the hand of Dioscurides."*

"Odd. Perhaps it was just that he wanted to have himself seen as the equal of Alexander, a PR thing," said Dan. "What else have you got."

"Well the next one is more of the PR type stuff, I think. *"Later, when Octavius was leading an army through remote parts of Thrace, and in the grove of Father Bacchus consulted the priests .... since such a pillar of flame sprang forth from the wine that was poured over the altar, that it rose above the temple roof and mounted to the very sky. Such an omen had befallen no one save Alexander the Great, when he offered sacrifice at the same altar."*

"Yeah, that sounds like spin. Either that or he really did have an Alexander fixation! Are there any more references to Alexander?" asked Elizabeth.

"Yes. There is the one we already know about, Caligula. Whether Caligula visited Alexander's tomb or he just had someone plunder it is hard to know. Suetonius certainly says that Caligula took the breastplate from the sarcophagus himself."

"So why did they all think that Alexander was so great? What did he do that made all these people want to be like him?" asked Elizabeth.

"Partly it was that he never lost a battle. Some of it had to do with the size of the enemy he defeated, and the speed with which he defeated them. Maybe part to do with the amount of territory he conquered. He started by re-conquering Greece. Then, in ten years, he conquered what is modern day Turkey, Syria, Lebanon, Egypt and Iraq. After that he headed off into modern day Pakistan and India. If his own men hadn't demanded to go home, he would have kept on going east until there was no one left to fight. He had almost finished preparations for a new campaign into Arabia when he died," said Charlotte.

"So, if we think that the potion was made by Aristotle for Alexander, how do we think it is possible that Hamilcar got the potion?" asked Alberto.

"Well, Hamilcar was born in around 275BCE in a place called Cyrene," said Charlotte, "which is about a thousand kilometres from Alexandria, and we know that big things were happening in Alexandria at that time. So it is quite possible that he visited Alexandria."

"What things?" asked Alberto.

"The building of the Pharos of Alexandria, the great lighthouse. Construction for that started in 280BCE and was finished in 247. It was considered one of the seven wonders of the ancient world. That would be reason enough to travel there. The great library had been established by then, so that might be another reason, and if your thing was music it was probably about that time that Ctesibius invented the progenitor of all keyboard instruments, his famous water organ. Of course it was also the capital of Ptolemaic Egypt, so it was an important place to visit."

"Hang on," said Elizabeth, "Why are we talking about going to Alexandria all of a sudden? Why is that important?"

"Because that is where Alexander the Great was." She replied.

"So we have enough reasons for Hamilcar to, at the very least, travel to Alexandria. What thoughts do we have about how he got hold of the blood of.... the potion?" asked Dan.

"Onesicritus of Astypalaea, who was a contemporary of Alexander and who accompanied him on his campaigns makes, what I have always thought, is a strange observation." Charlotte paused and tapped on her keyboard, "... Here it is! "...*Onesicritus informs us, that he constantly laid Homer's Iliads, according to the copy corrected by Aristotle, called the casket copy, with his dagger under his pillow, declaring that he esteemed it a perfect portable treasure of all military virtue and knowledge.*"

"Wow!" said Alberto. "That fits with the whole idea of Aristotle passing information on to Alexander. Why is it called the Casket Copy, though?"

"Ah!" said Charlotte, with another tap of her keyboard, "Plutarch wrote about that. He writes of the time after Alexander has defeated the Persian King, Darius. In this bit he says... *Among the treasures and other booty that was taken from Darius, there was a very precious casket, which being brought to Alexander for a great rarity, he asked those about him what they thought fittest to be laid up in it; and when they had delivered their various opinions, he told them he should keep Homer's Iliad in it."*

"Wow! So this really is all coming together," said Elizabeth. "If the copy of the Iliad, in its fancy casket, was so important, then it is quite possible that it was buried along with him in his tomb."

"Not only that," said Charlotte, "listen to this...

"This is attested by many credible authors, and if what those of Alexandria tell us, relying upon the authority of Heraclides, be true, Homer was neither an idle, nor an unprofitable companion to him in his expedition. For when he was master of Egypt, designing to settle a colony of Grecians there, he resolved to build a large and populous city, and give it his own name. In order to which, after he had measured and staked out the ground with the advice of the best architects, he chanced one night in his sleep to see a wonderful vision; a grey-headed old man, of a venerable aspect, appeared to stand by him, and pronounce these verses:—

An island lies, where loud the billows roar,
Pharos they call it, on the Egyptian shore.

Alexander upon this immediately rose up and went to Pharos, which, at that time, was an island lying a little above the Canobic mouth of the river Nile, though it has now been joined to the main land by a mole. As soon as he saw the commodious situation of the place, it being a long neck of land, stretching like an isthmus between large lagoons and shallow waters on one side, and the sea on the other, the latter at the end of it making a spacious harbour, he said, Homer, besides his other excellences, was a very good architect...."

"Really!" said Dan amazed, "So Alexander is actually known to have had visions and credited them with having something to do with his copy of the Iliad, given to him by Aristotle! Well I am gob-smacked! That is truly amazing!"

"So that means the box we are looking for is the casket that Alexander took from Darius?" asked Alberto. "For some reason I was imaging a wooden box!"

"Oh no. "said Charlotte shaking her head. "It would be a treasure in its own right, gold or silver and studded with precious stones, possibly with marvellous and mythical animals sculptured in to it. It would have to be a singularly remarkable piece of art to have got a mention when it was first brought to Alexander, let alone to have been a fact worth repeating for over two thousand years."

"But why was Alexander buried in Egypt?" asked Elizabeth. "Surely he should have been buried in the Royal Tomb in Macedon. The one they think belongs to Alexander's father."

"That," said Charlotte., " is a complicated story."

25. The road to Babylon - May 323 BCE

"Are you alright my lord?" asked Ptolemy as he and the King rode side by side.

Alexander put his hand to his head. "My head and back ache and my skin still itches from the bites of those mosquitoes that swarmed us in the marshes. I will be glad to get back to Babylon and be able to bathe and rest."

"It will be good to see how the preparations for the Arabian Campaign have progressed while we have been away," said Ptolemy.

A shout from further up the line drew their attention. "It seems that we are almost there! A messenger is approaching."

A few minutes later the messenger rode up. "My lord!" he said, bowing his head as he reined his horse in.

Alexander smiled. "Peucestas! Welcome back. How did your mission among the Persians go?"

"Well, my Lord," said Peucestas, bringing his horse alongside Alexander's. "I have brought you twenty thousand men, all trained and eager to fight."

"All Persians?" asked Alexander. Peucestas nodded. "And the triremes? How do the shipbuilders progress?"

"There has been some minor disputes among the builders, but there are over nine hundred ships riding at anchor awaiting your inspection, my lord. I have been told that by June the last hundred or so will have been completed."

Alexander nodded.

"There are a number of envoys awaiting your return. The Athenians and the Spartans have sent sacred envoys, my Lord. They wish to present you with golden crowns,"

"Ha!" said Alexander derisively. "They do it out of fear, not love. Still, they do me more honour than my own countrymen who have not yet recognised my divinity!"

Peucestas looked across at Ptolemy who did not react to Alexander's statement.

"How go the preparation for Hephaestion's funeral pyre, Peucestas?" asked Alexander, a note of sadness entering his voice.

"The structure is finished, my Lord. It is an absolute marvel. All who see it stop and gaze at it in speechless wonder. Deinocrates has created a structure the like of which no one has ever before imagined."

Alexander nodded.

As the sun began to set they finally caught sight of the City. Two Ziggurats now graced its skyline. Rising above the city Alexander could see the now familiar step pyramid shape of the tower of Babylon. Rising to almost the same height, just outside the city walls, another giant structure now loomed.

As he approached the new structure Alexander reined in his horse and sat looking up at the funeral pyre he had ordered built for Hephaestion. In the fading daylight he could see Homer's Sirens standing, seventy metres above him, at the top of the pyre, silhouetted against the darkening sky. He could just make out the shape of their folded wings and their seductively feminine bodies, illuminated by the flickering light of torches. Inside each of the Sirens a singer sang a mournful lament for his dead friend that now echoed out over the gently undulating hills around Babylon.

His eyes travelled to the next level of the funeral pyre, the sixth of the seven steps that mimicked the great tower whose eminence it now challenged. Around this level he could make out rows of Greek and Persian weapons. Swords, sarissas, shields, breast plates and helmets gleamed and reflected the light of the torches.

On the level below that he could see the shapes of gilded lions and bulls, prancing and parading around the step on which they had been placed and on the level below them he could see Peirithoüs, King of the Lapiths, and his warriors fighting the centaurs. The centaurs looked incredibly realistic, their muscled flanks seemed to twitch and move as the torch light flickered. They were beautifully carved, reminding him of the carved centaurs on the Parthenon in Athens.

On the level below these mighty beasts were depictions of hunting scenes. In a passionate display of man against beast, naked hunters, clad only in billowing cloaks, speared horned stags. Enraged lions turned on hunters, desperately trying to defend themselves. Hunting dogs valiantly nipped at the heels and flanks of the beasts.

Alexander smiled sadly. The scene was so life like it reminded him of all the times that, as young men, he and Hephaestion had gone with Ptolemy, Perdiccas and the others on hunting expeditions into the Macedonian highlands. The good natured rivalry, the excitement of the hunt, the satisfaction of the kill! The boasting and the storytelling around the fire in the evening. It all seemed so far away, now. Simple pleasures lost.

The level below the hunting scene was decorated with flaming torches, each one seemingly carried aloft by an eagle, its wings outstretched.

The last level, closest to the ground, was adorned with the prows of galleys. Alexander knew that there were two hundred and forty of them evenly spaced around the base of the funeral pyre. On the prow of each stood two hoplites and two kneeling archers, standing watchful guard. Between each ship a red felt banner hung limply.

Alexander bowed his head, momentarily overwhelmed by feelings of guilt. Hephaestion was the only one who knew about Aristotle's potion. He knew what it did and had desperately wanted to use it. The competition between his Generals, his childhood friends, had always been robust. He acknowledged to himself that he had fostered that competition, leading his friends on to greater and greater achievements. In the beginning it had been all about skill at arms and who fought best on the day. As time went on though, it became more about strategy and tactics.

Hephaestion was a brilliant fighter. No one was better to have by your side during a melee. He was also the most trusted second in command but when it came to strategy and tactics he could not compete with the natural brilliance of the likes of Ptolemy and Perdiccas. They had the ability see the bigger picture and spot the battlefield opportunities when they arose. Hephaestion was always being left behind, and felt his lack of ability keenly.

Alexander had thought that promoting him to the position of commander of the Companion Cavalry, the most senior post in his army, would be the ideal solution. There was no one that Alexander trusted more to follow his orders. Hephaestion was like his right arm.

It was not until he was forced to intervene in a quarrel between Hephaestion and one of his other Macedonian Generals, Craterus, that he realised how the others perceived Hephaestion. The Macedonians saw him for what he was, a great fighter but a second rate Commander.

It was a shock to realise that was how he too saw him. It rankled Hephaestion. He desperately wanted to be seen as a leader in his own right. He had continually badgered Alexander to let him use Aristotle's potion and to let him fight independently as the others did from time to time.

Alexander had said no. He had thought no more of it, but clearly Hephaestion had. His friend had fallen ill with a fever when they were in the city of Ectabana. The fever had broken after seven days and Alexander had thought that Hephaestion was getting better and had gone to the games that the city had put on to honour him. While he was gone Hephaestion had found the vial that Alexander kept in Aristotle's secret compartment inside the scroll of the Iliad, by his bed, and drunk it. He was dead before Alexander could be called from the games.

A quiet cough behind him broke into his sad reverie. Alexander turned and saw Ptolemy waiting respectfully for him. Alexander took a deep breath. He turned his horse towards the Ishtar Gate, its blue glazed bricks and images of dragons and lions now glowing in the light of a full moon, and headed into Babylon along the Processional Way.

26. Babylon 9th June 323

Ptolemy knelt by Alexander's bed. Alexander was bathed in sweat. His face looked greasy, his hair dank and lifeless. "Brother", he said in a quiet voice. "Would that I could save your life as you did mine in India, but I do not have your knowledge of medicine, and none of these doctors here understand what ails you."

Alexander, who had been lying with his eyes closed, rolled his head towards Ptolemy. "I am dying, brother. Promise me that you will take me to Egypt when I am done with this body. Entomb me in the temple of Ammon where I can rest amongst my own. Promise me Ptolemy," he said, a sudden urgency in his voice.

Tears welled up in Ptolemy's eyes. "I will brother," he said. As soon as he said this Alexander's body relaxed. His breathing became shallower.

Ptolemy leant close to him and asked in a hoarse whisper, "Who will lead us when you are gone?" Alexander did not reply.

Ptolemy stayed, kneeling at Alexander's bedside, listening to his breathing become shallower and shallower, until night fell and he retired to his own apartments.

He was woken the next morning with the news that Alexander had died.

27. Rome - Present day

"Here upon the palace was filled with cries and lamentations; and by and by, all was hushed again as if it had been some lonesome waste, their grief being now turned into a ferocious reflection on what would ensue. The young noblemen who used to guard his person, were no longer able to contain their grief, nor keep themselves within the entrance of the palace, but ran about like so many mad men, filling the whole city with sadness, and omitting no kind of complaint that sorrow can suggest. on such an occasion."

"The troops therefore that used to keep guard without the palace, as well as barbarians and Macedonians, flocked thither, nor was it possible in their common affliction to discern the vanquished from the victors. The Persians called him 'their just and merciful lord' and the Macedonians 'the best and bravest of kings."

"They were not contended to utter their mournful expressions, but also gave way to transports of indignation "that so young a prince, in the very flower of his age and fortune, should through the envy of the gods, be so suddenly snatched for life and government. That they now imagined they beheld that cheerful and resolute countenance with which he used to lead them to battle, besiege the towns, scale the walls, and reward the brave. Then the Macedonians repented they had ever denied him divine honours, and owned they were both impious and ungrateful to have denied his ears the satisfaction of a title that was so fully his due."

"So wrote Quintus Curtius Rufus," said Charlotte.

"So what did he actually die of?" asked Elizabeth.

"Well, there is a whole range of options from bad lifestyle choices and alcohol poisoning, through conspiracy theories that involve strychnine poisoning to typhoid fever, to malaria. Given the evidence in the source material, and not knowing about Aristotle's potion, and the fact that he had just spent a few weeks in the mosquito infested swamps south of Babylon just prior to falling ill, I would have put my money on falciparum malaria," said Charlotte. "Now I am not so sure."

"And what happened after he died. Who took over?" asked Elizabeth, intrigued with the story.

"Well, this is where it starts to get really interesting. " said Charlotte with a grin. "This was the ultimate, untimely, power vacuum. The sources say that Alexander gave his royal signet ring to Perdiccas and that, when he was asked to whom he bequeathed his kingdom he replied, 'To the strongest'.

"The back story is that, at the time, One of Alexander's, Dad's old Generals, Antipater, was back in Macedonia looking after the home front. Alexander's wife Roxane was pregnant. Perdiccas was Alexander's chiliarchos, his chief military officer, but he wasn't royal, so to speak, so if Alexander did give him his ring it would have been to signify that he was to be regent, not King."

"There is also a story that Alexander had a son, Heracles, with a mistress by the name of Barsine. The strange thing is that he doesn't come up as a possible successor until ten or so years later, when he becomes the centre of a later succession plot."

"That still hadn't been sorted out ten years after Alexander died?" asked Elizabeth, amazed.

"After ten years they were just warming up," said Charlotte enthusiastically. "World domination is a hell of a prize to fight for! The war of the Diadochi lasted for nearly fifty years!"

Diadochi?' asked Alberto.

"'The Diadochi were the successors, Alexander's Generals" answered Charlotte.

"Crumbs!" said Elizabeth. "So we've got Generals, old and new, unborn heirs and illegitimate heirs. It could hardly be more complicated!"

"It was," said Charlotte. "Do you remember that I told you about Alexander's father's other son, Philip Arrhidaeus? He was actually Alexander's older brother!"

"Remind me, why wasn't he King, rather than Alexander?" asked Alberto.

"Because, he wasn't very bright. Listen to this," she said tapping on her laptop keyboard. "*Arrhidaeus, who was Philip's son by an obscure woman of the name of Philinna, was himself of weak intellect, not that he had been originally deficient either in body or mind; on the contrary, in*

563

his childhood, he had showed a happy and promising character enough. But a diseased habit of body, caused by drugs which Olympias gave him, had ruined not only his health, but his understanding."

"Good God! A wicked stepmother as well! So what happened in Babylon?" said Elizabeth.

"There was a bit of a brawl. " said Charlotte, " but in the end Perdiccas was appointed regent for Philip Arrhidaeus and Alexander's unborn child."

"Philip Arrhidaeus was king, but Perdiccas pulled the strings. Antipater stayed as regent in Macedon, controlling the European army. Then, the evil step mother, Olympias, got involved again!"

"Those evil step mothers just can't leave it alone, can they?" said Elizabeth with a glance at Charlotte and a slightly self conscious laugh.

"Olympias offered her daughter, Cleopatra, in marriage, to Perdiccas. This would have been a game changer for Perdiccas, who then would have been Alexander's brother in law and part of the royal family. His path to world domination would have been assured."

"Sounds like a no brainer!" said Alberto. "But I'm guessing it was more complicated than that?"

"Charlotte nodded. Perdiccas was already engaged to a lady by the name of Nicaea, who happened to be the daughter of Antipater."

"The bloke controlling the armies back in Macedonia?" queried Elizabeth.

"The same. " said Charlotte."He was not a happy daddy when he heard that his little girl might be cast aside."

"Man what a soap opera!" exclaimed Elizabeth.

"It was all a bit of mess then, but back to topic, what about poor old Alexander, while all this was going on?" asked Dan.

"The sources say that they just left the body lying on his bed while they argued with one another. Then, five days later, the embalmers went in," said Charlotte.

"God, the stench must have been horrible! Babylon in June must have been stinking hot!" said Alberto. "It must have been at least in the high twenties every day!"

"Yeah, you'd think that the body would have started to putrefy by then, but people writing at the time actually wrote that they found the body uncorrupted!" said Charlotte.

"How is that possible?" said Elizabeth.

"It could suggest that Alexander didn't actually die when they thought he did. Cerebral malaria is one of the possible complications of falciparum malaria. Cerebral malaria almost always ends in the patient lapsing into a coma."

"So he could have been alive when they started embalming him?" said Elizabeth, horrified.

"I guess he could have been, but these were Egyptian and Chaldaean embalmers. They would have been the best in their business. They would have realised he was alive if they cut into him and he started to bleed everywhere," said Charlotte.

"His body was preserved in "island honey and hipatic aloe" according to one writer. Another said that a mixture of honey and spices were added to his coffin. Whatever it was we can be pretty certain that his body was well preserved."

"His body was placed in a coffin of hammered gold that was fitted to his body. I guess it was probably like an Egyptian sarcophagus. I'm thinking King Tut's mask on steroids! Unfortunately it was melted down by some Pharaoh in around 80 BCE to pay his army, so it no longer exists," said Charlotte shrugging.

"It took about a year for Alexander's brother to prepare a magnificent catafalque to move Alexander and his coffin," said Charlotte.

"A catflap?" asked Alberto, laughing.

"A cat-a-falque. It comes from the word catafalco," she said to Alberto, laughing. "It's a moveable platform in which to put a casket. Let me read this to you... I'll leave out the boring bits..."

"...they prepared a coffin of the proper size for the body, made of hammered gold, and the space about the body they filled with spices such as could make the body sweet smelling and incorruptible. Upon this chest there had been placed a cover of gold. .... Over this was laid a magnificent purple robe embroidered with gold, beside which they placed the arms of the deceased."

"Then it describes the catafalque... *At the top of the carriage was built a vault of gold, eight cubits wide and twelve long, which would be* about three and half metres by five and a half, *covered with overlapping scales set with precious stones.*"

"*Beneath the roof all along the work was a rectangular cornice of gold, from which projected heads of goat-stags in high relief. Gold rings, two palms broad were suspended from these, and through the rings there ran a festive garland beautifully decorated in bright colours of all kinds. At the ends there were tassels...suspending large bells, so that any who were approaching heard the sound from a great distance. On each corner of the vault on each side was a golden figure of Victory holding a trophy. The colonnade that supported the vault was of gold with Ionic capitals. Within the colonnade was a golden net, made of cords the thickness of a finger, which carried four long painted tablets, their ends adjoining, each equal in length to a side of the colonnade.*"

"Are you starting to get a picture of this thing?" asked Charlotte.

Alberto shook his head. "This thing must have weighed tons! How the hell did they move it?"

"Ah, it says here, hang on, let me find the bit....*the body of the chariot beneath the covered chamber had two axles upon which turned four Persian wheels, the naves and spokes of which were gilded, but the part that bore upon the ground was of iron.* "

"Blah blah, more gold, blah blah... and then .... *Along the middle of their length the axles had a bearing ingeniously fitted to the middle of the chamber in such a way that, thanks to it, the chamber could remain undisturbed by shocks from rough places....*They built shock absorbers into it.... *There were four poles, and to each of them were fastened four teams with four mules harnessed in each team, so that in all there were sixty-four mules, selected for their strength and size. Each of them was crowned with ...* more gold jewels and stuff... and ...*it was accompanied by a crowd of road menders and mechanics, and also by soldiers sent to escort it.*"

"Wow!' said Dan. "So we are talking about something bigger in size than a shipping container, requiring seventy or eighty horsepower to pull it, made of an absolute truck load of gold.

"There is a reference in one document, potentially faked, that says that Alexander's coffin alone weighed 200 talents, which would be about," Charlotte thought for a moment, "five thousand two hundred kilograms of pure gold."

"Man! At today's gold prices that would be worth somewhere in the region of three hundred million dollars!" exclaimed Dan. "And that was only the coffin. Add in the cat-flap and we are talking Fort Knox on wheels!"

"And get this for understatement. This is the same writer, Diodorus... *it appeared more magnificent when seen than when described....* and I left out half the description, most of the description which read gold, jewels, gold, gold gold and more gold!" said Charlotte shaking her head.

"Where were they taking this traveling show? Back to Macedon?" asked Elizabeth.

"Initially yes, but this is where the body snatching part of the story begins," said Charlotte sitting forward in her seat and grinning enthusiastically.

28. Northern Syria - 321 BCE

Ptolemy sat on the edge of his bed looking across at the small bust of Alexander he kept with him when he was away from home.

"Home." he whispered to himself. "Where is home?" He was now ruling Egypt on behalf of Philip Arrhidaeus and Alexander and Roxanne's infant son, named Alexander in memory of his father. Home had been the hills of Macedon. Now home was the Egyptian city of Memphis on the banks of the Nile River.

He stood up and walked across to the small bust and picked it up. He smiled. The sculptor had captured that look that Alexander had, head slightly tilted to one side. He fancied that he could see a little of himself in the features that the artist had captured in the hard cold marble. He placed the bust back on the table. "I will not let them take you back to Aegae. You will be buried as you wished in Egypt!" he promised, "Even though it will likely cause the world to fall apart!"

Ptolemy had been sent word that the grand army was heading north. Perdiccas was accompanying them, at least part of the way, honouring some of the older hands who would finally be returning home to Macedon.

The catafalque, with Alexander's body, was rumbling its way slowly North. It was only a half days ride away. Ptolemy knew that this was his best, perhaps only chance, to fulfil his promise to Alexander.

****

Arrhidaeus reigned in his horse as Ptolemy approached. "Greetings Ptolemy. I am surprised to see you here. You are a long way from your responsibilities in Egypt!"

"That may be true, Arrhidaeus," said Ptolemy as he brought his horse to a stop beside Arrhidaeus, "but I have a greater responsibility," he said nodding towards the catafalque in the distance. "As you know, Perdiccas has made a decision to take Alexander back to Macedon, against Alexander's express wishes. I made a promise to Alexander that I would look after his body and have it interred in the temple of Ammon in Egypt. It is a promise that I intend to keep!"

Arrhidaeus smiled. "I have no love for Perdiccas, but you know what will happen if I give you charge of Alexander's remains. It will mean war! Do you think you can stand against Perdiccas and the Grand Army?"

"Perhaps." smiled Ptolemy. "Their is little love lost between myself and Perdiccas, as you well know. There are few among us who would willingly follow him had it not been Alexander's explicit wish that he be Regent." He paused and thought for a moment. "I believe that war between myself and Perdiccas is inevitable. We have all heard the rumours of him planning to marry Cleopatra. That can only mean that he has ambitions beyond the regency. Antipater has already sent messages of goodwill from Macedon, suggesting an alliance, should I ever feel that I need support against Perdiccas. It is only a matter of time Arrhidaeus."

"If I need a reason to die, I would rather it be to fulfil a promise to a man like Alexander than to defend Egypt against the grubby ambitions of a man like Perdiccas," said Ptolemy, bitterly.

"Well said, Ptolemy," said Arrhidaeus, with a smile. "You also know that if I were to be...," he paused and looked at the small group of men that had accompanied Ptolemy, and then back at the honour guard of hardened Macedonian veterans that accompanied him. "... overwhelmed by your superior force, that I would have to send word to Perdiccas as fast as possible that the catafalque has been seized by you."

"I would expect nothing less," said Ptolemy, his expression deadpan.

"You will need to give me some time to consult with my men," said Arrhidaeus. Ptolemy nodded, and Arrhidaeus turned his horse around and walked it back towards the Macedonian officers waiting a short distance away.

A short while later Arrhidaeus returned. "It seems that my men feel that they are dishonouring their former King by going against his wishes. They wish you luck, Ptolemy, in your desire to fulfill your commitment to him. They insist that they too, must fulfill their commitment to see their King's body safely to its destination. They will stay with the catafalque, wherever it goes.

Ptolemy nodded, turned his horse back towards the south and began leading the procession towards Egypt. Behind him, two horsemen broke from the honour guard and galloped north.

29. Southern Syria - 321 BCE

Ptolemy had got into the habit of looking over his shoulder. He knew Perdiccas well enough to know that he would not be able to let his hijacking of Alexander's funeral procession go unchallenged. There was too much at stake.

Under the Macedonian constitution, it was the prerogative of the new monarch to bury his predecessor. Both he and Perdiccas were familiar with the prophecy that said that the royal line would end when the kings of Macedon were no longer buried in the royal cemetery at Aegae. More importantly, for the ambitions of Perdiccas, would be the likely reaction of Olympias, his potential future mother-in-law, if her son was not returned to Macedon to be buried in the Royal Tombs and was not cremated in accordance with Macedonian custom.

It had been almost a month since he had led the catafalque and its entourage on its journey South. He had travelled as fast as he could, but there was a limit to the speed at which the heavy and cumbersome vehicle could move. He had posted scouts to keep watch for an army coming from the North. He expected them any day now.

When the shout came that a cavalry troop were heading towards them it came almost as a relief. Ptolemy turned to the honour guard of Macedonians.

"Perdiccas has sent a troop of Macedonian cavalry to retrieve the catafalque. He knows the strength of arms that we have guarding this greatest of treasures and has sent a troop large enough to overwhelm us. I will talk to their commander. I do not want you to fight your brothers. I will try to persuade them to leave us in peace to continue the journey that Alexander wished to take."

The men nodded. A few shouted that they would fight to the death to ensure that Alexander's dying wish was kept.

Ptolemy glanced at Arrhidaeus, and turned his horse around. They rode out towards the approaching cavalry together.

****

Ptolemy and Arrhidaeus sat astride their horses watching as the men that had been sent in pursuit of the catafalque rode closer. Ptolemy recognised the leading horsemen, the brothers Polemon and Attalus. He gritted his teeth. He disliked both men, but Polemon particularly. Polemon had been implicated in the Philotas, affair, a plot to kill Alexander. When Philotas' treachery was exposed and he was put on trial, Polemon ran away. Had it not been for his older brother, Amyntas, defending him in court, Polemon would likely have shared Philotas' fate, being stoned and speared to death.

Ptolemy wasn't surprised to see Polemon and Attalus leading the troop. They were among Perdiccas closest friends, and, in his mind, like attracted like.

"Greetings Attalus. Greetings Polemon!" said Ptolemy politely when they approached.

Attalus returned his greeting, but Polemon just sat glaring at him. Seeing how it would be, Ptolemy ignored him.

"You know why we have come Ptolemy. We are prepared to fight you if you do not turn the catafalque over to us," said Attalus, bluntly.

"Could I not persuade you of the wrong you are doing our King by not honouring his wish that he be buried in Egypt?' asked Ptolemy.

"He's dead, Ptolemy," said Polemon sullenly. "We know why you are doing this. There is enough gold in that thing to pay a hundred thousand men at arms. Perdiccas will not give you the chance to build an army to stand against the rightful heirs of Macedon."

Ptolemy raised an eyebrow. "You think I do this for gold?"

Polemon stared balefully at him. "There is nothing else worth having on that cart!" he said, and then spat deliberately on the ground.

Ptolemy put his hand on the hilt of his sword. "You dishonour our King when he is unable to defend himself. You have no honour, Polemon. You were a coward when your friend Philotas was proven to be a treasonous bastard, and you are still a coward."

Attalus held up his arm. "Hold Ptolemy. My brother is tired from our long ride. He does not mean you or Alexander any disrespect!"

"Your brothers always seem to be making excuses for you Polemon!" spat Ptolemy. "I will not accept an apology from his brother. If you want the Catafalque then you will have to fight for it!" he said angrily, turning his horse away from Attalus.

"Hold Ptolemy. We are all Macedonians. It should not be necessary for us to fight. You can see that we outnumber you at least three to one. What would be the point of fighting?" said Attalus.

Ptolemy turned back to look at him.

Polemon grinned at him. "Come now brother, if Ptolemy wishes to fight then let us oblige him!" he said, then, turning to Ptolemy, "This is one fight that you can not win, Ptolemy" he sneered. "You are no Alexander! We will crush you!"

"I will make you a proposition Attalus," said Ptolemy. "Your brother has offended me and my king. For that I demand satisfaction. I propose that he and I fight tomorrow. Whoever is left alive can take the catafalque!'

The blood drained from Polemon's face. He looked horrified, but his brother nodded. "I would prefer that we settled this without resorting to a battle. So be it, Ptolemy. You and Polemon will fight tomorrow. I would ask though that the fight be left until the cool of the evening and that Polemon be given time to recuperate after our long ride."

Ptolemy nodded agreement. "We fight tomorrow evening, then." Ptolemy turned his horse back towards his camp. Polemon and Attalus turned in the opposite direction, back towards their own men.

****

Polemon leaned towards his brother. "Are you mad, brother? I am not going to fight Ptolemy. He will slaughter me!"

"Do not worry Polemon, I have no intention of letting you fight him, brother. By morning we will be gone and we will take the catafalque with us! If Ptolemy wants to chase us to recover it then we will be forced to do battle. He would be a fool if he did." Attalus slapped his brother on the back. "Come on little brother, let us go and get some rest. We have a long night ahead of us I am afraid."

That evening Arrhidaeus set a light guard on the catafalque. The fight between Ptolemy and Polemon had created a great deal of excitement among the men and a festive atmosphere had fallen over the camp. The festive mood was heightened when soldiers from Attalus and Polemon's cavalry troop joined them later in the evening. Many of the men had fought together under Alexander in both Persia and India and knew each other well. Lubricated with wine and gossip the revelry went on late into the evening.

****

Ptolemy awoke the next morning to the news that Polemon, Attalus and their men had disappeared. They had taken the catafalque with them.

Arrhidaeus looked crest fallen as he reported to Ptolemy the extent of the disaster. Ptolemy studied Arrhidaeus's face. He looked devastated by the loss of the catafalque. The two men stood, looking at each other for a few minutes, Ptolemy looking angry, Arrhidaeus looking despondent. A smile started to flicker at the corner of Arrhidaeus mouth. Ptolemy strained to maintain his angry expression. Arrhidaeus cracked first, bursting into laughter. Under such provocation Ptolemy let out a huge guffaw.

"Did you see Polemon's face when his brother agreed that you two should fight?" laughed Arrhidaeus. "I think that he thought his brother was serious!"

"I thought so too for a few moments, but I could see Attalus' scheming mind working away. With us off guard and looking forward to the fight he figured he could take the catafalque and be gone by the time we noticed. I imagine he and Polemon are probably still congratulating themselves on their cleverness."

"What I would really like to see is their faces when they realise that the coffin in the catafalque is not Alexander's." laughed Ptolemy.

Arrhidaeus chuckled. "Perdiccas will not be happy!" and then in a more sober tone. "You do realise that Perdiccas will not let this subterfuge go unchallenged. By this deception you have made it inevitable that Perdiccas will bring the Grand Army back to Egypt! You will have to fight him!"

"I know," said Ptolemy sadly. "But in this I had no choice. I gave Alexander my word that I word bury him in Egypt. Then, after a brief pause, "Gather up the men, Arrhidaeus, I would like to catch up with Alexander, before he reaches Memphis, and he has a good five days start on us.

30. Rome - Present day

"So Alexander's body went to Memphis, not Alexandria?" asked Elizabeth.

"Initially," said Charlotte. "Alexandria was less then ten years old at the time the coffin arrived in Egypt, and would still have been, pretty much, a building site. Rufius Curtius says that '*Alexander's body was taken to Memphis by Ptolemy, in whose power Egypt had fallen, and transferred thence a few years later to Alexandria, where every mark of respect continues to be paid to his memory.*'"

"In fact, it is more likely that it was Ptolemy's son, Ptolemy Philadelphus, who moved the coffin to Alexandria once a mausoleum had been built for it."

"And what happened to Perdiccas? Did he end up attacking Ptolemy?" asked Alberto.

"He did. He took the Grand Army and tried to cross the Nile, but failed, drowning many of his own men. In the end his own officers stabbed him to death in his tent. The old man, Antipater, ended up as the sole regent."

"Let us say that all this is true, and Alexander's body was in Alexandria," said Elizabeth. "That would mean that Aristotle makes this stuff for Alexander. Hamilcar must have stolen the, what did you call it, casket copy of the Iliad, and the casket itself from Alexander's tomb. Hamilcar must have then discovered the potion, and presumably how to make it, when he opened the casket. He then gives the potion to his son, who fights the Romans' but the recipe, and maybe some potion, is left in Spain where Julius Caesar finds it."

"So far so good!" said Dan, passing Elizabeth a fresh cup of coffee.

"Julius passes it on to his adopted son, Octavian, who becomes the first Emperor Augustus. Augustus doesn't have any children of his own, but passes the secret to his wife Livia. Livia doesn't trust her own children or her grandchildren, so she doles the stuff out carefully, keeping control of it. The potion doesn't have a good effect on those in her direct line, but she has died by the time that becomes really obvious.

576

Clever lady that she is though, she establishes a cult that holds the secret of the potion. The cult eventually identifies Constantine the Great as the one to whom they will pass the secret."

Elizabeth took a sip of coffee.

"Constantine, just like Augustus, discovers how the potion can be a focus for disunity and, before he dies decides that the secret needs to be protected, so he sends it away from the Imperial court, to one of the leaders of the new cult that he has adopted, the Bishop of Rome, the Pope."

Alberto nodded.

"While the secret recipe is sent to Rome inside its casket, presumably with some of the ingredients, vials of the potion still exist in Constantinople. Constantine is raised to Apostle status by the church in the east and the vials, which are believed to contain his blood, in accordance with the new religion, become venerated as sacred objects."

"We think that Attila the Hun got hold of one of the vials, probably from Honoria, the daughter of the Emperor Constantius and the fabulous Galla Placidia."

"Alaric must have heard about the potion from someone, perhaps Stilicho, and gone in search of it. He eventually finds it during the sack of Rome, and then dies after taking it."

"From what Alberto has uncovered, it is highly likely that a number of Popes used the potion over the years. Some it made great, others it turned mad or killed. Out of desperation, to save his fragmenting church, Pope Pius the sixth gives the potion to a young Napoleon Bonaparte, in exchange for a promise to restore the church in France. Napoleon uses the potion, giving a couple of people vials of the stuff for safe keeping. One he gets back while he is exiled on Elba, the other he gives to his Mamluk servant Roustam Raza. The first runs out before the Battle of Waterloo, the second ends up in the hands of Adolf Hitler." Elizabeth stopped and looked around the room.

"Pretty good summary, Liz!" said Charlotte. "But you have forgotten about the other part of this story. The Dragas part."

"Ah, yes!" said Dan. "This is the bit that touches on what I have been doing. From what Liz told us about the Dragas view of the world,

Constantine the eleventh escaped the sack of Constantinople with a vial of what he believed was the Blood of Constantine. At some stage, after escaping Constantinople, he must have taken the potion. He wrote down his experiences with the potion and described his vision for a future which focused on the restoration of Constantinople to its Christian origins, the restoration of his family to its heritage and the humiliation of the Saracens."

"Dragas said that he was the direct descendant of Constantine Palaiologos. That, however, is not strictly true. From what I have discovered, tracing his lineage back, the family Dragas has used that particularly Roman style of perpetuating a strong family, the adoption of heirs.

Andris Dragas was adopted by the previous patriarch of the family, who was an extremely capable, and incredibly influential, individual. He did have two children of his own, one daughter and one son. The son was a bit of a wastrel and was killed in a hit and run car accident in the early eighties. The daughter was a few years older and a bit of a wild child. She took an overdose and ended her days in a mental institution."

Dan looked at Elizabeth, who had gone pale. "Are you OK?" he asked.

"Keep going with the story. I am Ok!" she mumbled.

Dan gave her a questioning look, but continued. "Andris Dragas was in fact an executive in one of the Dragas businesses. He was a second cousin, until he was adopted."

"Tracing the family back, and I can tell you it was difficult, I found half a dozen adoptions over a dozen generations, always cousins, always the most capable individuals. This family is very secretive. They live below the radar and have massive wealth and massive influence. I wouldn't be surprised at all if what Dragas told Liz about being behind a couple of wars was perfectly true, and probably only the tip of the iceberg. These guys have been serious players for as far back as I could track them. I think we should take the threats he made extremely seriously."

There were all lost in their own thoughts when the intercom from the front door buzzed.

Dan looked up. "Who could that be?" he asked walking over to the screen. "Fuck! Its Thomas Malm, and he doesn't look happy!"

"Is he alone?" asked Alberto jumping to his feet and coming over to the security screen. He tapped at the controls and four separate views of the front door and its surrounds appeared on the single screen. "He's alone!" he said to Dan.

Dan thought for a moment, "I suppose we had better let him in!"

****

Thomas Malm entered the room. He was impeccably dressed, as always, and his demeanour was polite and reserved. "I am glad to see that you are all ... well," he said casting an eye over their various scrapes, bumps, bruises and bandages.

He turned to Alberto. "Ah! Mister Nardovino I have read your file with great interest. Very impressive! I am glad that you have ended up in league with my friends. I think had you not, they may all well be dead by now," he said without drama. "Although," he said turning to Dan, "Your rescue of Elizabeth from the Dragas' yacht was most...inventive! I had not anticipated such resourceful inventiveness! I understand that Andris Dragas is most annoyed at the damage that you inflicted on his home."

"Did he tell you that?" asked Elizabeth, her tone accusatory.

Thomas looked around at Elizabeth, a questioning look on his face. "Now why would you ask that question, Elizabeth?" He surveyed the faces of the people that stood around the room. The hostility and distrust was palpable.

"Why are you here Thomas, and what do you want?" asked Dan, bluntly.

Thomas looked at Dan, his head cocked to one side. "I had expected a more friendly reception, Daniel. I came, first of all, to see if you were alright. I also came to find out about the analysis of the potion. Thirdly I came to discuss what you have got yourselves involved in and to give you some information that you might not have discovered, although I am beginning to think that, perhaps, you may know more about what is going on than I do."

"How did you know that we had been analysing the potion?' asked Elizabeth, suspiciously.

Thomas looked surprised. "Because you told me! You even gave me some of the preliminary results!"

"When?" said Elizabeth.

"When you were in London. What is going on here?" asked Thomas, momentarily confused. Before he received an answer a thought flashed through his mind, "My God! You've found a sample of the original potion!" His surprise was so spontaneous that it was clear that he had not known.

The looks that passed between Dan, Charlotte, Alberto and Elizabeth confirmed it for him.

"Do you realise how much danger you are in? If Dragas finds out that you have the potion he would move heaven and earth, literally, to get it! Your lives would not be worth the cost of a cup of coffee!"

Then it struck him. "He has got it as well! But .... he doesn't know that you have it! If he did you wouldn't all be sitting here so calmly!" he said turning on Dan, who was never very good at disguising his emotions.

"Good gracious!" he said sitting down, uninvited. "This changes everything!" he had gone deathly white, all the blood drained from his face.

Elizabeth asked him if he was OK. He didn't hear her. He shook his head distractedly, lost in his own thoughts.

Dan poured him a glass of whiskey and passed it to him. Thomas took it automatically. He drank it in a single swallow.

Then the penny dropped. "... and you must have been watching Dragas' yacht in Amalfi when I got on board! Of course, you rang me and saw me answer my phone! You didn't even need to see my face!"

He looked at Elizabeth. "And now you think I am in league with Dragas. Of course you do," he said almost to himself. "Not surprising you blew me off in Amalfi the morning we were meant to have breakfast, and have not been in touch since. My behaviour must have seemed duplicitous at best, perhaps even traitorous."

No one spoke. They all just stared impassively at Thomas, who gave a sigh and said, "I think that I had better tell you a story. It may be hard for you to believe some aspects of it, but I believe that, what I am about to tell you, is essentially true."

"I was recruited to work with MI6 in the late 1970's, while I was still studying at Oxford. I was reading history, which didn't seem to me to be a discipline that would offer much to her Majesty's Secret Service, but I soon found out how wrong I could be!"

"After passing through basic training, and getting some field experience in East Germany, I was called into the office of the Chief. I was informed that I had been selected to work on a particularly sensitive assignment. He told me that I would have a bit of reading to do and set me up in an office connected to his. It took me nearly a month to work through the files that I was given to read. What I read, literally, changed my view of the world."

"The oldest file came from the time of Henry VIII. Did you know that Thomas Cromwell, Henry's Chief Minister, ran a network of spies throughout Europe? No? Neither did I! That was where the story started, with Thomas Cromwell."

"Cromwell was the son of a blacksmith from Putney. He spent some time in his youth in Europe, perhaps fighting as a mercenary, no one is really sure, but ended up living in the home of a Florentine banker by the name of Francesco Frescobaldi. There is some evidence of his activities documented in the Vatican Archives that indicate that Cromwell was working as an agent for the Archbishop of York."

"The thing about Thomas Cromwell, though, is how he transformed himself from a blacksmith's son who left England on an adventure, and returned as a worldly wise, sophisticated and well connected individual. Something happened in Europe, perhaps in Italy, which changed him. Someone spent a lot of time schooling him in the art of politics. Anyway, as most of you know, he became Henry's right arm, his Chief Minister, and incredibly influential. He was the one that effectively brought about the reformation of the Roman Catholic Church in England. He was eventually brought down, charged with treason, heresy and corruption.

He was executed, without trial. His head was placed on a spike on London Bridge."

"In hindsight, Thomas Cromwell, and his "European Education" was the first clue that an individual, a group of individuals or an organisation, were actively attempting to influence English foreign and domestic policy. It was the first real English spy master, Sir Francis Walsingham, Elizabeth the first's Principal Secretary, who was the first to properly investigate what Cromwell had been up to. He was the first to start to put together a realistic picture of what was going on."

"Walsingham discovered that someone was promoting the reformation of the church in England and in other parts of Europe, and working against the revival of the Roman Catholic Church. In some instances, he discovered, they were actively trying to corrupt and discredit the church. Now, this didn't really bother the Tudors, given their own ambitions. They didn't see these activities as a threat. If anything they were helping to advance the Tudor's own agenda, but it was certainly something to keep an eye on."

"Over the centuries the people behind this influence were identified. It turned out that they were a family that fled Constantinople following its sack in 1453. MI6 and its predecessors put a lot of work into keeping on eye on the family. Their aims were simple. The destruction of the Roman Catholic Church, the return of Constantinople to its place as the centre of the Christian Church and the humiliation of Islam. They have even been implicated in the actual, and attempted, assassinations of various Popes. The family name is Dragas!' he said dramatically. N-one reacted. They all just continued to stare at him.

"My God! You already know all this!"

Dan nodded. "Yes, we do Thomas. Nothing you have told us is new."

"Well, here is something you may not know. The Dragas family has been using the Blood of Constantine for centuries. Unfortunately for them they have gradually been running out of it. There is a tradition in the Dragas family that the chosen heir to the family legacy drinks the blood of Constantine on his fourteenth birthday. For the last few generations they have only had just enough to give the head of the family a few drops. It is apparently not enough to affect the mind."

"The relic, the one that Hitler was trying to replicate, comes from Constantinople. It has the power to enhance a person's mind! Hitler took it and nearly destroyed the world!" he said less dramatically this time. He looked at the faces around him,. "You know that too, huh?"

They all nodded.

"We, that is MI6, were told about this stuff by Rudolf Hess when he was first captured. That's how we got to know about the Hitler potion in the first place. It was why Churchill was so intransigent about any treaty with Hitler. He knew that Hitler had taken the potion and didn't have any more."

"Churchill knew that Hitler was trying to reproduce the stuff, but he gambled on the fact that he wouldn't be able to and therefore be unlikely to match the successes that he had in the first few years of the war."

"The people at MI6 thought, at the time, that the Blood of Constantine was a code name for a Nazi secret weapon, a mind-altering drug. It was the report on the Blood of Constantine that inspired the American's MKUltra program. They were, in part, trying to replicate the effects that Hess described for the drug. In their analysis of Morell's version of the drug, at least the one that Hess brought to England, they found traces of ergot in the potion."

"Ergot?" asked Alberto.

"Its a fungus found on rye grain. Its the source for LSD, Lysergic acid diethylamide," said Thomas. "The MKUltra program had a big focus on LSD.

"Did you know about how they persuaded Churchill to attack the Dardanelles during the First World War?" he asked cautiously.

They all nodded.

"The Mayerling incident?"

They all nodded.

"9/11?"

They all nodded.

"So you would also know about your wife's death then. I am so sorry, that must have been a dreadful shock for you." said Thomas looking regretful.

"What! No!" said Dan, shocked.

Thomas looked up. Elizabeth was staring at her hands resting in her lap. Alberto looked confused. Charlotte and Dan both looked shocked. Thomas suddenly realised that he had just been, inadvertently, extremely callous. He was thinking frantically how he could recover from this situation when Elizabeth spoke.

"Dragas had Sarah killed so that they could get Barry Critchley into your business. Dragas told me when I was on his boat," said Elizabeth in a quiet voice. Thomas could see tears rolling down her cheeks. She didn't look up.

Dan was staring at her, a look of total betrayal on his face. He turned to look out the window. "How could you know this and not tell me! How could you betray me like this!" he said in a cold, hard voice devoid of emotion.

Elizabeth kept looking down, unable to meet his gaze.

"Get out!" he said in a quiet flat voice. "Get out of my apartment!"

Charlotte gasped. She looked at her father. She had never seen him really angry, really hurt. His calmness was awful. "No, Dad!" she cried. You can't! Liz had nothing to do with it!"

Dan looked across at his daughter. He stared into her eyes for a few moments. Tears welled up in them. He turned away and walked out of the room. They all heard the front door slam as he left the apartment.

Charlotte turned to Alberto. "Go after him, please!" she begged, tears streaming down her face. "Keep him safe!" Alberto nodded. A few moments later the door of the apartment closed quietly as Alberto hurried after Dan.

Neither Charlotte nor Thomas spoke. Elizabeth sobbed quietly to herself. "I couldn't bring myself to tell him. I just couldn't...!"

Charlotte came and sat beside her. She put an arm around her shoulders.

****

Dan was angry. He knew that he had never really gotten over Sarah's death. It was still a wound very close to the surface.

The police had told him that the driver of the stolen car that had rammed Sarah's car had probably been drunk, or high on drugs. Sarah's killer had run off and had never been caught. In his mind he felt that there had never been any real closure. No-one had paid for her death, except for Charlotte and him. He paid for it every day. Every time he looked into Charlotte's face he could see Sarah staring back. Their eyes were the same shape and colour. Their faces were the same shape. They had the same smile. The only difference was the colour of their hair. As Charlotte had grown older the similarity had become even stronger. Now, as a twenty six year old, Charlotte was the age that Sarah had been when she was killed. They could have been twins.

The last few weeks with Liz had been amazing. He had thought he had finally moved on. Now she had betrayed him in the most profound way. He couldn't imagine how she could have kept something so important a secret. How could she be happy, cheerful, loving, knowing something that, she must have realised, was so important to him?

It didn't make sense.

Dan had walked away from the apartment, turning away from the Tiber and heading east. He just wanted to walk. He wanted to think. He wanted to get away.

His thoughts turned back to Dragas. He could feel a deep, burning hatred developing inside him for the man that had killed, no, murdered his wife. He realised that Dragas would not have been driving the car, but that, in a way, made him hate him even more. He was, in Dan's mind, a manipulative, gutless coward.

He walked for an hour before he realised that he had no idea where he was. He had been walking along a main road, but had turned down a smaller side road to get away from the incessant noise of the cars. He now found himself standing outside the iron gates of a church. Wanting somewhere quiet to sit, he went through the gates and across a small courtyard. The building itself was brick, with a large circular rotunda rising above an arched portico.

He entered the church and was surprised by its simplicity. It was circular with pairs of marble Corinthian columns holding up the central dome. The ceiling of the church was covered with beautiful mosaics while some of the arched niches around the walls and the dome itself were covered in frescoes. The rest of the walls were bare bricks. It reminded him of the mausoleum of Galla Placidia in Ravenna.

Dan sat down in one of the seats that were lined up against a wall. He was the only person in the church. It was quiet and cool. He leaned his back against the brick work and closed his eyes.

"Funny that you should stop here Dottore," said a voice beside him, a few minutes later. "Did you know that Constantine the Great had this building built as a mausoleum for his daughters Constantina and Helena? There is a magnificent, carved porphyry sarcophagus, that came from here, in the Vatican, that is supposed to be Constantina's."

Dan looked across at Alberto. He was sitting a couple of chairs away. He hadn't heard him come in.

"You followed me?" he asked, leaning his head back against the wall and closing his eyes.

"I did. Your daughter wanted me to make sure you were safe," said Alberto quietly.

They both sat, ignoring each other for some time. No-one came into the church.

"Do you remember Dottore, when we were having dinner in Amalfi, and I told you how my apartment was bombed?" Alberto said in a quiet voice.

Dan nodded, but kept his eyes closed.

"I did not tell you the whole truth. Some things, as a man, you keep to yourself. Some things cause too much pain if they are shared."

"Oh spare me the pop psychology Alberto!" Dan said dismissively.

Alberto didn't say anything for a few minutes. "When the bomb went off in my apartment I was not alone," he said almost in a whisper.

Dan turned to him. Tears were rolling down Alberto's cheeks.

"When I first joined the Carabinieri I worked in a unit that was trying to deal with the trafficking of young women, children really. They were being brought into Italy to work in the sex trade. There was a priest, Father Rodriguez, who had a network of safe houses and foster homes, that used to take in the girls. He was one of the only people that cared. Most of my colleagues were hardened to it. Most of the politicians didn't care because there were no votes in it. They all went through the motions, but not too much more. There were always other priorities."

"One day Father Rodriguez was badly beaten up outside one of the safe houses. I was the one who took his statement at the hospital. The poor old man had been so badly brutalised that he could hardly talk through the swelling on his face. After I took his statement, I was about to leave, when he grabbed my hand. He begged me to check on the girls in the safe house."

"I talked to my commander about it when I got back to work. He told me to write up the report and get on with proper work. He told me it wasn't our job to go checking on a bunch of illegal immigrant whores."

"When I finished work that day I went to check. I was young. I was naive. I had promised the Padre. When I got there a couple of thugs were hanging around the front door. I watched for a while. The scumbags had taken it over and were using the safe house as a brothel. I got so mad I just went up to the front door and smashed their faces in. I went through the building kicking the Johns out. There were fifteen girls in that building. The youngest was fourteen, the oldest twenty four. They were all terrified of what would happen to their families back home."

"With the padre's help I relocated the girls to a new safe house. That was the start of a long association with Father Rodriguez. I would help out when I could, usually after work. He was the one that got me into the job with the Vatican police, when I came back from Afghanistan."

"While I was helping out with the girls I met Francesca. She was a psychologist that helped with some of the more difficult cases. She got me interested in studying Psych at university. She was absolutely gorgeous, a vision, a Madonna. She was kind, generous, loving. She was unbelievable. I fell madly in love with her the moment I saw her. Everyone loved her. All the girls that she helped loved her."

"It must have been obvious that I had fallen for her, because I kept finding myself left in places alone with her. Somehow the girls would conspire to get us alone together. Even the Padre got in on the act, inviting us both for coffee at the same place at the same time and then not showing up. He usually had some feeble excuse ready when we confronted him about it."

"After I came back from Afghanistan I asked Francesca to marry me. At that time of my life she was the only thing in the world that I thought was worth living for. I was damaged goods, but she said yes. She didn't have any family, and my mother had passed away by then, but my brother and sister came to the wedding and so did all the girls we had helped. The church was full to overflowing with them. They called themselves our cousins.

"Then, to make things even better Francesca got pregnant. I was over the moon. I could not believe that anyone could be as happy as I was. When the bomb went off, in that single moment, I lost everything that was precious to me. I have no proof, but I know now, in my heart, that Dragas was behind it."

Dan looked at Alberto. "I'm so sorry Alberto. I didn't realise."

"No reason why you should, Dottore. Like I said, sometimes it is too painful, too difficult, to share things. Sometimes you worry about whether the sharing of the information will do more harm than good."

"You think that I was wrong to get angry with Elizabeth, don't you?" he said.

Alberto nodded. "Dan, she is your best friend. It is obvious you love each other. She is family. Your daughter adores her. Perhaps she should have told you what Dragas told her when we rescued her from the yacht, but try and see it from her perspective. She didn't know if it was true, or if Dragas was just making things up to upset her. She had no way of knowing. If it wasn't true, then telling you would only needlessly hurt you."

Dan sat looking down at his hands. He knew that Alberto was right. It wasn't Liz he was angry at. She was as much a victim in this situation as he was.

He looked up into Alberto's eyes. "We both owe this bastard, big time. I vote we take him down, once and for all," he said coldly.

****

When Dan and Alberto walked into the apartment Thomas Malm was still there, talking to Elizabeth and Charlotte.

Charlotte ran to her father and hugged him. "Are you OK?" she asked holding on to him tightly. He nodded.

As Charlotte released him he looked across to where Elizabeth was sitting. She hadn't moved. Seeing her sitting there, uncharacteristically uncertain, he realised how wrong he had been and how much his behaviour must have hurt her. He walked over to her and knelt down in front of her. She wasn't looking at him and he could see that she was defiantly holding back tears. In that moment he realised how truly wrong he had been.

He took her chin gently in his hand and turned her head to face him. "Please forgive me. I was so wrong to have turned on you you like that. I love you, and I am so sorry."

Elizabeth looked into Dan's eyes. He felt like a searchlight had turned on his soul. After what seemed like forever, she reached forward and hugged him. "I know." she whispered.

Eventually Elizabeth loosened her grip. Dan got off the floor and sat beside her on the couch, holding tightly on to her hand. "Thomas, perhaps, now that my histrionics are over, you could tell us what you know about Sarah's death," he said.

Thomas looked at Dan. "What I am about to tell you is all subject to the Official Secrets Act, and you may not be happy about it. It sounds like we have more information to share than I had at first imagined."

He paused, collecting his thoughts. "The British Government has known about the Dragas family and its objectives for many hundreds of years. Often the family's objectives and those of his or her Majesty's Government have even coincided."

"The world has, however changed. In these more enlightened times the idea of a modern day crusade against Islam is ludicrous, when nearly five percent of the UK's population are Muslims. The Dragas influence on the relationship between Islamic and Christian peoples throughout the world has been unbelievably divisive and is now at odds with the policies of the UK, and most other civilized countries."

"The idea of returning Istanbul to its former position as the centre of the Christian Church is also, in this day and age, bizarre. The

Constantinople of the fifteenth century is gone, swallowed up by a vibrant, modern, secular city."

"The problem is that logic is not something to which the Dragas family will listen. They believe, with all their hearts, that they have a sacred mission to turn back the clock. There is no logic that you could possibly use to convince them otherwise. Their belief in their mission is as strongly and deeply held as any fundamentalist Christian or Muslim believes in theirs.

"You can not argue with them. Believe me I have tried. In fact, that was exactly what I was doing when you saw me get on to Dragas' yacht in Amalfi. Her Majesty's Government had asked me to see if I could reason with Andris Dragas one more time."

"How did that go?" asked Alberto.

"Not well," said Thomas with a shake of his head. "He was very polite. We fenced around the issues for three or four hours, but it was clear to me that he, like his father before him, and no doubt every head of the family all the way back to Constantine the eleventh, was not going to change his mind."

"They are an immensely powerful family. Over the centuries they have focussed their time and energies on investments in arms manufacturing, printing and publishing. There is apparently a book, they call it the Palaiologos Codex that is supposed to have been started by Constantine Palaiologos, that describes the way they will achieve their objectives and what they have done over the centuries. It is their guide in those times when they have run out of the blood of Constantine."

"We discovered, from interrogating Rudolf Hess, and subsequent interrogations by the Americans of a number of German's after the second World War, including Hitler's physician, Theodor Morell, that the potion is more than likely not the actual blood of Constantine but some compound that massively enhances the capacity of the human brain."

"Knowing all this, our secret service continued to keep tabs on the activities of the Dragas family. We have also kept an eye on people in whom they have shown an interest, like the two of you," he said looking at Dan and Elizabeth.

"you first came up on our radar," he said, looking at Elizabeth "when you were approached by a head hunting firm which we knew was associated with the Dragas family. They had used the same firm a number of times to get people into high priority projects in which Her Majesty's Government had an interest, mostly in the defence area."

"When we looked into the circumstances surrounding your joining Dan's firm we brought Barry Critchley in for a chat. He'd made a submission to do some work for the DoD so a security vetting was required anyway. He told us that he had been persuaded to invest in Dan's firm by a merchant banking friend of his that he had asked for advice. He had, apparently received a significant inheritance from an aunt who had been tragically killed in a hit and run car accident."

"I am afraid to say that the sudden death in a motor vehicle accident of an innocent victim has, quite frequently, been the precursor to the introduction of a promising prospect into a business that the Dragas family has taken an interest in."

"My God! Couldn't you do something about it?" asked Charlotte.

"You would think so, wouldn't you? But every time we tried to we were confronted with dead end after dead end. Sarah's death was caused by an unknown driver who subsequently disappeared. The car was stolen. There was nothing on the car, no fingerprints or other evidence, that shouldn't have been there. It was the same with Barry's aunt."

"The head hunting firm said they had got Elizabeth's name from a copy of a newspaper article they had been sent, anonymously. The family nearly always works through others. Sometimes its organisations outside the law, like the mafia or the IRA, sometimes its organisations that are legit, like the head hunting firm. They have had, literally, centuries to perfect and establish their networks."

"The family works in very subtle ways, and usually keep themselves so far under the radar that it has proven impossible to pin anything on them. We often guess that they are behind things but proving it in a court of law would be impossible. It would just make us look paranoid."

"Why don't you just shoot him?" asked Charlotte. "That would fix the bastard!"

Thomas laughed. "It has actually been discussed! More than once! Unfortunatley Dragas is a very wealthy and influential man with contacts in the arms and media industries throughout the world. While he is not well known to the general public, he is very well known to decision makers around the world. There are quite a few countries, including some among our allies, that would be very upset if anything untoward happened to him."

"It is no secret among the world's power brokers that the relationship between MI6 and the family has become more and more strained over the past few years. Do you remember the rocket attack on the MI6 building in 2000? That was a warning shot from Andris Dragas' father."

"So, if he is so secretive, how come we got involved with him so easily?" asked Elizabeth.

"That is an interesting question, Elizabeth. Partly it is serendipitous. Partly you have been manipulated into acting as bait, I am afraid."

"Bait?" said Dan. "By who?"

"Initially by Victor Kachenko! Victor had his own axe to grind with the family. The family have been meddling in Russian affairs pretty well since the fall of Constantinople. They had more recently done some things that upset Victor. He knew that Dragas was manipulating you and your firm. He thought that if he could buy your company he could get the jump on Dragas. When you wouldn't sell, he thought that he would do some manipulating of his own. That is why he sent you the Hitler vial."

"The problem was that Dragas got to Victor first. Victor told me about his intention to send you the vial when I went to see him in hospital. It was, I am ashamed to say, MI6 that put the vial in your car!" he said looking suitably embarrassed.

"Why? Why would you do that?" asked Dan angrily.

Thomas held up his hands. "It wasn't my decision. In fact I argued against it. The idea of getting you involved in this was not right. Despite what you might think at the moment, I value our friendship very highly and did not want to see you, Elizabeth or Charlotte anywhere near Dragas and his schemes. In the end the arguments I put up were all over ruled, at the highest level."

"When I pushed hard I was told to back off. The only concession I could get was to be given a free hand to try and keep the three of you safe. A job which I have spectacularly botched, I am afraid to say."

"But what were your bosses trying to achieve?" asked Elizabeth

"The higher ups are getting increasingly concerned by the situation in the Middle East and Turkey. There are some very strange things going on in the world at the moment and our analysts are tearing their hair out trying to figure out what it all means. The feeling within MI6 is that the situation in Egypt, in Syria and in Turkey, as well as in the Ukraine, is all leading up to something big. They are worried, and I mean really worried, that Dragas is setting up for some sort of end game."

"We knew that the one thing that would be sure to attract Dragas' personal interest, perhaps the only thing, was the Blood of Constantine. What we didn't suspect was that your involvement would lead to him getting his hands on a vial of the actual, real Blood of Constantine, or whatever the hell it is. God knows what the implications of this are!"

"Well, it is not as bad as you might think," said Elizabeth. "He might have a version of the original potion but it is not active. My analysis shows that the potion is, at least in part, activated by a unique virus, but the virus in the sample we got from Alaric's tomb is dead. My guess would be that the seal on the vial that Alaric had was not airtight."

"Does that mean that the potion won't work?" asked Thomas.

"Yes. At least I think so. It is an incredibly complex mixture. The nootropics and hallucinogenics that are in it will obviously have an effect but if the modification of the users DNA is somehow important then I don't think it would work in the way it did for Alexander, or any of the others that took it successfully. I am assuming that the virus is the method by which this stuff modify's the user's DNA, but in reality I am just guessing," said Elizabeth.

"Well, let's say your guess is right. Where would Dragas go to get some active virus?" asked Thomas.

"Well, assuming that Dragas has figured out the Alexander connection from the information that bastard got from me," said Elizabeth with a shiver, " in theory, from the corpse of Alexander the Great, just like Augustus did!"

"And where do we find that?" he asked.

"No one knows," said Charlotte. "It's gone missing!"

"Really?" asked Thomas suddenly looking concerned.

"Sixteen hundred years ago!" she said with a reassuring smile.

"That's alright then!" said Thomas happily. "If Dragas can't get his hands on it, then it looks like it might, finally, be the end of the Dragas family. Game over!" He then had another thought. "Could Dragas know how important Alexander's corpse is to making the potion work?"

"No," said Dan dismissively.

"He might have figured it out," said Elizabeth in a quiet voice.

They all looked at her.

"He threatened to have Charlie beaten up, or worse. I had to tell him what I knew," she said, her voice trembling.

Charlotte came and sat beside her and put her arm around her.

"You did the right thing." said Thomas. "What did you tell him?"

"Everything really. At least everything I knew at that point. Charlie and Alberto had tracked the potion back to Julius Caesar, so he knew that. I also told him about the strands of ancient DNA we found in the Hitler potion."

"I would imagine that he has had an analysis done on the Alaric potion by now, and, to some extent, you gave him clues of what to look for."

"So what you're saying," said Dan, "is that he could have made the same guess that we did.

Thomas nodded. "Could he be searching for it in Alexandria? We have been tracking him, and that is currently where his yacht is."

"He could be," said Dan. "Lots of people have tried to find Alexander's tomb, but they have all failed. It's likely that, if the tomb still exists, it is probably buried under the modern city or underwater out in the bay."

"Good luck to him then!" said Thomas smiling. "Anyway it looks like he has got bored with the whole thing. He is off for a holiday in Venice."

"What!" said Charlotte, suddenly alarmed.

"He lodged a flight plan this morning to fly from Alexandria to Venice early tomorrow in his private jet," said Thomas, surprised by her reaction.

"Shit!" she said. "We have to go to Venice, now!"

"Do you want to tell us why?" asked Dan, surprised by her sudden insistence.

"Sure, but if Dragas is flying there tomorrow morning I think we should leave, immediately!" She turned to Thomas, "Thomas, do you have your car outside, and will it take five of us?"

"Yes, absolutely!" he said as confused as the others.

They all sat looking expectantly at Charlotte. "Well? Come on! If you want the best chance of finding Alexander's corpse before Dragas does we have to move now!"

Book 5

1. Italy - Present day

"Why Venice? asked Dan, turning to face Charlotte, as Thomas concentrated on driving them out of Rome.

"It's a bit of a long story, but it is one that an English Historian, by the name of Andrew Chugg, came up with a few years ago."

"Let's hear it," said Dan.

"We know that Alexander's body was in Alexandria in the time of Augustus. We also know that other Emperors went to see Alexander and his tomb. The last ancient sources we have that talks, specifically, about both the tomb and the body, say that the Emperor Antoninus, or Caracalla, as he is know these days, visited the tomb in 215AD. This is what Herodian, writing pretty close to the time, says about the visit, '*When he entered the city, accompanied by his entire army, he went first into the temple, where he sacrificed many hecatombs of cattle and heaped the altars with frankincense. Leaving the temple for the tomb of Alexander, he removed there his purple robe, his finger rings set with precious gems, together with his belts and anything else of value on his person, and placed them upon the tomb.'*"

"Caracalla was a nut job. He was another one who had a major Alexander complex. At one stage he wrote to the Roman Senate telling them that he was the re-incarnation of Alexander. He even had a phalanx of sixteen thousand Macedonians kitted out in old fashioned armour and with old fashioned weapons, to look like Alexander's men.

"He had been getting reports for years that the Alexandrian's were taking the piss out of him. Admittedly he was an easy target. He had assassinated his brother and rumours were floating around that he was sleeping with his mother, but the Alexandrians were particular nasty to him about the fact that he pretended to be Alexander all the time. In retaliation for their meanness, Cassius Dio says that, when he visited the city, Caracalla butchered some twenty thousand unarmed, Alexandrians, mostly young men,"

"He eventually got his comeuppance when he was stabbed to death while sitting on the toilet with a case of the runs a couple of years later."

"So no record of the body since 215AD?" asked Thomas from the driving seat.

"No. We do know that Herodian finished his History in about 238AD, a couple of years after the death of Caracalla. Apparently a guy by the name of Theodoret of Cyrus, a Christian Bishop writing in the middle of the fifth century, said that Alexander's resting place was unknown."

"So what happened between 238AD and 450AD in Alexandria that could possible make them forget where Alexander was buried?" asked Dan.

"A brilliant question!" said Charlotte, enthusiastically. "There was a rebellion in around 260AD, which probably led to the destruction of at least part of the city and which was closely followed by the plague, which killed around a third of the population."

"The Alexandrian's continued to be revolting and eventually they ran up against one of the great Emperors, Aurelian. By the time Aurelian had finished with them a big chunk of the city had been flattened."

"There was another period at the end of the third century when Diocletian had to quell an uprising. He was so ticked off with the Alexandrians that he is said to have commanded that everyone who had supported the uprising should be put to the sword, and that the killing shouldn't stop till the blood flowed above his horses knees."

"God, these Roman's were brutal," said Elizabeth, who was sitting in the back seat next to Charlotte.

"Brutal but superstitious!" Charlotte replied. "The story goes that his horse stumbled and fell to its knees, so he took this as an omen and stopped the killing. The granite column, known as Pompey's pillar, the one that is still standing in Alexandria, was actually set up by Diocletian at around that time."

"So," said Dan, "the chance of the tomb of Alexander being lost among the destruction of the city due to civil unrest and a couple of wars, a serious bout of the plague, followed no doubt by the scavenging of stone for the rebuilding of defences would have been pretty high?"

"Yup, but to add to all that, there is a story, corroborated by a number of sources, of a massive earthquake and tidal wave that hit the city in about 365AD."

"So, Alexander's corpse was probably sucked out to sea?" Elizabeth suggested.

"Possibly, but Andrew Chugg writes about a document that strongly suggests that Alexander's body was on display in Alexandria towards the end of the fourth century, which is quite plausible if Alexander's corpse was, as is suspected, in an underground crypt. By the end of the century the city had probably been repaired following the tsunami. Excavating a large, underground tomb might well have been part of the rebuilding work."

"The trouble was, that around this time, the end of the fourth century, the Emperor, Theodosius, starts to have a go at outlawing the pagan religion of the original Romans. This is a complete three hundred and sixty degree turn about on what Nero did. Now its the turn of the pagans to be put to death for following their religion. So the whole cult of Alexander would have been outlawed."

Charlotte paused, for a moment. "Imagine this situation. You've got a corpse that has been venerated as the founder of your city for over six hundred years. It is also the greatest tourist attraction you've got. Even Emperors made pilgrimages to come to see it! But now you've got a bunch of religious zealots tearing apart pagan temples and shrines and building churches where those shrines previously stood."

"So what do you do with your famous corpse? If you are open to the main chance you repurpose it! Andrew Chugg's theory is that some bright spark had the idea of changing the name on the corpse from Alexander, the founder of the city, to Mark, the founder of the church in the city."

"So who is Mark?" asked Elizabeth.

"Mark the Evangelist, the one that wrote the Gospel according to Saint Mark." Charlotte said with a grin. "Mark was supposedly the founder of the church in Alexandria. According to church tradition Saint Mark was buried in Alexandria. In fact Saint Jerome confirms that he was buried there in about 392AD. There is also an apocryphal account of the death and subsequent entombment of Saint Mark which said that the nasty pagans were trying to burn his corpse when, miraculously, a storm blew up, put out the fire and gave the Christians a chance to snatch back the body."

"The inconsistency that Chugg highlights, is that these stories of the entombment of the body of Saint Mark all start around the end of the fourth century. Prior to that there were a number of sources, like Dorotheus of Tyre and Eutychius, who state that Saint Mark's body was cremated."

"The story of him being burnt is older than the one of him being entombed?" asked Elizabeth.

"Exactly!" said Charlotte. "Chugg also suggests that the location of the tomb of Alexander and the Church of Saint Mark are, coincidentally, the same!"

"So they did a switch?" asked Elizabeth.

Charlotte nodded.

"So now we are looking for the body of Saint Mark, rather than Alexander? How does that help us?" asked Elizabeth.

"You don't know the story of Saint Mark's body?" Charlotte asked her. Elizabeth shook her head.

2. Alexandria - 828AD

Captain Buono laughed out loud as his dromon heeled over in the fresh breeze. To windward, and slightly behind, Captain Rustico was bearing down on him. Ahead of them Buono could see the Pharos lighthouse at the entrance to the harbour of Alexandria. First into the Portus magnus, over a line from the lighthouse to the opposite shore would win their wager. A gold solidus was at stake and Buono was determined, this time, to win it from his friend.

He looked back over his shoulder and saw that Rustico was coming dangerously close. He suddenly realised the danger he was in. Rustico was trying to force him to leeward, pushing him down below the point at which he could sail through the opening to the port on his current tack.

Buono shouted to his men to haul the great triangular sail in more tightly, as he tried to head his ship higher into the wind. In response his ship slowed slightly and Rustico's dromon edged closer. If he caught up any further Rustico would steal the wind from Buono's sail.

The two boats sped through the water as if they were tied together. After hundreds of miles of sailing, all the way from Venice, it was testament to the skill of both men as sailors that they crossed into the harbour together, with Buono only slightly in front.

Looking up at the lighthouse that towered above the harbour entrance, Buono could see that men were working on the repair of the top, round section that, he had been told by his father, collapsed after an earthquake some forty years before. He had never seen work being done on the lighthouse before, but he was pleased that someone cared enough to rebuild it. Every time he had sailed into Alexandria, from the first time with his father when he was ten years old, he had marvelled at the colossal structure. He had been stunned when his father had told him that the lighthouse had been built a thousand years before by the great Greek Pharaohs of Egypt. He had told him that, in ancient times, four tritons stood at each of the building's corners and that a giant statute of Poseidon had stood on its top. In his travels around the Mediterranean, he had seen old coins and mosaics that showed the giant statues in place so he knew it to be true.

Buono was still making his ship secure at the quay side when he heard Rustico hailing him from above. He looked up into the smiling face of his friend and waved. Two minutes later he was standing beside him on the dock.

"What do you have planned, my friend?' asked Buono as he gave Rustico a bear hug. "If we had raced to a Christian port I would be offering you a cup of wine to toast my win, but here..." he shrugged.

"The wine can wait Buono. I would like to pay my respects to Saint Mark while we are here. Bishop Orso has asked me to see what is going on here. He has heard some disturbing reports about what has been happening to the city's churches."

"What sort of reports?" asked Buono as the two men started walking along the waterfront, dodging the men loading and unloading the ships.

"There are stories that the Caliph has ordered the marble columns from the churches to be taken and used for his palace," said Rustico.

They walked into the city, pushing their way along narrow and crowded streets. The remains of a wall appeared to their right and they followed it for a short distance before it turned at right angles to the street on which they were walking. Continuing to follow the wall they came to a large rectangular gate. As they walked through it, Buono looked up and marveled at the workmanship. The stone work was incredibly precise and the stones themselves had been beautifully finished, a far cry from the rough stonework of more recent constructions around the city. On the inside wall an empty stone niche was built into the stonework on one side of the gate and Buono absently wondered if it had once held some pagan deity or noble hero. The Arabs didn't allow representations of gods, people, or even of animals so if there had once been one it would have been smashed to pieces long ago when the Muslims first took the city.

Just inside the gate they came to the Church of Saint Mark. Standing outside was a priest, talking to a small child, who scurried off as Buono and Rustico approached.

The priest bowed his head in greeting to the two Venetians as they approached. He introduced himself as Minos and offered them a place to sit in the shade. They gratefully accepted.

"My Bishop has asked me to see if the rumours he has been hearing about damage to your church are true." Rustico said, once they were comfortably seated in the shade of the small church.

"Life under the Caliphate is sometimes difficult," said Minos in a quiet voice, his eyes darting backwards and forwards to ensure they weren't being overheard. "The Arabs do not respect the relics of the church, or the sanctity of our buildings. There are many among our congregation that fear that the Caliph and his men will arrive one day to take away the relics of our founder."

"Would it be possible for us to see the body and the relics of Saint Mark?" asked Buono.

Minos nodded and led them into the church. It was cool inside. Buono admired the rows of marble columns that ran the length of the building, reaching out to touch the cold stone as they walked past. Minos led them towards the pulpit and then down a set of stone steps to a crypt.

Illuminated by the light of oil lamps a mummified body, wrapped in linen, and covered in a beautiful vestment, lay on a marble slab. The air in the crypt was redolent with the exotic smell of spices and Buono wondered whether there were incense burners hidden somewhere in the room.

They all knelt on the stone floor and bent their heads in prayer. When they had finished, each of them walked quietly back up the stone steps to the chapel above where Rustico and Buono thanked the priest and went back out into the warm Alexandrian afternoon.

As they walked back towards the harbour Rustico said casually. "It is a shame that one of the Apostles didn't establish a church in the lagoon."

Buono, used to his friend's manner, said encouragingly, "Why is that Rustico?"

"Just think how many people go on pilgrimage to the Holy Land, to Constantinople and Rome to pray before the relics of the apostles that are in those cities. What a wonderful thing to have one of the Apostles venerated in your church!"

"You are a mercenary bastard, Rustico! You think that it would be good to have one of the Apostles founding a church in the lagoon because you think that it would bring in money!" said Buono with a chuckle.

"There is that aspect," said Rustico innocently. Then he said after a thoughtful silence. "What would be terrible though, is if the holy remains of an Apostle fell into the hands of people who didn't respect and value it."

"If that were to happen, Rustico, are you suggesting that perhaps, it would be the duty of a good Christian to do everything in their power to save such a holy relic?"

"Yes, my dear Buono, I think that would indeed be the duty of a good Christian. It might even go some way to absolve some of the sins of a good Christian who has, occasionally, fallen by the wayside."

"Fallen into the arms of loose women, you mean!" laughed Buono.

"But seriously Buono, would it not be a great thing for the lagoon to be the resting place of Saint Mark? With a Saint's protection a truly great city might one day rise out of the lagoon!"

"What are you suggesting, that we steal the body of Saint Mark?" asked Buono, suddenly serious.

"Why not, Buono?" said Rustico excitedly. "We would be saving Saint Mark!"

"If we were caught the Caliph would have our hands cut off and then have us stoned! If he didn't kill us, the Christians of the city would tear us limb from limb! You can't seriously entertain the idea of stealing the founding father of their church from them?" said Buono horrified.

"But just imagine, Buono, with Saint Mark watching over us, how great we might become!" said Rustico, caught up in his own enthusiasm.

Buono rolled his eyes and kept on walking.

****

Several days later, as night fell, Buono was finishing supervising the loading of his ship. He had spent his time bartering for silk and for grain and had not seen his friend Rustico at all since their walk to the Church of Saint Mark, nor had he given much thought to their odd, and somewhat disturbing, conversation. Now that his ship was loaded and the cargo safely stowed away, he had time to spare. While he awaited the arrival of the customs officers for the final inspection and calculation of port taxes he climbed onto the wharf and walked to where Rustico's ship was moored.

He stood on the wharf and stared at the ship. It stood empty and unattended. He called out, but no one replied. While he was standing there, wondering what had happened to Rustico and his crew he felt something hit the side of his head. Turning quickly he caught site of an arm disappearing into the shadows at the back of the wharf where a row of crumbling warehouses stood. His hand went to the pommel of the dagger he wore in his belt.

He heard his name called out in a hoarse whisper. "Buono, in here, quick!"

Cautiously he stepped towards the shadows. "Buono, its me Rustico! Come on! Come quickly before you are noticed!"

This time Buono recognised the voice of his friend. He looked around quickly and, seeing that he was unobserved, ducked into the alcove in which Rustico was hiding. "What the hell is going on Rustico. Why is your ship not loaded? Where are your men."

"A few of them have run away, I am afraid. The rest are here behind me," said Rustico.

Buono sniffed the air. A strong smell of fragrant spices filled the space in which Rustico and his men were hiding. "Why would your men ru...." Buono started saying, and then he suddenly recognised the smell. He had smelt the same overpowering aroma of sweet spices only a couple of days before. "My God, Rustico! You haven't stolen the body of Saint Mark?!"

Buono's heart sank. "You idiot!" he said in a harsh whisper. "No wonder your men ran away. If they weren't scared that the Caliph would take their heads from their shoulders, then they should be terrified that

God will strike them down. You can't steal the body of one of Christ's Apostles! You will get us all killed! How, in God's name did you intend to get it out of here? How do you propose to get it onto your boat, without getting caught?"

"I don't" said Rustico. "My boat is empty and I don't have enough crew left to sail her back to Venice!"

At that moment Buono realised why he was standing in the gloom having this conversation. "Oh no! You can't ask me to do this Rustico! We have been friends for a long time, and I have played along with a lot of your hare-brained schemes, but this," he said gesturing to where he presumed the corpse was, "this is going too far!"

"This is for Venice, Buono! Imagine the rewards that the Doge will bestow on us when we bring this treasure home!" wheedled Rustico. "We can leave on the next tide, just after dawn."

"But you know they will inspect the cargo just before we sail. If they don't see that, ' he said nodding towards the darkness where he suspected the corpse was" they will definitely smell it. I'm carrying grain and silk, not frankincense and myrrh!"

"I've got a plan Buono! I guarantee we won't get caught!" said Rustico, with a touch of his usual bravado.

Buono shook his head. He knew that he couldn't leave Rustico and his men to face the Caliph and the irate Christians that were almost certainly about to descend on them, baying for blood.

"Alright!" he agreed. "I will tell the men to get the boat ready to sail on the next tide! But I warn you Rustico, if you get me killed, I will never forgive you!"

Two hours later Buono was standing on the deck of his ship with the two customs officers that had just checked his cargo. He paid across a small bag of gold when a commotion started on the wharf beside him.

"Captain Buono!" said a man leading a small troop of men carry a long woven basket that had been strung between two stout poles. "I would like to buy passage to venice, if you have room for me and my men!"

Buono did not recognise the man. He was dressed like a bedouin in a white cotton robe, and a colourful striped coat with a turban on his head. He almost burst out laughing, though when he recognised the voice. Before he could answer Rustico had jumped onto the deck and waved to his men to follow him.

The men, with their burden weighing them down, began to struggle over the rail of the boat and onto the deck. As soon as it was obvious that they were bringing their cargo on board the customers officer became very agitated. They had, after all, just finished their inspection.

Rustico, seeing their concern, immediately offered to open up the cargo he was bringing on board. Buono expected that this was part of Rustico's plan, a bluff. He guessed that Rustico had timed his arrival so the customs officers would just let him pass. Buono held his breath. It was, as were most of Rustico's plans, typically audacious. Nine out of ten times it would have worked, but for some reason the customs officers decided to search the late comer's cargo. Perhaps they thought it was an opportunity to extract a higher duty for whatever it contained.

Buono's hand went to his dagger. He had warned his men that there might be trouble. They moved into positions to be better able to defend themselves and their ship.

Rustico stood, relaxed and smiling beside his baggage. One of the customs officer indicated that he should open the basket for inspection. Rustico obliged. The look of disgust on the officer face when he peered into the basket was almost comical. He looked at Rustico like he would look at camel shit on his sandals. Without turning back he and his associate stepped off the boat, muttering to each other. The only word that Buono heard was "Kanzir!" The word for pig!

He walked across to look inside the basket and let out a laugh. It was full of sides of pork. When he turned to his friend he saw that Rustico was grinning at him. " I told you I had a plan!" he said. "Now, I think my men and I will find somewhere to have a rest while we wait for the tide to turn."

Buono laughed. "You and your men rest Rustico. I will wake you if we have need of another of your marvellous plans."

****

It was dawn when Rustico felt himself shaken awake. "We've got trouble friend," said Buono nodding towards the quay. Striding along the stone wharf were the two customs officers and Minos, the priest from the church. Behind them came a troop of soldiers.

Buono met them on the edge of the quay. Minos immediately accused Buono of sacrilege, and of stealing the body of Saint Mark. Buono looked astonished. "My God! Someone has stolen Saint Mark's sacred relics?" he said, sounding truly shocked.

Minos wavered for a moment, then turned to the customs officials. "You must search this boat!"

The customs official looked at the priest for a moment, then said. "You search the boat. We told you this boat is unclean!"

Minos jumped down onto the deck and then down into the cargo hold. Stretching out before him were the neatly stacked amphora full of grain and the bundles of silks. Ignoring Buono's cargoe, he went straight to Rustico's large basket that had been stowed below the previous evening.

Rustico's heart sank. He hadn't expected the priest to be brought to search the basket. He watched with growing apprehension as the priest removed each side of pork and laid it carefully next to the basket. His mood changed to wonder as he realised that the body wasn't there. His apprehension grew again as Minos clambered over Buono's cargo sniffing audibly as he went.

He was even more amazed when Minos carefully replaced all the pork in the basket and came up to where he and Buono were standing and sincerely apologised to them both, for doubting their honesty. A dark look crossed his face as he looked up at the customs officials.

He and Buono watched as the unhappy priest led the customs officers and their troop of soldiers back along the wharf.

"I feel sorry for poor old Minos," said Buono. "He is not going to have any easy time of it for the next little while." He then turned to his men and shouted, "Alright you men, let's cast off and get this cargo home!"

Rustico sat out of the way watching with admiration as Buono's well trained crew navigated his boat out of the harbour. As they cleared the port entrance and with the Pharos light house well behind them, Rustico's curiosity finally got the better of him. "Where is the body Buonos? Don't tell me that after all the trouble I went to you got rid of it?"

Buono looked at Rustico. "Do you not believe in miracles, my friend? Saint Mark is still among us. He is keeping watch over us as we sail home!" As he said this he brought his hands together in prayer and looked heavenward.

Understanding suddenly dawned on Rustico and he too looked towards the sky. There, strapped safely to the end of the long spar that carried the large triangular sail, high above them, was Saint Mark.

3. Italy - Present day

Thomas laughed. "So the Venetians stole the body of Saint Mark! What a hoot! But you're saying that it is possible that the body that they stole, the one that had been venerated as Saint Mark, was really the body of Alexander the Great, hidden in plain sight?"

"It is possible. Andrew Chugg may be wrong!' said Charlotte.

"But if he is right, then the corpse that has been in Venice for what, over a thousand years, is not really a Saint at all, but one of the greatest conquerors in history! Wow! What a story!" said Thomas, chuckling.

"How would you know if it is Alexander if you got a look at it?" asked Alberto. "DNA testing, carbon dating?"

"Oh, its probably much simpler than that. I don't think that it would be necessary to use those sort of techniques, at least not initially. If it is possible to inspect the skeleton, either directly or with an x-ray or cat scan, that would give us a pretty good idea if it was Alexander or not," said Charlotte.

"How so?" asked Thomas.

"Well, there is pretty good documentation of the injuries that Alexander had over the years. He got smacked in the head with a stone when he was fighting the Illyrians. At the battle of Granicus he was cut with a dagger or sword across the scalp. At the battle of Issus his thigh was pierced by a sword or dagger. When he was at the siege of Gaza he had his shoulder dislocated and some sort of wound on his leg, either an arrow strike or stone hitting it. Somewhere near Hyrcania he got another hit in the head or neck that left him, according to Plutarch, with 'dimmed sight for a good while'. There are two or three other references in the sources for arrow wounds to different parts of his body, but the two that will be the critical ones in identifying the body are a really bad arrow wound to the leg, that Arrian says broke his fibula. Plutarch says that it was so badly broken that splinters of bone were taken out. Unfortunately none of them say if it was the right or left leg. The real test though will be looking at his chest. While he was in India an arrow pierced his chest."

"Can I read you this description, from Arrian?" Charlotte asked. "It is just so fantastic!"

"Sure," said Dan. "Remind me, who was Arrian?"

"Arrian was a Roman, Flavius Arrianus Xenophon, who wrote his history of the campaigns of Alexander around the end of the first century AD. He says that he pulled together a whole lot of sources from the actual time of Alexander, most of which are lost to us now, but it included stuff that Ptolemy and Aristotle's nephew Calisthenes, wrote," said Charlotte, her face now illuminated by the glow from her laptop screen. "Just listen to this., This is what Arrian wrote based on the descriptions written by people that were actually in India, with Alexander, over two thousand years ago..."

"They could all hear the excitement in her voice as she began to read. "On *the next day, Alexander divided the army into two parts. He himself assaulted the wall at the head of one, and Perdiccas led the other. The Indians did not try to repel the attack of the Macedonians, but abandoned the walls of the city and fled for safety into the inner citadel.*

Alexander and his troops, wrenching a gate from its hinges, got within the city long before the others. Those who had been put under Perdiccas were behind time, having experienced difficulty in scaling the walls, as most of them did not bring ladders, thinking that the city had been captured, when they observed that the walls were deserted by the defenders.

When the citadel was seen to be still in the possession of the enemy, and many of them were observed drawn up in front of it to repel attacks, some of the Macedonians tried to force an entry by undermining the wall, and others by placing scaling ladders against it, wherever it was practical to do so.

Alexander, thinking that the men who carried the ladders were too slow, snatched one from a man who was carrying it in his impatience, placed it against the fortress wall himself, and, crouching under his shield, climbed the ladder. Peucestas followed him carrying the sacred shield which Alexander took from the temple of theTrojan Athena and had carried before him into battle.

After Peucestas, by the same ladder ascended Leonnatus the confidential body-guard; and up another ladder went Abreas, one of the soldiers who received double pay for distinguished services.

The king now reached the top of the battlement. Leaning his shield against the battlement he forced some of the defenders back into the fortress and cleared that part of the wall, by killing others with his sword till he stood on top of the battlement alone.

The sight of him standing alone filled the men of the guard with terror for his safety. They made a dash for the ladders, but under the excessive load, they broke and the climbers were hurled to the ground.

Alexander then, standing upon the wall, was being assailed all round from the adjacent towers. None of the Indians dared approach him. He was also being assailed by the men in the city, who were throwing darts at him from no great distance, for a mound of earth happened to have been heaped up there opposite the wall.

That it was indeed Alexander who stood atop that was plain to all. His legendary courage no less than his shining armour proclaimed him.

Alexander perceived that if he remained where he was, he would be incurring danger without being able to perform anything at all worthy of consideration. He leaped off the battlement down into the fort so that he might perhaps, by this very act, strike the Indians with terror, and if he did not, but should only thereby be incurring danger, at any rate he would die not ignobly after performing great deeds of valour worth hearing about by men of after times.

To think was to act. He leaped down from the wall into the citadel where, supporting himself against the wall, he struck with his sword and killed some of the Indians who came to close quarters with him, including their leader, who rushed upon him too boldly.

Another man who approached him he kept in check by hurling a stone at him, and a third in like manner. Another who advanced nearer to him he again kept off with his sword; so that the barbarians were no longer willing to approach him, but standing round him in a half circle, cast at him from all sides whatever missile any one happened to have or could get hold of at the time.

Meantime, Peucestras and Abreas, and after them Leonnatus, being the only men who happened to have scaled the walls before the ladders were broken, had leaped down and were fighting in front of the king. Abreas fell there, being shot with an arrow in the forehead. Alexander himself also was wounded with an arrow under the breast through his breastplate in the chest, so that Ptolemy says air was breathed out from the wound together with the blood.

Although he was faint with exhaustion, Alexander continued to defend himself, as long as his blood was still warm. But the blood streaming out copiously and without ceasing at every expiration of breath, he was seized with a dizziness and swooning, and bending over fell upon his shield.

After he had fallen Peucestas defended him, holding over him the sacred shield brought from Troy. On the other side he was defended by Leonnatus. Both these men were themselves wounded, and Alexander was now nearly fainting away from loss of blood.

The Macedonian assault upon the fortress was by now totally out of hand. The men had seen Alexander as he stood on the battlements, they had seen him leap down into the citadel and now, afraid lest his rash act should be the end of him, and eager to bring help in time, they rushed the citadel wall.

The ladders were smashed and useless, but on the spur of the moment they used whatever means they could to get up and over the wall. Some drove stakes into the clay of the walls and dragged themselves slowly and laboriously up. Others struggled up by standing on their comrade's shoulders.

The first man who got up threw himself down from the wall into the city, and so did they all, with a loud lamentation and howl of grief when they saw the king lying on the ground.

Now ensued a desperate conflict around his fallen body. One Macedonian after another held his shield in front of Alexander's prostrate body. In the meantime some of the soldiers having smashed to pieces the bar by which the gate in the space of wall between the towers was secured, entered the city a few at the time. Others, putting their shoulders under the gap made by the gate, forced their way into the space inside the wall, and thus laid the citadel open in that quarter.

Now the slaughter began. Neither woman nor child was spared.

A party of men carried off the king, who was lying in a faint condition, upon his shield; and they could not yet tell whether he was likely to survive.

Some authors have stated that Critodemus, a physician of Cos, an Asclepiad by birth, made an incision into the injured part and drew the weapon out of the wound. Other authors say that as there was no physician present at the critical moment, Perdiccas, the confidential body-guard, at Alexanders bidding, made an incision with his sword into the wounded part and removed the weapon. On its removal there was such a copious effusion of blood that Alexander swooned again, and the effect of the swoon was, that the effusion of blood was stanched."

Charlotte finished reading and they all sat silently, caught up in the images that Arrian's description had invoked.

"He certainly led from the front!" said Thomas to break the silence.

"It is so visceral, so intimate, so barbaric!" said Elizabeth with distaste.

"Getting back to topic though", said Dan thoughtfully, "if the skeleton in Saint Mark's Basilica has wounds to its lower leg and around the chest that have healed then we can be pretty sure that the body is that of Alexander!"

They were all silent again for a while, each thinking their own thoughts, when Thomas asked. "Given this theory is out there in the world, has anyone ever asked the Church for a peek at the body in Saint Mark's?"

"I understand that there have been a number of representations made, but, as you can imagine, given the importance of Saint Mark to both Venice and the Catholic Church, they have been politely refused," said Charlotte. "There was an inspection of the body in the eighteen hundreds when it was moved from the original crypt, which was subject to flooding, up into the altar of the Basilica itself, though."

"Did that offer any clues to whose body it really was?" asked Elizabeth.

"No, not really. The description was pretty sketchy. All it really says is that there was a body with a head. The description sort of suggests that maybe it is the remains of an embalmed mummy, but nothing conclusive," said Charlotte.

"So, our best guess then, is that Dragas has followed up whatever leads he had in Alexandria, has come up empty handed, and is now going to see if he can get access to the remains of Saint Mark, or Alexander, in Venice?" asked Thomas.

They all agreed that this seemed to be the most likely scenario.

Alberto, who had been quiet for most of the drive so far, said quietly. "I think I should ring the Bishop of Venice and warn him."

Dan, Charlotte, Elizabeth and Thomas, who had all been thinking that there might be some way that they could access the corpse without alerting the church, considered the consequences of what Alberto was saying.

"If we warn the Bishop then the chance of us getting access to the skeleton are practically nil!" said Dan. "We know the church position on inspecting the remains already."

"If we do not warn him, and the remains are stolen or destroyed, then one of the truly great treasures of the church will be lost," said Alberto. "If it is not Saint Mark, and it is indeed Alexander the Great, the loss would be no less tragic for the world."

"Despite anything we may wish to do, we have to remember that the remains in the altar have been the responsibility of the Bishop of Venice for over a thousand years and at the end of the day all we want to do is stop Dagras getting hold of the relic. The responsibility is his, not ours."

In the quietness of the big black BMW no one spoke.

Alberto pulled his phone out of his pocket and scrolled through his address book. Charlotte, sitting next to him watched as he scrolled through a very long list and then found the one he wanted. He touched the name and put the phone to his ear.

"You had the Bishop of Venice's phone number in your address book!" she said somewhat amazed.

Alberto nodded as he listened to the ringing of the phone. She heard a voice answer in the typically Italian style. "Pronto!" There followed a very rapid conversation in Italian that Charlotte found difficult to follow, but the gist of it was that there was a threat to the sacred remains and that a guard should be arranged for the Basilica.

Alberto paused and leaned forward. "Thomas, how long till we reach Venice?"

Thomas touched the car's GPS. "About an hour and a half."

Alberto arranged to meet the Bishop outside the Basilica and hung up. He caught Charlotte looking at him. "What?" he asked.

"I was just wondering how well connected you really are within the Church. Is there anyone that doesn't know you?" she asked.

Alberto didn't answer the question, but said to the car in general, "We are meeting the Bishop at Saint Mark's. I have told him what we have agreed, that there is a threat to the sacred remains. He is arranging for the local police to be brought in to guard the Basilica."

4. Venice - Present day

As the Motoscafi came in sight of Saint Marks Square, they could all see that something was terribly wrong. The sun was climbing above the horizon and a crowd of police were milling around the entrance to the Basilica in the cold grey dawn. The Motoscafi edged its way into the quayside and tied up next to four of Venice's orange and yellow water ambulances.

As they disembarked they saw a body being carried on a stretcher onto one of the ambulances. It was entirely covered with a blanket.

Alberto led the way. A uniformed and armed officer walked towards him as their small group approached the entrance to the Basilica. After a brief conversation with Alberto the officer spoke into a radio. He listened to the reply and respectfully led Alberto and his small band of followers, through the striped police tape that surrounded the area, to the doors of the Basilica, where the Bishop of Venice stood waiting.

Alberto greeted him respectfully and then introduced Dan, Elizabeth, Charlotte and Thomas. They all stood looking into the church. Paramedics were working in two different places, one near the entrance, the other closer to the altar. Portable lamps flooded the interior with light. Armed police were milling around both the inside and outside the basilica, clearly unsure whether there was still a threat to be dealt with.

"What happened?" Alberto asked the Bishop.

"After your phone call, Alberto, I rang the police and told them what you told me. They sent four men to guard the doors. About an hour ago one of the men radioed for help. He said that they were under attack and that someone had broken into the Basilica and was vandalising the high altar."

"By the time I arrived two of the Carabinieri were dead and the other two had been badly wounded. The police and the paramedics were already doing what they could," said the Bishop.

"And the attack on the high altar?" asked Dan.

"Come, see for yourselves what these vandals have done!" said the Bishop leading them up the central isle to the altar. As they approached the altar Charlotte was distracted by the play of light on the Pala D'Oro, the gold altarpiece that stood above and behind the high altar. She stepped around the altar and then gasped.

The entire back off the altar had been ripped away, exposing the marble sarcophagus inside it. The long side of it had been brutally smashed in and its contents pulled out.

Alberto knelt down to inspect more closely the damage that had been done. A layer of dust, dragged out of the sarcophagus when its contents had been removed through the gap the thieves had made, covered the floor.

A round wooden box, obviously also dragged from the sarcophagus, lay on its side, pushed out of the way by the thieves. Charlotte bent down to inspect it. She noticed some Greek letters on its lid.

Dan who had been watching Charlotte asked her what it said.

Charlotte twisted her head around to better be able to read the letters. "It looks like it says Sanctus Antonius, Saint Anthony. I have seen it described in the book that Leonardo Manin wrote after seeing the coffin opened in 1811. It was probably stolen by Rustico and Buono at the same time they took the corpse," she said.

Charlotte looked at the devastation that the thieves had left. They had smashed the sarcophagus open with a sledge hammer that now lay carelessly tossed aside. They had then cleared the broken marble out of the way and grabbed the corpse. Among the dust and debris, Charlotte could identify bits of decayed cloth.

Standing a little away from the altar Charlotte could see Thomas, Alberto and another man, an officer of the local police perhaps, talking earnestly to one another. They appeared to come to some sort of agreement and the officer and Alberto walked down the main aisle and out of the church.

Thomas came across to where Charlotte was now standing with Dan and Elizabeth. "The local police have closed all the exits to Venice. The road and the railway are being watched, as is the airport. All boats trying to leave the lagoon will also be stopped. If Dragas wants to get the corpse out of Venice then it will not be easy for him."

"Alberto has gone with the local guys to the airport to watch for Dragas' plane." Thomas looked at his watch. "It should be landing in the next twenty minutes or so if he keeps to his flight plan."

"So what do we do now?" asked Elizabeth.

"I think we go and find some breakfast. I'm starving!" said Thomas taking her arm and heading out of the Basilica. "Cafe Florian is just across the square. It is supposed to be the oldest restaurant in Venice and may even be the oldest coffee house in Europe, an amazing institution. A bit Disneyland these days, but worth a visit every now and then. Charge like wounded bulls. I think they charge you for the air you breathe while you are there, but lovely all the same and, of course, the coffee is good. Did you know that it is supposed to have been the haunt of Casanova, Lord Byron and Goethe?"

Dan and Charlotte followed them out into the bright morning sunshine.

5. Venice - Present day

Alberto, with two armed police, stood watching Dragas' jet touch down. They watched as it taxied back along the runway towards the western end of the airport where several other executive jets were parked.

They continued to watch as two men, both in pilot's uniforms, descended from the plane. A few minutes later Dragas disembarked. They followed him at a safe distance. He walked to the water taxi rank and stepped on to a Motoscafi. Alberto and the police officer hung back for about thirty seconds and then walked casually over to another Motoscafi set apart from the others. The owner seemed to be working on the engine, but as soon as Alberto and his companion approached he closed the engine bay hatch and started the motor.

They followed Dragas into the city. Keeping at a safe distance, so as not to alert him.

At the airport another figure, dressed in tight fitting jeans and an elegantly tailored jacket, her long blonde hair tied in a pony tail, disembarked from the plane. Two men carrying a long wooden packing case followed her. The three of them took the box through customs and then walked to the taxi stand and caught another Motoscafi into the city.

6. Venice - Present day

Dan put down his coffee cup among the debris of their breakfast and looked out across Saint Mark's Square. "What do we do now? I don't want to just sit here and wait to see if they find the body. How about we have a look around and see if we can see anything?"

"After that decadent breakfast I would sure like to walk off a few calories!' said Elizabeth.

"Ok, said Thomas. "It can't do any harm to have some more eyes on the ground, but to be on the safe side I think we should go in pairs. If you and Elizabeth work your way north on this side of the Grand Canal, Charlotte and I will have a look around on the other side. If anyone sees anything suspicious they let the other know, or get in touch with Alberto. Agreed?"

They all agreed. Thomas paid the bill, he and Charlotte headed off towards the Rialto Bridge, while Elizabeth and Dan headed in the other direction, towards the Arsenale di Venezia.

Elizabeth and Dan were walking hand in hand, pushing their way through the throngs of tourists that were crowding the waterfront when Dan suddenly stopped walking. Elizabeth turned to him. "What's up?"

"We are doing this all wrong," he said. "Randomly walking about hoping that we see someone we recognise is crazy. Logically Dragas will want to inspect the body, right?"

Elizabeth nodded.

"But we know he is a full-on Christian, so the last thing he will want to do is damage a relic as holy as the possible remains of Saint Mark," he said.

Elizabeth nodded again. "So he will need some fast, noninvasive way to check the body to determine whether it is Alexander or not."

"Of course!" said Elizabeth. "That has to be either a CT scanner or, at the very least, an x-ray machine! Now assuming he hasn't got one of his own, that will mean taking the remains to a hospital or clinic."

"I'm on it!" said Elizabeth taking out her smart phone and tapping quickly on the screen. "Nothing comes up under Venice Radiology, except on the mainland over in Mestre. Given how quickly the police set up road blocks I doubt they had a chance to get over there."

She tapped on the screen again. "There is a Hospital or nursing home on the other side of the Grand Canal where Charlie and Thomas are, and there are two Hospitals listed on this side. They are both over on the North east side of the island looking out towards Murano and the island with the San Michele cemetery on it!"

"Thats where we should head, then!" said Dan.

They walked along the narrow paths of Venice, gradually working their way to the path that ran along the outside of the Island.

"Do you think we are going the right way?" Elizabeth asked.

"Yup. Those look like the water ambulance we saw this morning up ahead, tied up to that landing. It looks like that is a cemetery over there," he said pointing across the water to a nearby island.

They loitered around the entrance to the hospital for about ten minutes before Elizabeth got bored and went inside. Five minutes later she came out shaking her head.

They continued to walk along the path on the edge of the island until it ran out and then turned inland until they found a bridge they could cross. Once again they tried to make their way to a path that led along the edge of the island, but there wasn't one, so they followed the nearest one.

The second hospital was on the end of a section of Island where the pedestrian path ended, so they could comfortably watch anyone coming or going while sitting in a small Piazza in front of a church, leaning up against a wall, a few hundred yards away from the entrance of the Hospital.

"What's this one called?" asked Dan nodding at the church. Elizabeth checked on her phone.

"Its called the Church of Madonna Dell'orto, built in the fourteenth Century, apparently," she said looking down at the screen.

"And has some outstanding paintings by Tintoretto that are well worth a look," said a voice that Elizabeth thought she recognised. "A bit dark for my liking, but it is one of his best!'

The woman, who was standing with the sun behind her so it wasn't easy to see anything but the svelte outline of her figure, looked down at Dan and Elizabeth.

"Julia?" asked Elizabeth getting to her feet. "Nice to see you again," she said politely. "Are you here alone or did your come with Andris?"

Julia stood looking at Elizabeth for a few moments. "I flew in with Andris this morning. I am just on my way to see him. Why don't you come with me? He would love to see you again."

Dan and Elizabeth looked at each other, unsure what to do. Julia smiled. "There are two men waiting by the canal who can be very persuasive if they are allowed to be. I think you have even met them before?" Julia asked.

Dan and Elizabeth looked towards the canal and saw the well remembered faces of Luigi and Paolo.

"I have told them to only shoot to wound you Elizabeth. Andris would like to have a talk to you about your work on the potion and when he has finished he says that I can play with you, so we don't want you to be too badly hurt," she said with a smile. "You on the other hand," she said turning to Dan with a look of distaste, "have caused too much inconvenience. I have told them to shoot you through the head if you try to run."

"Now, lets take a walk shall we? I believe you know the way to the hospital," she said putting an arm through Elizabeth's and leaving Dan to trail along behind with her two henchmen.

7. Venice - Present day

"Ah, Julia found you, how lovely!' said Dragas with mock sincerity as they were led into a glass fronted control booth that looked over a room containing a CT Scanner. On the bed of the scanner was what Dan presumed was the body taken from the Basilica.

"They were exactly where you said they would be, Andris," said Julia with a smirk.

"That, my dear Daniel and Elizabeth, is an example of the benefits of having taken the Blood of Constantine, or as I should perhaps now call it, the blood of Alexander!" said Dragas, "... or maybe the potion of Aristotle!"

"People are so incredibly predictable, especially intelligent ones! How obvious was it that you would realise that I would need to examine the corpse and that there are only two hospitals in Venice with the facilities to do so. The only question was whether it would be you or Thomas Malm who would think of it first!" he said with a laugh.

"Still, we are all together now and we have the opportunity to solve a real mystery! Luckily this is one of the many hospitals that the Dragas family has donated money to over the years. Since the mid 1700's in this instance. My forebears were always keen to help those poor fellows injured in war. It's not good for business to have too many injured ex-soldiers walking the streets, uncared for!"

"So you admit that your family deals in death, Dragas?" said Dan.

"Of course!" said Dragas, ignoring the obvious judgement in Dan's tone. "Constantine the eleventh didn't need to take the potion to realise that the future of his family fortunes lay in the new technologies of war. He had just seen cannons blow apart the impregnable walls of Constantinople!"

"Now, the Hospital has very kindly loaned me their brand new CT Scanner for a couple of hours. Why don't we see if this really is the body of Saint Mark or if it is the body of Alexander the Great?"

Dan and Elizabeth stood at the back of the room watching the corpse slide through the giant white doughnut of the scanner.

Once the body had passed through the scanner the technician operating it worked for a few minutes, typing on his keyboard and then stood up, nodded to Dragas and left the room.

"Ah! The moment of truth!" said Dragas rubbing his hands together and taking over the technician's chair. "Let us start by having a close look at the legs!"

Dragas touched a key and the external surface of the corpse was revealed. It was clear that the body had been wrapped in some sort of material and there were indications that there was a layer of desiccated flesh and muscle still clinging to the bones.

Dragas dragged and clicked the mouse and the skeleton of the body itself was revealed.

"Here we are, he said looking closely at the big monitor, "This is the left leg. If we travel up here we should see if there is any thickening in the density of the bone that might reveal a healed break."

They all watched enthralled as the image moved past on the screen.

"Looks perfectly normal!" said Dragas. "Let's have a look at the other leg."

Again the image moved slowly past on the screen. This time the image was very different. Rather than the smooth gentle curve of the tibia, the narrower calf bone had a significantly thicker area just above the ankle.

"There we go!" said Dragas, clapping his hands together. "Now let's see what has happened to the chest!"

The upper thigh and hip flashed on the screen and then it stabilised above the middle of the chest. Dragas moved the image so that it focused on the sternum.

"Son of a bitch!" said Elizabeth, involuntarily, caught up in the excitement, despite their predicament. "It really is Alexander the Great!"

They all looked in stunned silence. The damage to the sternum and the ribs around it was obvious.

"Well, imagine that!" said Dragas. "The long lost body of Alexander the Third of Macedon! Truly remarkable!"

Dragas turned to Luigi who had also been standing at the back of the room. "You know what to do!" he said shortly.

Dan and Elizabeth watched as Luigi led Paolo into the scanning room. They dragged a long wooden packing case out from beneath the observation window and opened it up. They then, very carefully, lifted out an Egyptian mummy case, which they placed on the floor beside the CT scanner. They lifted the lid from the sarcophagus and carefully lifted a mummy out.

The mummy was not in good shape, some of its bones were exposed where the wrappings had decayed. It looked, to the uninitiated, remarkably similar to the corpse that still rested on the bed of the CT Scanner.

It took Luigi and Paolo only a few minutes to swap the two corpses over and repack the sarcophagus with the corpse of Alexander.

Following Dragas, Elizabeth and Dan, with Julia and the coffin, carried by Paolo and Luigi, behind them, trooped through the hospital to the back entrance and into a waiting Motoscafi.

****

Twenty minutes later, Alberto and a team of Carabinieri burst into the radiology suite.

"All clear!" said Alberto. "It looks like they have left the relic!"

"Thank God!" said the Bishop of Venice, ten minutes later, when he walked over to the corpse lying on the CT Scanner table. After a brief inspection he knelt down beside the remains and prayed.

8. Dragas' jet - Present day

"So the world thinks that the remains of Saint Mark are all safe and sound! Another miracle!' said Dan, sarcastically.

"Oh, yes!" said Dragas. And not only that, but when they investigate the remains, if the Pope ever lets them, they will discover that they are the right age and the right ethnicity. I was very careful to make sure that 'Saint Mark" will always, from now on, be, unquestionably, Saint Mark."

"And what about Alexander?" asked Elizabeth.

"Alexander will be well looked after. Once you have isolated whatever it is in his genes that activate the Blood of Constantine his body will be respectfully interred in a safe place where my family will be sure to always have access to it," he said, smugly.

"And what happens to us?" asked Dan.

"For the moment I need you, or at least Elizabeth. Your old partner is still proving to be a big disappointment I am afraid. The poor man just didn't have the skills or the flair to solve this little problem of mine.'"

Once you have solved the riddle of the potion then I, personally, will have no more need of you. I understand that Julia has taken quite a fancy to Elizabeth," he said with a creepy smile. "but you, Daniel, have proven yourself way too resourceful."

"It is obviously important to keep you alive while Elizabeth works on the potion, should she need any encouragement to maintain focus on her task. I have always found that the screams of a loved one can be a very useful motivator. After the job is done the length of your lives will depend on your behaviour."

"I am not an uncivilised man!" said Dragas, after a pause. "If you do as you are told, you might live. If you try and escape or otherwise act in a manner that I find disagreeable you won't live. It is that simple." Dragas smiled politely. "Now if you will excuse me I need to get a few things done. This whole affair with the potion has been a significant distraction, and my other duties beckon," he said standing up and walking to the partitioned off section at the back of the plane. He closed the door behind him as he passed through it.

627

9. Location unknown - Present day

"How's it going?" Dan asked looking over Elizabeth's shoulder.

"I still haven't managed to find any of the virus alive," she said looking up from the microscope she had been looking through. "How about you dig a little deeper this time, perhaps try one of the vertebrae?"

"OK! You're the boss!" he said and walked back over to the table where Alexander's body lay. The skeleton lay open and exposed, its rotting wrappings cut away. Dan brought a spinning blade carefully into contact with one of the vertebrae below the rib cage, slicing off a section.

"I wish I knew more about how they mummified bodies. It might make it easier to figure out where there might be some dormant virus," said Elizabeth. "I'd look it up on the web, but Dragas still refuses to give me any access at all."

"Hang on! I've got a copy of Herodotus in that pile of books he put in our room. Herodotus wrote a description of seeing a mummy being worked on, I'm sure. That would have been a couple of hundred years before Alexander was embalmed, but I guess it would be pretty much the same process."

Dan retrieved the book from their room, which was accessed through an interconnected door to the modern well equipped laboratory in which they now spent most of their time. He sat at a work bench skimming through the paperback he held in his hand. "Here we go!" he said reading from the book. "It says that with a crooked iron tool they hooked the brains out through the nose and then dissolved whatever was left with drugs. It doesn't say what sort of drugs though. They then take all the guts and wash the cavity with palm wine before stuffing it full of spices. Then they shove it in natron for seventy days."

Elizabeth looked thoughtful. "The alcohol in the palm wine would probably kill most bacteria and possibly viruses. The natron would be a pretty difficult thing for a virus to survive in too."

"As well as the vertebrae, how about we take a slice out of the femur. Its the biggest bone in the body and potentially far enough away from all that basting in palm wine and herb stuffing!"

Dan laughed. "Your wish is my command."

A couple of hours later they were working together preparing cultures from scrapings taken from the interior of the bones that Dan had sliced up. Standing close together, with a tap left running in a nearby sink, to cover the sound of their voices, Elizabeth asked. "Had one of your ingenious brainwaves to get us out of here yet?"

"They are watching us a bit too closely this time," he said his eyes indicating one of the many cameras that seemed to cover every part of the laboratory. "They lock up all the useful chemicals every night before they let us out of here and they have only given us roll on deodorant in our bathroom. There are no windows in either the lab or the rooms they have let us use. In fact we've literally been kept in the dark since we were bundled off Dragas' plane into that van. I have no idea what country we are even in, let alone what city or town! I just haven't got anything to work with. I am really just praying that Charlotte is okay."

"I am sure that between them Thomas and Alberto will make sure nothing happens to her," said Elizabeth, consolingly. "Its us that I'm worried about."

"We really should have left this alone when we had the chance, shouldn't we? Even if we somehow get away now, I can't see how we will ever get Dragas off our backs, mine, yours, Charlotte's or Alberto's."

"You'll think of something, my love! You always do!" said Elizabeth giving him a peck on the cheek.

"I hope you are right, 'cos just at the moment I got nuffin!"

10. Rome - Present day

Alberto opened the door and let Thomas inside. "Any news?" he asked as Thomas shrugged off his coat and hung it on the stand by the door. He walked across to Charlotte, who had followed Alberto to the door, and gave her a kiss on both cheeks.

"We have tracked the plane to Rome, but of course no one saw any reason to keep an eye on the passengers or crew once they left the airport. They could be anywhere by now. There is no signal from either of their mobile phones."

"I have put out an alert through Interpol to look out for Daniel and Elizabeth, but it will be sheer luck if we hear anything back," he said as he sat down on one of the stools pulled up to the kitchen bench.

"Do you think they are all right?" Charlotte asked, the stress and worry of the last week starting to tell.

"If, as we suspect, Dragas grabbed them then he probably needs them to find a new way to make the potion work," said Thomas. "I am sure they are safe for the time being"

"I hope you are right," said Charlotte. "One small mercy is that they didn't find Alexander's body."

"Have you heard anything from your friends in the church about the corpse that they took from the Basilica?" Thomas asked Alberto.

"Yes. The initial analysis suggests that the remains are of a male, somewhere around sixty years old. They did something called a stable isotope analysis that has suggested that the man had grown up with a fish rich diet, consistent with the history of Mark who was supposed to have grown up on the Libyan coast."

"The vatican's archaeologist said that there is evidence of catastrophic trauma around the neck, suggesting that the story about Mark being dragged through the streets of Alexandria with a rope around his neck till he was dead is probably true. Everything is consistent with what the church understands about the life of Mark. Apparently there is even an area that shows some signs of scorching of some of the bones and flesh, as if the body has been pulled from a fire. The Patriarch of Venice is very happy!"

"Dragas must have been pissed after all his effort to get the body!" said Charlotte with a grin. "At least he doesn't always get everything he wants!"

"No, and I don't imagine that he is having an easy time with your father and Elizabeth. I can't imagine them being overly co-operative," said Thomas.

11. Location unknown - Present day

Elizabeth looked down the microscope and was just about to change the sample when she stopped. "Dan, could you come over here please."

Dan walked over to where she was sitting. "I am getting a bit tired. Could you take over looking at these next few slides?"

Dan nonchalantly took her place and looked down the microscope. In whispered conversation, in bed at night, they had agreed a signal that would alert the other that they had found a viable virus, without alerting Dragas. This was it.

Sure enough, he found himself looking at an active virus. The problem was what to do now. If they just kept working they could be held, wherever they were, for months. They guessed it had already been two weeks and they were both starting to get disorientated by the monotonous routine and not knowing what time of day it was.

On the other hand, if they let Dragas know that they had found the key component needed to reactivate the potion then things might actually change. They might get the opportunity to escape. Alternatively, he might consider their usefulness was at end and they might be killed.

Even if they did manage to escape, not knowing where they were was another major issue. For all they knew they could be out in the middle of a desert, or on an island somewhere. Planning to escape when you didn't know what you were escaping into was decidedly tricky.

Dan made a mental note of the slide that contained the live sample, and moved onto the next one, while Elizabeth prepared more samples.

Just as Dan leant forward to look down the microscope, the door opened and Dragas walked in, followed closely by Luigi who stood by the door, a gun held loosely in his hand.

"So, you have a live virus!" he said walking over to Dan and picking up the sample that he had just removed from the microscope. "Let me see it!" he demanded.

Elizabeth and Dan looked at each other, stunned, not sure how Dragas had found out about the virus and that they had just found a live version of it. They stood aside as Dragas took a turn at the microscope.

"Ah, fantastic!" he said, straitening up. "Now, I will give you some of the original potion that we took from the Alaric vial and you will make up an active batch."

"You will also need some appropriate blood to mix it with, which I will provide!' he said.

Elizabeth, hesitated, then said, "Really? Are you sure about that?"

Dragas looked irritated by her question. "You know so little!" he said arrogantly. "The blood of Con..." he paused for a moment, " ...the mixture has always been mixed with the blood of the man who is to drink it."

"That at least explains why Hitler's DNA was in the Hitler vial. He had probably got the same story from Hess and the apothecary in Alexandria. He was mixing his own blood with the brew that Morell was concocting," said Elizabeth.

"Once you have prepared an active sample of the potion, I want you to complete a full analysis of it. I want to know what all the original ingredients were! When that is done I will consider what to do with you!"

"You really are a prick, Dragas!" said Dan, knowing full well that he was not in a position to antagonise the man, but feeling frustrated and fed up with his arrogance. "I hope that, one day, someone gets to take you down in the most painful way possible!"

Dragas looked at Dan's face, suffused with anger and laughed."You are a child, Doctor Marsh. Despite your wealth and intelligence you have no idea how the world really works. It is the people that you no doubt call the 'pricks' of this world that actually run it!"

"People like you, who earn their money accidentally, and then stroke their own egos by engaging in altruistic philanthropy to give their lives meaning, never understand what wealth is really about. Money is about the creation of influence. With influence you can create a better world."

"A better world for who?" said Dan with a sneer. "People like you?"

"You are a heathen, Marsh. You are ignorant of the ways of the world and the ways of God. There is no redemption, no salvation for you. Once you pass through this life you have nothing to look forward to but the fires of hell!"

"Well I guess I will just see you there then, because there is no way your God is going to let you into heaven after the life you have led. Killing innocents like my family will ensure that."

"Your wife wasn't an innocent. She was a heathen like you. I don't kill innocents, only those that are beyond redemption!" said Dragas, contemptuously. "Only those that deserve it!"

Dan had been surreptitiously moving closer to Dragas as they had been arguing, making sure that Dragas was between his own position and Luigi. He could feel the anger and bitterness rising. "Sarah may have made a conscious decision to not believe the puerile religious crap that infects you, but even you have to admit that the baby inside her was, even by your distorted and corrupt thinking, truly innocent."

Dan saw doubt and confusion in Dragas eyes. He obviously hadn't know that Sarah had been pregnant when he had her killed. The moment of distraction was enough for Dan, he launched himself at Dragas, punching him as hard as he could in the face as he came within reach and pushing him backwards towards Luigi.

Luigi neatly sidestepped and Dragas and Dan hit the wall, hard. A brief moment of satisfaction washed through Dan as he saw Dragas eyes roll back into the top of his head. It was, however only a very brief moment of triumph as Luigi stepped forward and brought the but of his gun down hard on the back of Dan's head.

Dazed he felt himself pushed off Dragas and a sudden explosion of pain in this stomach as Luigi kicked him hard. Winded, Dan struggled for breath and consciousness. Another kick landed in his groin and another explosion of pain shot through his body. He didn't feel the third kick that snapped his head back and brought oblivion.

****

Elizabeth screamed and launched herself at Luigi's back. She grabbed on to him and dug her fingers in to his face. One finger pressed hard against his eyeball. Luigi spun around, smashing Elizabeth's body against the wall. She fell into a heap on the floor. Luigi, incandescent with rage, lifted his gun. He pointed it at Elizabeth's head, flicked off the safety catch and started to squeeze the trigger.

"No!" shouted Dragas desperately. "I need her alive!"

Luigi hesitated for a moment, then lowered his gun. He stepped over to where Dragas still slumped against the wall and helped him to his feet. He looked down at Dan and then across at Elizabeth. "Take him and put him in one of the cells. Don't bother about being gentle about it. I want him alive, but I don't care if he is living in pain."

Luigi grinned and grabbed Dan's arm. He dragged him across the floor to the door. Dragas opened it and then followed Luigi through the door, locking it after him.

Elizabeth lay where she had fallen, sobbing until she felt a gentle hand on her head. She flinched at the touch, turning to see who it was. Julia knelt beside her, a concerned smile on her face. "Don't worry" she said in a soothing voice. "I will look after you."

"I don't want you to look after me," said Elizabeth angrily. "Where is Dan? What has that psychopath done with him?"

"Dan is a little the worse for wear, I am afraid, but he's still alive. As long as you continue to cooperate he won't be hurt," she paused, "any more. It is entirely up to you." "And," Julia paused again as she ran her hand gently and slowly down Elizabeth's arm, "how cooperative you are."

Elizabeth flinched. Julia's eyes hardened for a moment, but then she smiled again. "Perhaps you need a little time to think about your predicament," she said standing up. "I'll just go and have a word with Luigi, shall I?"

"No!" said Elizabeth quickly. Then, more slowly "I just need a little time to .. recover"

Julia smiled. "That's the way. I look forward to seeing you later," she said as she tapped on the door. It opened and she walked out without looking back.

****

Dan woke up with a start. Pain shot through his body. He had a splitting headache. His face hurt, his lips were swollen and crusted in blood. He could only just open his eyes. His stomach ached and it felt like he had two tennis balls in his trousers. He groaned. He could taste vomit in his mouth.

He was lying on a steel cot on a dank smelling, stained mattress. A single light bulb hung, glowing dimly, from the ceiling. The walls of the room were bare concrete. They perfectly matched the floor which was covered in puddles of what he hoped, was just water. By twisting his head slightly he could see the door of the room. It was painted grey. Patches of rust showed through the flaking paint. There were no windows and it was cold. He was handcuffed to the steel cot. He pulled the one thin blanket that was on the bed around himself and curled into a ball.

12. Rome - Present day

Charlotte met Thomas at the door of the apartment "Any news?" she asked before he had even stepped over the threshold.

"Thomas shook his head. "It's like looking for a needle in a paddock full of haystacks. Dragas' plane touched down in four different cities. When he left Venice he flew to Zurich, then to Prague, on to Berlin and finally to Rome. Dan and Elizabeth could be in any of those cities, or none of them by now."

They walked into the living room where Alberto was already making coffee. He invited them to take a seat at the island bench.

"This is impossible!' said Charlotte tears starting to well up in her eyes. "However are we going to find them."

"I don't know," said Thomas. "I've tried everything I can think of. I've arranged alerts at airports and seaports. I've put a trace on Dragas' jet, but that is just sitting at the airport in Rome. His boat is still in Alexandria and hasn't moved since it arrived there a month ago. It looks like Dragas has gone to ground. That model friend of his has not turned up anywhere lately either. I've checked with as many people in the fashion industry as I can get to. No-one has seen her and she isn't booked for any modelling jobs that I can find."

"Modelling jobs," said Charlotte repeating part of Thomas' comment. "Modelling," she said again thoughtfully. "I wonder."

Alberto and Thomas stared at her.

"You have thought of something?" asked Alberto.

"Well, maybe," said Charlotte hesitantly. "If it was Dragas who kidnapped Liz and Dad to work on the potion, then one thing that Liz would need to do the job properly is modelling software to model the chemical reactions and the reactions of the potion on human cells."

"So?" said Thomas, "Dragas could afford to buy any software she needed."

"Yes, that's true, but this is a very specialised field. There aren't many people in the world using the sort of software that Liz used. It was one of her things. She was working with a bunch of colleagues from Oxford and MIT. They developed a suite of software programs that they were about to launch on to the market. Liz had our people in Sydney put together a web site that was going to be the portal through which they sold the software. The site was meant to go live a few weeks ago, but I am guessing, with Liz missing, it hasn't happened. Currently you would have to know the actual URL to get access to it. There would only be, maybe, a half dozen people in the world, at most, who know about the site!"

"So what are you saying? If we keep an eye on that site, we might be able to get a lead on where they are?" asked Thomas.

"It would be worth a try," said Charlotte. "Liz is unlikely to let Dragas, or any of his cronies know how few people have access to that site. Dragas would have to have someone go online and register, which he would undoubtedly do using a bogus email and probably pay for the software using some untraceable corporate credit card, but because so few people even know about the site, it might be possible to track him."

"The administrator is one of Dad's senior techs in Sydney. I could give him a ring and see if anyone has accessed the site lately. If someone has we might be able to get their IP address and track them through that!"

Twenty minutes later Charlotte put the phone down. "The site was accessed two days ago!" she said with a grin. "I've got the IP address. Thomas, do you think your gurus at MI6 could track its location?"

"We will give it a red hot go!" said Thomas reaching for the set of numbers that made up the address of the computer that had accessed the web site.

Three hours later Thomas' phone rang. After a brief conversation he turned to Charlotte and Alberto. "They're in Berlin! I've got the location within 600 meters!"

13. Berlin - Present day

Thomas had arranged an Interpol team to covertly watch the building that Charlotte's idea had pinpointed as the location from which the web site had been accessed. They had been watching for two days and as yet, no one that they recognised as being associated with Dragas had gone either in or out.

The building, a slightly ramshackle apartment building, was one of the many that had been built quickly in the East German sector of Berlin after the Second World War. It now appeared to be an artist's squat. The building was covered in colourful graffiti and street art and three huge pink pipes passed along the street about twenty feet off the ground in front of it. The whole area looked like one crazy modern art installation.

The ownership of the building itself had been impossible to trace. It was apparently owned by a property development company, but the contact details of anyone listed on any of the official documents appeared to be either missing or illegible.

Alberto, who had got tired of just sitting around and waiting for something to happen, sat on a street corner opposite the apartment building, at a cafe that one of the local artists had set up out the front of her flat. The tables and chairs were an eclectic mixture of styles and colours, scavenged from wherever the owner, Anna, could find them. She served great coffee, and a passable apple cake, which, at least to Alberto's eyes, made the place a worthwhile hangout. Anna was Italian and Alberto soon found himself showing her how he cooked his Nonna's favourite recipe.

Alberto had been happily working away, peeling apples, when Anna walked into the kitchen fuming. "Fuckin' arse-hole!" she said throwing a coffee cup and saucer so violently into the sink that chips of china bounced onto the floor.

While he had only known her for a few days, Alberto was surprised to see someone, normally so happy and amicable, so angry. "What is the problem?"

"Oh, it's nothing," she said, almost apologetically.

"Come on" wheedled Alberto with a smile. "What's made you so cross?"

"Oh it really is nothing. It's just that it was Italian men like that," she said indicating someone outside, "that made me leave home! Arrogant, opinionated, misogynistic bastardi!"

Suddenly alert, Alberto asked with a smile, "Another Italian, where?"

Anna opened the window of the kitchen and pointed to a man, dressed in scruffy jeans and a t-shirt, walking back towards the apartment building. He recognised him instantly, despite the crude attempt to blend in with the local artist community. Luigi!

Alberto excused himself and walked out into the street. He followed Luigi along one side of the building and then around a corner, keeping a respectful distance and always making sure that a number of other people where between them.

Luigi came to the front door of the building and let himself in. There was a keypad on the door, but it didn't work. Anyone could walk in. Alberto followed him into the building. There was a long hallway that led to a central courtyard. The courtyard was crowded with bikes in various states of repair and rubbish bins in various states of overflow. Alberto watched from the shadowy hallway as Luigi walked casually into another door across the far side of the courtyard and then let himself into a ground floor flat.

He waited a few minutes and then walked up the stairs that led to the flats opposite the one Luigi had walked into. He stopped at the first floor landing window, which had once been rippled glass, but was now broken. From this vantage point he could see easily see into Luigi's flat through the four windows that faced out onto the courtyard. The first window looked like it was the living room. Through it he could see an old worn-out couch and some mismatched armchairs. The second window was the bedroom that contained an unmade bed. The third window was narrower than the other two and looked like it was a small kitchen. The last window was very small and frosted, presumably the bathroom.

Alberto sat on the landing watching the flat for two hours. In all that time he did not see Luigi once. He knew that he had walked into the flat. He knew that he had not come out of the flat. If he had he would have seen him. As the afternoon wore on the other residents of the other flats started to turn their lights on. Alberto had almost dozed off when the bedroom light in the flat went on. He suddenly came alert. The light was on, but no one was there to turn it on. A few minutes later the living room light came on. Again, there was no sign of Luigi. Then the bedroom curtains were closed, as if by magic.

Alberto thoughtfully walked back to Anna's cafe.

As he walked in she gave him an odd look, shrugged and went back to making coffee. Alberto started peeling apples again. After a little while he asked. "The building across the way. How big are those apartments?'

"Why you thinking of moving in?' she asked with a sudden smile.

Alberto smiled back. "Maybe. Just wondering how many bedrooms they have."

"I've got a spare room here, if you need somewhere to stay," she said, flushing pink as she quickly turned back to the espresso machine. Then to cover her embarrassment, "They are all one bedroom over there. You just grab one when someone moves out."

Alberto nodded thoughtfully.

14. Berlin - Present day

That evening, Thomas, Alberto and Charlotte were sitting at a street restaurant a few blocks from the artists squat where Alberto had seen Luigi.

"My guys have set up surveillance systems all around the flat. Luigi has been in and out a few times. It is definitely him. What we can't figure out is what happens when he goes into the flat. We literally lose him!" said Thomas, clearly exasperated. "The only room we can't see into is the bathroom."

"Perhaps he spends his time in there, having long baths," said Charlotte.

"Where does he go?" asked Thomas. "The apartments on either side are legit, or at least as legit as a squatters place can be. The one above it is legit. It only leaves a basement, and as far as the plans show, incomplete as they are, they didn't build a basement to the building when it was put up in the early 1950's."

"What if, said Alberto who had been puzzling over this conundrum all afternoon, "the basement was already there?"

"You mean there could be a basement from an old building and they just built on top of it?" asked Charlotte.

"Or" said Thomas, leaning forward excitedly, "what if there was an air raid shelter under the building! They were built with massively thick concrete roofs. There would be no way the East German Authorities would have bothered digging up a bunker. They would have just built over it!"

"And the Dragas family could have taken the opportunity to purchase something as unique as an apartment with a subterranean shelter, figuring that Berlin would eventually become a wealthy city again and they might have a use for it!" said Charlotte. "God, if the Dragas family are always thinking with time horizons of hundreds of years the decisions they make must be totally different to the rest of us!"

"So, how do we flush them out of their underground hole without alerting them to the fact we are on to them?" asked Thomas.

"Exactly!" said Alberto, grinning. "Flush!"

****

Elizabeth hadn't seen Dan for two days, ever since he was dragged unconscious from the laboratory by Luigi.

Without Dan sharing her room, over the last couple of nights she had taken to chocking a chair under the door handle to make sure no one could get in while she was sleeping.

She had continued to work on the analysis of the potion and, now that she had the software that she had asked Dragas to get for her, building the computer model of its effect on the human body. The work distracted her from her predicament, and was also a distraction from worrying about what had happened to Dan.

She was concentrating so hard on her modelling work that she didn't notice Julia come into the laboratory. She had taken to dropping in at odd times. She would try and engage Elizabeth in conversation. Elizabeth would ignore her. She could tell that this infuriated Julia, who would eventually leave the laboratory in a huff.

The first she knew about Julia being in the room was when she was grabbed around the neck and pulled backwards so that she was balanced precariously on two legs of the high stool on which she was sitting. She could feel Julia's warm breath close to her ear.

"I have been very patient with you Lizzy." Julia whispered. "If you want to come out of this situation alive I think it is time that you stopped being mean to me." Elizabeth felt Julia kiss her gently on her cheek. "You know that I want you! I have since that first moment I saw you at the restaurant in Amalfi" she kissed Elizabeth on the cheek again.

Julia suddenly let the stool go. It dropped for a few centimetres before she caught it. Elizabeth gasped.

"Now, I am in control!" whispered Julia, as she leant in and kissed Elizabeth on the neck. She let the stool drop suddenly and before Elizabeth knew what was happening Julia had covered her mouth with her own. Elizabeth started to struggle, but realised if she did that Julia would drop the stool and she would very likely crack her skull on the hard polished concrete floor.

Elizabeth started to respond to Julia's advances. She brought her hands up and rested them on Julia's neck, gently stroking her warm flesh. After a short while Julia brought the stool up to its rightful position and let Elizabeth stand up. The two women stood locked in an embrace. Elizabeth gently moved Julia backwards so that she was pushing her against one of the laboratory work tables. Julia slid on to the table. Her legs parted and she pulled Elizabeth towards her as she leaned backward.

"I'm getting wet!" said Elizabeth suddenly pulling away from Julia. "Me too" said Julia, her eyes misty, reaching for Elizabeth.

"No. I mean I am getting wet. The laboratory is flooding, you stupid cow!" Around her feet dirty brown water swirled. "Jesus!" she said pulling Julia off the table. "It's rising fast." In the few seconds it had taken to realise what was going on the water had already risen a couple of inches. "We have to get out of here, quick!"

The laboratory door was pushed open and Luigi stood looking at them. The fly of his jeans was undone and his shirt was untucked. "We have to get out of here now!" he ordered, "before the weight of the water makes the doors impossible to open!"

Luigi grabbed Elizabeth's arm as she reached the door. He dragged her down a hallway to a steel door, which she had always assumed was the entrance to the building they were in. It opened into a short concrete corridor. Steel doors led off on either side of the hallway and, for the first time, Elizabeth realised that they were in some sort of bunker.

The water was now just below their knees. Wading through it was getting difficult. The current seemed to be getting stronger. Luigi dragged her though another steel door and then up a flight of concrete steps down which water was cascading.

Luigi pulled the steel door at the top of the steps open. All three of them were thrown down the steps by the rush of dirty brown water that poured through the entrance.

Caught by surprise Elizabeth fell backwards into Julia. They were both forced underwater and down the hallway. Elizabeth struggled to stand up, eventually grabbing on to the doorjamb of one of the rooms they had passed. She pulled herself to her feet, coughing and spluttering, and looked around her. Both Luigi and Julia were still struggling to stand against the flow of the water. Seeing her chance, she made her way to the steps and grabbed on to the rail that angled up beside them. As she got near the top of the steps an arm reached down and pulled her through the door.

To her amazement she was standing in a well lit apartment. Alberto was standing in front of her grinning, waist deep in muddy brown water that was still spilling out of a huge pink pipe that had somehow smashed through one of the flat's external windows.

Alberto pulled her out of the way of a small squad of armed men who waded through the door and down into the rapidly filling concrete corridor. Julia and Luigi were dragged through the door. Elizabeth watched as they were taken out to a group of waiting German policemen.

"Where's Dan?" asked Alberto looking into the corridor.

"I don't know!" said Elizabeth. "You mean he is not with you? I thought he had somehow escaped and that's why you were here!'

"No.' said Alberto looking concerned. "Charlotte tracked you down because you downloaded some piece of software or other. We thought the two of you were together."

Elizabeth shook her head. "Then he's still down there somewhere! They beat him up pretty badly a couple of days ago and then dragged him off somewhere. I haven't seen him for two days!"

"Fuck!" said Alberto. He dove for the door and splashed down the steps. The water was now above his waist and still rising. "See if you can get them to stop the water! I'll see if I can find him!" he shouted over his shoulder.

Alberto waded down the corridor, checking each of the rooms that led from it. Even though they were only dimly lit, he could see that they were all empty. He came to the door which led to the section of the bunker that had been done up for contemporary use. The walls were painted and it was well it. He found several bedrooms, a recreation room, the laboratory and a high tech surveillance centre with a bank of monitors showing images of the rooms he had just looked into as well as those of the flat above. Dan was not in any of them.

Alberto made his way back to the entrance. He retraced his steps. There had to be more rooms down here. The water was now almost up to the middle of his chest and it was getting harder to move around. With a crackle and flash the lights suddenly went out.

He pulled his wet smartphone out of his pocket and mentally crossed his fingers. It worked! He turned on the torch app. It wasn't a lot of light but it would be enough to search by.

A second door led from the opposite side of the entrance corridor. With difficulty, Alberto pushed it open. It was heavy to move, not just because he was pushing it through water, but because it had clearly not been used often.

This corridor was much colder than the renovated one. he could feel the chill on his skin as he entered. The smell of mould and neglect filled the air. As soon as he pushed open the door, Alberto could hear someone screaming.

****

Dan had been asleep when the water had started to seep in under the door of the cell they had thrown him into. He had only woken up when he had rolled over and his free arm had flopped off the edge of the metal cot.

It had taken him a few seconds to figure out what was going on. In the gloominess of his cell he had watched with growing terror as the water rose. He pulled at the metal handcuff that tethered him to the cot. It dug uncomfortably into his wrist. Standing next to the cot he tried to lift it up. It was bolted to the floor.

He squatted on the cot. The water swirled around his legs. He started to shout.

By the time the water was up to his neck he was freezing cold and shivering and his voice was getting hoarse. He was pulling hard against the handcuff. He could no longer feel the pain of it cutting into his wrist. His hand was numb. He continued to scream. Then the lights went out. He was in complete darkness. He screamed louder!

Dan struggled to keep his head above water. He tried to maintain a squatting position, but his legs were starting to cramp. He took a breadth and ducked his head under water so he could straighten out his leg and relieve the pain, but he was forced back into the uncomfortable squatting position to get his head above water again. He gasped for air. The water was lapping around his chin.

He shouted as loud as he could, swearing at Luigi and Dragas and demanding to be let out. He stopped to catch his breath. He thought he heard a noise. He started shouting again. Then he heard a voice. A wave of relief washed over him. It was Alberto, calling his name!

The water was now up to his ears. He shouted. "Alberto! I am tied to a bed! I am about to drown, help me!" By the time he had said it, his ears were under water. Now he couldn't hear anything, couldn't see anything, and was so cold he could hardly feel anything.

****

Elizabeth had run outside the flat to find Thomas. He was standing speaking to some of the local police. "Thomas, quick! We have to stop the water. Dan is still down there somewhere!"

Thomas looked at her. It took a moment to process the implications of what she had said. He talked into his radio. He listened for a few minutes and then started to get angry. He turned to Elizabeth. "It will take them an hour to get someone here from the piping company. Come on, lets get my chaps and we'll see if we can move that pipe by ourselves!"

Thomas yelled orders and four of his men ran back into the flat where the pipe had smashed through the window and part of the external wall. The water was still pouring in, unabated, through the large pink pipe.

Above the noise of the water flooding the flat Elizabeth, shouted, "Why can't they just turn the water off at the source?"

"This is all water from a construction site," shouted Thomas. "The groundwater round here is so high that when they build a new building they have to constantly pump water out of the foundations. If they stop pumping the water they will flood the construction site!"

The men were struggling to move the pipe.

"How did you get it in here to start with?" she shouted.

"You know how these pipes are all suspended in the air?" he asked. Elizabeth nodded. "Well, Alberto ran into it with a truck and pushed it through the wall!" he shouted back. Elizabeth and Thomas both stepped in to help the others try to move the pipe. "Why?" she shouted.

"We couldn't find the entrance to the bunker and we couldn't look for it without arousing suspicion. We had to flush you all out somehow. It seemed like a good idea at the time!" he shouted over the rush of the water.

A couple more people that had been passing by were dragooned in to help. Eventually the pipe began to shift.

With a final heave it moved out onto the footpath. The water continued to flood out of the pipe, only now it was flooding into the gutter and across the road.

****

Alberto put his shoulder against the door and pushed. He held his phone above his head and directed the light of the tiny torch into the room. Other than the water, which was now up to his armpits, it looked empty. He was just turning away to try the next room when he saw bubbles burst through the surface of the water.

He pushed his way into the room and, with his arms outstretched, began to feel his way around it. Something grabbed him. He reached down to feel what it was. He found an arm. He followed it. He found a head. It was just under the water.

Alberto took a deep breath and then grabbed the head with both hands. With one hand he felt for the nose. He pinched it shut. With the other he found the mouth. He put his own mouth over it. Dan knew immediately what he was doing, and let Alberto blow fresh air into his lungs.

Alberto waited for a few seconds and then repeated the exercise. He then ducked under water, following, with Dan's help, the direction that brought him to the handcuffs around Dan's wrist.

He felt to where the handcuffs connected to the metal cot and then felt all around the metal cot, visualising as he did so, the location of the bolts that held it to the floor. He braced his feet against the floor and pulled upwards. Try as he might, he couldn't budge it.

He felt around the cot itself. It seemed to be made of metal. There was a piece of curved metal tubing at either end making up the bed head and foot, and the interior part, that the mattress sat on, was made of square section metal tubing, welded at the corners, with the bed springs attached to it. Across the bed, bent slightly downwards were two cross members made of lighter weight steel. Dan was handcuffed to the square side section.

Starting to run out of breath, Alberto stood up and pushed his face above the surface. The water was now up to his shoulders. It was still rising. He gave Dan some air, then ducked under the water again.

He put his feet against the steel side of the bed but found that he couldn't reach the opposite wall to get enough purchase to try and shift it. Desperately he tried to think of a way to free Dan.

He climbed underneath the bed and braced himself against the wall behind the bed-head. He kicked at the lightweight cross pieces. They both broke away after a few blows . Reaching under the bed for them he twisted them both free and resurfaced. He gave Dan some more air and then hyperventilated. Sucking as much air into his own lungs as he could he dove back under the water.

With Dan's assistance he pulled the mattress off the bed and removed all of the wire springs that stretched across it.

He then took a deep breath, gave Dan some air, took a deep breath for himself and ducked under the water again.

This time he felt for Dan's leg and followed it up to his waist. He undid his belt and slid it off, doing the same with his own. He then connected the two belts together at one end, wrapped them around the bed so that they stretched between the two side rails and then connected the other ends of the belt together, pulling them as tight as he could. They were just long enough.

He surfaced for air again, gave Dan some and then ducked under water for what he hoped would be for the last time.

He took one of the steel struts he had broken from under the bed and slid it into the gap between the two belts and began to turn the bar, twisting the two belts together. He kept turning putting more and more pressure on the side bars. He prayed that one of the welds would break before one of the belts did.

The bar became harder and harder to turn. Alberto was running out of breath and about to resurface for air when he felt the bar suddenly give way. Something had snapped. He felt for the rail on the side that Dan was handcuffed. The weld had broken!

Alberto braced himself next to the rail and pulled upward. The rail twisted towards the roof. As it went up his own head broke the surface of the water in time to hear Dan take a huge, rasping breath of air.

"Are you Okay?" asked Alberto as soon as he got his breath back.

"Other than a couple of broken ribs," he gasped between coughs," a face that probably looks like a mandrill's backside and testicles the size of tennis balls, I think so! Oh, and Dragas shot me full of something an hour or so ago!" he said, still trying to catch his breath. "Is Liz Okay? Did she get out?"

"Yeah, she seemed fine," said Alberto. "And Charlotte is too!" he said, knowing what Dan's next question would be. "Now, this water is till rising. We have to get out of here now! Can you get that bedrail off the handcuff?"

Dan tried to slide the handcuff off the rail but the fittings on either end made it impossible. "No! Looks like I will have to bring it with me!"

The water, which was up to Dan's chin was still rising as they made there way out, through several doors and a couple of short corridors.

Dan was partially blinded as he stepped out into the brightly lit apartment. He stood, dazed, in the middle of the living room, wet, bruised, battered and handcuffed to a seven foot long length of steel.

Charlotte, who had arrived a few minutes before, saw him and gasped. She ran to him. "God Dad, what did they do to you!" she cried.

"Nothing that a whiskey and a hot meal won't fix," he said hugging her. He looked over her shoulder and saw Liz, wrapped in a towel, coming through the door of the apartment.

He smiled at her and collapsed.

15. Rome - Present day

"How is he?" asked Alberto as he walked into the apartment.

Charlotte looked drawn and tired. "No change. He still has a high fever, and he hasn't woken up."

"That's what, almost thirty-six hours!" said Alberto looking at his watch. "Did the MI6 medico arrive?"

"Yes. He has set up an intravenous drip to keep Dad's fluids up, but he says there is nothing else he can do. We just have to wait."

Charlotte sat down at the big island bench that separated the kitchen and living room.

"And how are you, *Tesoro*?" asked Alberto starting to make coffee.

"Worried. I don't know what I would do if anything happened to Dad! I can't believe that Dragas shot him full of that revolting potion! Why would he do that?"

"My guess would be to test it. He couldn't be certain that Liz had guessed correctly about the active component being a mutated virus that Alexander had picked up somewhere. He couldn't even be completely sure that the corpse we had was really Alexander." Alberto turned the gas on under the coffee pot came and sat beside Charlotte. "If the potion had worked, Dragas was quite prepared to murder your father. If it didn't work, then he would have your dad's body to do a post-mortem on."

"Oh God this is all so horrible!" said Charlotte. Tears welled in her eyes. Alberto put a comforting arm on her shoulder. Before he could react she had turned and wrapped her arms around his neck and buried her face in his shoulder.

Charlotte was still holding Alberto when she heard a cough and her father's voice. "What's all this then? Has there been a death in the family?" he said. He was standing at the bedroom door with his arm over Elizabeth's shoulder.

Charlotte jumped like she had been electrocuted. "Dad?!" She ran to her father and put her hands on either side of his head and stared into his eyes, trying to see if he was the same person he had always been.

"The one and only!" he said with a grin.

"How do you feel? Are you Okay? Can you still remember everything? Oh God, are you still you?" she said in a rush of words, disconcerted by the intense colour of his normally brown eyes which now almost seemed to glow golden with an inner light.

"I think so!" said Dan with a grin as Elizabeth led him over to the big settee and sat him down. "But I have to say that something has happened inside my head. It is almost like someone has gone through and done a major tidy up in there. I thought that I was a pretty intuitive person who could see connections in things that others couldn't. In fact, I have made my fortune doing exactly that. But now I can see that I was a babe in the woods compared to what I now realise is potentially possible."

"It is almost as if everything I look at I can see ways of making it better, more efficient, more functional, more beautiful. It is an amazing feeling," he said putting both hands up to his head.

The smell of freshly brewed coffee was filling the apartment. Alberto walked over to the kitchen and brought back the coffee pot and cups.

A few minutes later they were all sitting on the settee sipping coffee, except for Dan.

Wanting to catch up with what was happening in the world, he had picked up Charlotte's iPad. It had opened to a game of Words with Friends she had been playing. The game was almost finished. Charlotte was losing badly and there were only two letters left. He looked for a moment at the screen.

"Wow!" he said putting the iPad back on the coffee table and touching his forehead with his fingers.

"What's the matter?" said Elizabeth and Charlotte in unison.

"It's Ok," he said seeing their worried faces. "That has never happened to me before! I looked at your game of Words with Friends and saw immediately how you could beat your opponent. It was bizarre!"

Charlotte picked up the iPad and looked at the screen. "You're kidding! I am being annihilated! There are only two letters left! and I am eighty something points behind!"

Dan concentrated for a second, then said, without pause, "The two letters that are left are an 'e' and a 'b'. Your opponent has an 'e', 'f', 'i','n', 'h', t' and a 'p'. If you put the word 'qi' on the side of the word 'remit' that will give you 44 points. The logical thing for your opponent to do is to put the word 'finite' across where you have put the i of qi. He will think that is a good move because it gives him a score of 28. His pattern of words indicates that he tries to get scores in excess of twenty but doesn't try harder to maximise his score. That will then allow you to put in the word 'friable', using all your letters and getting a score of 70 points, which will mean you will win by 1 point!"

"You only looked at the screen for a couple of seconds!" she exclaimed.

"Like I said, it is like someone has reorganised my mind. Information just streams in! Its like there is no filter on information. I see and remember everything! I could tell you the placement of every item in this room! It is staggering! I don't know how to explain it!"

Charlotte tapped on the screen of her iPad and then put it back on the coffee table.

"It sounds like a variation of savant syndrome," said Alberto.

"You mean my Dad is now Rainman?" asked Charlotte.

"Yes. Savant syndrome is usually related to damage to the anterior temporal lobe of the brain. Savants seem to have sensory hypersensitivity. Often they have eidetic or photographic memories. This ability leads them to become very detail focused. The level of detail focus they achieve is very useful in developing skills in mathematics, music and art."

"Are you suggesting that the potion has damaged Dan's brain?" asked Elizabeth.

"I don't know, Elizabeth. I do know that researchers have temporarily replicated savant syndrome using trans-cranial magnetic stimulation. By simultaneously decreasing excitability of the left anterior temporal lobe and increasing the excitability of the right anterior temporal lobe they have got some remarkable results. We may be seeing a chemically induced version of the effects they produced in the lab. If that is the case it may not be a permanent change," said Alberto.

"I don't feel like my brain is damaged. It feels more like it has been supercharged! I agree with Alberto. We don't know whether the effect will last, so I need to get on with trying to figure out what Dragas is up to. Charlie, can you set me up with a couple of computers with big screens.

I need to access as much information as fast as possible. Given that the Dragas family has had centuries to work on their plan, the clues to it could be anywhere."

"Sure thing," said Charlotte reaching for her phone. As she did so her iPad made a sound.

"Hah! You were right Dad. He did go with 'finite'! She tapped on the screen. "Beat him by one point! That could be a really useful talent you have Daddy!" she said with grin.

"Liz, while I grab a shower, could you get in touch with Thomas? We need to see if we can get access to the MI6 files on Dragas and the work that his analysts have done. It will save a lot of time."

"I'm on it!" she said grabbing her phone out of her pocket.

"Alberto..." began Dan.

"I will make some food while you have a shower, Dottore. You can not save the world on an empty stomach!"

Dan smiled and nodded. "That would be great! Thanks!"

16. Rome - Present day

Thomas Malm walked into Dan's apartment and stopped. Dan was sitting at the dining room table. Four large screens, connected to four cylindrical black Apple Pro computers formed an arc around him. He was moving rapidly from one computer to another, twisting in a swivel chair. The screens flashed with information. He could see the familiar MI6 Intranet on one, with scanned documents flicking past, page after page, each with a faded, red 'Top Secret' stamp on them.

"Didn't have any trouble accessing the MI6 network?" he asked Charlotte as she led him into the room.

"No. Thank you for arranging that," she said sitting him down at the island bench and pouring him coffee.

"How long has he been at it?" he said nodding towards Dan.

"Four days now. He catnaps every afternoon for an hour or so and then works through until three or four in the morning. He is up again at eight. I can't keep up with him! He just doesn't seem to need as much sleep as he used to," said Charlotte.

"A biphasic sleep pattern! Winston Churchill is often cited as doing something similar. So is Thomas Edison. It would be interesting to know if it's a result of the potion or just Dan's desire to get as much done as he can, just in case the effects of the potion wear off," said Thomas in a quiet voice.

"Oh, don't worry about whispering. His powers of concentration were always good, but now you couldn't distract him if you let a bomb off under his chair! It is pretty scary to see someone so absolutely absorbed," she said.

"Where are the others?" asked Thomas looking around the apartment for Elizabeth and Alberto.

"Liz is off doing some work on the active potion. She wants to know as much as she can about its effects, just in case something goes wrong with Dad. She is trying to finish the computer simulation of the potion to see how it interacts with different gene types. She has been running the computer boffins in Sydney ragged."

"Alberto is at the Vatican finding documents for Dad. He should be back soon," she said looking at her watch.

****

"I think I've got it!" said Dan!"

They all looked up, expectantly, from what they were doing.

Dan stood up, stretched and then walked over and sat down beside Elizabeth on the couch.

"Out with it Dad. What are the Dragas family really up to?" asked Charlotte.

"Okay, we know they want to pay back the Roman Catholic Church for shafting them, make the Orthodox Christian Church the number one religion in the world, get their city back and take down the infidels."

"Big ask!" said Elizabeth.

"It sure is!" said Dan "To do this they have been working over the centuries to build up their influence. That means they have plenty of money and power. So far they have managed to keep an incredibly low profile. Unless there is an institution, like the English secret service and its antecedents, that has taken a long term watching brief, you would hardly notice their activities. Even then, because of the way they work through others, it is almost impossible to discern any specific patterns."

"Their one major weaknesses is their reliance on the Blood of Constantine. We know through the work that Alberto did on the sacred relics, that they have periodically found vials of the potion. Every few generations they need a review of their strategy. The world changes and random events can, and do, derail their plans from time to time. This has been even more important since the Industrial Revolution because the pace of change has sped up so much."

"The Pope giving Napoleon the potion must have been unexpected and upset their plans for destabilising the Roman Catholic Church in France. The fact that Hitler got hold of a vial must have been a shock as well."

"Our involvement," he said waving his hand between himself and Elizabeth, "only came about because they have run so low on the potion

656

that they can no longer get the insights they need to continue their struggle. Their sponsorship of various scientists and promising PhD students through various scholarship programs was a tactic to try and accelerate the science that they needed to analyse the compound."

"Money wise they are loaded. Numbered bank accounts in Switzerland and Trusts setup in Liechtenstein are just the tip of the iceberg. It would be nearly impossible to trace the full extent of the Dragas fortune."

"On the power front, the patriarch, who is usually the only visible member of the family, is always well connected. He mostly tends to use his influence through personal contacts. Everything is done in the back rooms and the clubs of the wealthy and powerful. I could detect a Dragas influence in quite a few countries just through the pattern of political donations. Because they have such a long time horizon they can cultivate a large number of aspiring politicians and always end up with one or two who reach the highest levels. I could give you a list of extremely well known, and powerful politicians, who are effectively in the Dragas family pocket, although they would probably never know it themselves."

"So they don't want to restore themselves as Emperors?" asked Charlotte.

"I can't find any indication of that in their plans. In a way they are incredibly altruistic. All of this accumulation of power and influence is focused on their main objectives. There doesn't seem to be any personal gain involved. It almost seems to go against human nature."

"So what are they going to do Daniel?" asked Thomas.

"Well, as we all know there has been an increase in the level of militancy in the Islamic world. We already know that they have been stoking the fire, so to speak. What I believe is that Dragas has been working to set the Muslim world up as the fall guy. At the end of the day, whatever happens, it will be the Muslims of the world that will be blamed."

"But blamed for what?" asked Thomas.

"For the destruction of the Roman Catholic Church! The Dragas family have been setting up a situation that will lead to the complete destruction of the Roman Catholic Church."

"How could they do that? The Church is huge. It has over a billion people in its congregation! How do you destroy something like that?" asked Thomas.

"Let me ask you a question, Thomas. What happens when the Pope dies?" asked Dan.

"They have a conclave and all the Cardinals get together and elect a new one," he said.

"Not all the Cardinals." interrupted Alberto. "The College of Cardinals is limited to those Cardinals that are under eighty years old when the Pope dies."

"Ok," said Thomas, "The Cardinals who are under eighty get together and vote in a new Pope."

"And how many Cardinals are there?" Dan asked looking at Alberto.

"It depends on who has passed on. There are always quite a few over eighty. The Cardinal Electors though are limited to 120. So effectively 120 have to be under eighty."

"So the Cardinals elect a new Pope," said Dan. "Who elects a new Cardinal?"

"They are not elected. Cardinals are created by the Pope," said Alberto.

"Can anyone else create a new Cardinal?" he asked.

"No. Even during the period after a Pope's death, and before the election of a new Pope, when the Cardinals are running the church, they can not appoint a new Cardinal," said Alberto. "It is forbidden!"

"So what would happen if the Pope died and, before there was an election, all the Cardinal's died?" asked Dan.

Alberto looked shocked. "What all of them?"

Dan nodded.

"It couldn't happen!" said Alberto.

"But if it did?" insisted Dan.

Alberto just stared at him. After some time, shaking his head, he said. "I have no idea. There would be no one to elect a new Pope and no one to elevate new cardinals that could elect a new Pope so no one to elect a new Pope and no one to elevate anyone in the church to be a Cardinal!"

"A classic Catch 22 situation!" said Dan.

"So you think that is what Dragas is planning? To take out the Pope and all the Cardinals?" asked Thomas.

"I don't think he is going to do it. I know that he has already started doing it!" said Dan.

"No! That would be worldwide headline news! He can't have!" said Elizabeth, shocked.

"Its not a case of can't have, Liz. Like I said, he has already started. The election of a new Pope is governed by the Apostolic constitution 'Universi Dominici Gregis' which limits the size of the conclave to one hundred and twenty Cardinals, as Alberto said. This puts an effective limit on the actual number of Cardinals. Fifteen years ago there were two hundred and fifteen cardinals. Of those one hundred and eighteen were eligible to vote in conclaves. There were ninety seven who were over eighty and wouldn't be part of a conclave if a Pope died or resigned."

"Today there are one hundred and thirty five Cardinals, total. Only fifteen are over eighty. The likelihood of the number of Cardinals over eighty reducing so quickly due to natural causes is astronomical. Someone has been systematically killing the older Cardinals!"

"But why? Assuming that is true, they are a bunch of old men! Why would any one want to kill them?" asked Charlotte.

"My guess is so that when the next Pope dies, and a conclave is called, all, or at least most, of the hierarchy of the church will be in one spot. Take them out in one hit and there is no one left to elect a new Pope! Get rid of all the Cardinals that are too old to be at a conclave, and there is absolutely no-one left to elect a Pope!"

"If there were Cardinals over eighty still alive then it wouldn't be a stretch to believe that they could form a new conclave and elect a new Pope. If there are no Cardinals, period, then there is no one to elect a new Pope."

"Good God!" said Elizabeth.

"But how has he managed to kill that many cardinals?" asked Charlotte.

"He hasn't had to kill them all. Many of them have died naturally, but the number of cardinals who have had 'accidents' and subsequently died, has increased incredibly from what it was. Old men have falls, and slip over, but an analysis of the causes of death of cardinals makes them the clumsiest old men on earth!"

"But why hasn't anyone noticed?" asked Alberto.

"Because it has been happening over such a long period of time and all over the world. There is no reason why anyone would pick it up," said Dan.

"It is such a preposterous notion!" said Thomas. "Do you have any idea who Dragas will use to do this heinous thing?"

Dan frowned. "Not specifically. What I have identified is an increase in social media and other web traffic that is focussing more and more on Yawm ad-Dīn, the Islamic day of judgement."

"You'll have to explain that one!" said Elizabeth.

"Islamic scholars, using the Qur'an and the narratives that document the words and deeds of Muhammad, the Hadith, have identified twelve major signs that indicate the end of time. I believe that Dragas, and his family, is actively trying to manipulate situations to convince gullible and radicalized Muslims that the end of days is upon them," said Dan. "By misleading the faithful, he can increase the level of militancy among those who are more extreme in their views. We already know that he has connections in that world."

"What are the signs?' asked Elizabeth.

"Roughly, they are the appearance of the redeemer of Islam. The appearance of the false messiah, Masih ad-Dajjal. The return of Jesus. The ravaging of the earth, the drinking of all its water and the destruction of all life. The desertion of Medina. An attack on Mecca and the destruction of the Kaaba. A pleasant breeze blowing from Yemen that will cause all believers to die peacefully. The Quran will be forgotten and no one will remembers its verses. The sun rising from the west and black smoke enveloping the earth. Oh, and the beast will appear out of the earth."

"They are the major signs, but there is a list a mile long of minor signs. If you look on the internet there is a proliferation of sites using the minor ones to predict the end of days."

Like what?" asked Charlotte.

"Well, some of them are a bit easy to suggest like, 'Good deeds will decrease', and 'There will be much killing and murder.' One I particularly like, "Power and authority will be given to the wrong people.' would seem to happen on a regular basis. Others are a bit more difficult for the internet looneys to claim have occurred like the one that says a mountain of gold will be disclosed from beneath the River Euphrates. Many of them could be claimed to have already occurred such as the one that says that 'Female singers and musical instruments will become popular.' and 'the consumption of intoxicants will be widespread.'"

"OK, I agree that some of those minor signs could be argued to have occurred, but the major ones you mentioned certainly haven't," said Elizabeth.

"I don't think Dragas aim is to actually bring about the end of days! It seems to me he has been playing a long con. If you think of the steps of a classic confidence trick then you can see what he is doing."

"Hey! You will need to explain that as well!" said Charlotte.

"First, there is the foundation work, setting up the scam. Over the years the Dragas family has built contacts with fundamentalist Islamic groups. They have suggested ideas that , from their point of view, have been spectacularly successful, like 9/11 and no doubt others that we don't know about. I would bet that he has even put some of his own money, suitably laundered, into the pot, to support some of their activities. I would imagine he has become a trusted partner, perhaps even a confidant of some very dangerous, very radical people."

"That covers both the foundation work and the approach stages of a classical confidence trick. The next stage would be the 'build up'. This is where the grifter builds up the interest of the mark. In this case, convincing fundamentalists that the end of days is coming, hence the use of the internet and other media over a long period of time."

"That's what we have been picking up!" said Thomas. "Our analysts have been constantly on about the proliferation of web sites that talk about the end of time, or the end of days, or whatever it is. They have been desperate to try and understand who or what is driving it."

"Dragas, through a variety of methods, has been promoting increased social media chatter about the end of days, sucking people in to

661

thinking that something is really going to happen. That the end of days are really upon us. That is the build up."

"So do you think he has employed people to keep it going?" asked Thomas.

"No. I wouldn't think so. The increase started a good while back with some well placed stories and now it has its own momentum. We have all seen how fast a video, photo or news story goes viral these days. It just needs to catch a few people's imaginations and the new meme takes off, and don't forget, he has had a long time to bring this about. After a while the whole mythology starts to have a life of its own, so he doesn't even need to put any effort into it."

"Or from what I have seen, any truth," said Elizabeth

"That's right. These things tend to work best on uninformed people who are using their ignorance to fuel their prejudices. The web sites that go viral aren't the ones that have a detailed analysis of the sources and the pros and cons of arguments," said Charlotte. "You can see that in the amount of misinformation that is out there on historical subjects. A little bit of knowledge is a scary thing in the modern world!"

"The next stage of the big con, " said Dan, " will be the convincer. He needs a couple of events to convince the mark that what he has almost been convinced to believe is really happening. In this case I believe he will make one of the major signs happen."

"How is he possibly going to do that? Its not like he can arrange the second coming!" said Elizabeth.

"No. That's right. But he is so unscrupulous he could engineer the destruction of the Kaaba or...

"... the desertion of Medina!!" said Alberto who had glanced at the television that had been running silently on one of the news channels.

He turned up the volume. They all watched in stunned silence as the news reporter announced the evacuation of Medina due to the explosion of an Industrial Gas plant near the town and the simultaneous escape of a cloud of deadly chlorine gas from a newly commissioned water plant near the town.

17. Medina - Present day

Dragas looked out the window of his private jet. He had just taken off from Prince Mohammad Bin Abdulaziz Airport.

It had taken a long time, he thought to himself, as he looked down towards the centre of Medina as the plane rose into the clear blue sky, to find an opportunity that might let him progress his plans. The development of the gas business and the construction of a new water plant near the city had finally given him that opportunity.

In the end it was simple. Evacuate the city. It didn't even need to be for long. Just enough time to say that it had occurred. Most of the idiots that believed all that gibberish on the internet about the end of days wouldn't bother to read any further than the simplistic lists that he had made sure proliferated across the world wide web.

Scholars that really studied Islamic eschatology would not be fooled. They were not his target. He just had to convince the lunatic fringe that the time had come for drastic action. Serious students of Islam wouldn't go for it, but the fanatics, who believed anything they were told, would be convinced. It was so easy to stir up and perpetuate religious bigotry. The Internet had just made the task almost too easy.

As Medina disappeared in the distance, he sighed. He consoled himself that his plan would not damage the buildings, nor take many lives. In fact, within a few weeks, everything in Medina would, probably, return to normal.

"Penny for your thoughts," said the beautiful, leggy brunette that sat opposite him.

Dragas looked back at her, his latest companion, admiring her understated elegance.

He felt a little bad that Julia had ended up in a German prison. They were such dangerous places. He consoled himself with the knowledge that he had sent a good lawyer in to talk to her. She wouldn't be a problem.

Luigi's escape, on the other hand, had come as a nice bonus.

Below the plane and far to the south a small incendiary device flared near a cylinder of inflammable gas. Some distance away, in another part of the outskirts of Medina, a small explosion dislodged a pipe at a water plant. Yellow, chlorine gas started to billow into the still afternoon air.

18. Rome - Present day

"If this was Dragas' work then we have to stop him. He is a lunatic!" said Elizabeth, desperately upset by the scenes of men, women and children fleeing Medina.

"That is surprisingly difficult to do. He is incredibly well connected, and respected, around the world. For all his anonymity to the public he is exceedingly well known to many powerful and influential people," said Thomas. "What do you think he is going to do next Dan?" he asked.

"Like I said, as melodramatic as it sounds, I think Dragas is setting up a situation that will end up in the destruction of the Vatican, and the death of all the cardinals. In one stroke he plans to destroy the hierarchy of the church, undermine the apostolic progression and, at the same time, destroy the Vatican bank and throw the finances of the Roman Catholic Church into absolute, total disarray. It is a blow from which they may never recover."

"Not only that, but I think that this scenario is the one that the Dragas family has been setting up for a very, very, long time. Have any of you heard about the Prophecy of the Popes?" he asked.

Charlotte and Elizabeth shook their heads. Alberto and Thomas nodded.

"The prophecy of the Popes is attributed to Saint Malachy, a twelfth century Irish Archbishop. The prophesies supposedly predict all the future Popes, starting with Celestine the second, up to the present day, including the final Pope. The thing is, though, that they weren't published until 1595. So they are very accurate up until 1590 and then become a little more flakey."

"The prophecies say that the final Pope, named as Peter the Roman, *will pasture his sheep in many tribulations, and when these things are finished, the city of seven hills will be destroyed, and the dreadful judge will judge his people.*"

"If the Dragas family started this game a little while after Constantine the eleventh left Constantinople, then all the dates fit. I think that the Prophecy of the Popes was one of the first pieces they played in this very long game."

"But that would imply a plan that had been in play for what? Four hundred years!" said Alberto.

"Why not?" asked Dan. "The Catholic Church has been following their plan for what? Two thousand years?"

"About the same time as Malachy's prophecies were published, the writings of Nostradamus appear. Most of his mishmash of mumbo jumbo can be interpreted in so many ways that almost any event can be worked in to them, but a number of his statements specifically mention Rome. There is one that goes,

The movement of sense, heart, feet, and hand
Shall be in one accord, Naples, Lyon, Sicille
Sword, fire, water, then the noble Romans
Drowned, killed, dead because of their weak brain."

"This has been interpreted, somehow, as meaning that Russia and the Muslims will attack Europe, most notably France and Italy, with great surprise and swiftness. They will kill many including the clergy. They will destroy Rome and the blame will be laid at the feet of the Romans who bring this tragedy upon themselves because of their heretical and false beliefs."

"Then there is the one that supposedly predicts the destruction of the Vatican by fire.

Near the Tiber, the goddess of death threatens
A little before the great flood
The master of the ship being taken, put in a well
His castle and palace being burnt down."

"There are other prophesiers of the doom of Rome. I haven't even touched on the many interpretations that have been made about the Book of Revelations and the supposed destruction of Rome that they are supposed to include."

"There is, more importantly, a pattern to all this, but it has been accomplished over such a long period of time that it is almost impossible to detect. A bit like Nostradamus' predictions, you can't see it until the events have passed!"

"So you think the Dragas family has been planting suggestions about what the future will hold since as far back as the 1500s?" asked Thomas.

"I do," said Dan. "By taking the potion after the traumatic events of 1453, Constantine Dragas saw a future where not only would he restore Constantinople's position in the world, but he and his family could redeem themselves in the eyes of the Orthodox Christian world by bringing the Roman Catholic Church to its knees and restoring the power of the his Church. At the same time he could deal a potential death blow to Islam, by making them the fall guy. His guilt over the fall of Constantinople, and all the events surrounding it, must have been all consuming."

"You have to remember that Constantine had no love for the Latin Church given what they had done during the fourth crusade, and no love for the Muslims, given what Mehmed had done to him in 1453."

"So what do you think he is going to do next?" asked Thomas.

"What I think he is working towards is convincing someone to destroy the Vatican at the time of the next conclave and he needs to manipulate the situation such that the blame falls unequivocally on the Muslims, and it all needs to have a semblance of historical legitimacy!"

"To bring about such a dramatic event he needs to finish his long con. My guess is that, after Medina," he said nodding towards the television, "he will have a go at either destroying the Kaaba or setting up some sort of accident that fits the prophecy about a pleasant wind from Yemen that kills people. Either of those two events would convince the more gullible that the end of days has finally arrived."

"Then, sometime soon, he has to make a move that will focus Islamic disapprobation on the Roman Catholic Church, sufficient to convince the fanatics he has been cultivating to take extreme, unprecedented action against the Church."

"How the hell is he going to do that?" asked Thomas. "The last few Popes has been credited with improving the dialogue between Islam and the Roman Catholic Church. I read a very positive article in the Saudi Gazette just the other day that said something about this Pope being a welcome relief against the West's supposed Islamophobia."

"I don't know, Thomas. Perhaps he will engineer some sort of media beat up. That has been done before," said Dan.

"I'll have our analysts have a look at that, and see if they can come up with anything, but given what you can now do with those four screens, I doubt they will have any better luck than you have," said Thomas.

"In the mean time I will get on to our guys in the Middle East and get them to word up the Saudis and their contacts in Yemen. This bastard is not going to get away with killing thousands of innocent people or destroying a world renowned cultural icon, if I can help it. Its just not on!" said Thomas passionately. " The pleasant wind scenario could be some sort of wind borne attack, like Medina. Our boys are pretty familiar with the sorts of options in that area. Do you have any thoughts on how he might take out the Kaaba?"

"Not really. It has actually been damaged in the past, to a greater or lesser extent. In the six hundreds AD it was damaged by fire , bombarded by rocks and then rebuilt, twice. It was desecrated in the nine hundreds and collapsed and rebuilt again after heavy rains in the sixteen hundreds."

"Why is it so important," asked Elizabeth.

"The Quran says that the foundations of the Kaaba were laid by Abraham and Ishmael, and in a way they are the most significant part of the building. I am guessing that, given that history, for Muslims to believe that it has actually been irrevocably destroyed, it would mean everything was gone, including those foundations. It would have to be a pretty big explosion!"

"I don't know enough about explosives to give you any insights on how it might be done. What I would say, though, is that he couldn't use a Muslim to do it. There is no way, under normal circumstances, that a Muslim would intentionally damage the Kaaba, and there is no way a non-muslim could normally get anywhere near it. Mecca is like Medina. Non-muslims aren't allowed anywhere near the Kaaba. Everyone gets checked."

"There is however an Hadith that makes reference to the destroyer of the Kaaba being Ethiopian, and that he will destroy it block by block using a steel shovel and an axe that cuts through rock, but how much

Dragas wants to stick to the actual word, rather than the intent, I don't know. I would definitely follow the Ethiopian angle though."

"Why Ethiopia?" asked Thomas.

"Ethiopia has had a Christian community since the first century AD. There are something like forty million Christians in Ethiopia. In that part of the world that makes them pretty unique. As Christians in an Islamic world perhaps they have always been considered a threat. Bear in mind too that it is also, quite literally, only a stone's throw across the red sea to the Arabian Peninsular. From Addis Ababa to Jeddah is less than a three hour flight."

"It is probably worth at least one of my guys working on the Ethiopian connection then. I'll get on it," said Thomas, picking up his coat and walking to the door.

19. Sydney - Present day

Elizabeth dumped the last box of crockery on Dan's kitchen table and wiped her brow. A minute later Dan walked through the door carrying a large painting of an archway with autumn leaves entwined around it. Where shall we put this?' he asked, lowering the painting to the ground so it rested on his foot.

"How about in Charlotte's room?" she said. "It would look nice in there." Dan nodded.

"Okey-Dokey!" he said happily, heading off in the direction of Charlotte's old bedroom with the painting.

It had taken them a couple of weeks to sort out Elizabeth's apartment, clear out some room in Dan's house and finally move Elizabeth's stuff in.

Charlotte had gone back to England to continue her work on her Phd thesis and Alberto had decided that he needed a holiday. His job with the Vatican was finished. He had solved the riddle of the systemic theft of stolen relics and passed on his findings to his boss, along with Dan's suspicions about the threat to the church.

They heard regular updates from Thomas Malm, but so far nothing had happened that would indicate that Dragas was moving on, what they suspected, were his next objectives.

Dan walked back into the kitchen and opened the big two door refrigerator. Beer?" he asked.

"Oh yes please!" said Elizabeth. "I'll meet you on the deck as soon as I have put the last of these plates away.

Five minutes later they were both sitting, with feet propped up on the verandah rail and beer in hand, looking out at Sydney Harbour.

Elizabeth looked across at Dan, who had his eyes closed. He looked relaxed, tanned and happy. She had been keeping a close eye on him since the day he took the potion and she was pretty sure that it hadn't damaged him permanently in any way.

She had convinced him, soon after they got back to Australia, to do some benchmark tests to see if they could detect any change over time.

As a scientist, as his business partner, and now as his lover, she wouldn't take no for an answer. She had even convinced him to have a cat scan of his brain to be really sure. Her conclusions were that the effects of the potion were slowly wearing off. While he still seemed to have his newly acquired eidetic memory, and his enhanced ability to detect patterns and determine strategy, there was a gradual, but noticeable reduction in his abilities in those areas. She estimated, if the decline continued, that he would be back to normal within a year, with maybe some residual permanent improvement in brain function.

She closed her own eyes. She realised that she too, was happy, happier than she could ever remember being. She took a sip of her drink just as Dan's phone rang.

Dan looked at his phone as he picked it up and smiled. "Hello Professori Pellegrini!"

Dan listened for a few minutes. "We would love to Professor. Let me just check with Liz!"

"Professor Pelegrini has invited us to the hand over of the capitoline wolf to the city of Rome at the end of May. What do you think?"

Elizabeth nodded. "You bet!" she said, smiling. "Rome in spring would be fantastic! How about we see if Charlie could meet us there?"

Dan enthusiastically nodded his agreement.

20. Rome - Present day

As Dan and Elizabeth walked out of the Arrivals gate they could see Charlotte waving madly at them and standing behind her, grinning, was Alberto.

"Hey, you two!" said Dan as he walked up and hugged his daughter. He then turned to Alberto, hand outstretched ready to shake hands, but was suddenly enveloped in a bear hug.

"It is good to see you again, Dottore!' he said smiling down at Dan." I have arranged a car to take us to your apartment!"

Dan stopped and laughed when he saw the car that Alberto had arranged. It was a stretch limo made from one of the modern Fiat 500's. Standing beside the beautiful black car was an equally beautiful uniformed Chauffeur.

"Cousin?" Dan asked Alberto.

"Indeed!" said Alberto with a straight face.

As they approached the front door of the apartment they were surprised to see Thomas Malm standing waiting for them.

"Still keeping tabs on us, Thomas?" asked Elizabeth, remembering the last time she had arrived in Italy and feeling somewhat irritated that MI6 were apparently still watching her.

Thomas chose to ignore the remark. "I am glad you are all here." he said. "I have some information that I would like to discuss with you."

Five minutes later, the smell of warm apple cake and coffee filling the air, they were all comfortably seated in the living room.

"First thing," said Thomas, "It looks like you were right about the Ethiopian connection, Dan. Two days ago an Ethiopian Airlines pilot, on a flight to Riyadh, shot his co-pilot and then attempted to shoot his flight engineer. It was sheer luck that the Flight Engineer managed to overpower him and land the plane safely."

"He was taken into custody by the Ri'āsat Al-Istikhbārāt Al-'Āmah and..."

The what?" interrupted Charlotte.

"The Ri'āsat Al-Istikhbārāt Al-'Āmah, the Saudi General Intelligence Presidency. Secret Service to you." he replied with a smile. "They had a bit of a stern word to the pilot and he admitted to planning to fly his plane into the Kaaba. He claimed that he was on a divine mission to destroy it."

"Why?" asked Elizabeth. "Did he give any reasons?"

"He said that he believed the devil lived in the Kaaba and that it was a symbol of darkness. He said that the bible says that God hates idols and the Kaaba is worshipped by Muslims as an idol."

"Our guys did a little more digging and it turns out that the pilot's sister was the woman that was whipped and then hung in Sudan a few years ago."

"The one that was eight months pregnant?" said Charlotte.

"That's the one. Her father was a Sudanese Muslim who deserted the family when she was a baby. She, and her brother, were raised by their Ethiopian mother as orthodox Christians. The woman married an engineer who had emigrated to the UK when he was a child. He was a Christian. They both returned to Sudan to work on an aid project. Someone, no one really seems to know who, accused her of adultery," said Thomas.

"But she was married!" said Charlotte, indignantly.

"Under Sudan's Islamic Shari'a law, a Muslim woman cannot marry a man who is not a Muslim. Because her father was a Muslim, she was considered to be a Muslim," said Thomas. "She refused to renounce her Christian faith, so they charged her with apostasy."

"Her majesty's government, like many other government's around the world, protested vociferously at the treatment of the woman, but the Sudanese government would not budge. We had quite a lot of diplomatic contact with the husband and the woman. It was an horrific situation."

"I read a report from one of our diplomats who went with the husband to see her in prison. She was eight months pregnant and they had chained her to the wall of her cell. It was barbarous!"

"Anyway, long story short, she was whipped, then hung. You can imagine the effect on the family. Her brother, the pilot, was beside himself. He fell in with a small group of fundamentalist Christians who persuaded him that he should take extreme action against the people that murdered his sister. The rest you can guess."

"Can you track down this fundamentalist Christian group?" asked Dan

"Unlikely," said Thomas. "A cursory check has shown that the three people in the group have suddenly disappeared. There appear to be no records of any of them, at least under the names that the pilot knew."

"What's going to happen to him?" asked Alberto.

Thomas just shook his head.

"So he has done it again!' said Elizabeth with disgust. "That bastard has used people as pawns in his game and this time he has destroyed at least five people's lives in the process. Somebody has to do something to stop this immoral mongrel!" she said angrily.

"We would if we could Elizabeth, but his plots and plans are all over such a long time scale. We never know what's going on until it happens. Not only that, but given the Dragas family's dedication to their objectives they literally think nothing of taking someone's life, or of losing their own, in the pursuit of their aims!"

"The only way Dragas might make a mistake and expose himself is if something absolutely unexpected occurred that would give him an opportunity to advance his plans. On a smaller time scale he might end up taking greater risks than he would normally," said Dan thoughtfully.

"Like what Daniel?" asked Thomas, leaning forward, interested.

"Oh, I don't know, say like a vote in the Turkish parliament to turn Hagia Sofia back into a church, or the Pope suddenly dying and there having to be another conclave. No, scratch that, he would have to have already done something to give the fundamentalist Muslims some reason to believe that destroying the Roman Catholic Church was necessary."

"Would something like the announcement of a third Vatican Council be significant enough?" asked Alberto.

"What!?" exclaimed Thomas.

"It is a rumour that I have heard whispered around the Vatican over the last few days, while I have been doing some research there. The Holy Father has apparently been giving it consideration as a way of renewing the church after all the issues of the last few decades."

"When would it start?" asked Dan.

"It would be a couple of years, if the time taken to setup Vatican II is anything to go by. From memory Vatican II was first announced in early 1959, but the actual ecumenical council was not convened until late 1962."

"If you wanted to destroy the Roman Catholic Church, then that would be an even more opportune time than a conclave. I would imagine that every Cardinal of the Church and every Bishop who could make it would be there, all in one place. The perfect target!"

"Not only that, but the announcement itself would offer an unparalleled opportunity to get world wide coverage for whatever Dragas had in mind to discredit the church. When do you think the announcement will be made?" Dan asked, turning to Alberto.

"I get the impression that it will be soon, perhaps even this Sunday. My guess is that it would be announced at Saint Peter's square, after the Angelus. Around midday," said Alberto.

"That will be on the 29th May," said Dan almost to himself. Then he turned to Charlotte. "Charlie, the 29th of May. Do you remember what happened on the 29th May?"

Charlotte thought for a moment. "Oh my God!" she exclaimed. "The fall of Constantinople!"

"It must be just a coincidence, but it is one that a psycho like Dragas would just love! This could be it. This could be the opportunity we have been waiting for to grab that son of a bitch!" said Dan.

21. Rome - Present day

The rumour mill had been running hot for the last few days that something special would be happening at the Vatican so when Dan and Elizabeth walked into Saint Peters square on Sunday morning it was already crowded.

Dan had spent the last few days and nights in front of his computer screens trying to find some clue as to what Dragas might be planning. He had come up with nothing.

Elizabeth had finally dragged him away from the screens with a promise to wake him early enough so they could walk around the Square before it became too crowded. She had woken him early but the crowds were up earlier.

They hurried past some roadworks just before the entrance to Saint Peters Square. An excavator stood idle beside a deep hole in the pavement. A couple of living statues, buskers trying to attract the attention of tourists, stood nearby, crowded out of the square itself by the crowd. Dan admired a rather convincing and curvaceous Greek statue. The woman, dressed all in white, was holding an amphora. He was less convinced by a copper coloured cowboy who winked at Elizabeth as they walked past.

"I'll never be able to figure anything out with all these people in the way!" Dan grumbled irritably as they got pushed and jostled towards the front of the basilica. "I need inspiration! I need a clue! A sign! Something! Anything!"

Elizabeth had been in this situation before. She knew from years of working with him that Dan's mind, before he was forced to take the potion, worked best at solving intractable problems if she could provide him with, what Edward de Bono had called, a provocation, a way of derailing his current thought processes so that his mind could follow a new and different path. She didn't really know how his mind worked now, but decided to give it a try. The downside was that, if it didn't work, he would be come progressively more irritable.

"He'll probably just shoot the Pope," she said conversationally.

"Don't be ridiculous," said Dan shortly. "That wouldn't achieve anything! Dead Pope's attract sympathy!"

"What about wounding him?" she asked, trying not to show her own irritation at his manner.

"No. If someone just injured him that would have the same sort of results! Sympathy."

"Ok. What if the Pope said something that made Muslims hate him. That might be it!"

"How could they do that?"

"Put an impostor in his place," she said, taking inspiration from the living statues they had just passed. "A good makeup artist could create a double. Dragas is about the same build. He could have already kidnapped the real Pope!"

"Possible but unlikely. Don't forget that Alberto has warned the Vatican. They have been on high alert for days. Have you noticed the number of fit looking young men among the crowd? The Swiss Guard are out here in plain clothes. In force."

As they had been talking they had been gradually pushed further and further away from the centre of the square, and now stood with their backs against the plinth of a statue, close to the bottom of the steps that led up to the front entrance of Saint Peter's Basilica.

"At least we can't be pushed further away!" grumbled Dan, looking up at the statue that rested on the plinth. His eye caught a flash of gold.

"So what is he going to do?" Elizabeth continued. "Turn the Pope into some sort of monster. Have the Pope abuse a child in front of all these people, or have him grow horns out of the top of his head?"

Dan stared at her. "What did you say?"

"I said turn him into a monster," she said.

"That's it!" said Dan, his mood suddenly changing. "He is going to turn the Pope into a monster! Quick, we have got to find Alberto!" He grabbed Liz's hand and pushed his way back into the crowd, pulling out his phone as he did so.

Ten minutes later they were standing at the entrance to the Bernini colonnade where Alberto and Charlotte were waiting for them. A line of

677

angry Italians and tourists marked their passage through the crowd from the other side of the square.

"What's happened? Have you figured out his plan?" asked Charlotte as they approached.

Dan nodded. "I think he is somehow going to try and blind the Pope in one eye. That's his master stroke. That's how he is going to convince his fanatical friends that the Roman Catholic Church needs to be destroyed!"

"What? Why? How would that work?" asked Charlotte, confused.

"Remember the signs marking the end of days? The one about Masih- ad-Dajjal, the false Messiah who will deceive people with his supernatural powers. What better way to discredit a charismatic pope working to bring peace between the world's great religions than to brand him as the great deceiver." Said Dan. "Did you read the description of him?"

Charlotte shook her head.

"The description of the false messiah says that his right eye would be punctured, or that he has one good eye and one blind eye. The other bit talked about him having the keys to heaven and hell. "

"But I thought Saint Peter has the keys to heaven.....oh God, he is going to use their own beliefs against them!" said Charlotte.

Dan nodded. "Dragas is going to turn the Pope into, the anti-christ!!"

"How do you figure all this out?" asked Alberto.

"I was thinking about the statue over there, the one with Saint Peter holding the keys to heaven," he said pointing back over his shoulder. "Then Liz asked me if Dragas was going to turn the Pope into a monster. Then it hit me. That is exactly what he is going to do."

"Do you remember the big round section of mosaic floor that Dragas had on his boat? The one that he said had special significance to his family?" he asked Elizabeth.

"The mosaic that told the story of Theseus and the Minotaur?" she said.

He nodded. "Do you remember where he said it came from?"

"Crete wasn't it?"

"Yes, but remember he also said it was a copy of the one from the house of Sergius Paulus. Sergius Paulus was the Pro-Consul that asked to see Saint Paul and Saint Bartholomew when they arrived from the holy land. He was the one that witnessed Saint Paul blind the sorcerer Elymas who was trying to turn the Pro-Consul away from the true faith!"

"Ok," said Alberto. "Say that I am convinced. How the hell is he going to do it?"

""I don't know," said Dan. "shaking his head, shoot him with some sort of projectile, maybe? Hatever he intends to use it would have to be sufficiently strong to damage the Popes eye, but not so strong that he will do any other permanent damage."

"Shit!" said Alberto, looking up at statues that stood on top of the colonnade surrounding the piazza. "Could he use a mobile platform, a light plane or a drone or quadcopter?"

"I don't think so, said Dan. "I think that he would require a very stable platform, otherwise he might do more damage than he wants to. My guess is that he would prefer that this all happens without any evidence that there was human intervention. Ideally he wants people to believe that this is the hand of God striking down the false prophet."

"What sort of distance are we talking about?" asked Alberto.

"I would guess pretty close. The greater the distance the more force you have to use and the better the optics would have to be," said Dan.

"Right, its eleven fifteen. We know the Pope has refused to be put off. We only have forty-five minutes to find this bastard. It will take me five minutes to brief the Commander of the Swiss Guard. You and Elizabeth see if you can figure out where he might be operating from. Charlotte, will you come with me?"

Charlotte nodded.

"Hang on!" said Dan as a thought struck him. He grabbed a small notebook from his jacket pocket. He scribbled something and handed it to Alberto. "Get your guys to arrange this and can you get us up to the top of the Dome quickly, and maybe find us a pair of binoculars?"

"Sure. We can ask the guard near the elevator. Come on," he said leading them around the colonnade and through a doorway near the entrance to the Basilica. Alberto had a brief conversation with the guard on duty. He nodded and looked towards Dan and Elizabeth, waving them forwards to the front of a queue that ended at a set of elevator doors.

Dan looked back to thank Alberto, but he and Charlotte had already disappeared, lost amongst the crowd.

The elevator took them to the base of the Cupola, high above the floor of the Basilica. The guard asked them to wait, and disappeared for a few minutes. When he returned he was carrying a small pair of binoculars that he handed to Elizabeth with a bow of his head. He then led them through a doorway and up inside the cupola. They moved quickly up the narrow staircase, the guard asking politely but insistently for the people already on their way up to step aside.

Ten minutes later, breathing heavily, they emerged on to the small balcony that surrounded the lantern on top of the dome.

Elizabeth immediately lifted the binoculars to her eyes and started to scan the surrounding area. Dan stood looking out over Saint Peters square, trying to figure out the most likely location for the positioning of a laser.

He knew that the Pope would be standing in the second window from the right hand end of the Apostolic Palace. A maroon coloured banner emblazoned with the papal insignia already hung below the window. He could see that the window was already open.

He scanned the crowd, but realised that no one would be able to aim anything at the Pope from down there without the risk of being continually bumped and jostled. He lifted his eyes higher, to the top of the colonnade and followed the curved line it traced around Saint Peters Square. Other than the statues that were arrayed around the top of the colonnade on either side of the square, he couldn't see anyone, or anywhere among the hundred or so statues, where someone could easily hide.

He lifted his eyes still higher. He could see the giant statues of Christ and his Disciples that stood at the top of the facade of Saint Peters itself. From the back they looked to him like a rock band waving at the crowd. Again, given that the Swiss Guard and the Vatican Police had cleared tourists away from those areas, there didn't seem to be anywhere that someone could hide on the roof of the basilica.

He turned to Elizabeth who still had the binoculars pressed to her eyes. "See anything?" he asked.

"I don't know," she said. "Nothing obvious." There is a guy on the roof of that building over there, the one on the right side of that quadrangle before you get to the colonnade. I think he is just a photographer though, with one of those long telephoto lenses. I thought I maybe saw something in the top floor window of that place over there to the right of that building. Just there behind the colonnade."

Dan took the binoculars and pointed them at the two possibilities that Elizabeth had seen. "I see the photographer, if he is a photographer. I guess Dragas could have made a laser look like that, but he's not using a tripod. I reckon it would be almost impossible to hold a laser steady enough without some sort of stand. I can't see anything in that window you were talking about."

He turned to the Swiss Guard who was still standing beside them. "What's that building?" he said pointing at the one near the entrance to the Square where they had seen the photographer.

"That is the Libreria Ancora. The bookshop," he said following Dans gesture.

"And that one there, over a bit further," he asked.

"That is the Residenza Paolo VI. It is a hotel."

Dan looked at his watch and then at Elizabeth. "We've got twenty minutes to stop this madman. Come on, I think I know where he could be."

22. Rome - Present day

Dan burst through the door with Elizabeth hard on his heels. Dragas turned casually away from the window that looked out on the Apostolic Palace. Beside him was what looked like a long, square lensed camera. He did not look at all surprised to have someone burst into his room. At that moment Dan realised that he had just blundered into a trap. His heart sank. He turned slowly around and saw two men, Luigi and Paolo, standing against either side of the door with guns in their hands. Paolo pushed the door shut behind Elizabeth.

"I'm a bit surprised you didn't see that one coming, Doctor Marsh," said Dragas, "especially given you have the Blood of Constantine flowing through your veins. Perhaps it just doesn't work as well on ordinary people." Then he paused. "I really should stop calling it that. I will have to think of a more appropriate name."

"Now, we have a few minutes before the Pope steps up to the window, so let me tell you how this is going to go."

"First, you will both remain quiet while I use this," he said putting his hand on a long rectangular tube mounted on a tripod and connected by a cable to a large box on the floor. A telescopic sight from a rifle was attached to the tube. "This is a very difficult shot to make so I really cannot afford any distractions. The last thing I want to do is to injure the Pope more than required. I don't want a brain damaged Pontiff, just one who has been blinded in one eye by the hand of God."

"Second, as you deprived me of my opportunity to keep possession of Alexander's corpse, I will need another source of that unusual virus that seems to be so important to the potion. Given that you appear to have survived taking it I must assume that the virus has successfully transferred to you. The other ingredients of the potion I can reconstitute from the remnants that I have from the Alaric vial. Now, ideally I would like to keep you alive for a while to ensure that I have sufficient quantity of the virus, but that is not completely necessary. Carrying a dead body out of this hotel is merely inconvenient, not impossible. As for your lover here," he said nodding towards Elizabeth. "She is no longer necessary to my plans. Her only use now is as leverage. Luigi and Paolo would be quite happy to take her into another room and play with her if you do not cooperate with me."

A loud cheer erupted from the crowd outside the window. Dragas smiled. "I feel a bit like Doctor Frankenstein," he said, with a laugh as he lifted the heavy blackout curtain covering the window. He looked out to see if the Pope was standing at the window of the Apostolic Palace. "Oh!", he said, still looking through the window. "You thought I was going to shoot him? That piece of bullet proof glass won't stop my laser I'm afraid." He dropped the curtain. "It is not every day that you get to create a monster from legend."

"This is madness!" said Elizabeth. "That man has done nothing to you. He does not deserve what you are going to do to him."

Dragas turned on Elizabeth, scowling. "Doesn't deserve it! How naive! This is not about the man. It is about the symbol. He is just unlucky to have the job today. The Pope has become, over the centuries, the embodiment of deceit and duplicity! He leads a church that is corrupt, abusive and heretical. It is time that the Roman Catholic Church finally reaped what it has sown."

There was another noise from outside the window, not a cheer this time, more of a rumble. Dragas didn't seem to notice.

"What gives you the right to meddle in the affairs of the church?' asked Dan, provocatively.

"Divine right!" he said, arrogantly. "I can trace my family line directly back to Constantine the eleventh, the last Emperor of the Romans. I have more right to meddle in the affairs of the Church than anyone alive! More than that, I have an obligation to put right what has been done by these degenerate Bishops of Rome!"

The rumbling outside the window got louder. Dragas started to look around, but Dan forestalled him by saying aggressively, "Bullshit, Dragas! That is history. The Roman Catholic Church, despite its faults, is a power for good in the world now. You can't judge it on the basis of what happened hundreds of years ago."

"Why not?" said Dragas, bluntly. "The Christian church is not one of your modern day corporations that can change its missions statement to suit the whim of its customers. Christianity is the accumulated wisdom of two millennia of discussion and debate among the faithful of the church, based on the infallible decisions of seven ecumenical councils and made into law by the Emperor of the Romans. It is certainly not the heretical ramblings of the Bishop of Rome! And it is certainly not something that people can pick and choose from like some breakfast buffet in an hotel dining room!"

Dragas turned away from Dan and back to his laser. The noise of the crowd outside in the square had erupted. Dragas looked at his watch. "Just on time!" he said pulling back the curtain.

"What the fuck!" he said as he stared at the dirty steel bucket of an excavator that now blocked his view.

"You bastard!" he said turning on Dan. "You will regret meddling in my affairs," he said starting to unhook the laser from its power supply.

"You two," Dragas said turning to Luigi and Paolo. "Lock these two in the bathroom, then one of you give me a hand to get this stuff up to the roof garden." He paused, then as an afterthought said maliciously. "Put a bullet in each of their legs to make sure they can't do any more meddling."

Luigi and Paulo pushed Dan and Elizabeth into the bathroom and before they had a chance to react they both felt their legs pushed out from under them as Luigi, smirking, put a bullet into Dan's thigh and into Elizabeth's calf. Elizabeth screamed as the bone in her lower leg shattered. Luigi stepped forward and slapped her hard with the back of his hand, knocking her to the ground. Dazed and only semi-conscious she collapsed onto the pristine white tiles.

Dan knelt down beside her, cradling her head in his hands. "You bastard. You will pay for this," he said looking up at Luigi.

"Fuck off loser," said Luigi as he turned to follow Paolo out of the bathroom. "I'll be back to finish you two off later. I am looking forward to finally getting some hands on time with your girlfriend," he said with a salacious leer.

****

Dragas hurried up the stairs to the roof garden. He had hoped to be able to do this from the privacy of his room. The last thing he wanted was for it to get out that the Pope's sudden blindness was caused by a human agency. That would spoil the whole effect.

As he walked out onto the terrace he could see Saint Peter's Basilica and the Apostolic Palace spread out before him. He could hear the Pope's voice praying through the loud speakers set around the square. He would need to hurry.

Half a dozen people sat at the tables on the terrace watching what was happening. Dragas turned to them and said, "Ladies and Gentlemen, I am afraid we have detected a gas leak. I will be testing for it, but for your own safety., I would suggest you vacate the building as soon as possible."

All of the people on the terrace, including the staff, hurriedly left. Dragas indicated to Paolo that he should guard and lock the door. It took only a couple of minutes for him, with Luigi's help, to set up the laser. He aimed it towards the Apostolic Palace and then bent over to look through the sight mounted on top of it.

Paolo shouted. "They are coming!" He could see a group of men, led by Thomas Malm, coming towards the glass door to the roof terrace. Paolo ducked down behind some flower boxes and let loose a shot. The glass door to the rooftop shattered. The men behind it dived for cover.

"Keep them busy you two." Dragas shouted.

Luigi, crouched down behind a row of tables and flower boxes, where he could help Paolo cover the door.

Dragas quickly checked the power settings and, satisfied, concentrated on aiming the laser. As he focused in on the Pope he detected a movement in his peripheral vision. He looked over his shoulder to where Luigi and Paolo were still trading shots with whoever was trying to get on to the roof terrace.

He went back to adjusting the laser. The Pope's face appeared in his sights. Again he caught something out the corner of his eye, but it was too late to worry about distractions, now. He adjusted his magnification and suddenly the pope's eye was caught clearly in the telescopic lens of his sight.

He took a deep breath. This, he thought to himself, is the beginning of the end! He pressed the trigger on the laser and as he did so a blinding pain erupted in his eye. He staggered back holding his face.

At that same moment he heard a burst of automatic gunfire behind him and then a crash as two heavily armoured policemen crashed through the terrace door.

Dragas was grabbed and forced onto the ground. A refined English voice said, "Got you, you prick! There is no way you will get out of this one. We've got the whole thing on video! You're nicked!"

Above them, an unusual looking quadcopter hovered over the rooftop its camera staring directly at Dragas.

Thomas Malm waved at the quadcopter, which waggled in the air and then lifted away into the clear blue Roman sky.

Thomas Malm lifted Andris Dragas roughly to his feet. Dragas was still holding his eye and groaning. "Take him away!" he said to a young Italian police officer. "He's all yours. Be sure to let your comrade's know he just tried to kill the Pope!"

Thomas let go of Dragas and looked away. Two seconds later he heard a shout, turned back, and was in time to see Dragas leap off the roof terrace. By the time they had reached the edge themselves, he and the young Italian police officer, could see a crowd gathering around the lifeless body spread-eagled on the cobbles below therm.

The young officer looked at Thomas, horrified. He started to say something, but Thomas put a hand on his shoulder. "Don't worry about it. Best thing that could have happened," he said to him in a kind voice.

He looked up and saw Dan and Elizabeth being helped through the door to the roof. Both had bandages around their legs and both looked pale and shaken.

Thomas walked across to them, smiling.

"It's over!" he said as he came close to them. "The Pope is fine, no harm done. That sheet of perspex stopped the laser beam, just like you said it would. It also had the added advantage that it gave Dragas a taste of his own medicine."

"Where is the bastard?" asked Elizabeth looking around the rooftop.

Thomas pointed.

"Your guesses were spot on, Daniel. You were right about everything. What he was doing, where he would be, how he would react when Charlotte blocked his view with the excavator. The whole thing was very impressive. Can I offer you a job with Her Majesty's secret service?" asked Thomas with a smile.

Dan laughed. "My days as an action man are over, I think," he said looking down at the blood soaked bandage around his leg. "I'm just glad it was this scenario that Dragas took not the other one."

"What other one?" asked Elizabeth, holding tightly on to his arm.

"Well you know the other sign of the end of days where the sun rises in the west," said Dan.

"Pretty tough to organize that I would have thought, unless you reverse the rotation of the earth. Wasn't superman the last one to do that?" said Elizabeth flippantly. "And clearly Dragas couldn't fly!" she added casually, looking over the edge at the body on the ground below.

Dan laughed, "Yeah, so he was! But thinking through the outcome of all this, he could have just as easily gone with that one."

"How would he have done that?" asked Thomas.

"Well, let me ask you a question. If the west is a place, and not a direction, and a nuclear bomb went off here...."

" ... it would look like the sun rising in the west! That is horrible!" said Elizabeth.

Thomas had gone pale.

****

Charlotte looked down at the lifeless body that had fallen close to where she had been sitting in the seat of the excavator. She was still staring at it, and the crowd that had gathered around it as the police arrived and started to move everyone back.

She felt a hand on her arm. She turned to see the grim face of Alberto. He was still carrying the iPad that he had used to control the quadcopter.

"Is it over?" she asked him. He nodded. "We got video of everything. By this time tomorrow the world will know what he was trying to do." She threw her hands around his neck and hugged him tightly.

23. Texas - Present day

Vanessa Spotswood looked through the glass walls of her office at the young man working in the office opposite. They had been at university together and she had often caught herself watching him out of the corner of her eye. He was tall, handsome and extremely clever. They had graduated at the same time and both been awarded their doctorates on the same day.

They had been at a few social events together, both during their time at university and since they graduated. At one time she thought that he would ask her out. He never did. They had remained more than acquaintances, but less than friends.

From their sporadic conversations over the years she had discovered that he was European, born somewhere in the Balkans. He had been adopted by a very wealthy, distant cousin and that his adopted father wanted him to gain experience working for other people before getting involved in the family businesses, whatever that was.

As she was watching he picked up his phone. He talked for a few moments and then put the phone back in it's cradle. She could tell immediately that he had just received some bad news. He unconsciously reached for something that was hanging around his neck.

She stood up and walked across the hall to his office, picking up a report that sat on her desk as she walked past it.

She tapped on his open door and walked in. Feigning surprise at the way he looked she asked, "Constantine, are you Okay? You look like you have just seen a ghost!"

He turned to look at her. "My father has just been killed," he said in a monotone. Kirsten suddenly felt out of her depth. "Oh, I am so sorry," she said, as sympathetically as she could.

Constantine looked at her, noticing her properly for the first time. "What do you have there?" he asked indicating the papers in her hand.

"Oh, its just the repot on the decommissioning of the M388 nuclear projectiles, you know, the portable nukes that were deployed in Germany during the Cold War, the ones that went with the Davy Crockett

Weapons System. You mentioned that you wanted to have a look at it when it came in. But you probably don't want to bother with it at the moment!" she mumbled.

Constantine Dragas nodded, an odd smile on his face. "Life must go on Vanessa." he said, reaching for the report.

As he leant towards her she saw the light glance off the pendant that hung around his neck. It seemed to be a small glass and gold vial. She had not seen him wearing jewelry before. It must be new, she thought. Perhaps he did have a girlfriend after all.

Printed in Australia
Ingram Content Group Australia Pty Ltd
AUHW021204150124
389101AU00001B/1

9 798215 961995